S0-EJH-707

THE MUSIC BOX

WITHDRAWN

written by Carbone

illustrated by Gijé

STONE ARCH BOOKS
a capstone imprint

Compilation first published in the United States in 2024
Individual titles first published in the United States in 2023
by Stone Arch Books, an imprint of Capstone
1710 Roe Crest Drive, North Mankato, Minnesota 56003
capstonepub.com

Individual titles first published in French in 2018, 2019, 2020,
and 2021 by Editions Dupuis s.a,
52 rue Destrée
6001 Marcinelle,
Belgium

Original titles: La boîte à musique 1 – Bienvenue à Pandorient; La
boîte à musique 2 – Le secret de Cyprien; La boîte à musique 3 – À
la recherche des origines; La boîte à musique 4 – La mystérieuse
disparition; La boîte à musique 5 – Les plumes d'aigle douce

Text and illustration copyright © DUPUIS 2018, 2019, 2020, and
2021, by Gijé, Carbone
www.dupuis.com
All rights reserved

English translation: Original titles 1 and 2 2018 by Mercedes Claire
Gilliom; original titles 3, 4, and 5 2019, 2022 by Jessie Aufiery

All rights reserved. No part of this publication may be
reproduced in whole or in part, or stored in a retrieval system,
or transmitted in any form or by any means, electronic,
mechanical, photocopying, recording, or otherwise, without
written permission of the publisher.

Library of Congress Cataloging-in-Publication Data is available
on the Library of Congress website.
ISBN: 9781669080190 (paperback)
ISNB: 9781669080206 (ebook PDF)

Summary: For her eighth birthday, Nola receives a marvelous
present: her late mother's music box. What an enchanted melody
it plays! But looking closer, Nola discovers there is a little girl
waving inside—and she's calling for help! Wasting no time,
Nola follows the tiny girl's instructions and shrinks down to
enter the music box. There, she discovers Pandorient, a world as
extraordinary as it is dangerous. Can Nola unravel the mysteries
of this magical realm and reveal her mother's connection to it?

Printed and bound in China. 5834

TABLE OF CONTENTS

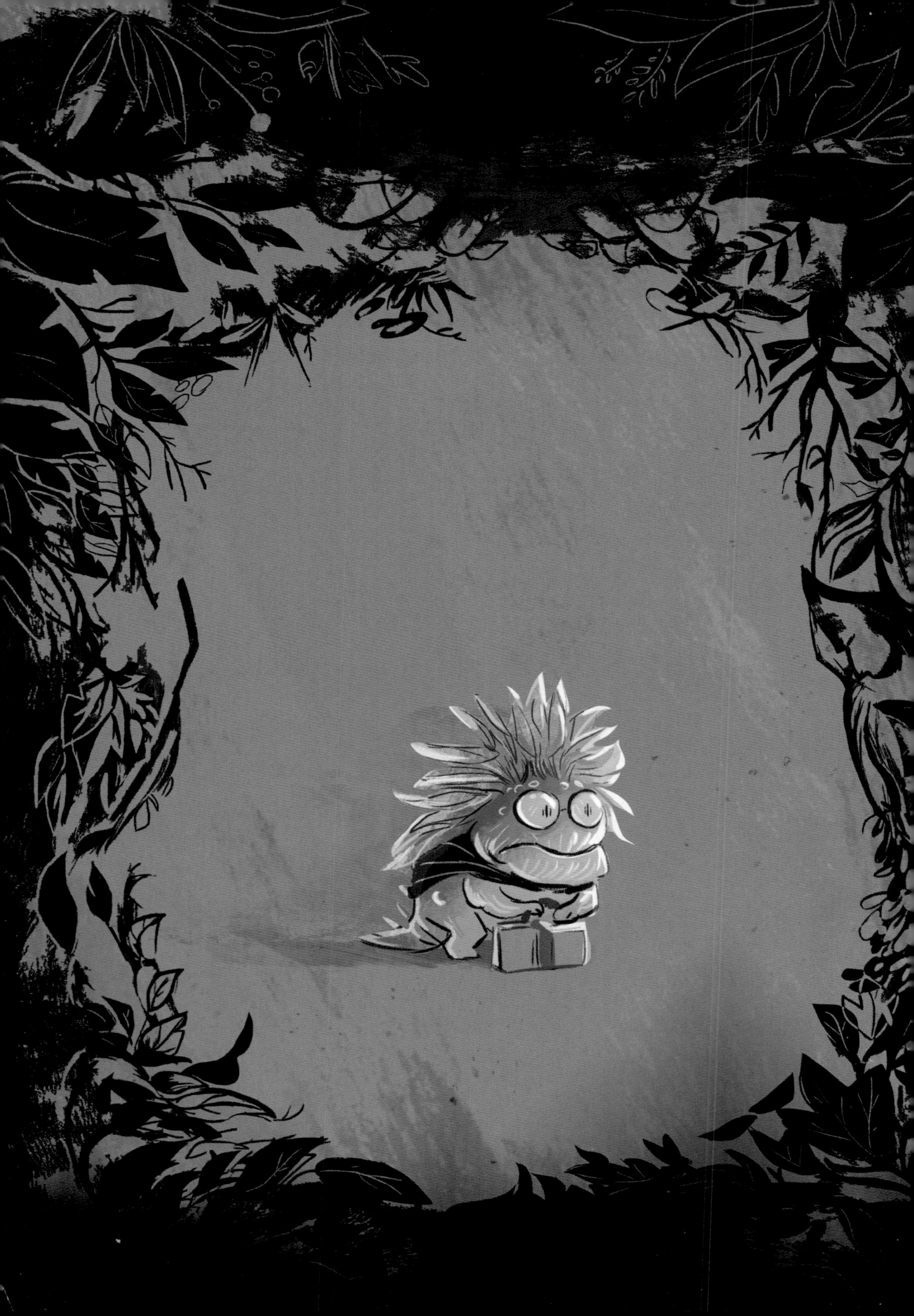

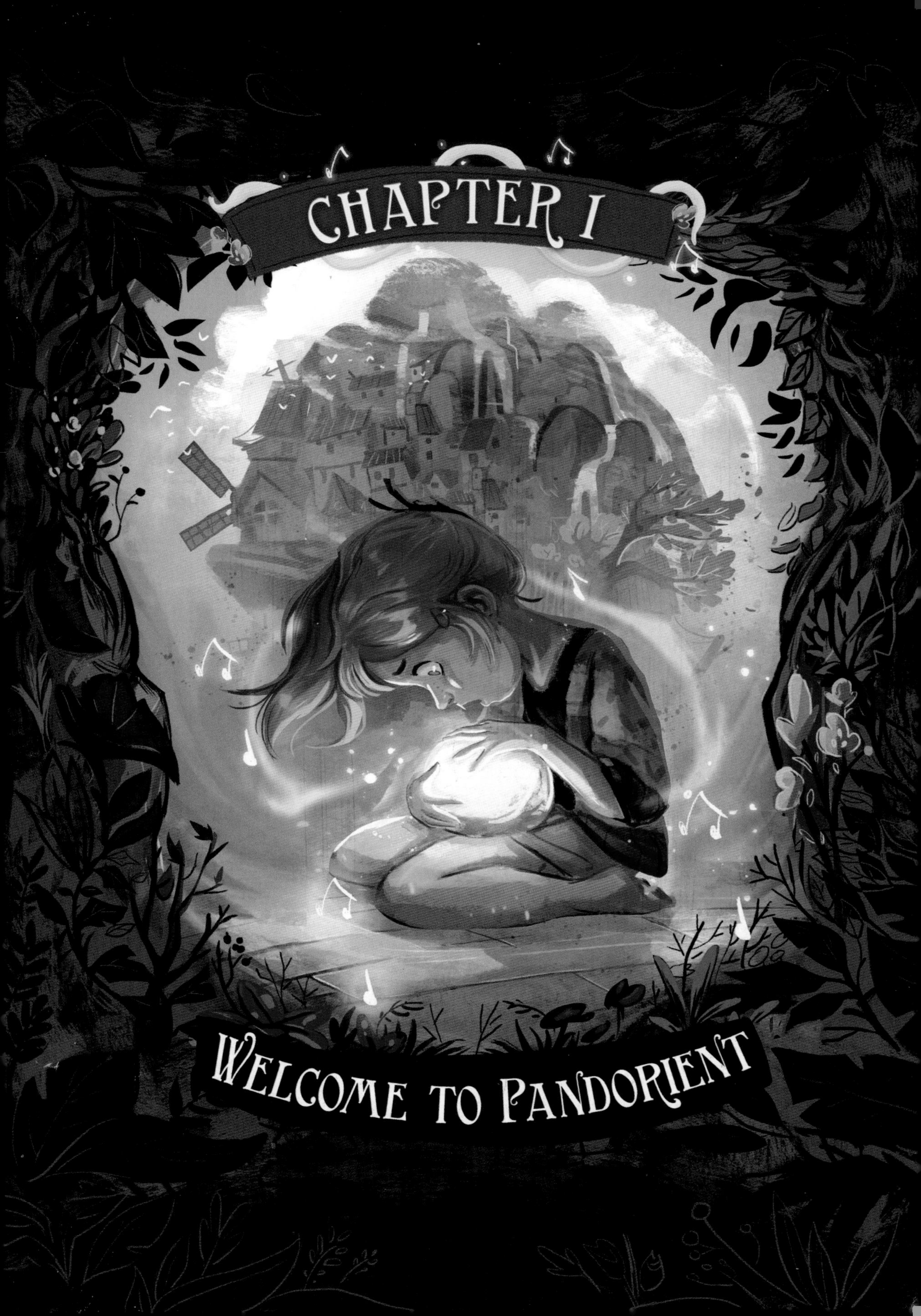
CHAPTER I
WELCOME TO PANDORIENT

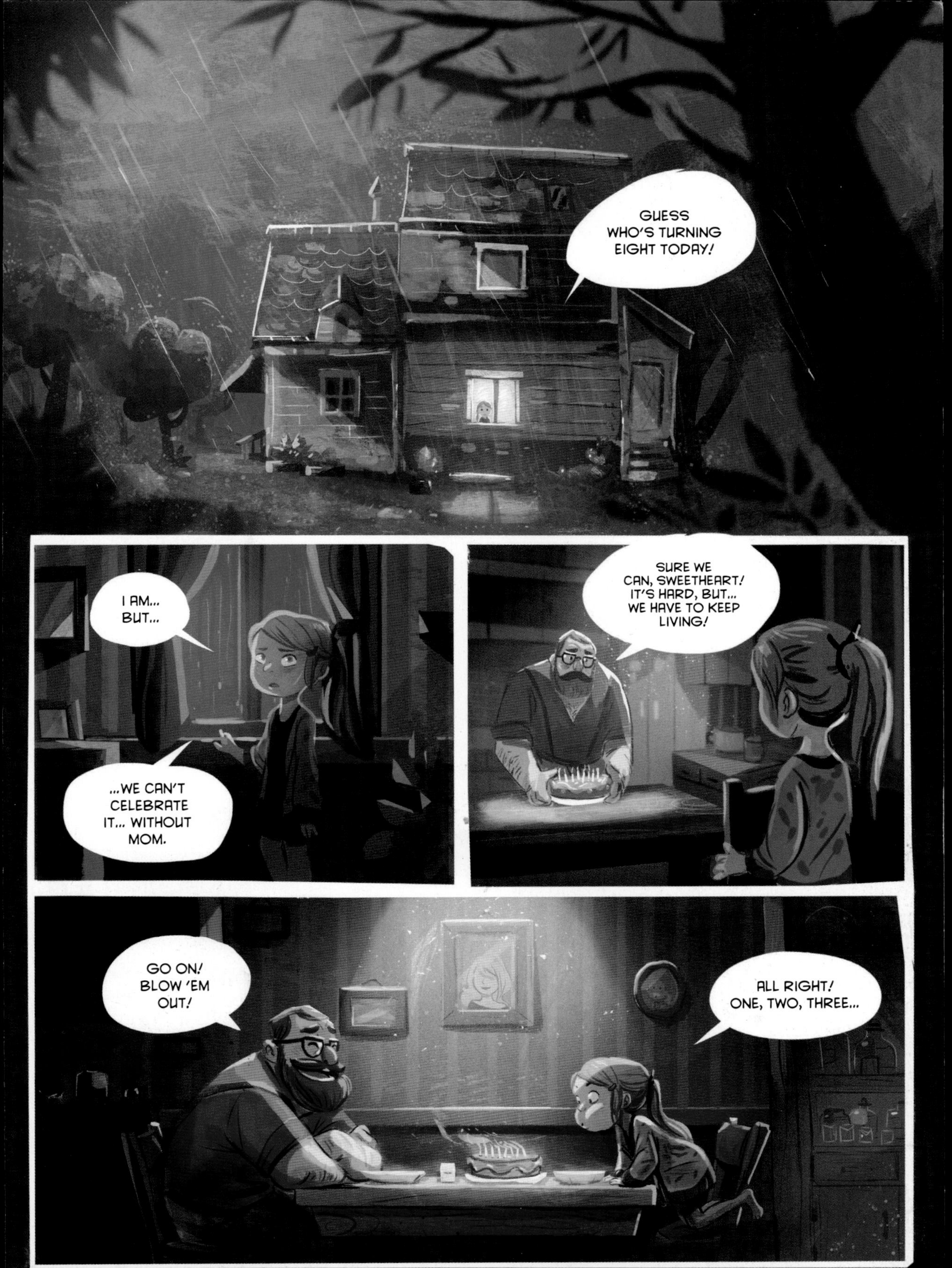
GUESS WHO'S TURNING EIGHT TODAY!
I AM... BUT...
...WE CAN'T CELEBRATE IT... WITHOUT MOM.
SURE WE CAN, SWEETHEART! IT'S HARD, BUT... WE HAVE TO KEEP LIVING!
GO ON! BLOW 'EM OUT!
ALL RIGHT! ONE, TWO, THREE...

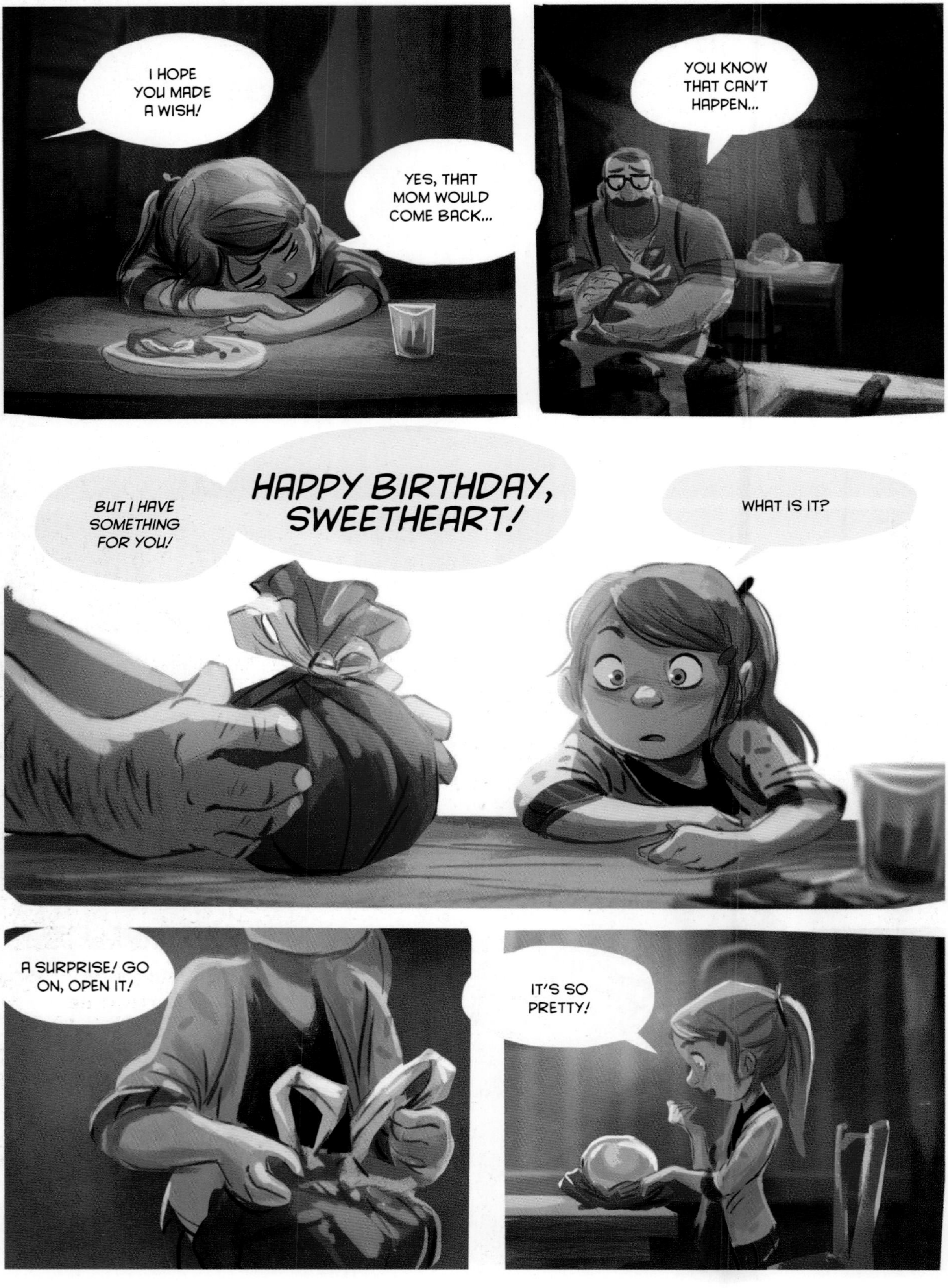
I HOPE YOU MADE A WISH!
YES, THAT MOM WOULD COME BACK...
YOU KNOW THAT CAN'T HAPPEN...
BUT I HAVE SOMETHING FOR YOU!
HAPPY BIRTHDAY, SWEETHEART!
WHAT IS IT?
A SURPRISE! GO ON, OPEN IT!
IT'S SO PRETTY!

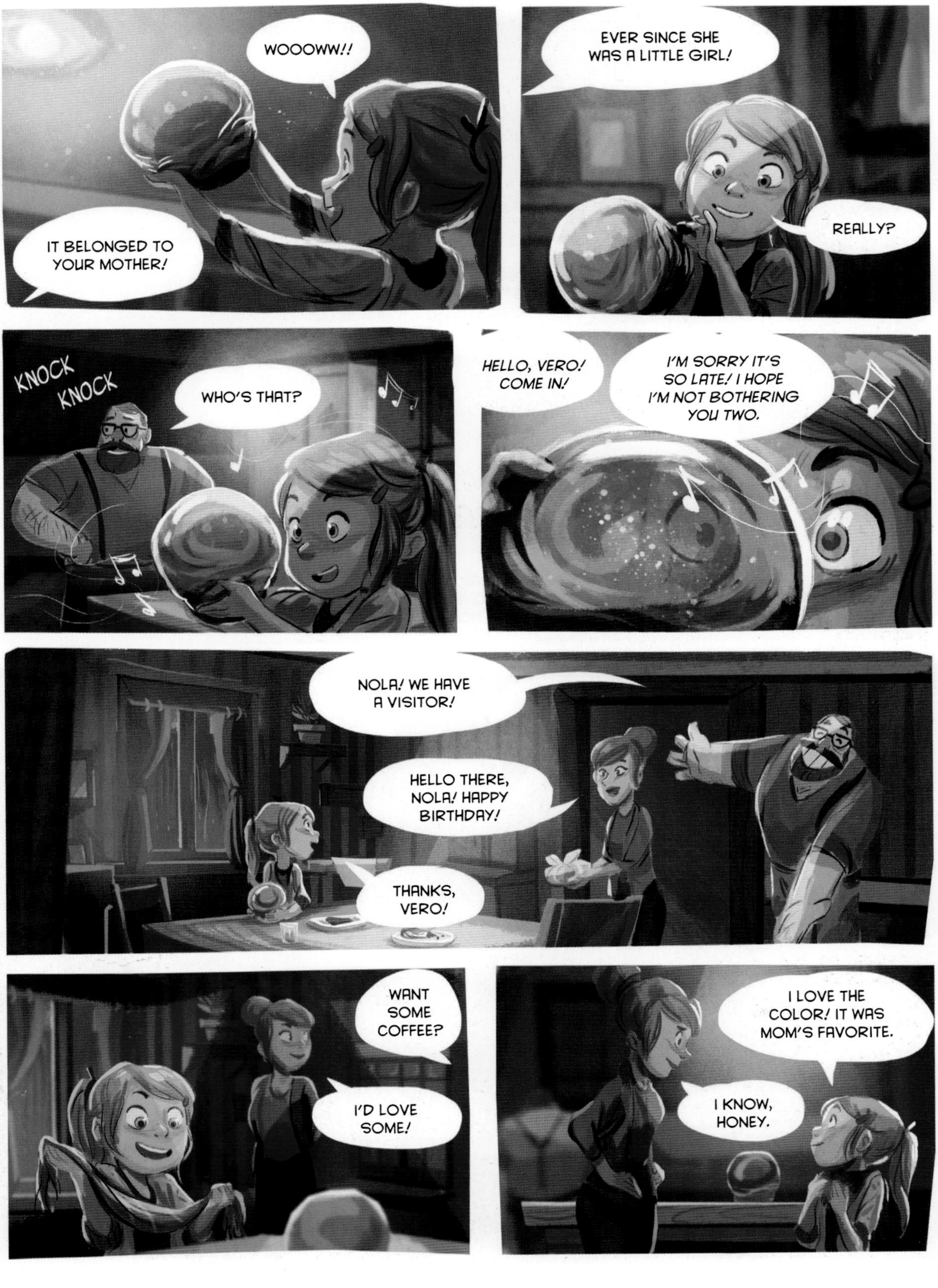

WOOOWW!!
IT BELONGED TO YOUR MOTHER!
EVER SINCE SHE WAS A LITTLE GIRL!
REALLY?
KNOCK KNOCK
WHO'S THAT?
HELLO, VERO! COME IN!
I'M SORRY IT'S SO LATE! I HOPE I'M NOT BOTHERING YOU TWO.
NOLA! WE HAVE A VISITOR!
HELLO THERE, NOLA! HAPPY BIRTHDAY!
THANKS, VERO!
WANT SOME COFFEE?
I'D LOVE SOME!
I LOVE THE COLOR! IT WAS MOM'S FAVORITE.
I KNOW, HONEY.

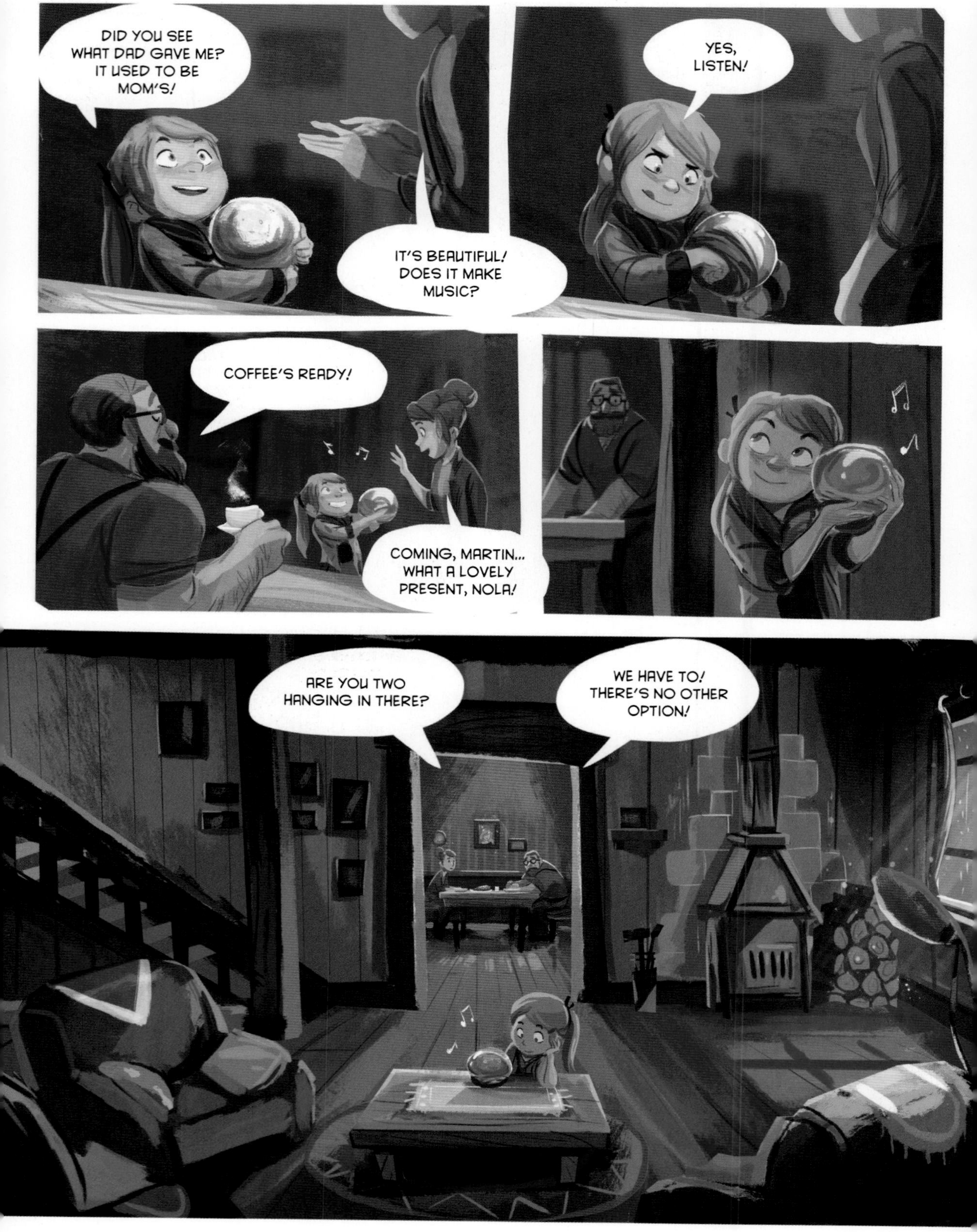
DID YOU SEE WHAT DAD GAVE ME? IT USED TO BE MOM'S!
IT'S BEAUTIFUL! DOES IT MAKE MUSIC?
YES, LISTEN!
COFFEE'S READY!
COMING, MARTIN... WHAT A LOVELY PRESENT, NOLA!
ARE YOU TWO HANGING IN THERE?
WE HAVE TO! THERE'S NO OTHER OPTION!

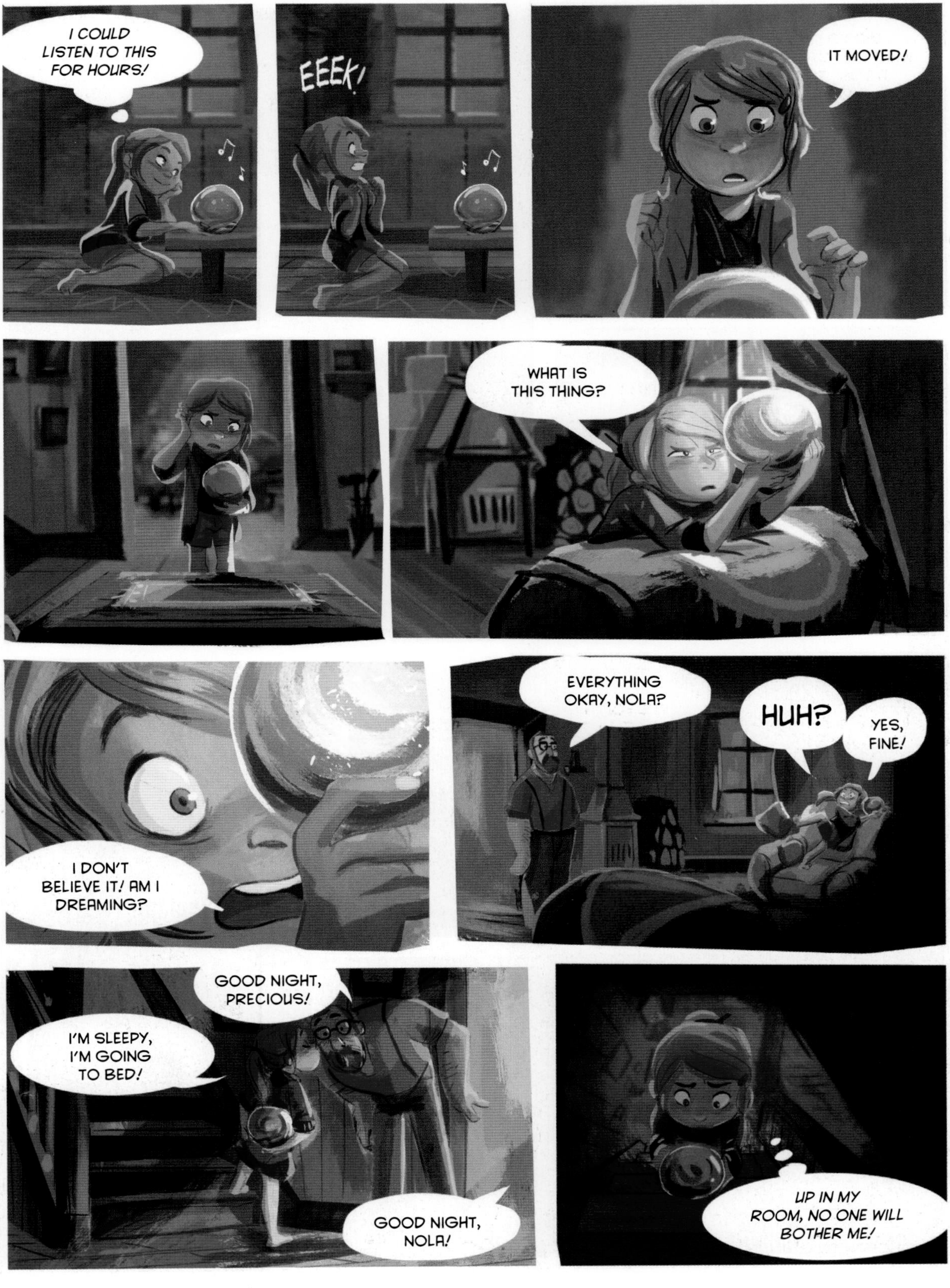
I COULD LISTEN TO THIS FOR HOURS!
EEEK!
IT MOVED!
WHAT IS THIS THING?
I DON'T BELIEVE IT! AM I DREAMING?
EVERYTHING OKAY, NOLA?
HUH?
YES, FINE!
GOOD NIGHT, PRECIOUS!
I'M SLEEPY, I'M GOING TO BED!
GOOD NIGHT, NOLA!
UP IN MY ROOM, NO ONE WILL BOTHER ME!

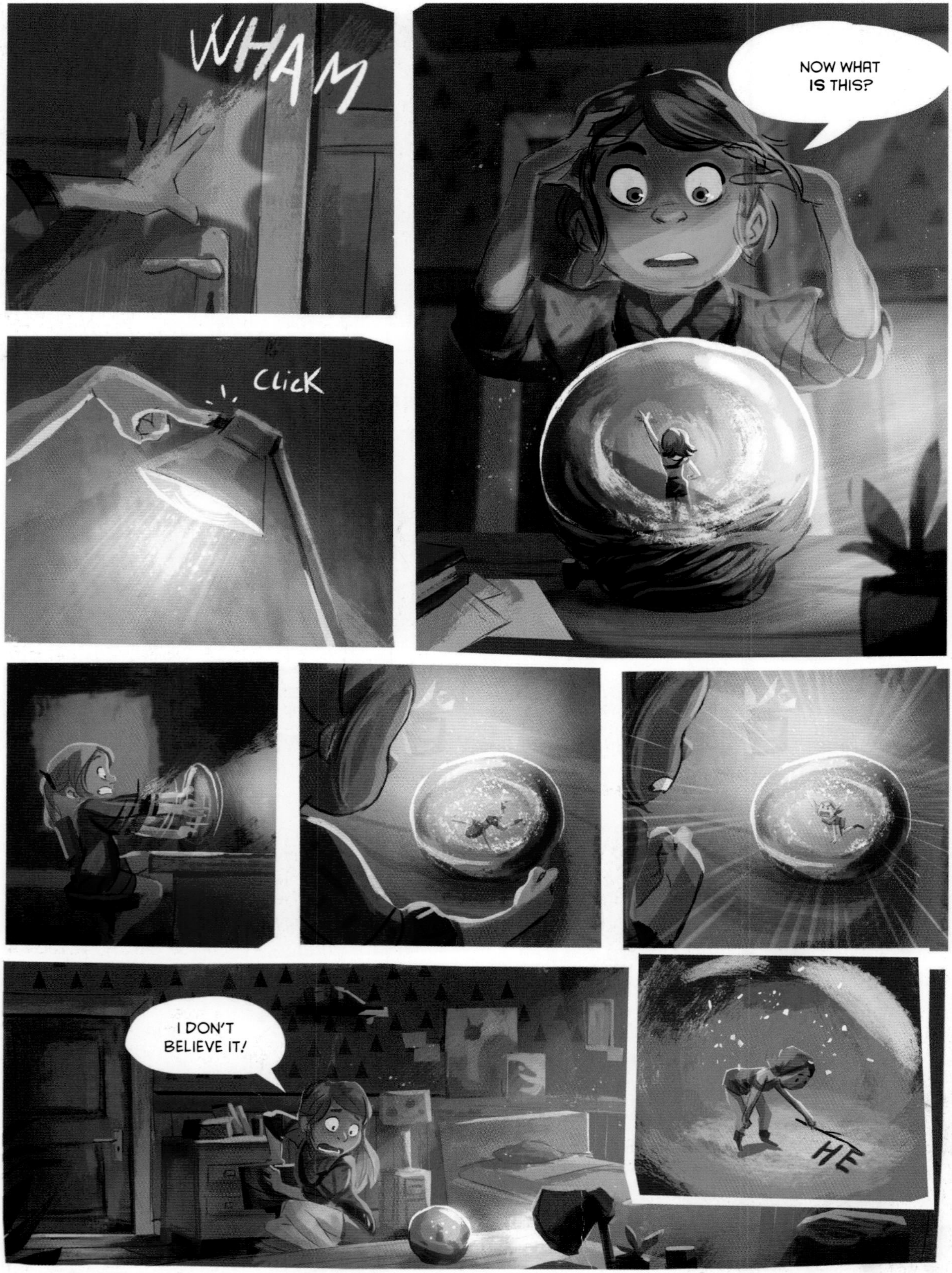
WHAM
NOW WHAT IS THIS?
CLICK
I DON'T BELIEVE IT!
HE

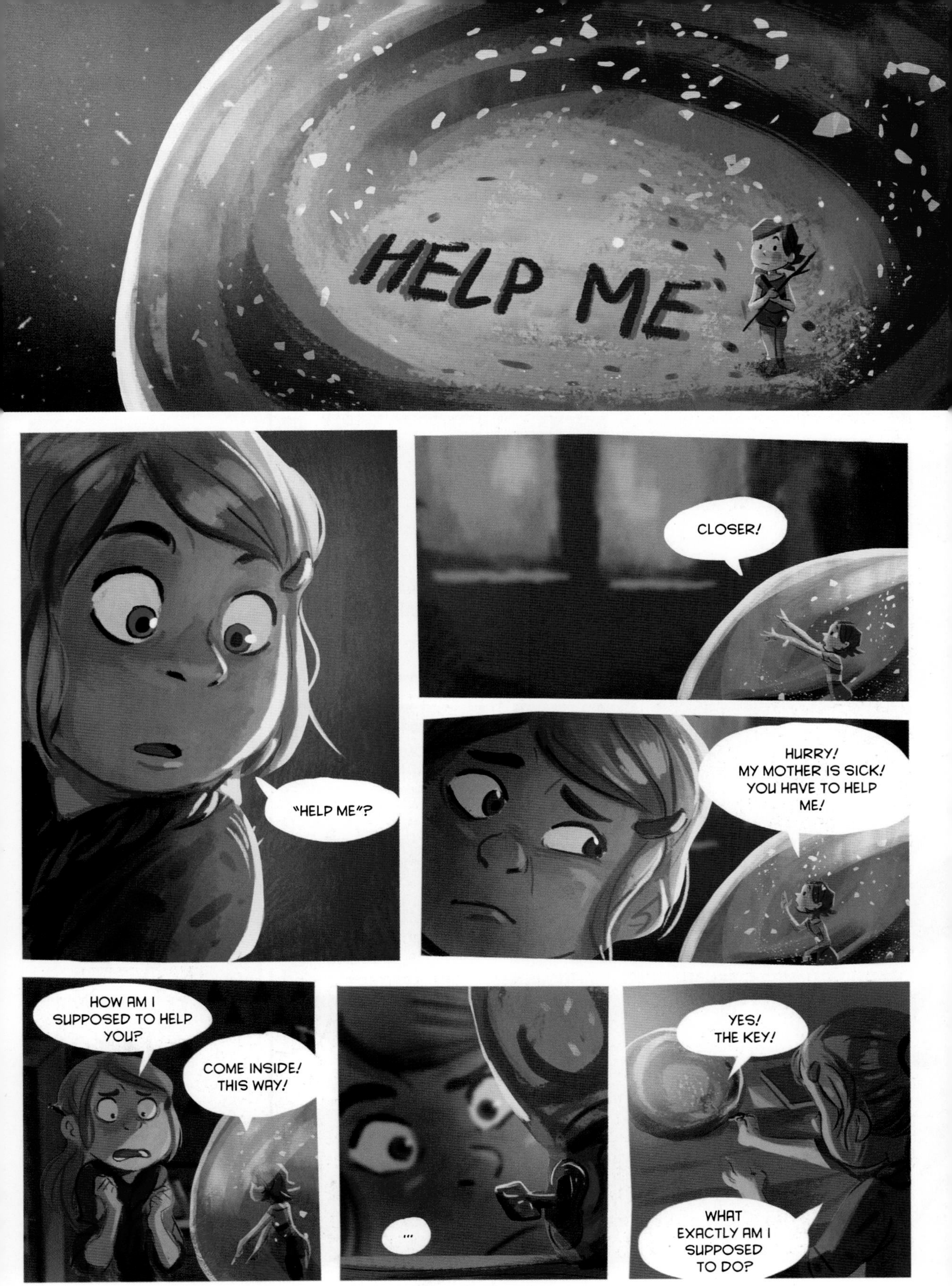
HELP ME
"HELP ME"?
CLOSER!
HURRY! MY MOTHER IS SICK! YOU HAVE TO HELP ME!
HOW AM I SUPPOSED TO HELP YOU?
COME INSIDE! THIS WAY!
...
YES! THE KEY!
WHAT EXACTLY AM I SUPPOSED TO DO?

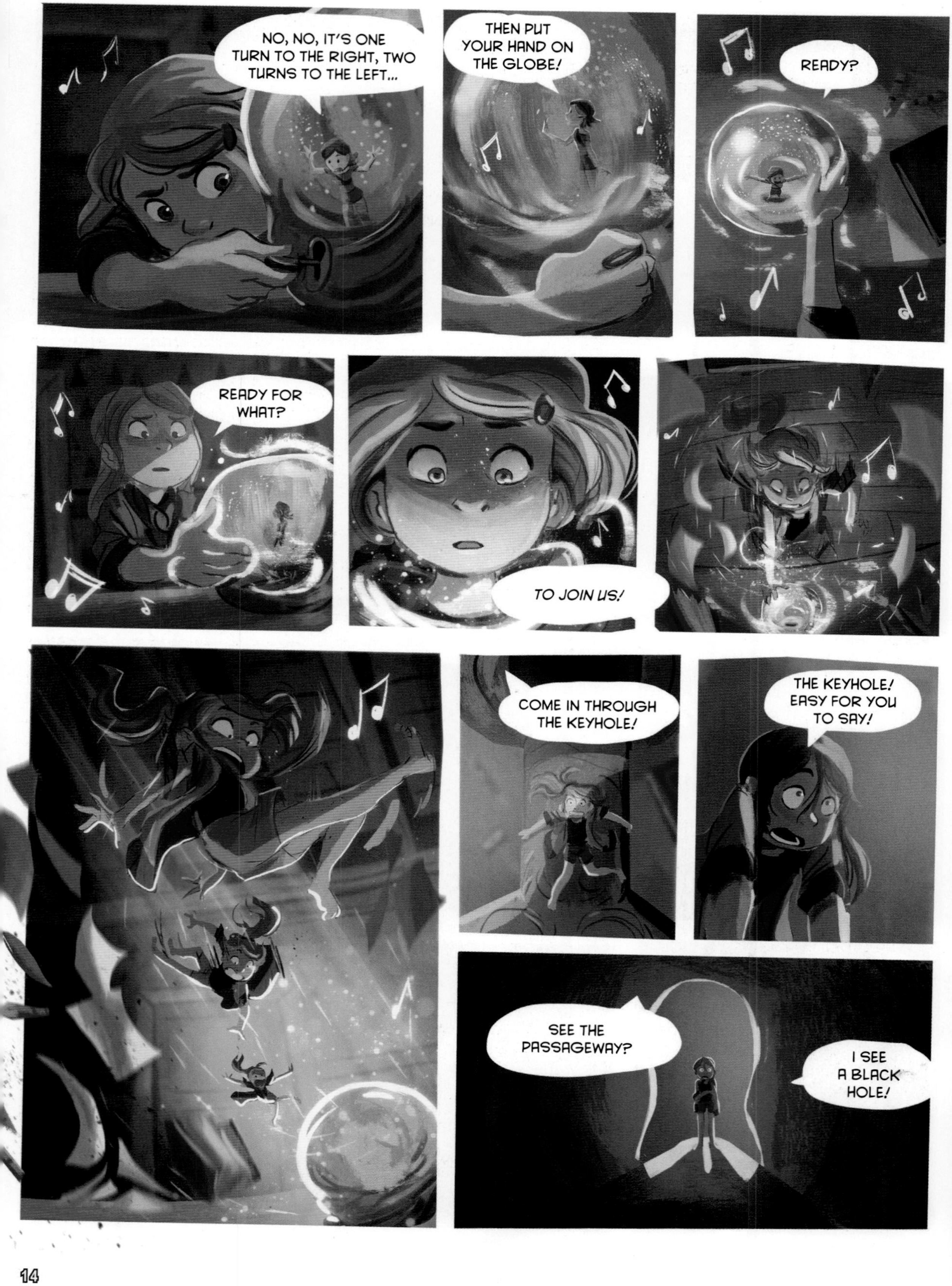
NO, NO, IT'S ONE TURN TO THE RIGHT, TWO TURNS TO THE LEFT...
THEN PUT YOUR HAND ON THE GLOBE!
READY?
READY FOR WHAT?
TO JOIN US!
COME IN THROUGH THE KEYHOLE!
THE KEYHOLE! EASY FOR YOU TO SAY!
SEE THE PASSAGEWAY?
I SEE A BLACK HOLE!

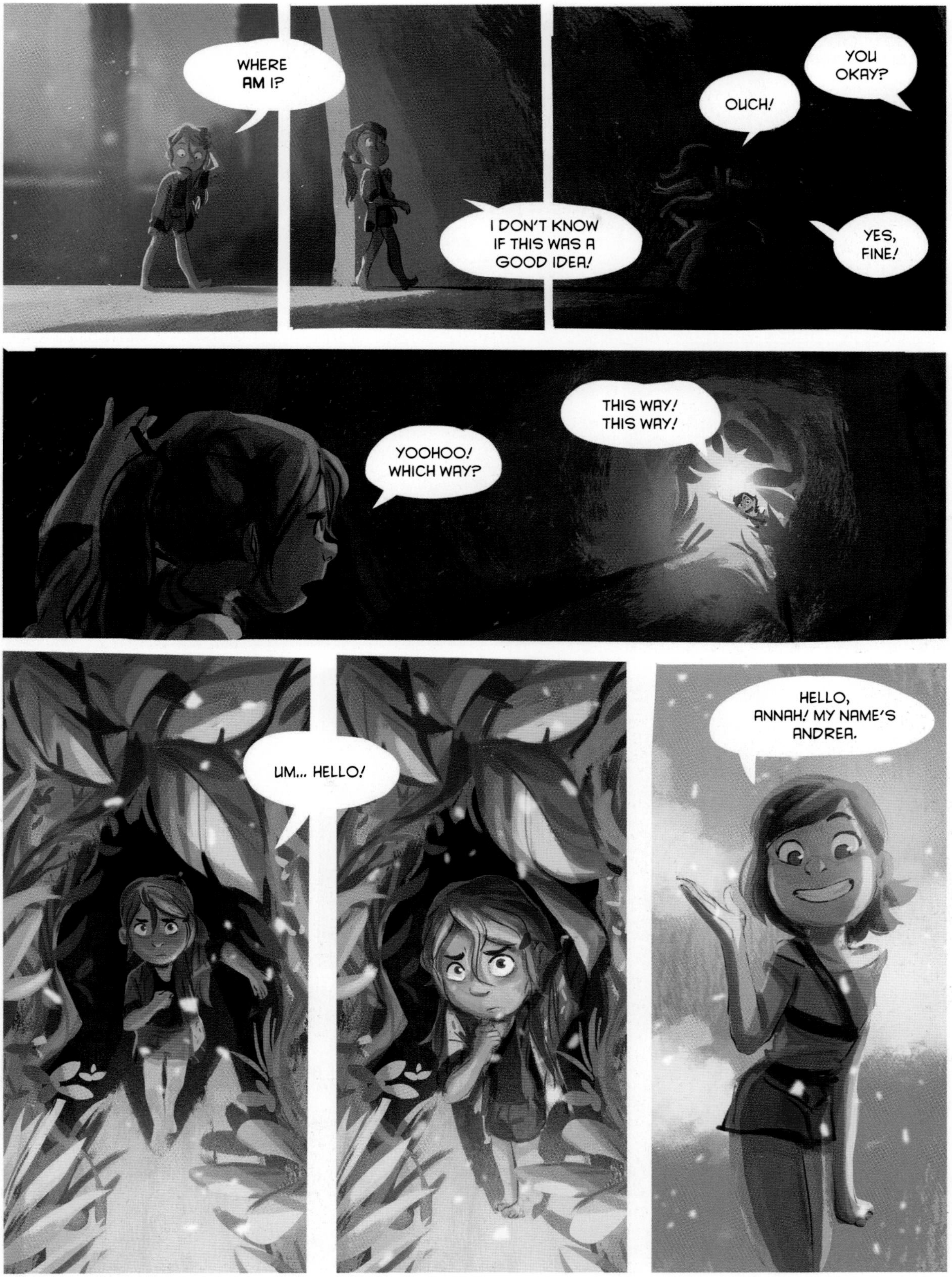
WHERE AM I?
I DON'T KNOW IF THIS WAS A GOOD IDEA!
OUCH!
YOU OKAY?
YES, FINE!
YOOHOO! WHICH WAY?
THIS WAY! THIS WAY!
UM... HELLO!
HELLO, ANNAH! MY NAME'S ANDREA.

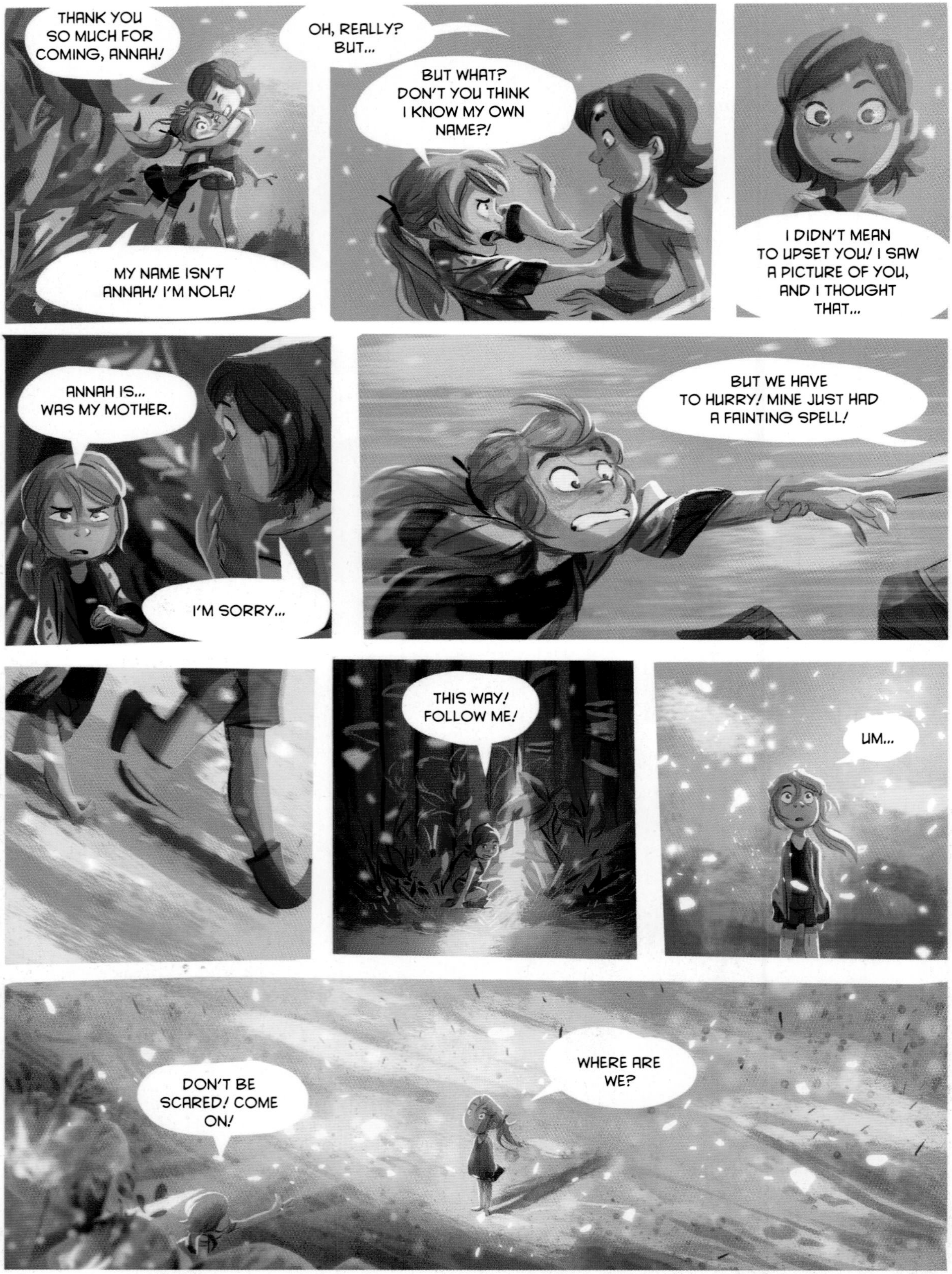
THANK YOU SO MUCH FOR COMING, ANNAH!
MY NAME ISN'T ANNAH! I'M NOLA!
OH, REALLY? BUT...
BUT WHAT? DON'T YOU THINK I KNOW MY OWN NAME?!
I DIDN'T MEAN TO UPSET YOU! I SAW A PICTURE OF YOU, AND I THOUGHT THAT...
ANNAH IS... WAS MY MOTHER.
I'M SORRY...
BUT WE HAVE TO HURRY! MINE JUST HAD A FAINTING SPELL!
THIS WAY! FOLLOW ME!
UM...
WHERE ARE WE?
DON'T BE SCARED! COME ON!

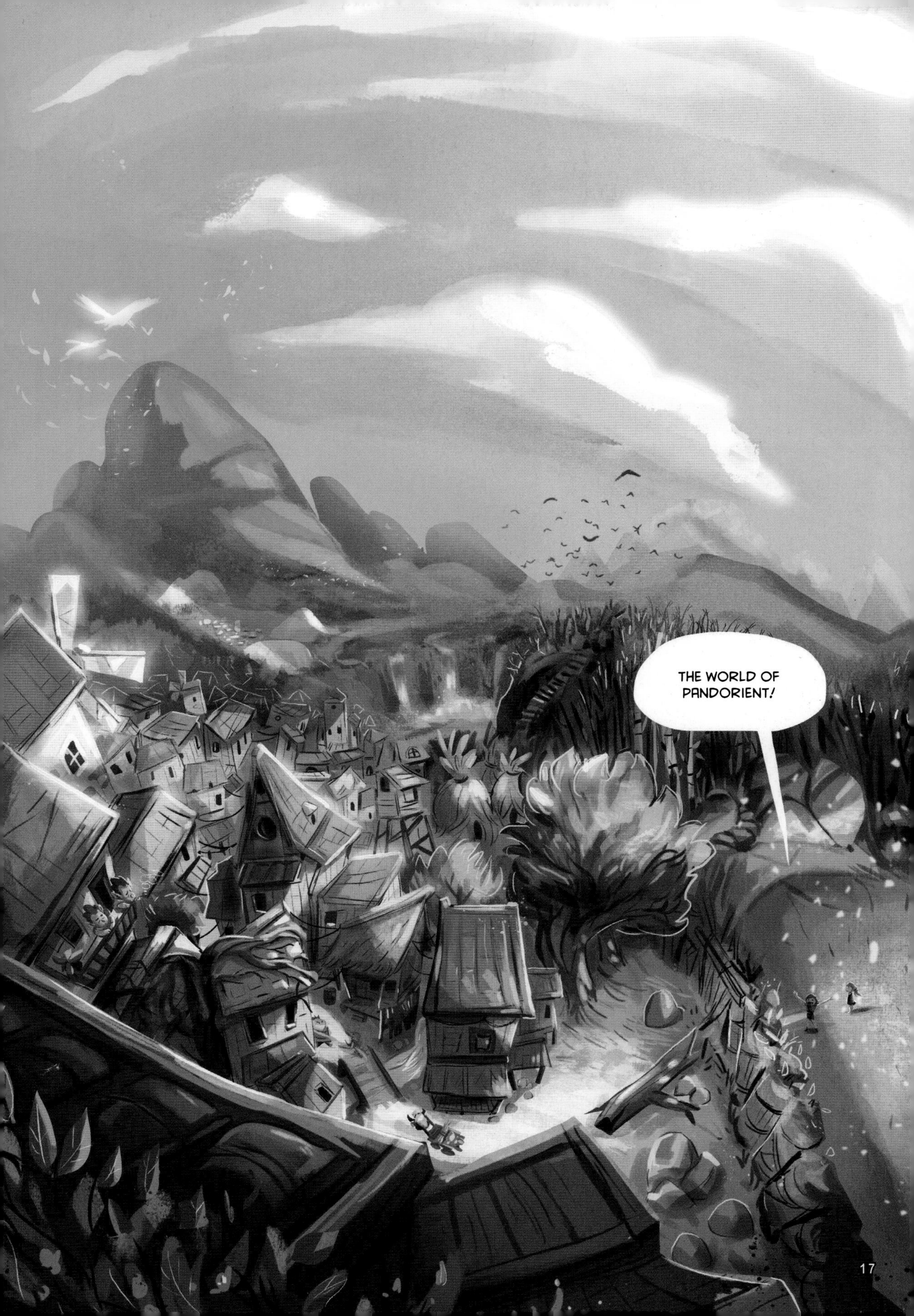
THE WORLD OF PANDORIENT!

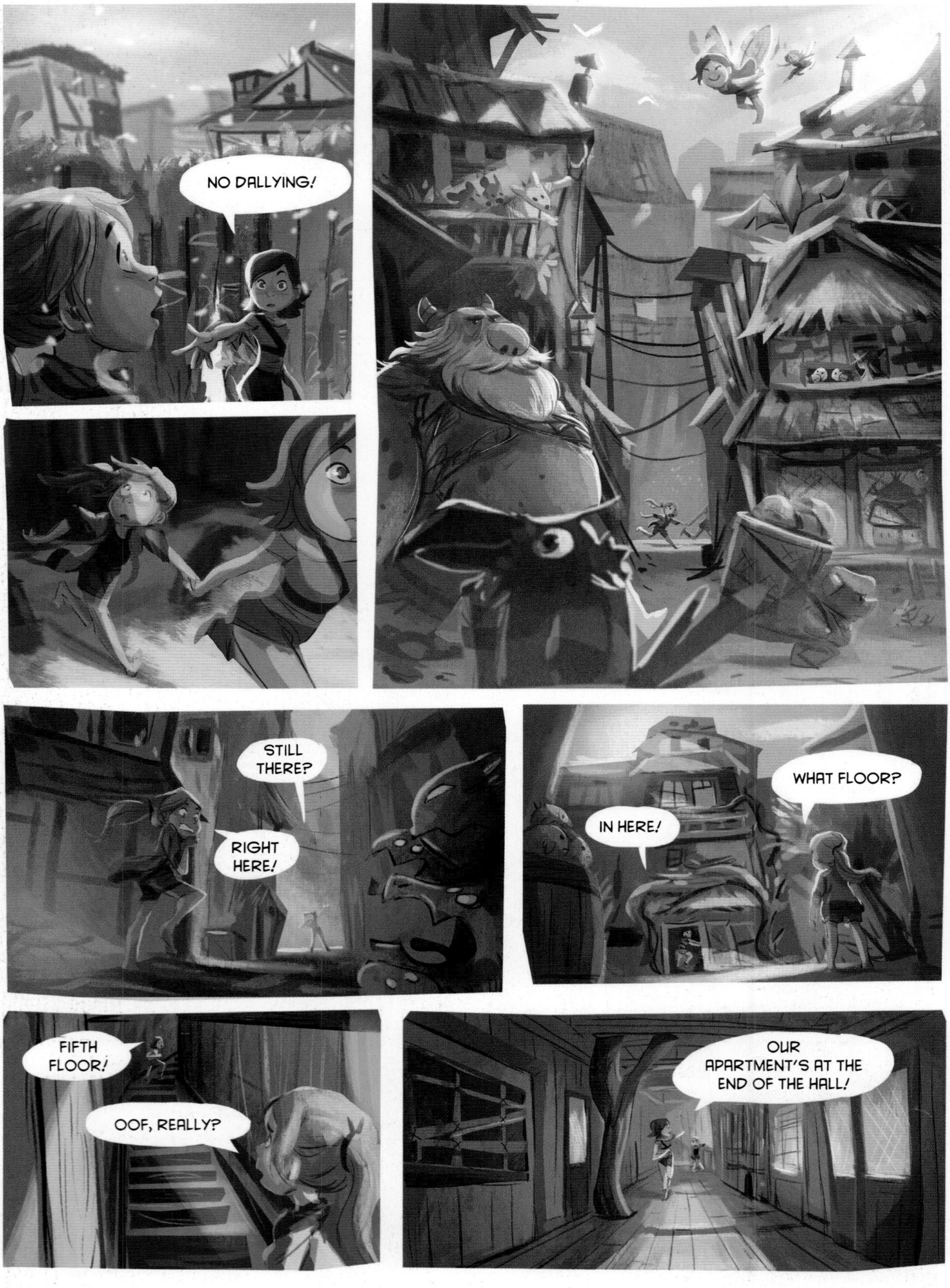
NO DALLYING!
STILL THERE?
RIGHT HERE!
WHAT FLOOR?
IN HERE!
FIFTH FLOOR!
OOF, REALLY?
OUR APARTMENT'S AT THE END OF THE HALL!

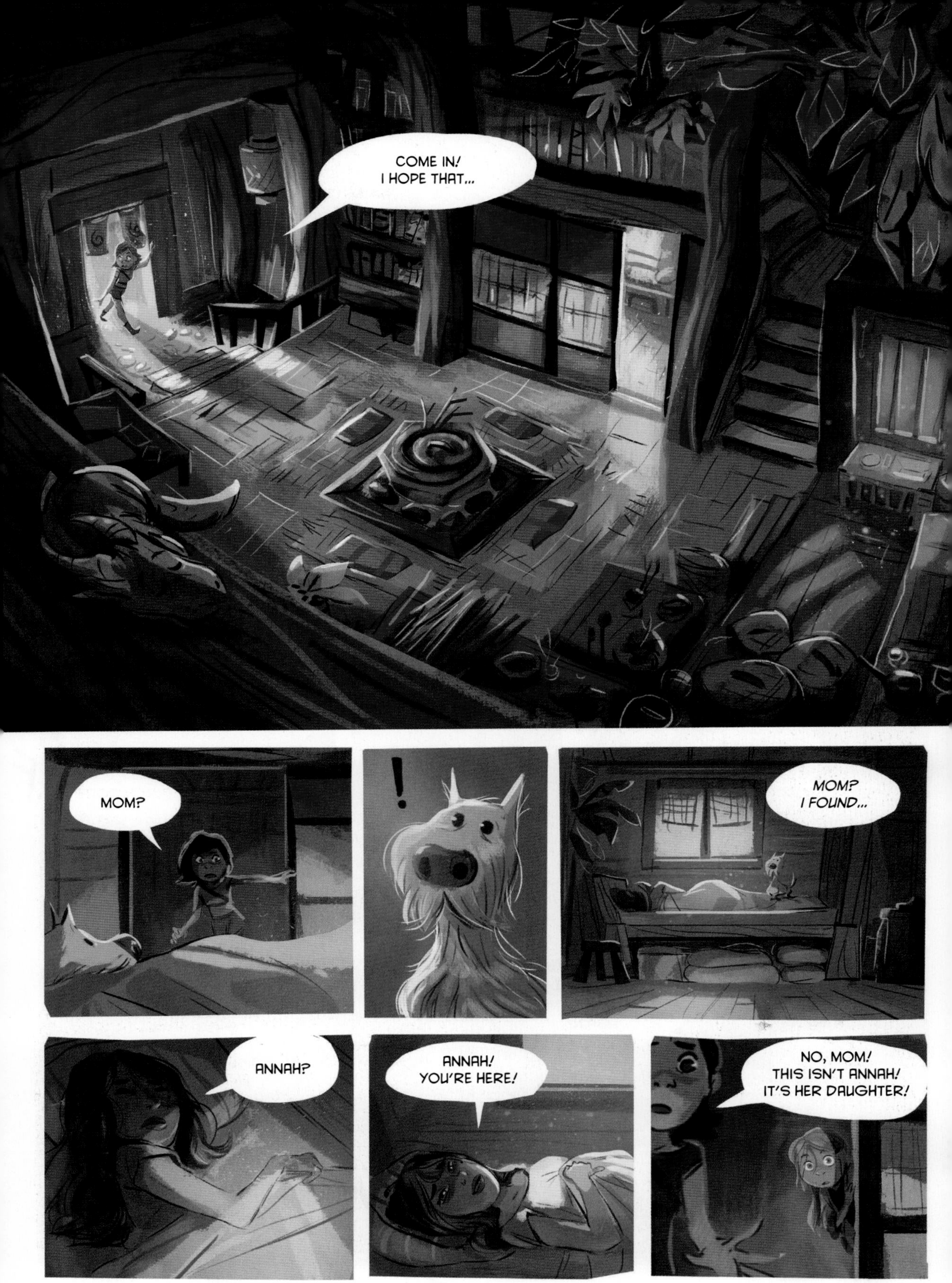
COME IN!
I HOPE THAT...
MOM?
!
MOM?
I FOUND...
ANNAH?
ANNAH!
YOU'RE HERE!
NO, MOM!
THIS ISN'T ANNAH!
IT'S HER DAUGHTER!

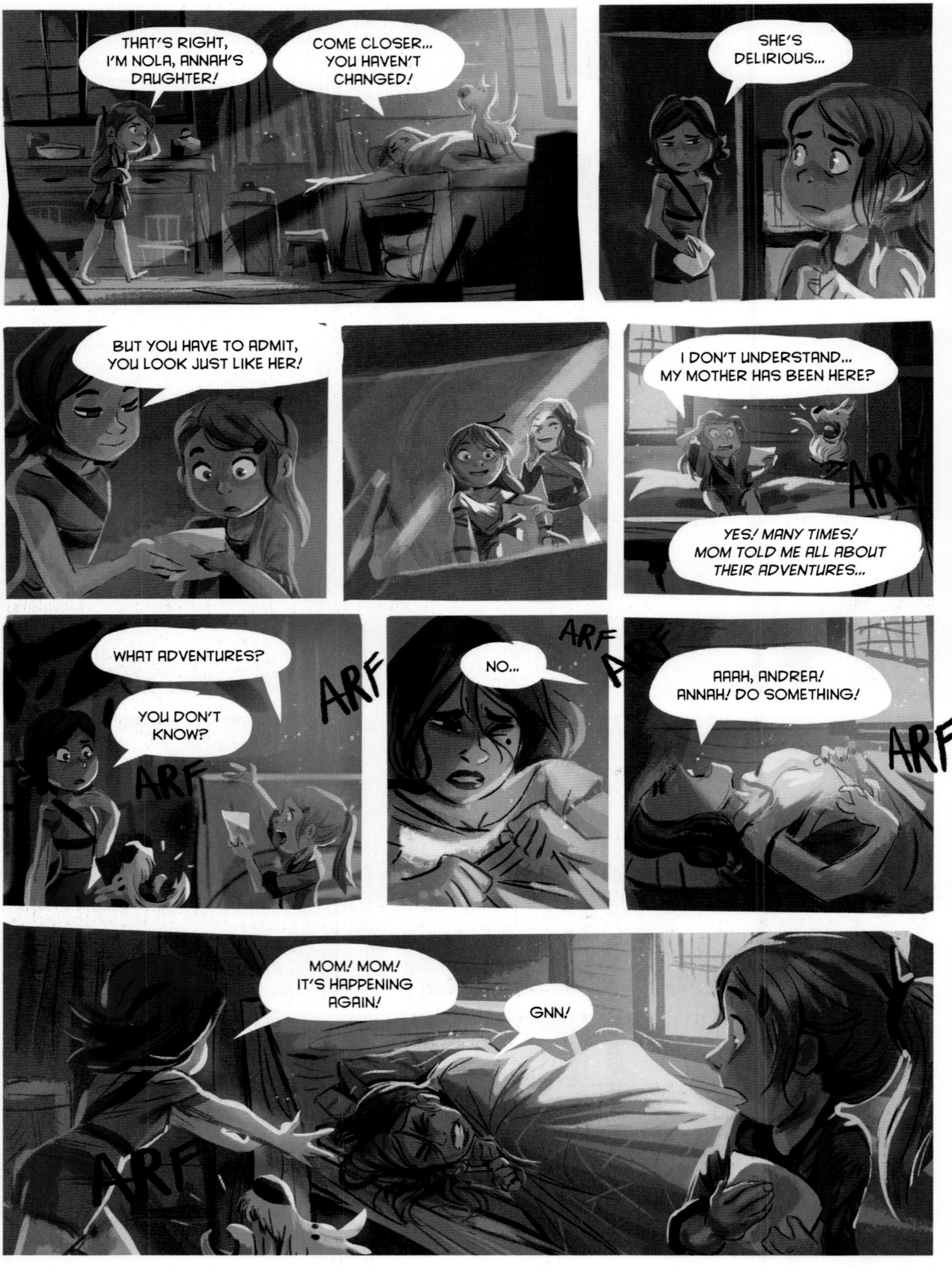
THAT'S RIGHT, I'M NOLA, ANNAH'S DAUGHTER!
COME CLOSER... YOU HAVEN'T CHANGED!
SHE'S DELIRIOUS...
BUT YOU HAVE TO ADMIT, YOU LOOK JUST LIKE HER!
I DON'T UNDERSTAND... MY MOTHER HAS BEEN HERE?
ARF
YES! MANY TIMES! MOM TOLD ME ALL ABOUT THEIR ADVENTURES...
WHAT ADVENTURES?
ARF
YOU DON'T KNOW?
ARF
NO...
ARF
ARF
AAAH, ANDREA! ANNAH! DO SOMETHING!
ARF
MOM! MOM! IT'S HAPPENING AGAIN!
GNN!
ARF

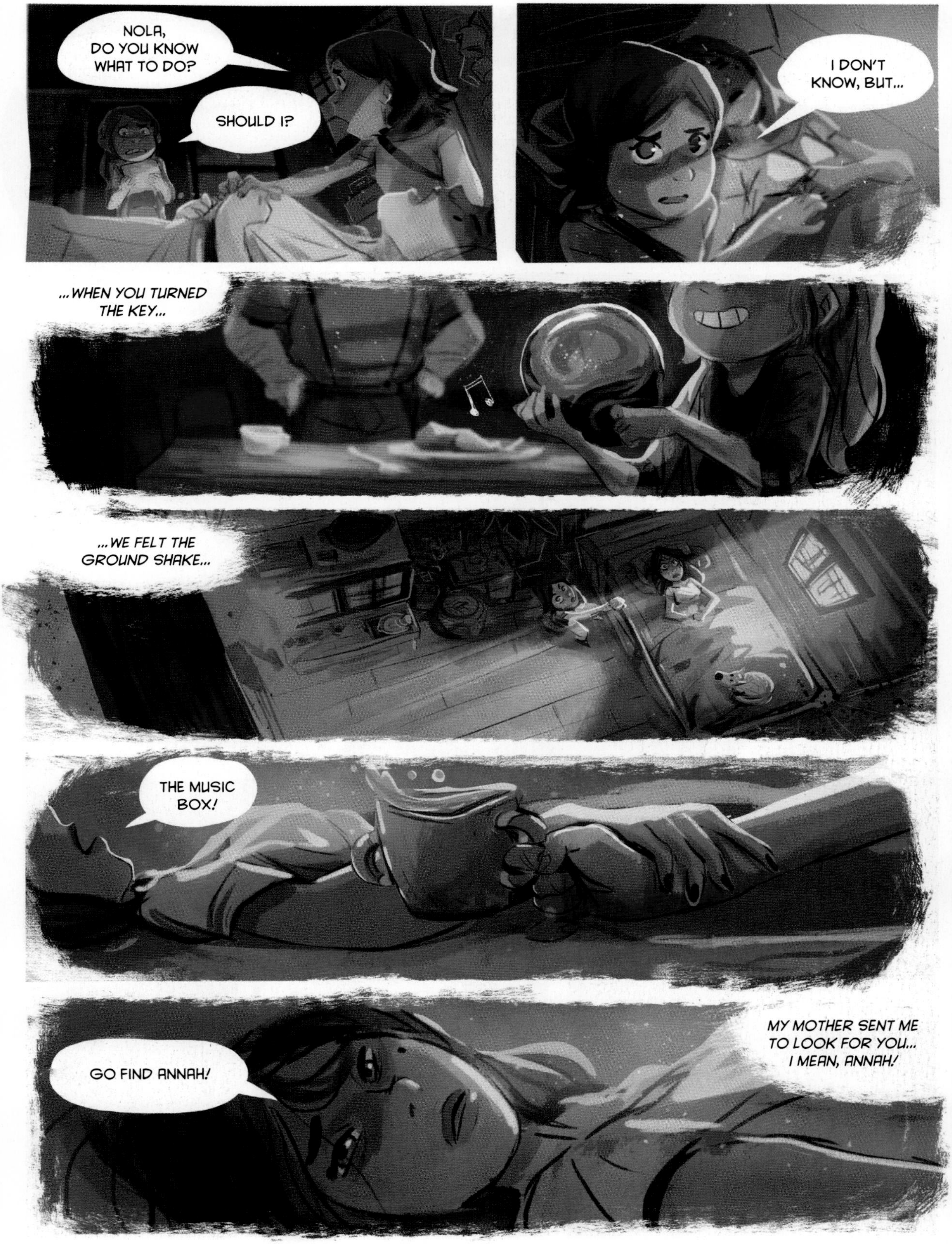
NOLA, DO YOU KNOW WHAT TO DO?
SHOULD I?
I DON'T KNOW, BUT...
...WHEN YOU TURNED THE KEY...
...WE FELT THE GROUND SHAKE...
THE MUSIC BOX!
MY MOTHER SENT ME TO LOOK FOR YOU... I MEAN, ANNAH!
GO FIND ANNAH!

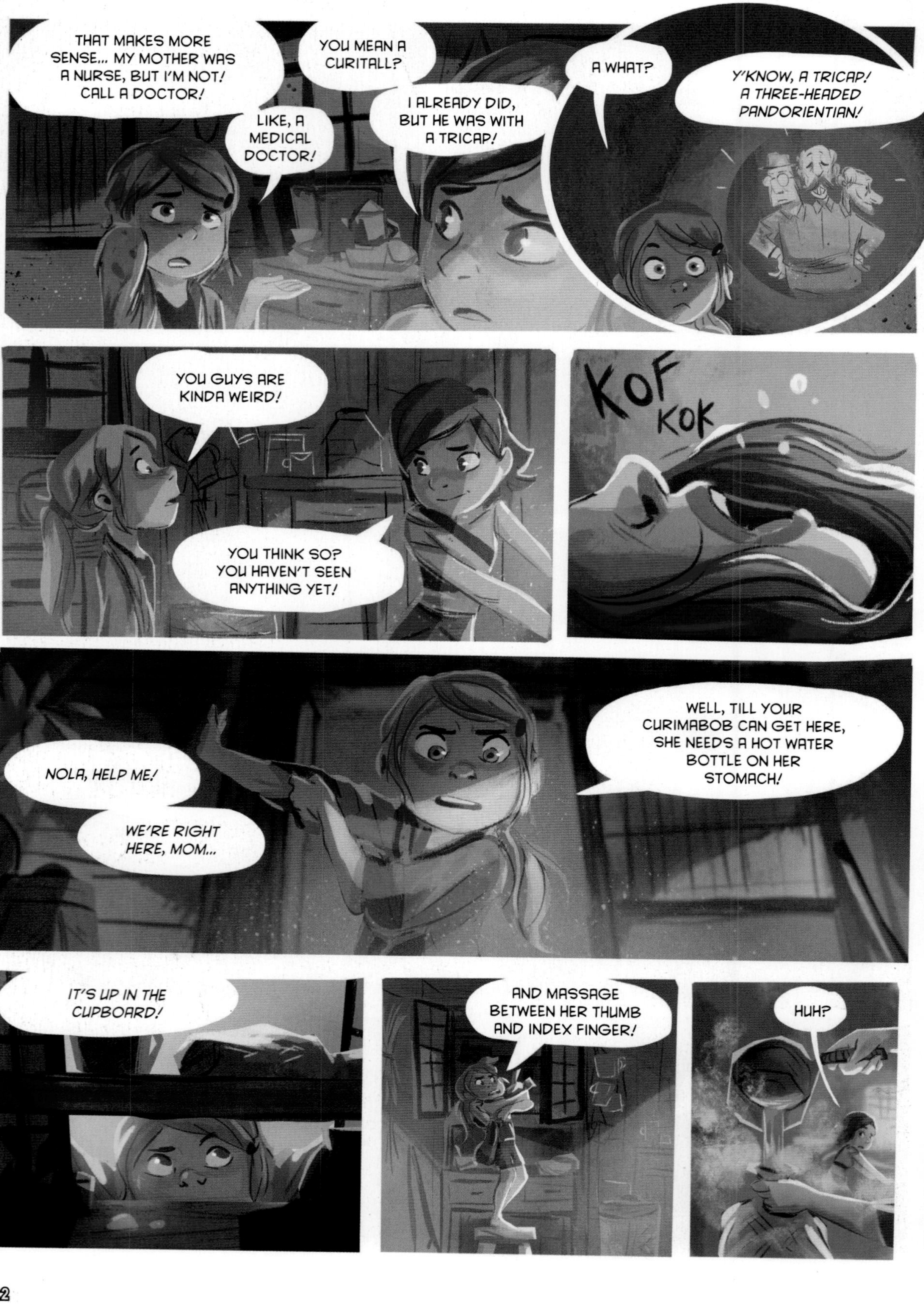

THAT MAKES MORE SENSE... MY MOTHER WAS A NURSE, BUT I'M NOT! CALL A DOCTOR!
YOU MEAN A CURITALL?
LIKE, A MEDICAL DOCTOR!
I ALREADY DID, BUT HE WAS WITH A TRICAP!
A WHAT?
Y'KNOW, A TRICAP! A THREE-HEADED PANDORIENTIAN!
YOU GUYS ARE KINDA WEIRD!
YOU THINK SO? YOU HAVEN'T SEEN ANYTHING YET!
KOF
KOK
NOLA, HELP ME!
WE'RE RIGHT HERE, MOM...
WELL, TILL YOUR CURIMABOB CAN GET HERE, SHE NEEDS A HOT WATER BOTTLE ON HER STOMACH!
IT'S UP IN THE CUPBOARD!
AND MASSAGE BETWEEN HER THUMB AND INDEX FINGER!
HUH?

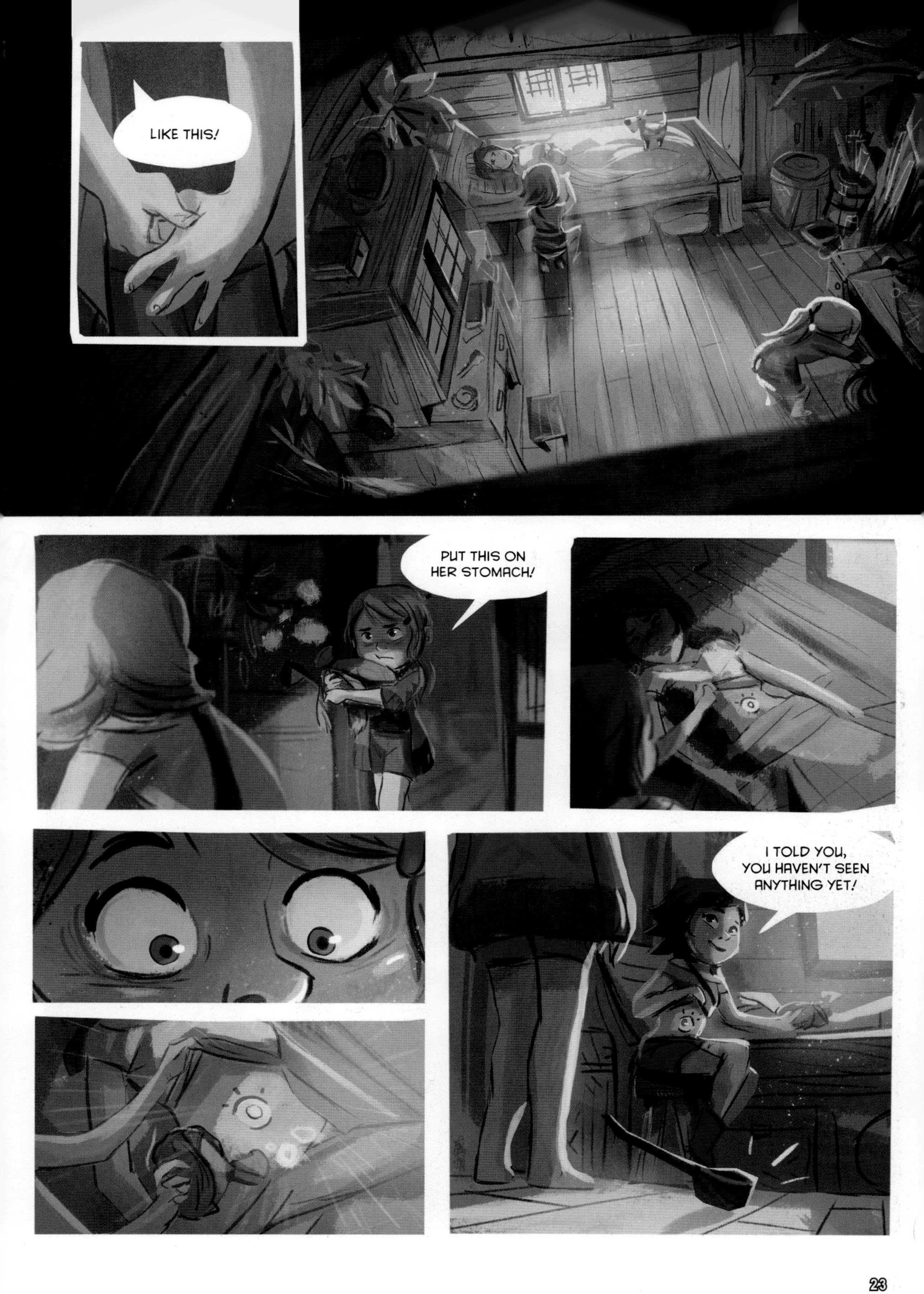
LIKE THIS!
PUT THIS ON HER STOMACH!
I TOLD YOU, YOU HAVEN'T SEEN ANYTHING YET!

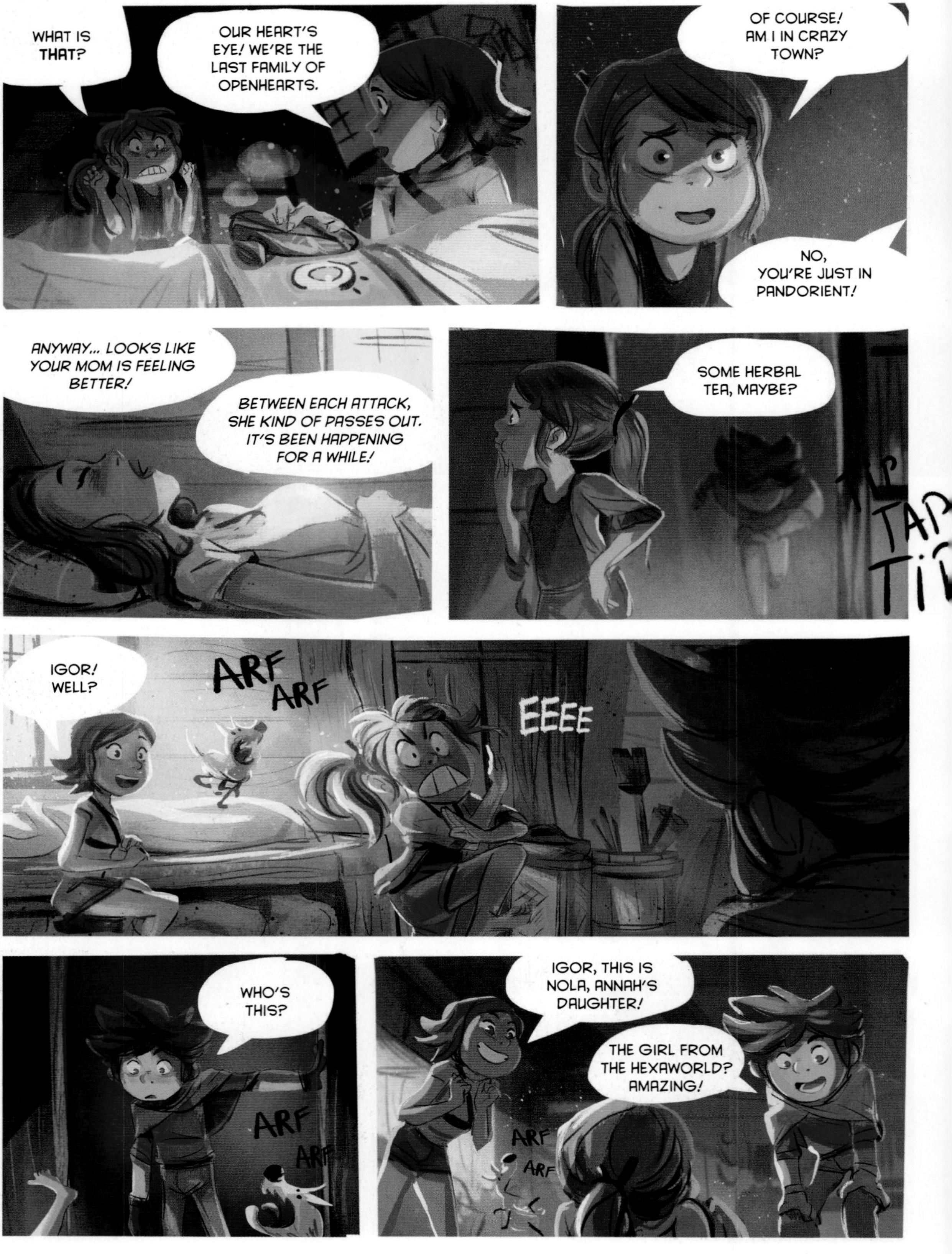
WHAT IS THAT?
OUR HEART'S EYE! WE'RE THE LAST FAMILY OF OPENHEARTS.
OF COURSE! AM I IN CRAZY TOWN?
NO, YOU'RE JUST IN PANDORIENT!
ANYWAY... LOOKS LIKE YOUR MOM IS FEELING BETTER!
BETWEEN EACH ATTACK, SHE KIND OF PASSES OUT. IT'S BEEN HAPPENING FOR A WHILE!
SOME HERBAL TEA, MAYBE?
IGOR! WELL?
ARF ARF
EEEE
WHO'S THIS?
ARF ARF
IGOR, THIS IS NOLA, ANNAH'S DAUGHTER!
THE GIRL FROM THE HEXAWORLD? AMAZING!
ARF ARF

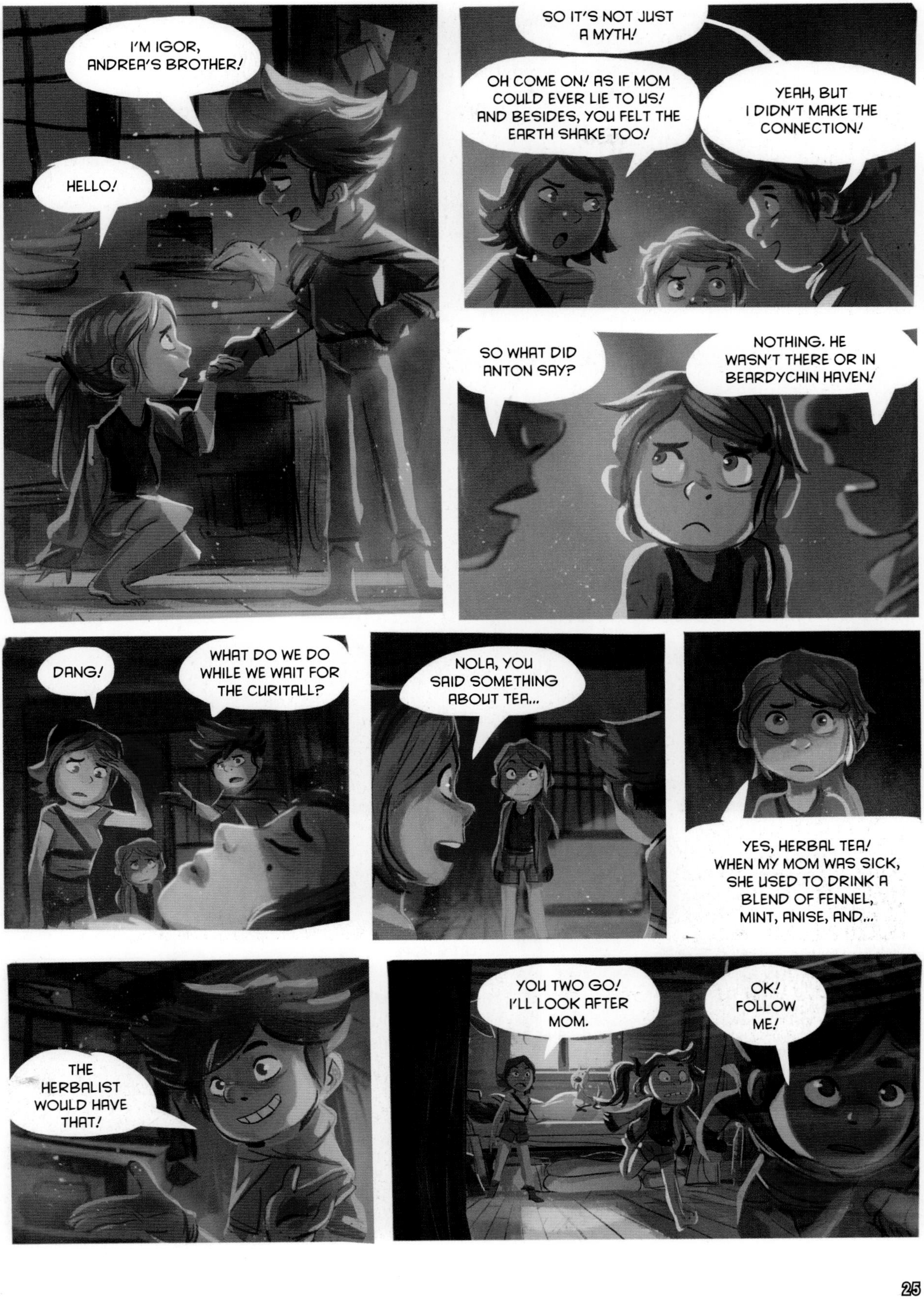
I'M IGOR, ANDREA'S BROTHER!
HELLO!
SO IT'S NOT JUST A MYTH!
OH COME ON! AS IF MOM COULD EVER LIE TO US! AND BESIDES, YOU FELT THE EARTH SHAKE TOO!
YEAH, BUT I DIDN'T MAKE THE CONNECTION!
SO WHAT DID ANTON SAY?
NOTHING. HE WASN'T THERE OR IN BEARDYCHIN HAVEN!
DANG!
WHAT DO WE DO WHILE WE WAIT FOR THE CURITALL?
NOLA, YOU SAID SOMETHING ABOUT TEA...
YES, HERBAL TEA! WHEN MY MOM WAS SICK, SHE USED TO DRINK A BLEND OF FENNEL, MINT, ANISE, AND...
THE HERBALIST WOULD HAVE THAT!
YOU TWO GO! I'LL LOOK AFTER MOM.
OK! FOLLOW ME!

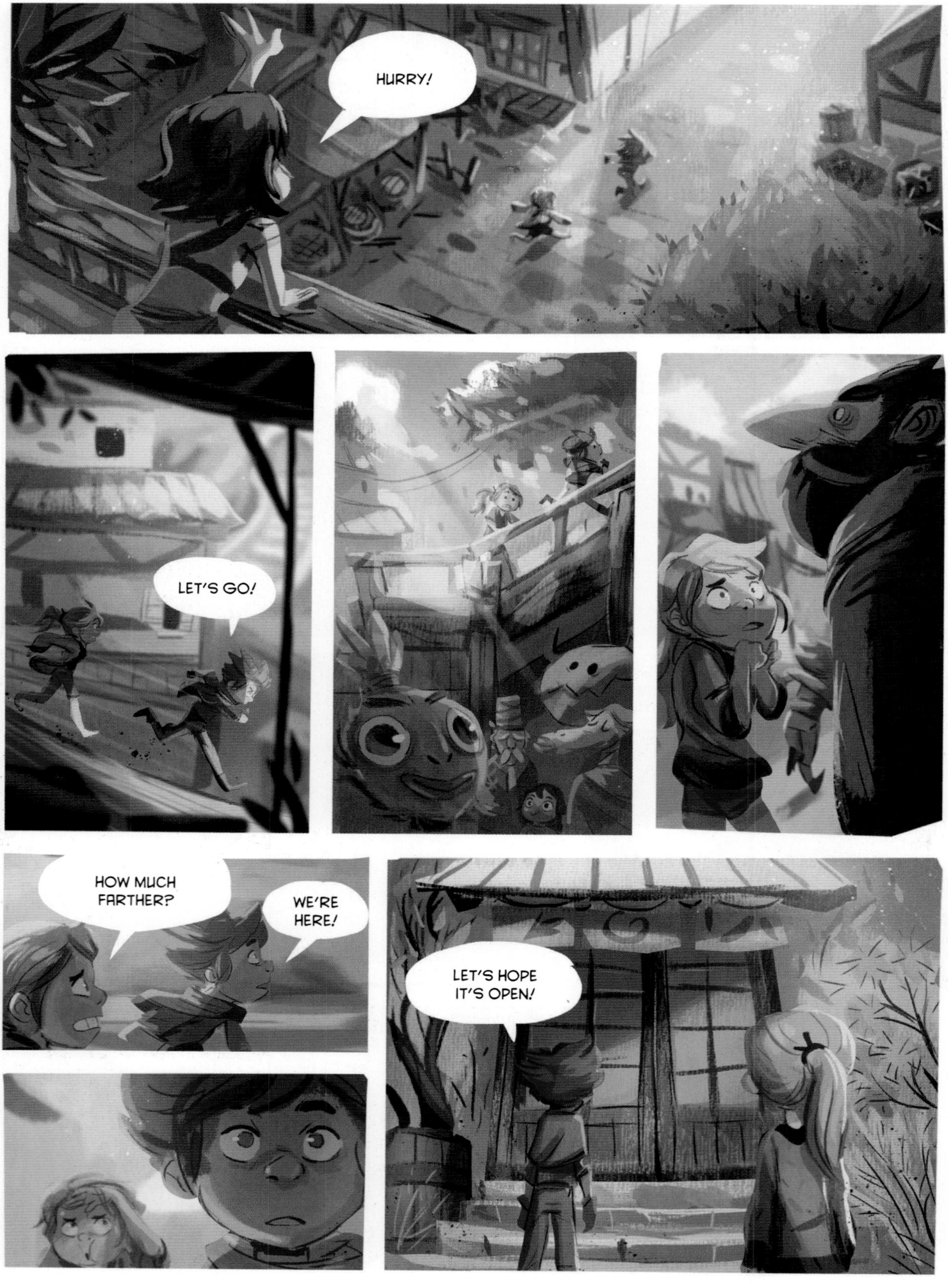
HURRY!
LET'S GO!
HOW MUCH FARTHER?
WE'RE HERE!
LET'S HOPE IT'S OPEN!

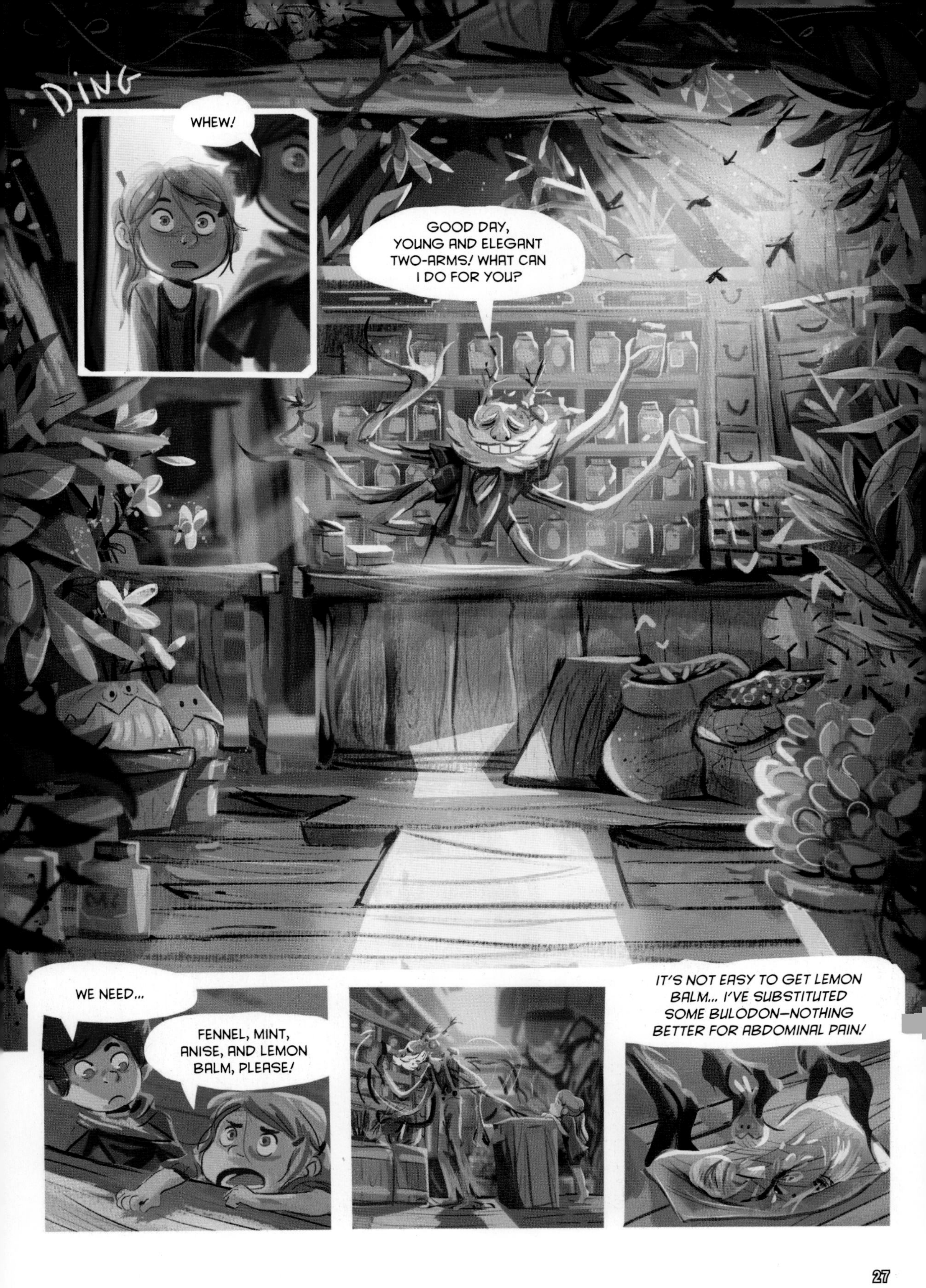
DING
WHEW!
GOOD DAY, YOUNG AND ELEGANT TWO-ARMS! WHAT CAN I DO FOR YOU?
WE NEED...
FENNEL, MINT, ANISE, AND LEMON BALM, PLEASE!
IT'S NOT EASY TO GET LEMON BALM... I'VE SUBSTITUTED SOME BULODON—NOTHING BETTER FOR ABDOMINAL PAIN!

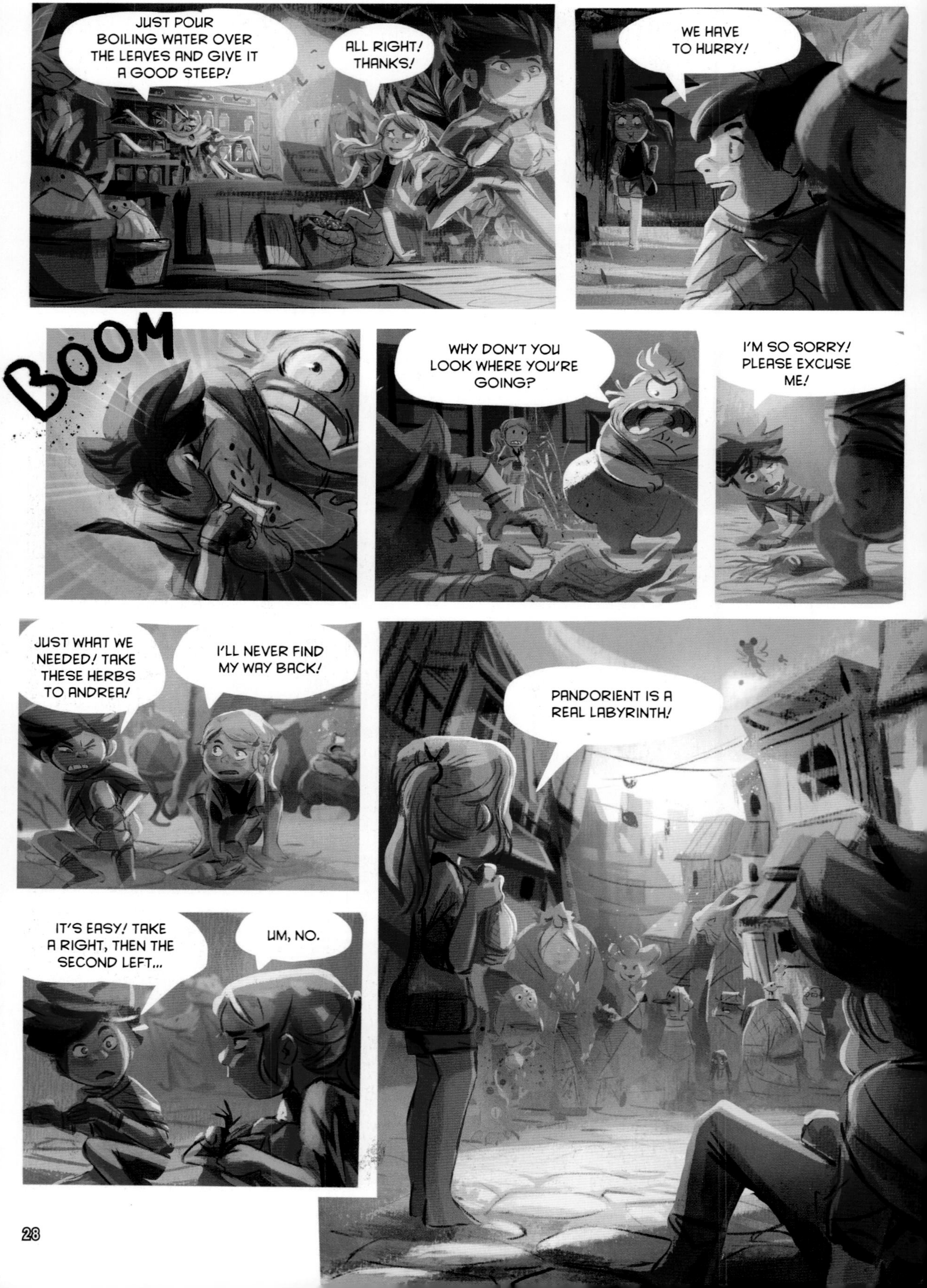
JUST POUR BOILING WATER OVER THE LEAVES AND GIVE IT A GOOD STEEP!
ALL RIGHT! THANKS!
WE HAVE TO HURRY!
BOOM
WHY DON'T YOU LOOK WHERE YOU'RE GOING?
I'M SO SORRY! PLEASE EXCUSE ME!
JUST WHAT WE NEEDED! TAKE THESE HERBS TO ANDREA!
I'LL NEVER FIND MY WAY BACK!
IT'S EASY! TAKE A RIGHT, THEN THE SECOND LEFT...
UM, NO.
PANDORIENT IS A REAL LABYRINTH!

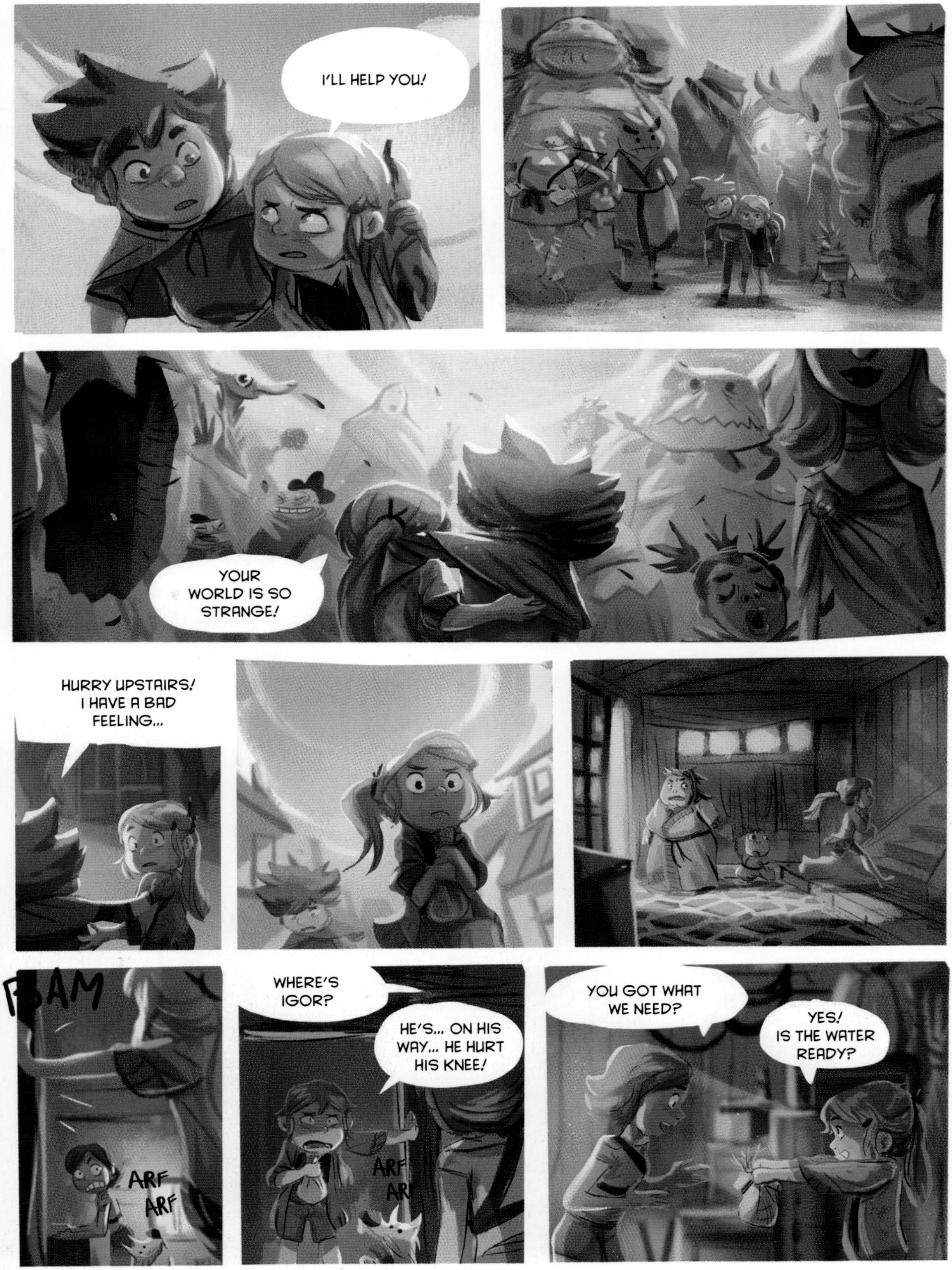
I'LL HELP YOU!
YOUR WORLD IS SO STRANGE!
HURRY UPSTAIRS! I HAVE A BAD FEELING...
BAM
ARF ARF
WHERE'S IGOR?
HE'S... ON HIS WAY... HE HURT HIS KNEE!
ARF ARF
YOU GOT WHAT WE NEED?
YES! IS THE WATER READY?

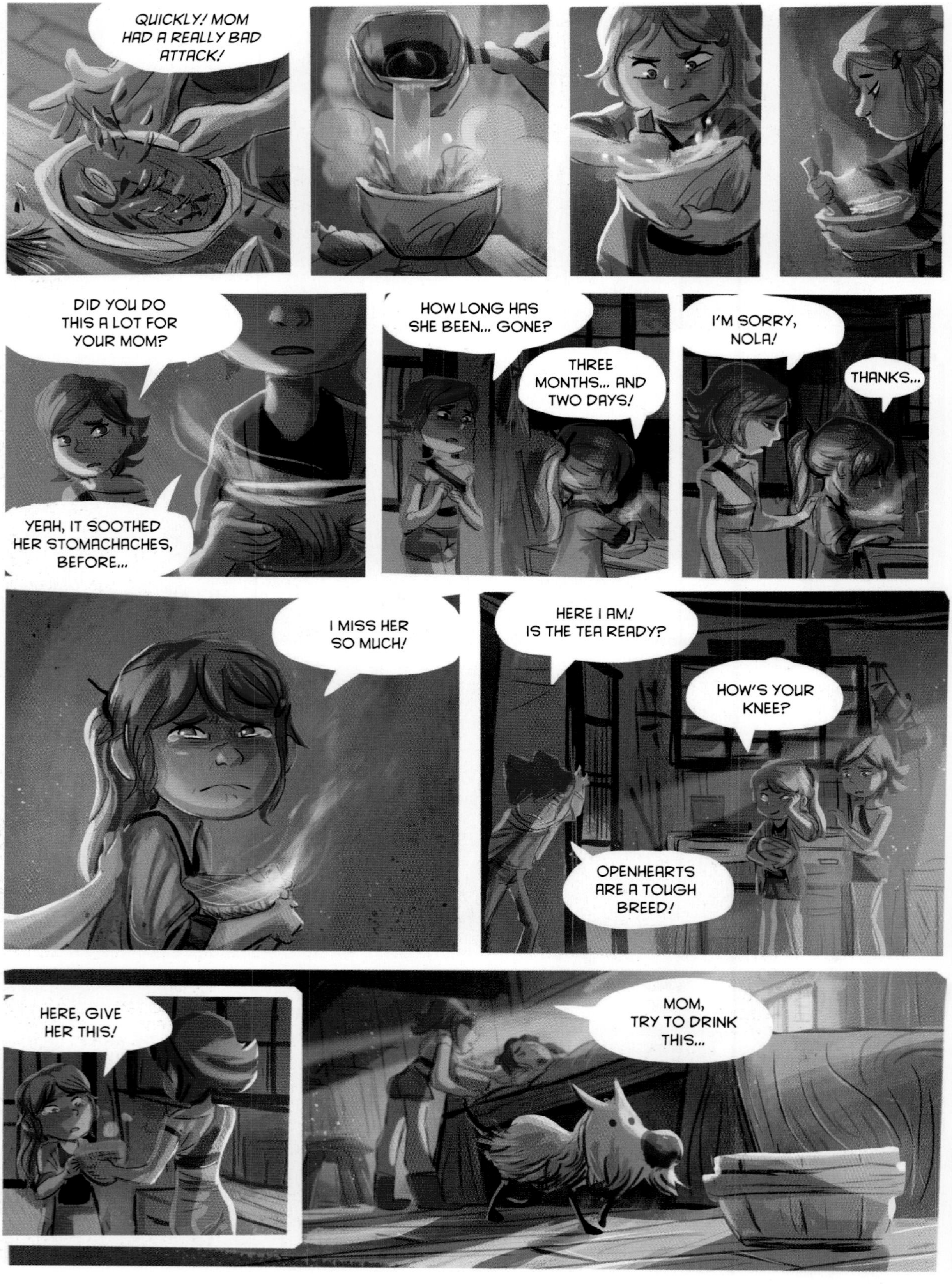

QUICKLY! MOM HAD A REALLY BAD ATTACK!
DID YOU DO THIS A LOT FOR YOUR MOM?
YEAH, IT SOOTHED HER STOMACHACHES, BEFORE...
HOW LONG HAS SHE BEEN... GONE?
THREE MONTHS... AND TWO DAYS!
I'M SORRY, NOLA!
THANKS...
I MISS HER SO MUCH!
HERE I AM! IS THE TEA READY?
HOW'S YOUR KNEE?
OPENHEARTS ARE A TOUGH BREED!
HERE, GIVE HER THIS!
MOM, TRY TO DRINK THIS...

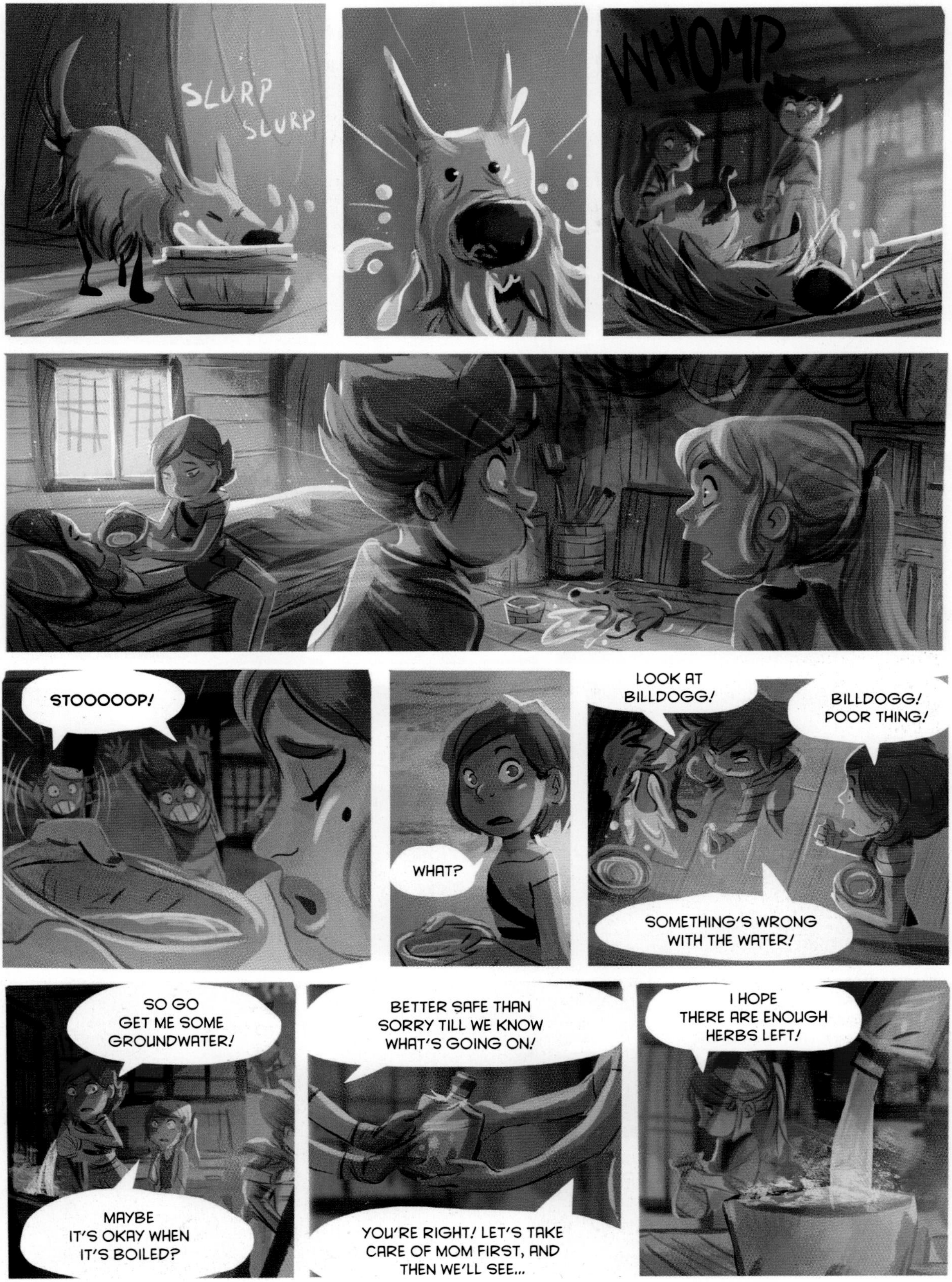
SLURP
SLURP
WHOMP
STOOOOOP!
WHAT?
LOOK AT BILLDOGG!
BILLDOGG! POOR THING!
SOMETHING'S WRONG WITH THE WATER!
SO GO GET ME SOME GROUNDWATER!
MAYBE IT'S OKAY WHEN IT'S BOILED?
BETTER SAFE THAN SORRY TILL WE KNOW WHAT'S GOING ON!
YOU'RE RIGHT! LET'S TAKE CARE OF MOM FIRST, AND THEN WE'LL SEE...
I HOPE THERE ARE ENOUGH HERBS LEFT!

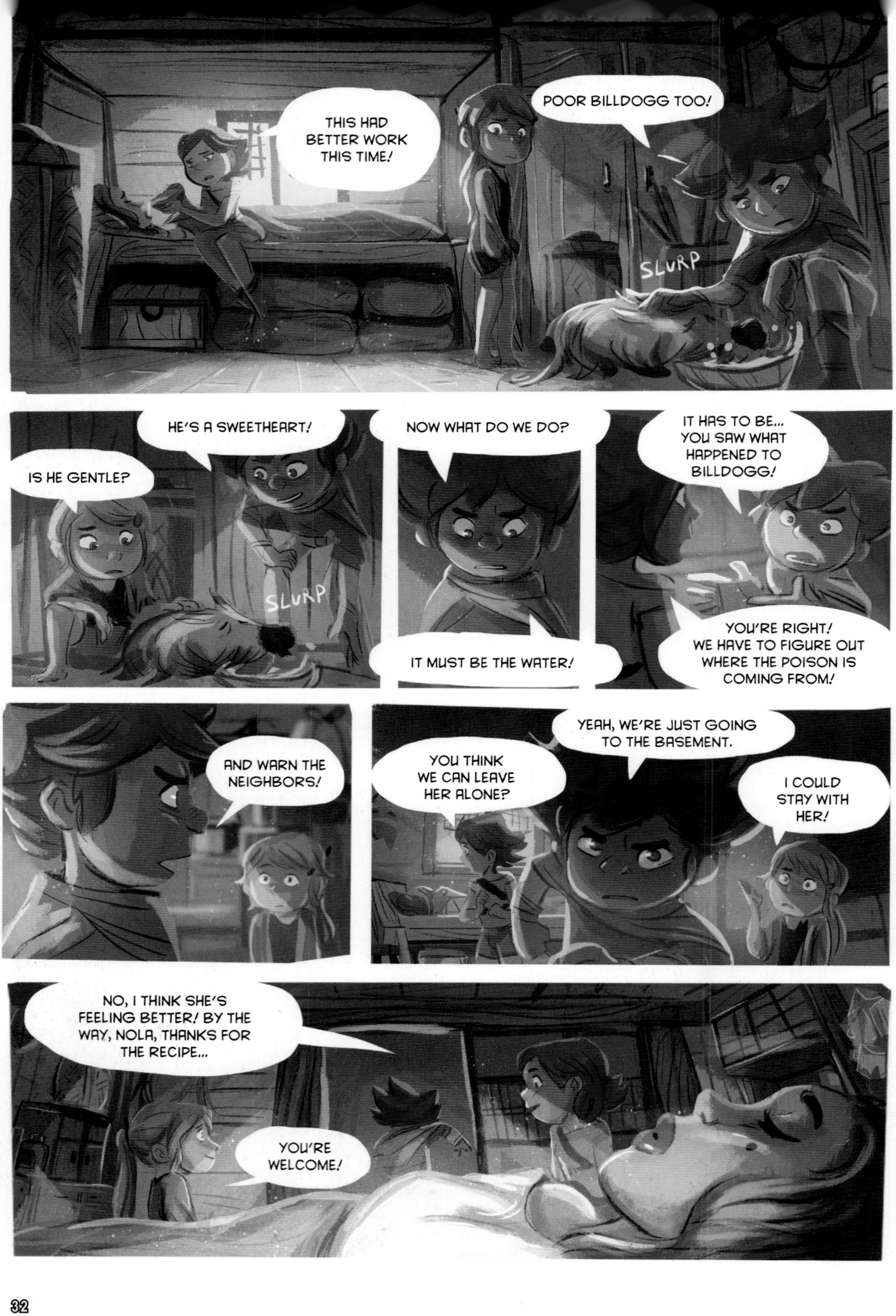
THIS HAD BETTER WORK THIS TIME!
POOR BILLDOGG TOO!
SLURP
IS HE GENTLE?
HE'S A SWEETHEART!
SLURP
NOW WHAT DO WE DO?
IT MUST BE THE WATER!
IT HAS TO BE... YOU SAW WHAT HAPPENED TO BILLDOGG!
YOU'RE RIGHT! WE HAVE TO FIGURE OUT WHERE THE POISON IS COMING FROM!
AND WARN THE NEIGHBORS!
YOU THINK WE CAN LEAVE HER ALONE?
YEAH, WE'RE JUST GOING TO THE BASEMENT.
I COULD STAY WITH HER!
NO, I THINK SHE'S FEELING BETTER! BY THE WAY, NOLA, THANKS FOR THE RECIPE...
YOU'RE WELCOME!

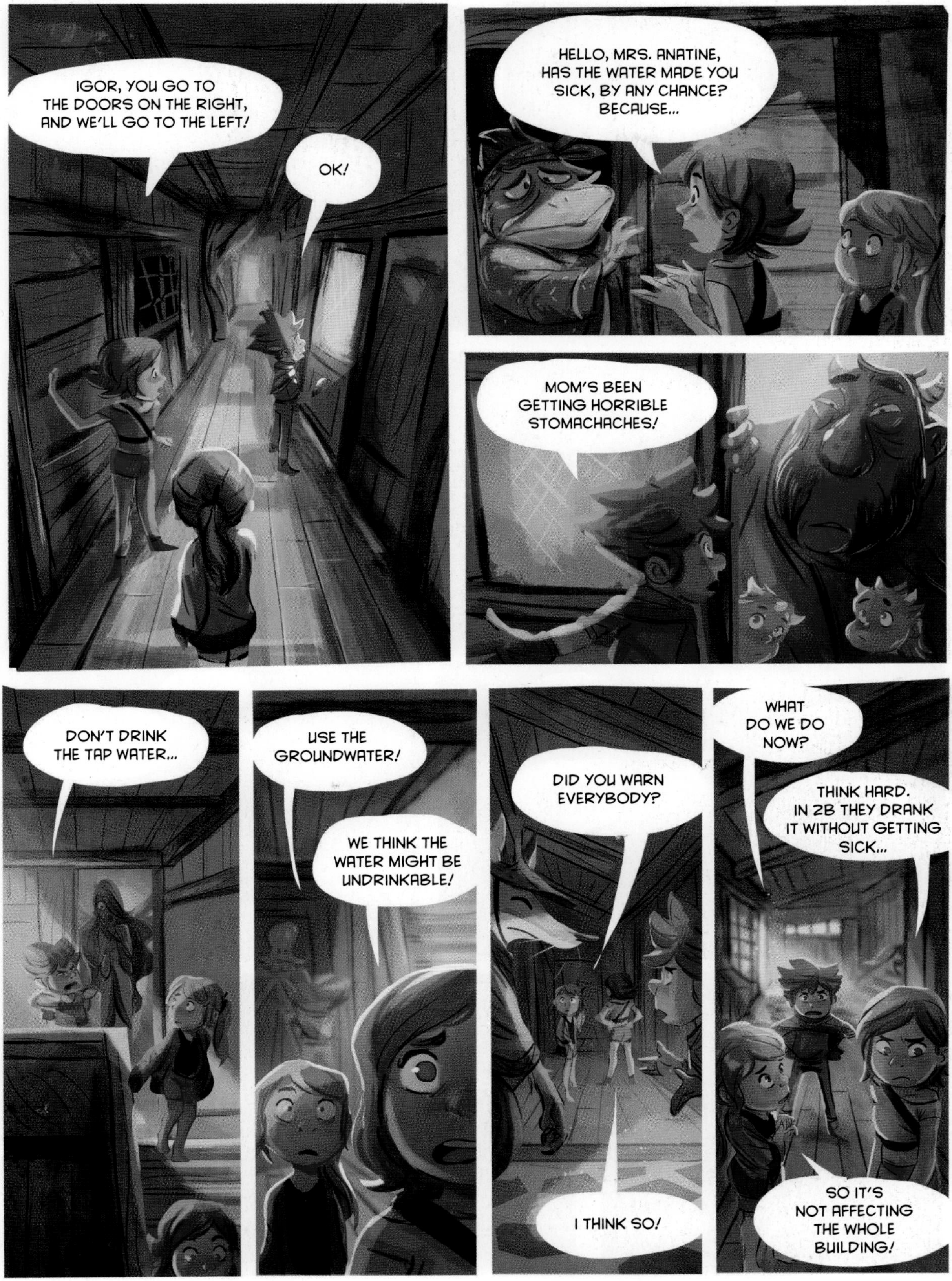
IGOR, YOU GO TO THE DOORS ON THE RIGHT, AND WE'LL GO TO THE LEFT!
OK!
HELLO, MRS. ANATINE, HAS THE WATER MADE YOU SICK, BY ANY CHANCE? BECAUSE...
MOM'S BEEN GETTING HORRIBLE STOMACHACHES!
DON'T DRINK THE TAP WATER...
USE THE GROUNDWATER!
WE THINK THE WATER MIGHT BE UNDRINKABLE!
DID YOU WARN EVERYBODY?
I THINK SO!
WHAT DO WE DO NOW?
THINK HARD. IN 2B THEY DRANK IT WITHOUT GETTING SICK...
SO IT'S NOT AFFECTING THE WHOLE BUILDING!

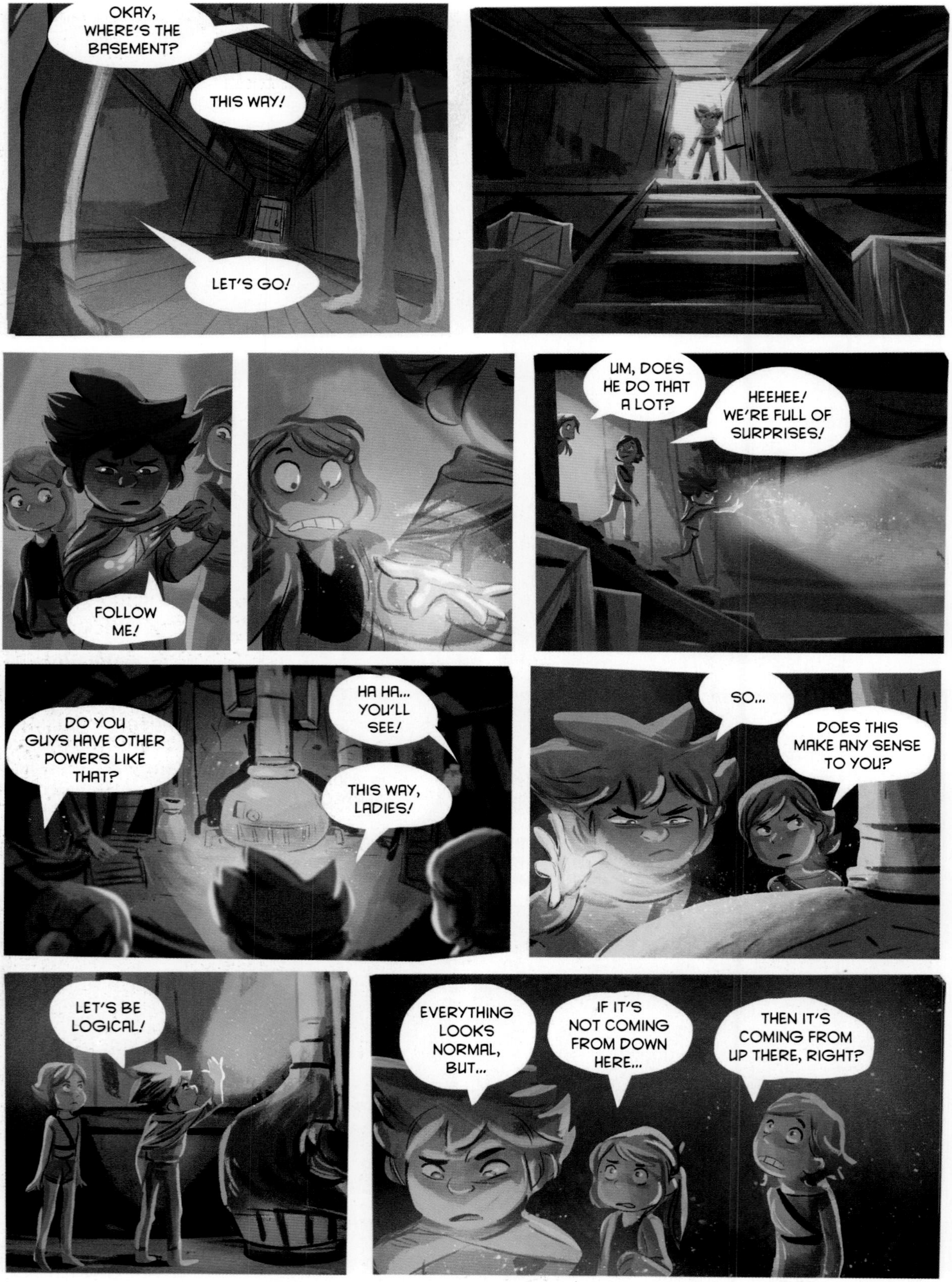
OKAY, WHERE'S THE BASEMENT?
THIS WAY!
LET'S GO!
FOLLOW ME!
UM, DOES HE DO THAT A LOT?
HEEHEE! WE'RE FULL OF SURPRISES!
DO YOU GUYS HAVE OTHER POWERS LIKE THAT?
HA HA... YOU'LL SEE!
THIS WAY, LADIES!
SO...
DOES THIS MAKE ANY SENSE TO YOU?
LET'S BE LOGICAL!
EVERYTHING LOOKS NORMAL, BUT...
IF IT'S NOT COMING FROM DOWN HERE...
THEN IT'S COMING FROM UP THERE, RIGHT?

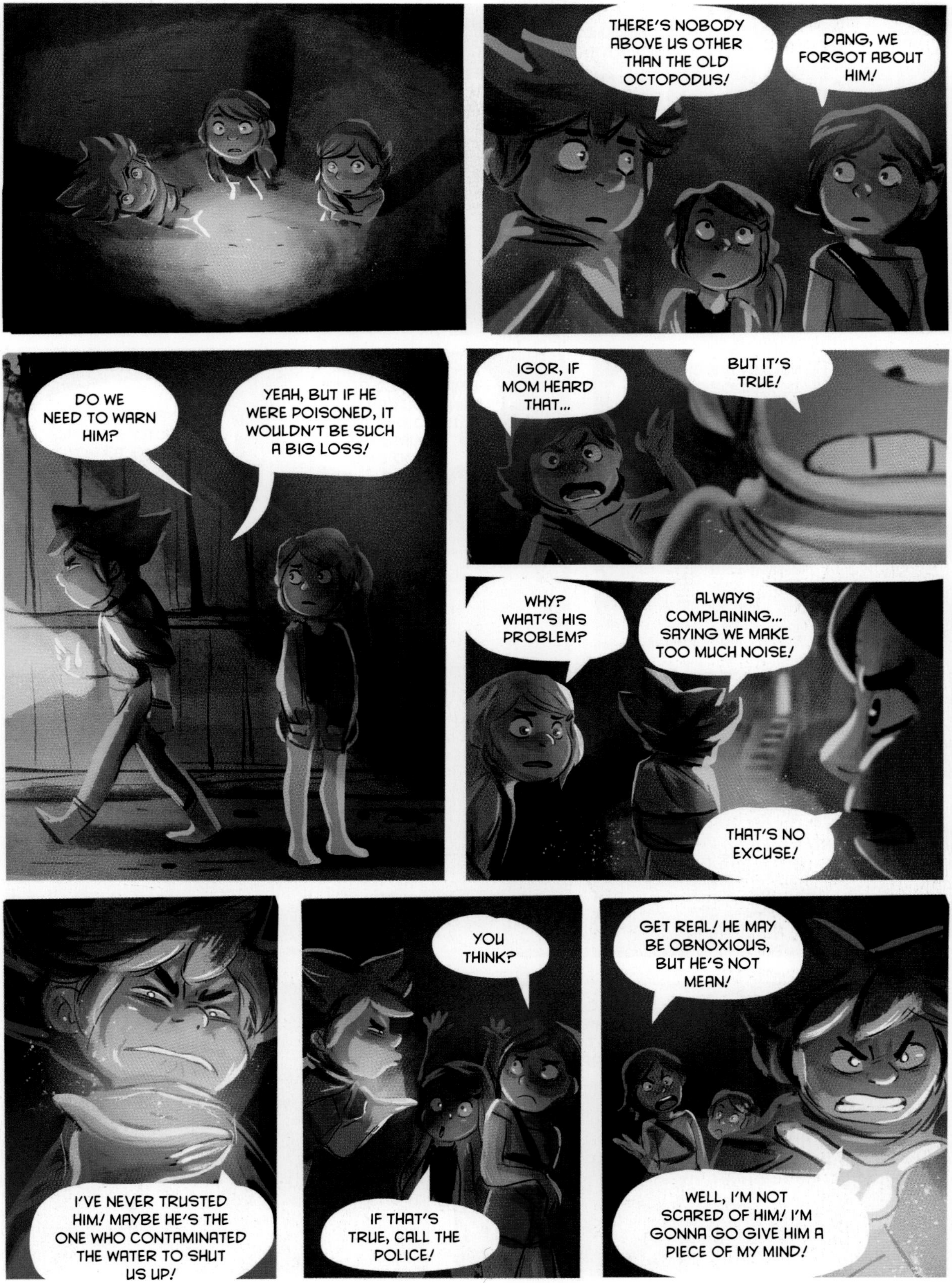

THERE'S NOBODY ABOVE US OTHER THAN THE OLD OCTOPODUS!
DANG, WE FORGOT ABOUT HIM!
DO WE NEED TO WARN HIM?
YEAH, BUT IF HE WERE POISONED, IT WOULDN'T BE SUCH A BIG LOSS!
IGOR, IF MOM HEARD THAT...
BUT IT'S TRUE!
WHY? WHAT'S HIS PROBLEM?
ALWAYS COMPLAINING... SAYING WE MAKE TOO MUCH NOISE!
THAT'S NO EXCUSE!
I'VE NEVER TRUSTED HIM! MAYBE HE'S THE ONE WHO CONTAMINATED THE WATER TO SHUT US UP!
YOU THINK?
IF THAT'S TRUE, CALL THE POLICE!
GET REAL! HE MAY BE OBNOXIOUS, BUT HE'S NOT MEAN!
WELL, I'M NOT SCARED OF HIM! I'M GONNA GO GIVE HIM A PIECE OF MY MIND!

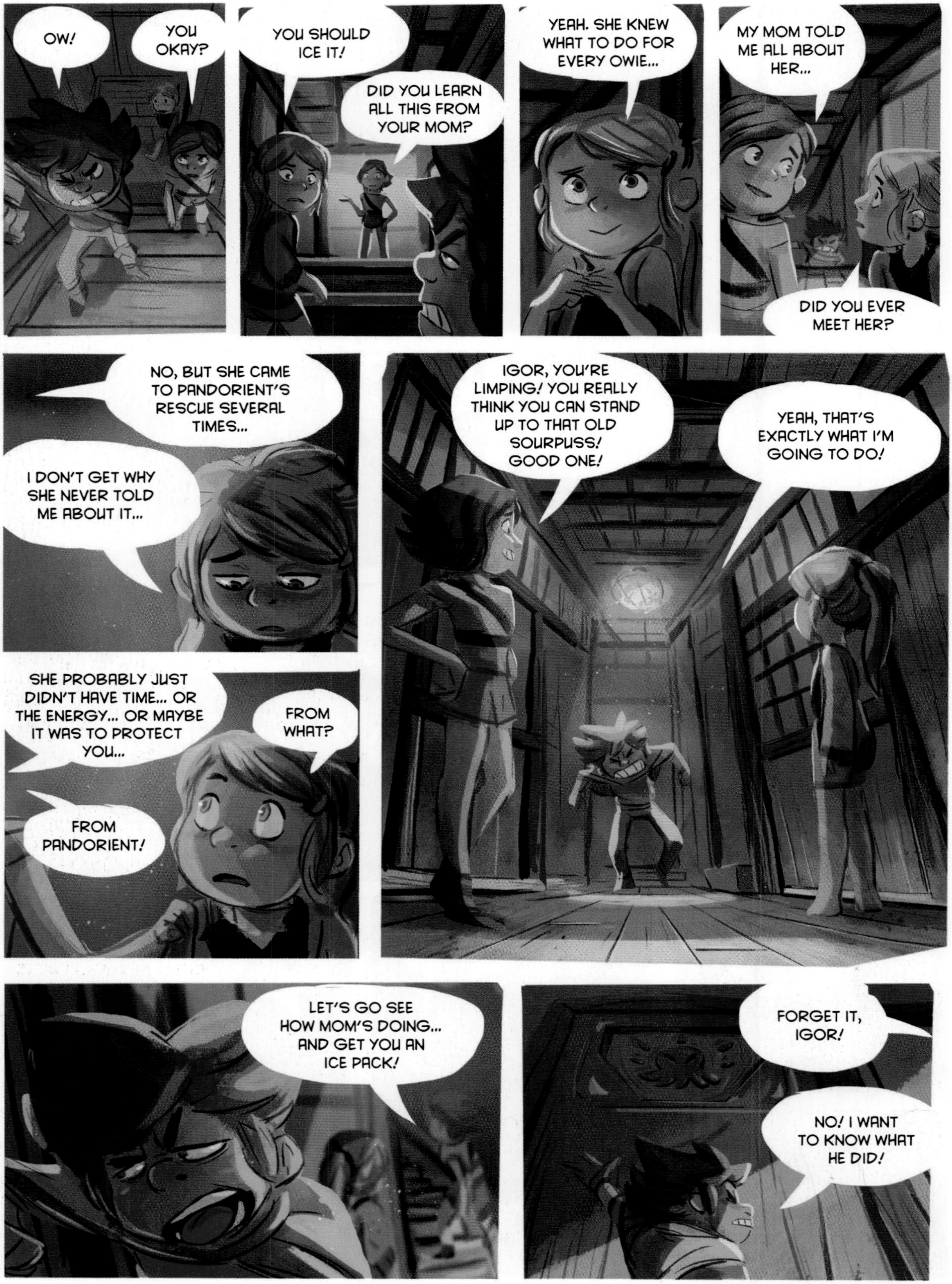
OW!
YOU OKAY?
YOU SHOULD ICE IT!
DID YOU LEARN ALL THIS FROM YOUR MOM?
YEAH. SHE KNEW WHAT TO DO FOR EVERY OWIE...
MY MOM TOLD ME ALL ABOUT HER...
DID YOU EVER MEET HER?
NO, BUT SHE CAME TO PANDORIENT'S RESCUE SEVERAL TIMES...
I DON'T GET WHY SHE NEVER TOLD ME ABOUT IT...
SHE PROBABLY JUST DIDN'T HAVE TIME... OR THE ENERGY... OR MAYBE IT WAS TO PROTECT YOU...
FROM WHAT?
FROM PANDORIENT!
IGOR, YOU'RE LIMPING! YOU REALLY THINK YOU CAN STAND UP TO THAT OLD SOURPUSS! GOOD ONE!
YEAH, THAT'S EXACTLY WHAT I'M GOING TO DO!
LET'S GO SEE HOW MOM'S DOING... AND GET YOU AN ICE PACK!
FORGET IT, IGOR!
NO! I WANT TO KNOW WHAT HE DID!

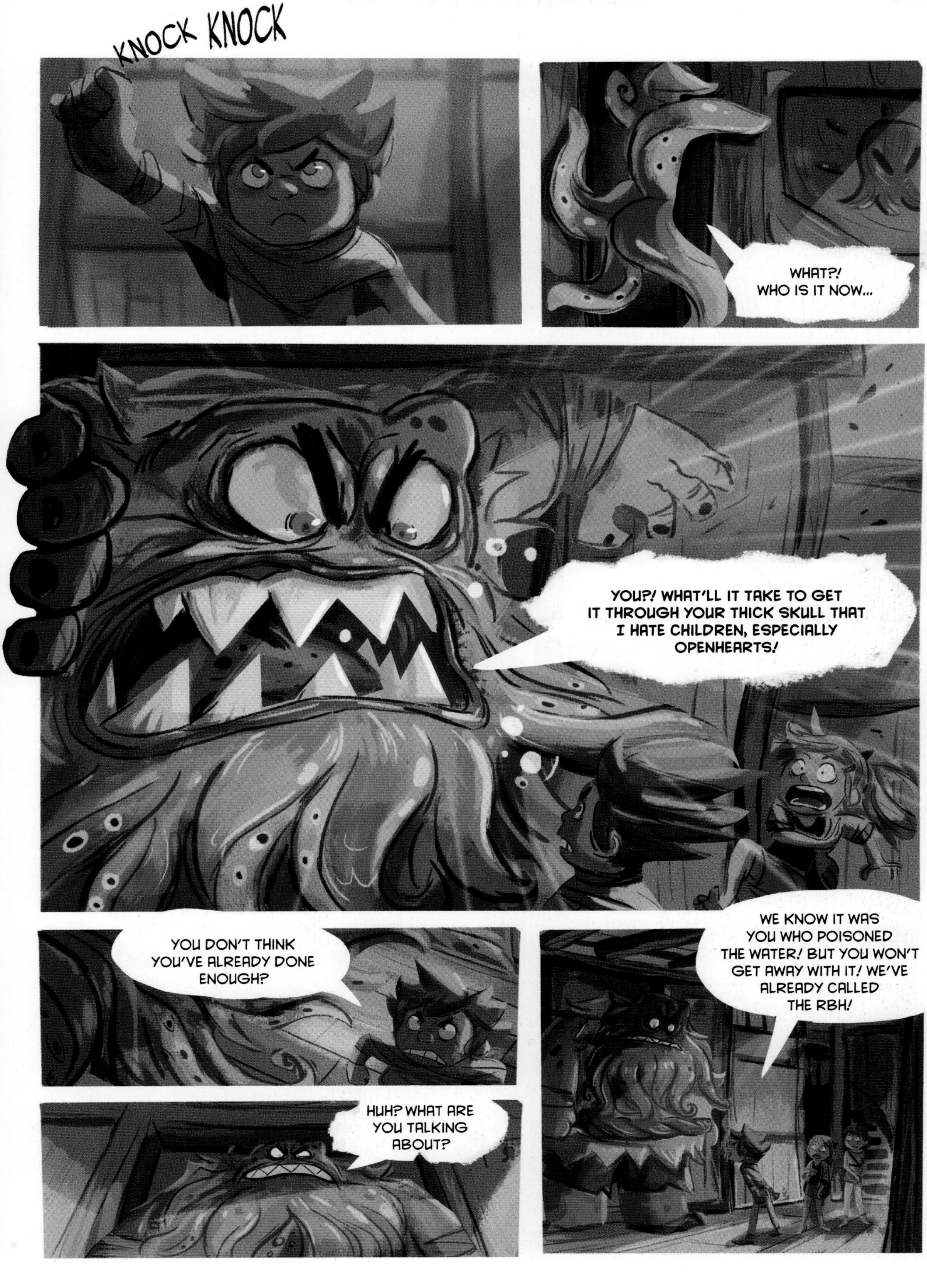
KNOCK KNOCK
WHAT?! WHO IS IT NOW...
YOU?! WHAT'LL IT TAKE TO GET IT THROUGH YOUR THICK SKULL THAT I HATE CHILDREN, ESPECIALLY OPENHEARTS!
YOU DON'T THINK YOU'VE ALREADY DONE ENOUGH?
HUH? WHAT ARE YOU TALKING ABOUT?
WE KNOW IT WAS YOU WHO POISONED THE WATER! BUT YOU WON'T GET AWAY WITH IT! WE'VE ALREADY CALLED THE RBH!

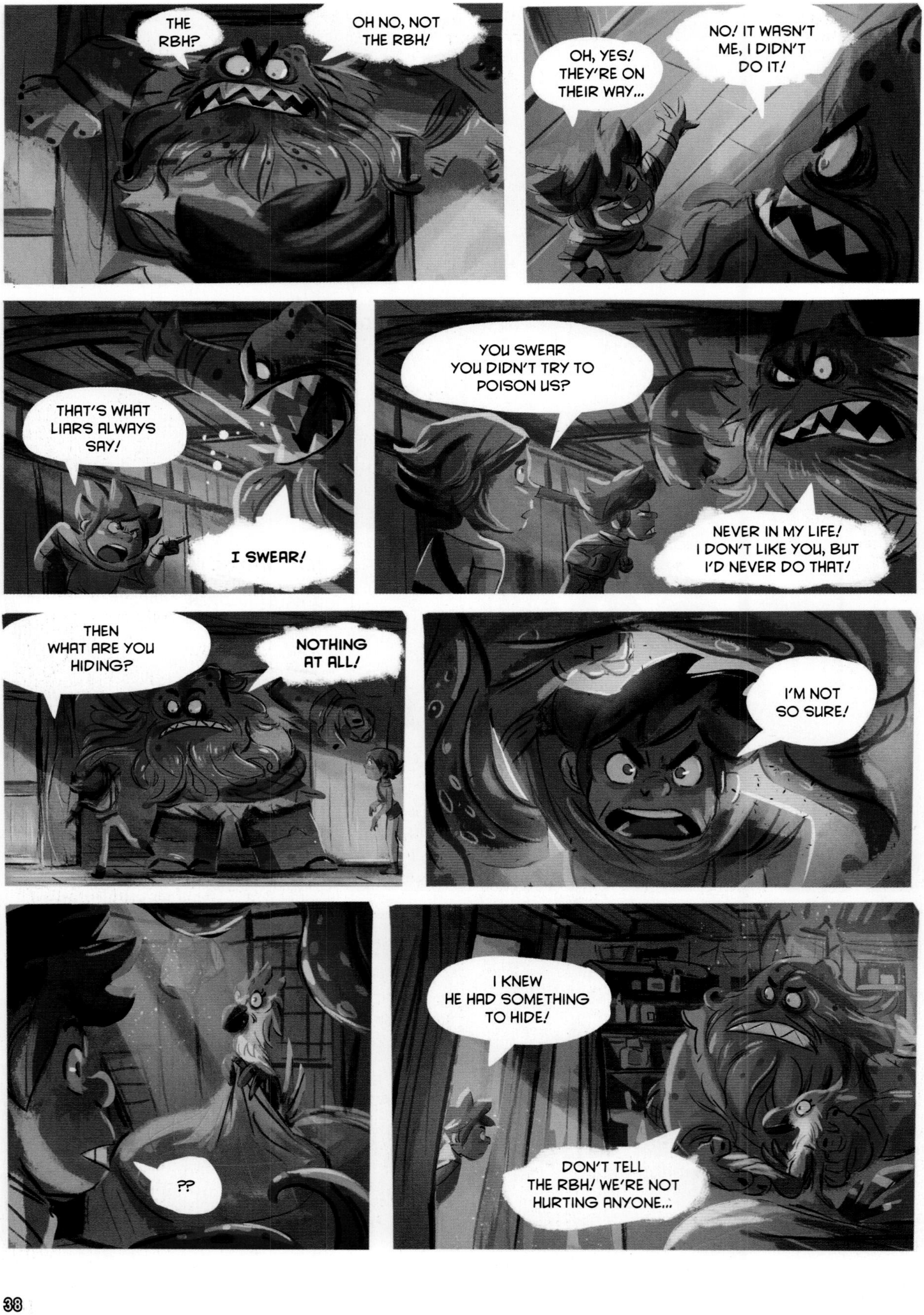
THE RBH?
OH NO, NOT THE RBH!
OH, YES! THEY'RE ON THEIR WAY...
NO! IT WASN'T ME, I DIDN'T DO IT!
THAT'S WHAT LIARS ALWAYS SAY!
I SWEAR!
YOU SWEAR YOU DIDN'T TRY TO POISON US?
NEVER IN MY LIFE! I DON'T LIKE YOU, BUT I'D NEVER DO THAT!
THEN WHAT ARE YOU HIDING?
NOTHING AT ALL!
I'M NOT SO SURE!
??
I KNEW HE HAD SOMETHING TO HIDE!
DON'T TELL THE RBH! WE'RE NOT HURTING ANYONE...

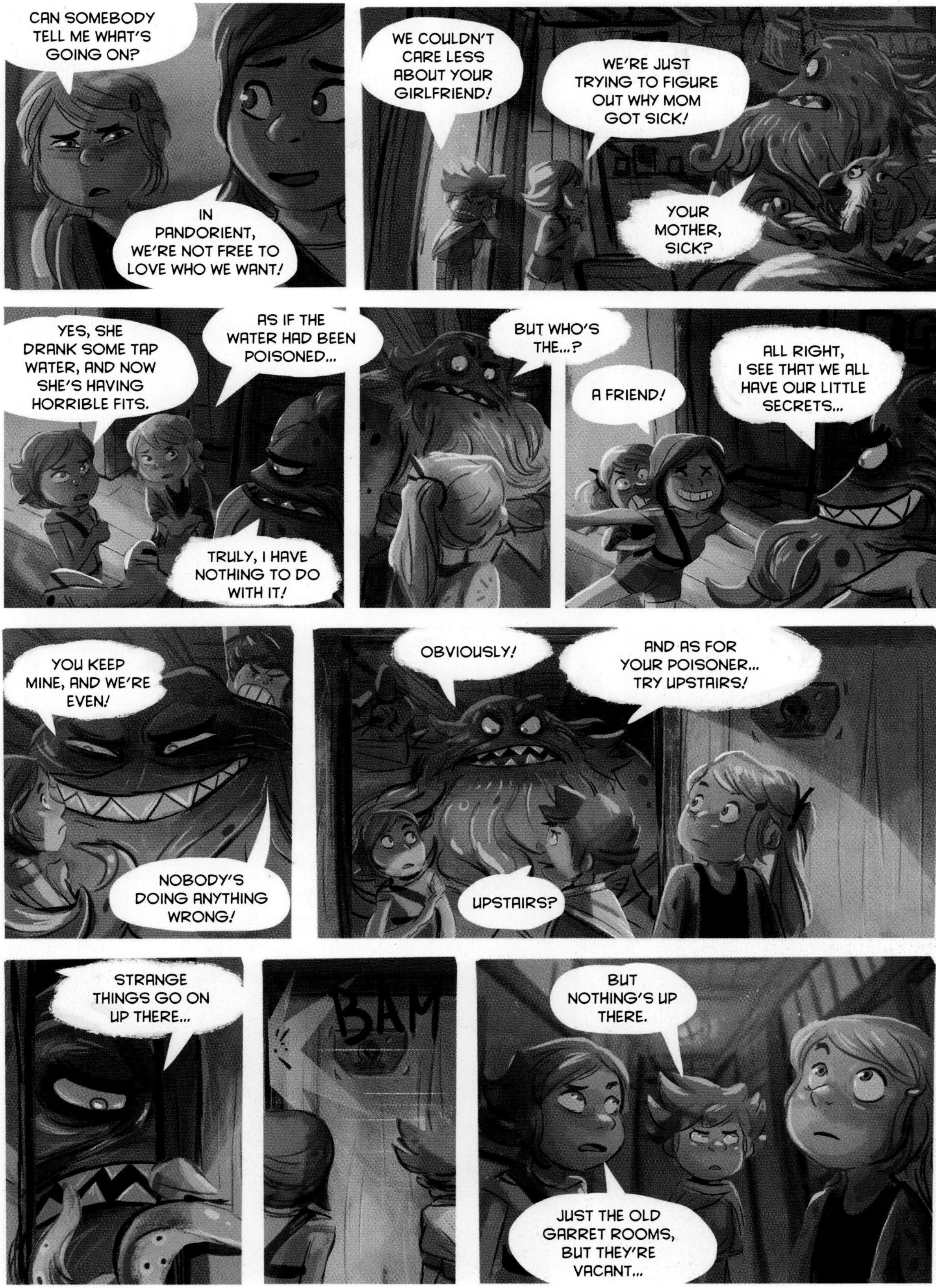
CAN SOMEBODY TELL ME WHAT'S GOING ON?
IN PANDORIENT, WE'RE NOT FREE TO LOVE WHO WE WANT!
WE COULDN'T CARE LESS ABOUT YOUR GIRLFRIEND!
WE'RE JUST TRYING TO FIGURE OUT WHY MOM GOT SICK!
YOUR MOTHER, SICK?
YES, SHE DRANK SOME TAP WATER, AND NOW SHE'S HAVING HORRIBLE FITS.
AS IF THE WATER HAD BEEN POISONED...
TRULY, I HAVE NOTHING TO DO WITH IT!
BUT WHO'S THE...?
A FRIEND!
ALL RIGHT, I SEE THAT WE ALL HAVE OUR LITTLE SECRETS...
YOU KEEP MINE, AND WE'RE EVEN!
NOBODY'S DOING ANYTHING WRONG!
OBVIOUSLY!
AND AS FOR YOUR POISONER... TRY UPSTAIRS!
UPSTAIRS?
STRANGE THINGS GO ON UP THERE...
BAM
BUT NOTHING'S UP THERE.
JUST THE OLD GARRET ROOMS, BUT THEY'RE VACANT...

DID YOU REALLY CALL THE RBH?

NAH. DID YOU SEE ME CALL THEM?

UM... WHAT'S THE RBH?

YOU DON'T KNOW ANYTHING!

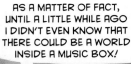

AS A MATTER OF FACT, UNTIL A LITTLE WHILE AGO I DIDN'T EVEN KNOW THAT THERE COULD BE A WORLD INSIDE A MUSIC BOX!

RELAX, I WAS JOKING!

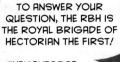

TO ANSWER YOUR QUESTION, THE RBH IS THE ROYAL BRIGADE OF HECTORIAN THE FIRST!

THEY ENFORCE THE LAWS IN PANDORIENT!

OKAY, SO WHAT DO THEY DO?

YOU DON'T MESS AROUND WITH HECTORIAN'S LAWS...

AND HE'S ALWAYS ADDING NEW ONES!

SERIOUSLY? THERE SHOULDN'T BE ANYONE UP HERE...

YEAH, BUT YOU HEARD WHAT THE OCTOPODUS SAID.

YOU REALLY WANT TO GO UP THERE?

WHAT IF THE POISONER'S THERE?

THEN WE REALLY WILL CALL THE RBH!

SO?

NOTHING SO FAR...

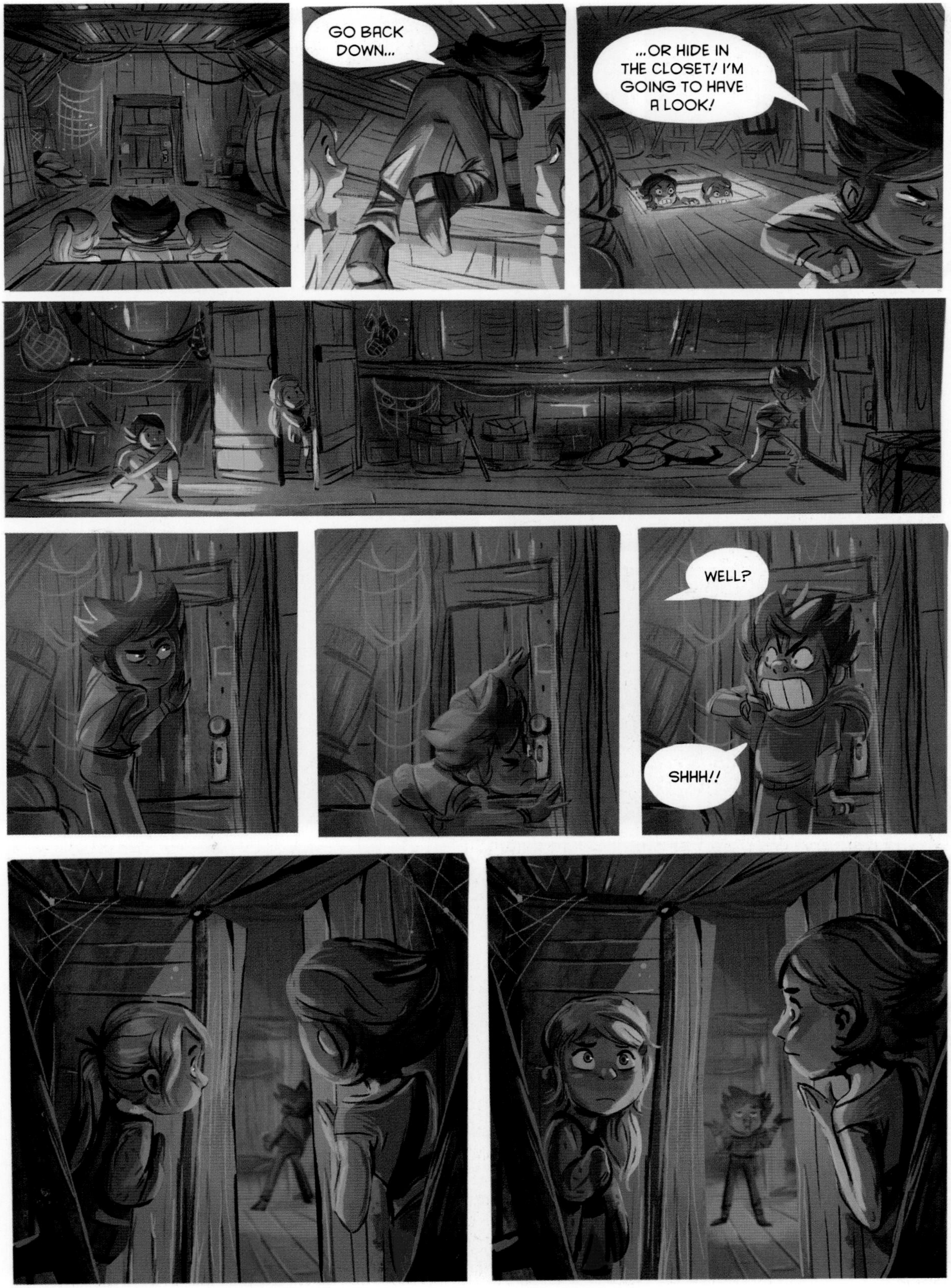
GO BACK DOWN...
...OR HIDE IN THE CLOSET! I'M GOING TO HAVE A LOOK!
WELL?
SHHH!!

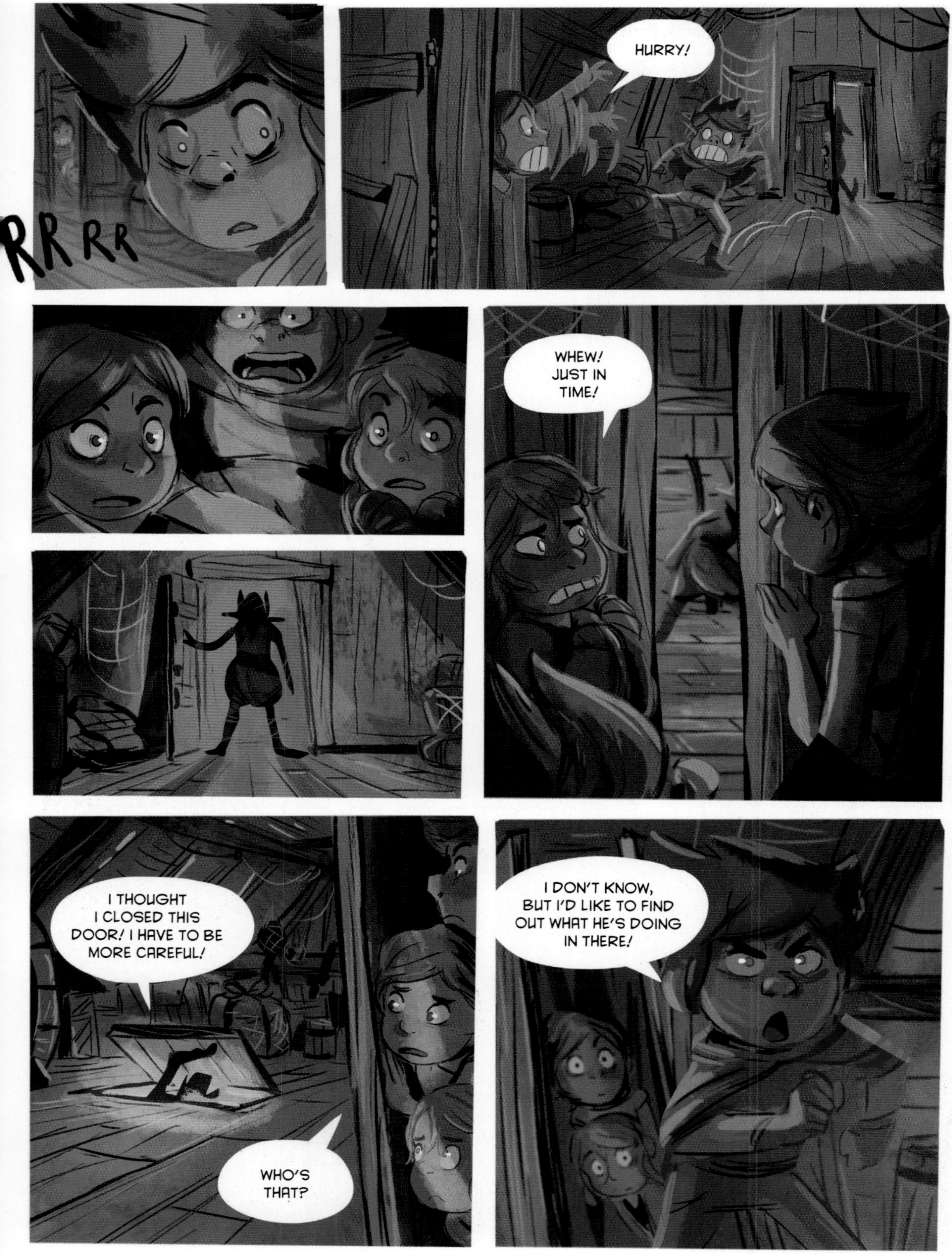
RRRRR
HURRY!
WHEW! JUST IN TIME!
I THOUGHT I CLOSED THIS DOOR! I HAVE TO BE MORE CAREFUL!
WHO'S THAT?
I DON'T KNOW, BUT I'D LIKE TO FIND OUT WHAT HE'S DOING IN THERE!

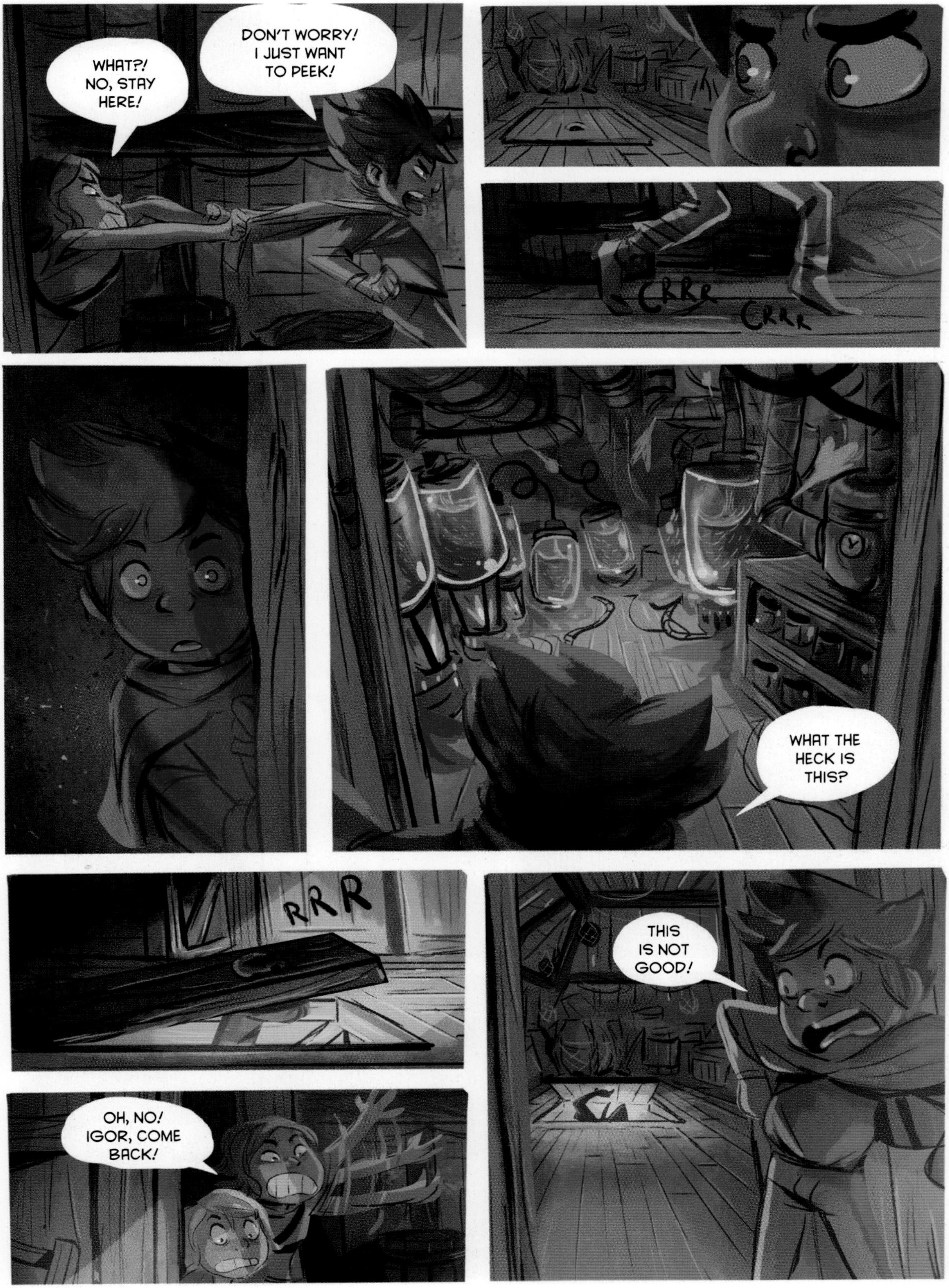
WHAT?! NO, STAY HERE!
DON'T WORRY! I JUST WANT TO PEEK!
CRRR
CRRR
WHAT THE HECK IS THIS?
RRR
OH, NO! IGOR, COME BACK!
THIS IS NOT GOOD!

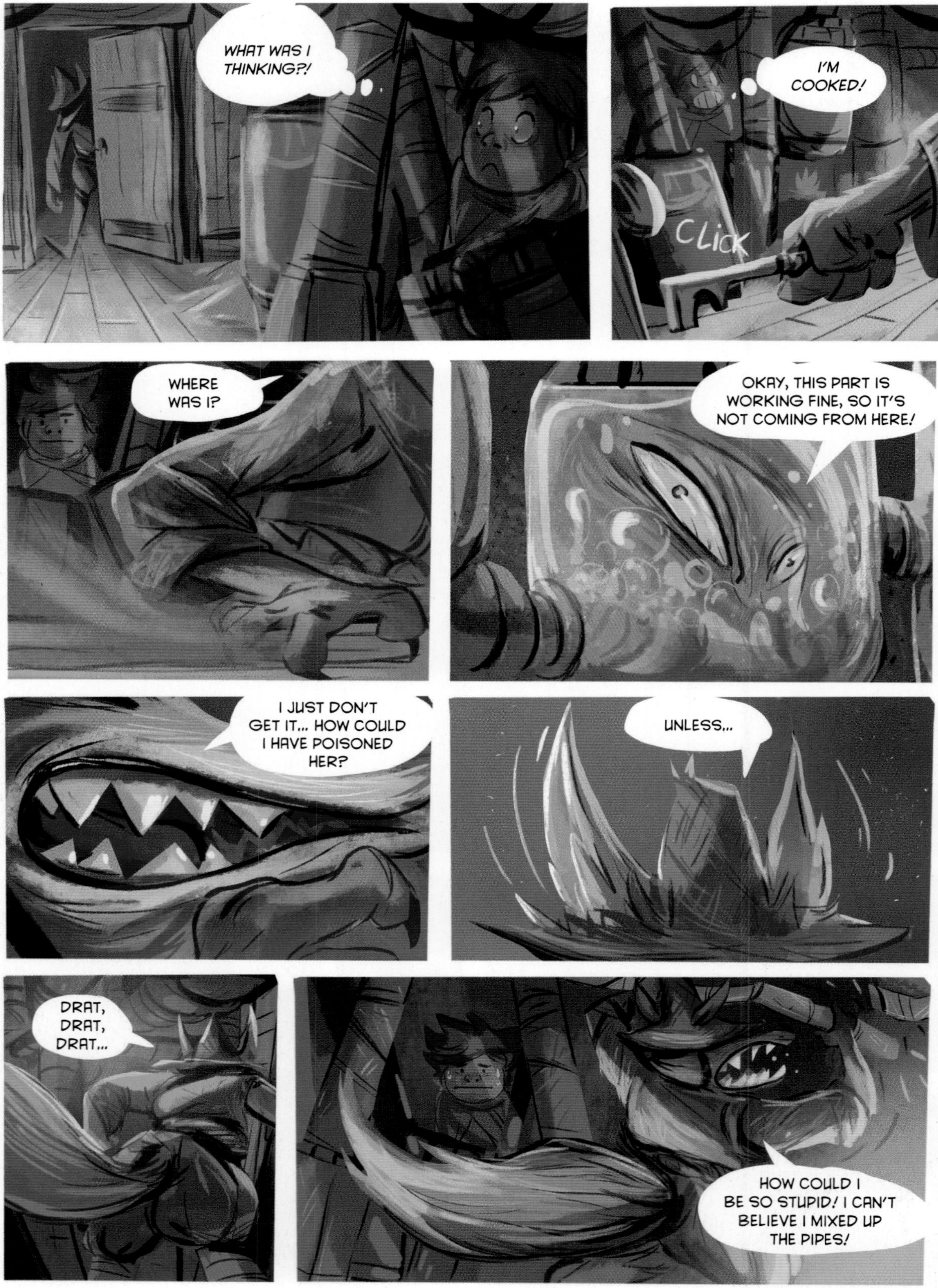
WHAT WAS I THINKING?!
I'M COOKED!
CLICK
WHERE WAS I?
OKAY, THIS PART IS WORKING FINE, SO IT'S NOT COMING FROM HERE!
I JUST DON'T GET IT... HOW COULD I HAVE POISONED HER?
UNLESS...
DRAT, DRAT, DRAT...
HOW COULD I BE SO STUPID! I CAN'T BELIEVE I MIXED UP THE PIPES!

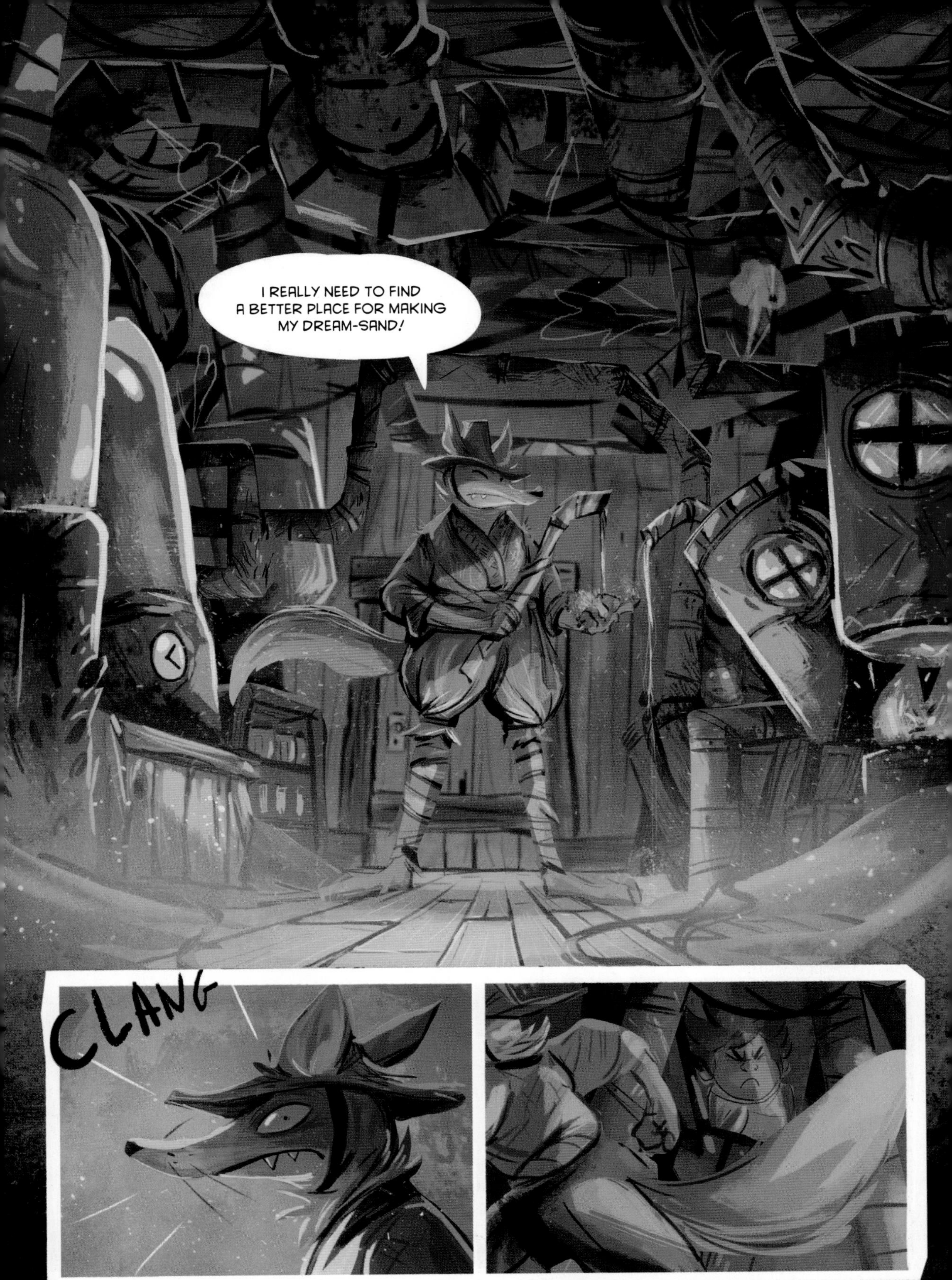
I REALLY NEED TO FIND A BETTER PLACE FOR MAKING MY DREAM-SAND!
CLANG

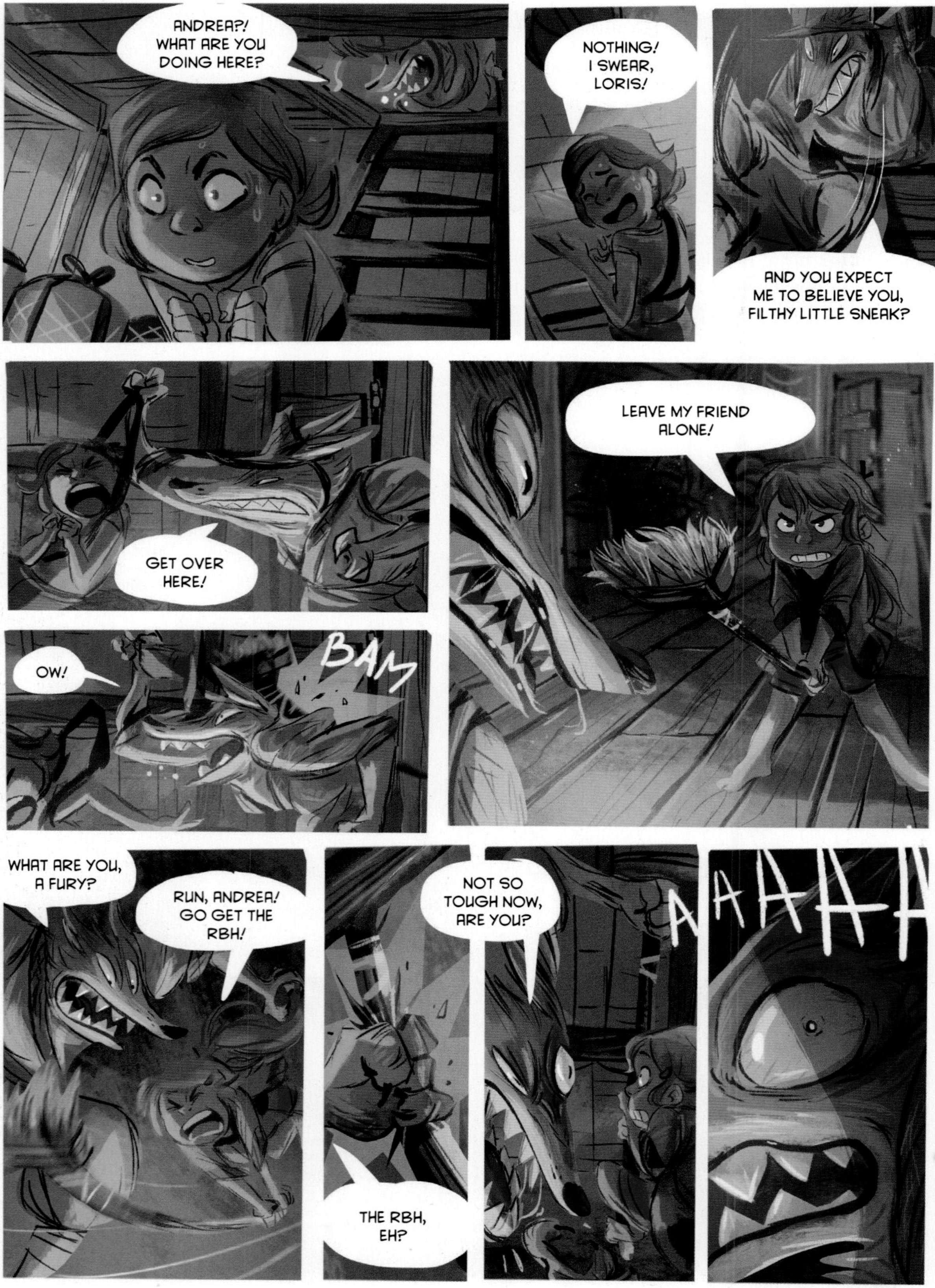
ANDREA?! WHAT ARE YOU DOING HERE?
NOTHING! I SWEAR, LORIS!
AND YOU EXPECT ME TO BELIEVE YOU, FILTHY LITTLE SNEAK?
GET OVER HERE!
LEAVE MY FRIEND ALONE!
OW!
BAM
WHAT ARE YOU, A FURY?
RUN, ANDREA! GO GET THE RBH!
THE RBH, EH?
NOT SO TOUGH NOW, ARE YOU?
AAAAAA

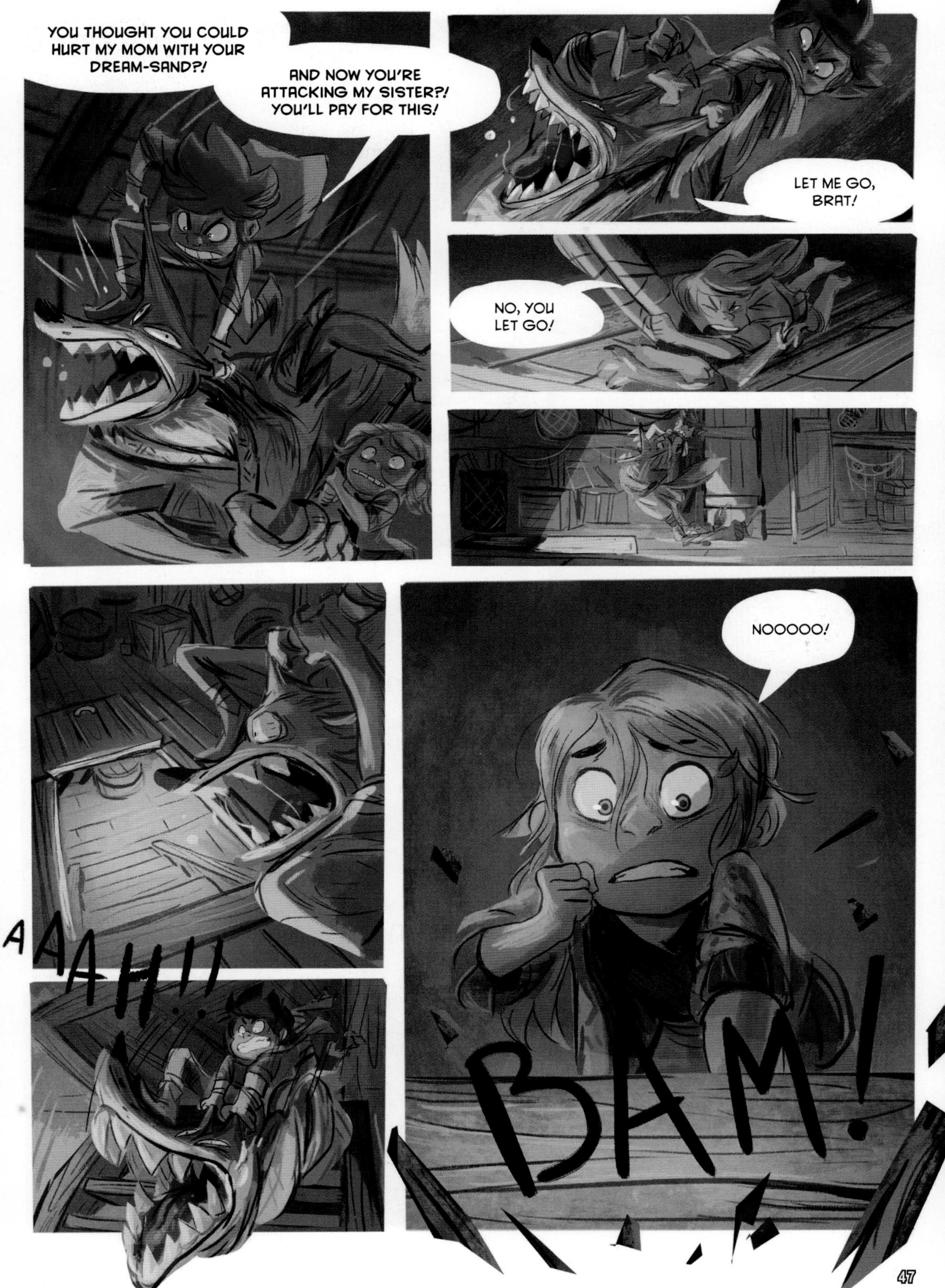
YOU THOUGHT YOU COULD HURT MY MOM WITH YOUR DREAM-SAND?!
AND NOW YOU'RE ATTACKING MY SISTER?! YOU'LL PAY FOR THIS!
LET ME GO, BRAT!
NO, YOU LET GO!
AAAH!!!
NOOOOO!
BAM!

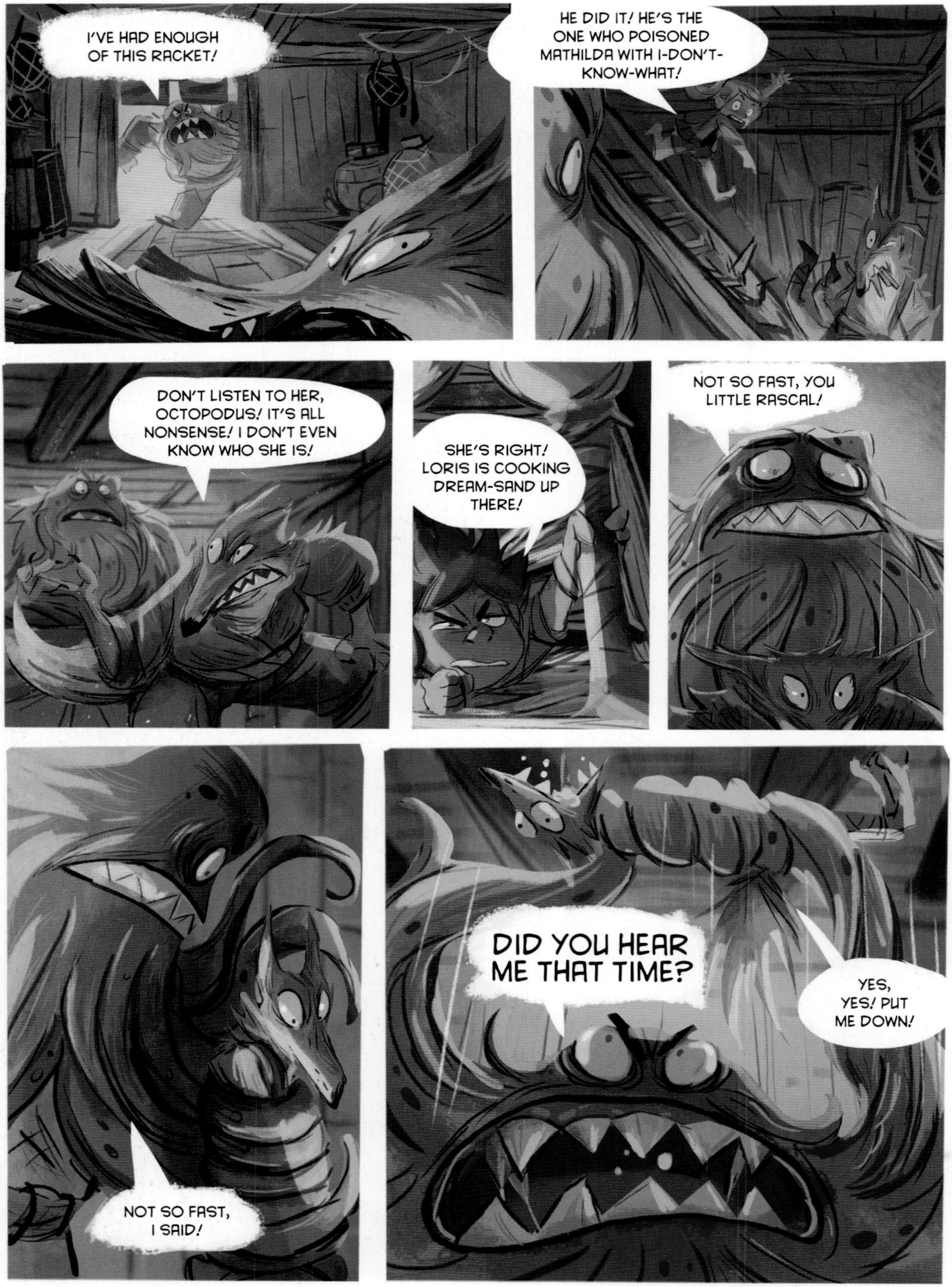
I'VE HAD ENOUGH OF THIS RACKET!
HE DID IT! HE'S THE ONE WHO POISONED MATHILDA WITH I-DON'T-KNOW-WHAT!
DON'T LISTEN TO HER, OCTOPODUS! IT'S ALL NONSENSE! I DON'T EVEN KNOW WHO SHE IS!
SHE'S RIGHT! LORIS IS COOKING DREAM-SAND UP THERE!
NOT SO FAST, YOU LITTLE RASCAL!
NOT SO FAST, I SAID!
DID YOU HEAR ME THAT TIME?
YES, YES! PUT ME DOWN!

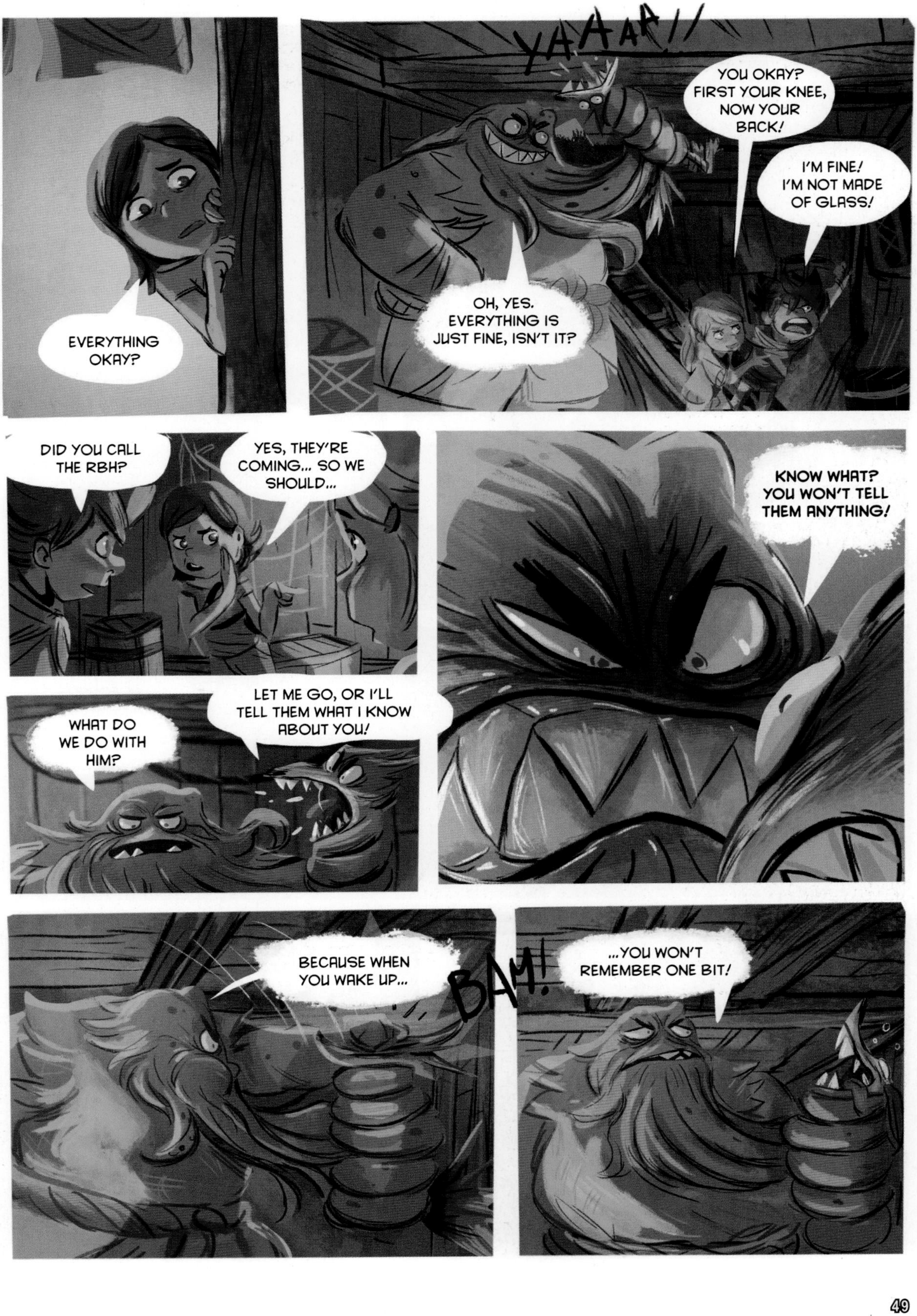
EVERYTHING OKAY?
YAAAA!!
OH, YES. EVERYTHING IS JUST FINE, ISN'T IT?
YOU OKAY? FIRST YOUR KNEE, NOW YOUR BACK!
I'M FINE! I'M NOT MADE OF GLASS!
DID YOU CALL THE RBH?
YES, THEY'RE COMING... SO WE SHOULD...
WHAT DO WE DO WITH HIM?
LET ME GO, OR I'LL TELL THEM WHAT I KNOW ABOUT YOU!
KNOW WHAT? YOU WON'T TELL THEM ANYTHING!
BECAUSE WHEN YOU WAKE UP...
BAM!
...YOU WON'T REMEMBER ONE BIT!

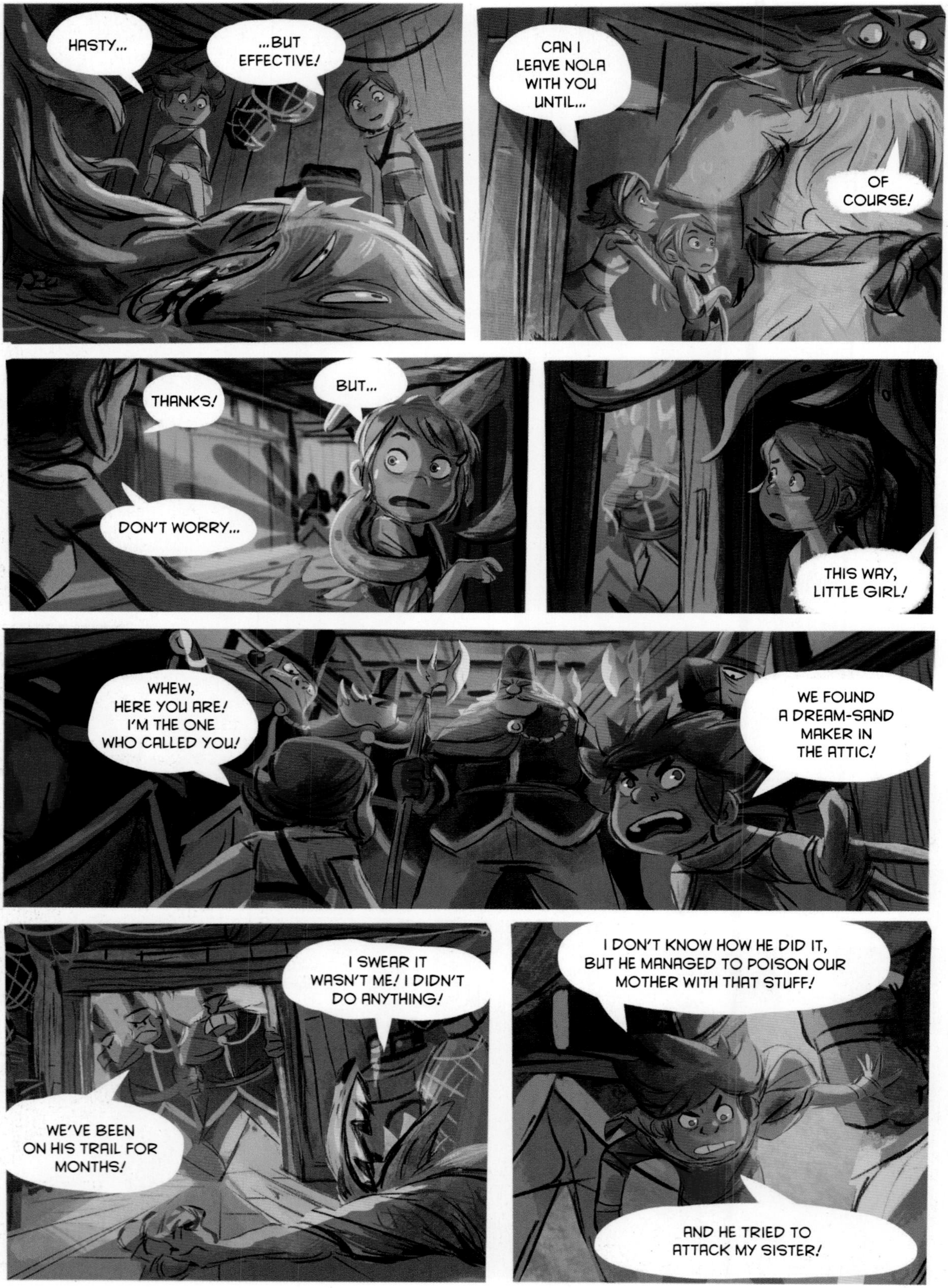
HASTY...
...BUT EFFECTIVE!
CAN I LEAVE NOLA WITH YOU UNTIL...
OF COURSE!
THANKS!
DON'T WORRY...
BUT...
THIS WAY, LITTLE GIRL!
WHEW, HERE YOU ARE! I'M THE ONE WHO CALLED YOU!
WE FOUND A DREAM-SAND MAKER IN THE ATTIC!
I SWEAR IT WASN'T ME! I DIDN'T DO ANYTHING!
WE'VE BEEN ON HIS TRAIL FOR MONTHS!
I DON'T KNOW HOW HE DID IT, BUT HE MANAGED TO POISON OUR MOTHER WITH THAT STUFF!
AND HE TRIED TO ATTACK MY SISTER!

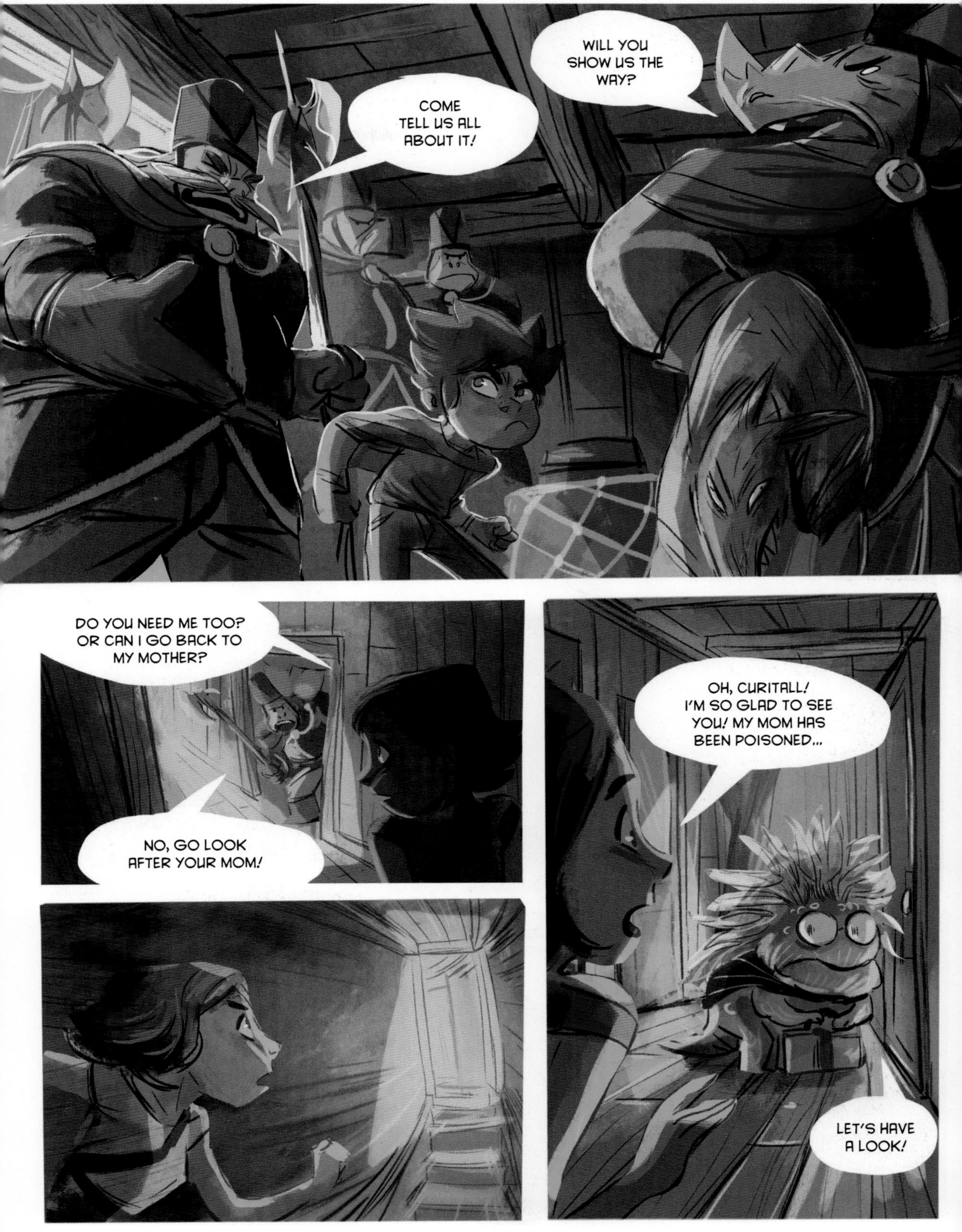
COME TELL US ALL ABOUT IT!
WILL YOU SHOW US THE WAY?
DO YOU NEED ME TOO? OR CAN I GO BACK TO MY MOTHER?
NO, GO LOOK AFTER YOUR MOM!
OH, CURITALL! I'M SO GLAD TO SEE YOU! MY MOM HAS BEEN POISONED...
LET'S HAVE A LOOK!

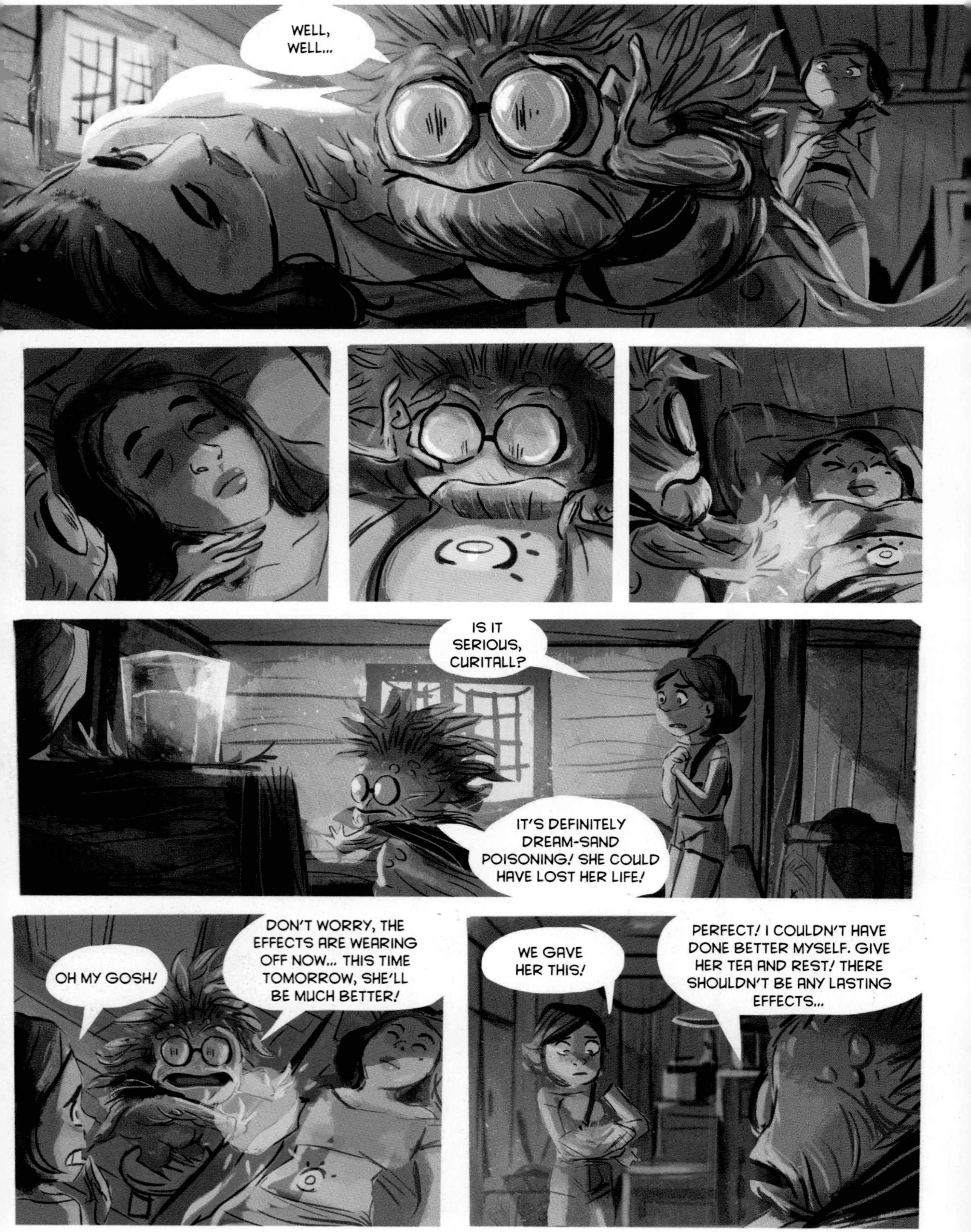
WELL, WELL...
IS IT SERIOUS, CURITALL?
IT'S DEFINITELY DREAM-SAND POISONING! SHE COULD HAVE LOST HER LIFE!
OH MY GOSH!
DON'T WORRY, THE EFFECTS ARE WEARING OFF NOW... THIS TIME TOMORROW, SHE'LL BE MUCH BETTER!
WE GAVE HER THIS!
PERFECT! I COULDN'T HAVE DONE BETTER MYSELF. GIVE HER TEA AND REST! THERE SHOULDN'T BE ANY LASTING EFFECTS...

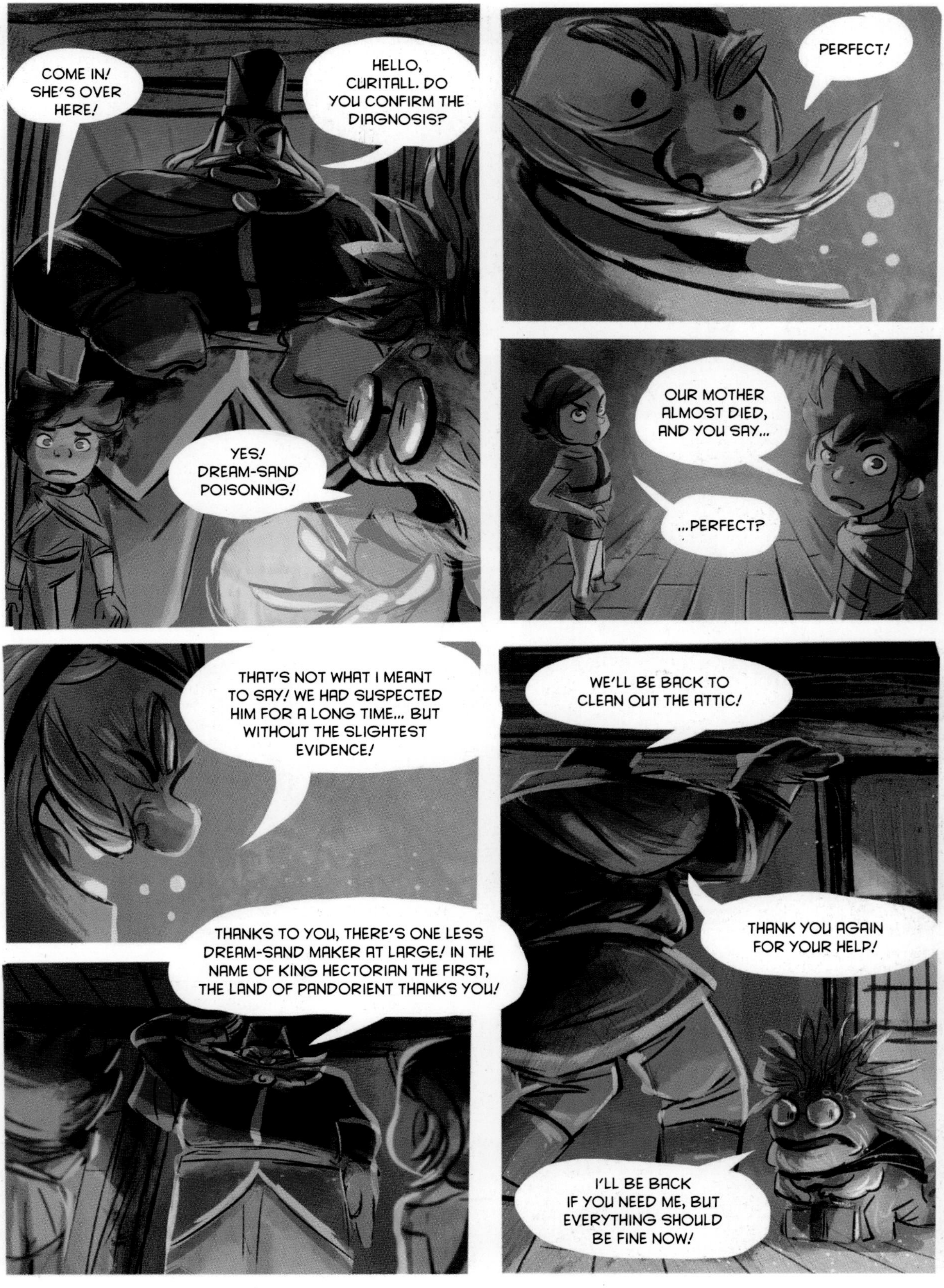
COME IN! SHE'S OVER HERE!
HELLO, CURITALL. DO YOU CONFIRM THE DIAGNOSIS?
YES! DREAM-SAND POISONING!
PERFECT!
OUR MOTHER ALMOST DIED, AND YOU SAY...
...PERFECT?
THAT'S NOT WHAT I MEANT TO SAY! WE HAD SUSPECTED HIM FOR A LONG TIME... BUT WITHOUT THE SLIGHTEST EVIDENCE!
THANKS TO YOU, THERE'S ONE LESS DREAM-SAND MAKER AT LARGE! IN THE NAME OF KING HECTORIAN THE FIRST, THE LAND OF PANDORIENT THANKS YOU!
WE'LL BE BACK TO CLEAN OUT THE ATTIC!
THANK YOU AGAIN FOR YOUR HELP!
I'LL BE BACK IF YOU NEED ME, BUT EVERYTHING SHOULD BE FINE NOW!

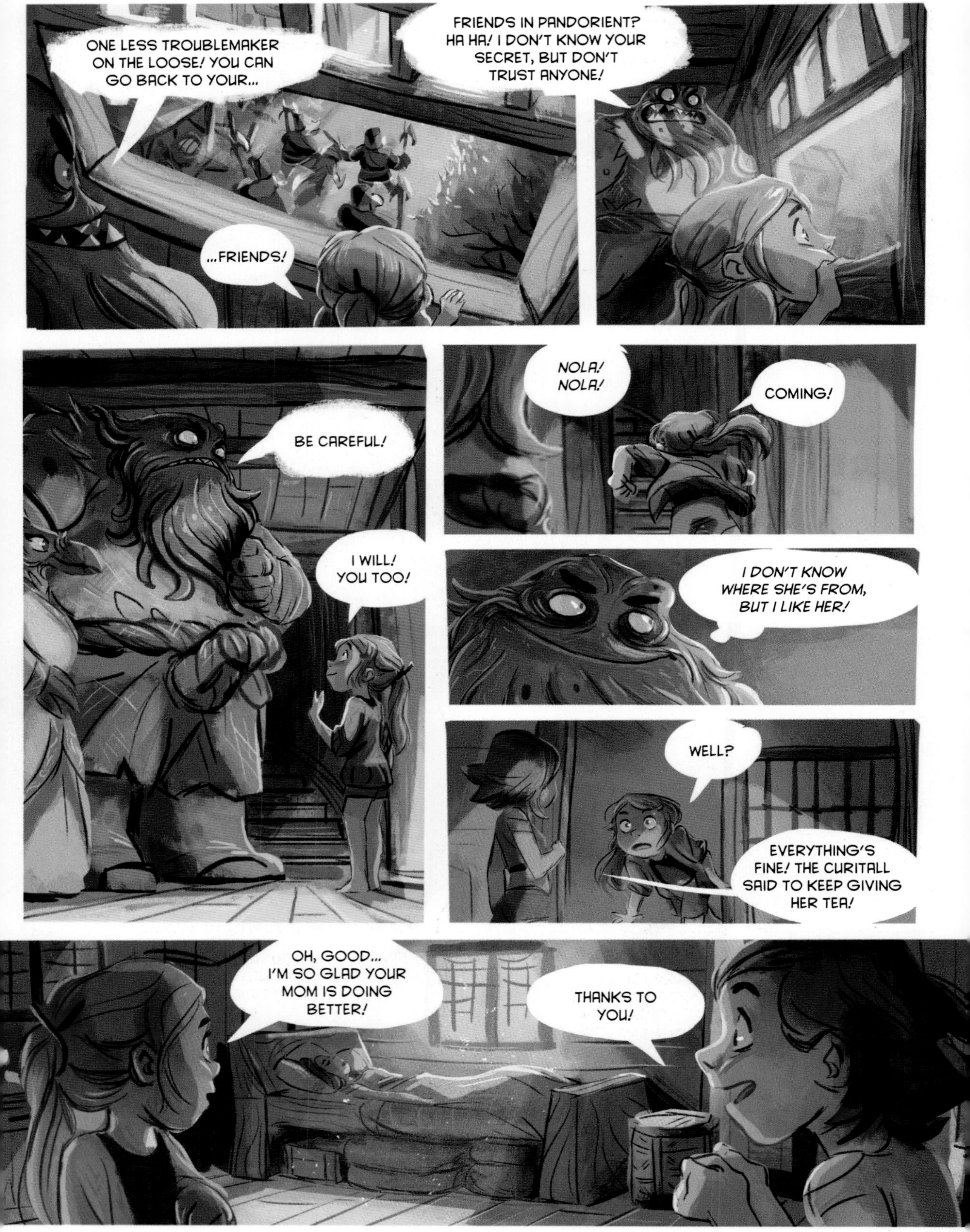
ONE LESS TROUBLEMAKER ON THE LOOSE! YOU CAN GO BACK TO YOUR...
...FRIENDS!
FRIENDS IN PANDORIENT? HA HA! I DON'T KNOW YOUR SECRET, BUT DON'T TRUST ANYONE!
BE CAREFUL!
I WILL! YOU TOO!
NOLA! NOLA!
COMING!
I DON'T KNOW WHERE SHE'S FROM, BUT I LIKE HER!
WELL?
EVERYTHING'S FINE! THE CURITALL SAID TO KEEP GIVING HER TEA!
OH, GOOD... I'M SO GLAD YOUR MOM IS DOING BETTER!
THANKS TO YOU!

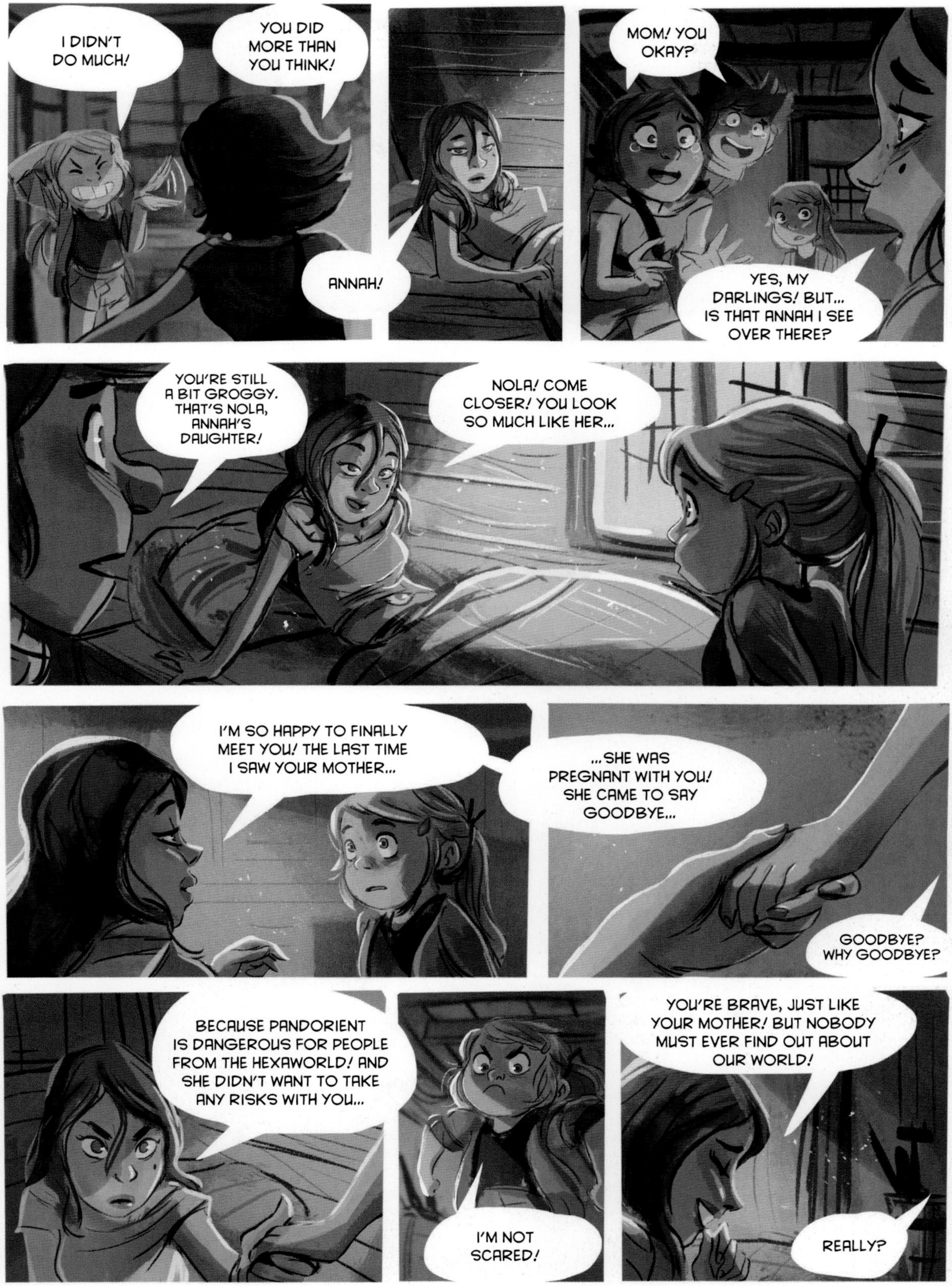
I DIDN'T DO MUCH!
YOU DID MORE THAN YOU THINK!
ANNAH!
MOM! YOU OKAY?
YES, MY DARLINGS! BUT... IS THAT ANNAH I SEE OVER THERE?
YOU'RE STILL A BIT GROGGY. THAT'S NOLA, ANNAH'S DAUGHTER!
NOLA! COME CLOSER! YOU LOOK SO MUCH LIKE HER...
I'M SO HAPPY TO FINALLY MEET YOU! THE LAST TIME I SAW YOUR MOTHER...
...SHE WAS PREGNANT WITH YOU! SHE CAME TO SAY GOODBYE...
GOODBYE? WHY GOODBYE?
BECAUSE PANDORIENT IS DANGEROUS FOR PEOPLE FROM THE HEXAWORLD! AND SHE DIDN'T WANT TO TAKE ANY RISKS WITH YOU...
I'M NOT SCARED!
YOU'RE BRAVE, JUST LIKE YOUR MOTHER! BUT NOBODY MUST EVER FIND OUT ABOUT OUR WORLD!
REALLY?

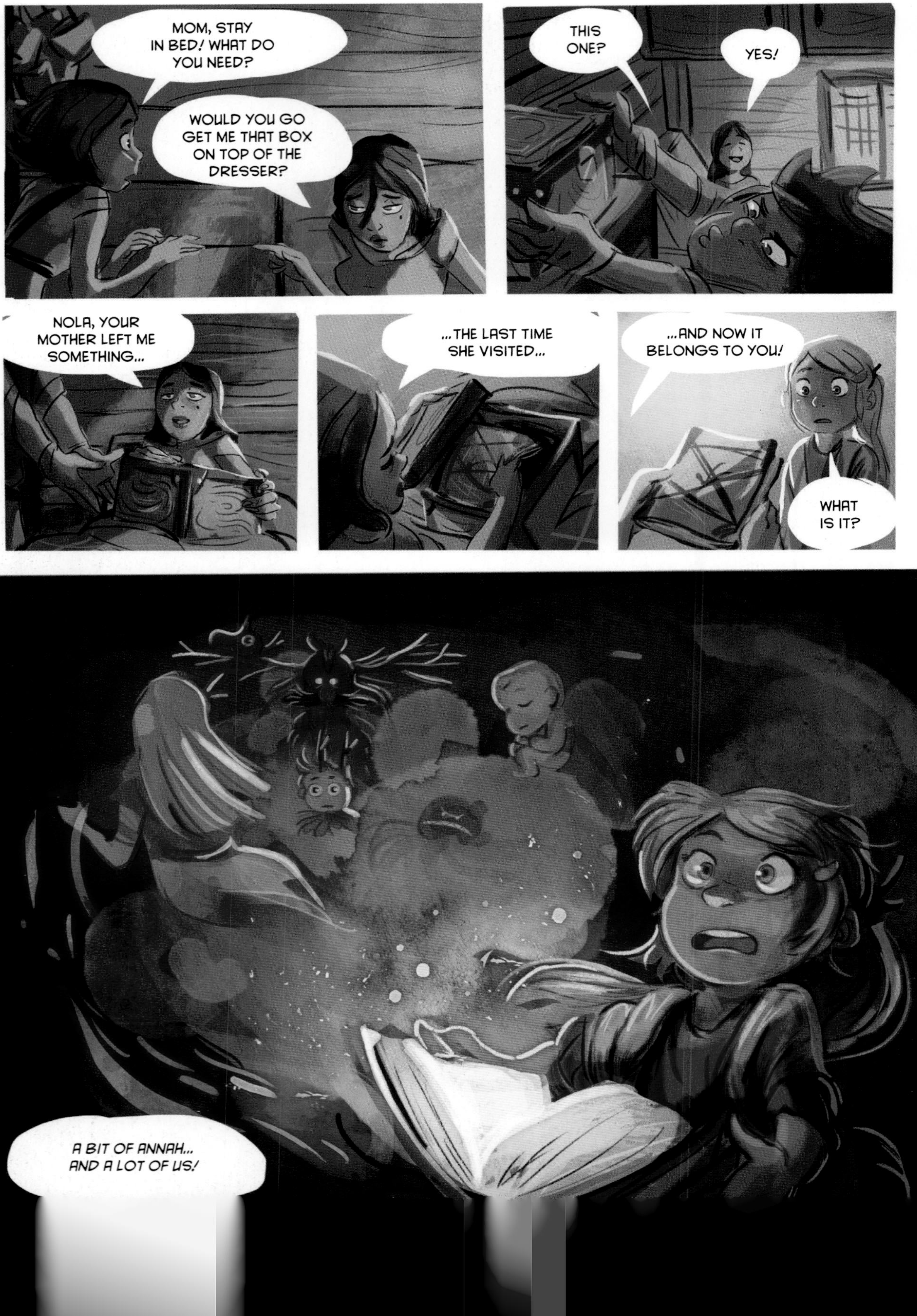
MOM, STAY IN BED! WHAT DO YOU NEED?
WOULD YOU GO GET ME THAT BOX ON TOP OF THE DRESSER?
THIS ONE?
YES!
NOLA, YOUR MOTHER LEFT ME SOMETHING...
...THE LAST TIME SHE VISITED...
...AND NOW IT BELONGS TO YOU!
WHAT IS IT?
A BIT OF ANNAH... AND A LOT OF US!

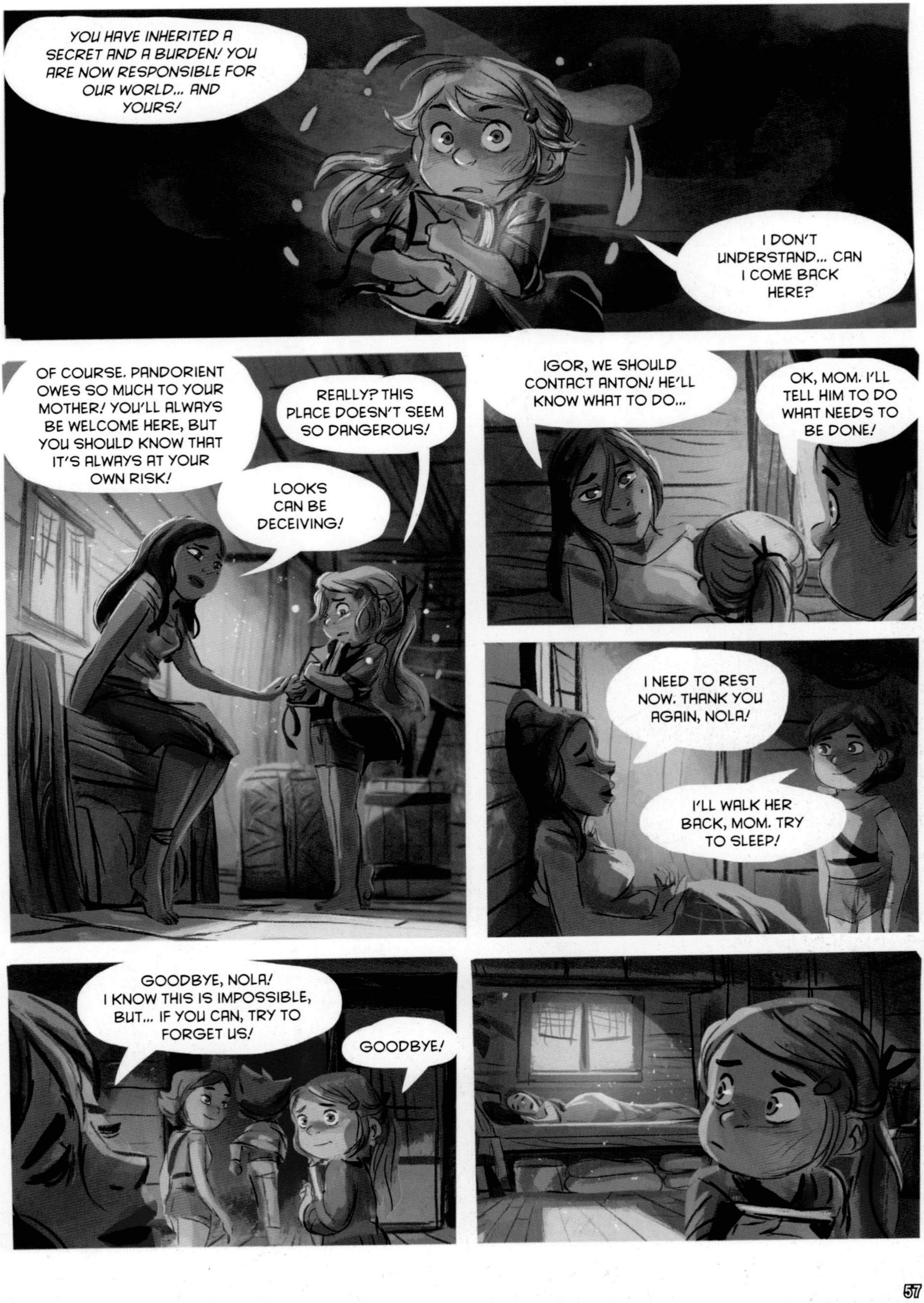
YOU HAVE INHERITED A SECRET AND A BURDEN! YOU ARE NOW RESPONSIBLE FOR OUR WORLD... AND YOURS!
I DON'T UNDERSTAND... CAN I COME BACK HERE?
OF COURSE. PANDORIENT OWES SO MUCH TO YOUR MOTHER! YOU'LL ALWAYS BE WELCOME HERE, BUT YOU SHOULD KNOW THAT IT'S ALWAYS AT YOUR OWN RISK!
REALLY? THIS PLACE DOESN'T SEEM SO DANGEROUS!
LOOKS CAN BE DECEIVING!
IGOR, WE SHOULD CONTACT ANTON! HE'LL KNOW WHAT TO DO...
OK, MOM. I'LL TELL HIM TO DO WHAT NEEDS TO BE DONE!
I NEED TO REST NOW. THANK YOU AGAIN, NOLA!
I'LL WALK HER BACK, MOM. TRY TO SLEEP!
GOODBYE, NOLA! I KNOW THIS IS IMPOSSIBLE, BUT... IF YOU CAN, TRY TO FORGET US!
GOODBYE!

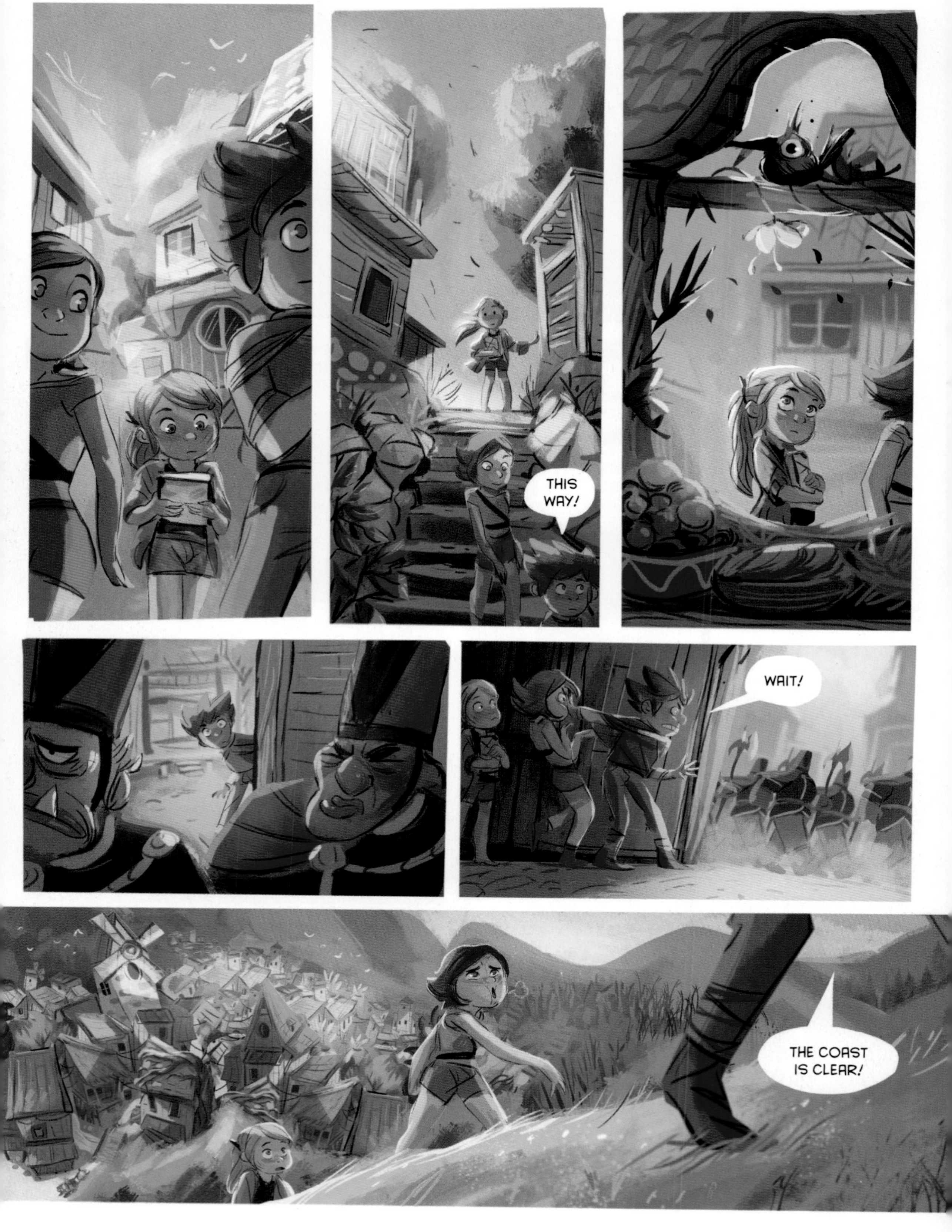
THIS WAY!
WAIT!
THE COAST IS CLEAR!

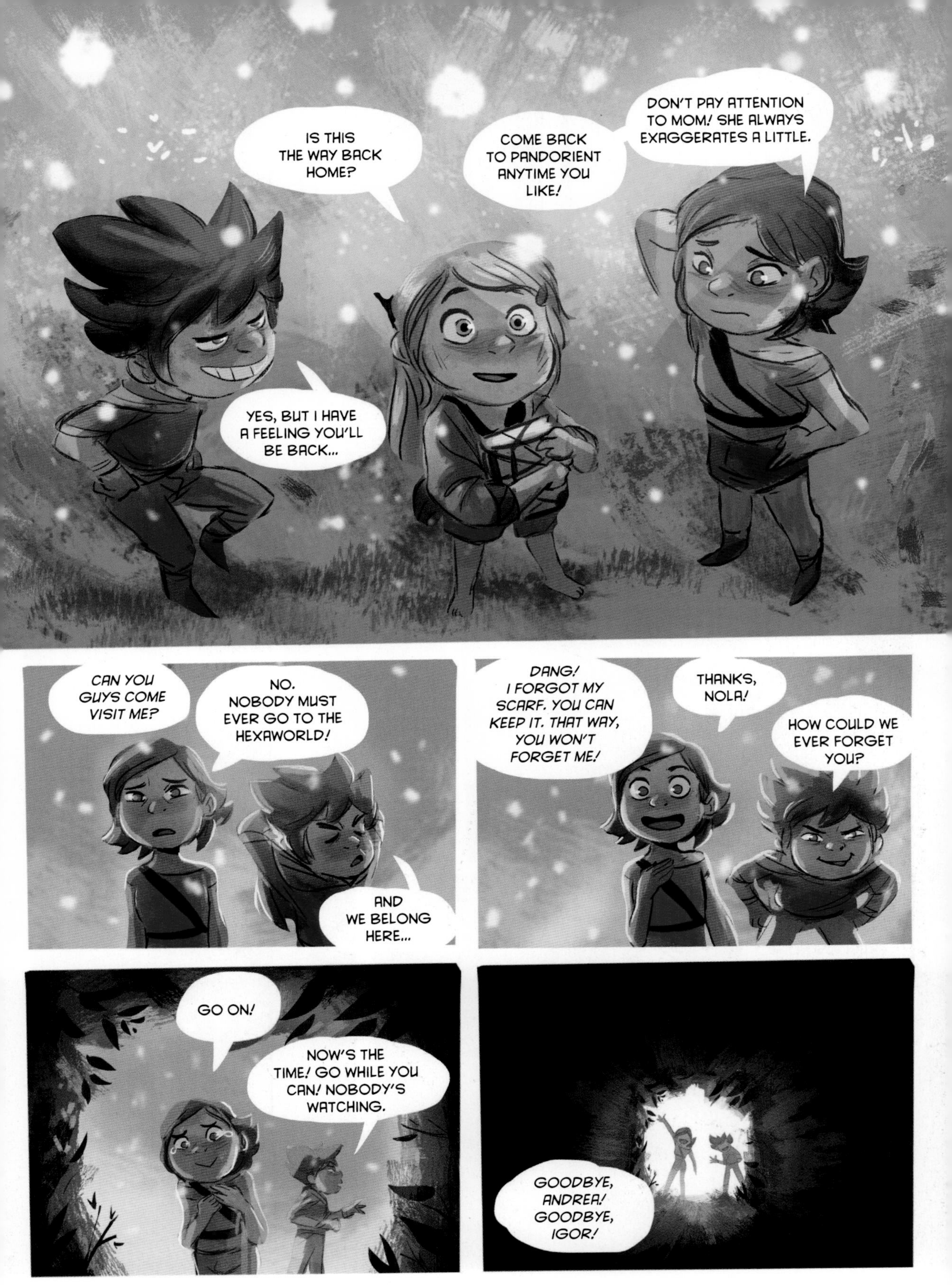
IS THIS THE WAY BACK HOME?
COME BACK TO PANDORIENT ANYTIME YOU LIKE!
DON'T PAY ATTENTION TO MOM! SHE ALWAYS EXAGGERATES A LITTLE.
YES, BUT I HAVE A FEELING YOU'LL BE BACK...
CAN YOU GUYS COME VISIT ME?
NO. NOBODY MUST EVER GO TO THE HEXAWORLD!
AND WE BELONG HERE...
DANG! I FORGOT MY SCARF. YOU CAN KEEP IT. THAT WAY, YOU WON'T FORGET ME!
THANKS, NOLA!
HOW COULD WE EVER FORGET YOU?
GO ON!
NOW'S THE TIME! GO WHILE YOU CAN! NOBODY'S WATCHING.
GOODBYE, ANDREA! GOODBYE, IGOR!

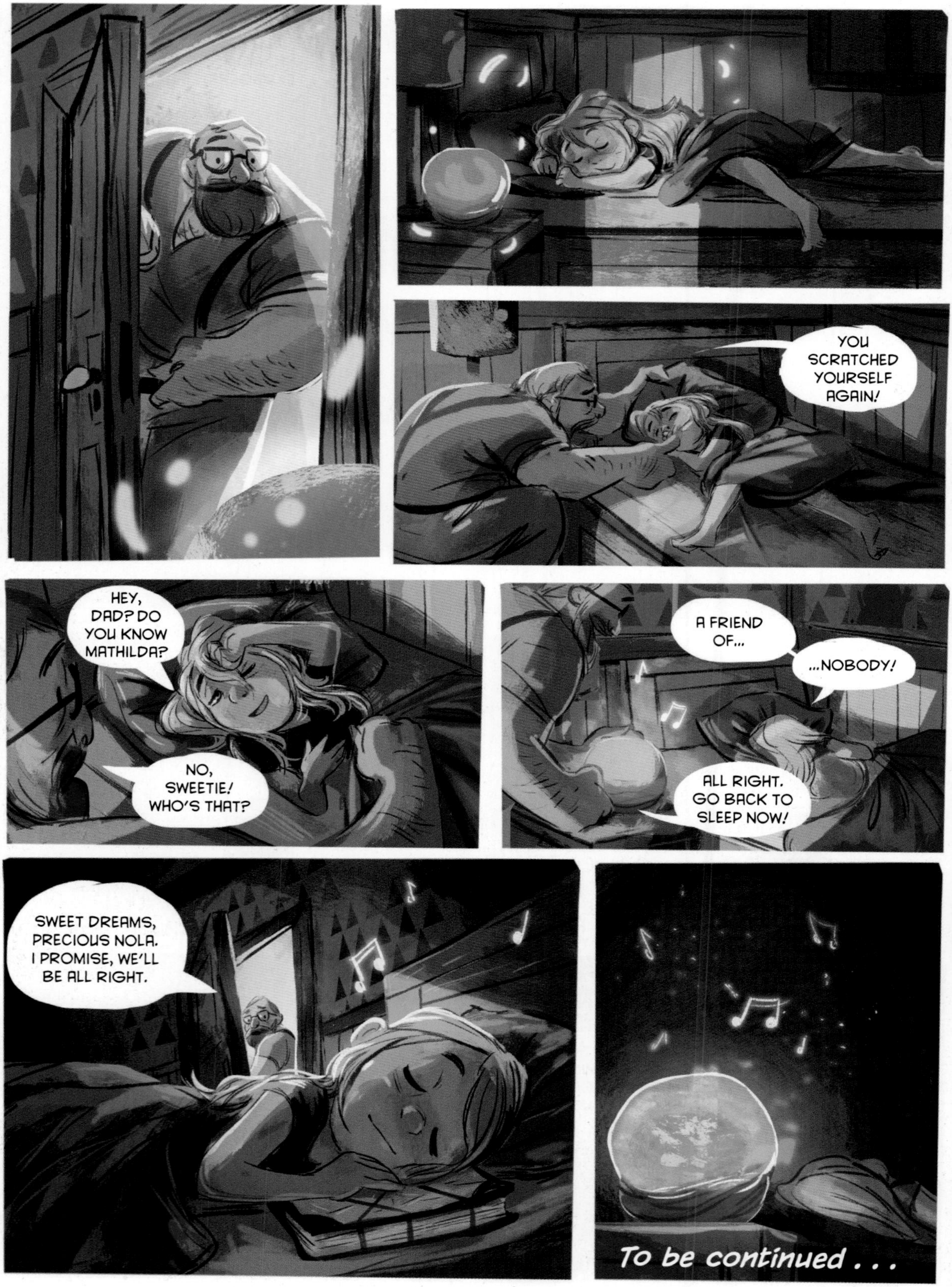
YOU SCRATCHED YOURSELF AGAIN!
HEY, DAD? DO YOU KNOW MATHILDA?
NO, SWEETIE! WHO'S THAT?
A FRIEND OF...
...NOBODY!
ALL RIGHT. GO BACK TO SLEEP NOW!
SWEET DREAMS, PRECIOUS NOLA. I PROMISE, WE'LL BE ALL RIGHT.
To be continued . . .

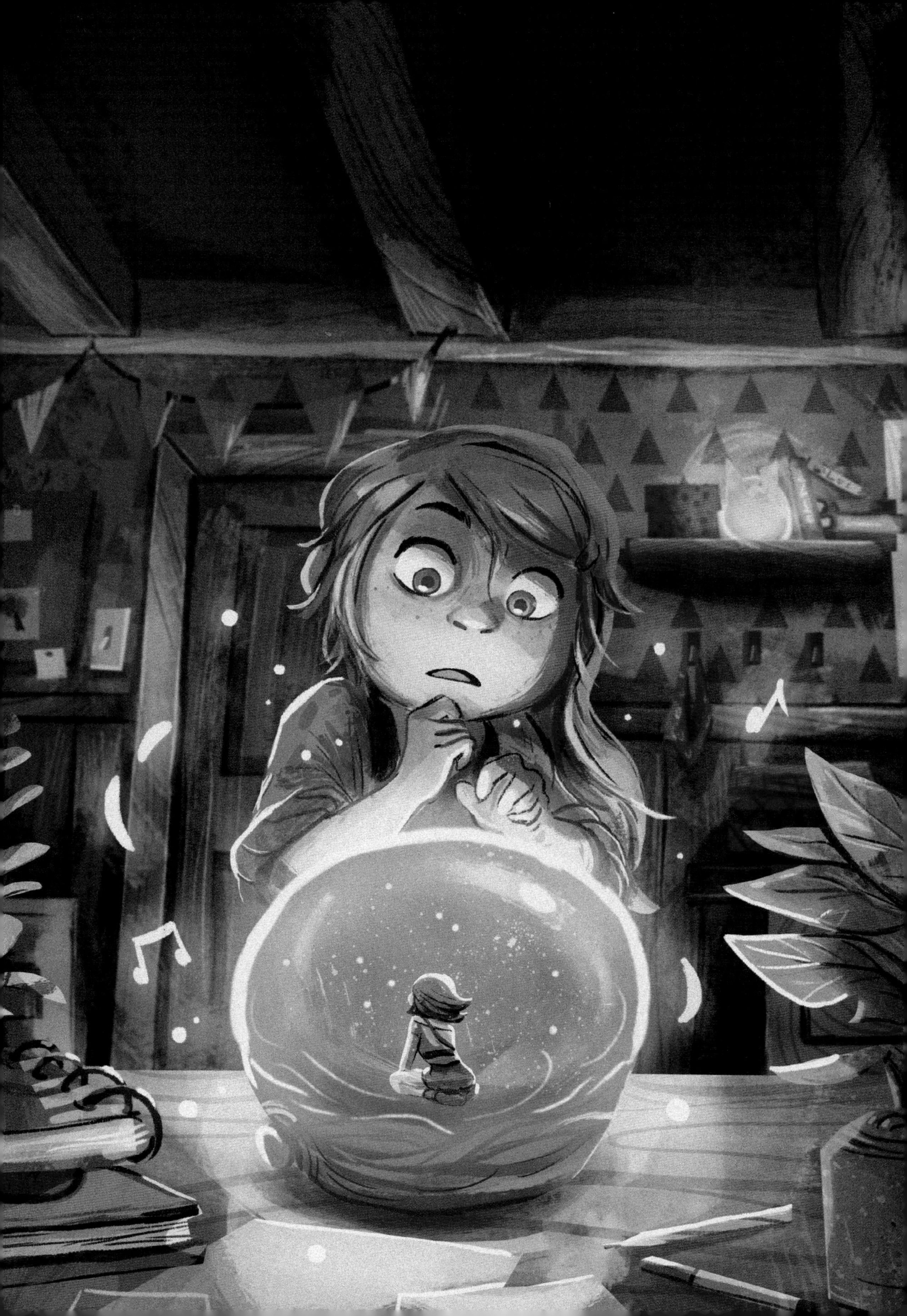

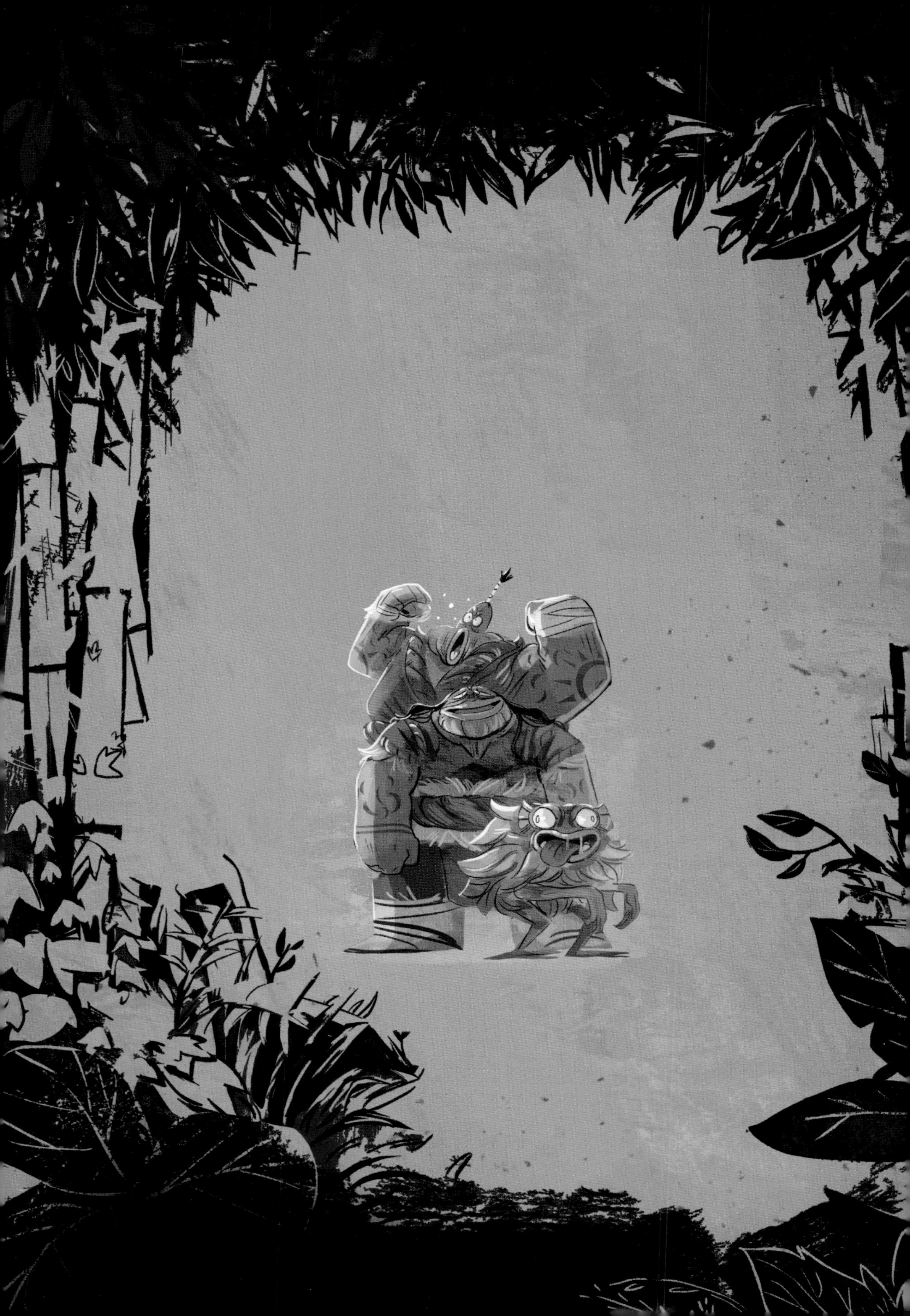

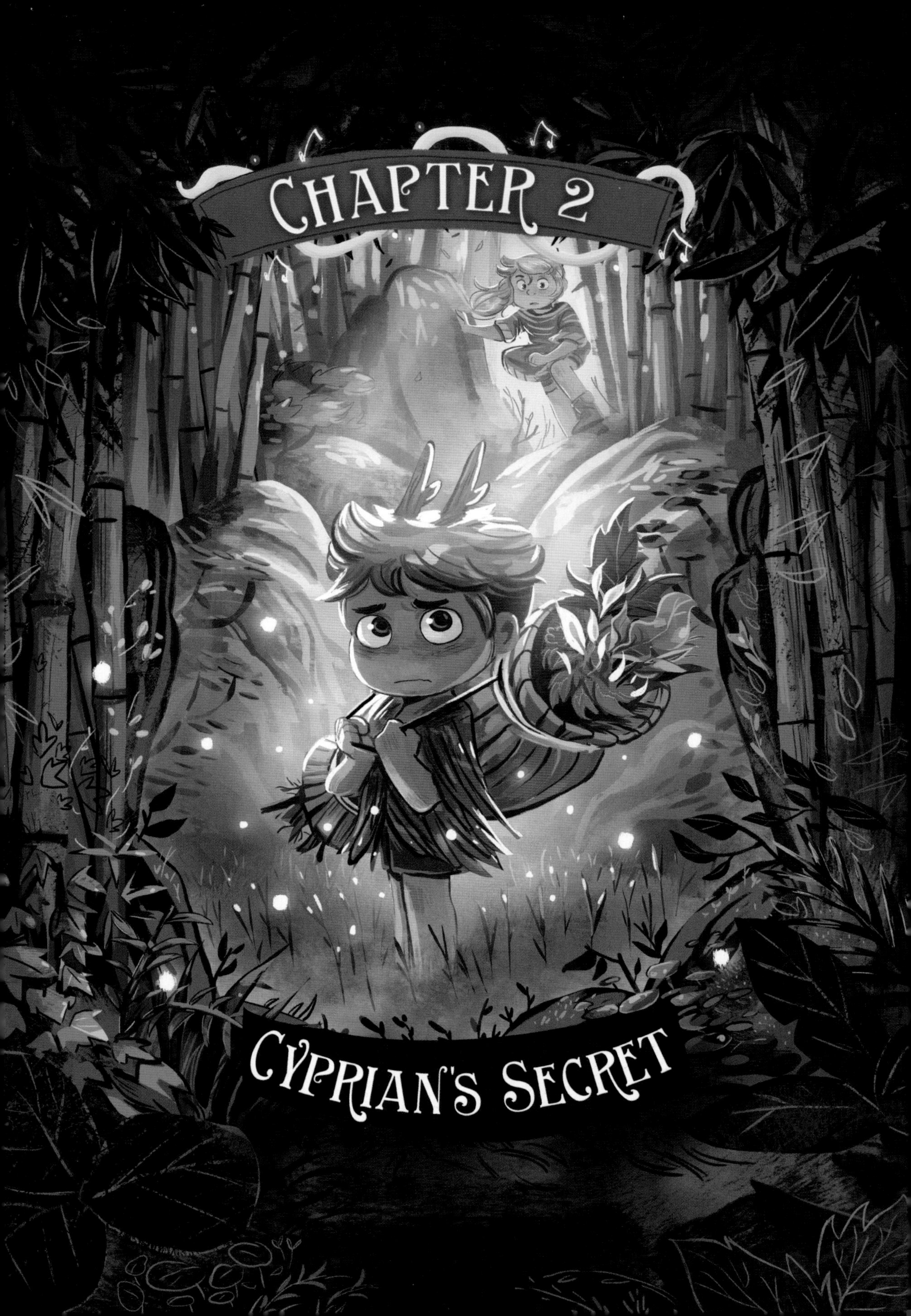
CHAPTER 2
CYPRIAN'S SECRET

I STILL JUST CAN'T BELIEVE IT! MOM WAS IN PANDORIENT... INCREDIBLE!

WHAT IS THAT? IT LOOKS LIKE A KEY.

MOM WAS GOOD AT DRAWING!

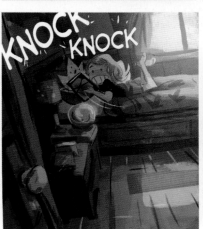

KNOCK KNOCK

EXCUSE ME, SWEETIE! YOU AWAKE?

YEP!

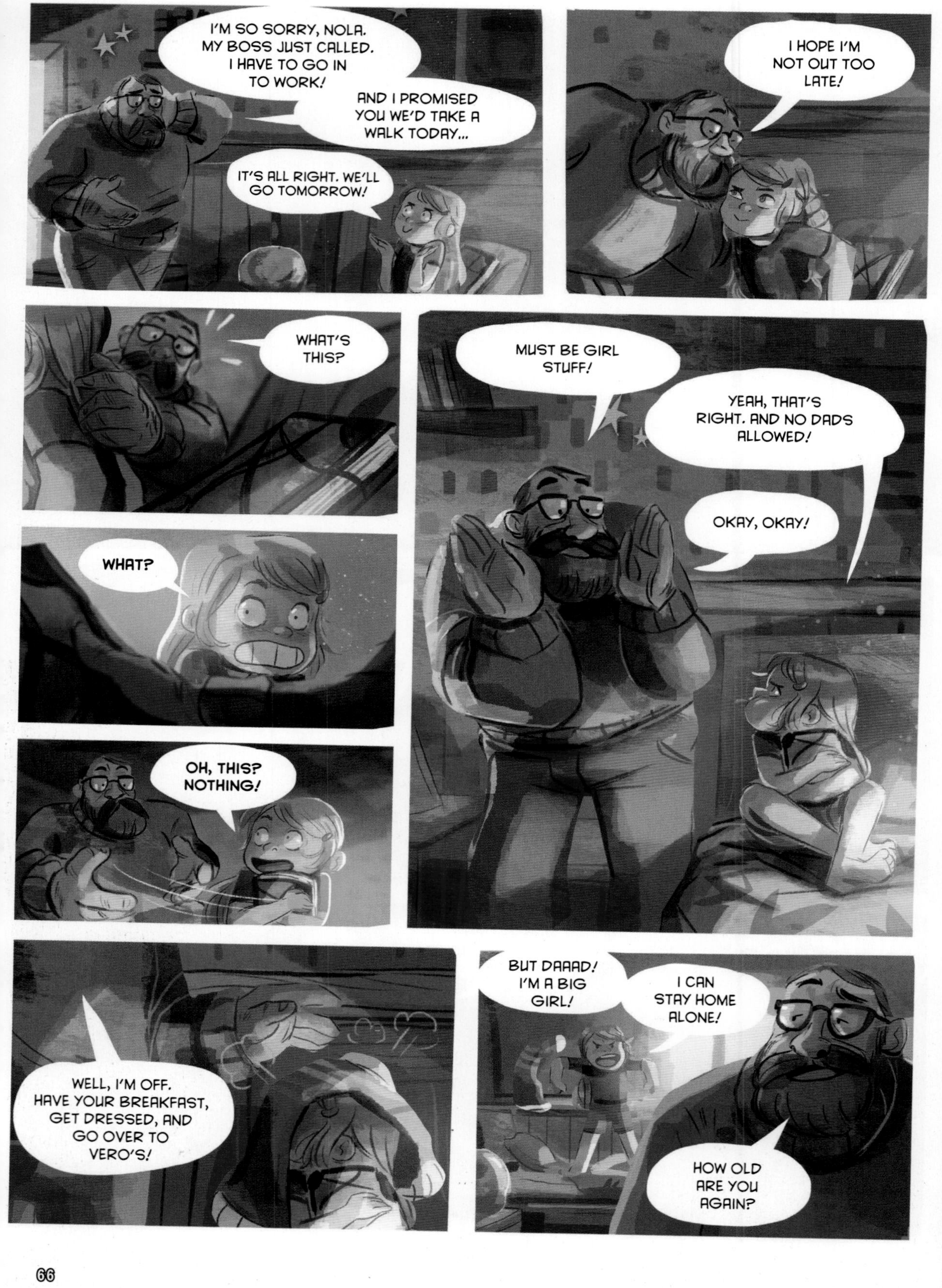
I'M SO SORRY, NOLA. MY BOSS JUST CALLED. I HAVE TO GO IN TO WORK!
AND I PROMISED YOU WE'D TAKE A WALK TODAY...
IT'S ALL RIGHT. WE'LL GO TOMORROW!
I HOPE I'M NOT OUT TOO LATE!
WHAT'S THIS?
WHAT?
OH, THIS? NOTHING!
MUST BE GIRL STUFF!
YEAH, THAT'S RIGHT. AND NO DADS ALLOWED!
OKAY, OKAY!
WELL, I'M OFF. HAVE YOUR BREAKFAST, GET DRESSED, AND GO OVER TO VERO'S!
BUT DAAAD! I'M A BIG GIRL!
I CAN STAY HOME ALONE!
HOW OLD ARE YOU AGAIN?

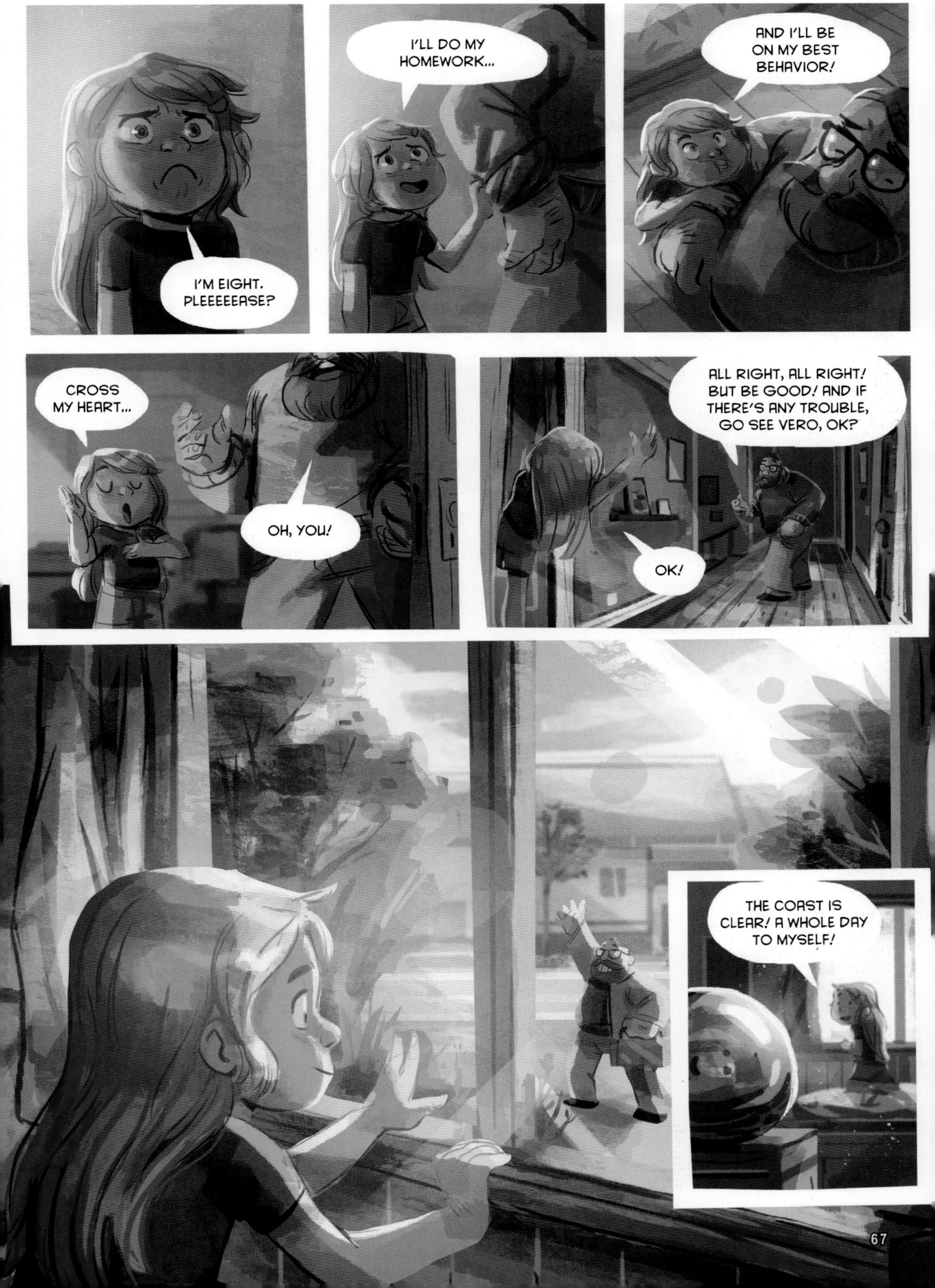
I'M EIGHT. PLEEEEEASE?
I'LL DO MY HOMEWORK...
AND I'LL BE ON MY BEST BEHAVIOR!
CROSS MY HEART...
OH, YOU!
ALL RIGHT, ALL RIGHT! BUT BE GOOD! AND IF THERE'S ANY TROUBLE, GO SEE VERO, OK?
OK!
THE COAST IS CLEAR! A WHOLE DAY TO MYSELF!

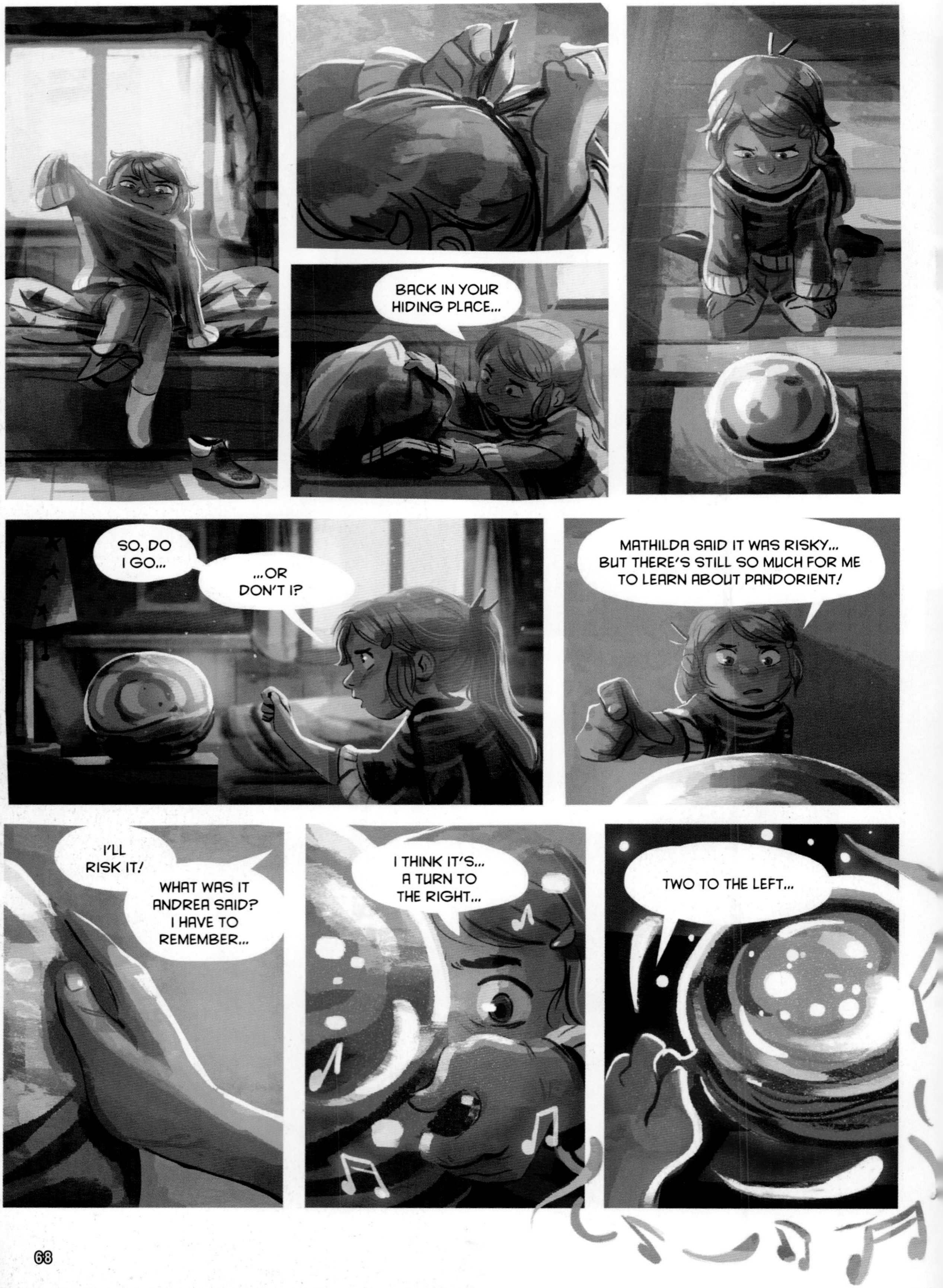
BACK IN YOUR HIDING PLACE...
SO, DO I GO...
...OR DON'T I?
MATHILDA SAID IT WAS RISKY... BUT THERE'S STILL SO MUCH FOR ME TO LEARN ABOUT PANDORIENT!
I'LL RISK IT!
WHAT WAS IT ANDREA SAID? I HAVE TO REMEMBER...
I THINK IT'S... A TURN TO THE RIGHT...
TWO TO THE LEFT...

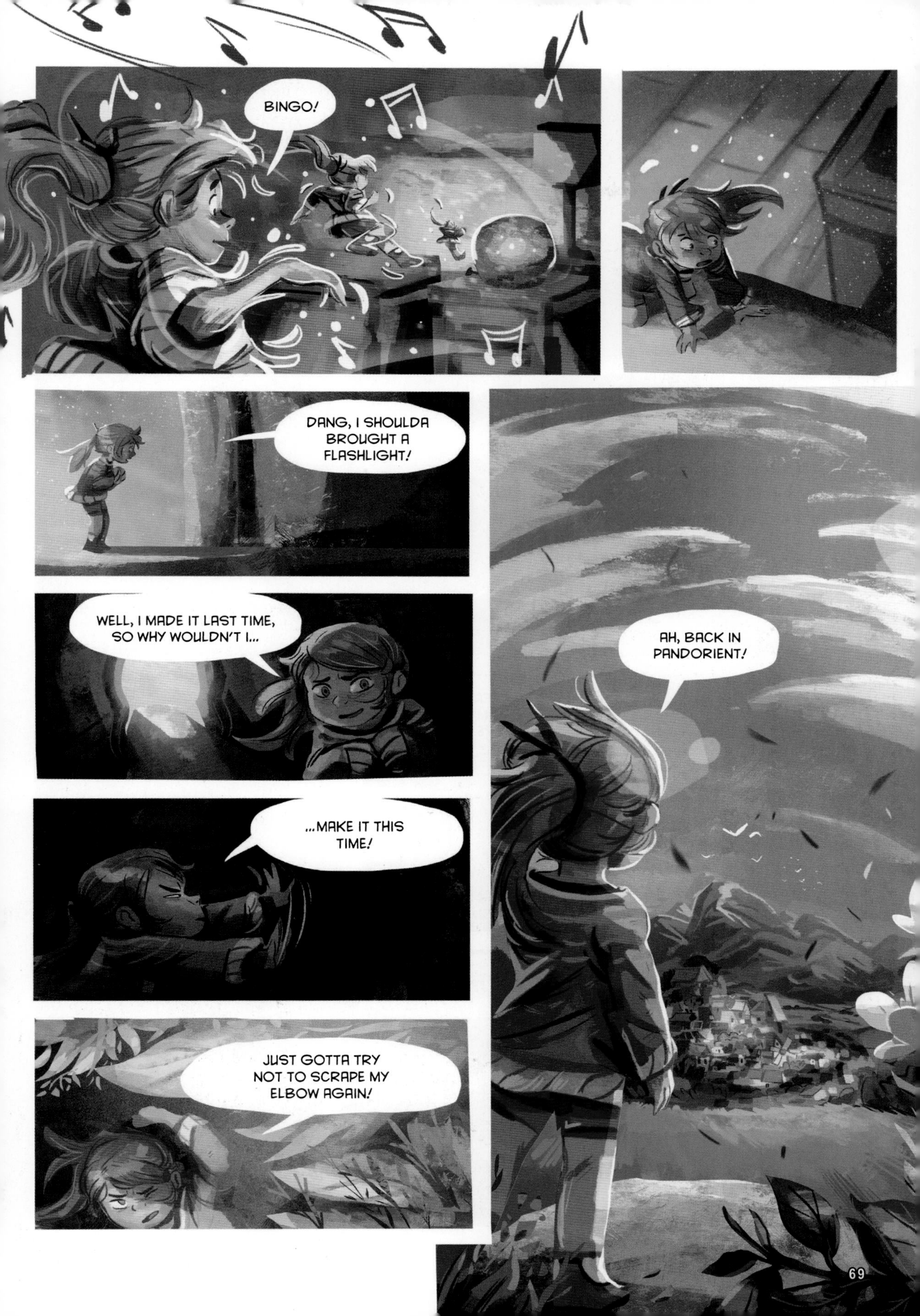
BINGO!
DANG, I SHOULDA BROUGHT A FLASHLIGHT!
WELL, I MADE IT LAST TIME, SO WHY WOULDN'T I...
...MAKE IT THIS TIME!
JUST GOTTA TRY NOT TO SCRAPE MY ELBOW AGAIN!
AH, BACK IN PANDORIENT!

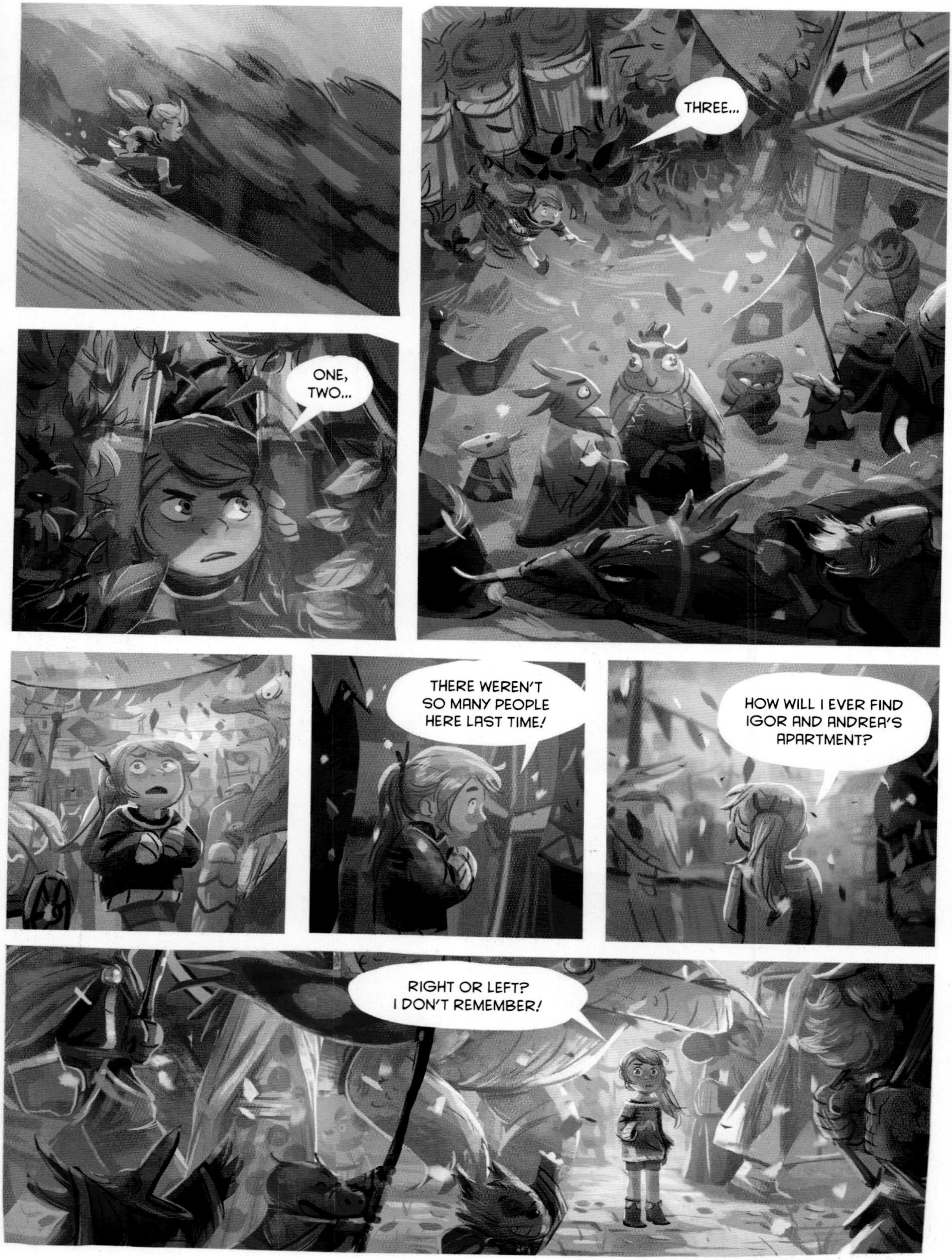

ONE, TWO...
THREE...
THERE WEREN'T SO MANY PEOPLE HERE LAST TIME!
HOW WILL I EVER FIND IGOR AND ANDREA'S APARTMENT?
RIGHT OR LEFT? I DON'T REMEMBER!

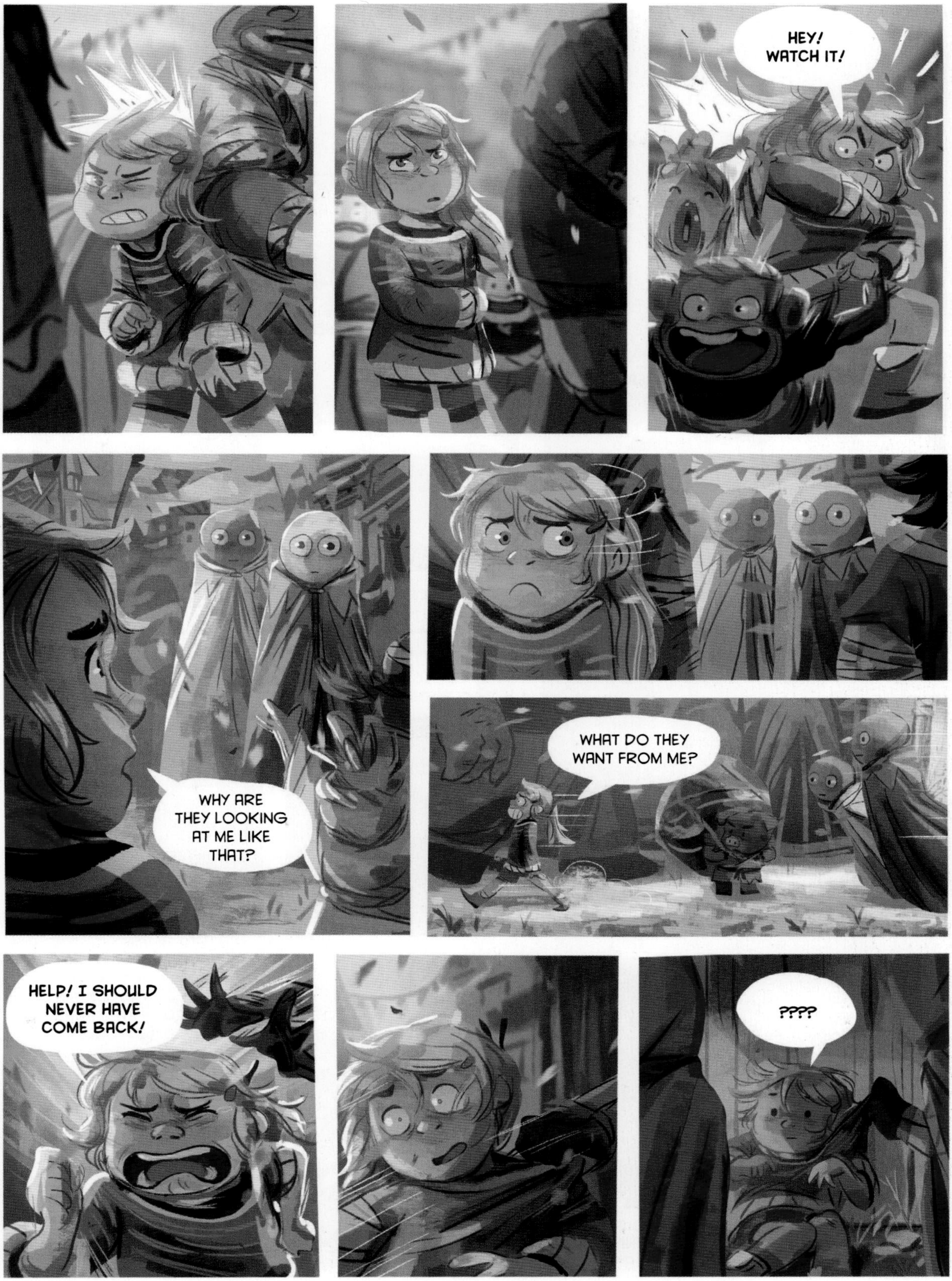

HEY! WATCH IT!
WHY ARE THEY LOOKING AT ME LIKE THAT?
WHAT DO THEY WANT FROM ME?
HELP! I SHOULD NEVER HAVE COME BACK!
????

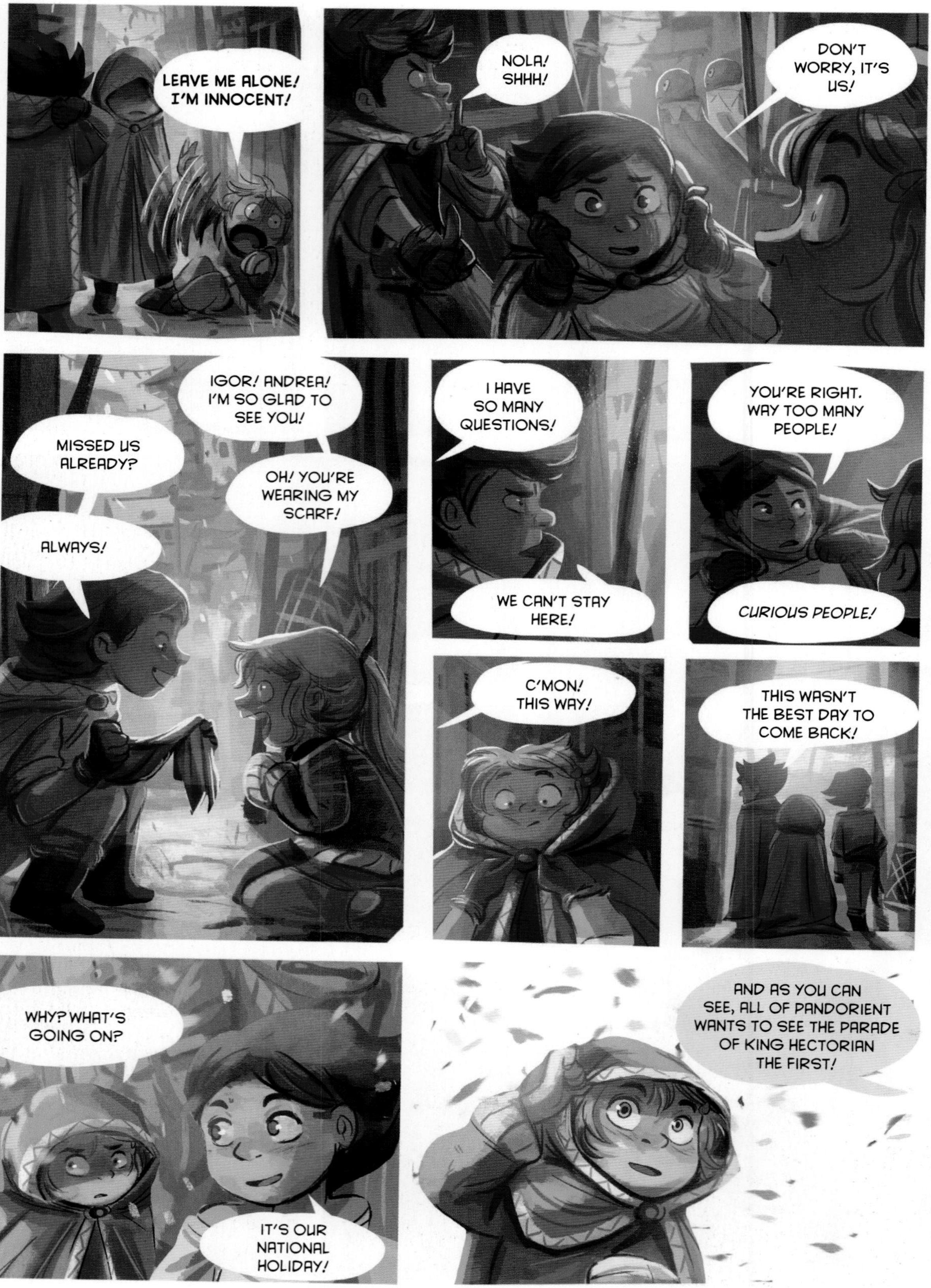

LEAVE ME ALONE! I'M INNOCENT!
NOLA! SHHH!
DON'T WORRY, IT'S US!
IGOR! ANDREA! I'M SO GLAD TO SEE YOU!
MISSED US ALREADY?
OH! YOU'RE WEARING MY SCARF!
ALWAYS!
I HAVE SO MANY QUESTIONS!
WE CAN'T STAY HERE!
YOU'RE RIGHT. WAY TOO MANY PEOPLE!
CURIOUS PEOPLE!
C'MON! THIS WAY!
THIS WASN'T THE BEST DAY TO COME BACK!
WHY? WHAT'S GOING ON?
IT'S OUR NATIONAL HOLIDAY!
AND AS YOU CAN SEE, ALL OF PANDORIENT WANTS TO SEE THE PARADE OF KING HECTORIAN THE FIRST!

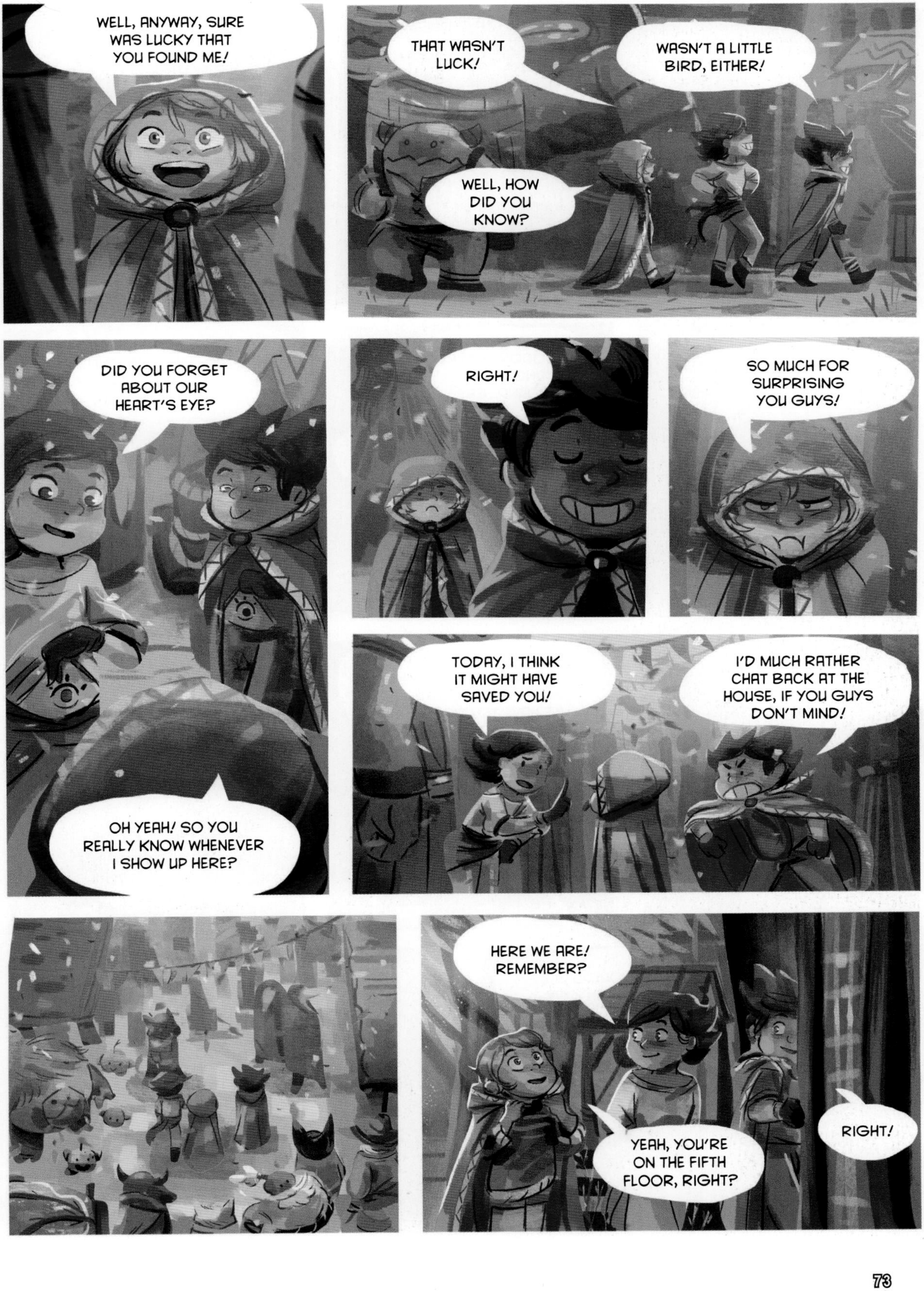

WELL, ANYWAY, SURE WAS LUCKY THAT YOU FOUND ME!
THAT WASN'T LUCK!
WASN'T A LITTLE BIRD, EITHER!
WELL, HOW DID YOU KNOW?
DID YOU FORGET ABOUT OUR HEART'S EYE?
OH YEAH! SO YOU REALLY KNOW WHENEVER I SHOW UP HERE?
RIGHT!
SO MUCH FOR SURPRISING YOU GUYS!
TODAY, I THINK IT MIGHT HAVE SAVED YOU!
I'D MUCH RATHER CHAT BACK AT THE HOUSE, IF YOU GUYS DON'T MIND!
HERE WE ARE! REMEMBER?
YEAH, YOU'RE ON THE FIFTH FLOOR, RIGHT?
RIGHT!

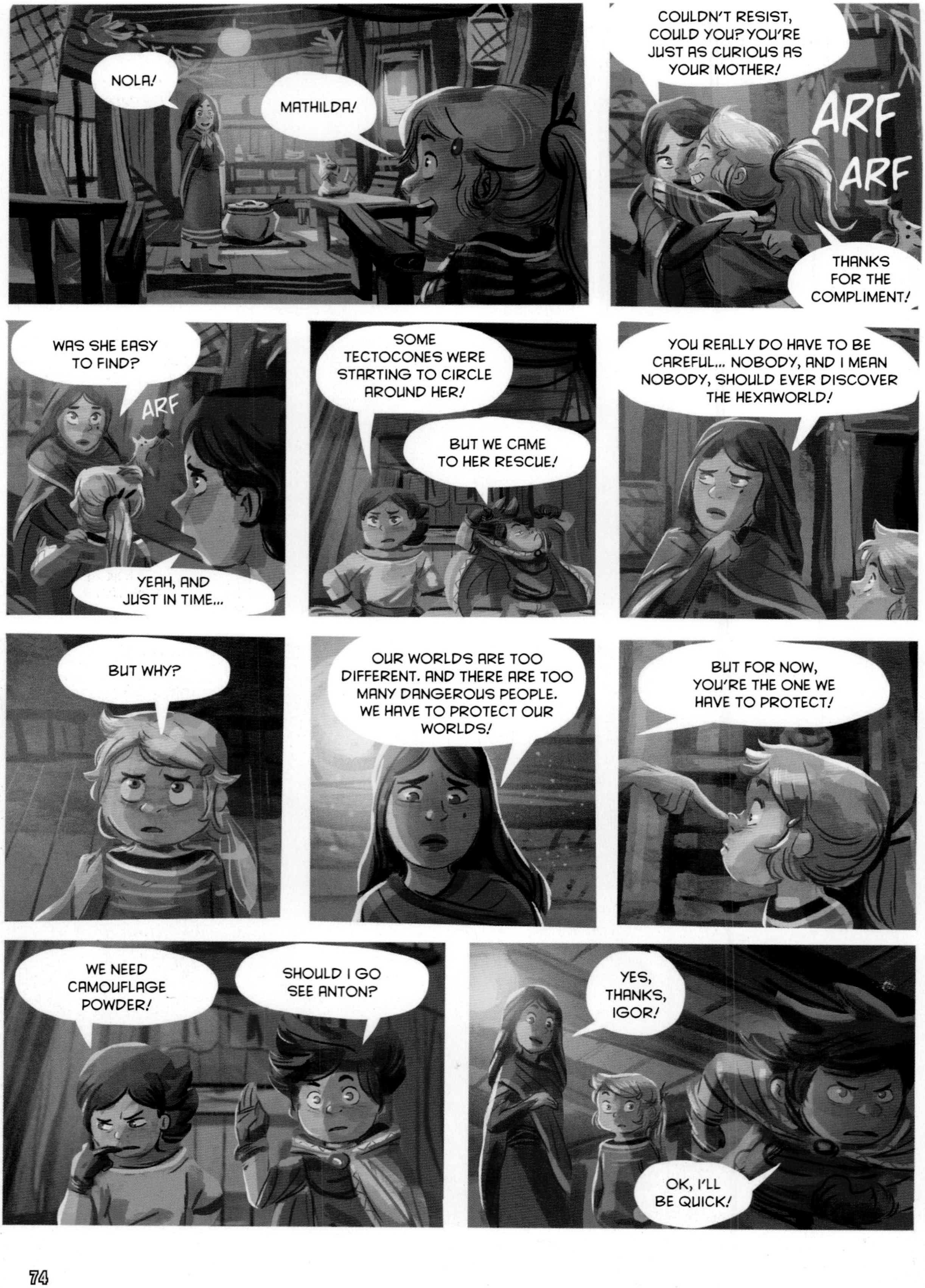
NOLA!
MATHILDA!
COULDN'T RESIST, COULD YOU? YOU'RE JUST AS CURIOUS AS YOUR MOTHER!
ARF
ARF
THANKS FOR THE COMPLIMENT!
WAS SHE EASY TO FIND?
ARF
YEAH, AND JUST IN TIME...
SOME TECTOCONES WERE STARTING TO CIRCLE AROUND HER!
BUT WE CAME TO HER RESCUE!
YOU REALLY DO HAVE TO BE CAREFUL... NOBODY, AND I MEAN NOBODY, SHOULD EVER DISCOVER THE HEXAWORLD!
BUT WHY?
OUR WORLDS ARE TOO DIFFERENT. AND THERE ARE TOO MANY DANGEROUS PEOPLE. WE HAVE TO PROTECT OUR WORLDS!
BUT FOR NOW, YOU'RE THE ONE WE HAVE TO PROTECT!
WE NEED CAMOUFLAGE POWDER!
SHOULD I GO SEE ANTON?
YES, THANKS, IGOR!
OK, I'LL BE QUICK!

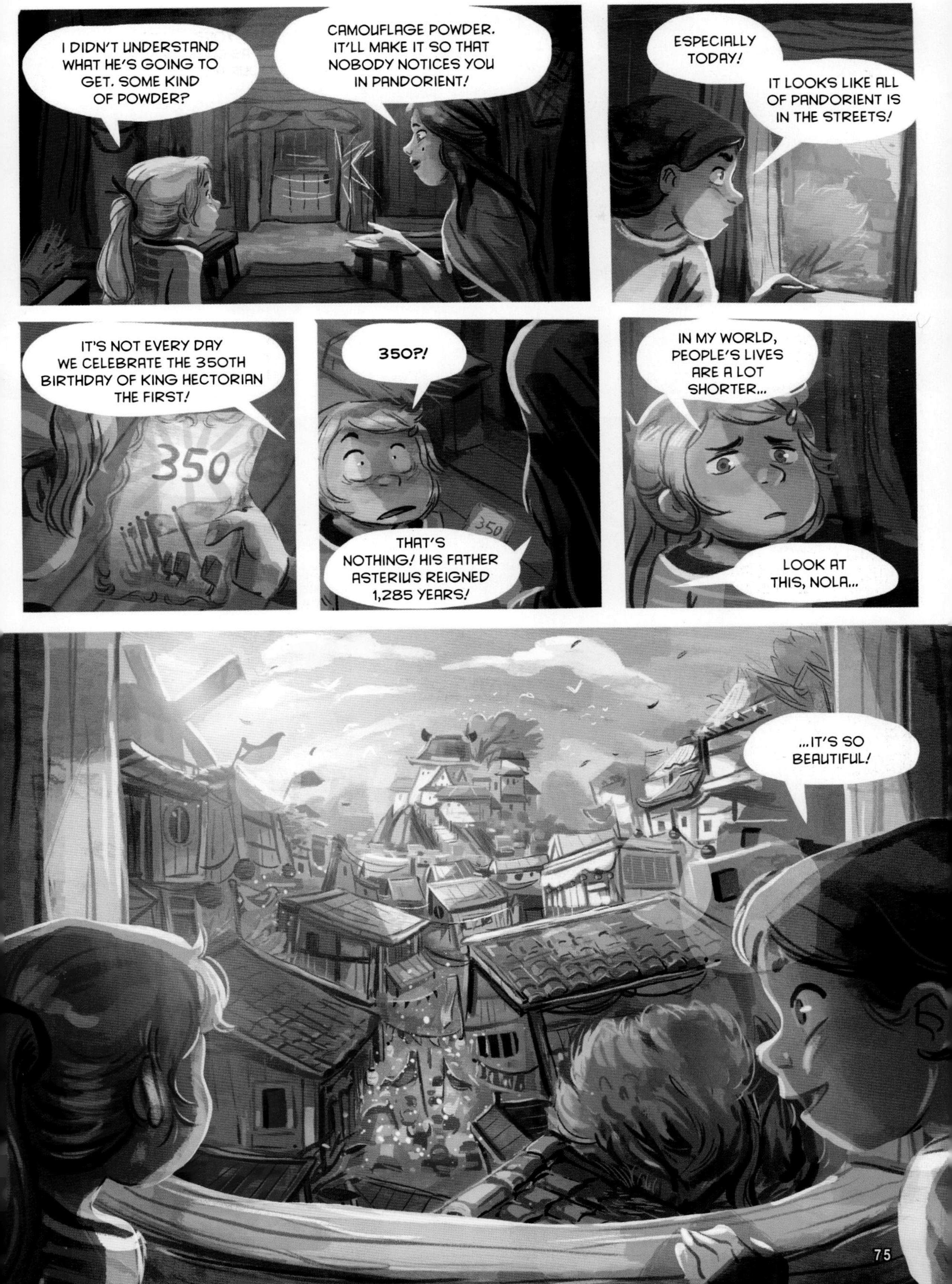
I DIDN'T UNDERSTAND WHAT HE'S GOING TO GET. SOME KIND OF POWDER?
CAMOUFLAGE POWDER. IT'LL MAKE IT SO THAT NOBODY NOTICES YOU IN PANDORIENT!
ESPECIALLY TODAY!
IT LOOKS LIKE ALL OF PANDORIENT IS IN THE STREETS!
IT'S NOT EVERY DAY WE CELEBRATE THE 350TH BIRTHDAY OF KING HECTORIAN THE FIRST!
350
350?!
350
THAT'S NOTHING! HIS FATHER ASTERIUS REIGNED 1,285 YEARS!
IN MY WORLD, PEOPLE'S LIVES ARE A LOT SHORTER...
LOOK AT THIS, NOLA...
...IT'S SO BEAUTIFUL!

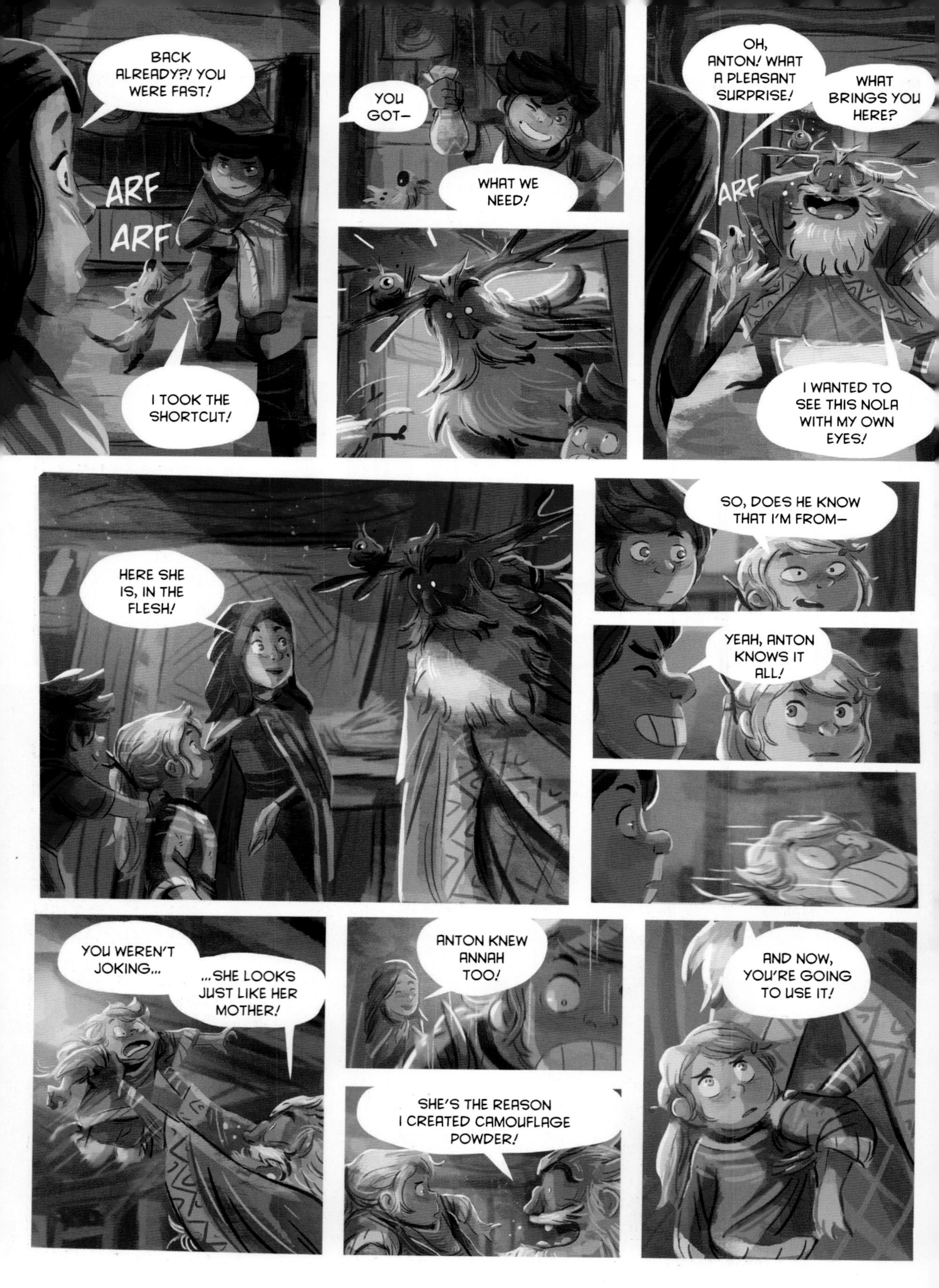

BACK ALREADY?! YOU WERE FAST!
ARF
ARF
I TOOK THE SHORTCUT!
YOU GOT—
WHAT WE NEED!
OH, ANTON! WHAT A PLEASANT SURPRISE!
WHAT BRINGS YOU HERE?
ARF
I WANTED TO SEE THIS NOLA WITH MY OWN EYES!
HERE SHE IS, IN THE FLESH!
SO, DOES HE KNOW THAT I'M FROM—
YEAH, ANTON KNOWS IT ALL!
YOU WEREN'T JOKING...
...SHE LOOKS JUST LIKE HER MOTHER!
ANTON KNEW ANNAH TOO!
SHE'S THE REASON I CREATED CAMOUFLAGE POWDER!
AND NOW, YOU'RE GOING TO USE IT!

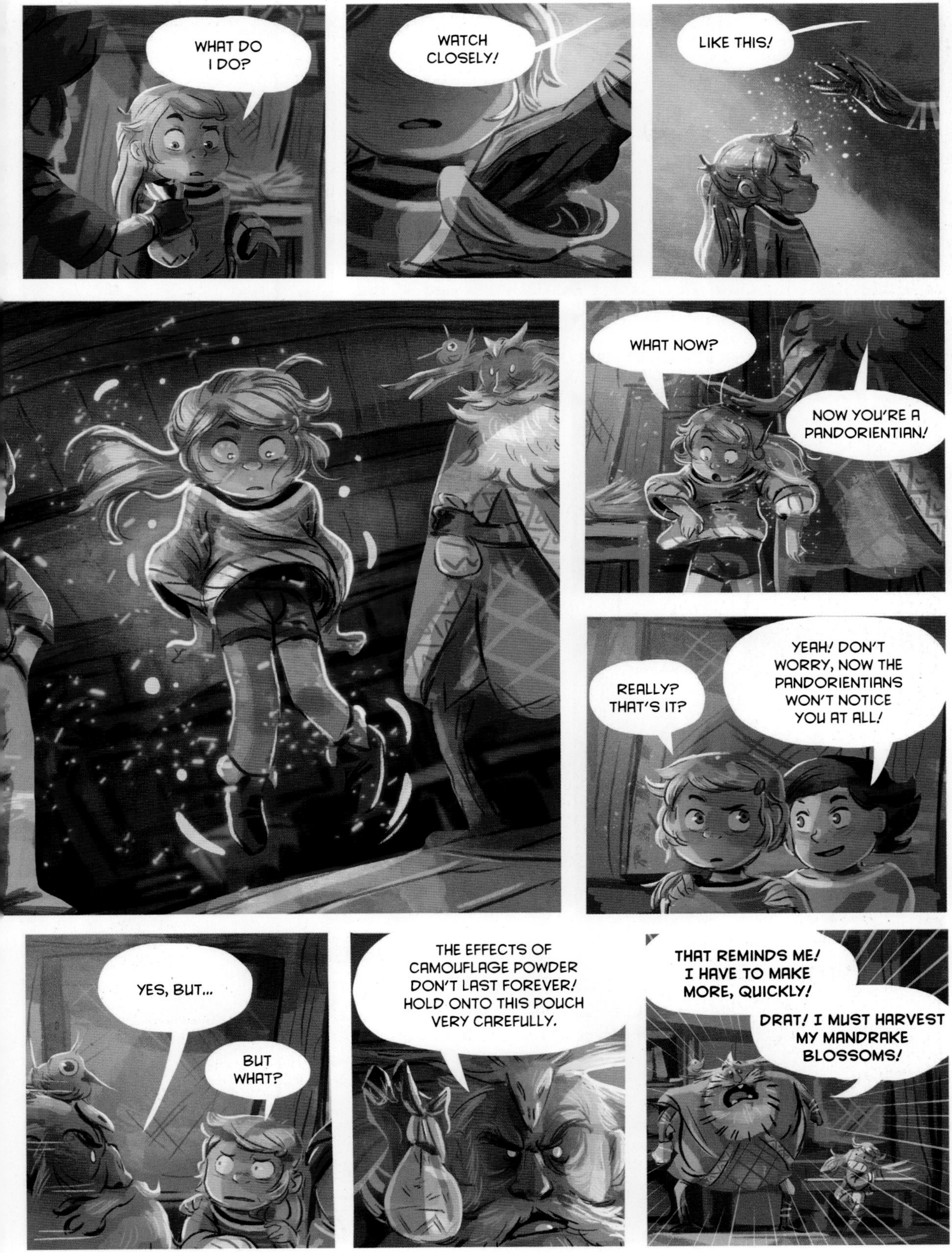
WHAT DO I DO?
WATCH CLOSELY!
LIKE THIS!
WHAT NOW?
NOW YOU'RE A PANDORIENTIAN!
REALLY? THAT'S IT?
YEAH! DON'T WORRY, NOW THE PANDORIENTIANS WON'T NOTICE YOU AT ALL!
YES, BUT...
BUT WHAT?
THE EFFECTS OF CAMOUFLAGE POWDER DON'T LAST FOREVER! HOLD ONTO THIS POUCH VERY CAREFULLY.
THAT REMINDS ME! I HAVE TO MAKE MORE, QUICKLY!
DRAT! I MUST HARVEST MY MANDRAKE BLOSSOMS!

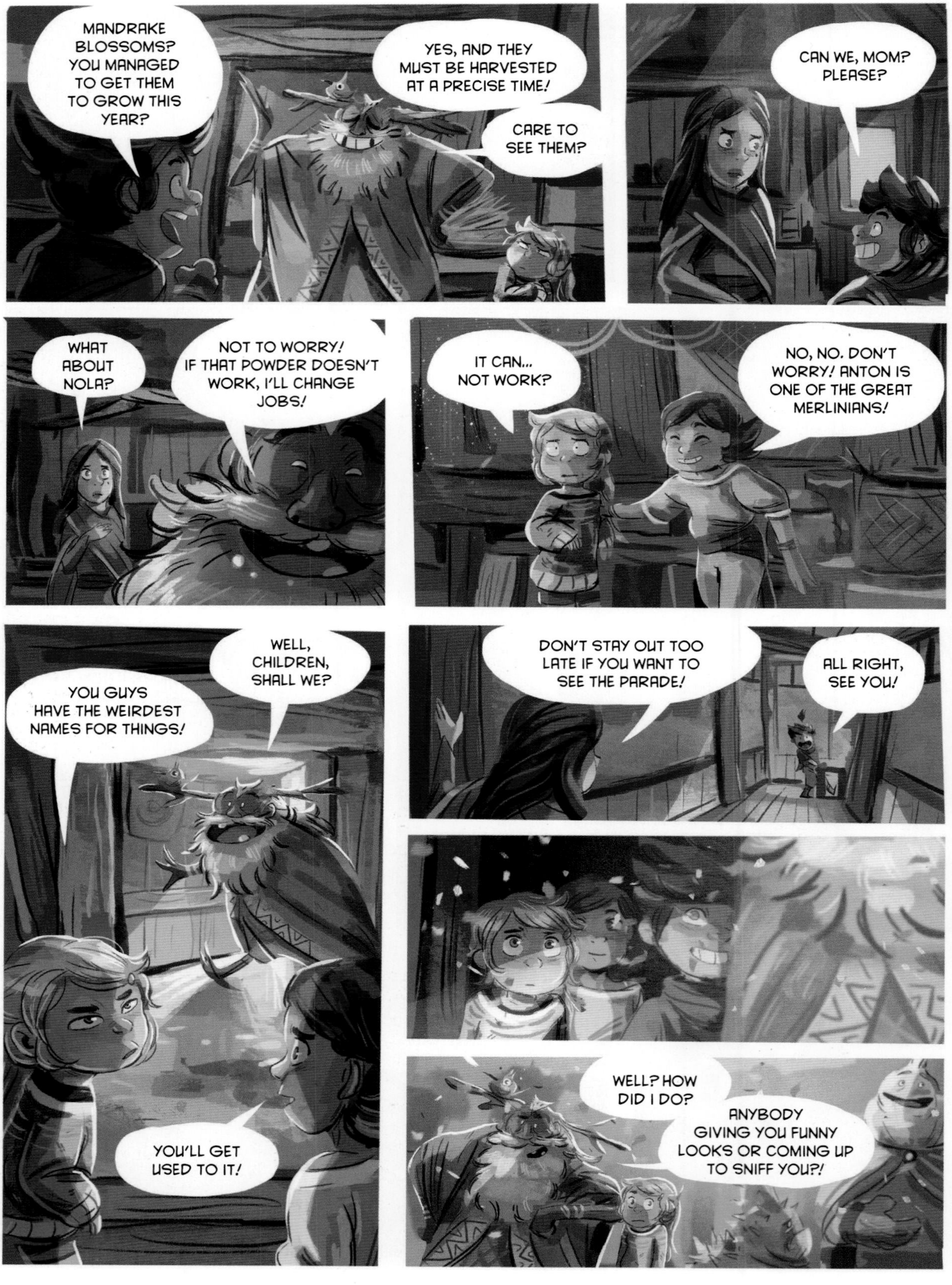
MANDRAKE BLOSSOMS? YOU MANAGED TO GET THEM TO GROW THIS YEAR?
YES, AND THEY MUST BE HARVESTED AT A PRECISE TIME!
CARE TO SEE THEM?
CAN WE, MOM? PLEASE?
WHAT ABOUT NOLA?
NOT TO WORRY! IF THAT POWDER DOESN'T WORK, I'LL CHANGE JOBS!
IT CAN... NOT WORK?
NO, NO. DON'T WORRY! ANTON IS ONE OF THE GREAT MERLINIANS!
YOU GUYS HAVE THE WEIRDEST NAMES FOR THINGS!
WELL, CHILDREN, SHALL WE?
YOU'LL GET USED TO IT!
DON'T STAY OUT TOO LATE IF YOU WANT TO SEE THE PARADE!
ALL RIGHT, SEE YOU!
WELL? HOW DID I DO?
ANYBODY GIVING YOU FUNNY LOOKS OR COMING UP TO SNIFF YOU?!

MY MY MY! WHAT A CROWD THERE IS TODAY!

RELAX! YOU'RE JUST ANOTHER PANDORIENTIAN NOW!

I HEAR THERE'S GOING TO BE FIREWORKS!

YOU KNOW KING HECTORIAN THE FIRST ALWAYS DOES THINGS RIGHT!

I LOVE FIRE-WORKS!

DARN! I'LL BE GONE BY THEN!

I DON'T WANT MY DAD TO WORRY!

YES, HE MUSTN'T SUSPECT THE SLIGHTEST THING!

I'LL MAKE SURE HE DOESN'T!

COME ON, LET'S TAKE THE SHORTCUT...

...OR ELSE MY BLOSSOMS WILL WILT BEFORE WE GET THERE!

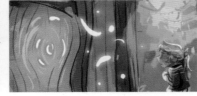

READY?

??

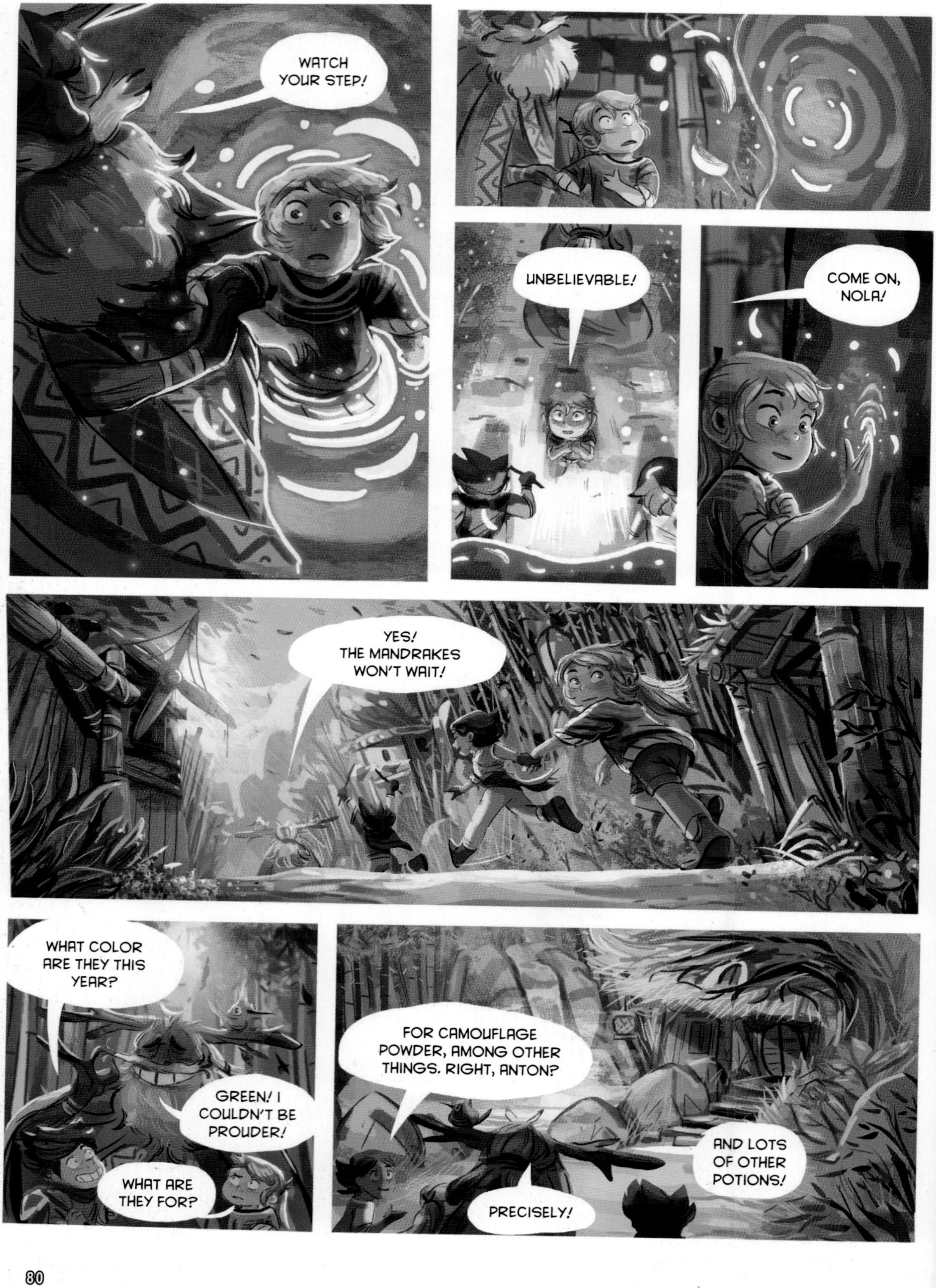
WATCH YOUR STEP!
UNBELIEVABLE!
COME ON, NOLA!
YES! THE MANDRAKES WON'T WAIT!
WHAT COLOR ARE THEY THIS YEAR?
GREEN! I COULDN'T BE PROUDER!
WHAT ARE THEY FOR?
FOR CAMOUFLAGE POWDER, AMONG OTHER THINGS. RIGHT, ANTON?
PRECISELY!
AND LOTS OF OTHER POTIONS!

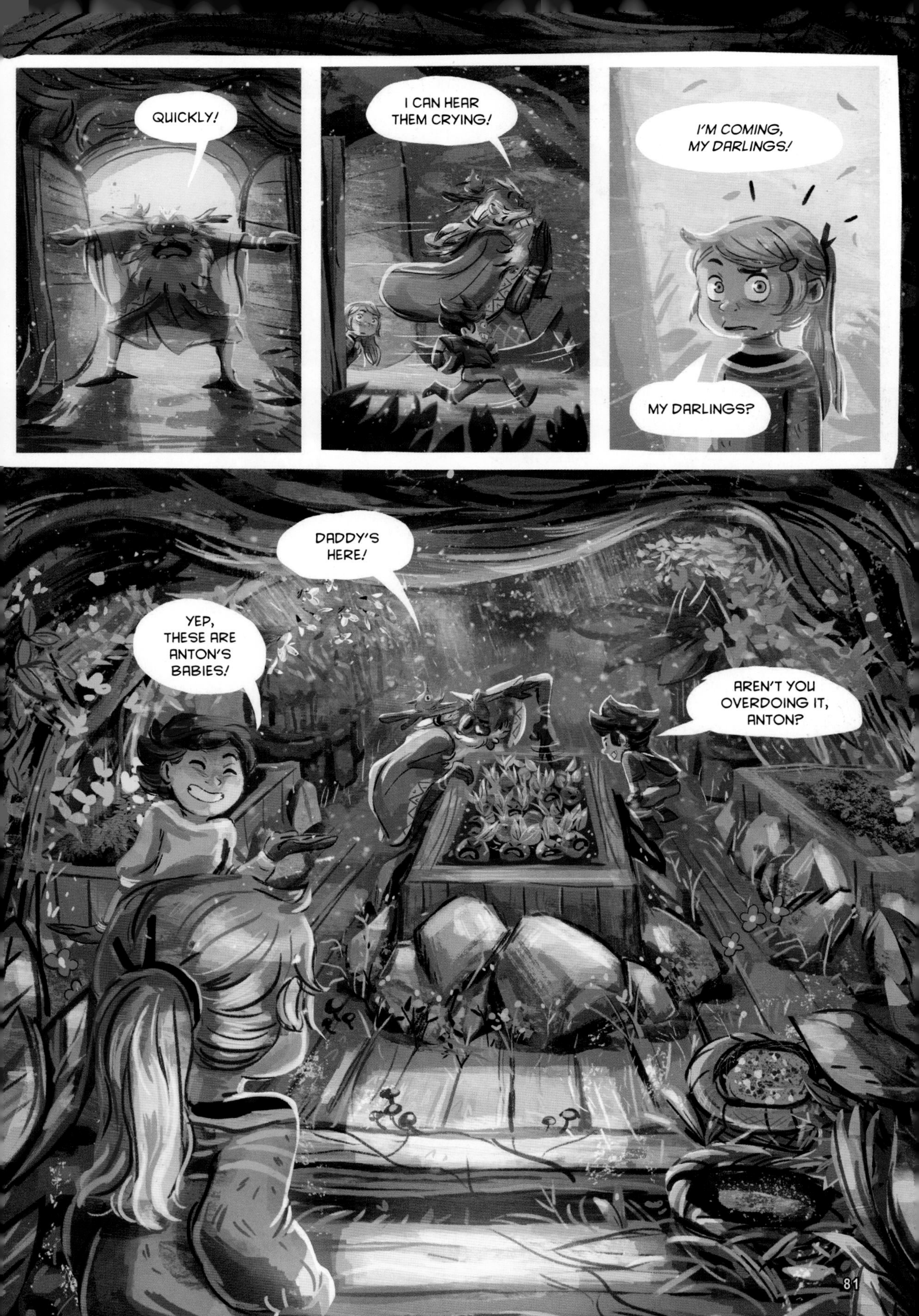
QUICKLY!
I CAN HEAR THEM CRYING!
I'M COMING, MY DARLINGS!
MY DARLINGS?
DADDY'S HERE!
YEP, THESE ARE ANTON'S BABIES!
AREN'T YOU OVERDOING IT, ANTON?

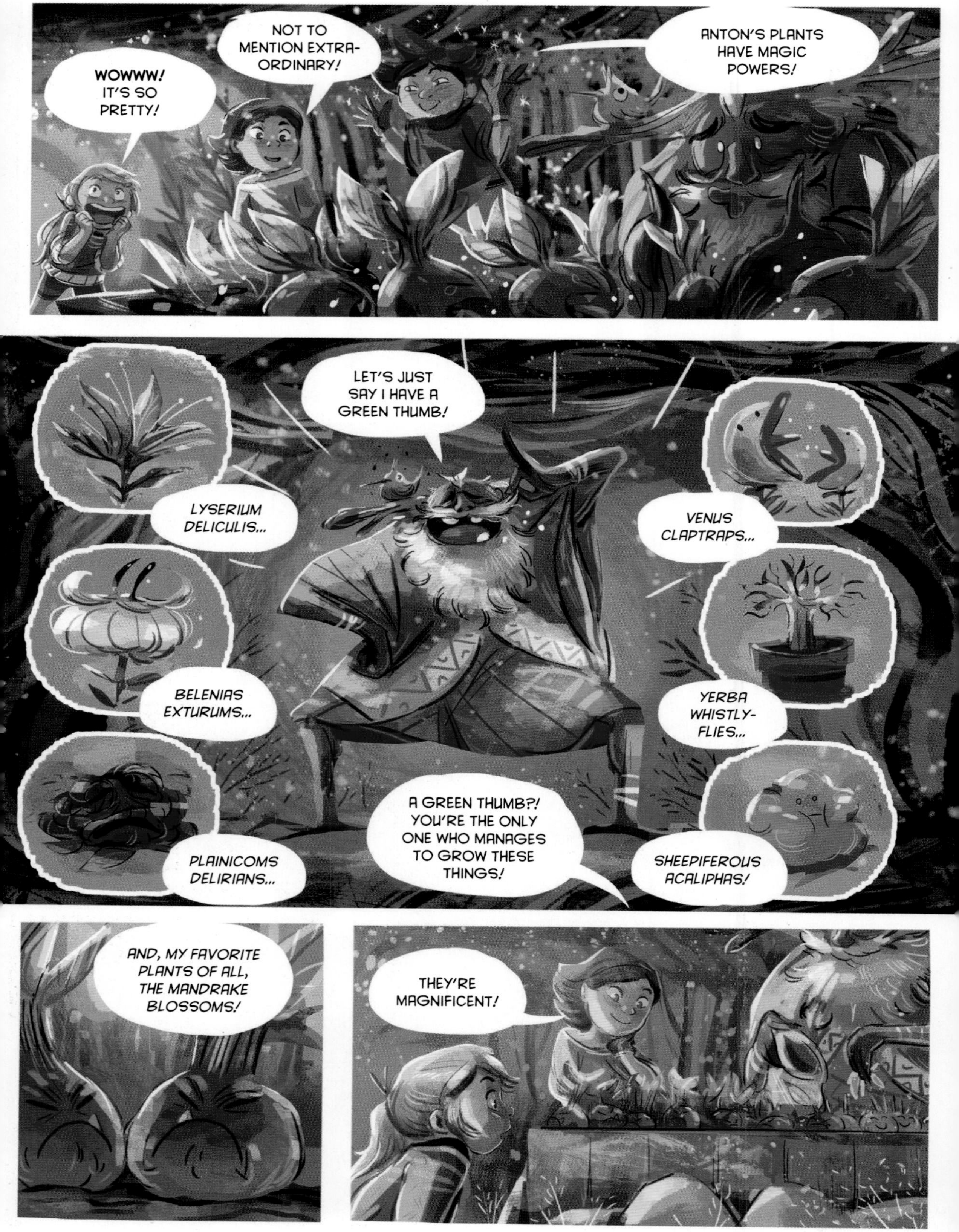

WOWWW! IT'S SO PRETTY!
NOT TO MENTION EXTRA-ORDINARY!
ANTON'S PLANTS HAVE MAGIC POWERS!
LET'S JUST SAY I HAVE A GREEN THUMB!
LYSERIUM DELICULIS...
VENUS CLAPTRAPS...
BELENIAS EXTURUMS...
YERBA WHISTLY-FLIES...
PLAINICOMS DELIRIANS...
A GREEN THUMB?! YOU'RE THE ONLY ONE WHO MANAGES TO GROW THESE THINGS!
SHEEPIFEROUS ACALIPHAS!
AND, MY FAVORITE PLANTS OF ALL, THE MANDRAKE BLOSSOMS!
THEY'RE MAGNIFICENT!

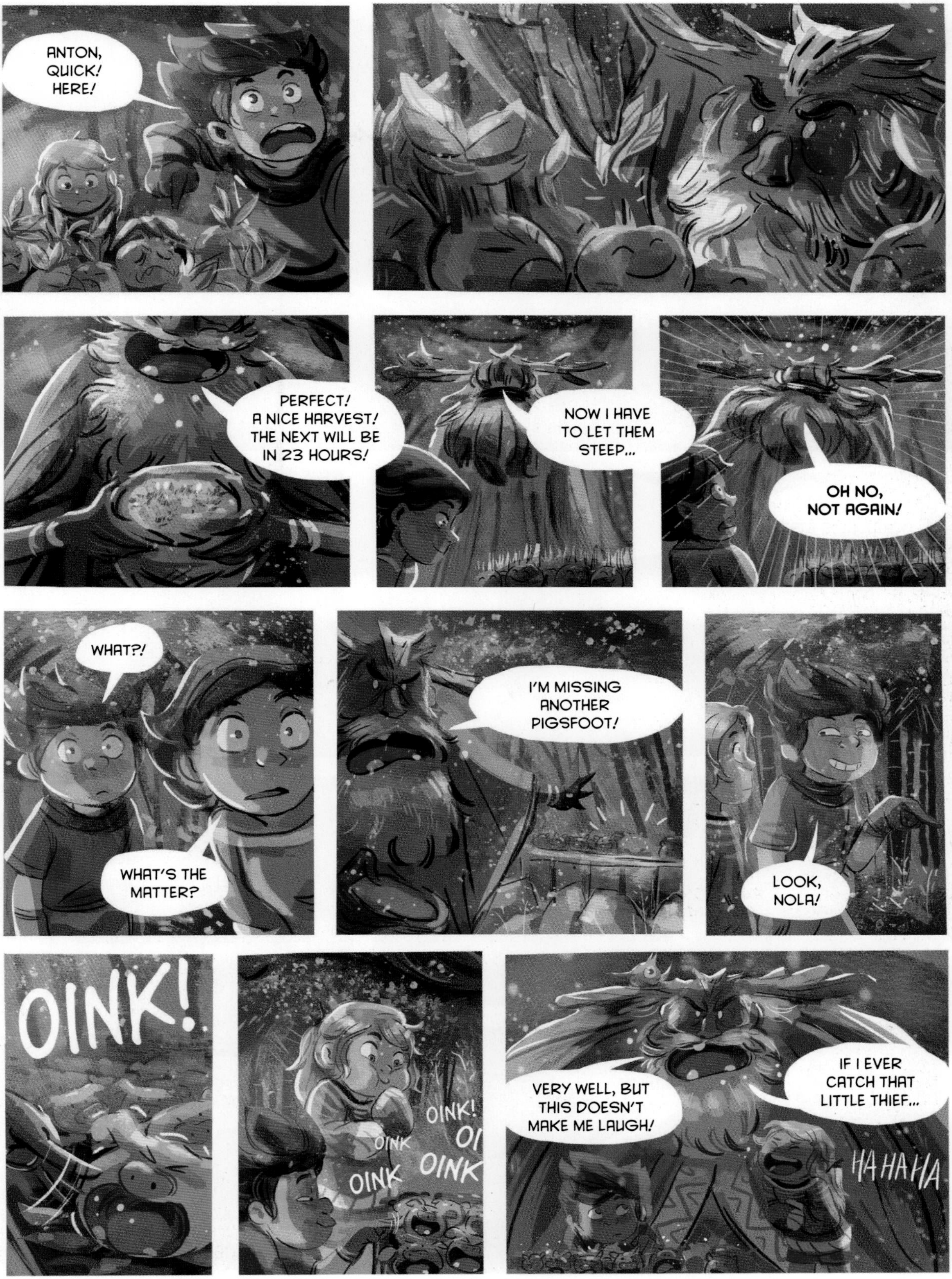
ANTON, QUICK! HERE!
PERFECT! A NICE HARVEST! THE NEXT WILL BE IN 23 HOURS!
NOW I HAVE TO LET THEM STEEP...
OH NO, NOT AGAIN!
WHAT?!
WHAT'S THE MATTER?
I'M MISSING ANOTHER PIGSFOOT!
LOOK, NOLA!
OINK!
OINK!
OINK
OINK
OINK
VERY WELL, BUT THIS DOESN'T MAKE ME LAUGH!
IF I EVER CATCH THAT LITTLE THIEF...
HA HA HA

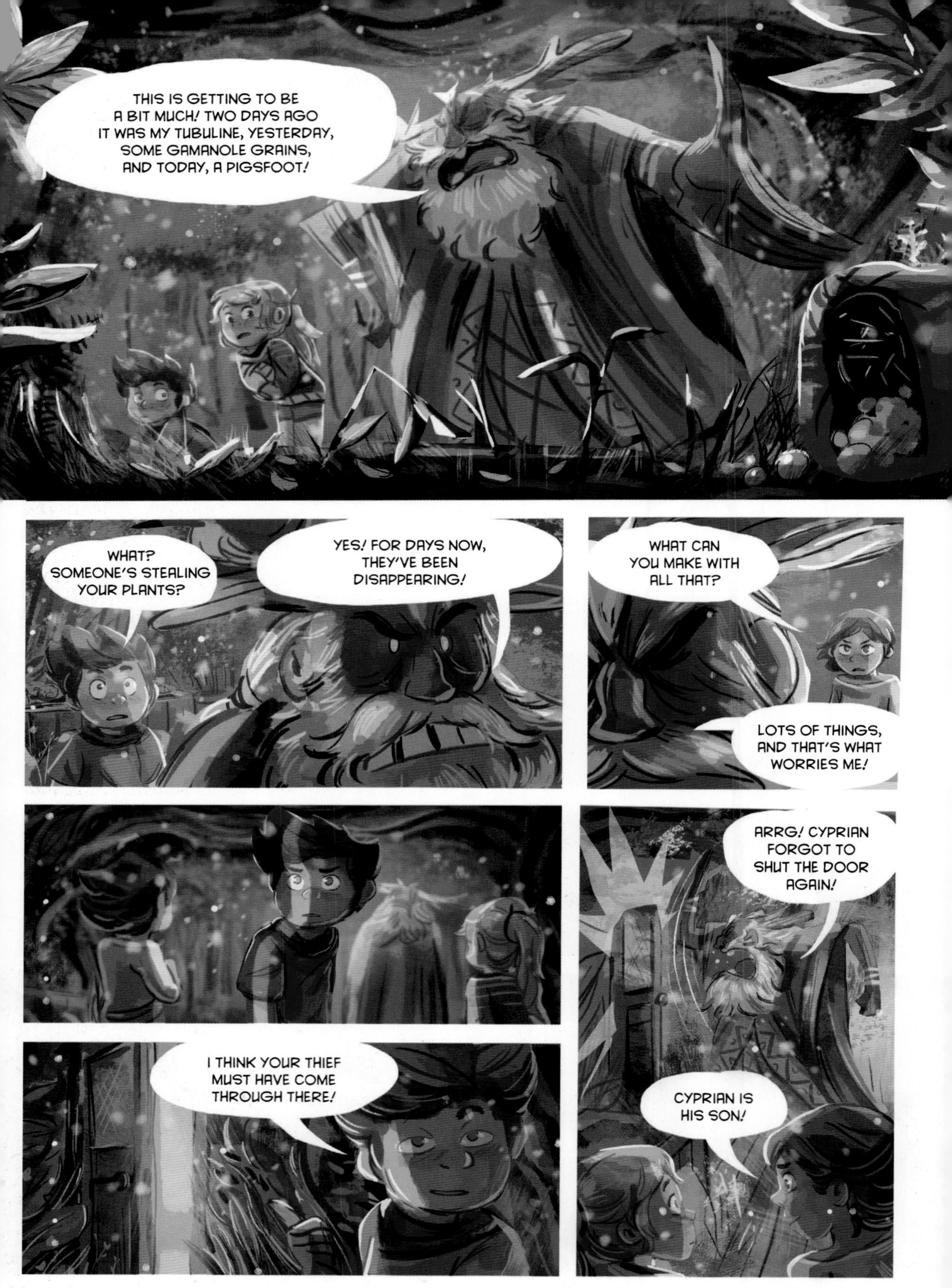
THIS IS GETTING TO BE A BIT MUCH! TWO DAYS AGO IT WAS MY TUBULINE, YESTERDAY, SOME GAMANOLE GRAINS, AND TODAY, A PIGSFOOT!
WHAT? SOMEONE'S STEALING YOUR PLANTS?
YES! FOR DAYS NOW, THEY'VE BEEN DISAPPEARING!
WHAT CAN YOU MAKE WITH ALL THAT?
LOTS OF THINGS, AND THAT'S WHAT WORRIES ME!
ARRG! CYPRIAN FORGOT TO SHUT THE DOOR AGAIN!
I THINK YOUR THIEF MUST HAVE COME THROUGH THERE!
CYPRIAN IS HIS SON!

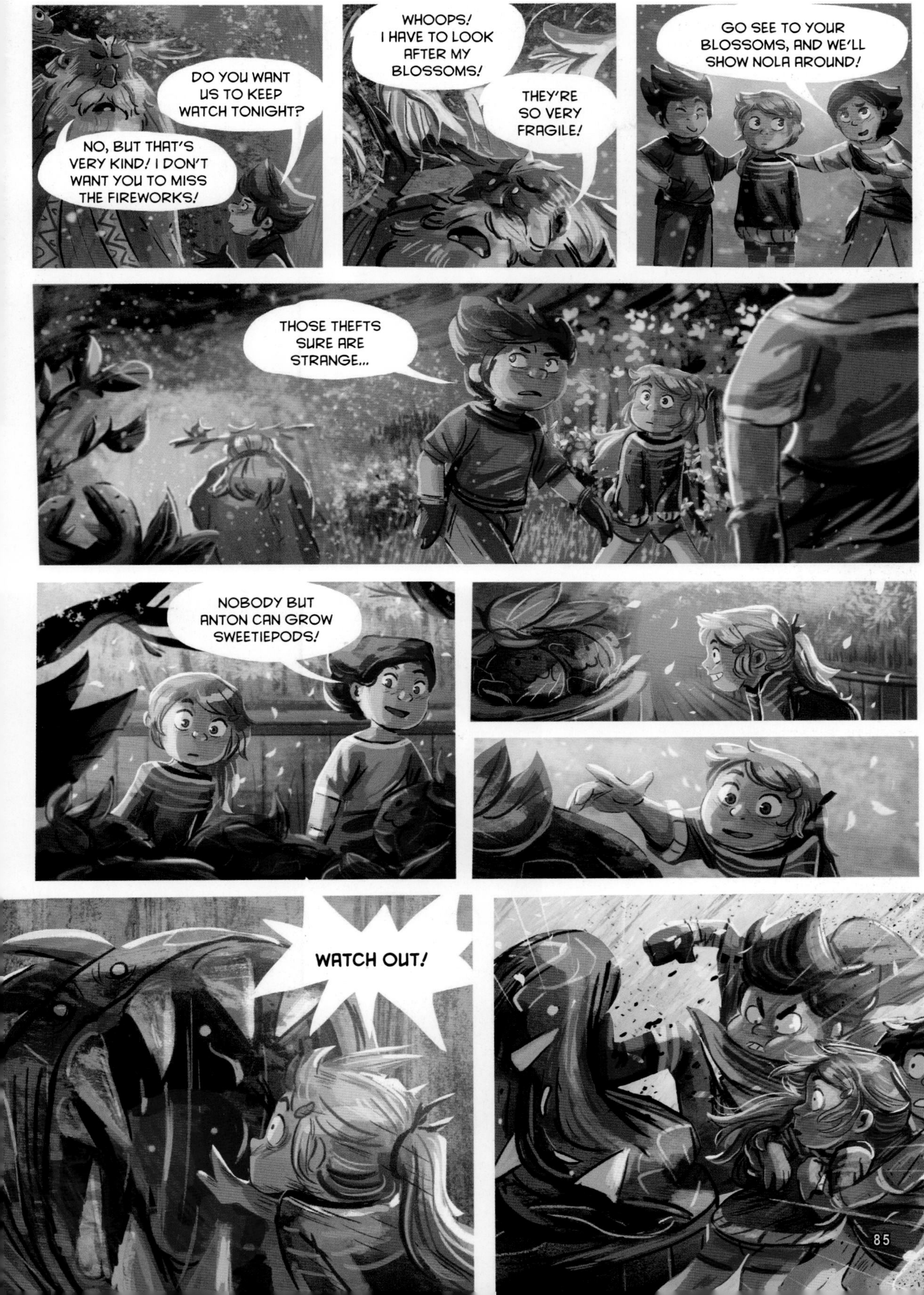
DO YOU WANT US TO KEEP WATCH TONIGHT?
NO, BUT THAT'S VERY KIND! I DON'T WANT YOU TO MISS THE FIREWORKS!
WHOOPS! I HAVE TO LOOK AFTER MY BLOSSOMS!
THEY'RE SO VERY FRAGILE!
GO SEE TO YOUR BLOSSOMS, AND WE'LL SHOW NOLA AROUND!
THOSE THEFTS SURE ARE STRANGE...
NOBODY BUT ANTON CAN GROW SWEETIEPODS!
WATCH OUT!

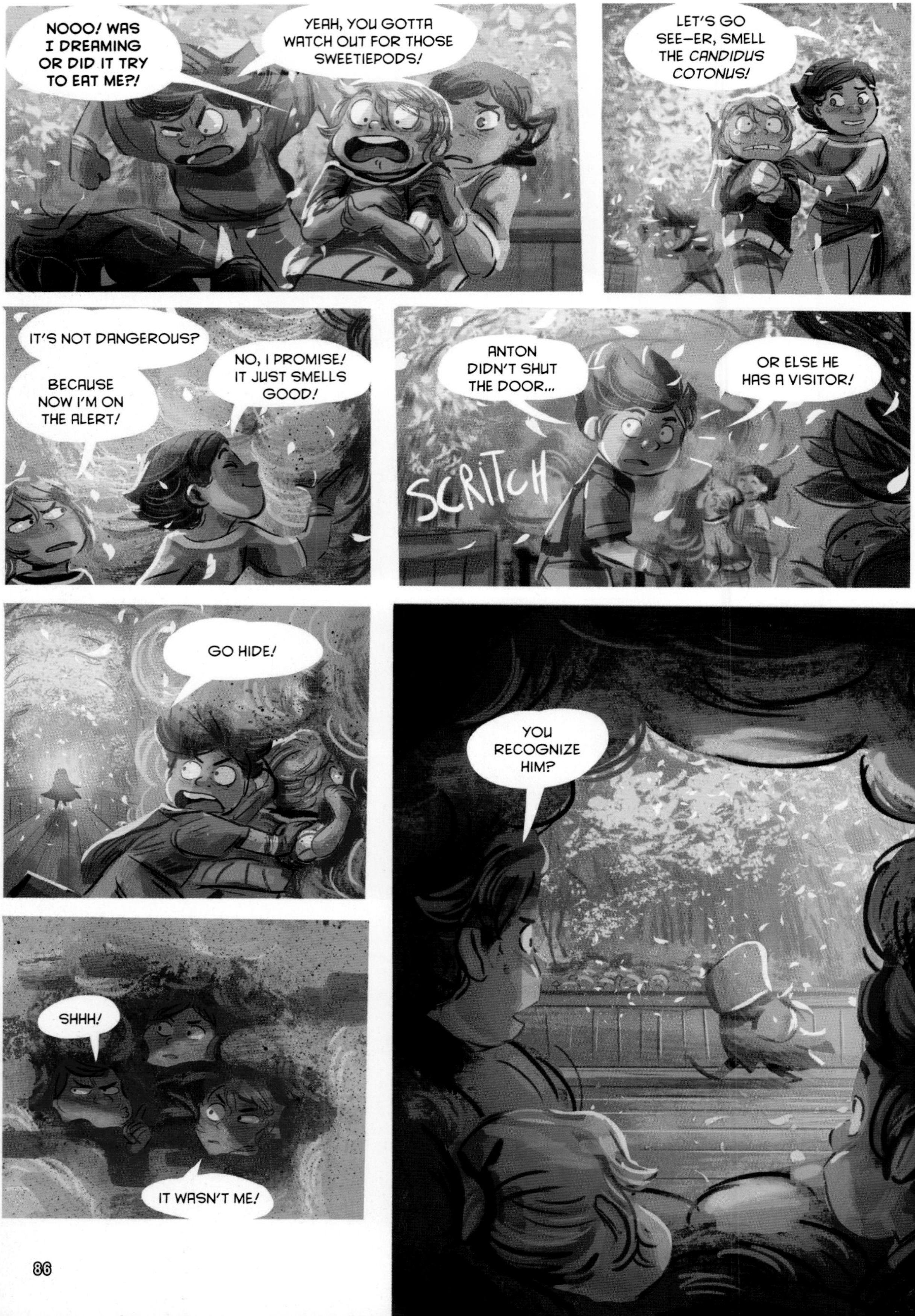
NOOO! WAS I DREAMING OR DID IT TRY TO EAT ME?!
YEAH, YOU GOTTA WATCH OUT FOR THOSE SWEETIEPODS!
LET'S GO SEE—ER, SMELL THE *CANDIDUS COTONUS!*
IT'S NOT DANGEROUS?
BECAUSE NOW I'M ON THE ALERT!
NO, I PROMISE! IT JUST SMELLS GOOD!
ANTON DIDN'T SHUT THE DOOR...
OR ELSE HE HAS A VISITOR!
SCRITCH
GO HIDE!
SHHH!
IT WASN'T ME!
YOU RECOGNIZE HIM?

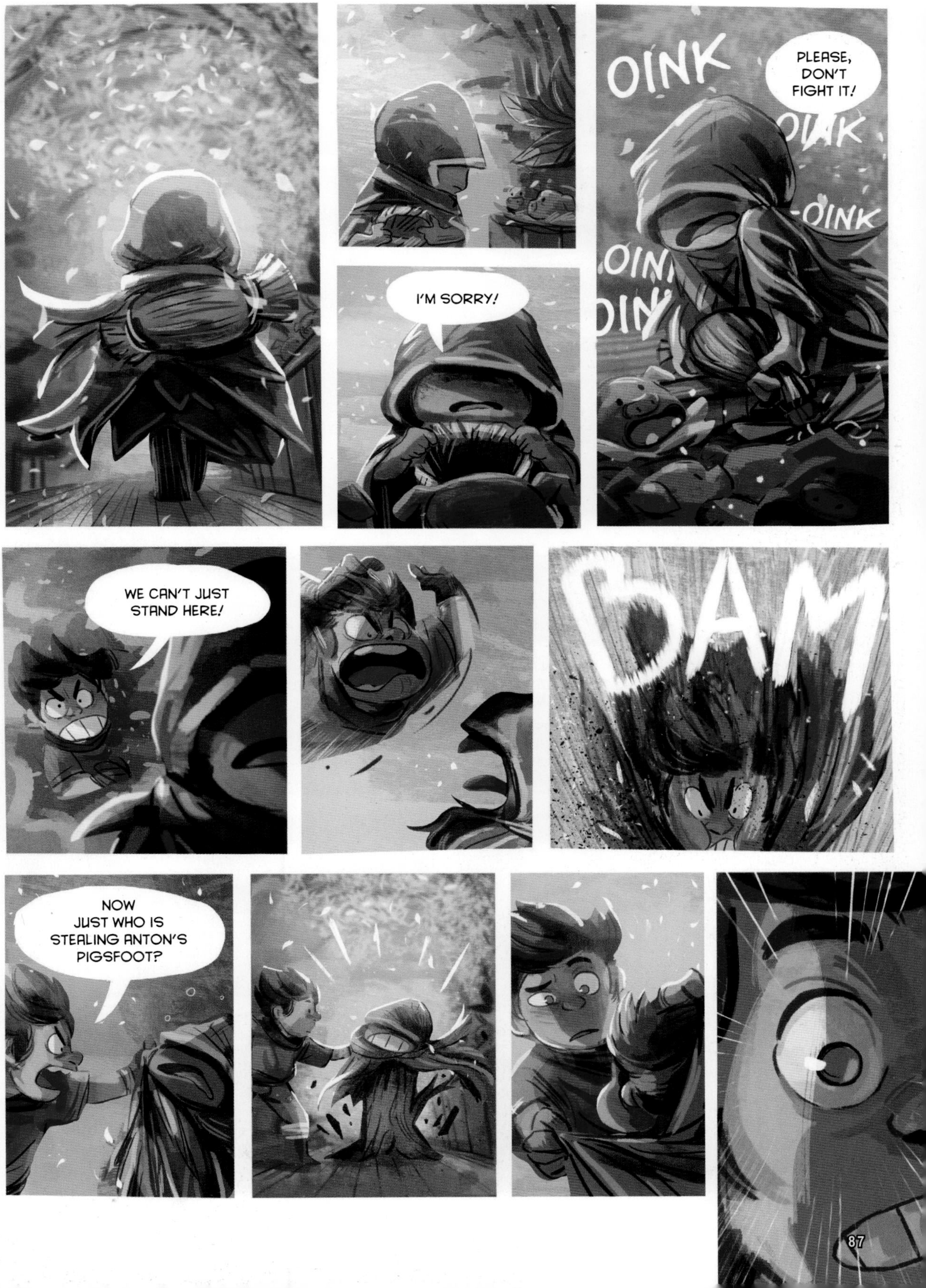
OINK
PLEASE, DON'T FIGHT IT!
I'M SORRY!
WE CAN'T JUST STAND HERE!
BAM
NOW JUST WHO IS STEALING ANTON'S PIGSFOOT?

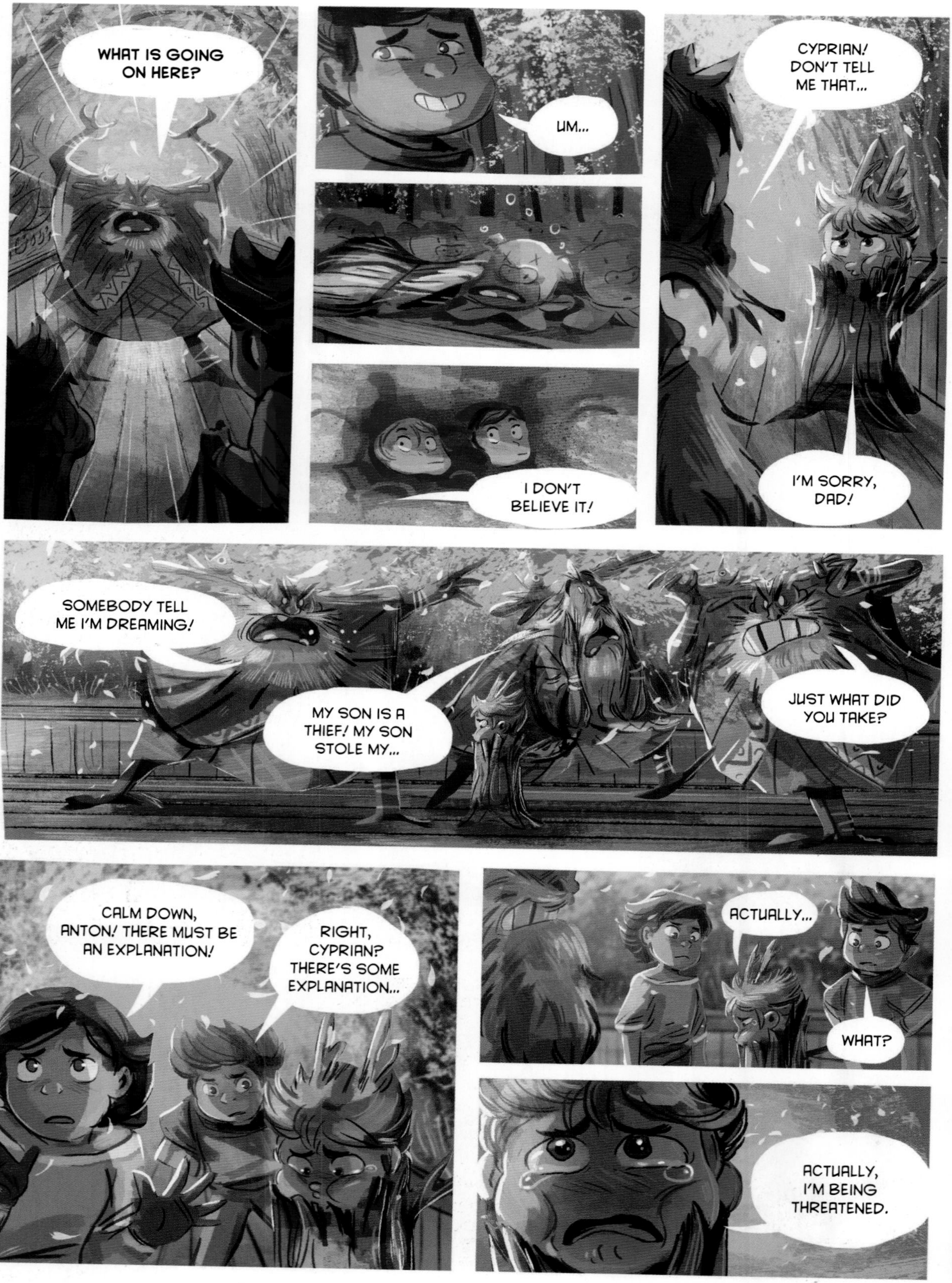
WHAT IS GOING ON HERE?
UM...
I DON'T BELIEVE IT!
CYPRIAN! DON'T TELL ME THAT...
I'M SORRY, DAD!
SOMEBODY TELL ME I'M DREAMING!
MY SON IS A THIEF! MY SON STOLE MY...
JUST WHAT DID YOU TAKE?
CALM DOWN, ANTON! THERE MUST BE AN EXPLANATION!
RIGHT, CYPRIAN? THERE'S SOME EXPLANATION...
ACTUALLY...
WHAT?
ACTUALLY, I'M BEING THREATENED.

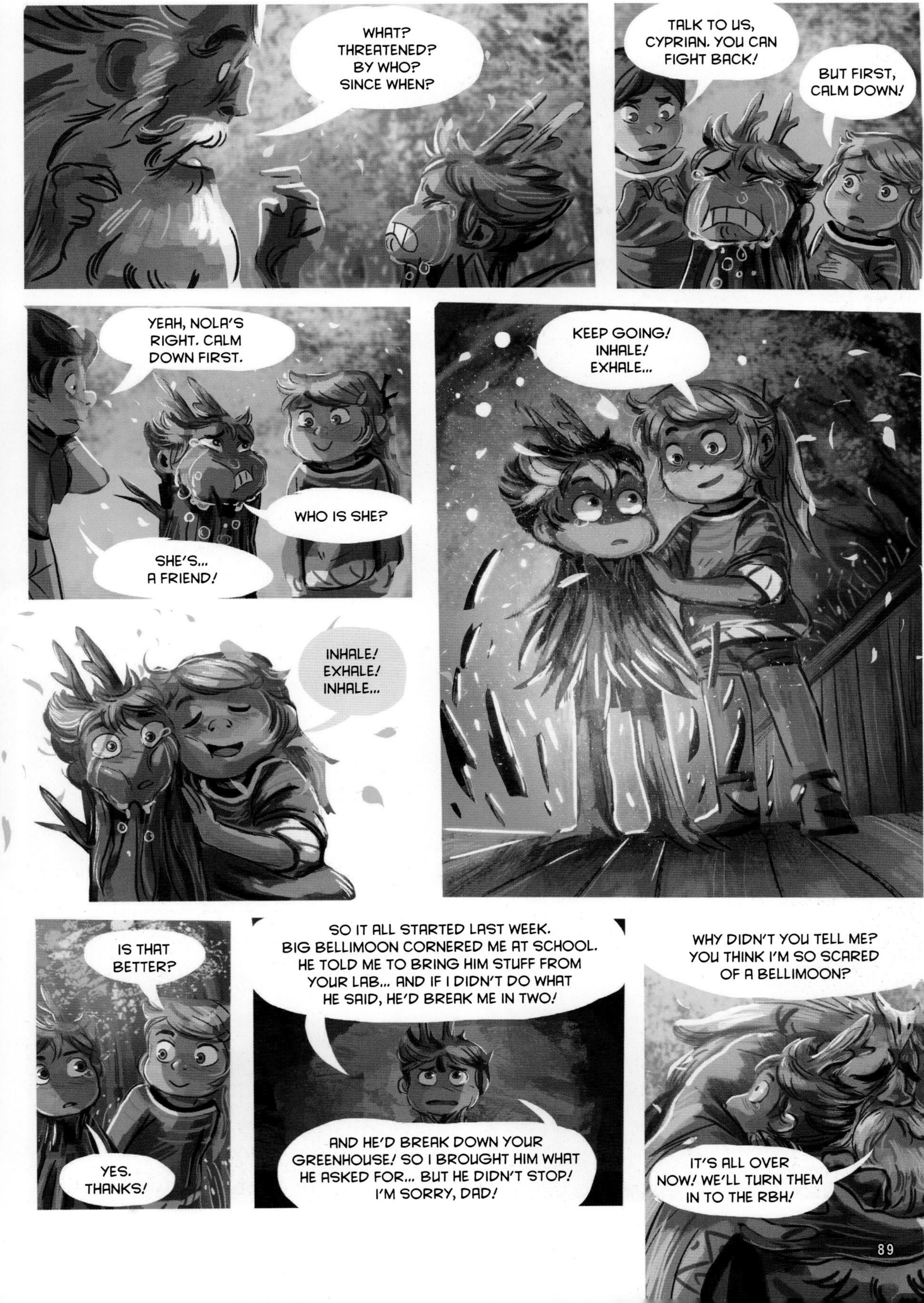

WHAT? THREATENED? BY WHO? SINCE WHEN?
TALK TO US, CYPRIAN. YOU CAN FIGHT BACK!
BUT FIRST, CALM DOWN!
YEAH, NOLA'S RIGHT. CALM DOWN FIRST.
WHO IS SHE?
SHE'S... A FRIEND!
KEEP GOING! INHALE! EXHALE...
INHALE! EXHALE! INHALE...
IS THAT BETTER?
YES. THANKS!
SO IT ALL STARTED LAST WEEK. BIG BELLIMOON CORNERED ME AT SCHOOL. HE TOLD ME TO BRING HIM STUFF FROM YOUR LAB... AND IF I DIDN'T DO WHAT HE SAID, HE'D BREAK ME IN TWO!
AND HE'D BREAK DOWN YOUR GREENHOUSE! SO I BROUGHT HIM WHAT HE ASKED FOR... BUT HE DIDN'T STOP! I'M SORRY, DAD!
WHY DIDN'T YOU TELL ME? YOU THINK I'M SO SCARED OF A BELLIMOON?
IT'S ALL OVER NOW! WE'LL TURN THEM IN TO THE RBH!

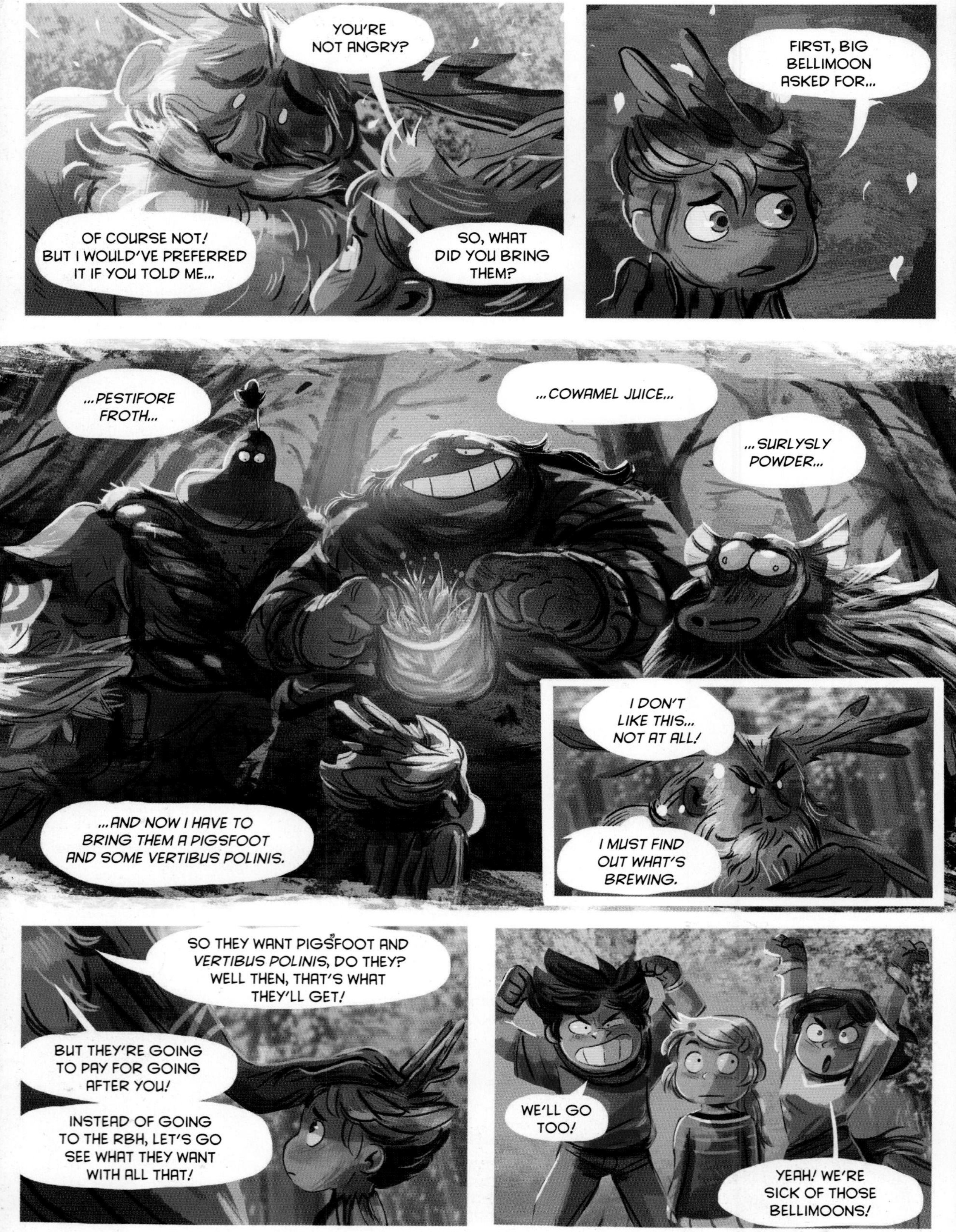
YOU'RE NOT ANGRY?
OF COURSE NOT! BUT I WOULD'VE PREFERRED IT IF YOU TOLD ME...
SO, WHAT DID YOU BRING THEM?
FIRST, BIG BELLIMOON ASKED FOR...
...PESTIFORE FROTH...
...COWAMEL JUICE...
...SURLYSLY POWDER...
...AND NOW I HAVE TO BRING THEM A PIGSFOOT AND SOME VERTIBUS POLINIS.
I DON'T LIKE THIS... NOT AT ALL!
I MUST FIND OUT WHAT'S BREWING.
SO THEY WANT PIGSFOOT AND VERTIBUS POLINIS, DO THEY? WELL THEN, THAT'S WHAT THEY'LL GET!
BUT THEY'RE GOING TO PAY FOR GOING AFTER YOU!
INSTEAD OF GOING TO THE RBH, LET'S GO SEE WHAT THEY WANT WITH ALL THAT!
WE'LL GO TOO!
YEAH! WE'RE SICK OF THOSE BELLIMOONS!

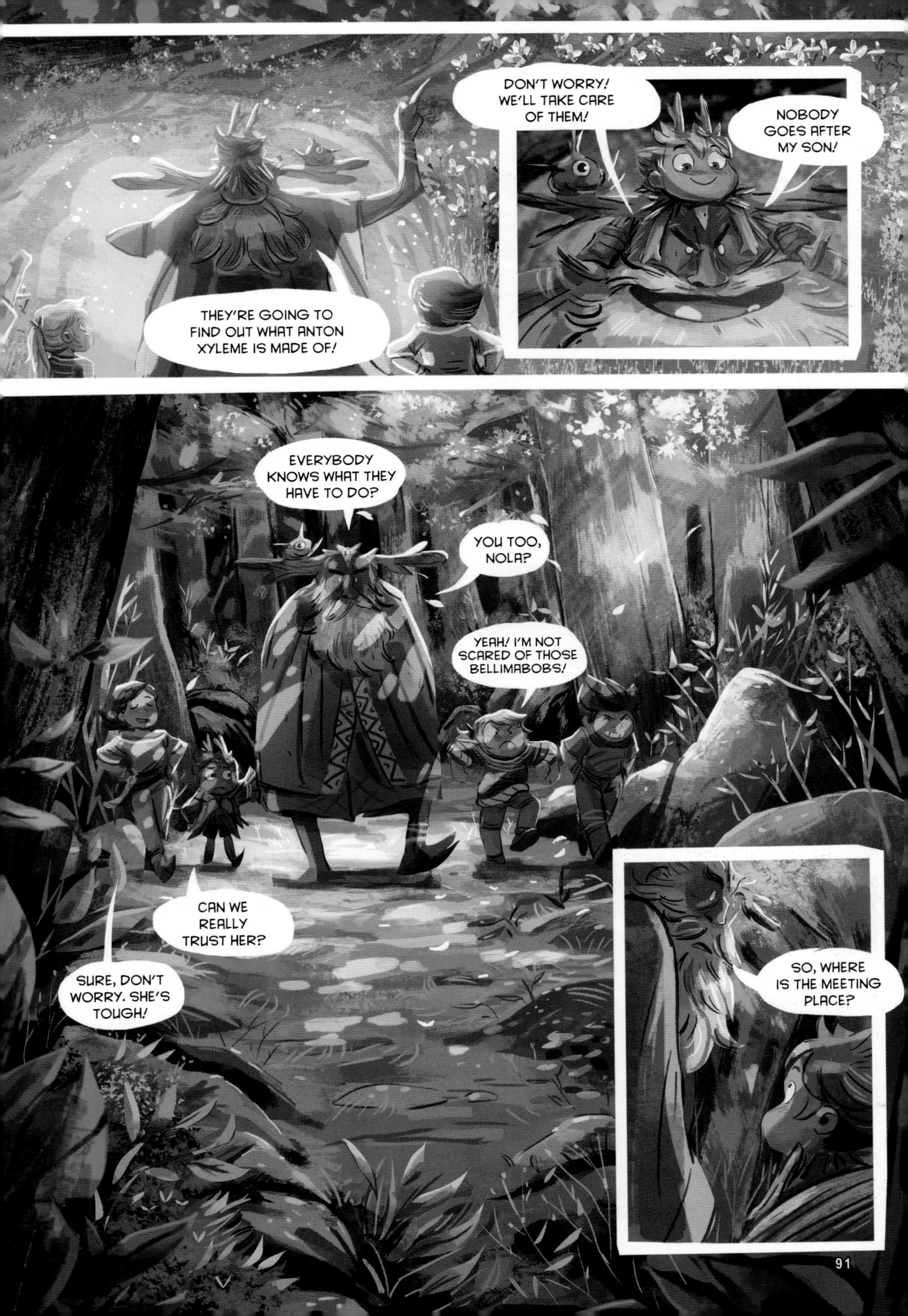
THEY'RE GOING TO FIND OUT WHAT ANTON XYLEME IS MADE OF!
DON'T WORRY! WE'LL TAKE CARE OF THEM!
NOBODY GOES AFTER MY SON!
EVERYBODY KNOWS WHAT THEY HAVE TO DO?
YOU TOO, NOLA?
YEAH! I'M NOT SCARED OF THOSE BELLIMABOBS!
CAN WE REALLY TRUST HER?
SURE, DON'T WORRY. SHE'S TOUGH!
SO, WHERE IS THE MEETING PLACE?

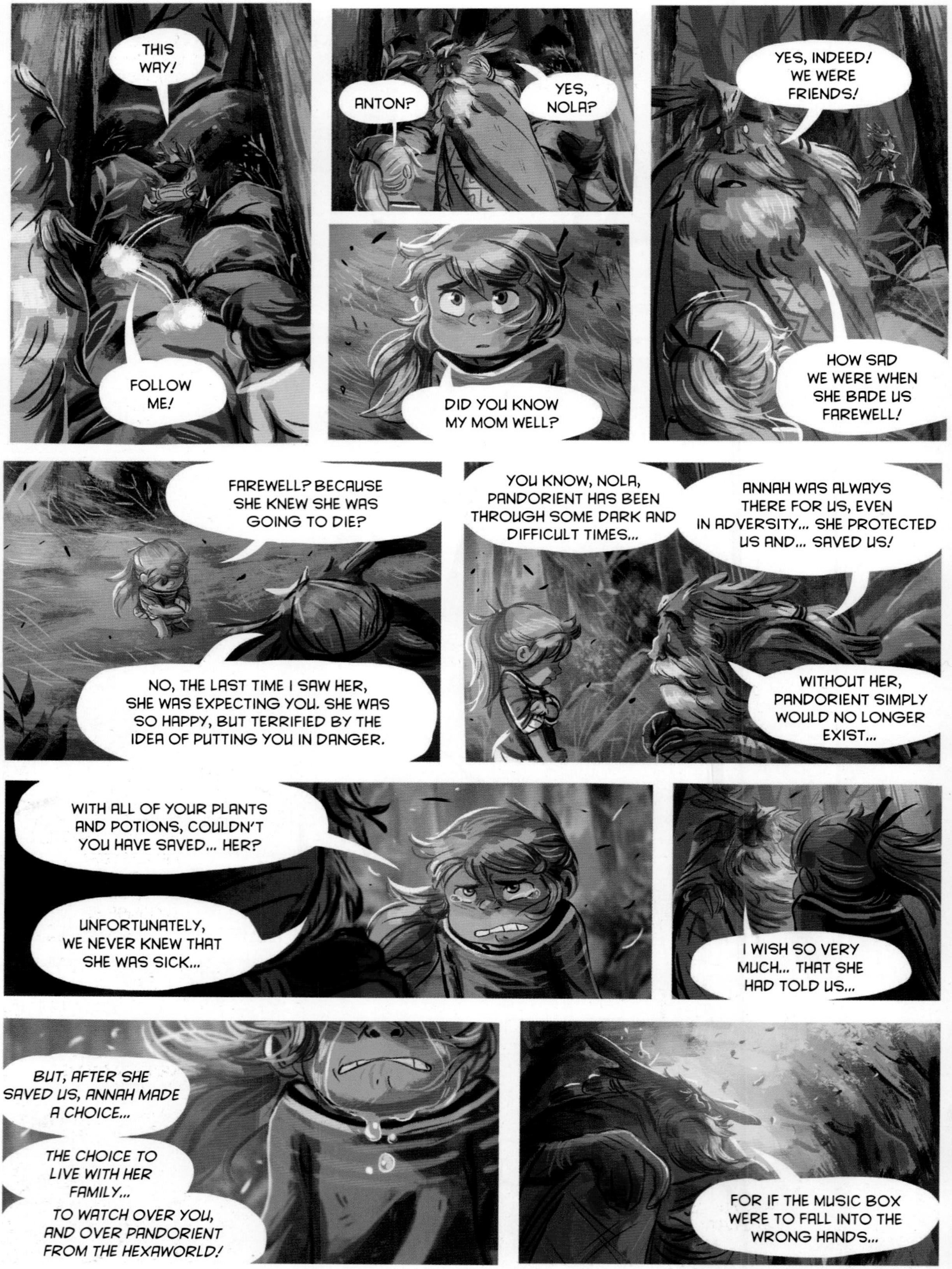
THIS WAY!
FOLLOW ME!
ANTON?
YES, NOLA?
DID YOU KNOW MY MOM WELL?
YES, INDEED! WE WERE FRIENDS!
HOW SAD WE WERE WHEN SHE BADE US FAREWELL!
FAREWELL? BECAUSE SHE KNEW SHE WAS GOING TO DIE?
NO, THE LAST TIME I SAW HER, SHE WAS EXPECTING YOU. SHE WAS SO HAPPY, BUT TERRIFIED BY THE IDEA OF PUTTING YOU IN DANGER.
YOU KNOW, NOLA, PANDORIENT HAS BEEN THROUGH SOME DARK AND DIFFICULT TIMES...
ANNAH WAS ALWAYS THERE FOR US, EVEN IN ADVERSITY... SHE PROTECTED US AND... SAVED US!
WITHOUT HER, PANDORIENT SIMPLY WOULD NO LONGER EXIST...
WITH ALL OF YOUR PLANTS AND POTIONS, COULDN'T YOU HAVE SAVED... HER?
UNFORTUNATELY, WE NEVER KNEW THAT SHE WAS SICK...
I WISH SO VERY MUCH... THAT SHE HAD TOLD US...
BUT, AFTER SHE SAVED US, ANNAH MADE A CHOICE...
THE CHOICE TO LIVE WITH HER FAMILY...
TO WATCH OVER YOU, AND OVER PANDORIENT FROM THE HEXAWORLD!
FOR IF THE MUSIC BOX WERE TO FALL INTO THE WRONG HANDS...

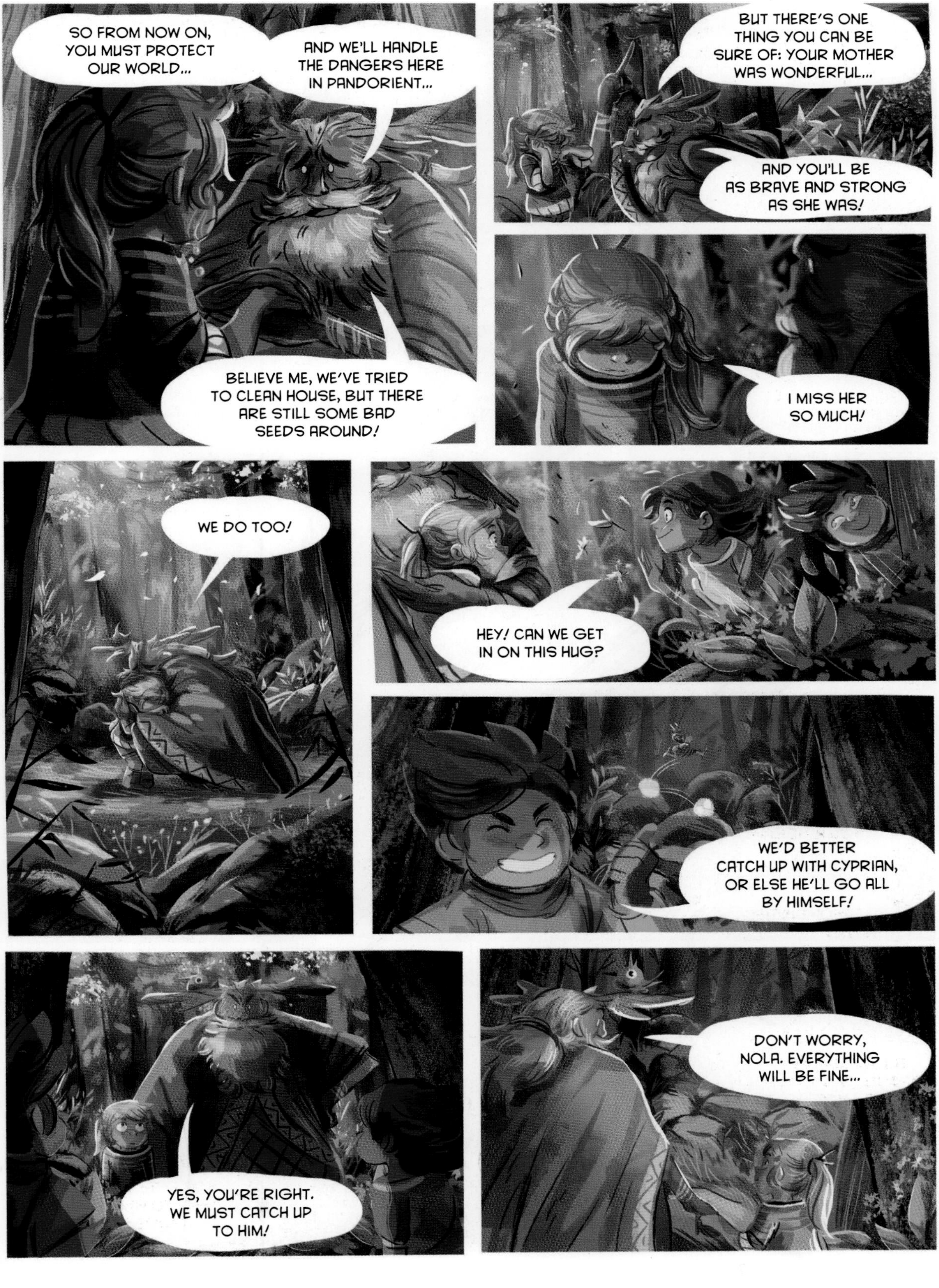
SO FROM NOW ON, YOU MUST PROTECT OUR WORLD...
AND WE'LL HANDLE THE DANGERS HERE IN PANDORIENT...
BELIEVE ME, WE'VE TRIED TO CLEAN HOUSE, BUT THERE ARE STILL SOME BAD SEEDS AROUND!
BUT THERE'S ONE THING YOU CAN BE SURE OF: YOUR MOTHER WAS WONDERFUL...
AND YOU'LL BE AS BRAVE AND STRONG AS SHE WAS!
I MISS HER SO MUCH!
WE DO TOO!
HEY! CAN WE GET IN ON THIS HUG?
WE'D BETTER CATCH UP WITH CYPRIAN, OR ELSE HE'LL GO ALL BY HIMSELF!
YES, YOU'RE RIGHT. WE MUST CATCH UP TO HIM!
DON'T WORRY, NOLA. EVERYTHING WILL BE FINE...

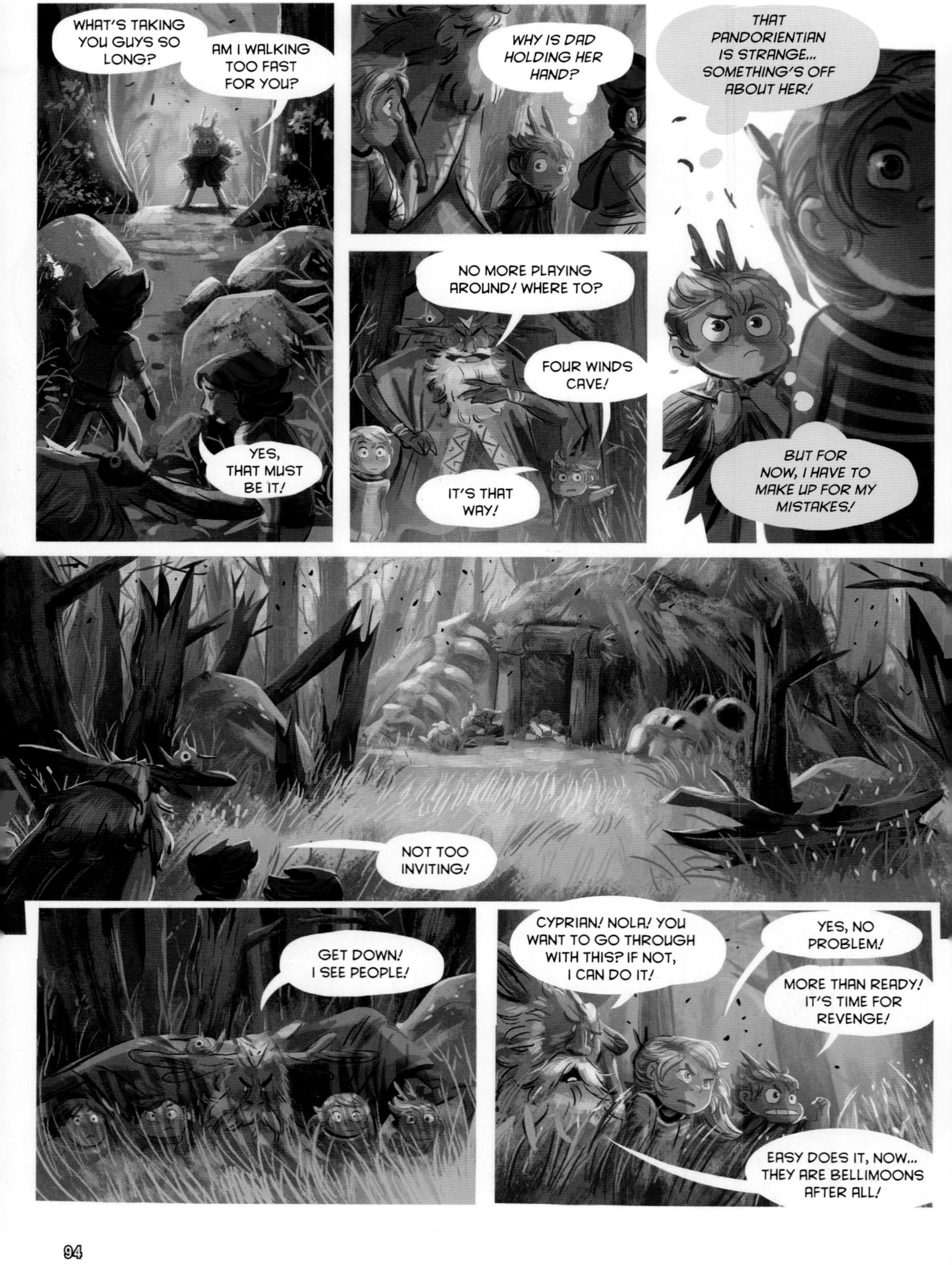
WHAT'S TAKING YOU GUYS SO LONG?
AM I WALKING TOO FAST FOR YOU?
YES, THAT MUST BE IT!
WHY IS DAD HOLDING HER HAND?
NO MORE PLAYING AROUND! WHERE TO?
FOUR WINDS CAVE!
IT'S THAT WAY!
THAT PANDORIENTIAN IS STRANGE... SOMETHING'S OFF ABOUT HER!
BUT FOR NOW, I HAVE TO MAKE UP FOR MY MISTAKES!
NOT TOO INVITING!
GET DOWN! I SEE PEOPLE!
CYPRIAN! NOLA! YOU WANT TO GO THROUGH WITH THIS? IF NOT, I CAN DO IT!
YES, NO PROBLEM!
MORE THAN READY! IT'S TIME FOR REVENGE!
EASY DOES IT, NOW... THEY ARE BELLIMOONS AFTER ALL!

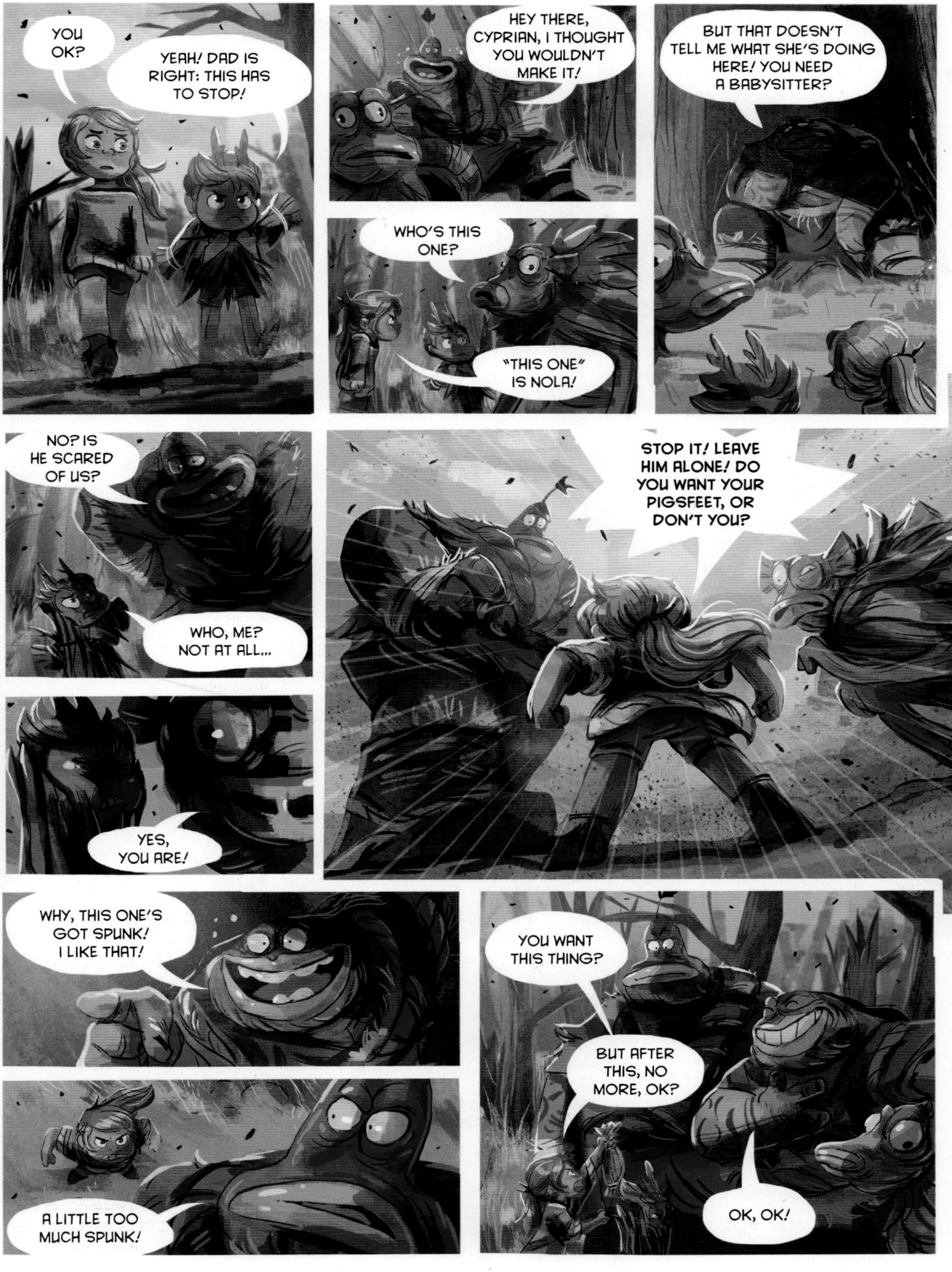

YOU OK?
YEAH! DAD IS RIGHT: THIS HAS TO STOP!
HEY THERE, CYPRIAN, I THOUGHT YOU WOULDN'T MAKE IT!
WHO'S THIS ONE?
"THIS ONE" IS NOLA!
BUT THAT DOESN'T TELL ME WHAT SHE'S DOING HERE! YOU NEED A BABYSITTER?
NO? IS HE SCARED OF US?
WHO, ME? NOT AT ALL...
YES, YOU ARE!
STOP IT! LEAVE HIM ALONE! DO YOU WANT YOUR PIGSFEET, OR DON'T YOU?
WHY, THIS ONE'S GOT SPUNK! I LIKE THAT!
A LITTLE TOO MUCH SPUNK!
YOU WANT THIS THING?
BUT AFTER THIS, NO MORE, OK?
OK, OK!

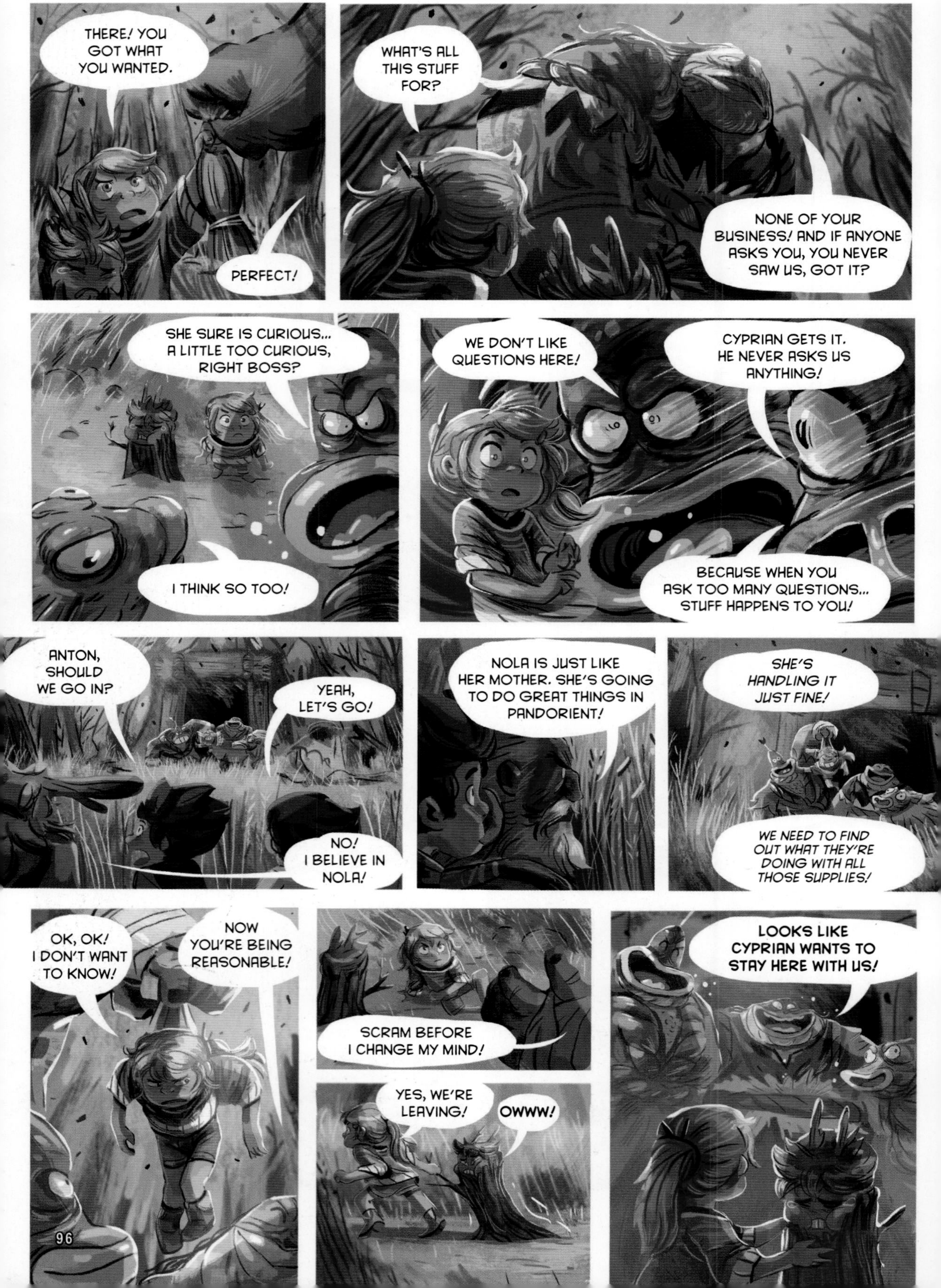
THERE! YOU GOT WHAT YOU WANTED.
PERFECT!
WHAT'S ALL THIS STUFF FOR?
NONE OF YOUR BUSINESS! AND IF ANYONE ASKS YOU, YOU NEVER SAW US, GOT IT?
SHE SURE IS CURIOUS... A LITTLE TOO CURIOUS, RIGHT BOSS?
I THINK SO TOO!
WE DON'T LIKE QUESTIONS HERE!
CYPRIAN GETS IT. HE NEVER ASKS US ANYTHING!
BECAUSE WHEN YOU ASK TOO MANY QUESTIONS... STUFF HAPPENS TO YOU!
ANTON, SHOULD WE GO IN?
YEAH, LET'S GO!
NO! I BELIEVE IN NOLA!
NOLA IS JUST LIKE HER MOTHER. SHE'S GOING TO DO GREAT THINGS IN PANDORIENT!
SHE'S HANDLING IT JUST FINE!
WE NEED TO FIND OUT WHAT THEY'RE DOING WITH ALL THOSE SUPPLIES!
OK, OK! I DON'T WANT TO KNOW!
NOW YOU'RE BEING REASONABLE!
SCRAM BEFORE I CHANGE MY MIND!
YES, WE'RE LEAVING!
OWWW!
LOOKS LIKE CYPRIAN WANTS TO STAY HERE WITH US!

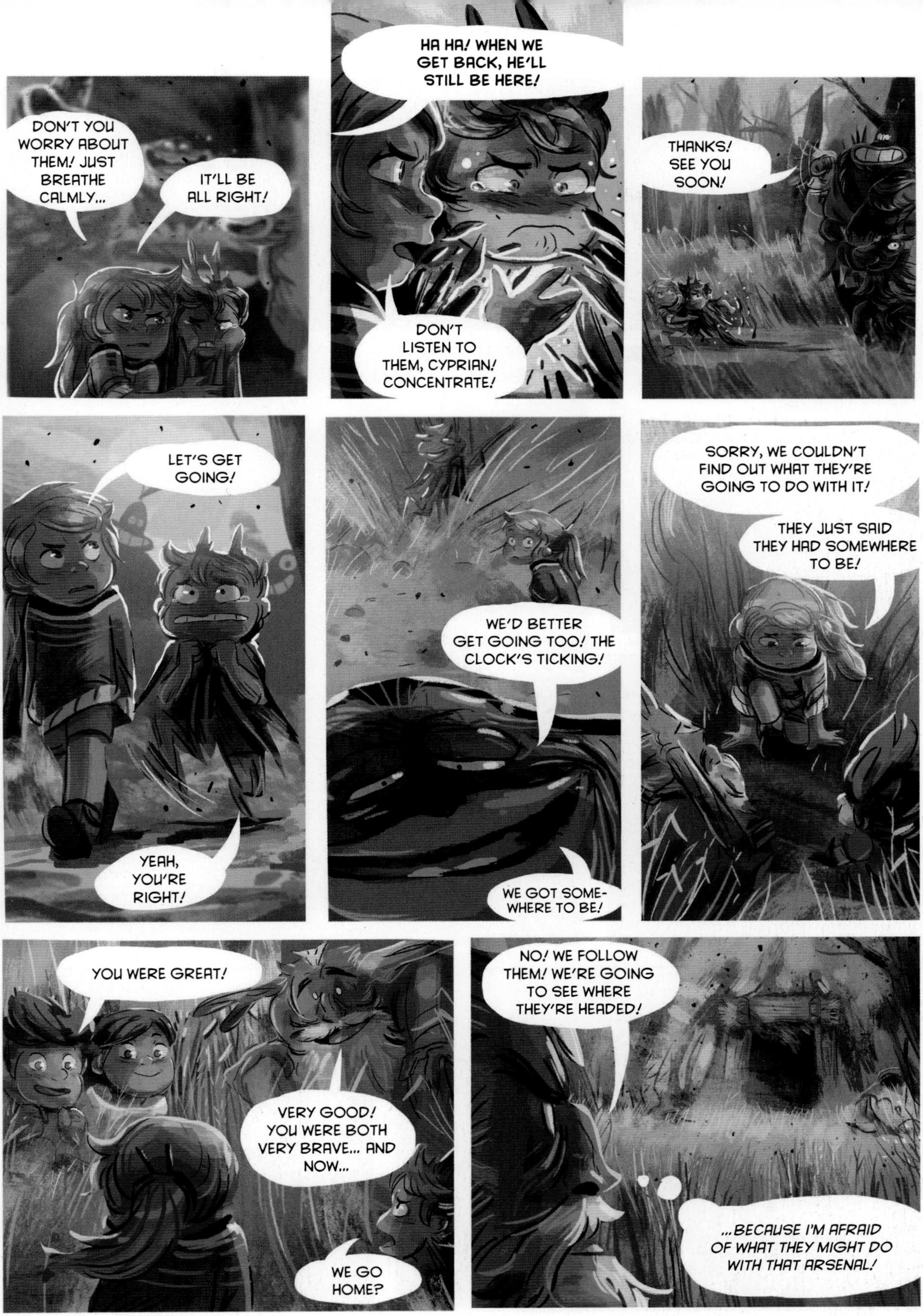
DON'T YOU WORRY ABOUT THEM! JUST BREATHE CALMLY...
IT'LL BE ALL RIGHT!
HA HA! WHEN WE GET BACK, HE'LL STILL BE HERE!
DON'T LISTEN TO THEM, CYPRIAN! CONCENTRATE!
THANKS! SEE YOU SOON!
LET'S GET GOING!
YEAH, YOU'RE RIGHT!
WE'D BETTER GET GOING TOO! THE CLOCK'S TICKING!
WE GOT SOME-WHERE TO BE!
SORRY, WE COULDN'T FIND OUT WHAT THEY'RE GOING TO DO WITH IT!
THEY JUST SAID THEY HAD SOMEWHERE TO BE!
YOU WERE GREAT!
VERY GOOD! YOU WERE BOTH VERY BRAVE... AND NOW...
WE GO HOME?
NO! WE FOLLOW THEM! WE'RE GOING TO SEE WHERE THEY'RE HEADED!
...BECAUSE I'M AFRAID OF WHAT THEY MIGHT DO WITH THAT ARSENAL!

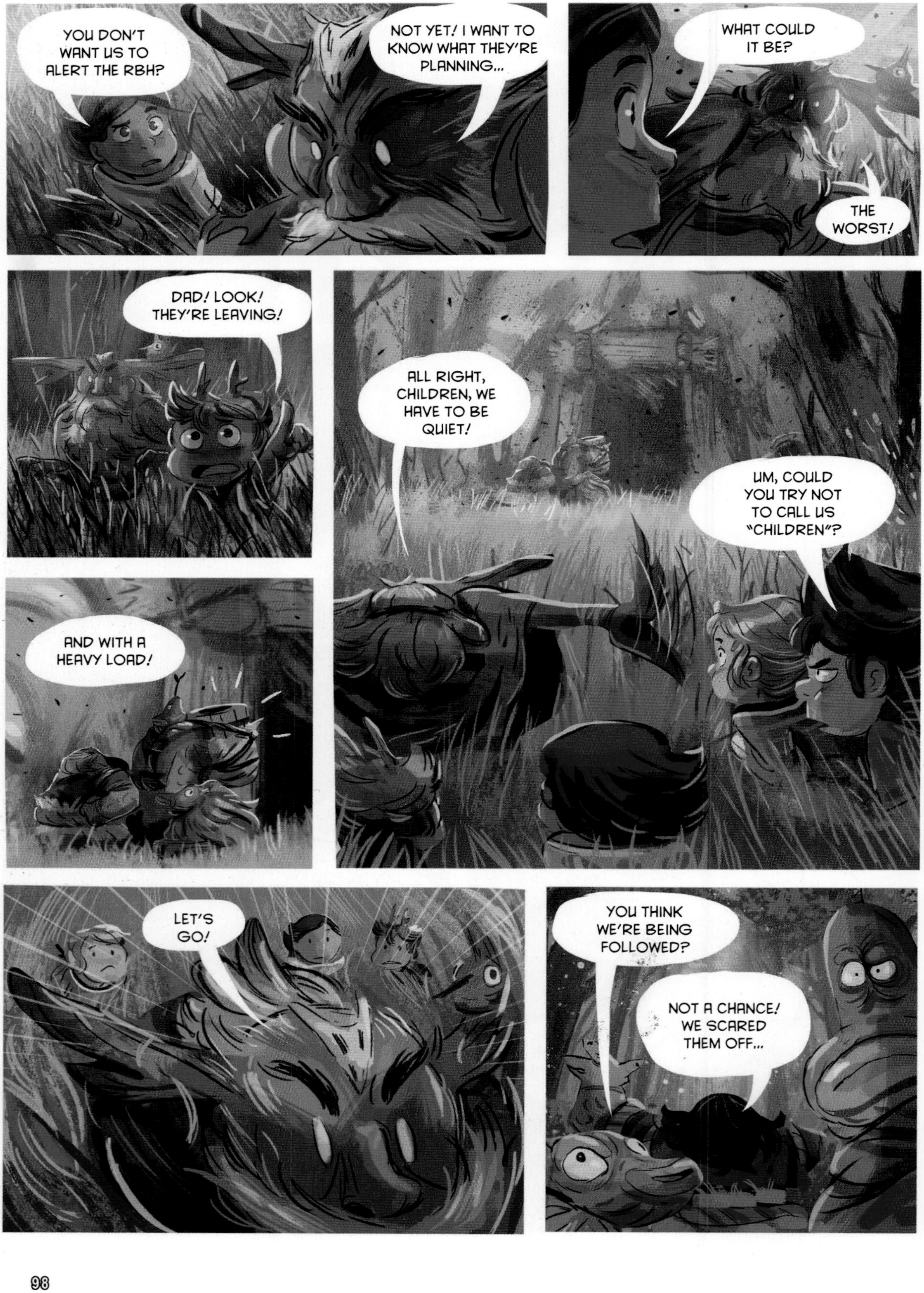
YOU DON'T WANT US TO ALERT THE RBH?
NOT YET! I WANT TO KNOW WHAT THEY'RE PLANNING...
WHAT COULD IT BE?
THE WORST!
DAD! LOOK! THEY'RE LEAVING!
AND WITH A HEAVY LOAD!
ALL RIGHT, CHILDREN, WE HAVE TO BE QUIET!
UM, COULD YOU TRY NOT TO CALL US "CHILDREN"?
LET'S GO!
YOU THINK WE'RE BEING FOLLOWED?
NOT A CHANCE! WE SCARED THEM OFF...

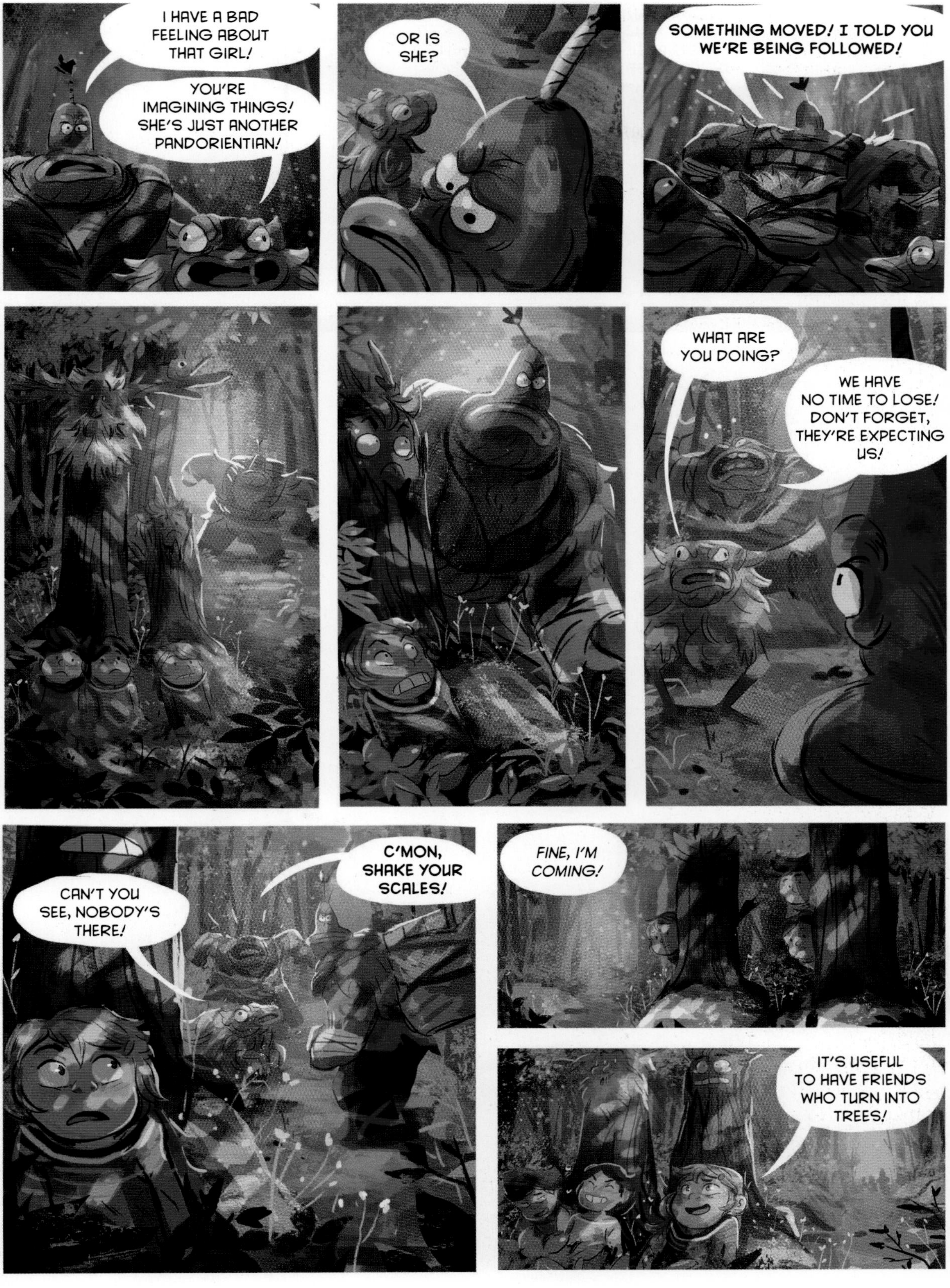
I HAVE A BAD FEELING ABOUT THAT GIRL!
YOU'RE IMAGINING THINGS! SHE'S JUST ANOTHER PANDORIENTIAN!
OR IS SHE?
SOMETHING MOVED! I TOLD YOU WE'RE BEING FOLLOWED!
WHAT ARE YOU DOING?
WE HAVE NO TIME TO LOSE! DON'T FORGET, THEY'RE EXPECTING US!
CAN'T YOU SEE, NOBODY'S THERE!
C'MON, SHAKE YOUR SCALES!
FINE, I'M COMING!
IT'S USEFUL TO HAVE FRIENDS WHO TURN INTO TREES!

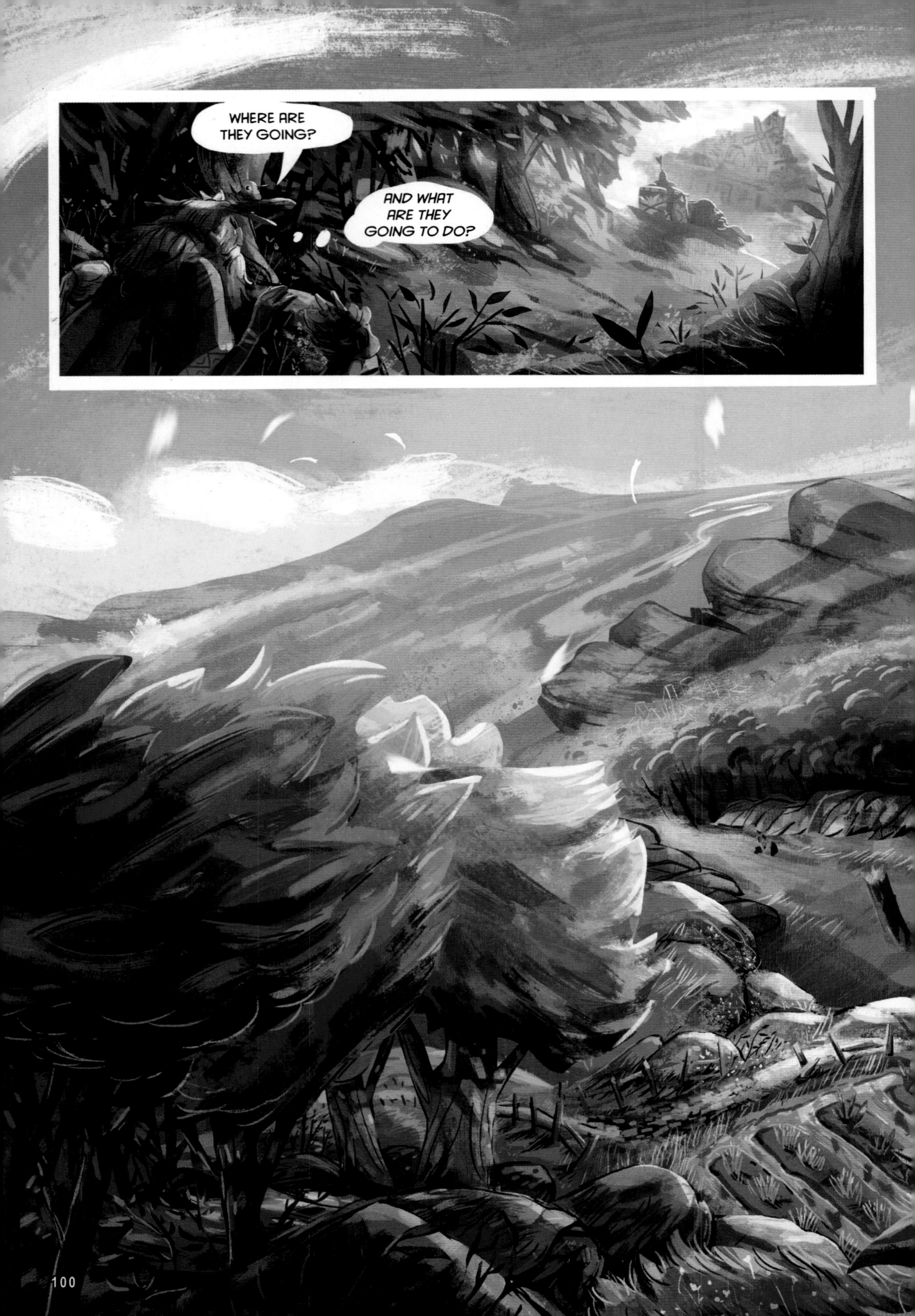
WHERE ARE THEY GOING?
AND WHAT ARE THEY GOING TO DO?

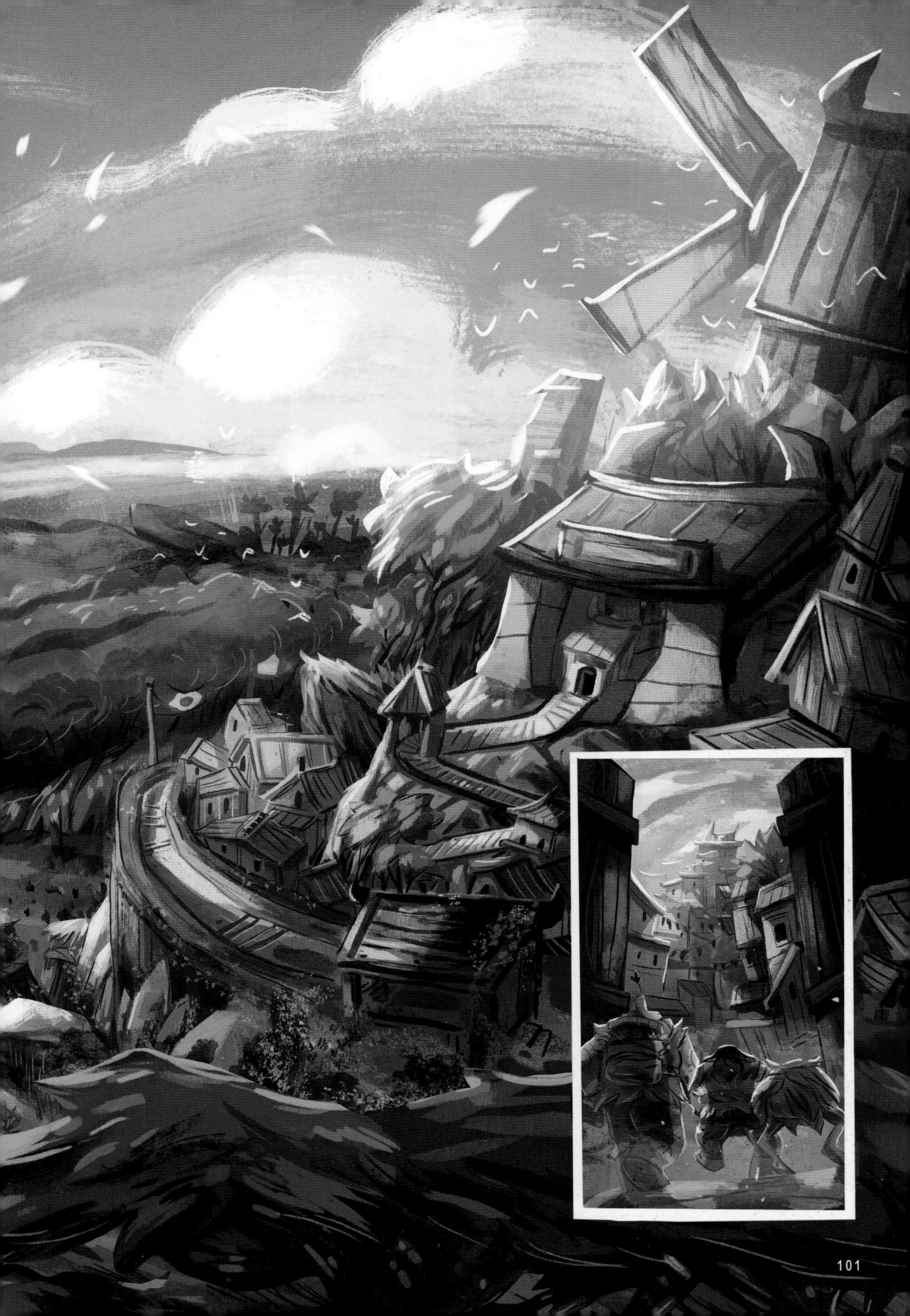

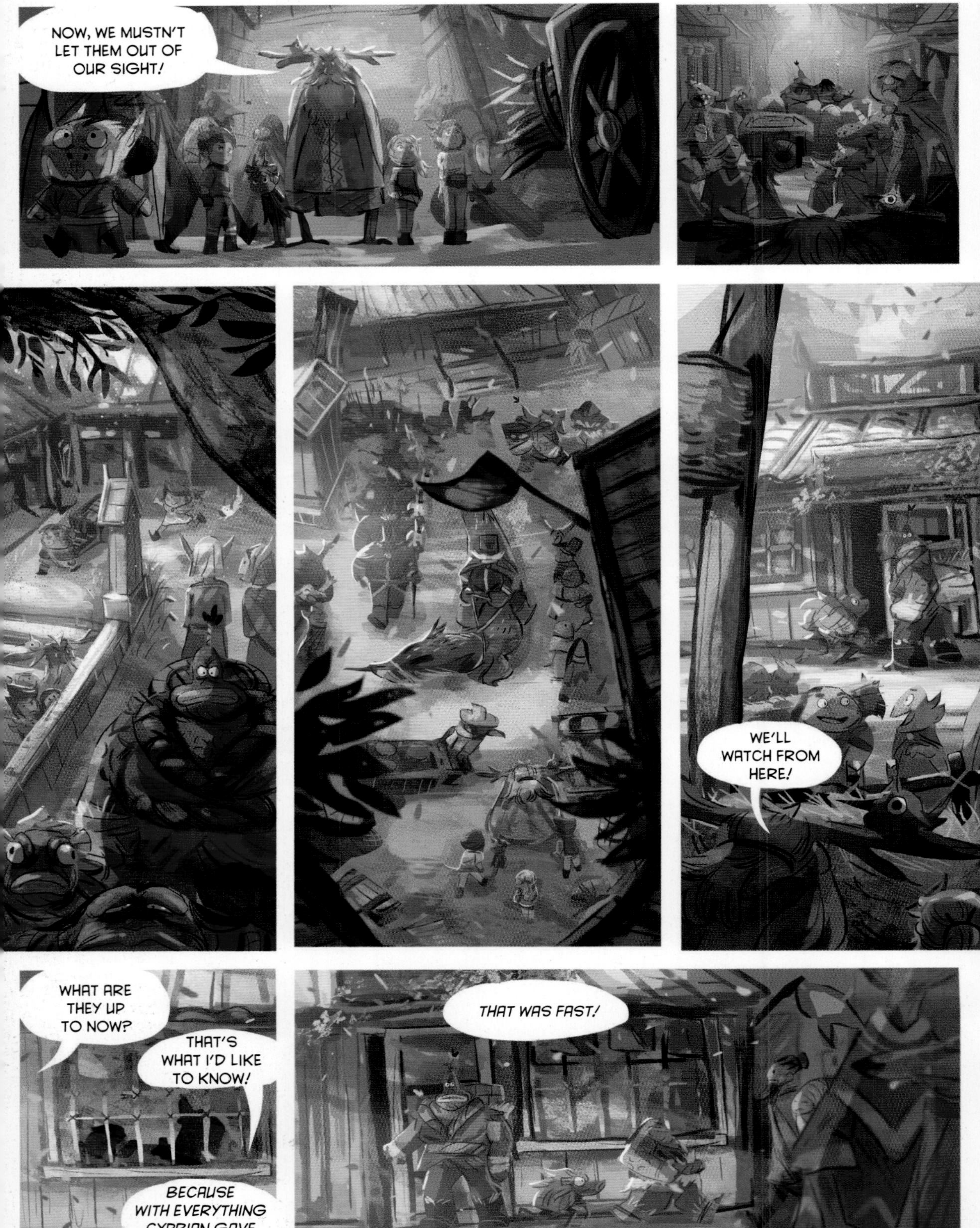
NOW, WE MUSTN'T LET THEM OUT OF OUR SIGHT!
WE'LL WATCH FROM HERE!
WHAT ARE THEY UP TO NOW?
THAT'S WHAT I'D LIKE TO KNOW!
BECAUSE WITH EVERYTHING CYPRIAN GAVE THEM...
THAT WAS FAST!

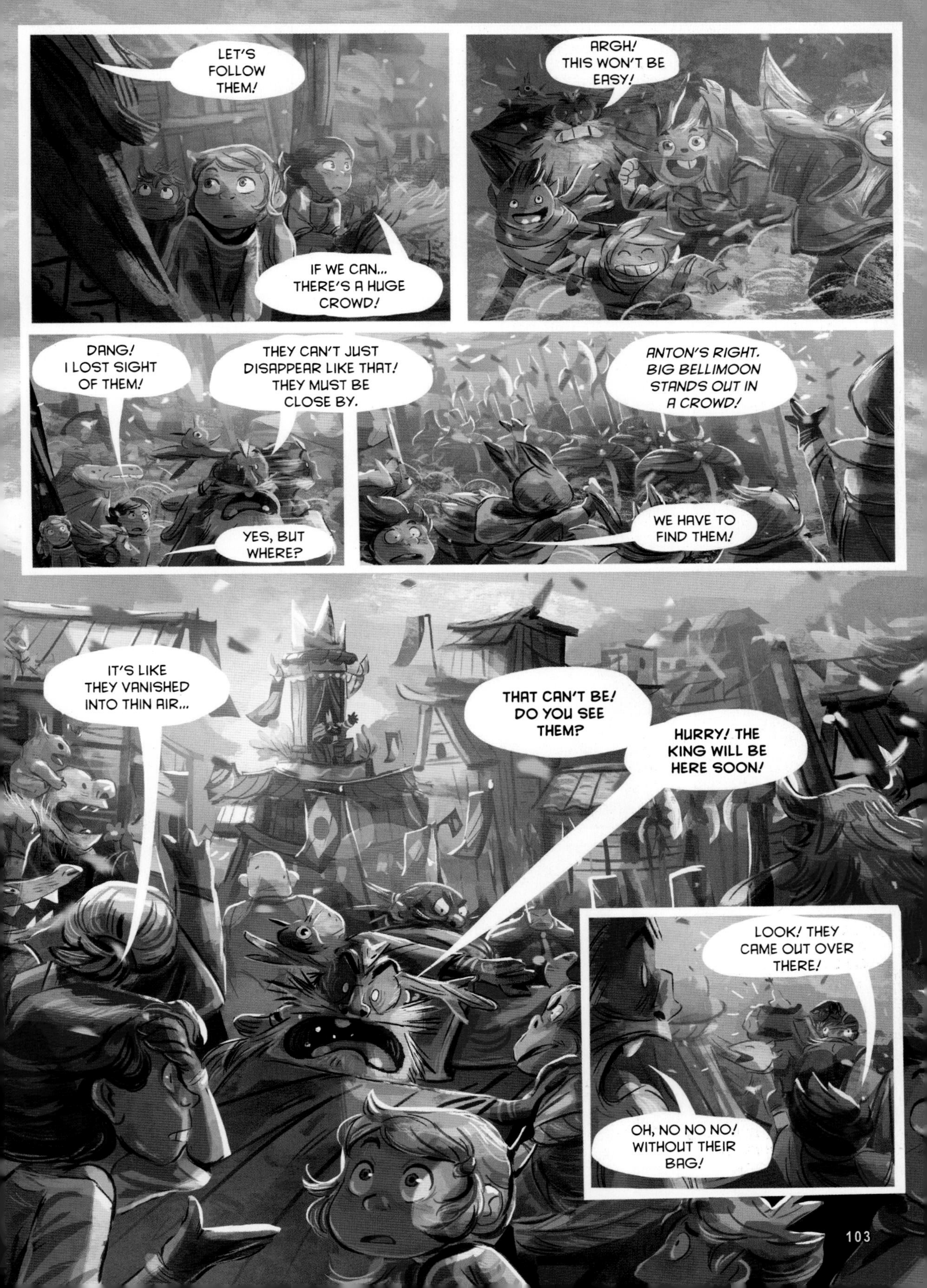
LET'S FOLLOW THEM!
IF WE CAN... THERE'S A HUGE CROWD!
ARGH! THIS WON'T BE EASY!
DANG! I LOST SIGHT OF THEM!
THEY CAN'T JUST DISAPPEAR LIKE THAT! THEY MUST BE CLOSE BY.
YES, BUT WHERE?
ANTON'S RIGHT. BIG BELLIMOON STANDS OUT IN A CROWD!
WE HAVE TO FIND THEM!
IT'S LIKE THEY VANISHED INTO THIN AIR...
THAT CAN'T BE! DO YOU SEE THEM?
HURRY! THE KING WILL BE HERE SOON!
LOOK! THEY CAME OUT OVER THERE!
OH, NO NO NO! WITHOUT THEIR BAG!

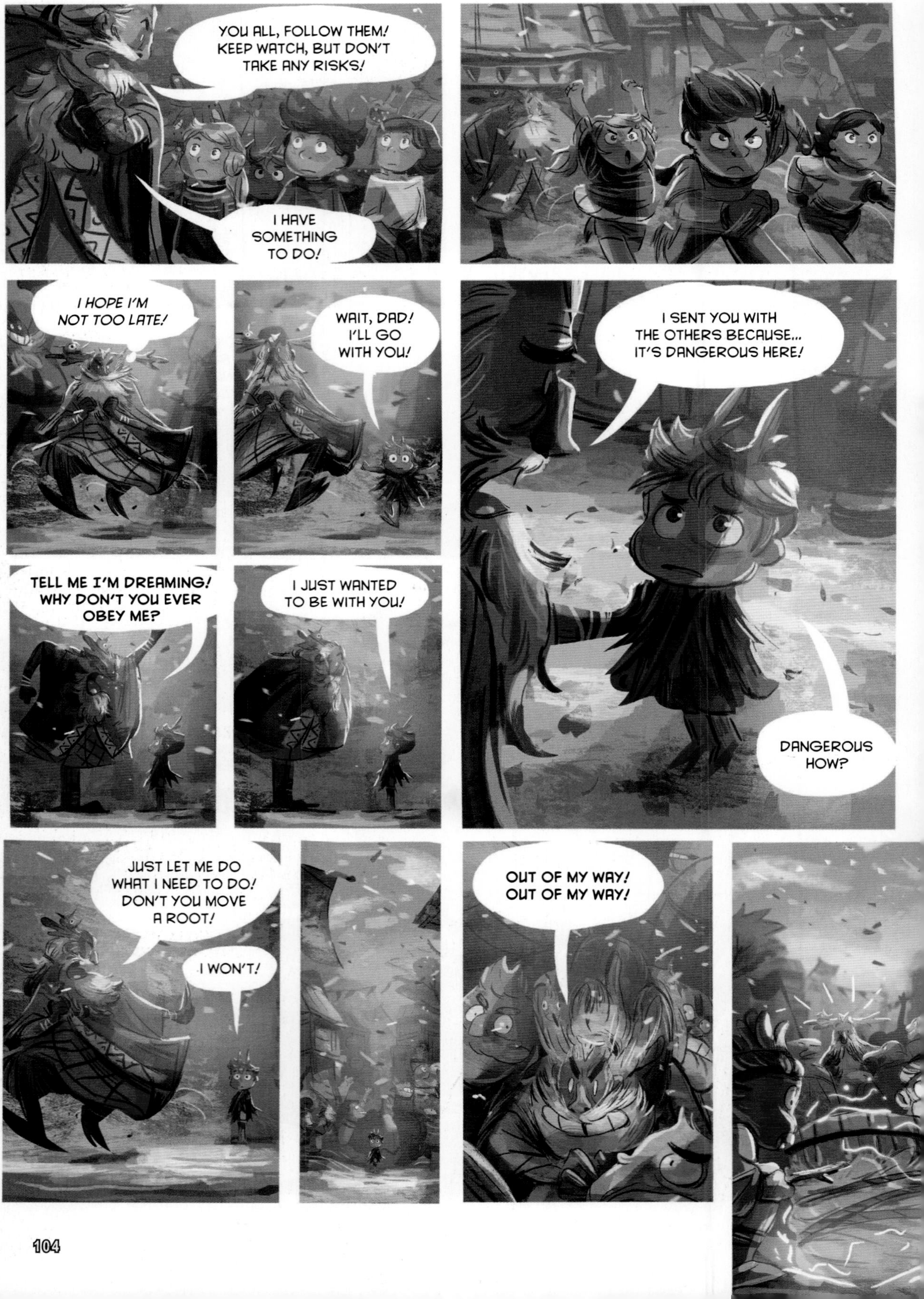
YOU ALL, FOLLOW THEM! KEEP WATCH, BUT DON'T TAKE ANY RISKS!
I HAVE SOMETHING TO DO!
I HOPE I'M NOT TOO LATE!
WAIT, DAD! I'LL GO WITH YOU!
I SENT YOU WITH THE OTHERS BECAUSE... IT'S DANGEROUS HERE!
TELL ME I'M DREAMING! WHY DON'T YOU EVER OBEY ME?
I JUST WANTED TO BE WITH YOU!
DANGEROUS HOW?
JUST LET ME DO WHAT I NEED TO DO! DON'T YOU MOVE A ROOT!
I WON'T!
OUT OF MY WAY! OUT OF MY WAY!

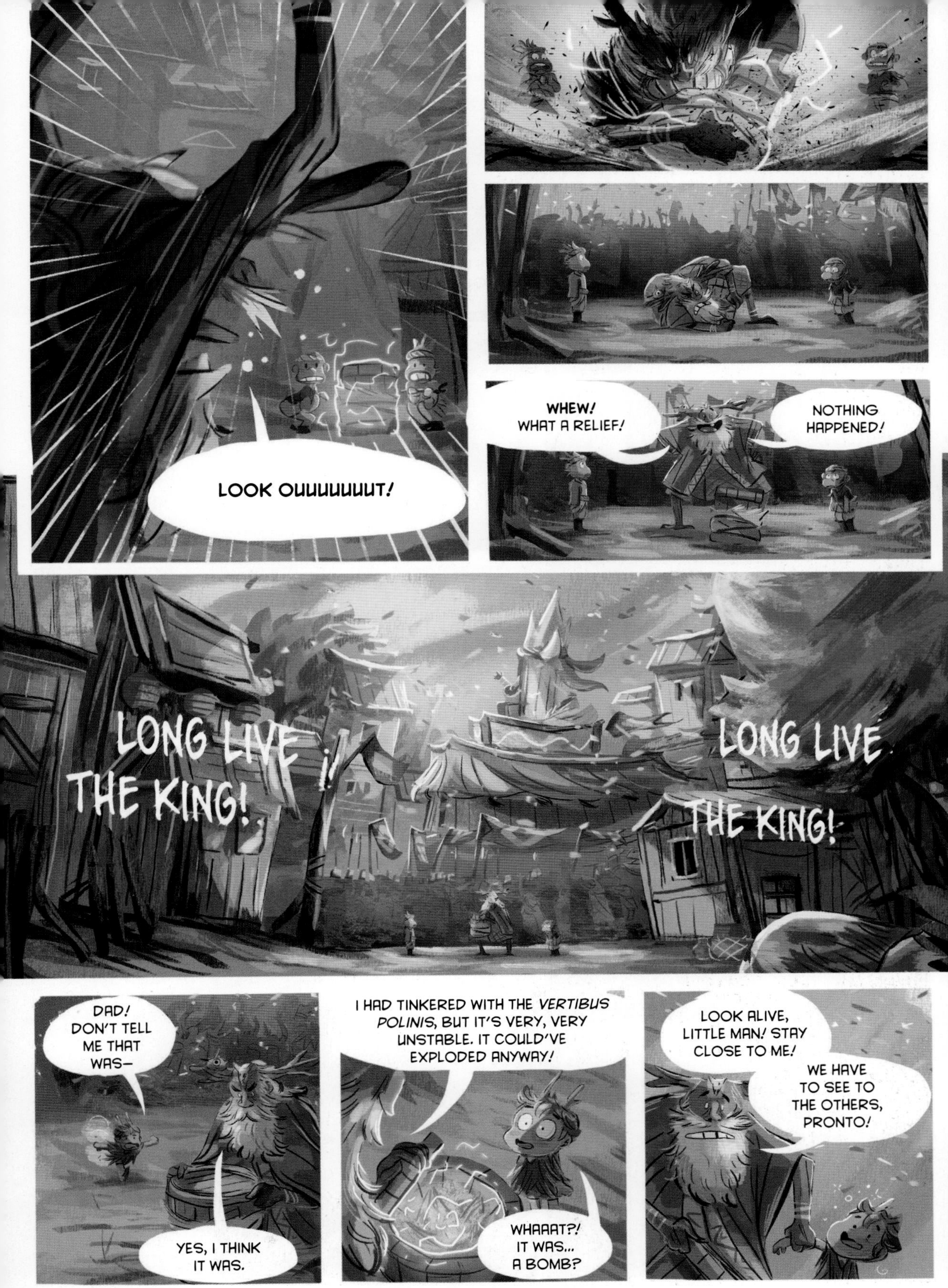
LOOK OUUUUUUUT!
WHEW! WHAT A RELIEF!
NOTHING HAPPENED!
LONG LIVE THE KING!
LONG LIVE THE KING!
DAD! DON'T TELL ME THAT WAS—
YES, I THINK IT WAS.
I HAD TINKERED WITH THE *VERTIBUS POLINIS*, BUT IT'S VERY, VERY UNSTABLE. IT COULD'VE EXPLODED ANYWAY!
WHAAAT?! IT WAS... A BOMB?
LOOK ALIVE, LITTLE MAN! STAY CLOSE TO ME!
WE HAVE TO SEE TO THE OTHERS, PRONTO!

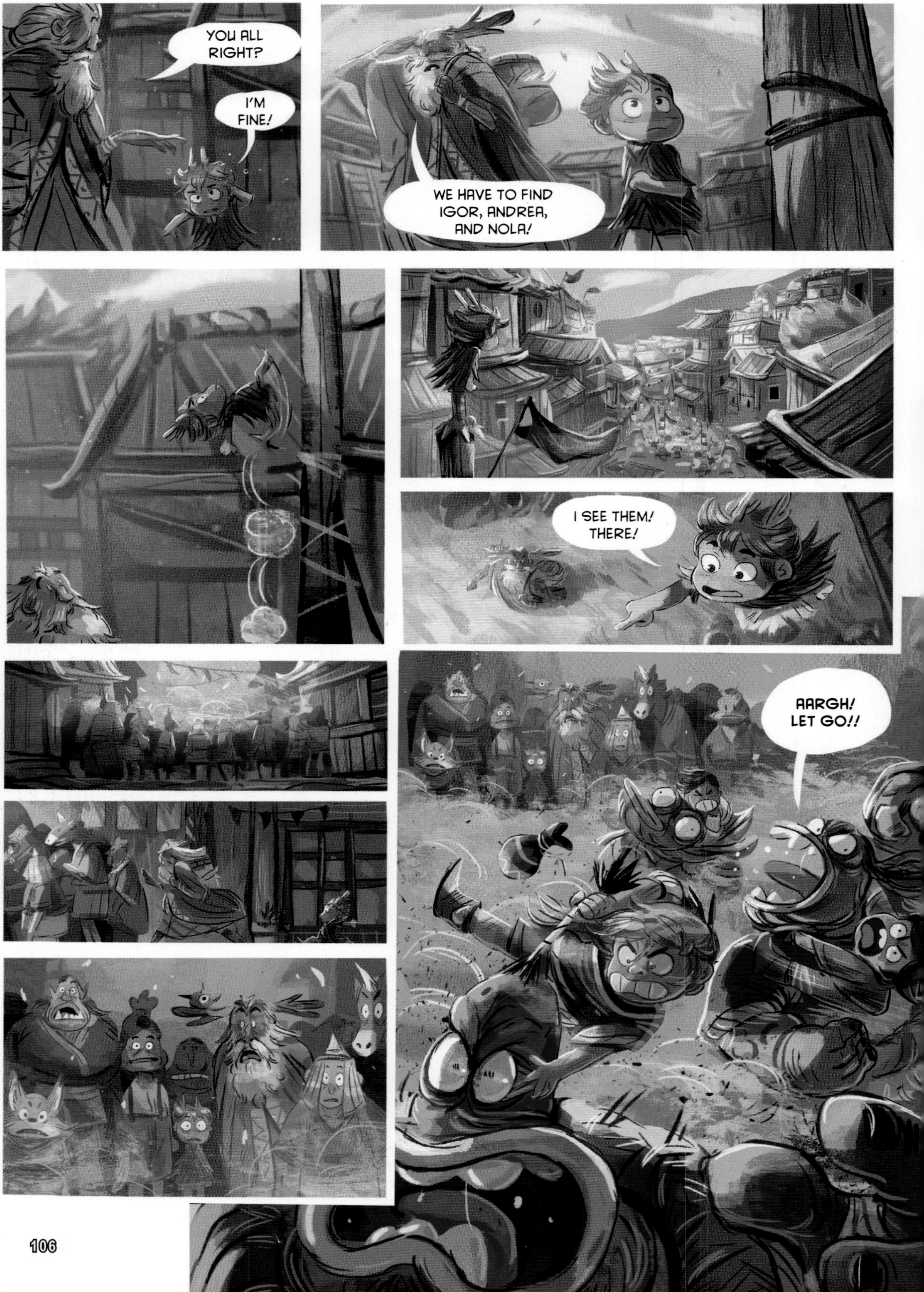
YOU ALL RIGHT?
I'M FINE!
WE HAVE TO FIND IGOR, ANDREA, AND NOLA!
I SEE THEM! THERE!
AARGH! LET GO!!

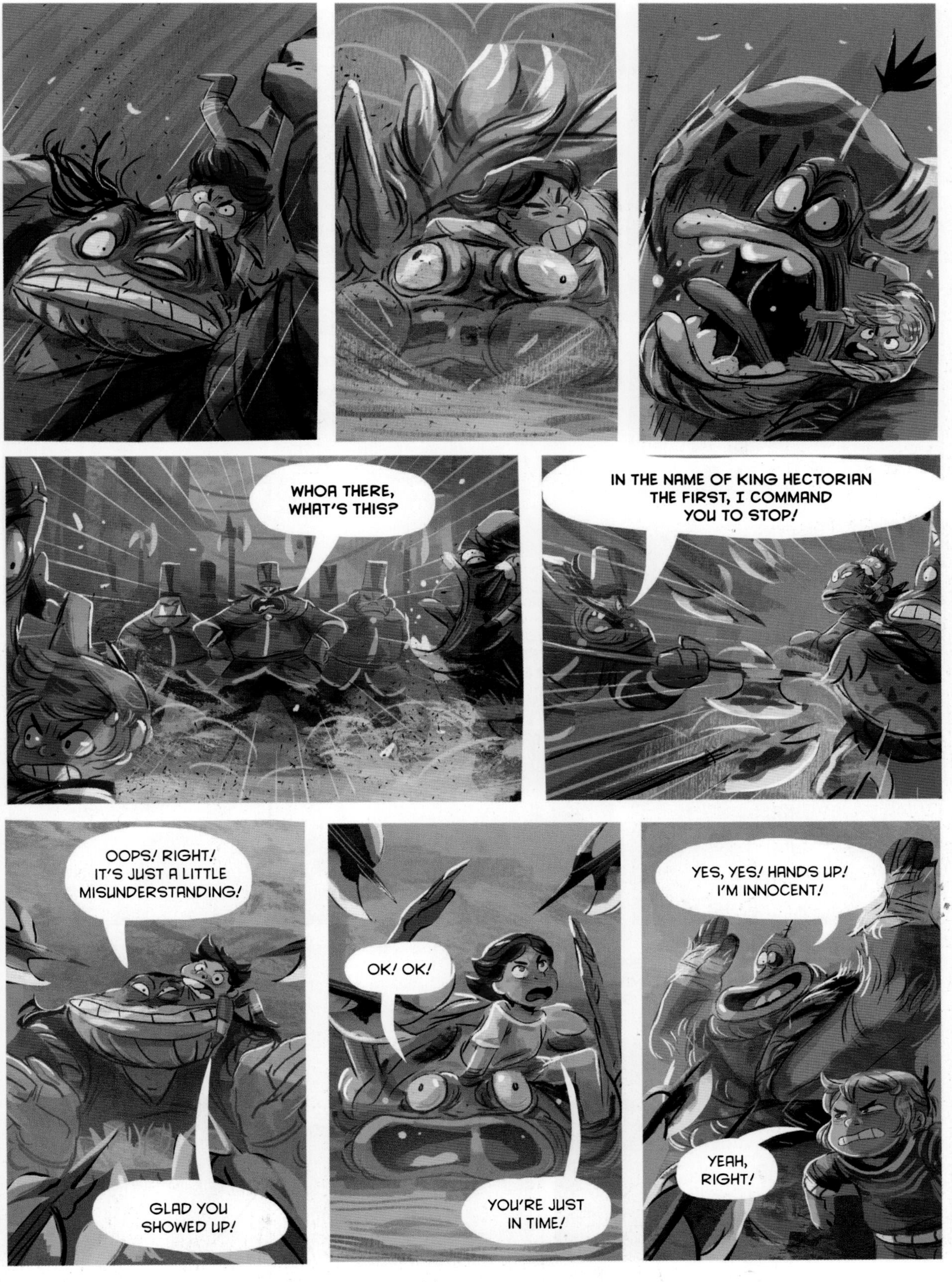
WHOA THERE, WHAT'S THIS?
IN THE NAME OF KING HECTORIAN THE FIRST, I COMMAND YOU TO STOP!
OOPS! RIGHT! IT'S JUST A LITTLE MISUNDERSTANDING!
GLAD YOU SHOWED UP!
OK! OK!
YOU'RE JUST IN TIME!
YES, YES! HANDS UP! I'M INNOCENT!
YEAH, RIGHT!

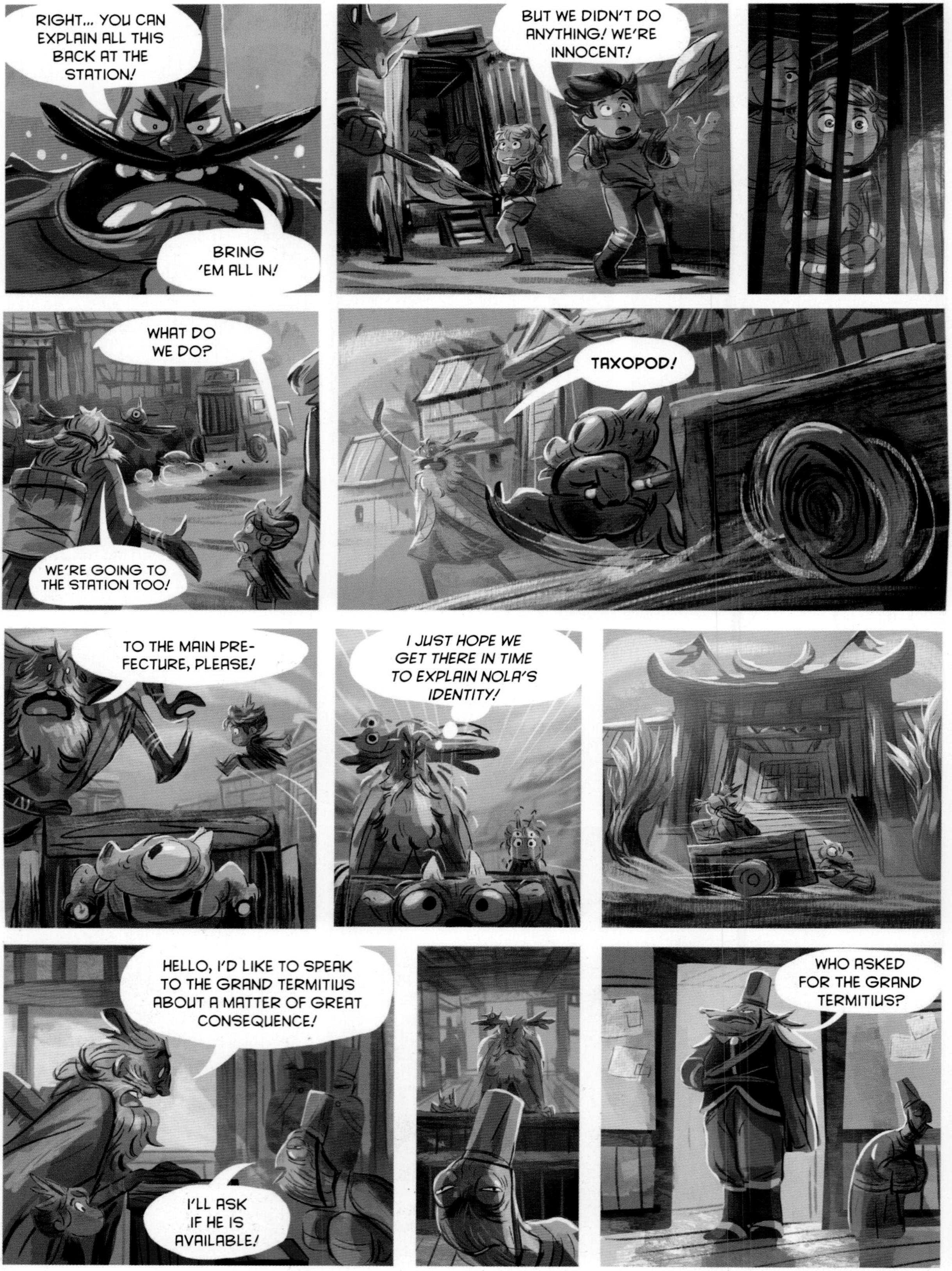
RIGHT... YOU CAN EXPLAIN ALL THIS BACK AT THE STATION!
BRING 'EM ALL IN!
BUT WE DIDN'T DO ANYTHING! WE'RE INNOCENT!
WHAT DO WE DO?
WE'RE GOING TO THE STATION TOO!
TAXOPOD!
TO THE MAIN PRE-FECTURE, PLEASE!
I JUST HOPE WE GET THERE IN TIME TO EXPLAIN NOLA'S IDENTITY!
HELLO, I'D LIKE TO SPEAK TO THE GRAND TERMITIUS ABOUT A MATTER OF GREAT CONSEQUENCE!
I'LL ASK IF HE IS AVAILABLE!
WHO ASKED FOR THE GRAND TERMITIUS?

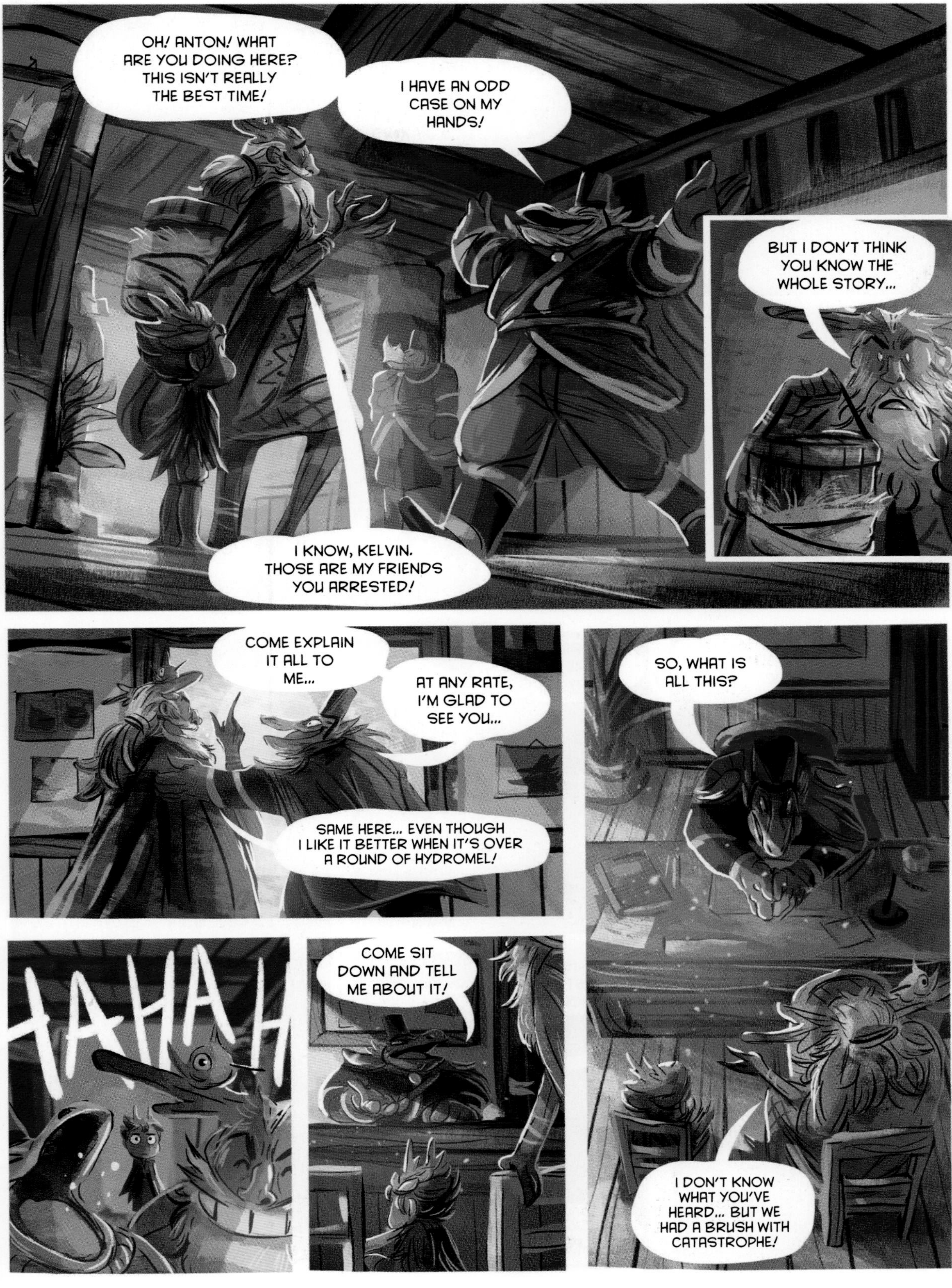
OH! ANTON! WHAT ARE YOU DOING HERE? THIS ISN'T REALLY THE BEST TIME!
I HAVE AN ODD CASE ON MY HANDS!
I KNOW, KELVIN. THOSE ARE MY FRIENDS YOU ARRESTED!
BUT I DON'T THINK YOU KNOW THE WHOLE STORY...
COME EXPLAIN IT ALL TO ME...
AT ANY RATE, I'M GLAD TO SEE YOU...
SAME HERE... EVEN THOUGH I LIKE IT BETTER WHEN IT'S OVER A ROUND OF HYDROMEL!
HAHAH
COME SIT DOWN AND TELL ME ABOUT IT!
SO, WHAT IS ALL THIS?
I DON'T KNOW WHAT YOU'VE HEARD... BUT WE HAD A BRUSH WITH CATASTROPHE!

A FEW EXPLANATIONS LATER...

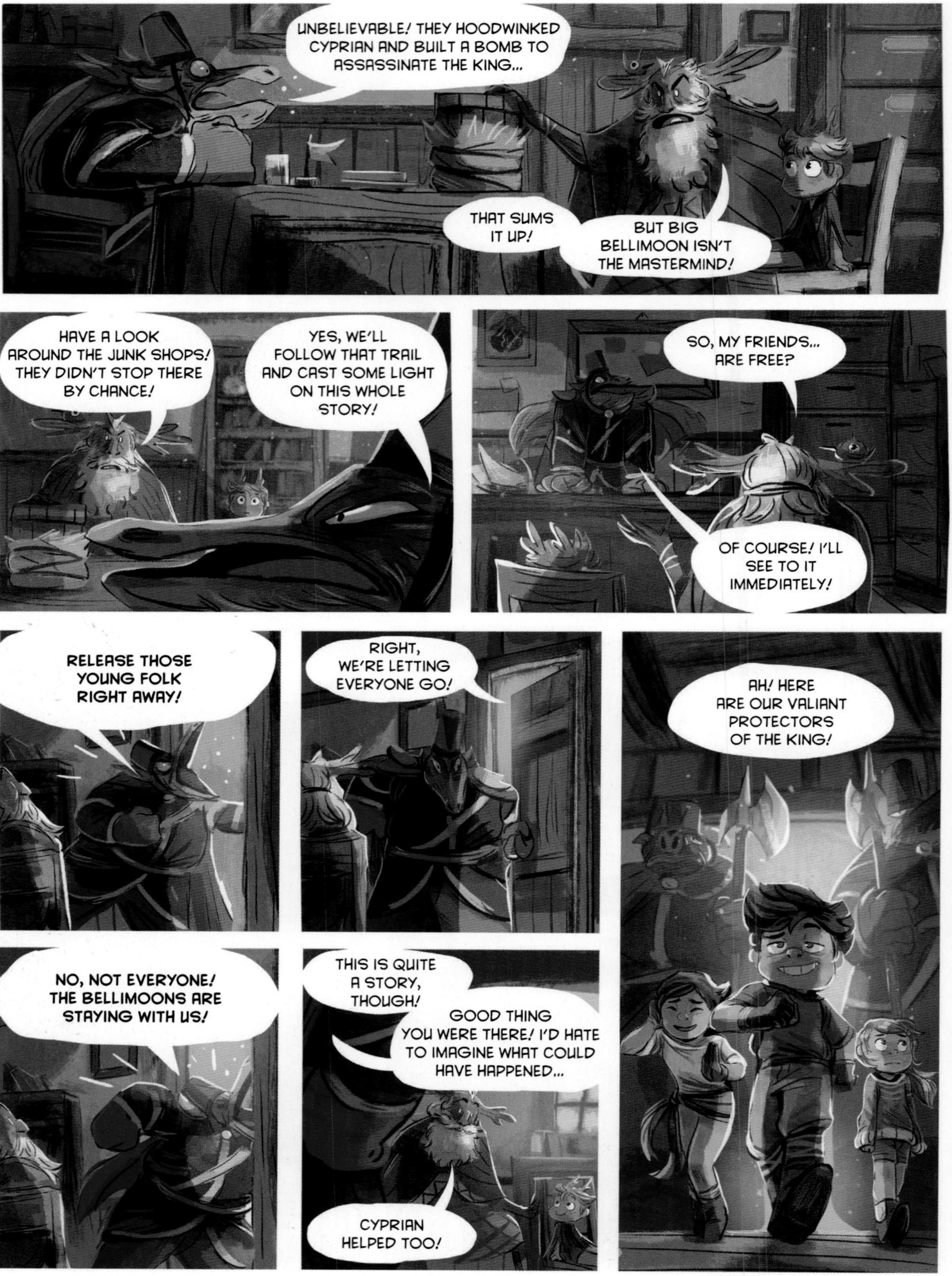
UNBELIEVABLE! THEY HOODWINKED CYPRIAN AND BUILT A BOMB TO ASSASSINATE THE KING...
THAT SUMS IT UP!
BUT BIG BELLIMOON ISN'T THE MASTERMIND!
HAVE A LOOK AROUND THE JUNK SHOPS! THEY DIDN'T STOP THERE BY CHANCE!
YES, WE'LL FOLLOW THAT TRAIL AND CAST SOME LIGHT ON THIS WHOLE STORY!
SO, MY FRIENDS... ARE FREE?
OF COURSE! I'LL SEE TO IT IMMEDIATELY!
RELEASE THOSE YOUNG FOLK RIGHT AWAY!
RIGHT, WE'RE LETTING EVERYONE GO!
NO, NOT EVERYONE! THE BELLIMOONS ARE STAYING WITH US!
THIS IS QUITE A STORY, THOUGH!
GOOD THING YOU WERE THERE! I'D HATE TO IMAGINE WHAT COULD HAVE HAPPENED...
CYPRIAN HELPED TOO!
AH! HERE ARE OUR VALIANT PROTECTORS OF THE KING!

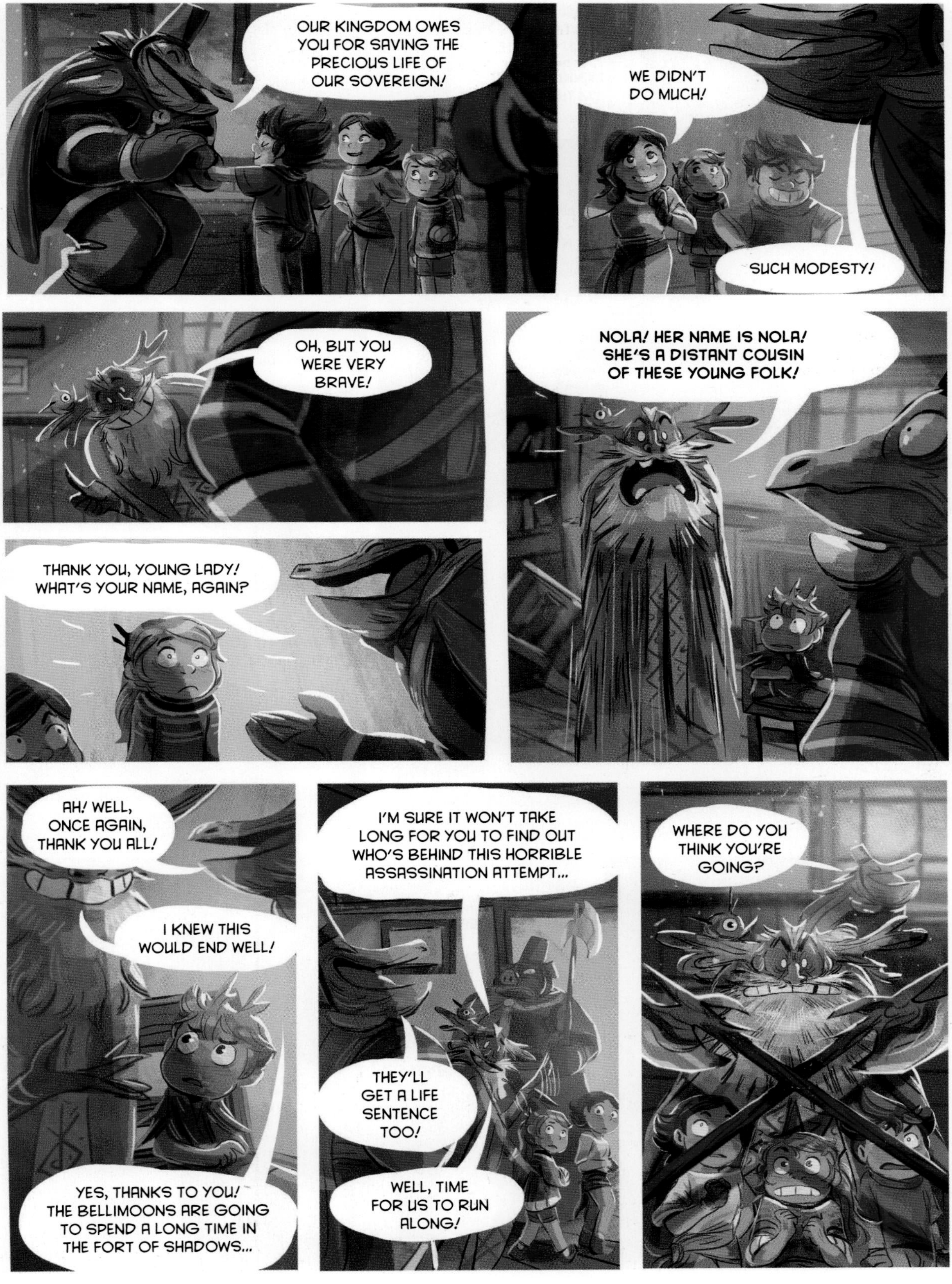
OUR KINGDOM OWES YOU FOR SAVING THE PRECIOUS LIFE OF OUR SOVEREIGN!
WE DIDN'T DO MUCH!
SUCH MODESTY!
OH, BUT YOU WERE VERY BRAVE!
THANK YOU, YOUNG LADY! WHAT'S YOUR NAME, AGAIN?
NOLA! HER NAME IS NOLA! SHE'S A DISTANT COUSIN OF THESE YOUNG FOLK!
AH! WELL, ONCE AGAIN, THANK YOU ALL!
I KNEW THIS WOULD END WELL!
YES, THANKS TO YOU! THE BELLIMOONS ARE GOING TO SPEND A LONG TIME IN THE FORT OF SHADOWS...
I'M SURE IT WON'T TAKE LONG FOR YOU TO FIND OUT WHO'S BEHIND THIS HORRIBLE ASSASSINATION ATTEMPT...
THEY'LL GET A LIFE SENTENCE TOO!
WELL, TIME FOR US TO RUN ALONG!
WHERE DO YOU THINK YOU'RE GOING?

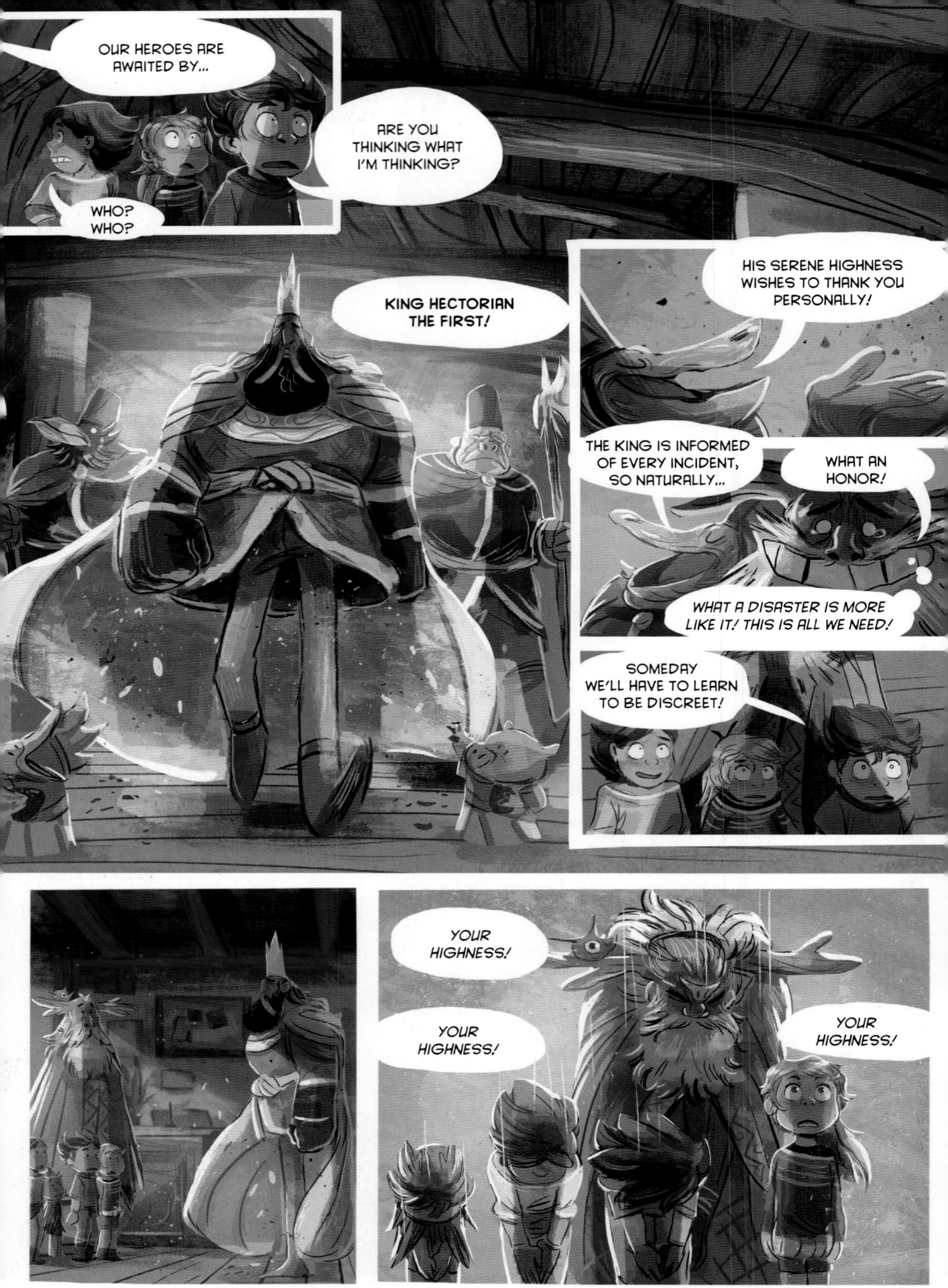
OUR HEROES ARE AWAITED BY...
ARE YOU THINKING WHAT I'M THINKING?
WHO? WHO?
KING HECTORIAN THE FIRST!
HIS SERENE HIGHNESS WISHES TO THANK YOU PERSONALLY!
THE KING IS INFORMED OF EVERY INCIDENT, SO NATURALLY...
WHAT AN HONOR!
WHAT A DISASTER IS MORE LIKE IT! THIS IS ALL WE NEED!
SOMEDAY WE'LL HAVE TO LEARN TO BE DISCREET!
YOUR HIGHNESS!
YOUR HIGHNESS!
YOUR HIGHNESS!

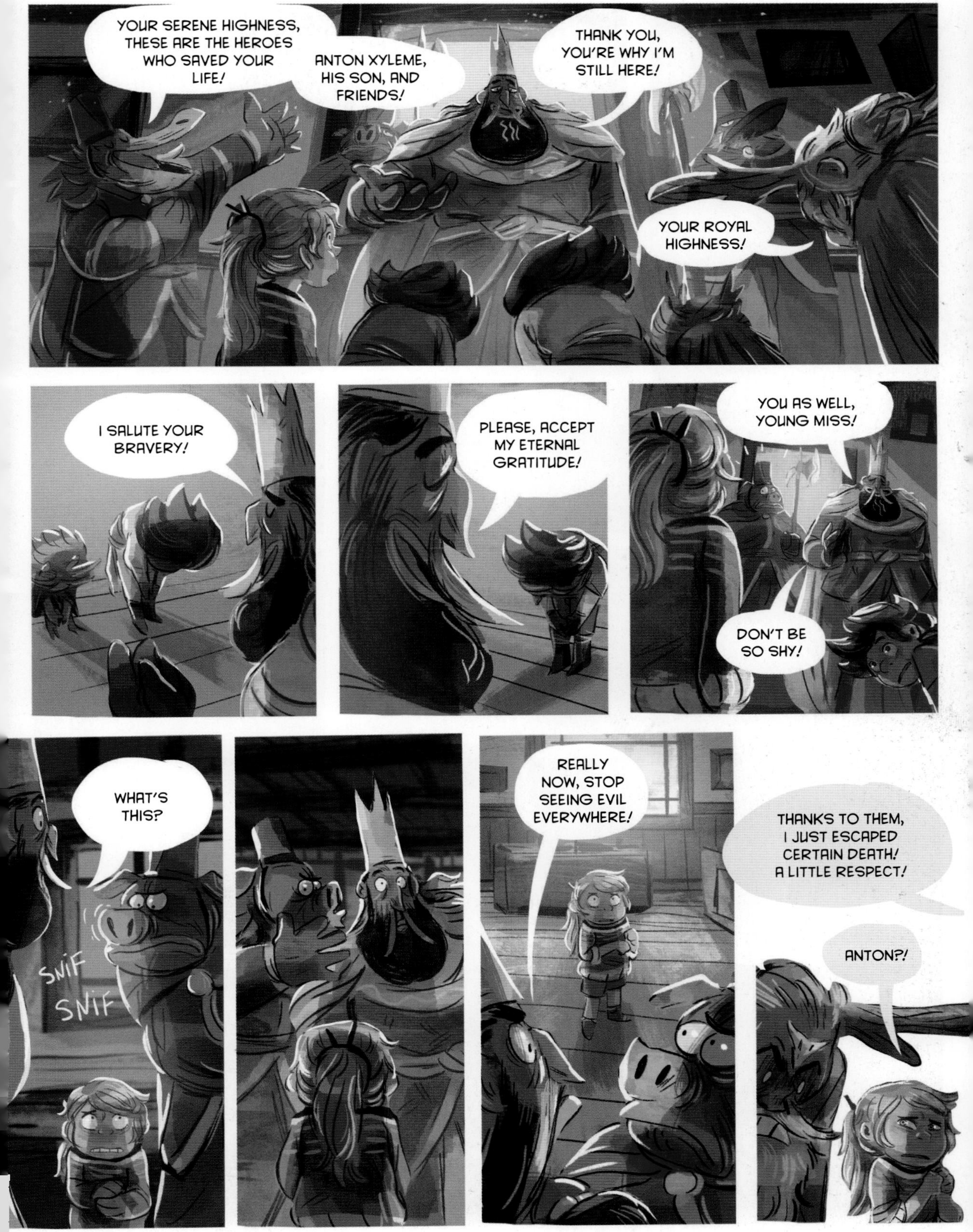

YOUR SERENE HIGHNESS, THESE ARE THE HEROES WHO SAVED YOUR LIFE!
ANTON XYLEME, HIS SON, AND FRIENDS!
THANK YOU, YOU'RE WHY I'M STILL HERE!
YOUR ROYAL HIGHNESS!
I SALUTE YOUR BRAVERY!
PLEASE, ACCEPT MY ETERNAL GRATITUDE!
YOU AS WELL, YOUNG MISS!
DON'T BE SO SHY!
WHAT'S THIS?
SNIF
SNIF
REALLY NOW, STOP SEEING EVIL EVERYWHERE!
THANKS TO THEM, I JUST ESCAPED CERTAIN DEATH! A LITTLE RESPECT!
ANTON?!

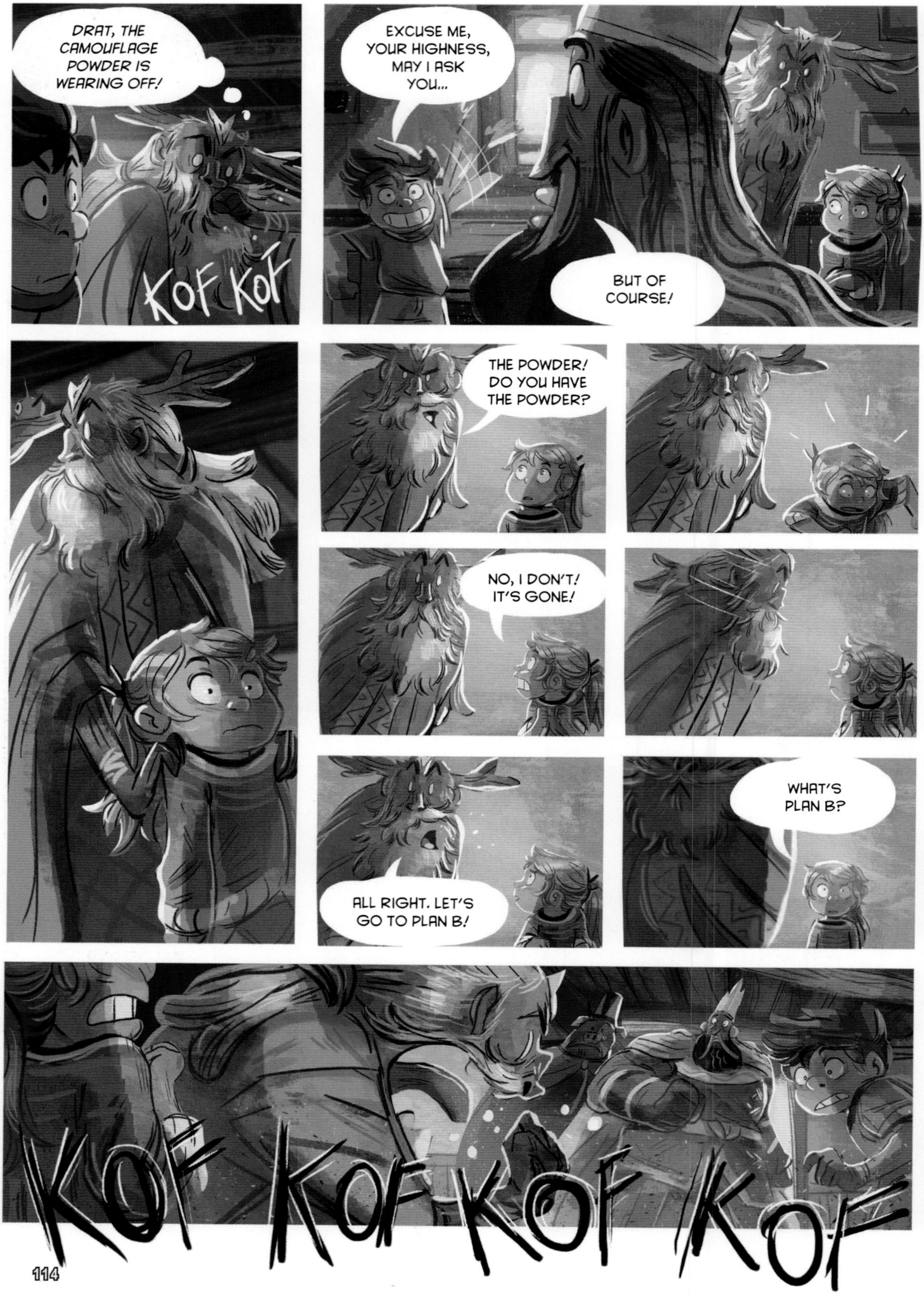
DRAT, THE CAMOUFLAGE POWDER IS WEARING OFF!
KOF KOF
EXCUSE ME, YOUR HIGHNESS, MAY I ASK YOU...
BUT OF COURSE!
THE POWDER! DO YOU HAVE THE POWDER?
NO, I DON'T! IT'S GONE!
ALL RIGHT. LET'S GO TO PLAN B!
WHAT'S PLAN B?
KOF KOF KOF KOF

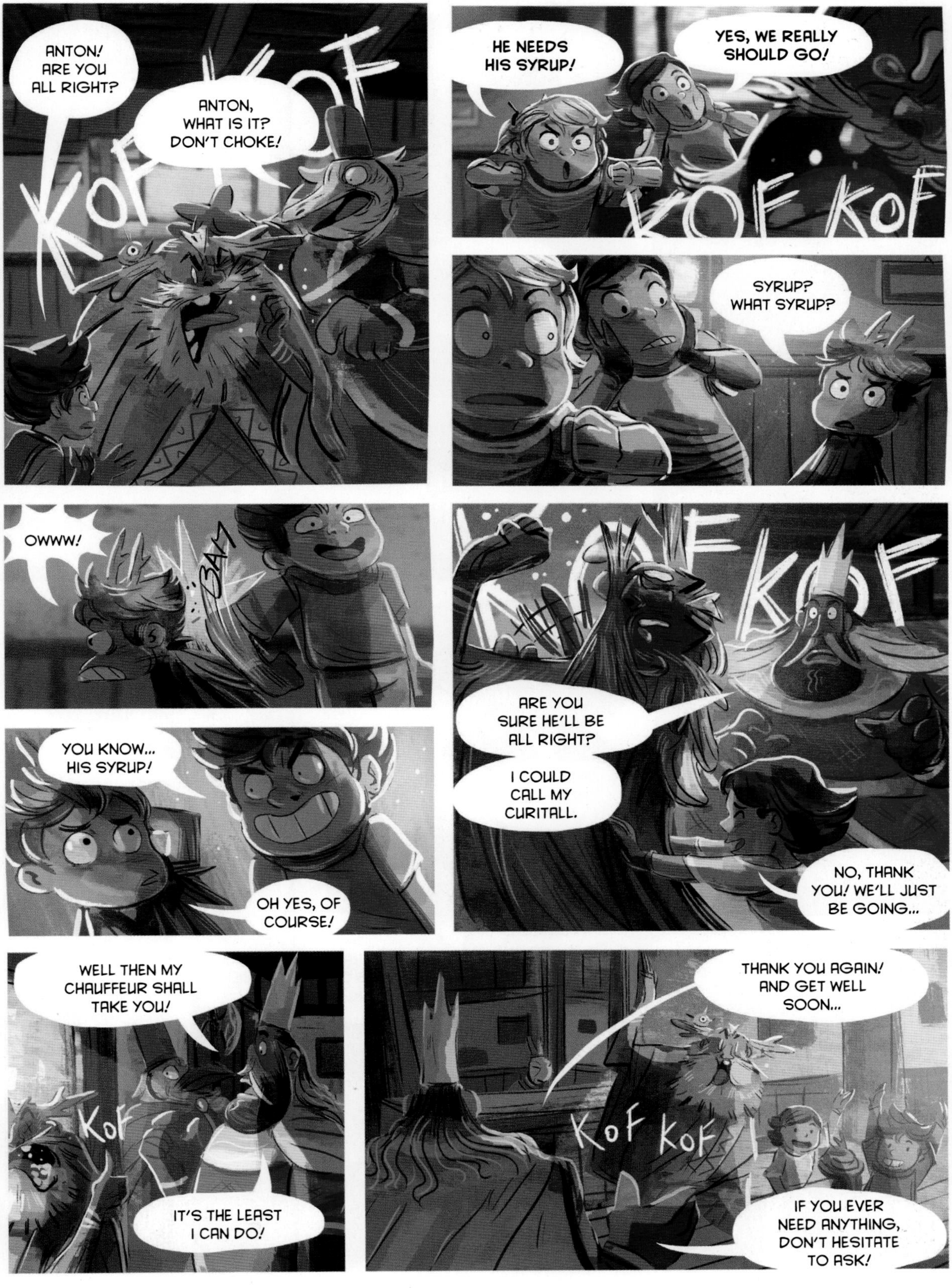
ANTON! ARE YOU ALL RIGHT?
ANTON, WHAT IS IT? DON'T CHOKE!
KOF KOF
HE NEEDS HIS SYRUP!
YES, WE REALLY SHOULD GO!
KOF KOF
SYRUP? WHAT SYRUP?
OWWW!
BAM
YOU KNOW... HIS SYRUP!
OH YES, OF COURSE!
KOF KOF
ARE YOU SURE HE'LL BE ALL RIGHT?
I COULD CALL MY CURITALL.
NO, THANK YOU! WE'LL JUST BE GOING...
WELL THEN MY CHAUFFEUR SHALL TAKE YOU!
KOF
IT'S THE LEAST I CAN DO!
THANK YOU AGAIN! AND GET WELL SOON...
KOF KOF
IF YOU EVER NEED ANYTHING, DON'T HESITATE TO ASK!

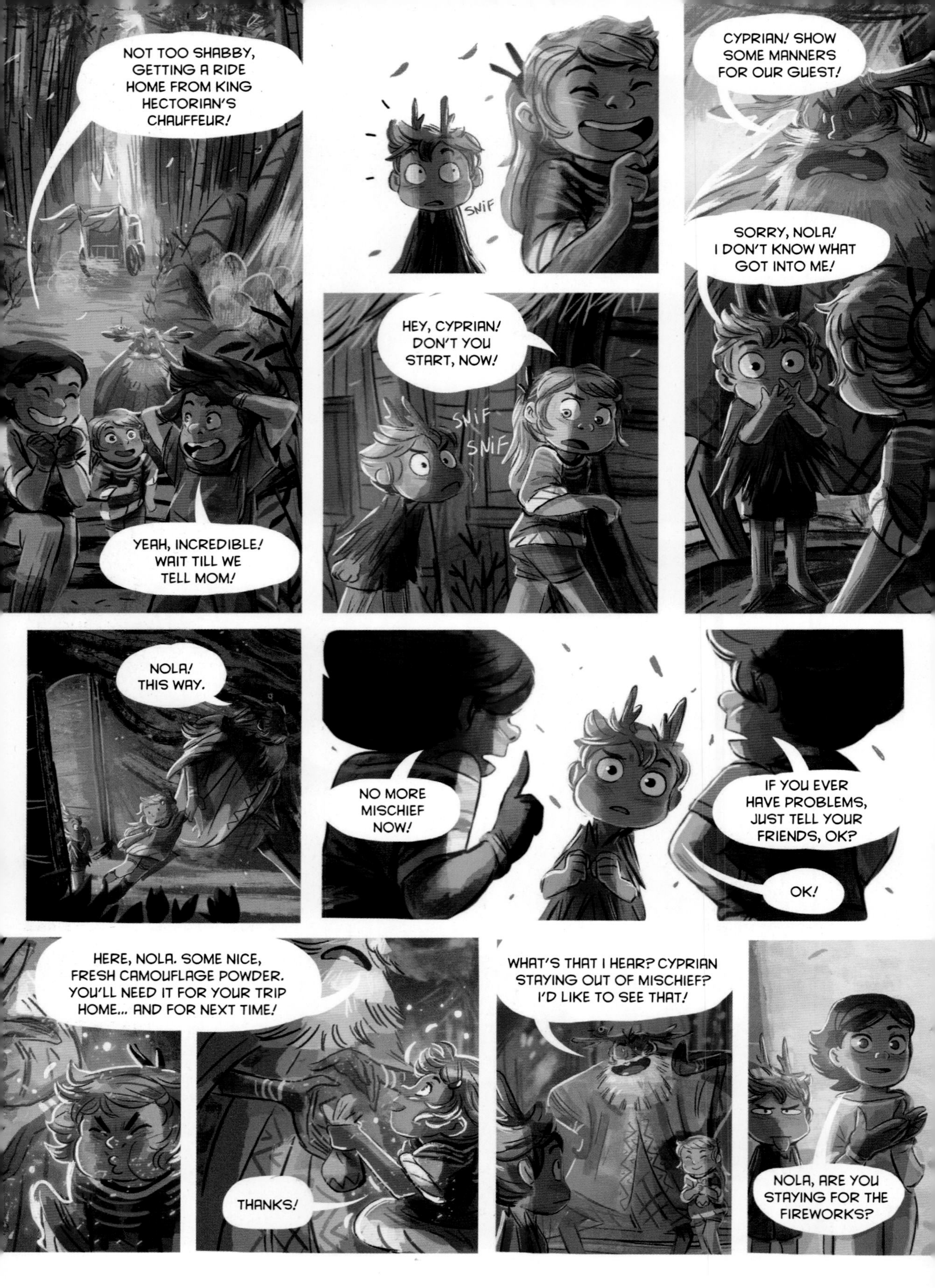
NOT TOO SHABBY, GETTING A RIDE HOME FROM KING HECTORIAN'S CHAUFFEUR!
YEAH, INCREDIBLE! WAIT TILL WE TELL MOM!
SNIF
HEY, CYPRIAN! DON'T YOU START, NOW!
SNIF
SNIF
CYPRIAN! SHOW SOME MANNERS FOR OUR GUEST!
SORRY, NOLA! I DON'T KNOW WHAT GOT INTO ME!
NOLA! THIS WAY.
NO MORE MISCHIEF NOW!
IF YOU EVER HAVE PROBLEMS, JUST TELL YOUR FRIENDS, OK?
OK!
HERE, NOLA. SOME NICE, FRESH CAMOUFLAGE POWDER. YOU'LL NEED IT FOR YOUR TRIP HOME... AND FOR NEXT TIME!
THANKS!
WHAT'S THAT I HEAR? CYPRIAN STAYING OUT OF MISCHIEF? I'D LIKE TO SEE THAT!
NOLA, ARE YOU STAYING FOR THE FIREWORKS?

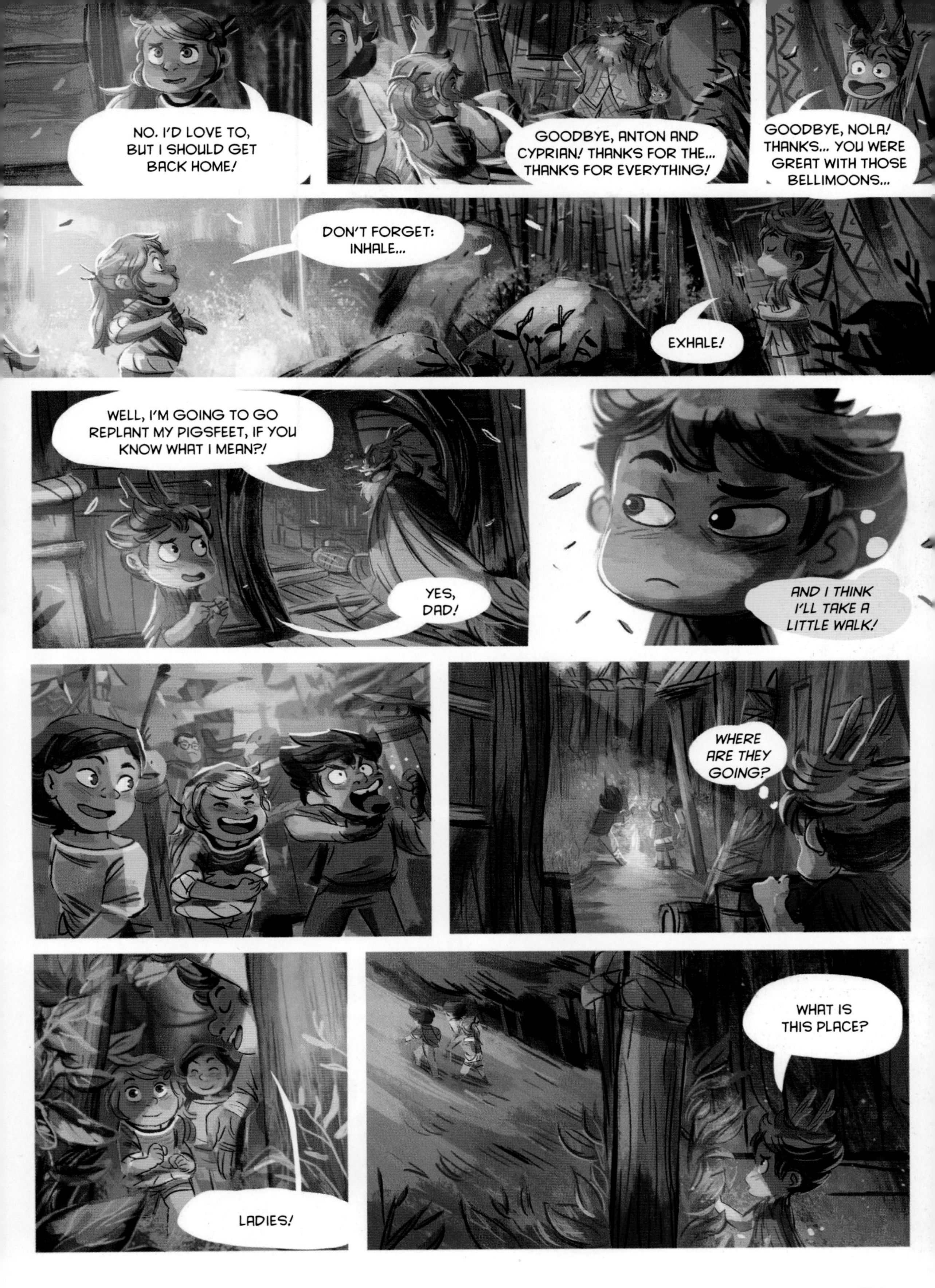

NO. I'D LOVE TO, BUT I SHOULD GET BACK HOME!
GOODBYE, ANTON AND CYPRIAN! THANKS FOR THE... THANKS FOR EVERYTHING!
GOODBYE, NOLA! THANKS... YOU WERE GREAT WITH THOSE BELLIMOONS...
DON'T FORGET: INHALE...
EXHALE!
WELL, I'M GOING TO GO REPLANT MY PIGSFEET, IF YOU KNOW WHAT I MEAN?!
YES, DAD!
AND I THINK I'LL TAKE A LITTLE WALK!
WHERE ARE THEY GOING?
LADIES!
WHAT IS THIS PLACE?

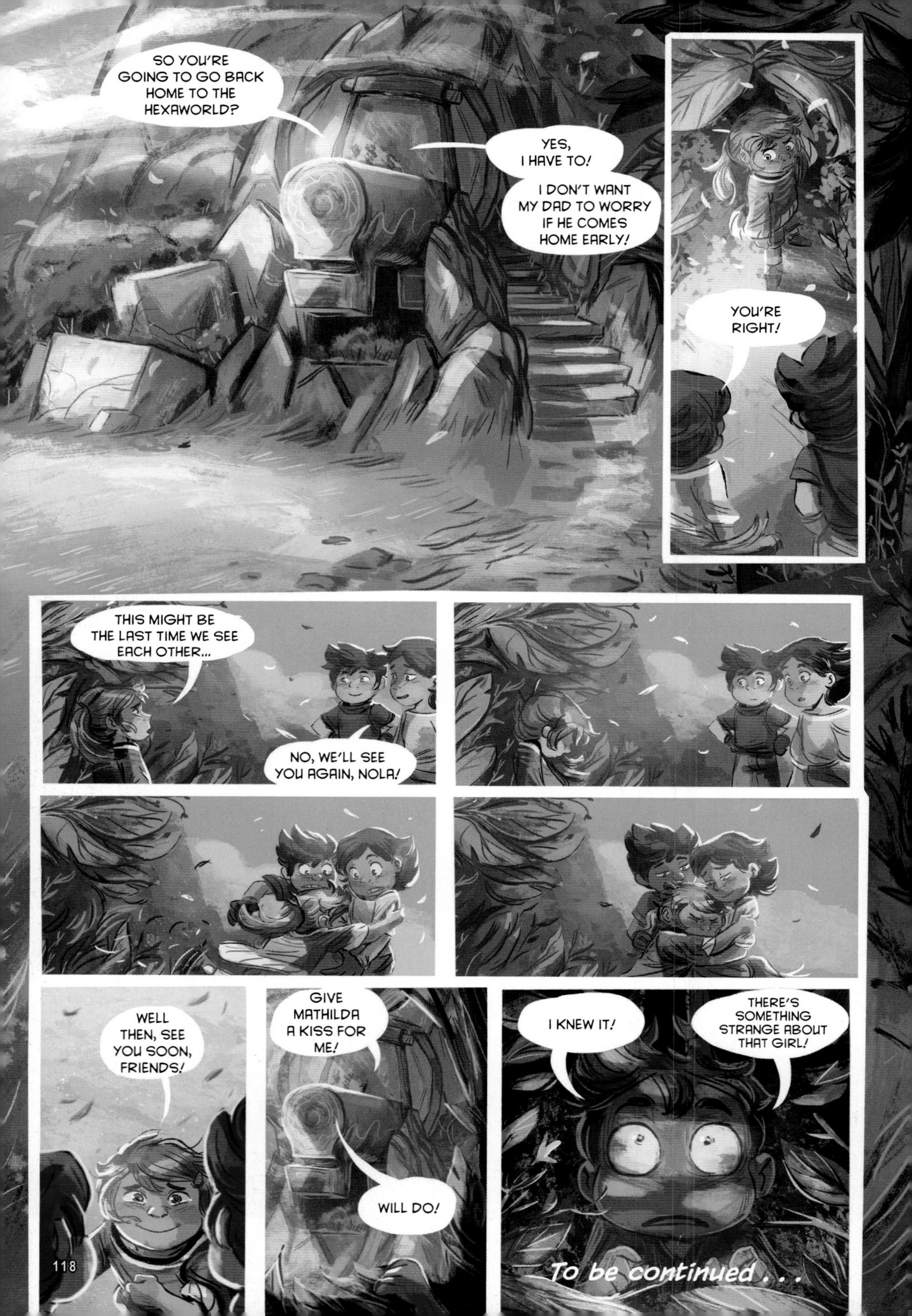
SO YOU'RE GOING TO GO BACK HOME TO THE HEXAWORLD?
YES, I HAVE TO!
I DON'T WANT MY DAD TO WORRY IF HE COMES HOME EARLY!
YOU'RE RIGHT!
THIS MIGHT BE THE LAST TIME WE SEE EACH OTHER...
NO, WE'LL SEE YOU AGAIN, NOLA!
WELL THEN, SEE YOU SOON, FRIENDS!
GIVE MATHILDA A KISS FOR ME!
WILL DO!
I KNEW IT!
THERE'S SOMETHING STRANGE ABOUT THAT GIRL!
To be continued . . .

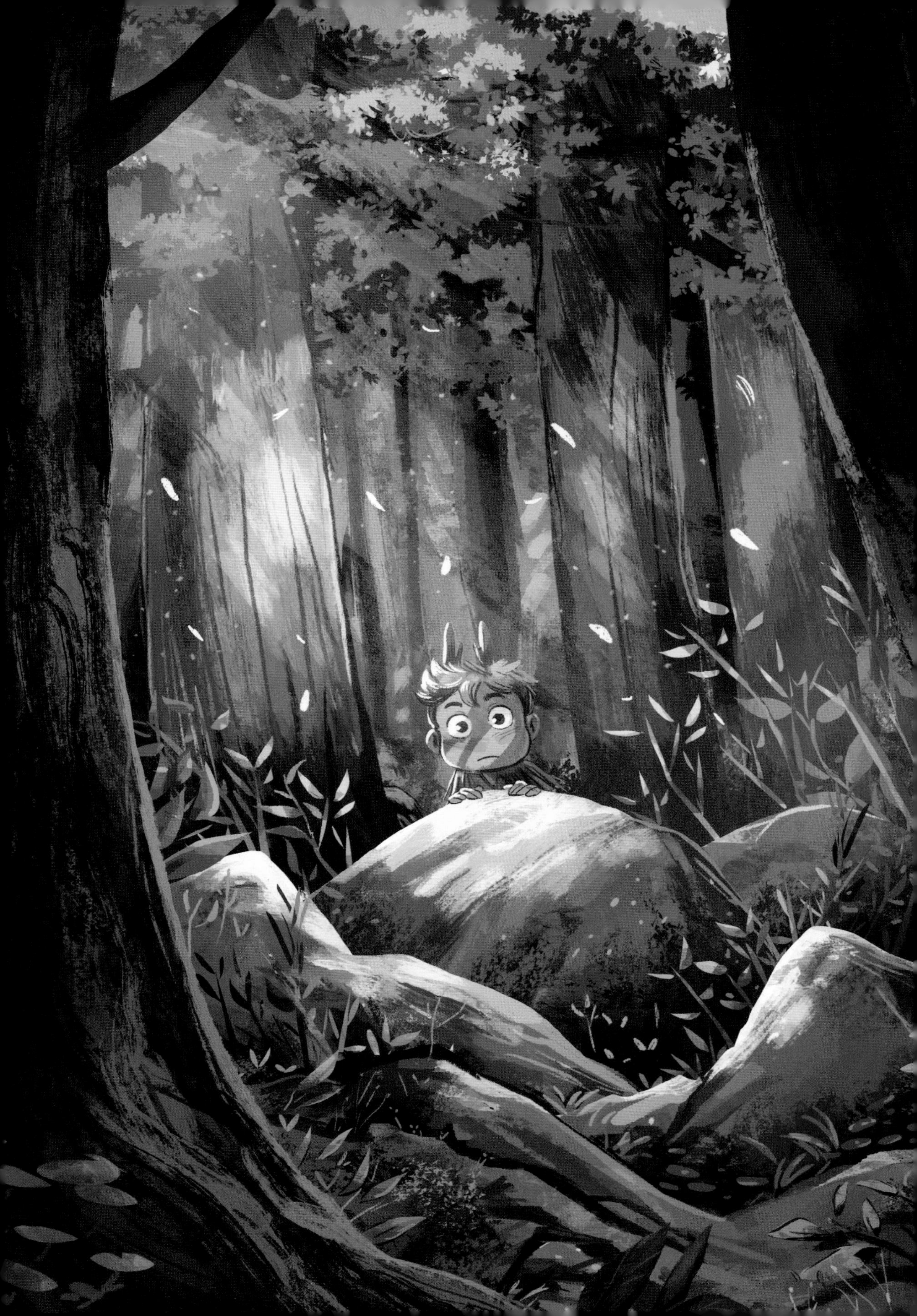

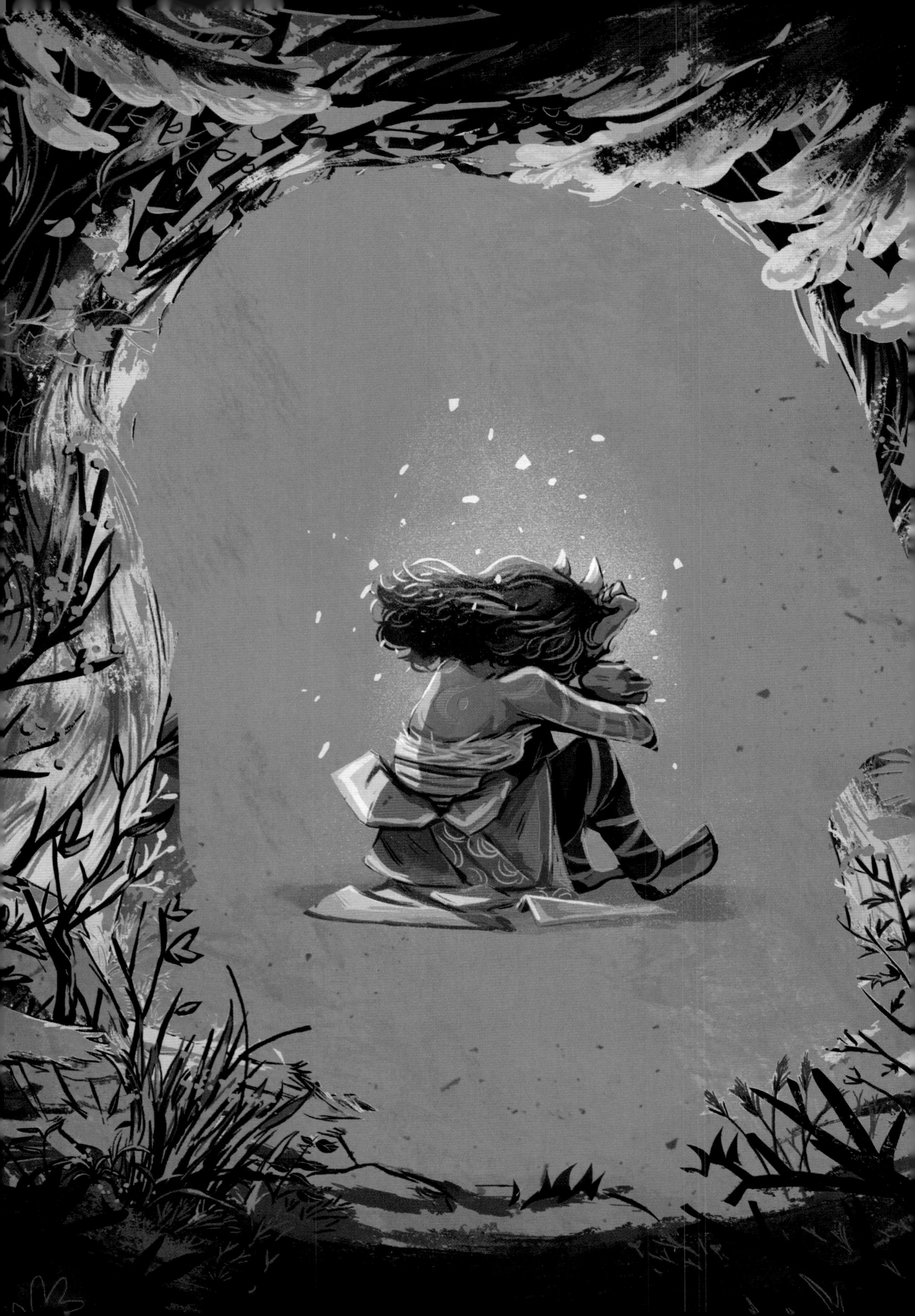

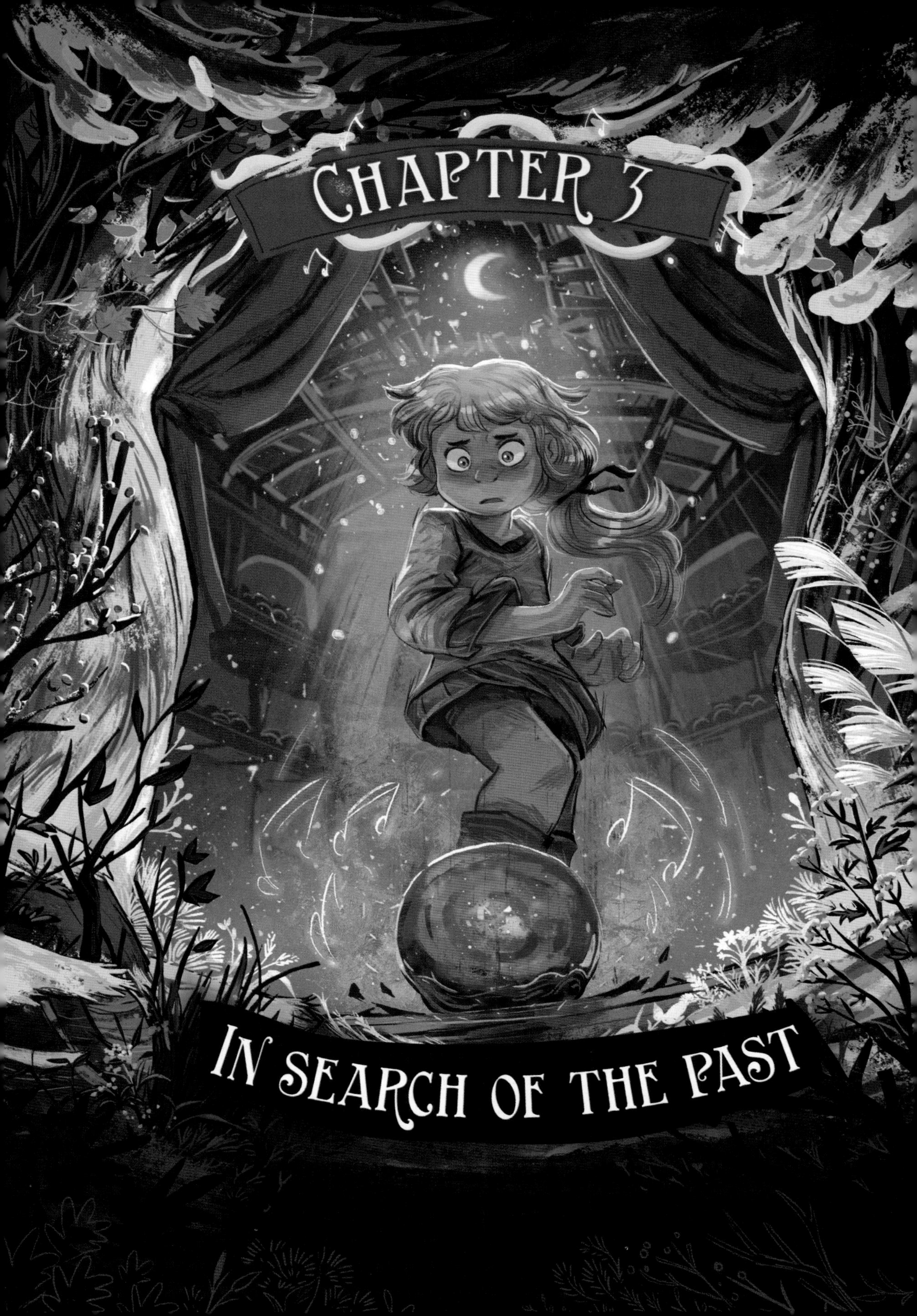
CHAPTER 3
IN SEARCH OF THE PAST

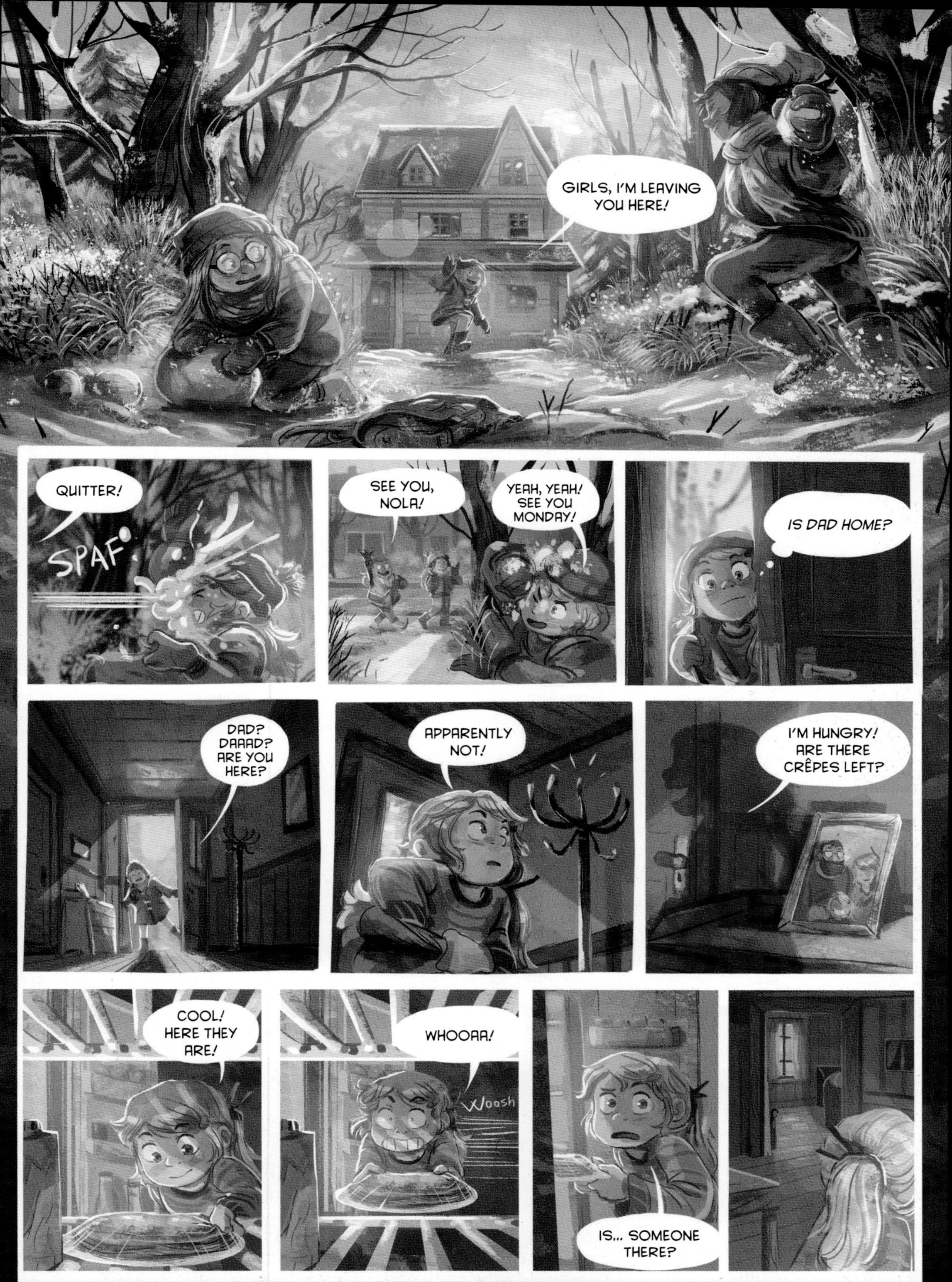

GIRLS, I'M LEAVING YOU HERE!
QUITTER!
SPAF
SEE YOU, NOLA!
YEAH, YEAH! SEE YOU MONDAY!
IS DAD HOME?
DAD? DAAAD? ARE YOU HERE?
APPARENTLY NOT!
I'M HUNGRY! ARE THERE CRÊPES LEFT?
COOL! HERE THEY ARE!
WHOOAA!
Woosh
IS... SOMEONE THERE?

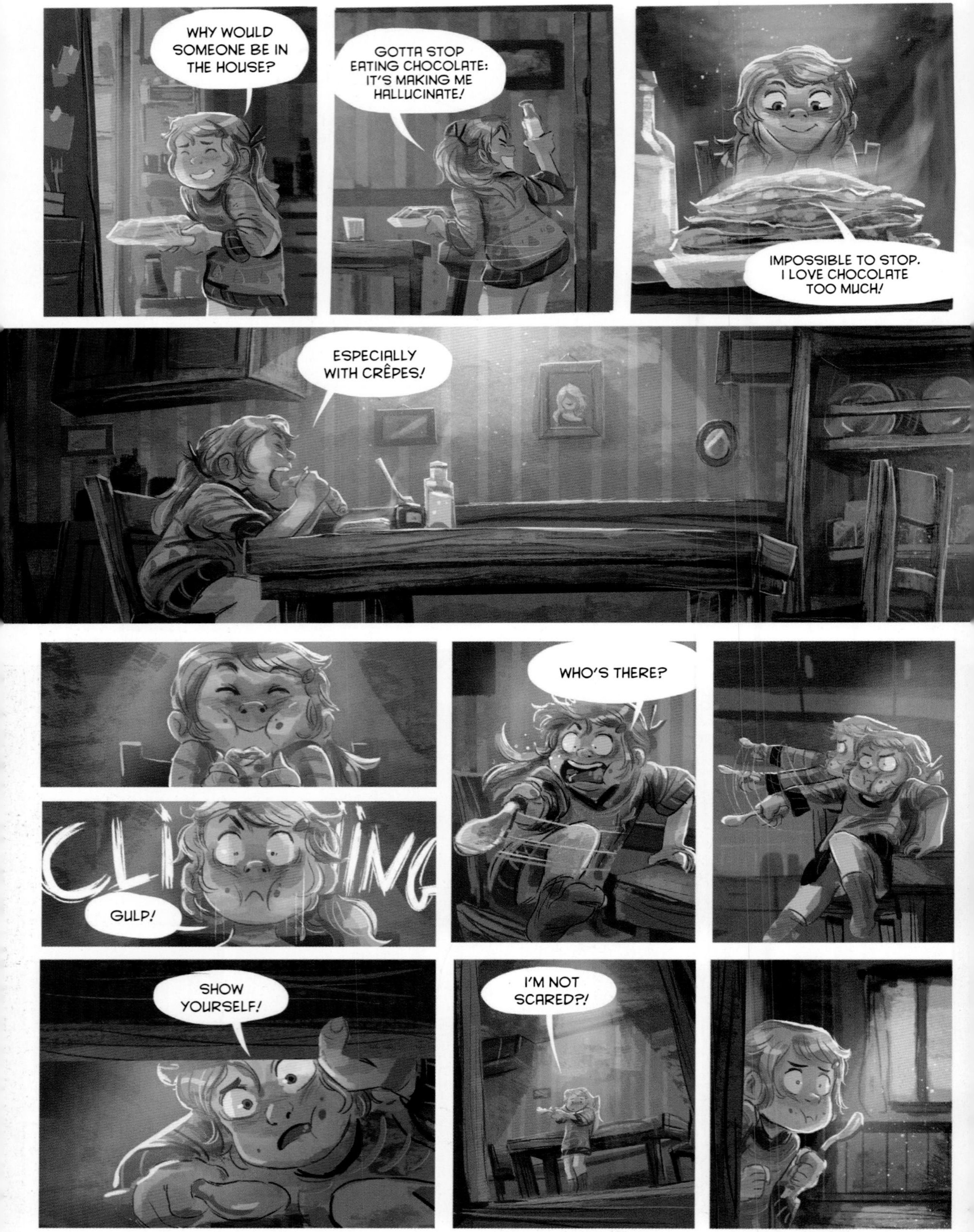
WHY WOULD SOMEONE BE IN THE HOUSE?
GOTTA STOP EATING CHOCOLATE: IT'S MAKING ME HALLUCINATE!
IMPOSSIBLE TO STOP. I LOVE CHOCOLATE TOO MUCH!
ESPECIALLY WITH CRÊPES!
GULP!
WHO'S THERE?
SHOW YOURSELF!
I'M NOT SCARED?!

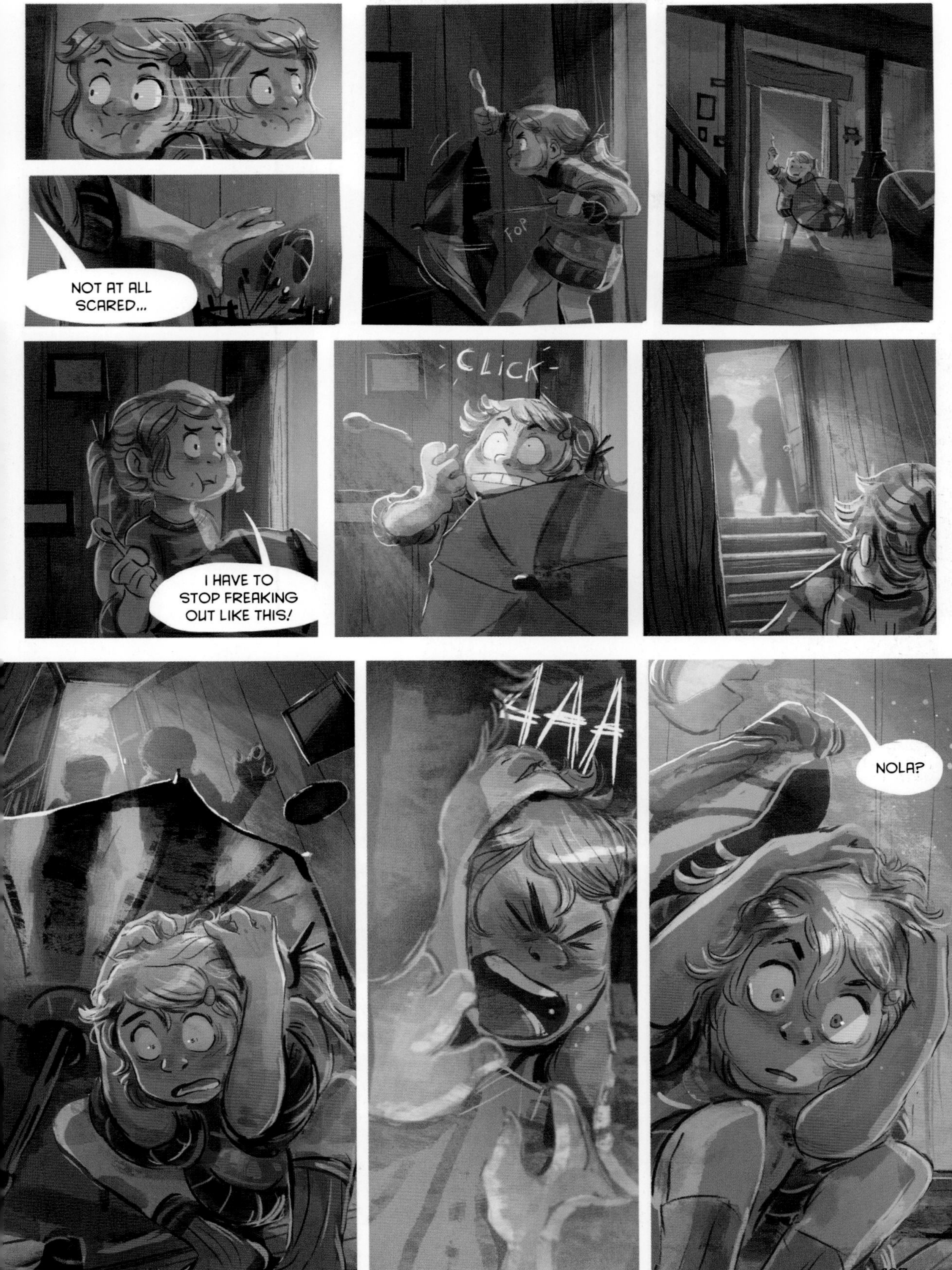
NOT AT ALL SCARED...
FOP
I HAVE TO STOP FREAKING OUT LIKE THIS!
CLICK
AAA
NOLA?

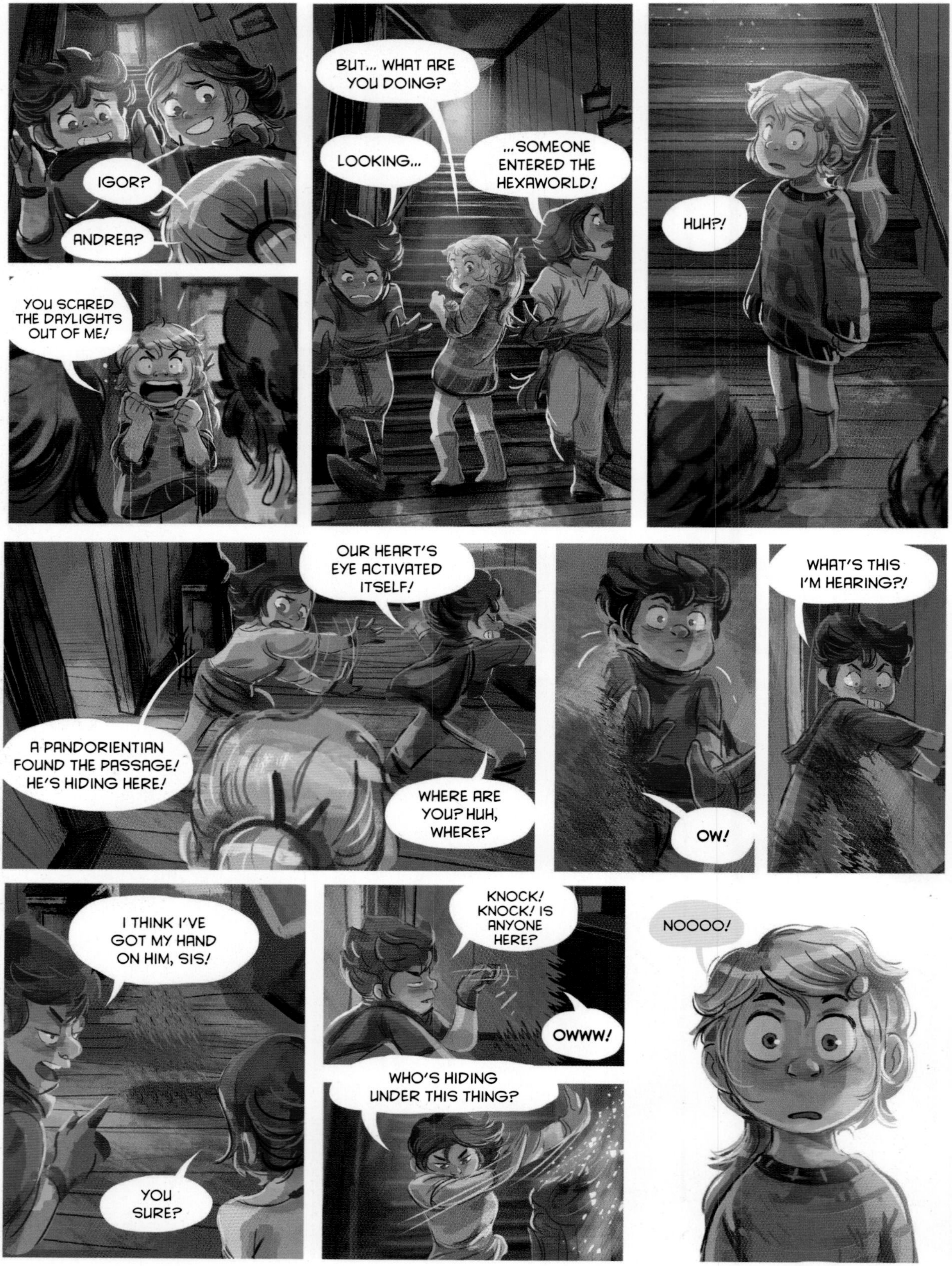
IGOR?
ANDREA?
YOU SCARED THE DAYLIGHTS OUT OF ME!
BUT... WHAT ARE YOU DOING?
LOOKING...
...SOMEONE ENTERED THE HEXAWORLD!
HUH?!
OUR HEART'S EYE ACTIVATED ITSELF!
A PANDORIENTIAN FOUND THE PASSAGE! HE'S HIDING HERE!
WHERE ARE YOU? HUH, WHERE?
OW!
WHAT'S THIS I'M HEARING?!
I THINK I'VE GOT MY HAND ON HIM, SIS!
YOU SURE?
KNOCK! KNOCK! IS ANYONE HERE?
OWWW!
WHO'S HIDING UNDER THIS THING?
NOOOO!

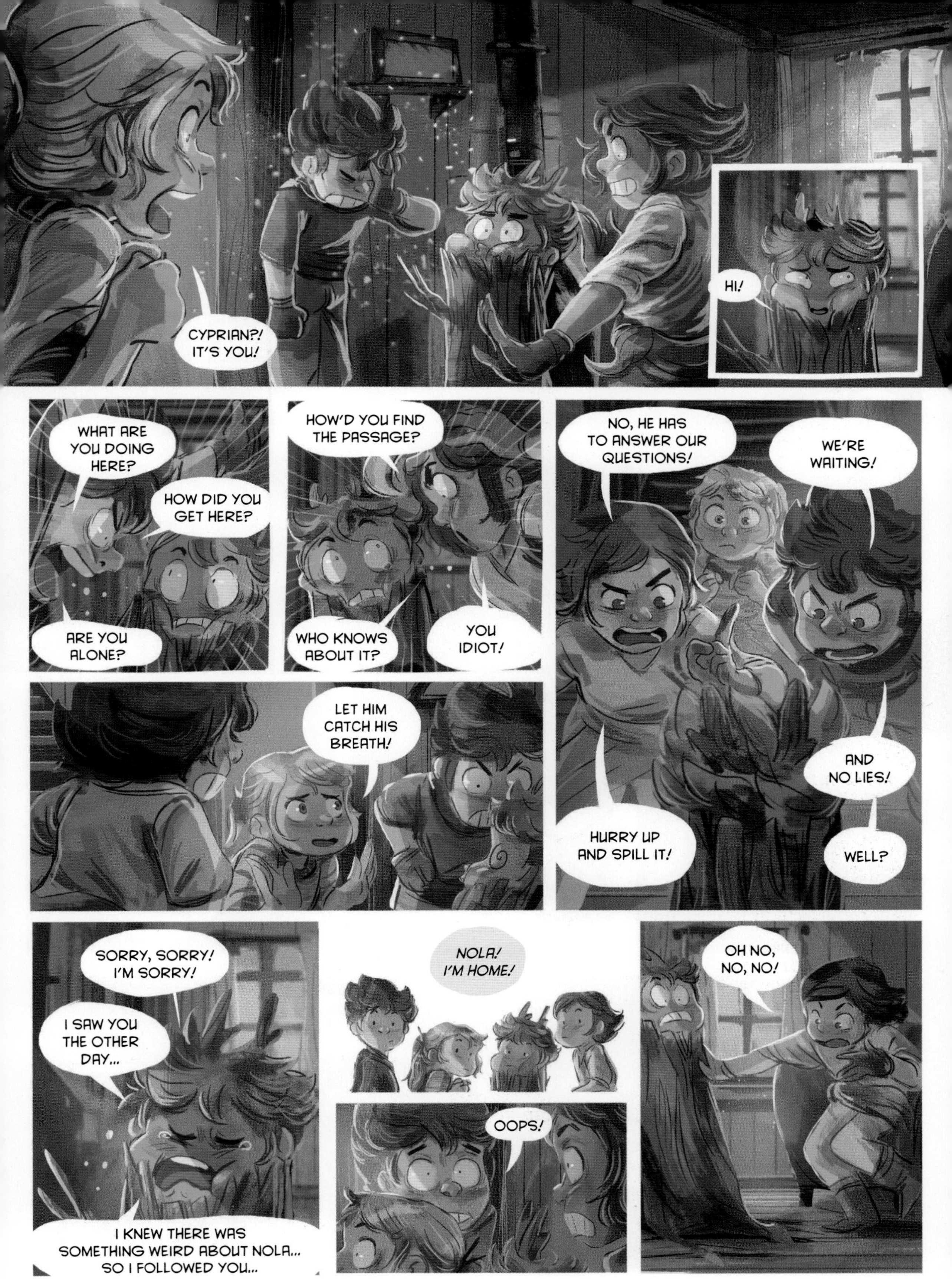
CYPRIAN?! IT'S YOU!
HI!
WHAT ARE YOU DOING HERE?
HOW DID YOU GET HERE?
ARE YOU ALONE?
HOW'D YOU FIND THE PASSAGE?
WHO KNOWS ABOUT IT?
YOU IDIOT!
NO, HE HAS TO ANSWER OUR QUESTIONS!
WE'RE WAITING!
AND NO LIES!
HURRY UP AND SPILL IT!
WELL?
LET HIM CATCH HIS BREATH!
SORRY, SORRY! I'M SORRY!
I SAW YOU THE OTHER DAY...
I KNEW THERE WAS SOMETHING WEIRD ABOUT NOLA... SO I FOLLOWED YOU...
NOLA! I'M HOME!
OOPS!
OH NO, NO, NO!

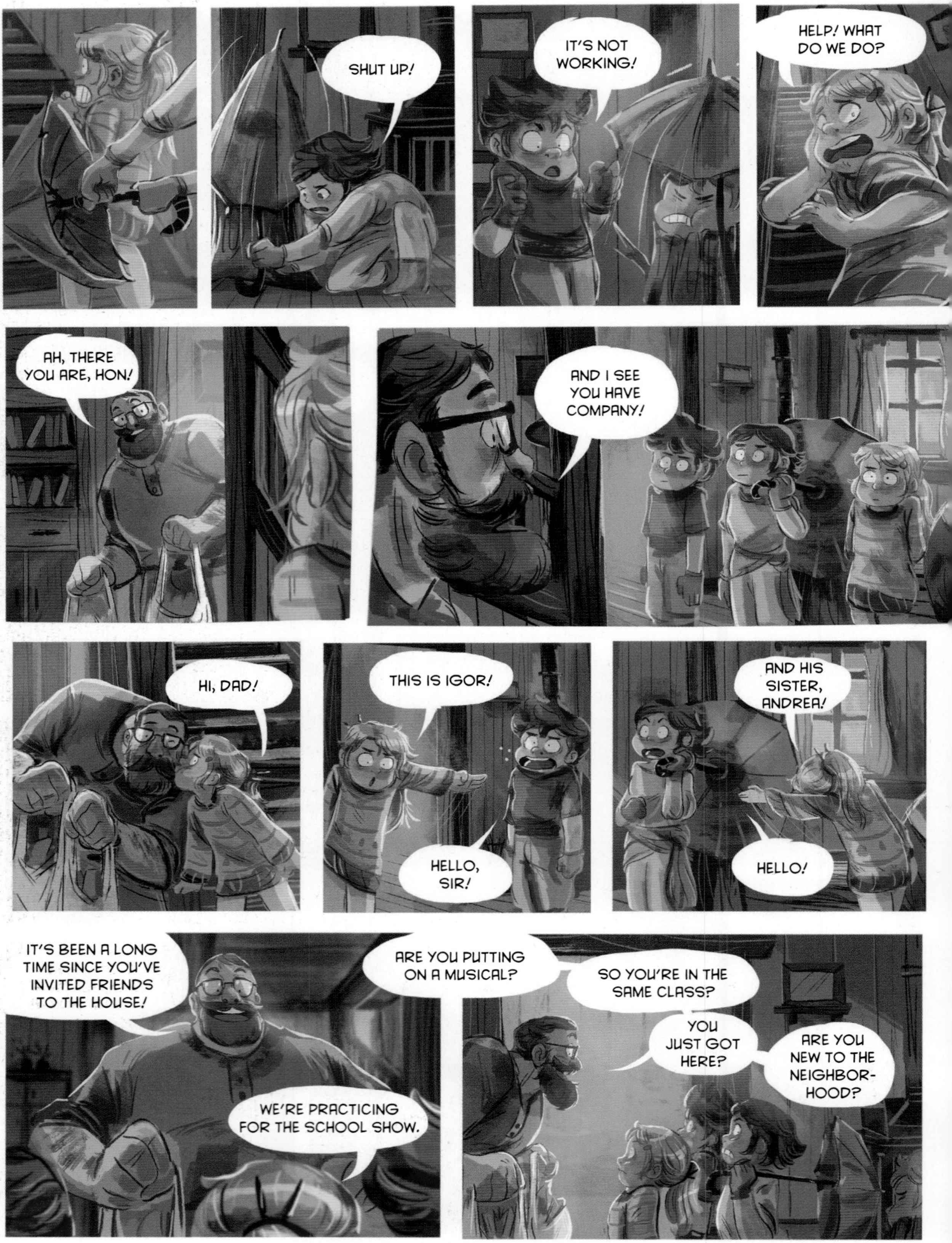
SHUT UP!
IT'S NOT WORKING!
HELP! WHAT DO WE DO?
AH, THERE YOU ARE, HON!
AND I SEE YOU HAVE COMPANY!
HI, DAD!
THIS IS IGOR!
HELLO, SIR!
AND HIS SISTER, ANDREA!
HELLO!
IT'S BEEN A LONG TIME SINCE YOU'VE INVITED FRIENDS TO THE HOUSE!
WE'RE PRACTICING FOR THE SCHOOL SHOW.
ARE YOU PUTTING ON A MUSICAL?
SO YOU'RE IN THE SAME CLASS?
YOU JUST GOT HERE?
ARE YOU NEW TO THE NEIGHBOR-HOOD?

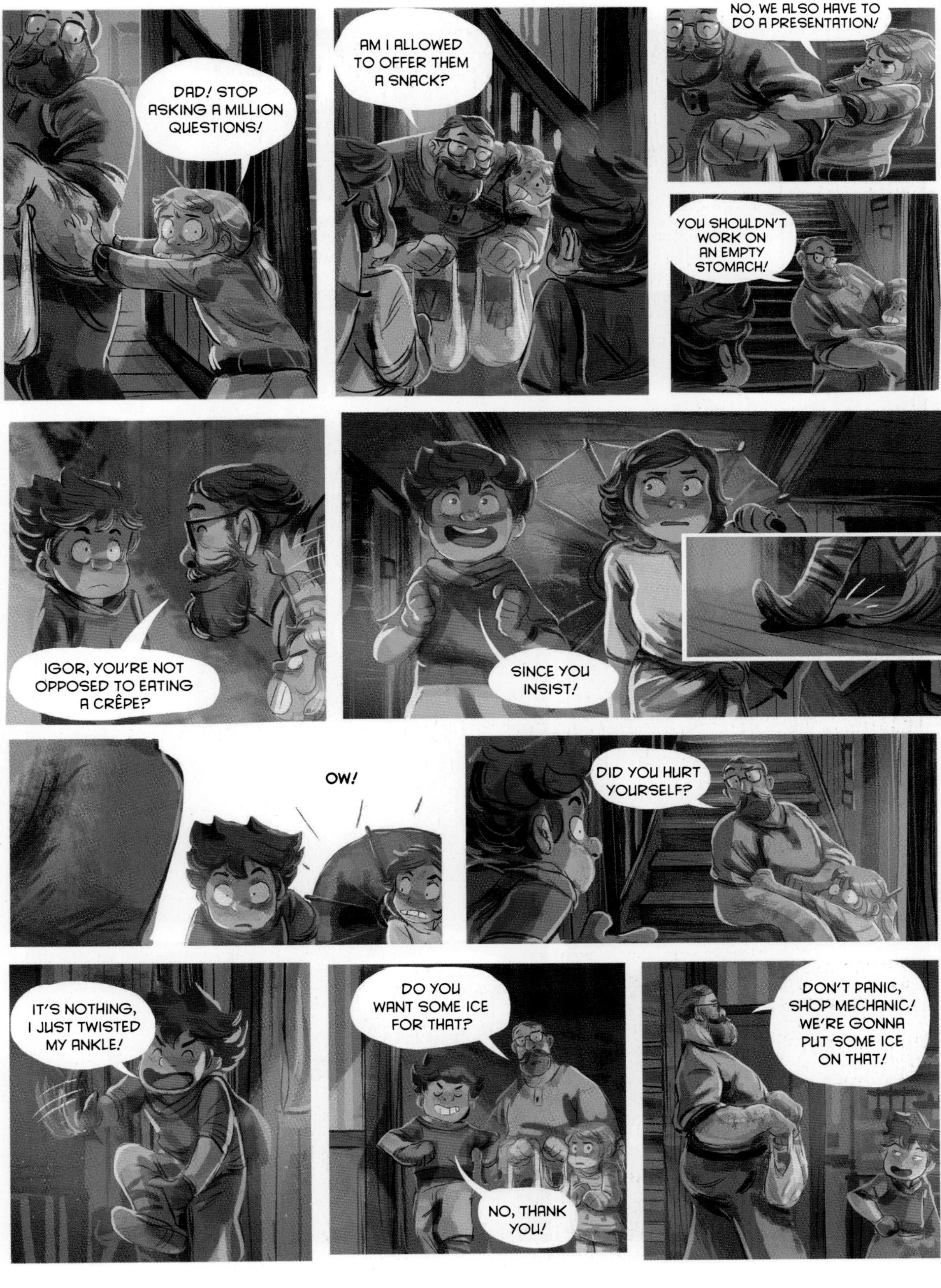
DAD! STOP ASKING A MILLION QUESTIONS!
AM I ALLOWED TO OFFER THEM A SNACK?
NO, WE ALSO HAVE TO DO A PRESENTATION!
YOU SHOULDN'T WORK ON AN EMPTY STOMACH!
IGOR, YOU'RE NOT OPPOSED TO EATING A CRÊPE?
SINCE YOU INSIST!
OW!
DID YOU HURT YOURSELF?
IT'S NOTHING, I JUST TWISTED MY ANKLE!
DO YOU WANT SOME ICE FOR THAT?
NO, THANK YOU!
DON'T PANIC, SHOP MECHANIC! WE'RE GONNA PUT SOME ICE ON THAT!

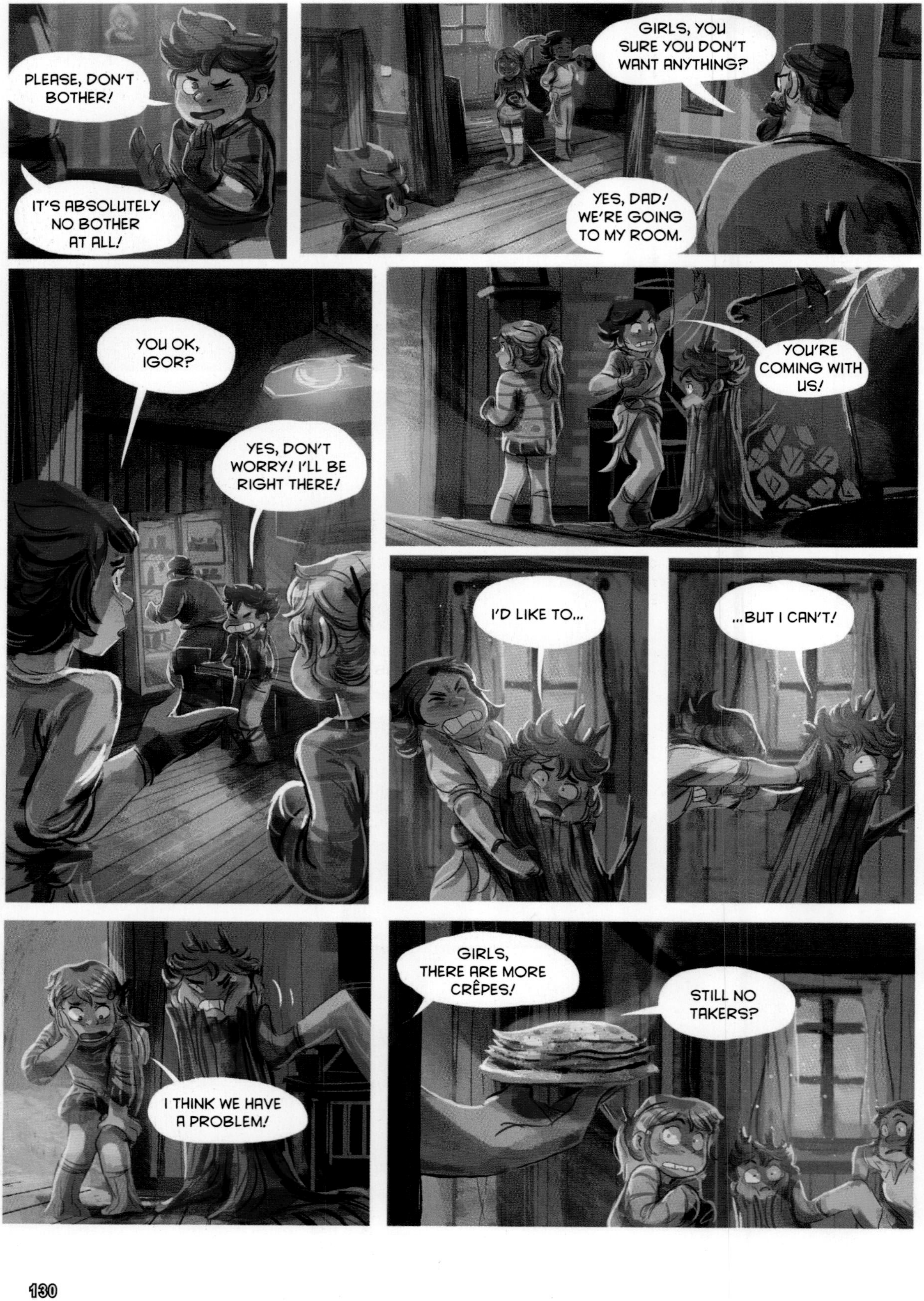
PLEASE, DON'T BOTHER!
IT'S ABSOLUTELY NO BOTHER AT ALL!
GIRLS, YOU SURE YOU DON'T WANT ANYTHING?
YES, DAD! WE'RE GOING TO MY ROOM.
YOU OK, IGOR?
YES, DON'T WORRY! I'LL BE RIGHT THERE!
YOU'RE COMING WITH US!
I'D LIKE TO...
...BUT I CAN'T!
I THINK WE HAVE A PROBLEM!
GIRLS, THERE ARE MORE CRÊPES!
STILL NO TAKERS?

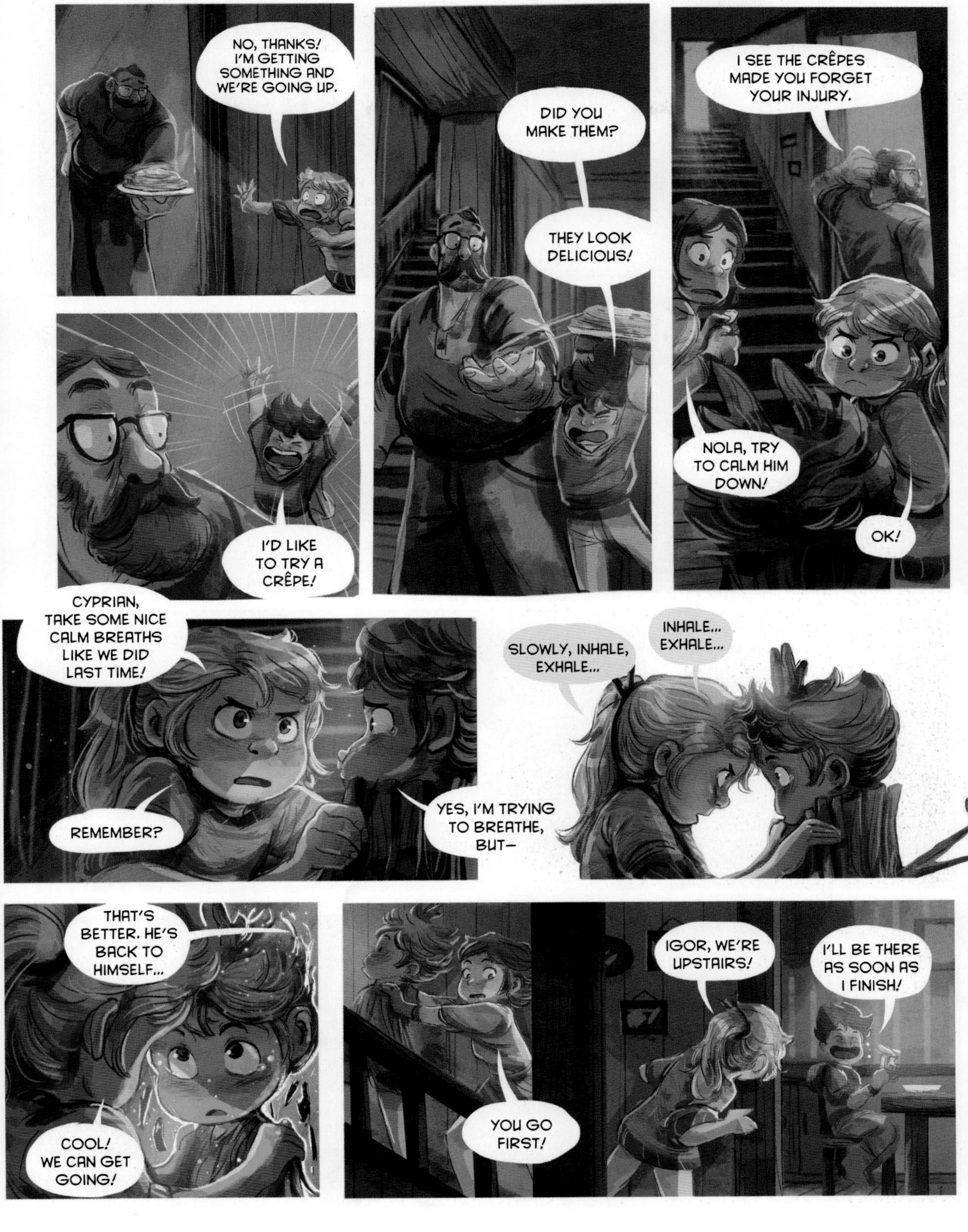
NO, THANKS! I'M GETTING SOMETHING AND WE'RE GOING UP.
I'D LIKE TO TRY A CRÊPE!
DID YOU MAKE THEM?
THEY LOOK DELICIOUS!
I SEE THE CRÊPES MADE YOU FORGET YOUR INJURY.
NOLA, TRY TO CALM HIM DOWN!
OK!
CYPRIAN, TAKE SOME NICE CALM BREATHS LIKE WE DID LAST TIME!
REMEMBER?
YES, I'M TRYING TO BREATHE, BUT–
SLOWLY, INHALE, EXHALE...
INHALE... EXHALE...
THAT'S BETTER. HE'S BACK TO HIMSELF...
COOL! WE CAN GET GOING!
YOU GO FIRST!
IGOR, WE'RE UPSTAIRS!
I'LL BE THERE AS SOON AS I FINISH!

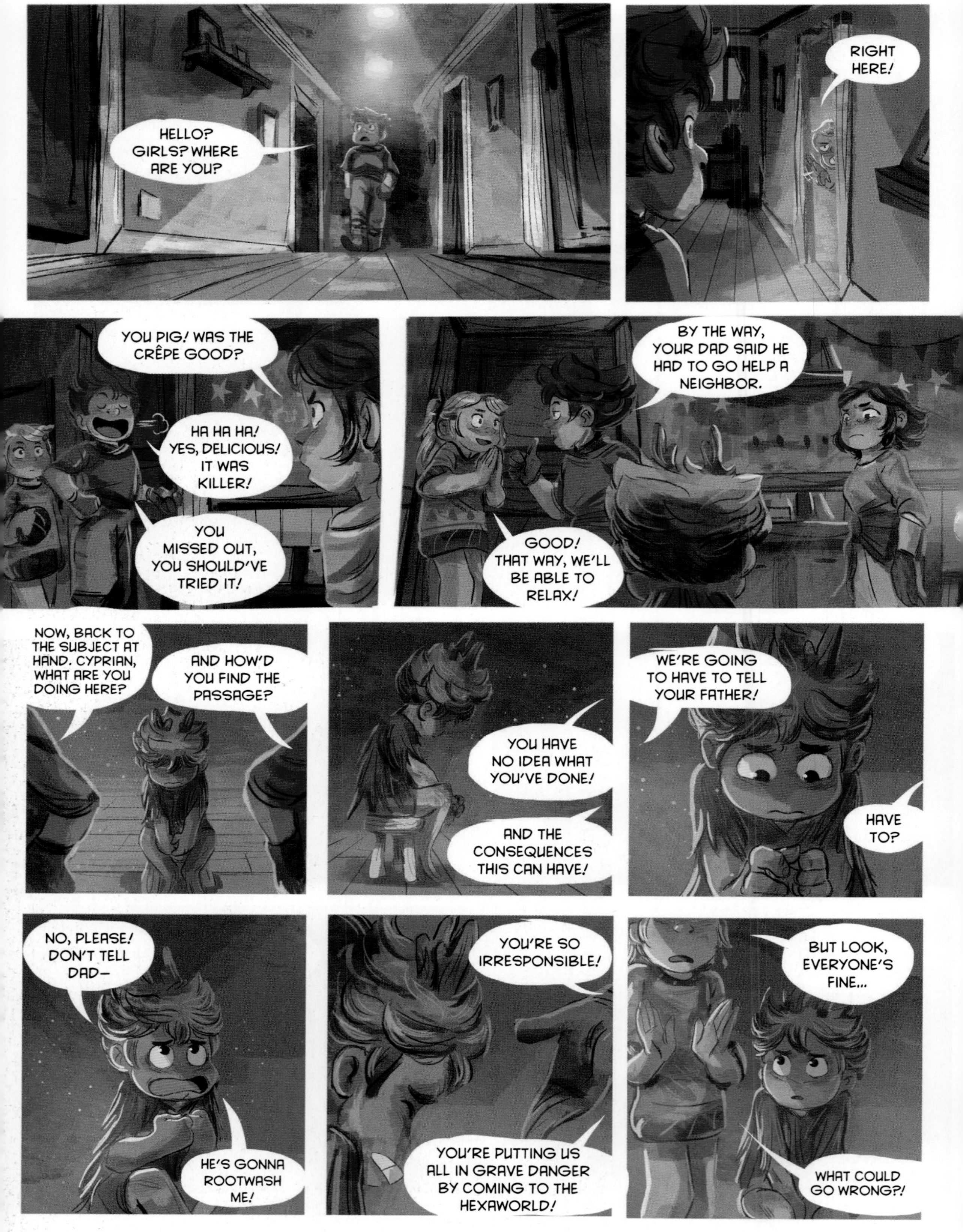
HELLO? GIRLS? WHERE ARE YOU?
RIGHT HERE!
YOU PIG! WAS THE CRÊPE GOOD?
HA HA HA! YES, DELICIOUS! IT WAS KILLER!
YOU MISSED OUT, YOU SHOULD'VE TRIED IT!
BY THE WAY, YOUR DAD SAID HE HAD TO GO HELP A NEIGHBOR.
GOOD! THAT WAY, WE'LL BE ABLE TO RELAX!
NOW, BACK TO THE SUBJECT AT HAND. CYPRIAN, WHAT ARE YOU DOING HERE?
AND HOW'D YOU FIND THE PASSAGE?
YOU HAVE NO IDEA WHAT YOU'VE DONE!
AND THE CONSEQUENCES THIS CAN HAVE!
WE'RE GOING TO HAVE TO TELL YOUR FATHER!
HAVE TO?
NO, PLEASE! DON'T TELL DAD—
HE'S GONNA ROOTWASH ME!
YOU'RE SO IRRESPONSIBLE!
YOU'RE PUTTING US ALL IN GRAVE DANGER BY COMING TO THE HEXAWORLD!
BUT LOOK, EVERYONE'S FINE...
WHAT COULD GO WRONG?!

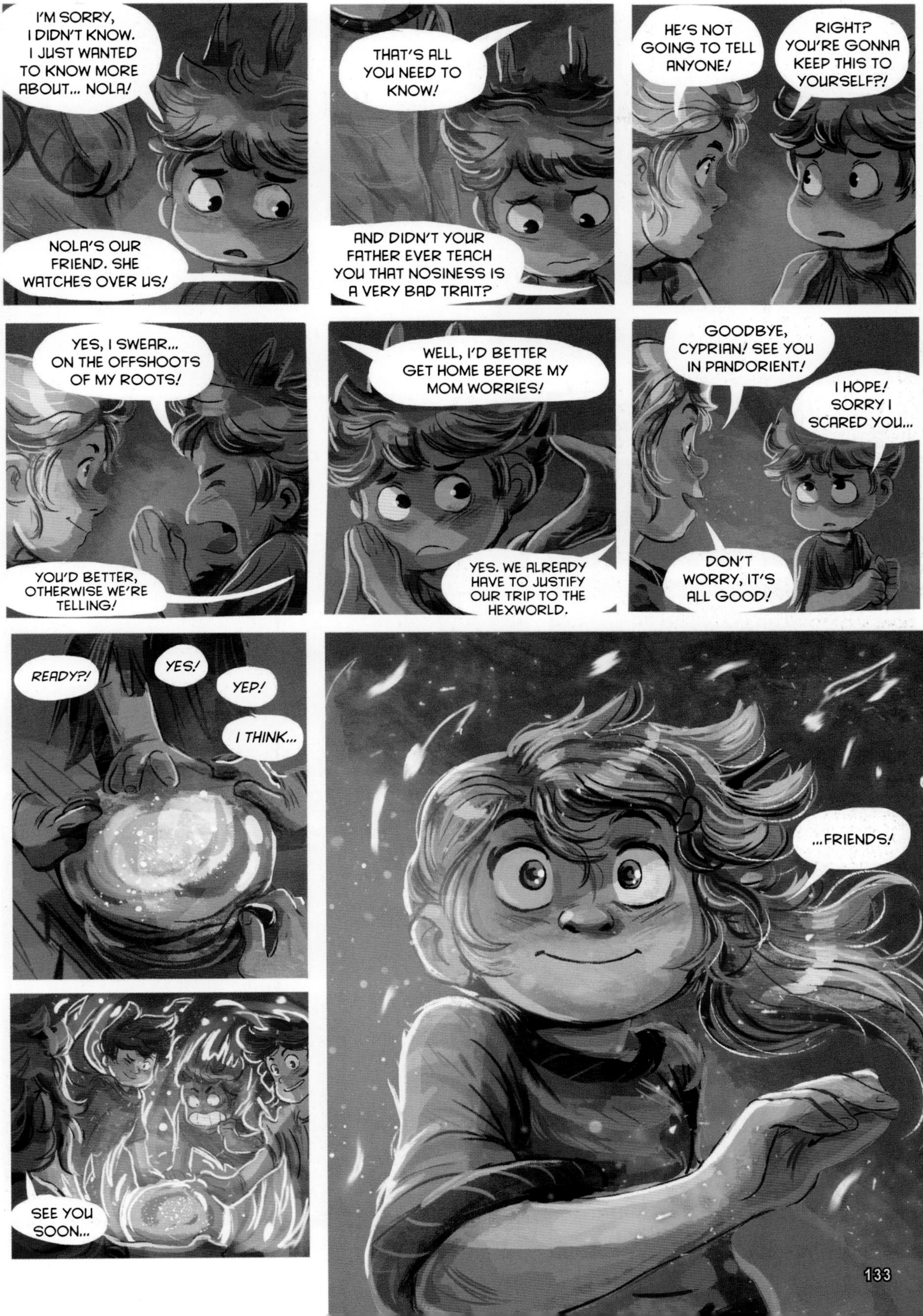
I'M SORRY, I DIDN'T KNOW. I JUST WANTED TO KNOW MORE ABOUT... NOLA!
NOLA'S OUR FRIEND. SHE WATCHES OVER US!
THAT'S ALL YOU NEED TO KNOW!
AND DIDN'T YOUR FATHER EVER TEACH YOU THAT NOSINESS IS A VERY BAD TRAIT?
HE'S NOT GOING TO TELL ANYONE!
RIGHT? YOU'RE GONNA KEEP THIS TO YOURSELF?!
YES, I SWEAR... ON THE OFFSHOOTS OF MY ROOTS!
YOU'D BETTER, OTHERWISE WE'RE TELLING!
WELL, I'D BETTER GET HOME BEFORE MY MOM WORRIES!
YES. WE ALREADY HAVE TO JUSTIFY OUR TRIP TO THE HEXWORLD.
GOODBYE, CYPRIAN! SEE YOU IN PANDORIENT!
I HOPE! SORRY I SCARED YOU...
DON'T WORRY, IT'S ALL GOOD!
READY?!
YES!
YEP!
I THINK...
SEE YOU SOON...
...FRIENDS!

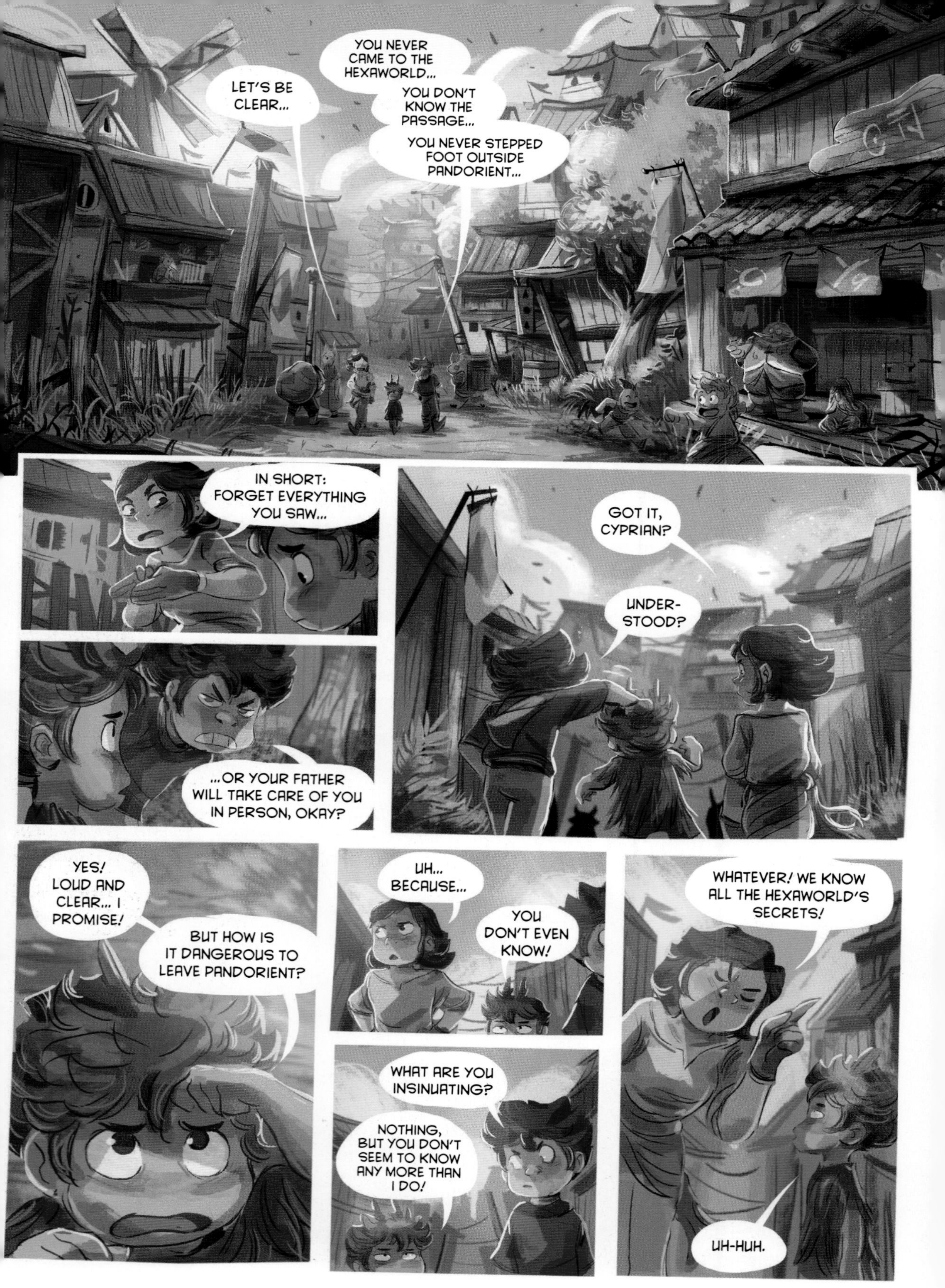
LET'S BE CLEAR...
YOU NEVER CAME TO THE HEXAWORLD...
YOU DON'T KNOW THE PASSAGE...
YOU NEVER STEPPED FOOT OUTSIDE PANDORIENT...
IN SHORT: FORGET EVERYTHING YOU SAW...
...OR YOUR FATHER WILL TAKE CARE OF YOU IN PERSON, OKAY?
GOT IT, CYPRIAN?
UNDER-STOOD?
YES! LOUD AND CLEAR... I PROMISE!
BUT HOW IS IT DANGEROUS TO LEAVE PANDORIENT?
UH... BECAUSE...
YOU DON'T EVEN KNOW!
WHAT ARE YOU INSINUATING?
NOTHING, BUT YOU DON'T SEEM TO KNOW ANY MORE THAN I DO!
WHATEVER! WE KNOW ALL THE HEXAWORLD'S SECRETS!
UH-HUH.

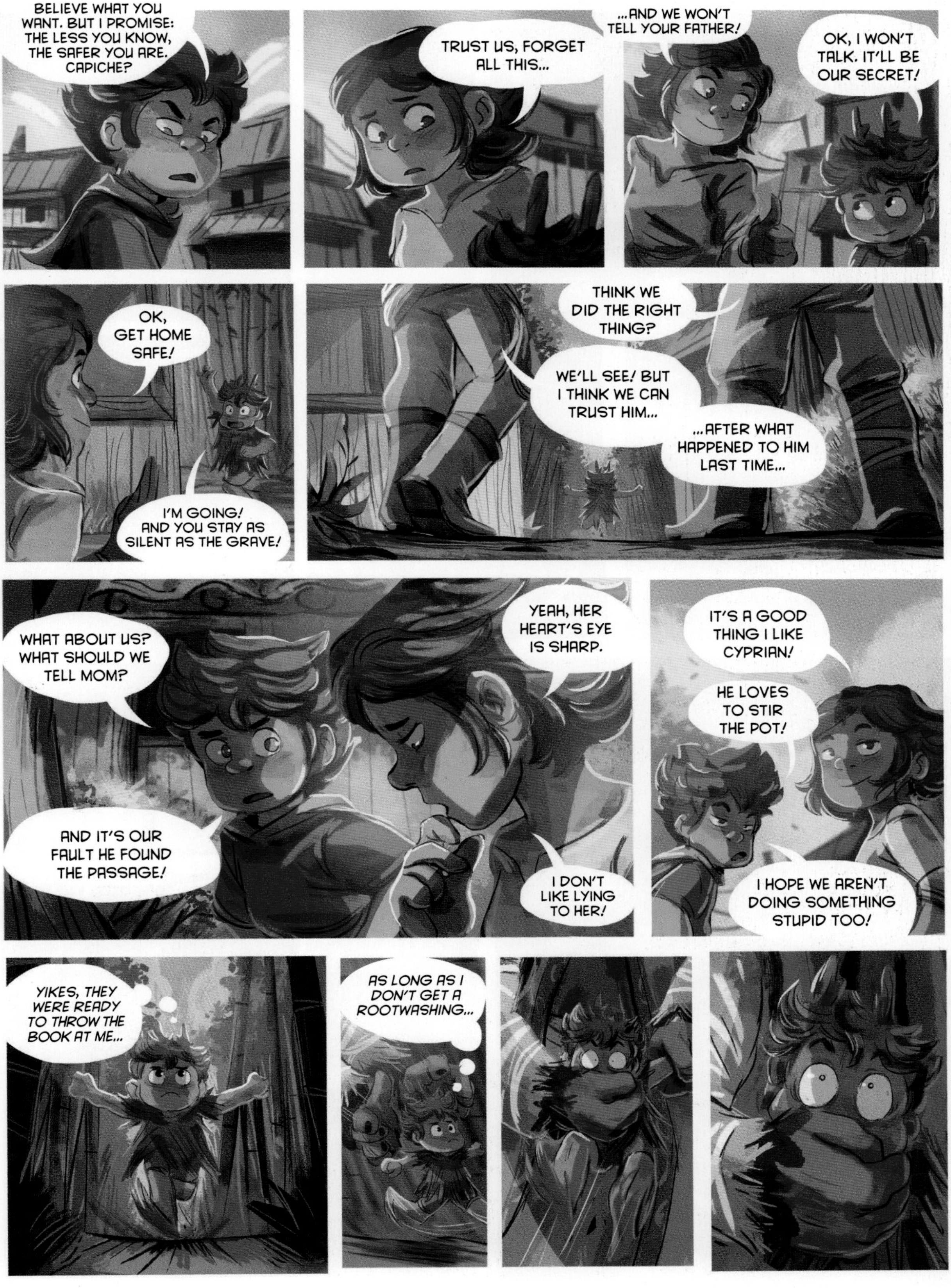

BELIEVE WHAT YOU WANT. BUT I PROMISE: THE LESS YOU KNOW, THE SAFER YOU ARE. CAPICHE?
TRUST US, FORGET ALL THIS...
...AND WE WON'T TELL YOUR FATHER!
OK, I WON'T TALK. IT'LL BE OUR SECRET!
OK, GET HOME SAFE!
I'M GOING! AND YOU STAY AS SILENT AS THE GRAVE!
THINK WE DID THE RIGHT THING?
WE'LL SEE! BUT I THINK WE CAN TRUST HIM...
...AFTER WHAT HAPPENED TO HIM LAST TIME...
WHAT ABOUT US? WHAT SHOULD WE TELL MOM?
YEAH, HER HEART'S EYE IS SHARP.
AND IT'S OUR FAULT HE FOUND THE PASSAGE!
I DON'T LIKE LYING TO HER!
IT'S A GOOD THING I LIKE CYPRIAN!
HE LOVES TO STIR THE POT!
I HOPE WE AREN'T DOING SOMETHING STUPID TOO!
YIKES, THEY WERE READY TO THROW THE BOOK AT ME...
AS LONG AS I DON'T GET A ROOTWASHING...

SEVERAL HOURS LATER...

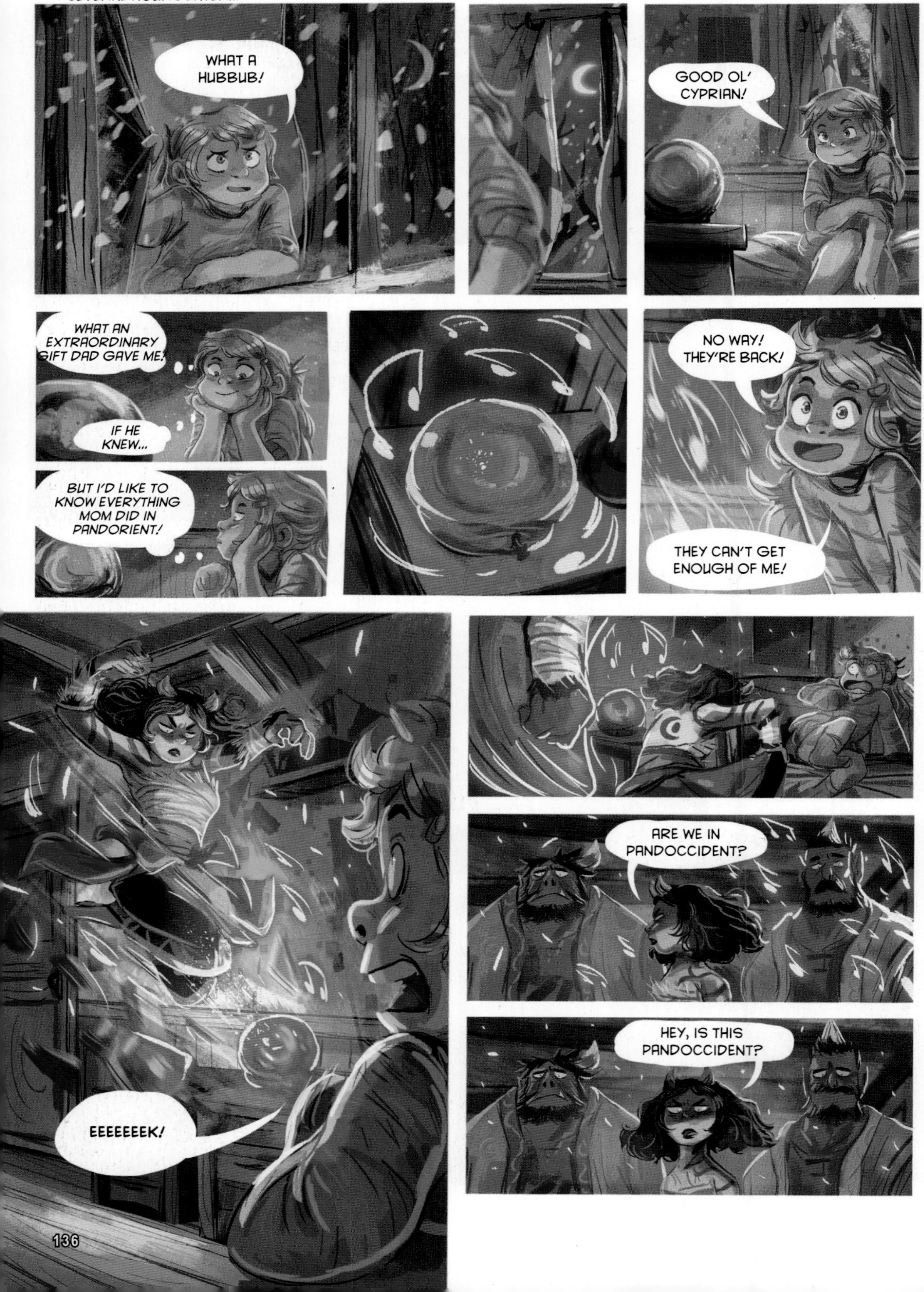
WHAT A HUBBUB!
GOOD OL' CYPRIAN!
WHAT AN EXTRAORDINARY GIFT DAD GAVE ME!
IF HE KNEW...
BUT I'D LIKE TO KNOW EVERYTHING MOM DID IN PANDORIENT!
NO WAY! THEY'RE BACK!
THEY CAN'T GET ENOUGH OF ME!
EEEEEEEK!
ARE WE IN PANDOCCIDENT?
HEY, IS THIS PANDOCCIDENT?

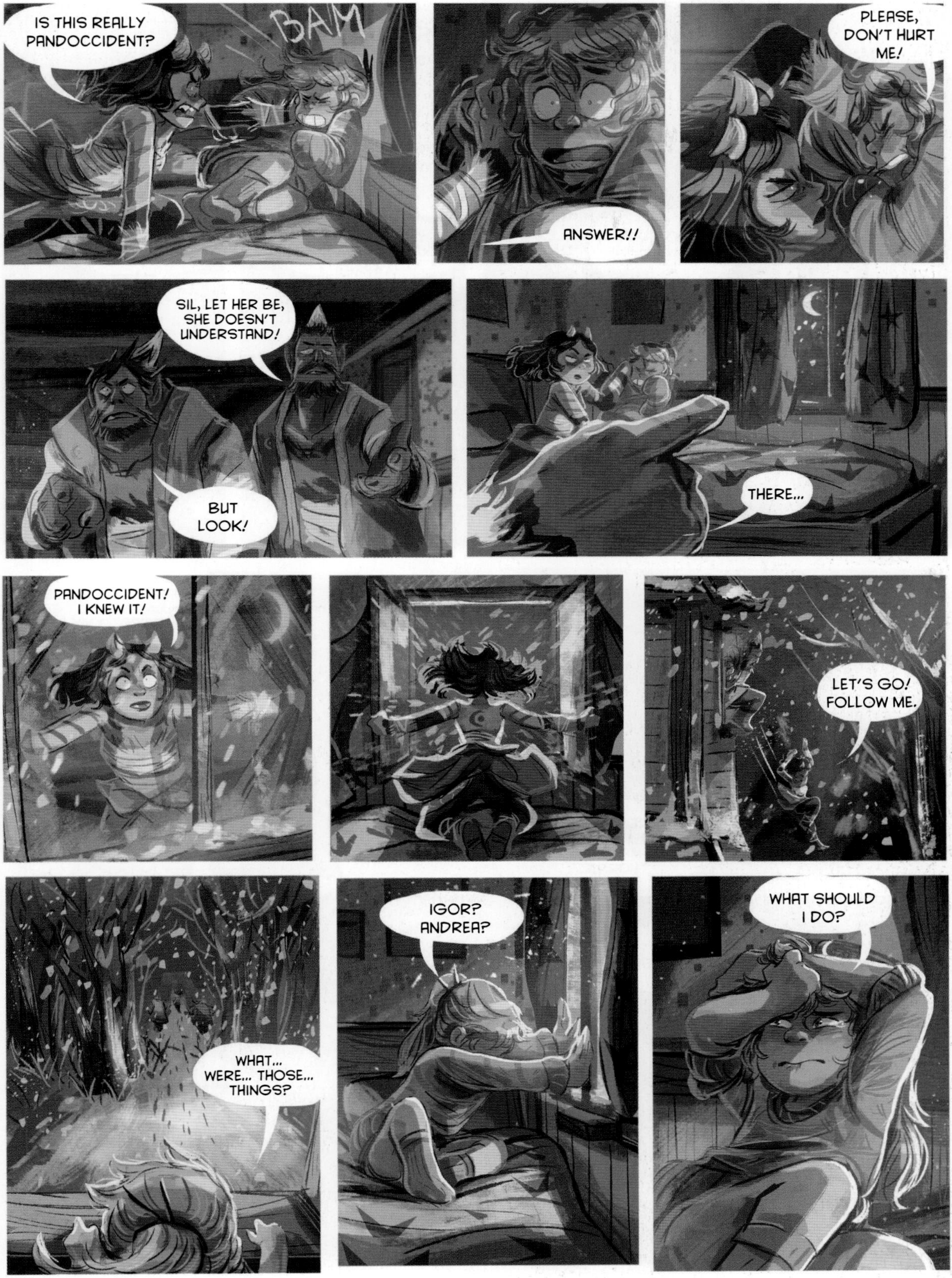
IS THIS REALLY PANDOCCIDENT?
BAM
ANSWER!!
PLEASE, DON'T HURT ME!
SIL, LET HER BE, SHE DOESN'T UNDERSTAND!
BUT LOOK!
THERE...
PANDOCCIDENT! I KNEW IT!
LET'S GO! FOLLOW ME.
WHAT... WERE... THOSE... THINGS?
IGOR? ANDREA?
WHAT SHOULD I DO?

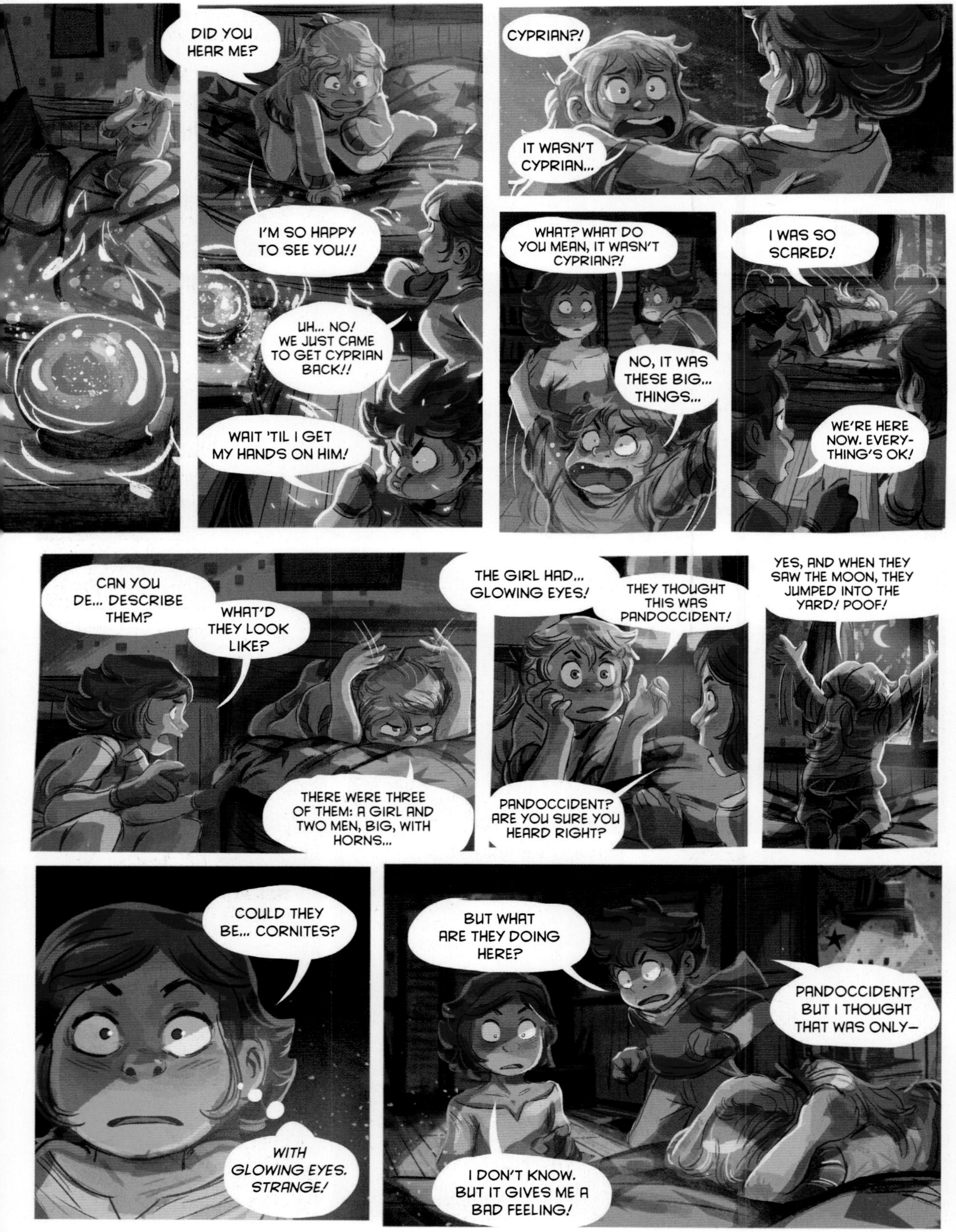
DID YOU HEAR ME?
I'M SO HAPPY TO SEE YOU!!
UH... NO! WE JUST CAME TO GET CYPRIAN BACK!!
WAIT 'TIL I GET MY HANDS ON HIM!
CYPRIAN?!
IT WASN'T CYPRIAN...
WHAT? WHAT DO YOU MEAN, IT WASN'T CYPRIAN?!
NO, IT WAS THESE BIG... THINGS...
I WAS SO SCARED!
WE'RE HERE NOW. EVERY-THING'S OK!
CAN YOU DE... DESCRIBE THEM?
WHAT'D THEY LOOK LIKE?
THERE WERE THREE OF THEM: A GIRL AND TWO MEN, BIG, WITH HORNS...
THE GIRL HAD... GLOWING EYES!
THEY THOUGHT THIS WAS PANDOCCIDENT!
PANDOCCIDENT? ARE YOU SURE YOU HEARD RIGHT?
YES, AND WHEN THEY SAW THE MOON, THEY JUMPED INTO THE YARD! POOF!
COULD THEY BE... CORNITES?
WITH GLOWING EYES. STRANGE!
BUT WHAT ARE THEY DOING HERE?
PANDOCCIDENT? BUT I THOUGHT THAT WAS ONLY—
I DON'T KNOW. BUT IT GIVES ME A BAD FEELING!

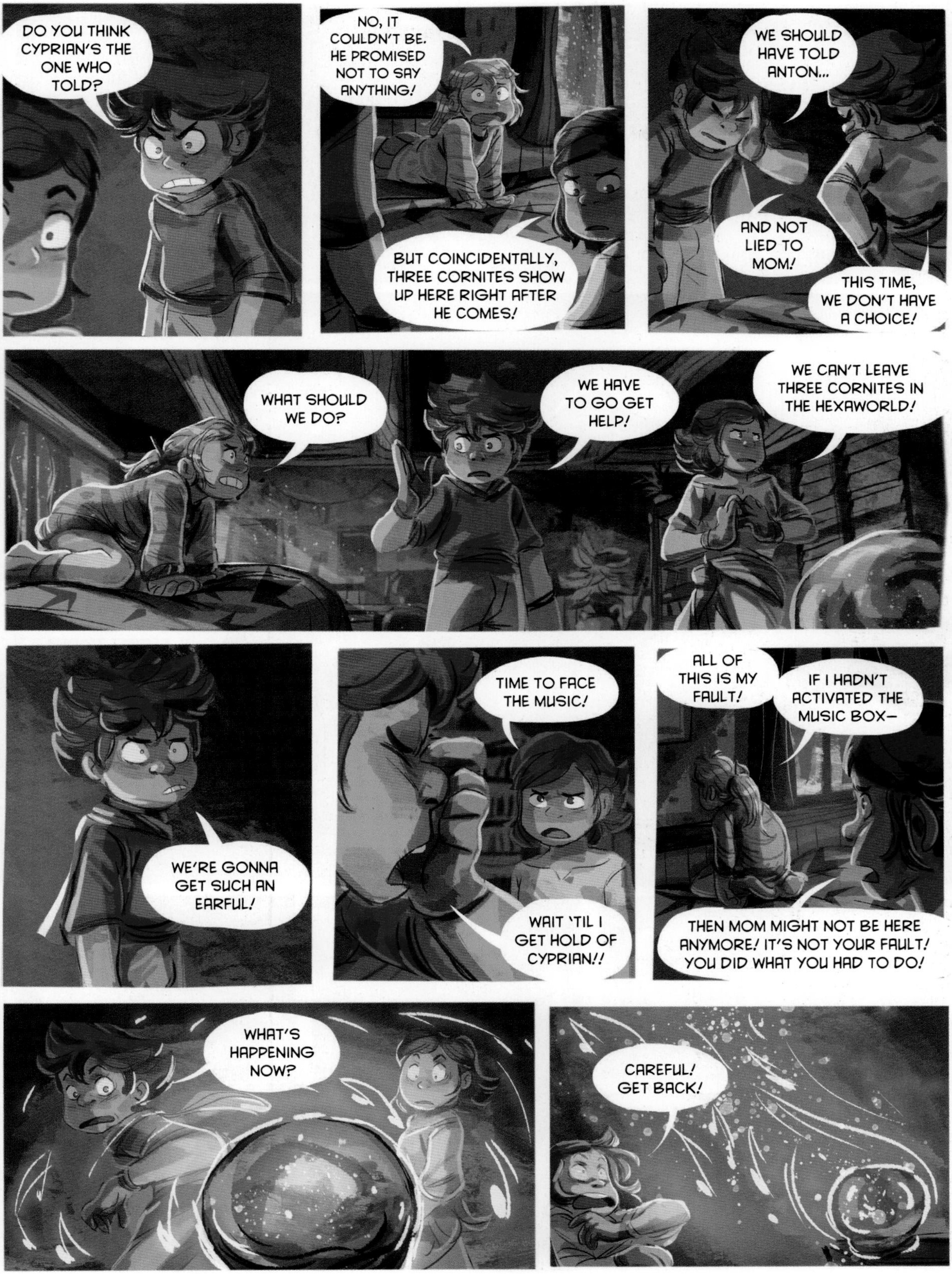
DO YOU THINK CYPRIAN'S THE ONE WHO TOLD?
NO, IT COULDN'T BE. HE PROMISED NOT TO SAY ANYTHING!
BUT COINCIDENTALLY, THREE CORNITES SHOW UP HERE RIGHT AFTER HE COMES!
WE SHOULD HAVE TOLD ANTON...
AND NOT LIED TO MOM!
THIS TIME, WE DON'T HAVE A CHOICE!
WHAT SHOULD WE DO?
WE HAVE TO GO GET HELP!
WE CAN'T LEAVE THREE CORNITES IN THE HEXAWORLD!
WE'RE GONNA GET SUCH AN EARFUL!
TIME TO FACE THE MUSIC!
WAIT 'TIL I GET HOLD OF CYPRIAN!!
ALL OF THIS IS MY FAULT!
IF I HADN'T ACTIVATED THE MUSIC BOX—
THEN MOM MIGHT NOT BE HERE ANYMORE! IT'S NOT YOUR FAULT! YOU DID WHAT YOU HAD TO DO!
WHAT'S HAPPENING NOW?
CAREFUL! GET BACK!

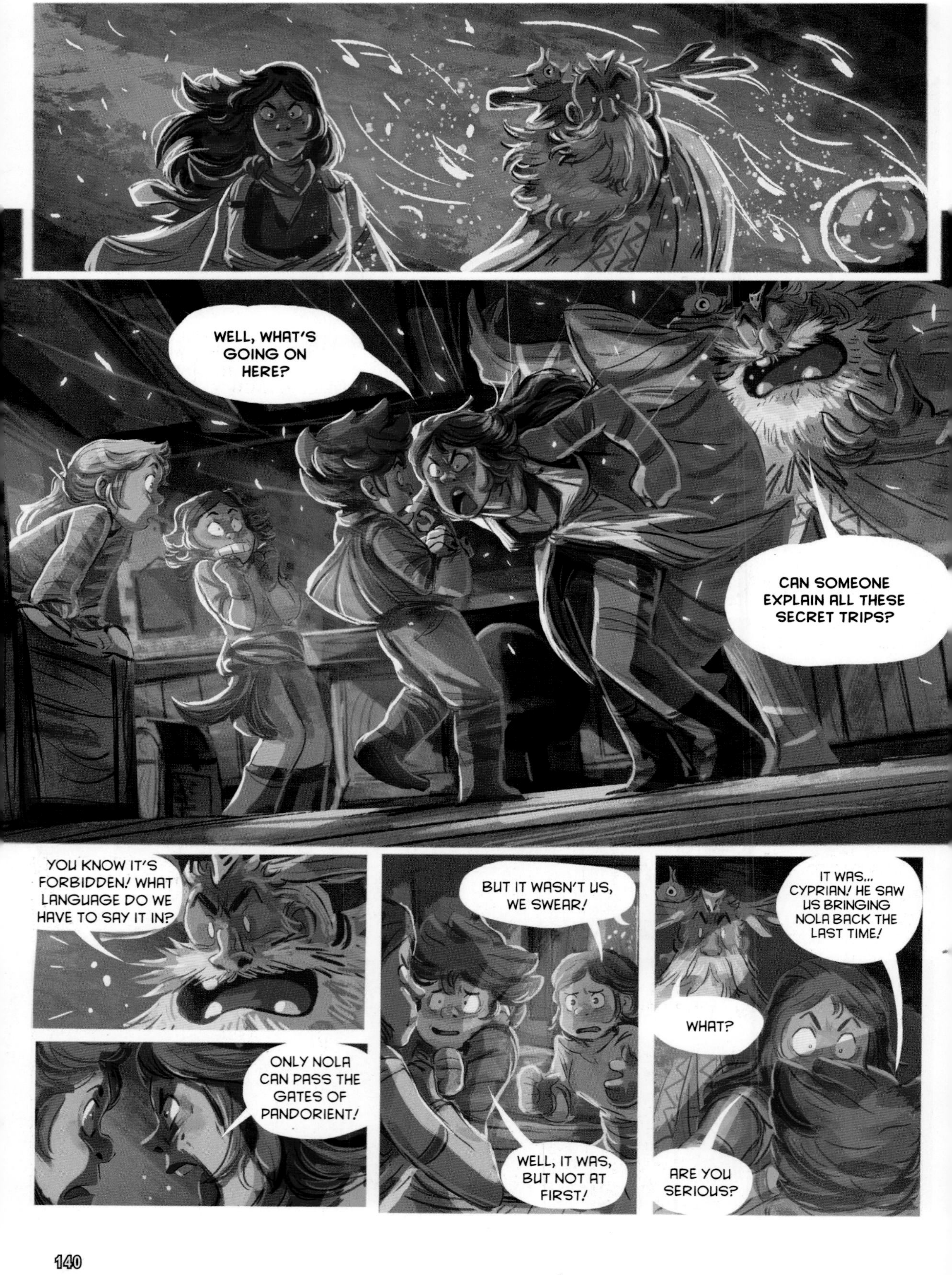
WELL, WHAT'S GOING ON HERE?
CAN SOMEONE EXPLAIN ALL THESE SECRET TRIPS?
YOU KNOW IT'S FORBIDDEN! WHAT LANGUAGE DO WE HAVE TO SAY IT IN?
ONLY NOLA CAN PASS THE GATES OF PANDORIENT!
BUT IT WASN'T US, WE SWEAR!
WELL, IT WAS, BUT NOT AT FIRST!
IT WAS... CYPRIAN! HE SAW US BRINGING NOLA BACK THE LAST TIME!
WHAT?
ARE YOU SERIOUS?

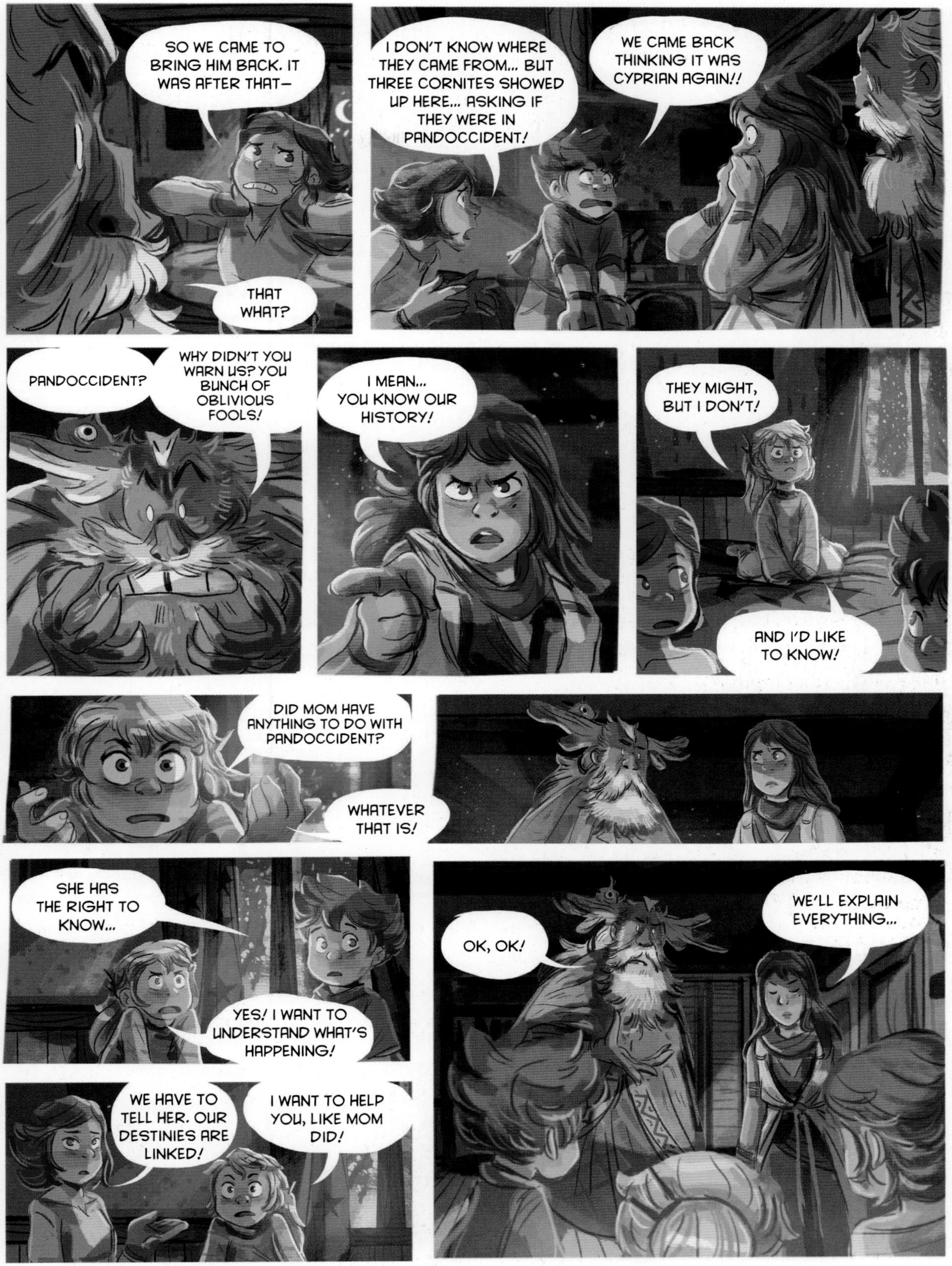
SO WE CAME TO BRING HIM BACK. IT WAS AFTER THAT—
THAT WHAT?
I DON'T KNOW WHERE THEY CAME FROM... BUT THREE CORNITES SHOWED UP HERE... ASKING IF THEY WERE IN PANDOCCIDENT!
WE CAME BACK THINKING IT WAS CYPRIAN AGAIN!!
PANDOCCIDENT?
WHY DIDN'T YOU WARN US? YOU BUNCH OF OBLIVIOUS FOOLS!
I MEAN... YOU KNOW OUR HISTORY!
THEY MIGHT, BUT I DON'T!
AND I'D LIKE TO KNOW!
DID MOM HAVE ANYTHING TO DO WITH PANDOCCIDENT?
WHATEVER THAT IS!
SHE HAS THE RIGHT TO KNOW...
YES! I WANT TO UNDERSTAND WHAT'S HAPPENING!
WE HAVE TO TELL HER. OUR DESTINIES ARE LINKED!
I WANT TO HELP YOU, LIKE MOM DID!
OK, OK!
WE'LL EXPLAIN EVERYTHING...

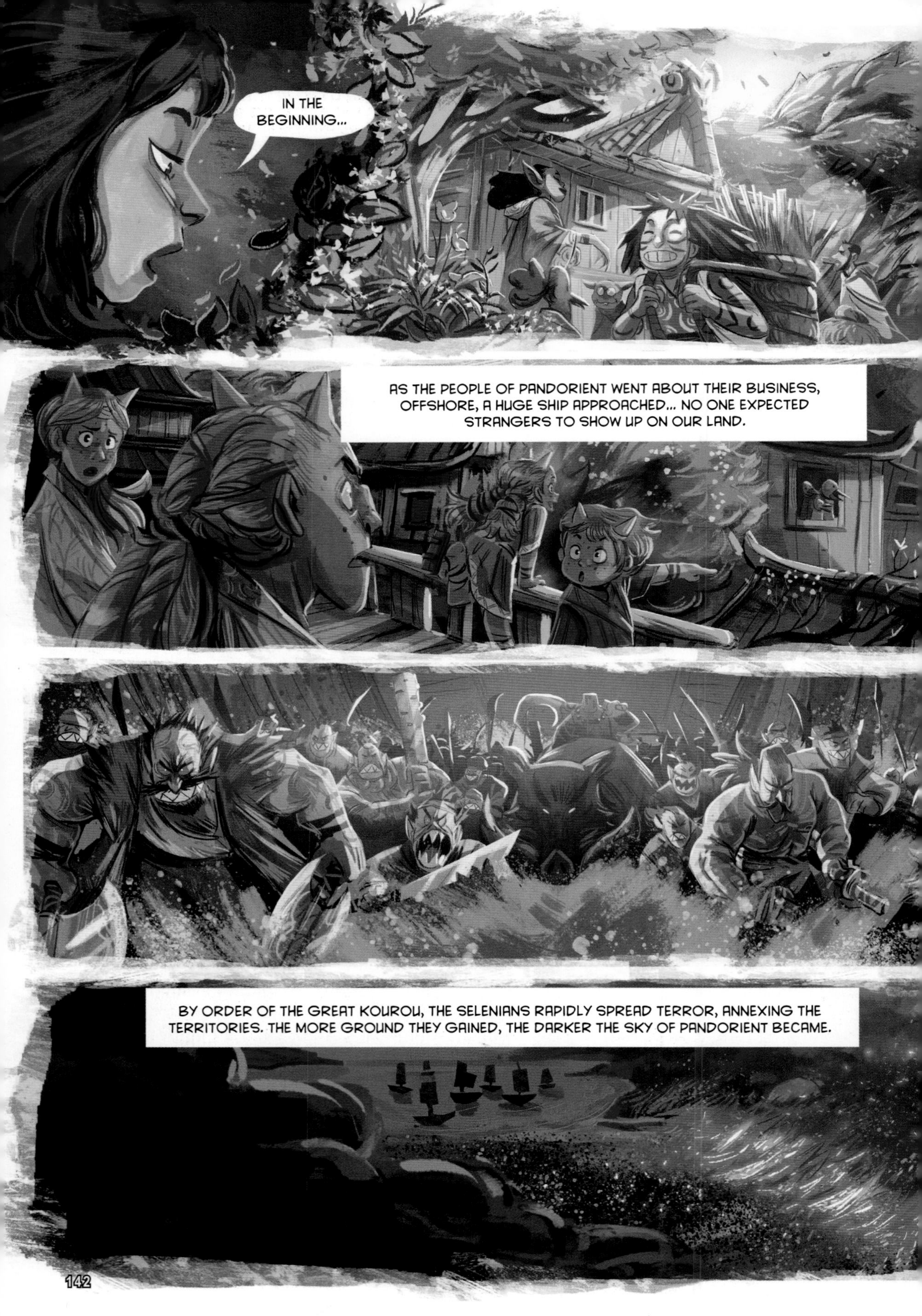
IN THE BEGINNING...
AS THE PEOPLE OF PANDORIENT WENT ABOUT THEIR BUSINESS, OFFSHORE, A HUGE SHIP APPROACHED... NO ONE EXPECTED STRANGERS TO SHOW UP ON OUR LAND.
BY ORDER OF THE GREAT KOUROU, THE SELENIANS RAPIDLY SPREAD TERROR, ANNEXING THE TERRITORIES. THE MORE GROUND THEY GAINED, THE DARKER THE SKY OF PANDORIENT BECAME.

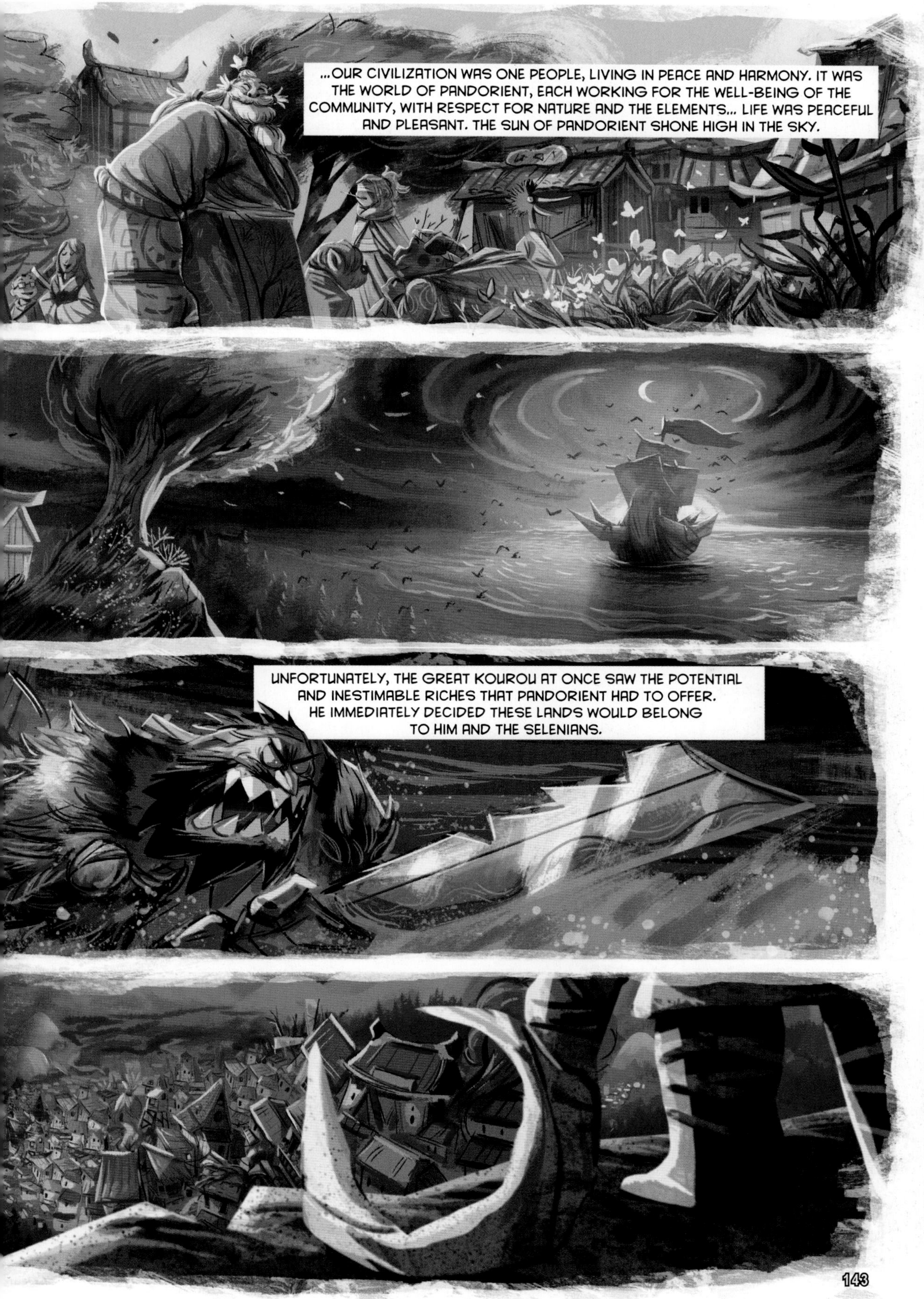
...OUR CIVILIZATION WAS ONE PEOPLE, LIVING IN PEACE AND HARMONY. IT WAS THE WORLD OF PANDORIENT, EACH WORKING FOR THE WELL-BEING OF THE COMMUNITY, WITH RESPECT FOR NATURE AND THE ELEMENTS... LIFE WAS PEACEFUL AND PLEASANT. THE SUN OF PANDORIENT SHONE HIGH IN THE SKY.
UNFORTUNATELY, THE GREAT KOUROU AT ONCE SAW THE POTENTIAL AND INESTIMABLE RICHES THAT PANDORIENT HAD TO OFFER. HE IMMEDIATELY DECIDED THESE LANDS WOULD BELONG TO HIM AND THE SELENIANS.

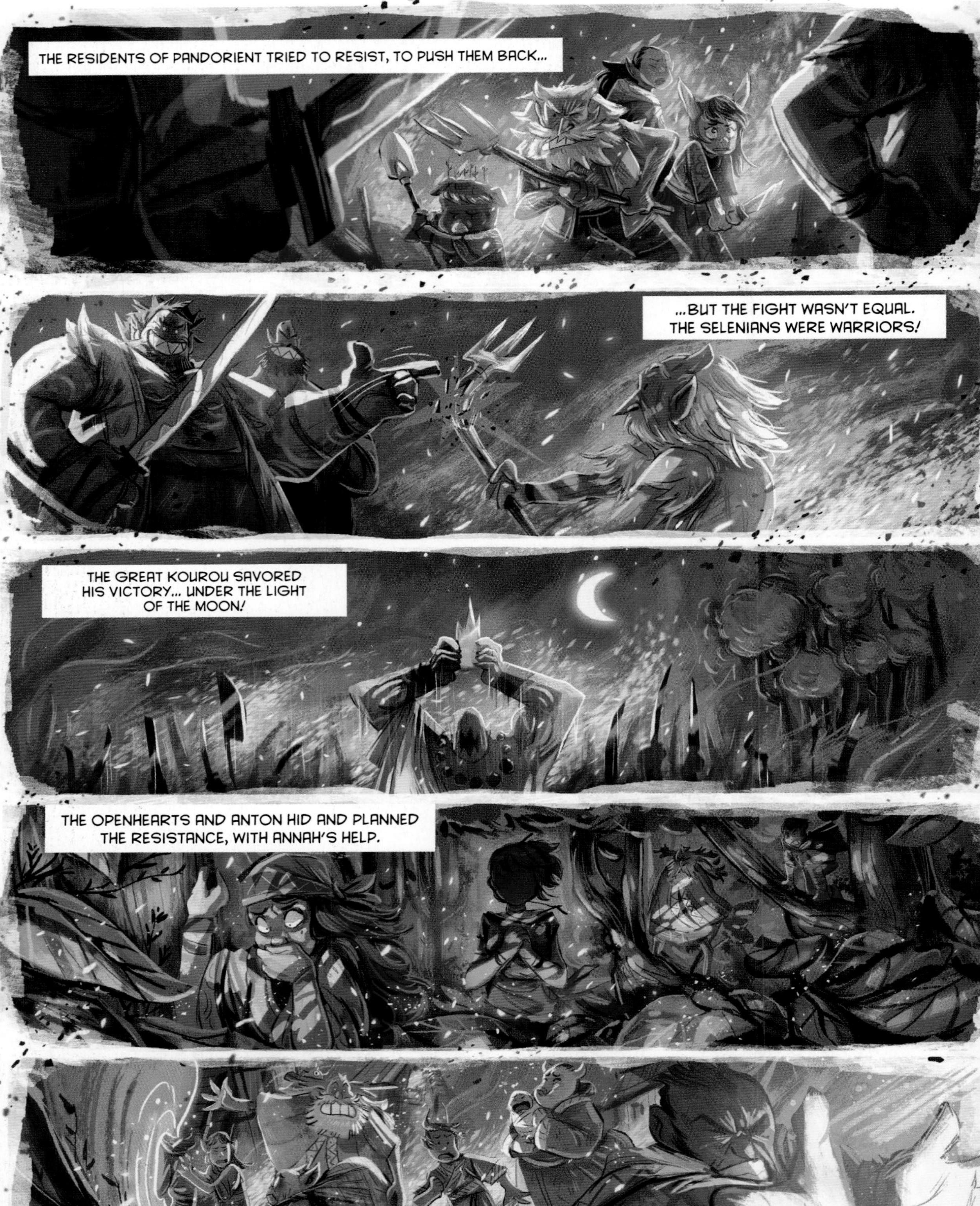
THE RESIDENTS OF PANDORIENT TRIED TO RESIST, TO PUSH THEM BACK...
...BUT THE FIGHT WASN'T EQUAL. THE SELENIANS WERE WARRIORS!
THE GREAT KOUROU SAVORED HIS VICTORY... UNDER THE LIGHT OF THE MOON!
THE OPENHEARTS AND ANTON HID AND PLANNED THE RESISTANCE, WITH ANNAH'S HELP.
THEY WERE LOOKING FOR A WAY TO PROTECT THE INHABITANTS OF PANDORIENT AND STOP THE SELENIANS' INEXORABLE PROGRESS.

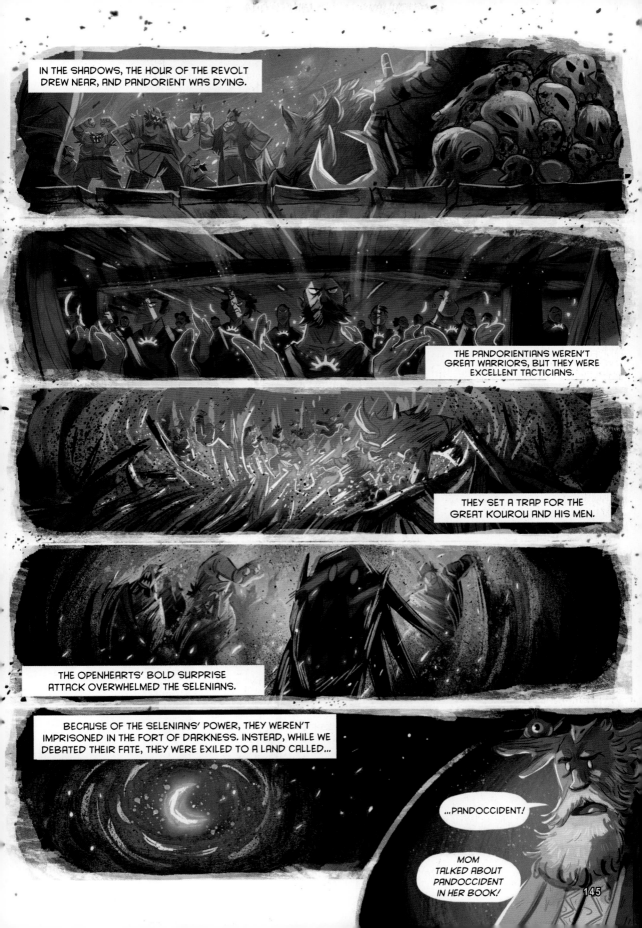

IN THE SHADOWS, THE HOUR OF THE REVOLT DREW NEAR, AND PANDORIENT WAS DYING.

THE PANDORIENTIANS WEREN'T GREAT WARRIORS, BUT THEY WERE EXCELLENT TACTICIANS.

THEY SET A TRAP FOR THE GREAT KOUROU AND HIS MEN.

THE OPENHEARTS' BOLD SURPRISE ATTACK OVERWHELMED THE SELENIANS.

BECAUSE OF THE SELENIANS' POWER, THEY WEREN'T IMPRISONED IN THE FORT OF DARKNESS. INSTEAD, WHILE WE DEBATED THEIR FATE, THEY WERE EXILED TO A LAND CALLED...

...PANDOCCIDENT!

MOM TALKED ABOUT PANDOCCIDENT IN HER BOOK!

145

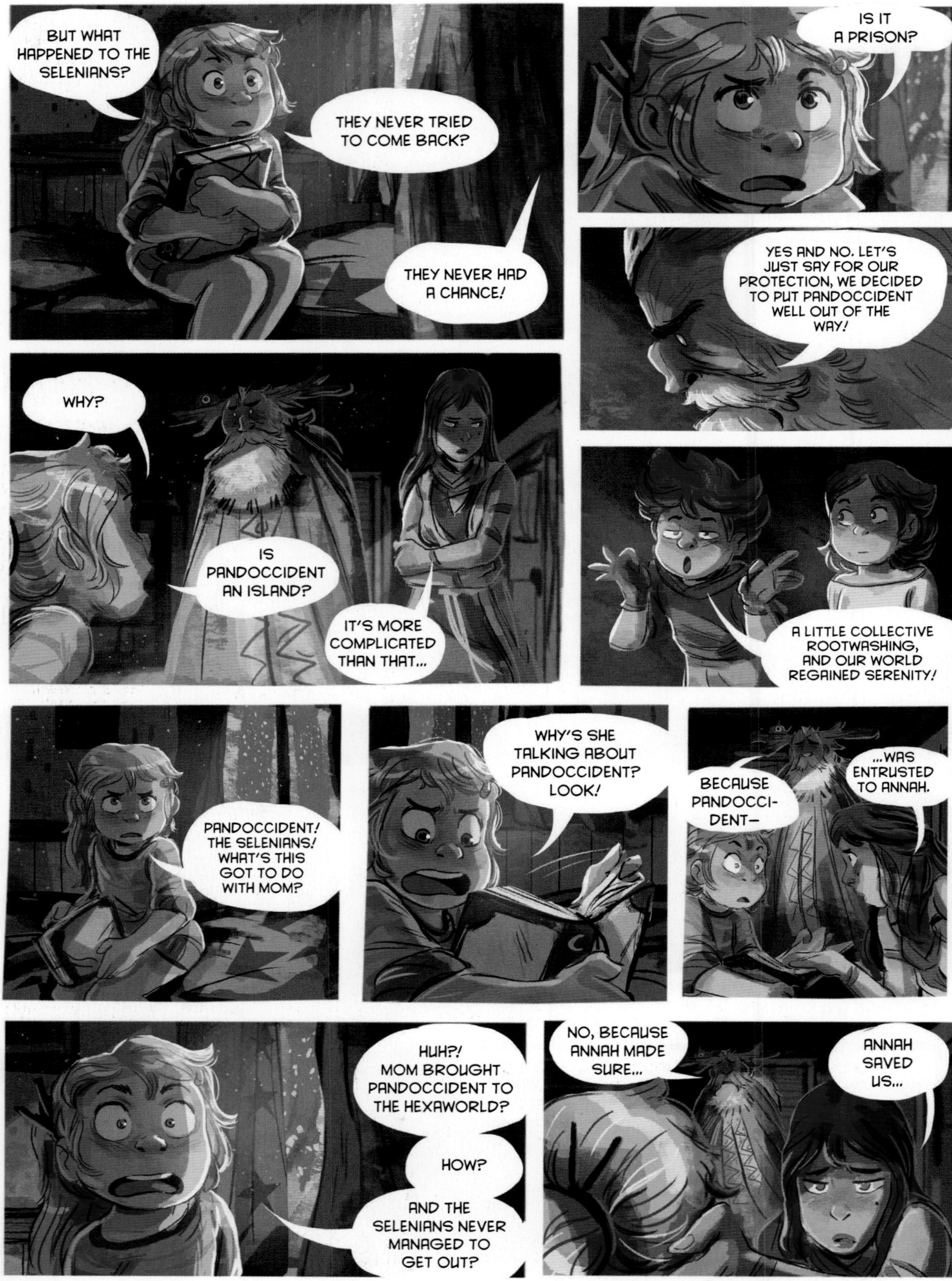

BUT WHAT HAPPENED TO THE SELENIANS?
THEY NEVER TRIED TO COME BACK?
THEY NEVER HAD A CHANCE!
IS IT A PRISON?
YES AND NO. LET'S JUST SAY FOR OUR PROTECTION, WE DECIDED TO PUT PANDOCCIDENT WELL OUT OF THE WAY!
WHY?
IS PANDOCCIDENT AN ISLAND?
IT'S MORE COMPLICATED THAN THAT...
A LITTLE COLLECTIVE ROOTWASHING, AND OUR WORLD REGAINED SERENITY!
PANDOCCIDENT! THE SELENIANS! WHAT'S THIS GOT TO DO WITH MOM?
WHY'S SHE TALKING ABOUT PANDOCCIDENT? LOOK!
BECAUSE PANDOCCI-DENT—
...WAS ENTRUSTED TO ANNAH.
HUH?! MOM BROUGHT PANDOCCIDENT TO THE HEXAWORLD?
HOW?
AND THE SELENIANS NEVER MANAGED TO GET OUT?
NO, BECAUSE ANNAH MADE SURE...
ANNAH SAVED US...

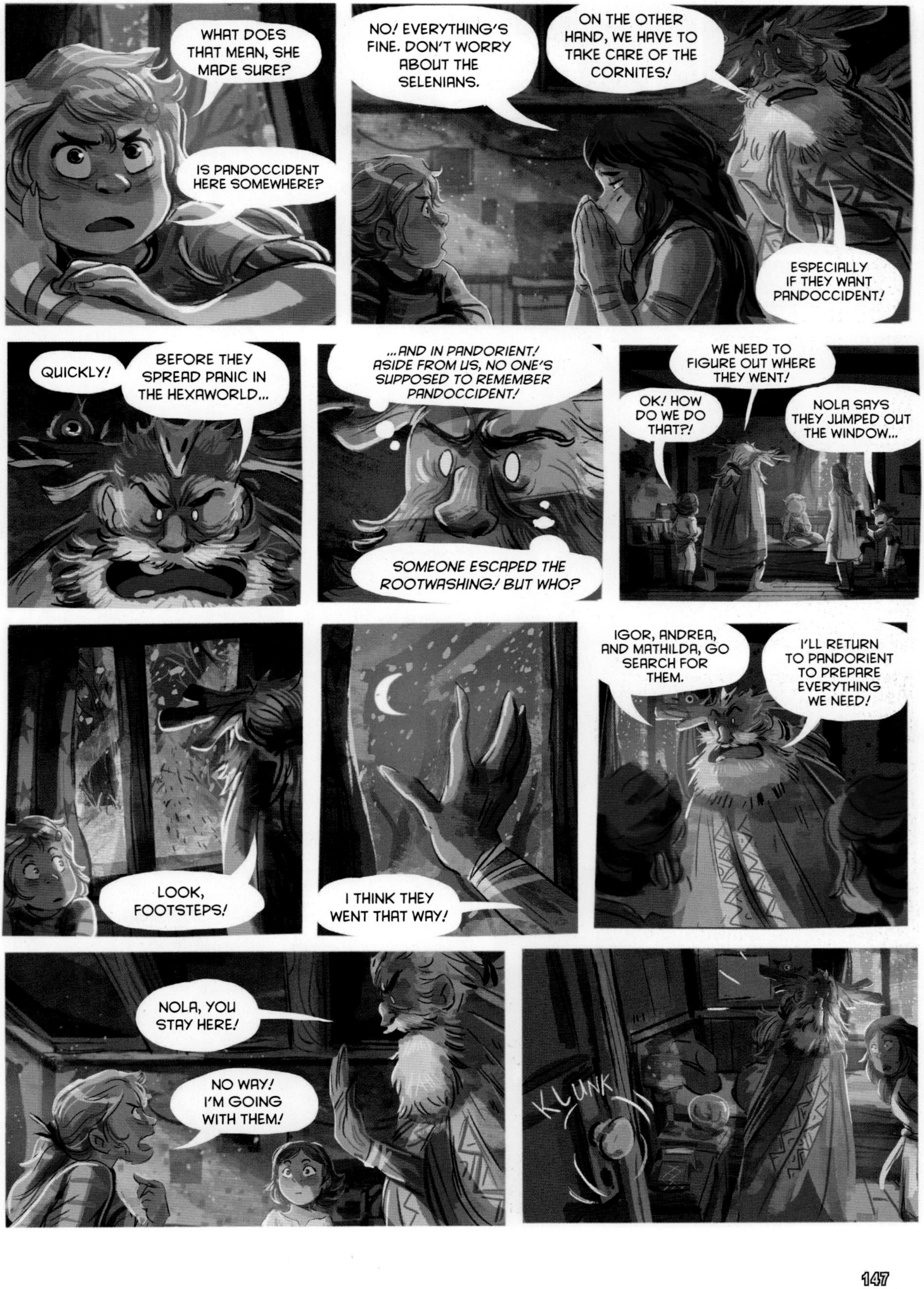
WHAT DOES THAT MEAN, SHE MADE SURE?
IS PANDOCCIDENT HERE SOMEWHERE?
NO! EVERYTHING'S FINE. DON'T WORRY ABOUT THE SELENIANS.
ON THE OTHER HAND, WE HAVE TO TAKE CARE OF THE CORNITES!
ESPECIALLY IF THEY WANT PANDOCCIDENT!
QUICKLY!
BEFORE THEY SPREAD PANIC IN THE HEXAWORLD...
...AND IN PANDORIENT! ASIDE FROM US, NO ONE'S SUPPOSED TO REMEMBER PANDOCCIDENT!
SOMEONE ESCAPED THE ROOTWASHING! BUT WHO?
WE NEED TO FIGURE OUT WHERE THEY WENT!
OK! HOW DO WE DO THAT?!
NOLA SAYS THEY JUMPED OUT THE WINDOW...
LOOK, FOOTSTEPS!
I THINK THEY WENT THAT WAY!
IGOR, ANDREA, AND MATHILDA, GO SEARCH FOR THEM.
I'LL RETURN TO PANDORIENT TO PREPARE EVERYTHING WE NEED!
NOLA, YOU STAY HERE!
NO WAY! I'M GOING WITH THEM!
KLUNK

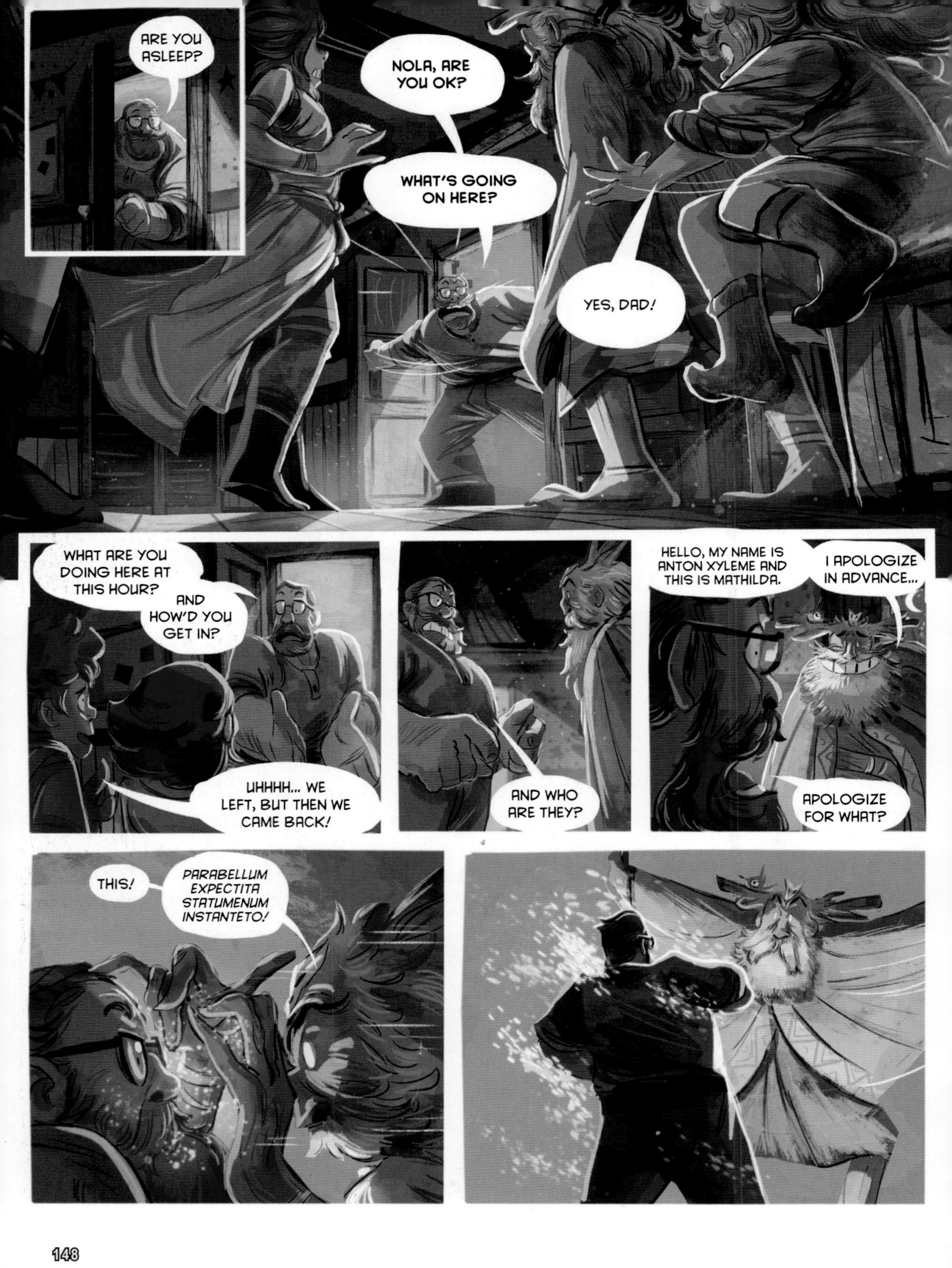
ARE YOU ASLEEP?
NOLA, ARE YOU OK?
WHAT'S GOING ON HERE?
YES, DAD!
WHAT ARE YOU DOING HERE AT THIS HOUR?
AND HOW'D YOU GET IN?
UHHHH... WE LEFT, BUT THEN WE CAME BACK!
AND WHO ARE THEY?
HELLO, MY NAME IS ANTON XYLEME AND THIS IS MATHILDA.
I APOLOGIZE IN ADVANCE...
APOLOGIZE FOR WHAT?
THIS!
PARABELLUM EXPECTITA STATUMENUM INSTANTETO!

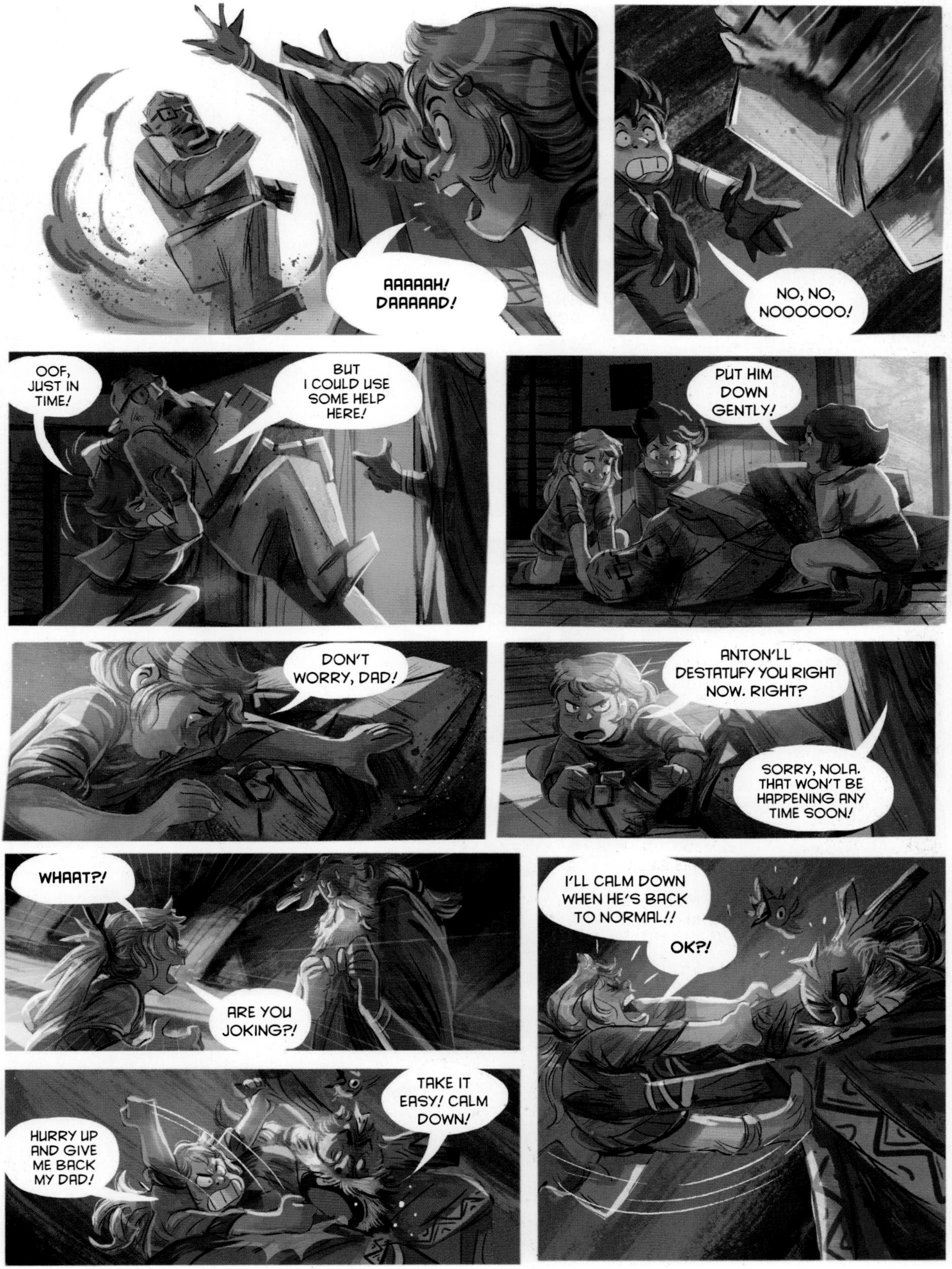

AAAAAH! DAAAAAD!
NO, NO, NOOOOOO!
OOF, JUST IN TIME!
BUT I COULD USE SOME HELP HERE!
PUT HIM DOWN GENTLY!
DON'T WORRY, DAD!
ANTON'LL DESTATUFY YOU RIGHT NOW. RIGHT?
SORRY, NOLA. THAT WON'T BE HAPPENING ANY TIME SOON!
WHAAT?!
ARE YOU JOKING?!
TAKE IT EASY! CALM DOWN!
HURRY UP AND GIVE ME BACK MY DAD!
I'LL CALM DOWN WHEN HE'S BACK TO NORMAL!!
OK?!

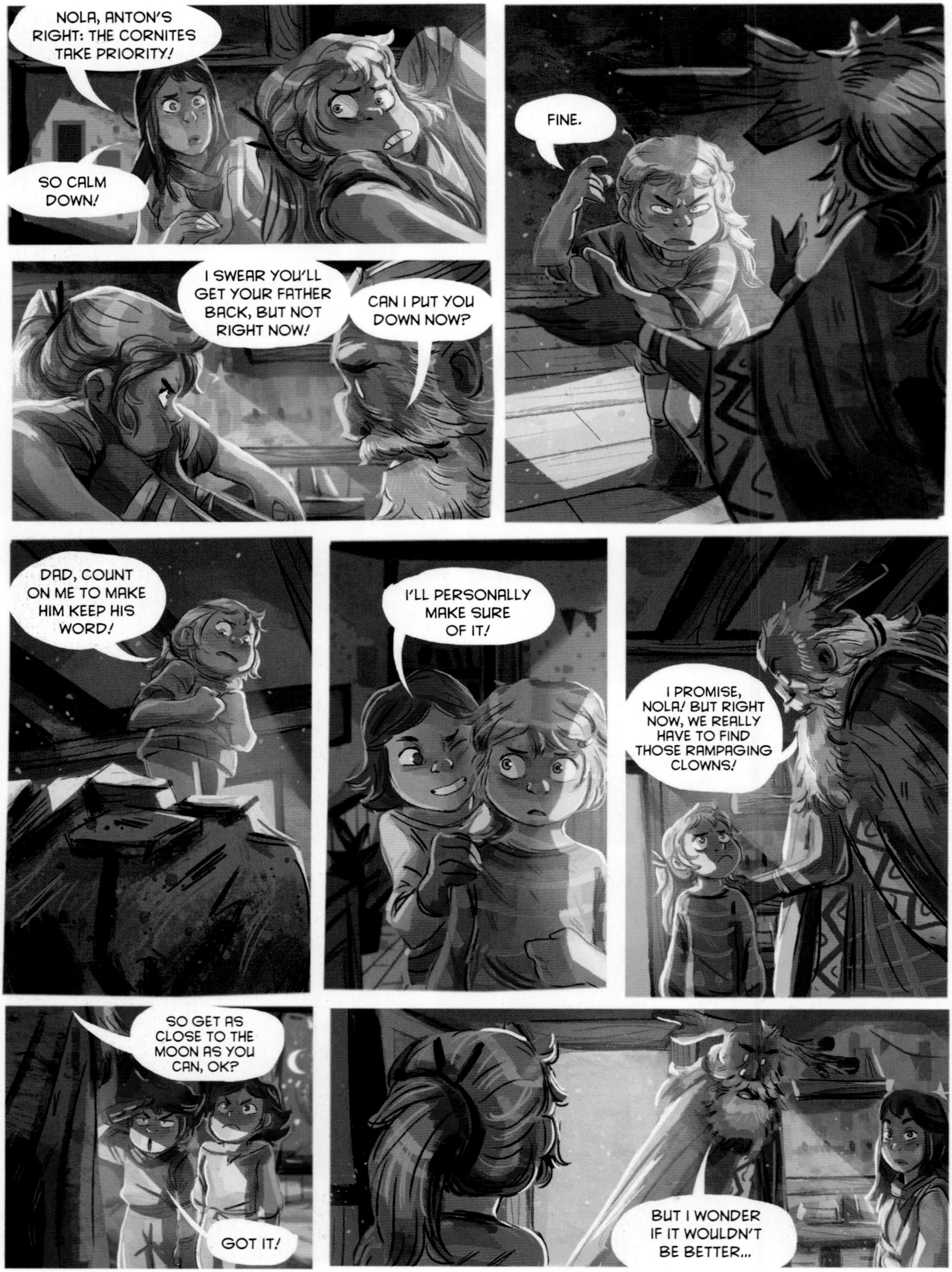
NOLA, ANTON'S RIGHT: THE CORNITES TAKE PRIORITY!
SO CALM DOWN!
FINE.
I SWEAR YOU'LL GET YOUR FATHER BACK, BUT NOT RIGHT NOW!
CAN I PUT YOU DOWN NOW?
DAD, COUNT ON ME TO MAKE HIM KEEP HIS WORD!
I'LL PERSONALLY MAKE SURE OF IT!
I PROMISE, NOLA! BUT RIGHT NOW, WE REALLY HAVE TO FIND THOSE RAMPAGING CLOWNS!
SO GET AS CLOSE TO THE MOON AS YOU CAN, OK?
GOT IT!
BUT I WONDER IF IT WOULDN'T BE BETTER...

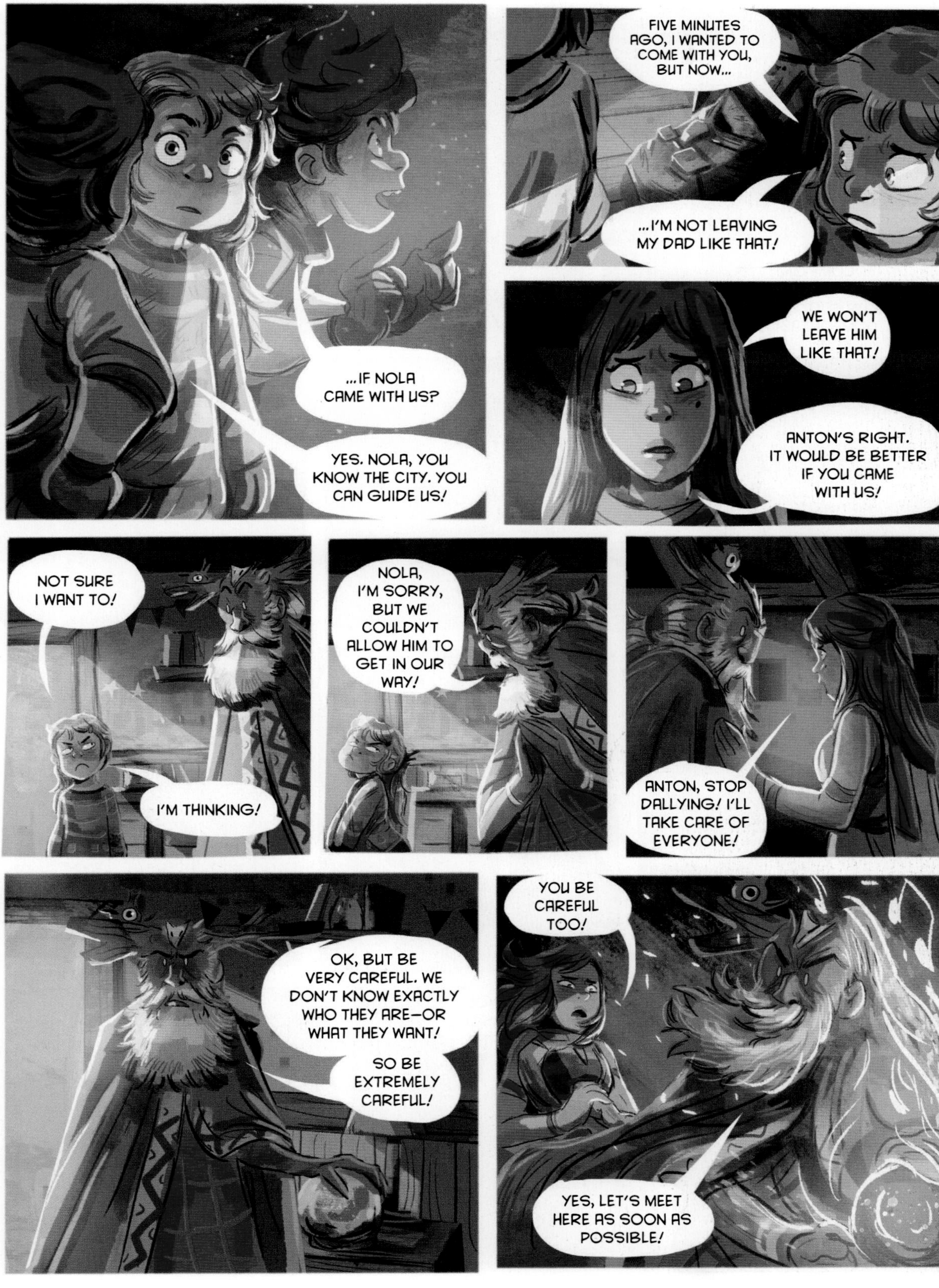
...IF NOLA CAME WITH US?
YES. NOLA, YOU KNOW THE CITY. YOU CAN GUIDE US!
FIVE MINUTES AGO, I WANTED TO COME WITH YOU, BUT NOW...
...I'M NOT LEAVING MY DAD LIKE THAT!
WE WON'T LEAVE HIM LIKE THAT!
ANTON'S RIGHT. IT WOULD BE BETTER IF YOU CAME WITH US!
NOT SURE I WANT TO!
I'M THINKING!
NOLA, I'M SORRY, BUT WE COULDN'T ALLOW HIM TO GET IN OUR WAY!
ANTON, STOP DALLYING! I'LL TAKE CARE OF EVERYONE!
OK, BUT BE VERY CAREFUL. WE DON'T KNOW EXACTLY WHO THEY ARE—OR WHAT THEY WANT!
SO BE EXTREMELY CAREFUL!
YOU BE CAREFUL TOO!
YES, LET'S MEET HERE AS SOON AS POSSIBLE!

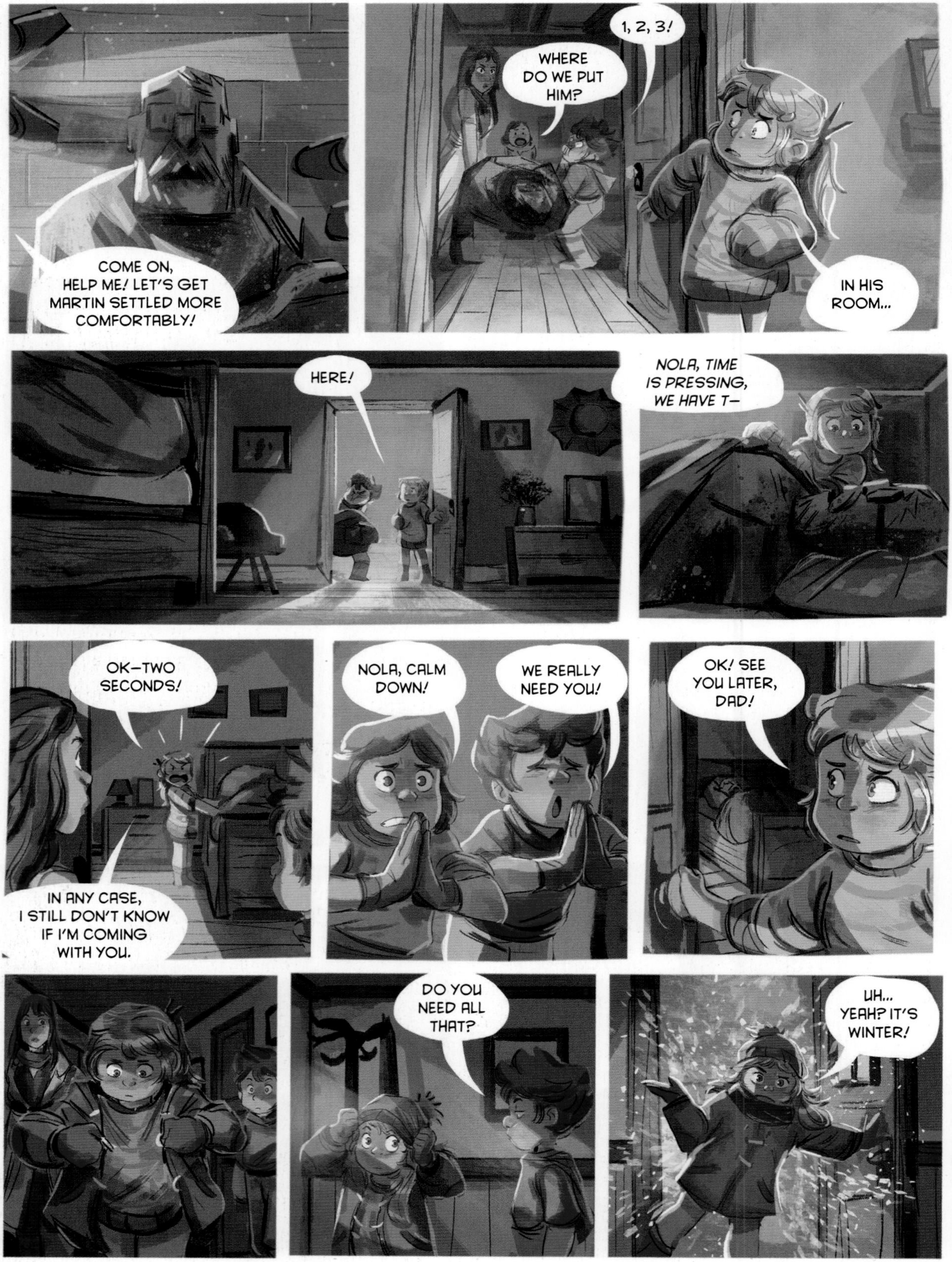
COME ON, HELP ME! LET'S GET MARTIN SETTLED MORE COMFORTABLY!
WHERE DO WE PUT HIM?
1, 2, 3!
IN HIS ROOM...
HERE!
NOLA, TIME IS PRESSING, WE HAVE T—
OK—TWO SECONDS!
IN ANY CASE, I STILL DON'T KNOW IF I'M COMING WITH YOU.
NOLA, CALM DOWN!
WE REALLY NEED YOU!
OK! SEE YOU LATER, DAD!
DO YOU NEED ALL THAT?
UH... YEAH? IT'S WINTER!

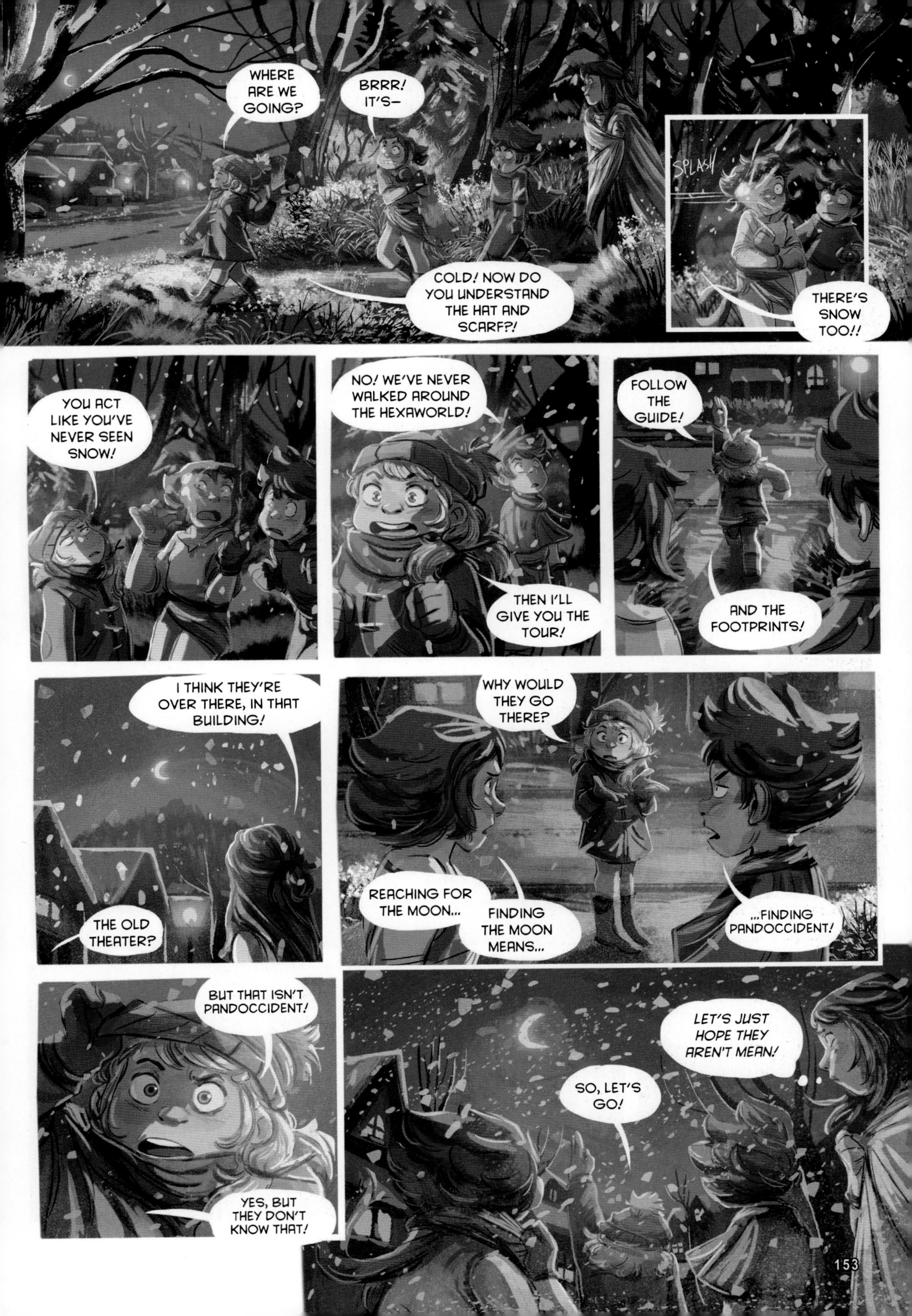

WHERE ARE WE GOING?
BRRR! IT'S—
COLD! NOW DO YOU UNDERSTAND THE HAT AND SCARF?!
SPLASH
THERE'S SNOW TOO!!
YOU ACT LIKE YOU'VE NEVER SEEN SNOW!
NO! WE'VE NEVER WALKED AROUND THE HEXAWORLD!
THEN I'LL GIVE YOU THE TOUR!
FOLLOW THE GUIDE!
AND THE FOOTPRINTS!
I THINK THEY'RE OVER THERE, IN THAT BUILDING!
THE OLD THEATER?
WHY WOULD THEY GO THERE?
REACHING FOR THE MOON...
FINDING THE MOON MEANS...
...FINDING PANDOCCIDENT!
BUT THAT ISN'T PANDOCCIDENT!
YES, BUT THEY DON'T KNOW THAT!
LET'S JUST HOPE THEY AREN'T MEAN!
SO, LET'S GO!

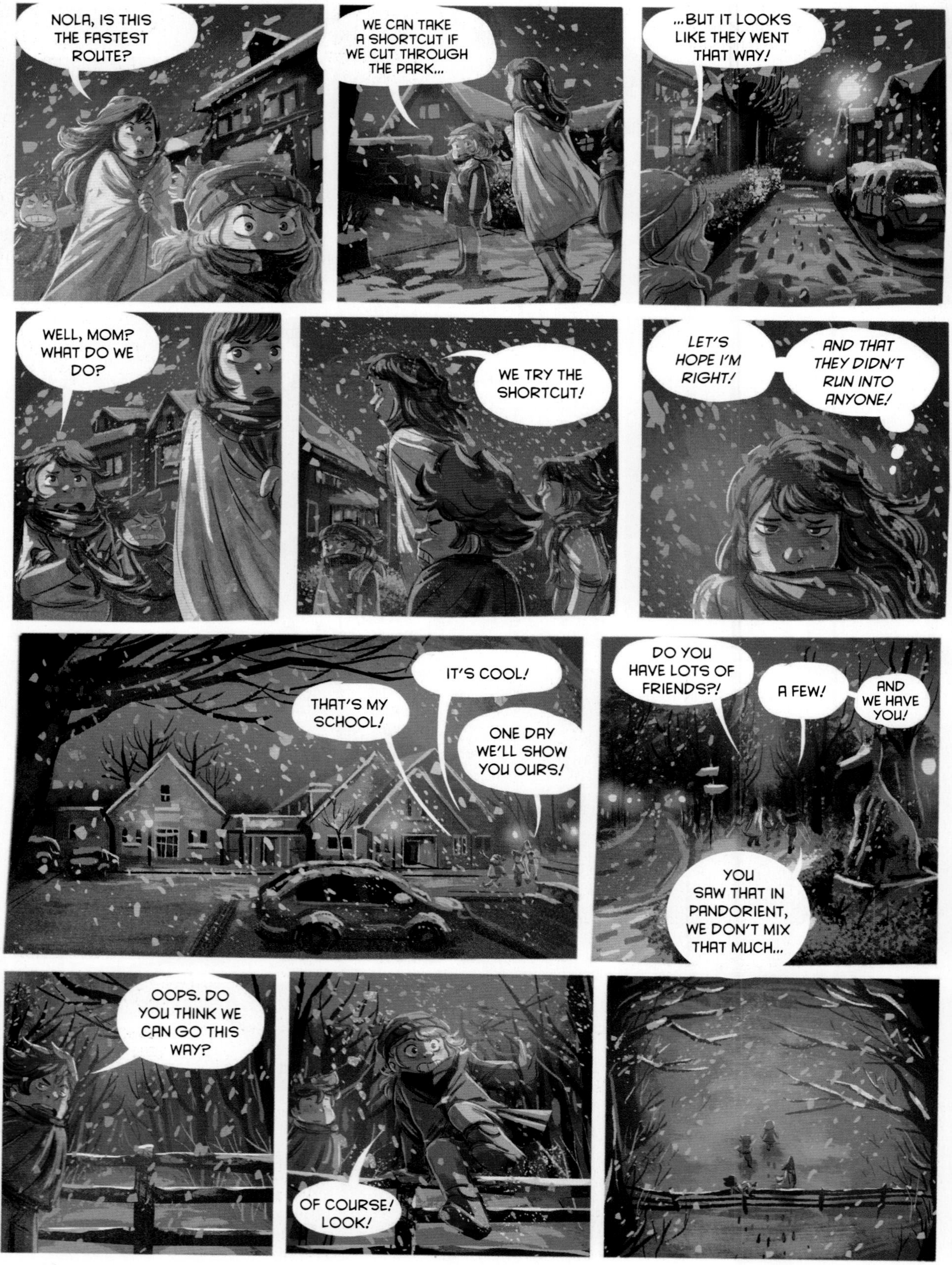
NOLA, IS THIS THE FASTEST ROUTE?
WE CAN TAKE A SHORTCUT IF WE CUT THROUGH THE PARK...
...BUT IT LOOKS LIKE THEY WENT THAT WAY!
WELL, MOM? WHAT DO WE DO?
WE TRY THE SHORTCUT!
LET'S HOPE I'M RIGHT!
AND THAT THEY DIDN'T RUN INTO ANYONE!
THAT'S MY SCHOOL!
IT'S COOL!
ONE DAY WE'LL SHOW YOU OURS!
DO YOU HAVE LOTS OF FRIENDS?!
A FEW!
AND WE HAVE YOU!
YOU SAW THAT IN PANDORIENT, WE DON'T MIX THAT MUCH...
OOPS. DO YOU THINK WE CAN GO THIS WAY?
OF COURSE! LOOK!

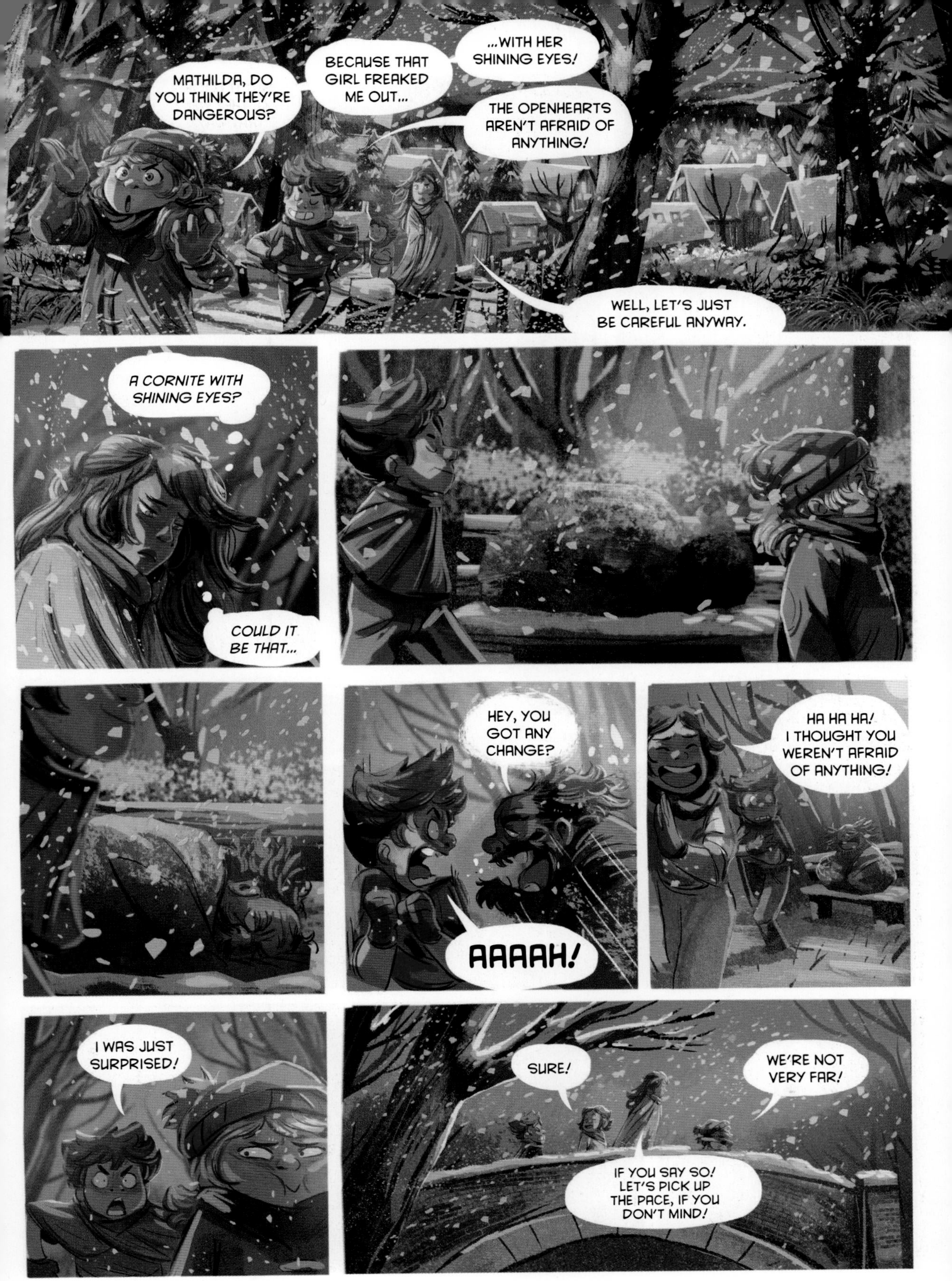
MATHILDA, DO YOU THINK THEY'RE DANGEROUS?
BECAUSE THAT GIRL FREAKED ME OUT...
...WITH HER SHINING EYES!
THE OPENHEARTS AREN'T AFRAID OF ANYTHING!
WELL, LET'S JUST BE CAREFUL ANYWAY.
A CORNITE WITH SHINING EYES?
COULD IT BE THAT...
HEY, YOU GOT ANY CHANGE?
AAAAH!
HA HA HA! I THOUGHT YOU WEREN'T AFRAID OF ANYTHING!
I WAS JUST SURPRISED!
SURE!
WE'RE NOT VERY FAR!
IF YOU SAY SO! LET'S PICK UP THE PACE, IF YOU DON'T MIND!

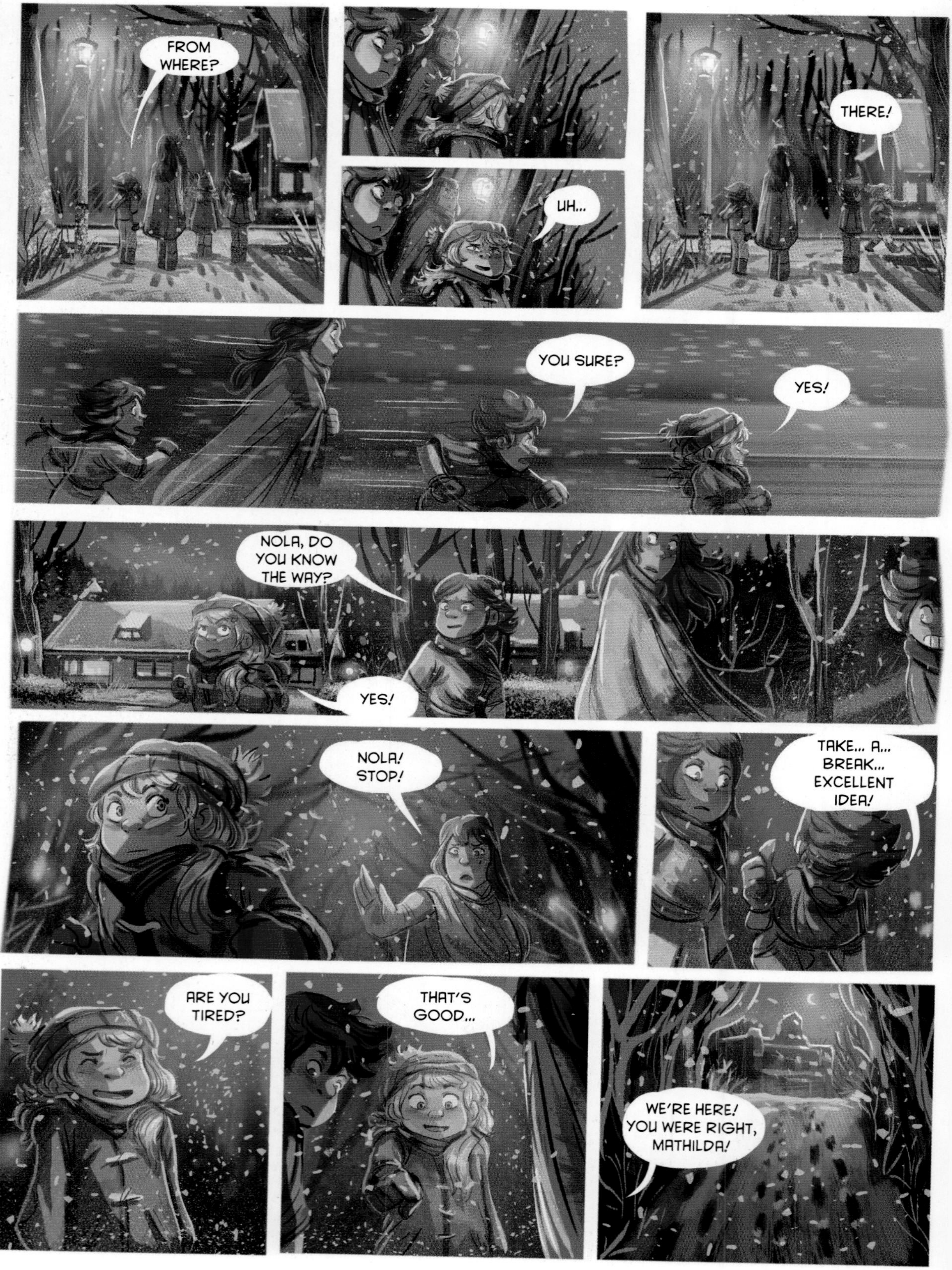
FROM WHERE?
UH...
THERE!
YOU SURE?
YES!
NOLA, DO YOU KNOW THE WAY?
YES!
NOLA! STOP!
TAKE... A... BREAK... EXCELLENT IDEA!
ARE YOU TIRED?
THAT'S GOOD...
WE'RE HERE! YOU WERE RIGHT, MATHILDA!

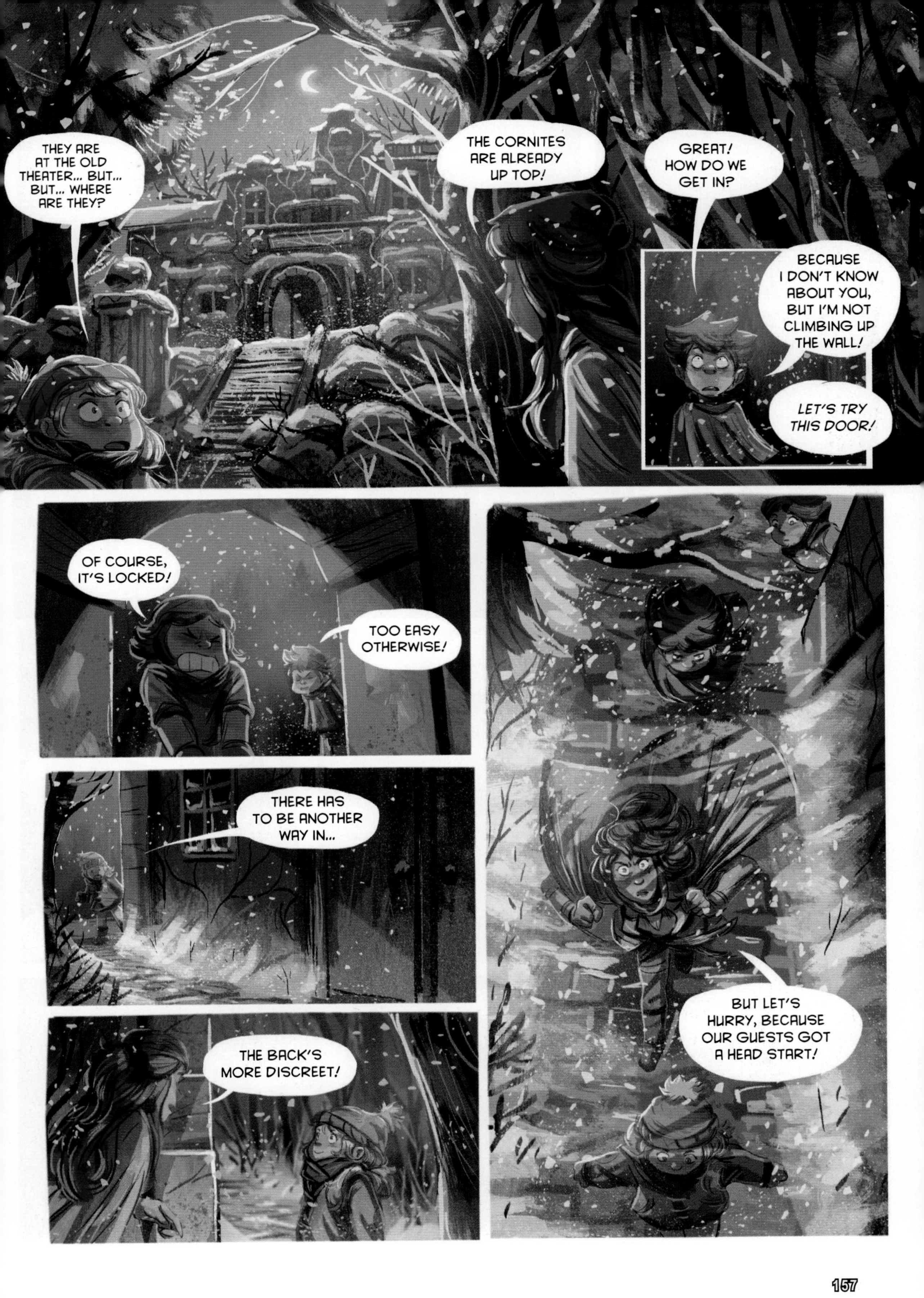
THEY ARE AT THE OLD THEATER... BUT... BUT... WHERE ARE THEY?
THE CORNITES ARE ALREADY UP TOP!
GREAT! HOW DO WE GET IN?
BECAUSE I DON'T KNOW ABOUT YOU, BUT I'M NOT CLIMBING UP THE WALL!
LET'S TRY THIS DOOR!
OF COURSE, IT'S LOCKED!
TOO EASY OTHERWISE!
THERE HAS TO BE ANOTHER WAY IN...
THE BACK'S MORE DISCREET!
BUT LET'S HURRY, BECAUSE OUR GUESTS GOT A HEAD START!

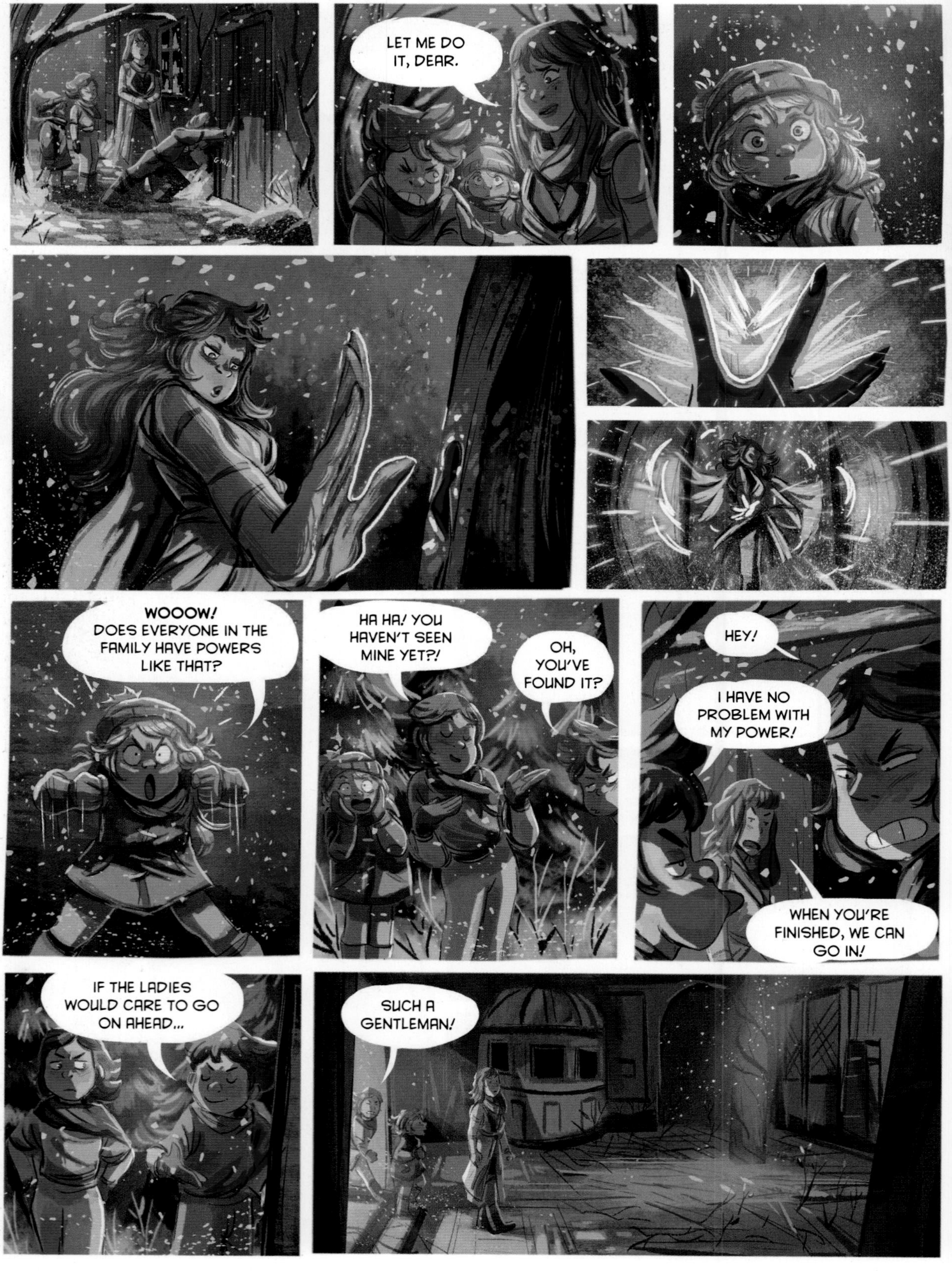
LET ME DO IT, DEAR.
WOOOW! DOES EVERYONE IN THE FAMILY HAVE POWERS LIKE THAT?
HA HA! YOU HAVEN'T SEEN MINE YET?!
OH, YOU'VE FOUND IT?
HEY!
I HAVE NO PROBLEM WITH MY POWER!
WHEN YOU'RE FINISHED, WE CAN GO IN!
IF THE LADIES WOULD CARE TO GO ON AHEAD...
SUCH A GENTLEMAN!

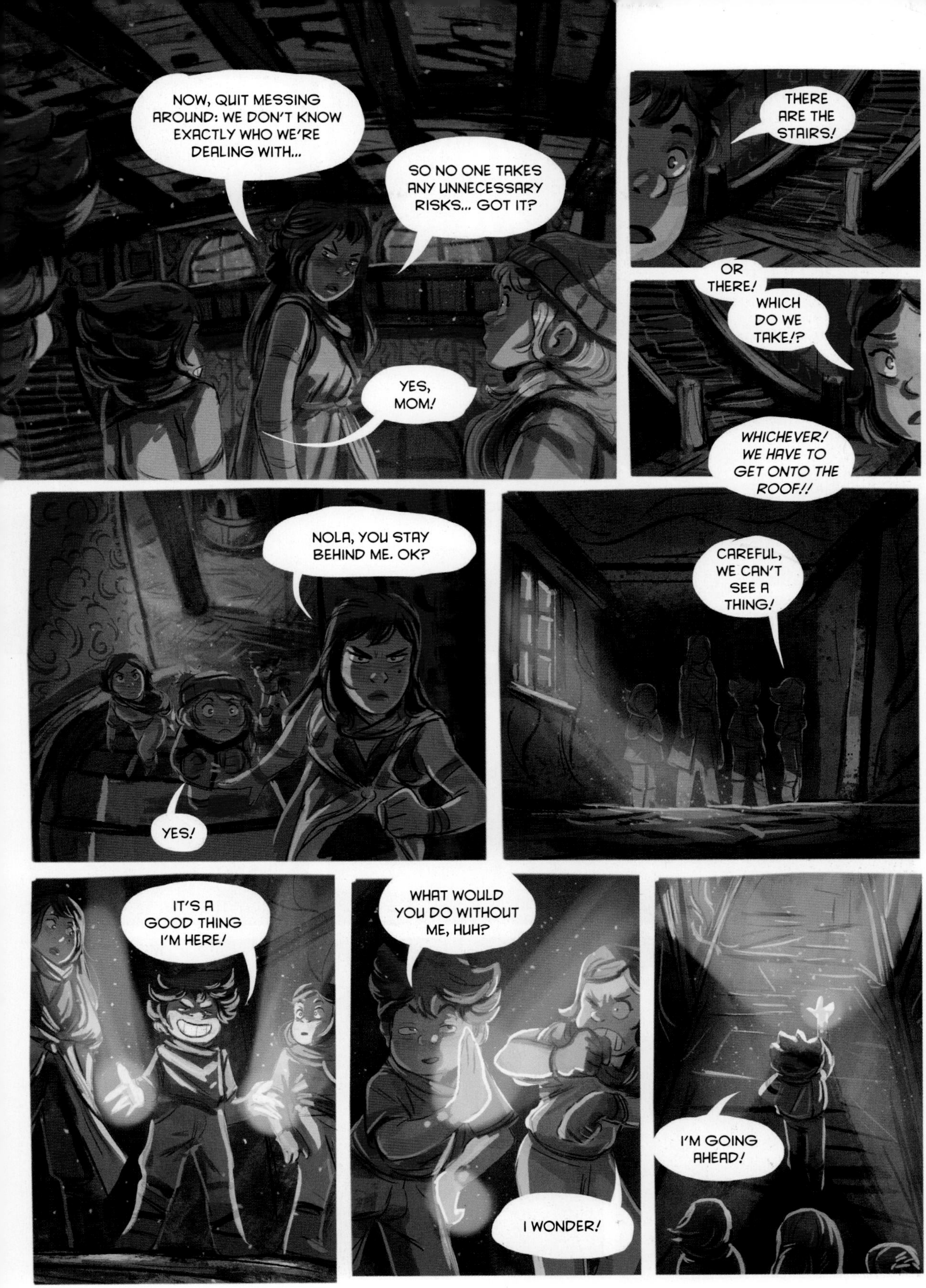
NOW, QUIT MESSING AROUND: WE DON'T KNOW EXACTLY WHO WE'RE DEALING WITH...
SO NO ONE TAKES ANY UNNECESSARY RISKS... GOT IT?
YES, MOM!
THERE ARE THE STAIRS!
OR THERE!
WHICH DO WE TAKE!?
WHICHEVER! WE HAVE TO GET ONTO THE ROOF!!
NOLA, YOU STAY BEHIND ME. OK?
YES!
CAREFUL, WE CAN'T SEE A THING!
IT'S A GOOD THING I'M HERE!
WHAT WOULD YOU DO WITHOUT ME, HUH?
I WONDER!
I'M GOING AHEAD!

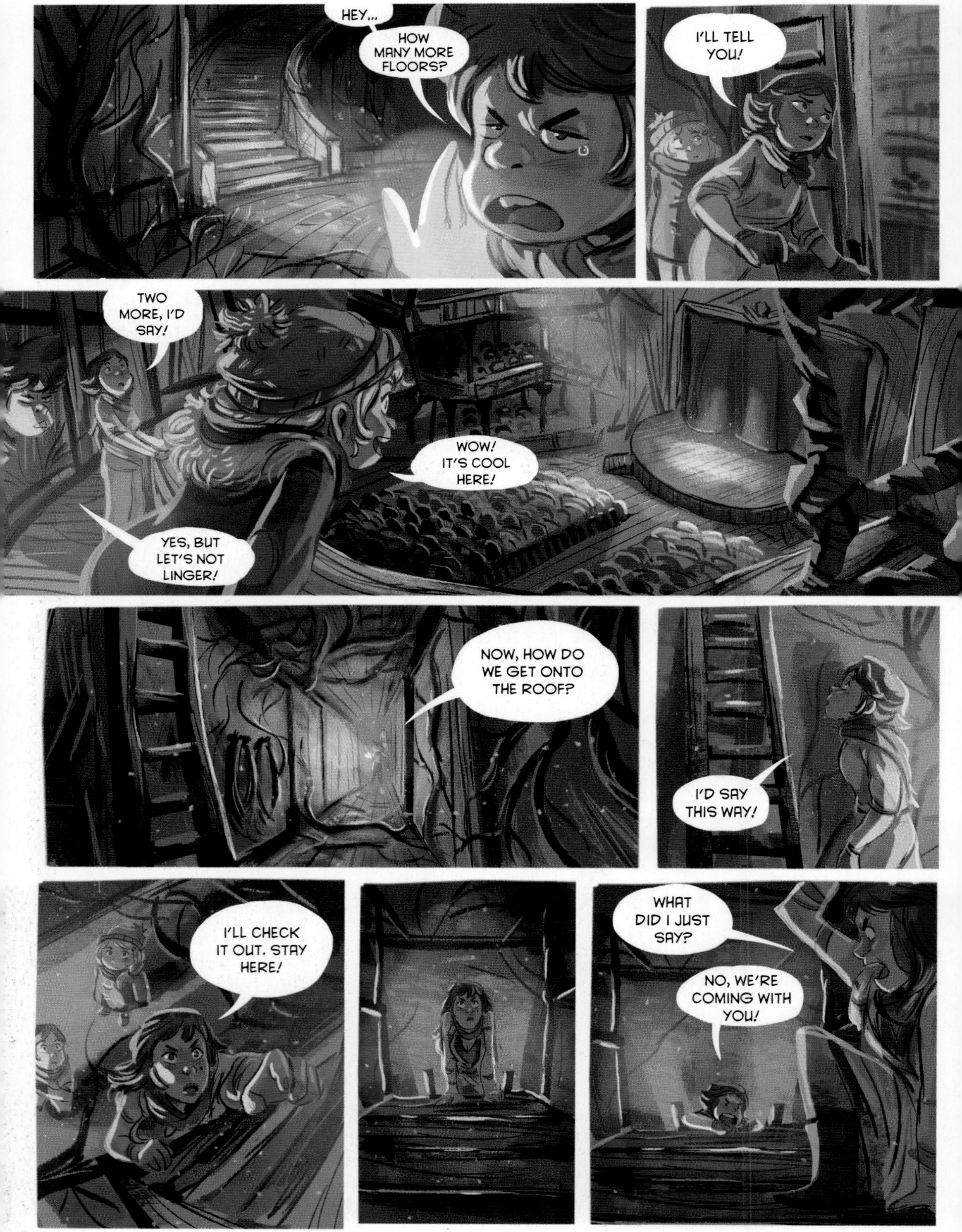
HEY...
HOW MANY MORE FLOORS?
I'LL TELL YOU!
TWO MORE, I'D SAY!
WOW! IT'S COOL HERE!
YES, BUT LET'S NOT LINGER!
NOW, HOW DO WE GET ONTO THE ROOF?
I'D SAY THIS WAY!
I'LL CHECK IT OUT. STAY HERE!
WHAT DID I JUST SAY?
NO, WE'RE COMING WITH YOU!

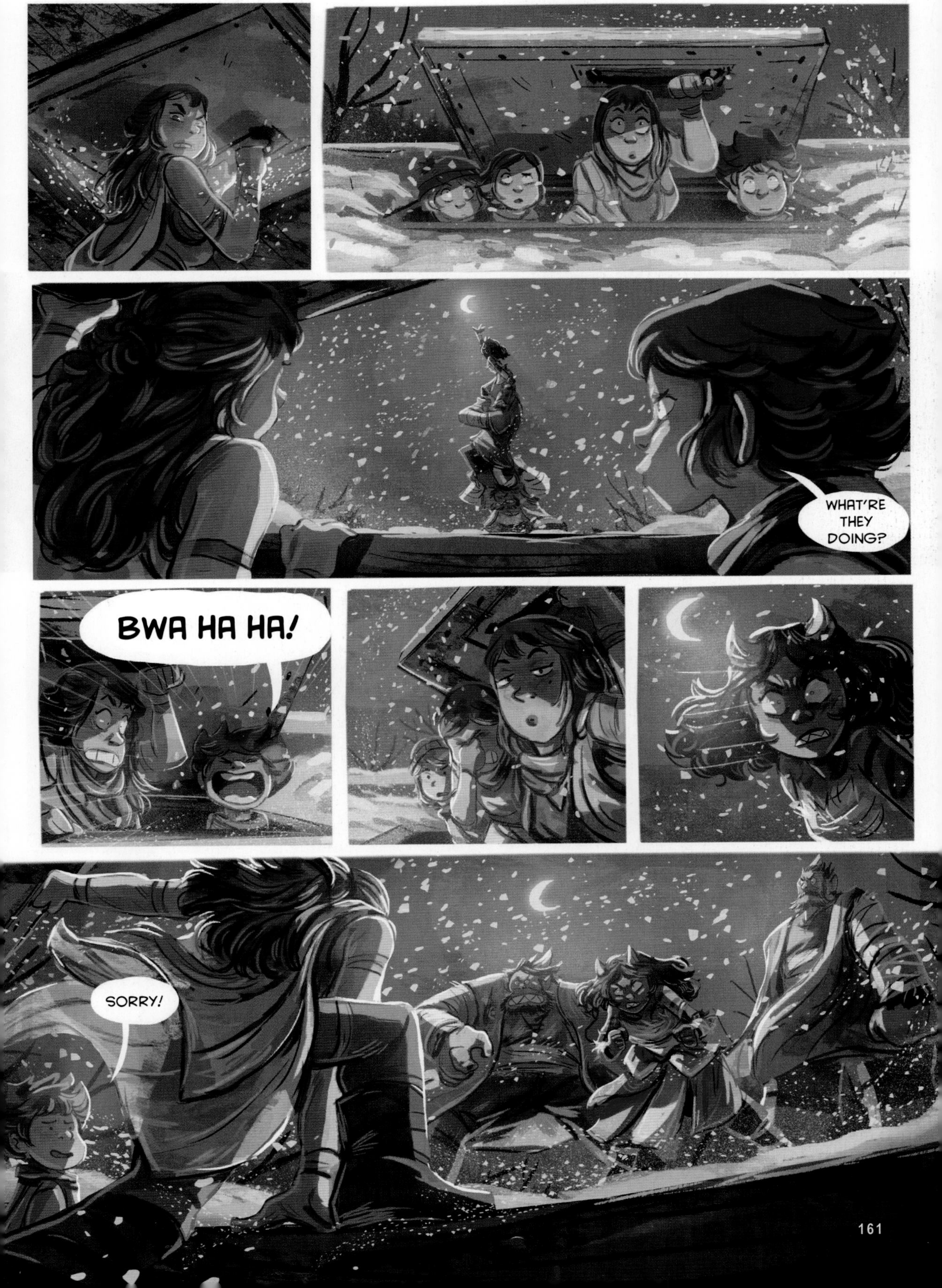
WHAT'RE THEY DOING?
BWA HA HA!
SORRY!

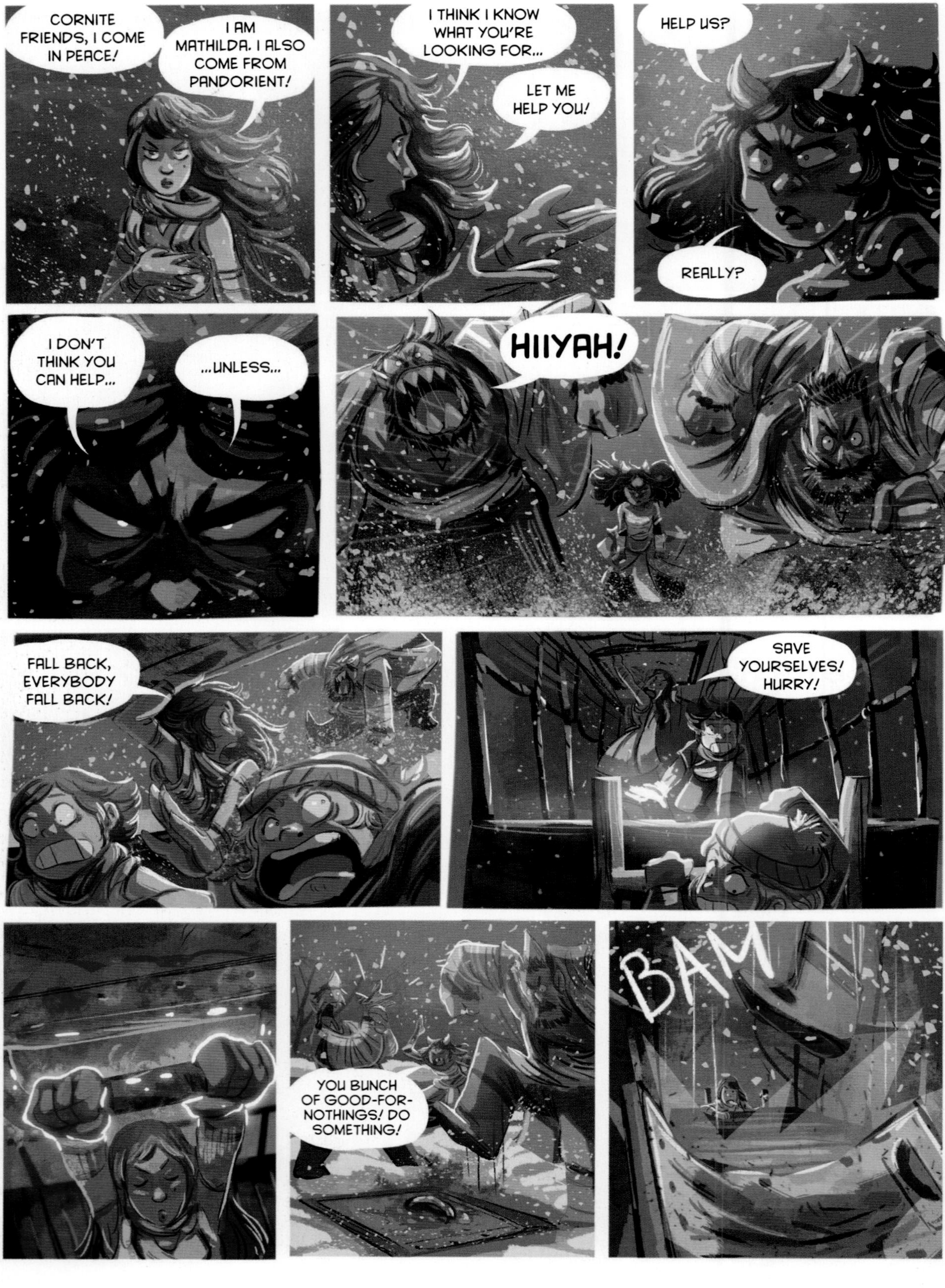
CORNITE FRIENDS, I COME IN PEACE!
I AM MATHILDA. I ALSO COME FROM PANDORIENT!
I THINK I KNOW WHAT YOU'RE LOOKING FOR...
LET ME HELP YOU!
HELP US?
REALLY?
I DON'T THINK YOU CAN HELP...
...UNLESS...
HIIYAH!
FALL BACK, EVERYBODY FALL BACK!
SAVE YOURSELVES! HURRY!
YOU BUNCH OF GOOD-FOR-NOTHINGS! DO SOMETHING!
BAM

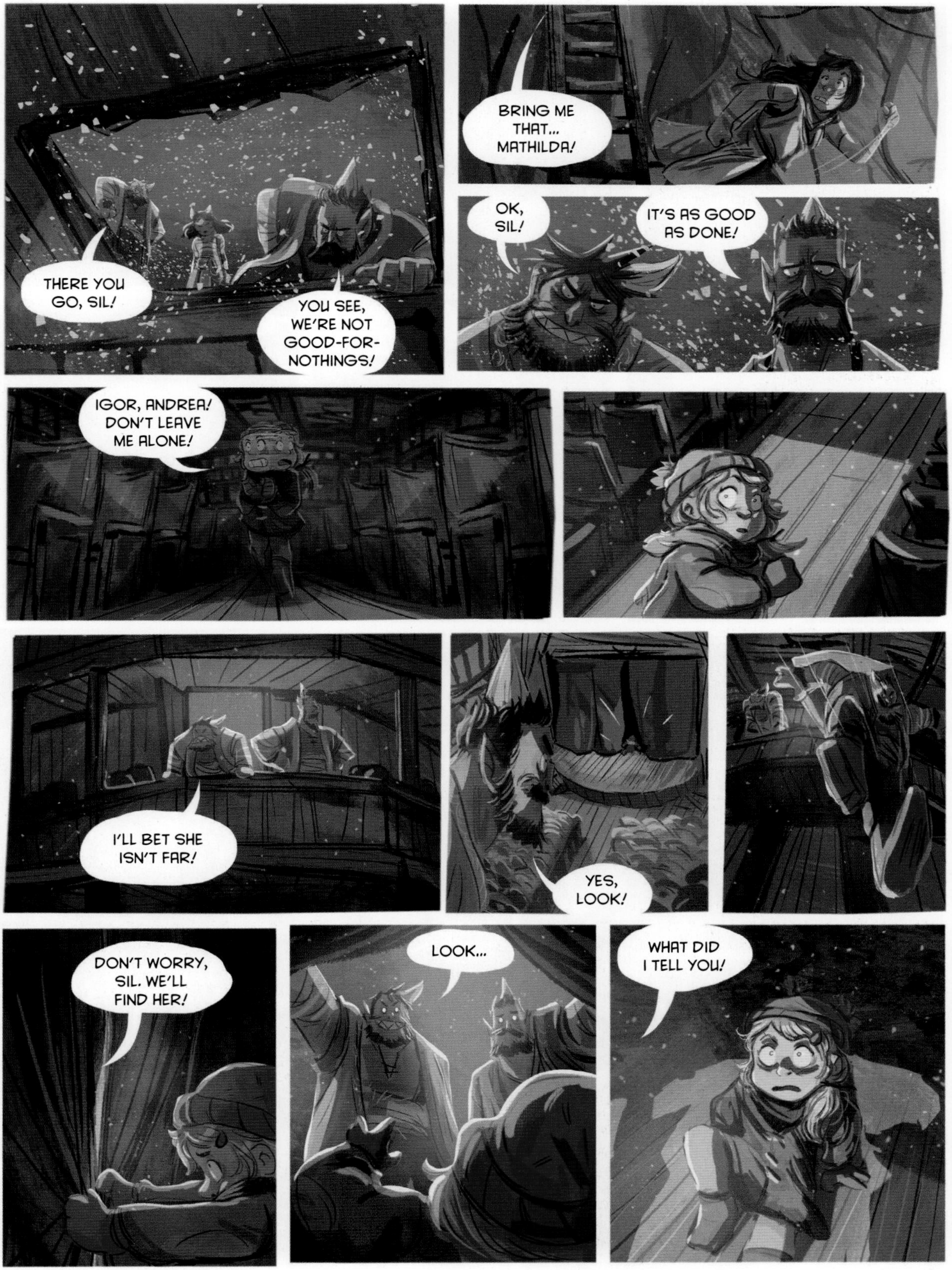

THERE YOU GO, SIL!
YOU SEE, WE'RE NOT GOOD-FOR-NOTHINGS!
BRING ME THAT... MATHILDA!
OK, SIL!
IT'S AS GOOD AS DONE!
IGOR, ANDREA! DON'T LEAVE ME ALONE!
I'LL BET SHE ISN'T FAR!
YES, LOOK!
DON'T WORRY, SIL. WE'LL FIND HER!
LOOK...
WHAT DID I TELL YOU!

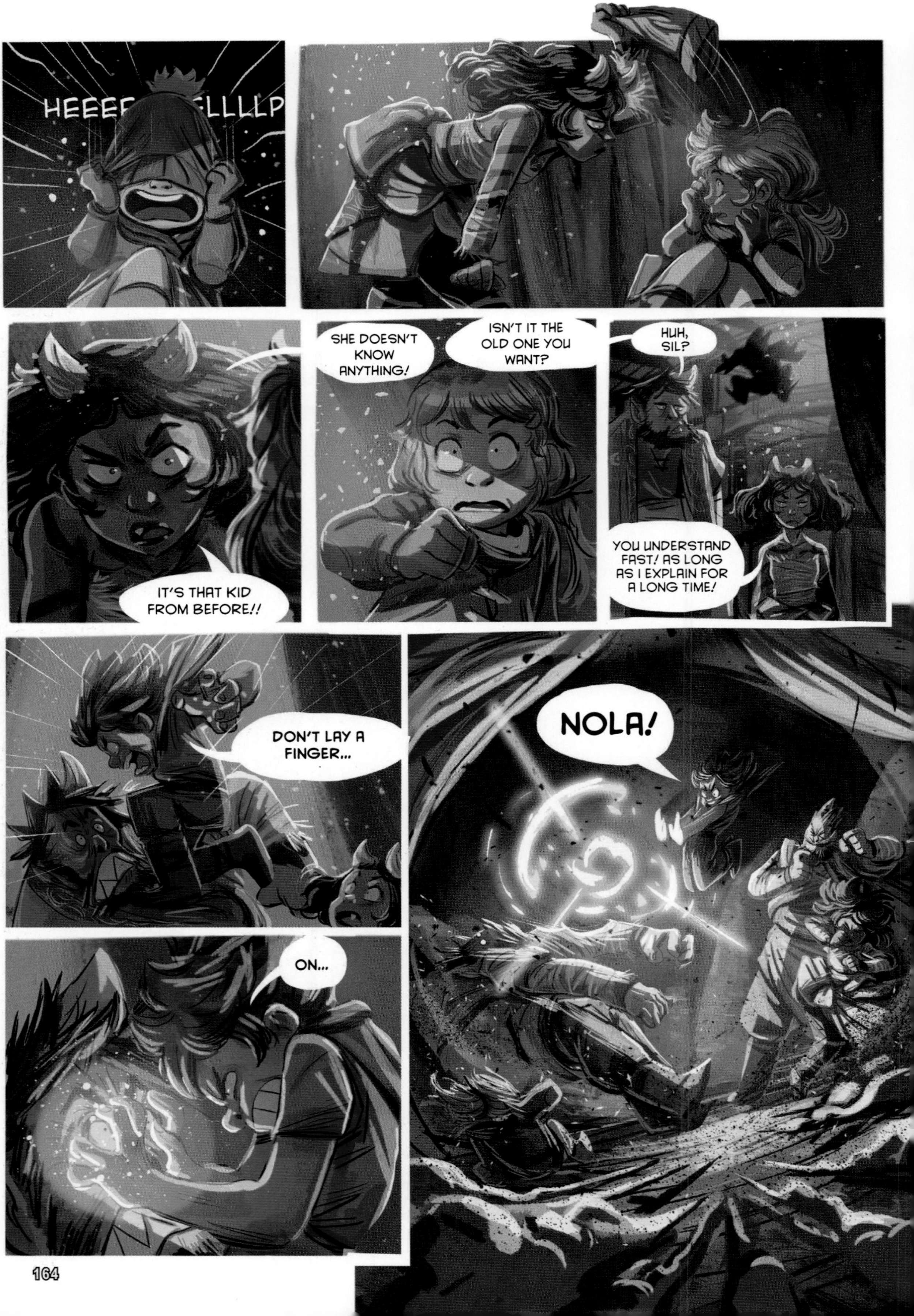
HEEEEELLLLP
IT'S THAT KID FROM BEFORE!!
SHE DOESN'T KNOW ANYTHING!
ISN'T IT THE OLD ONE YOU WANT?
HUH, SIL?
YOU UNDERSTAND FAST! AS LONG AS I EXPLAIN FOR A LONG TIME!
DON'T LAY A FINGER...
ON...
NOLA!

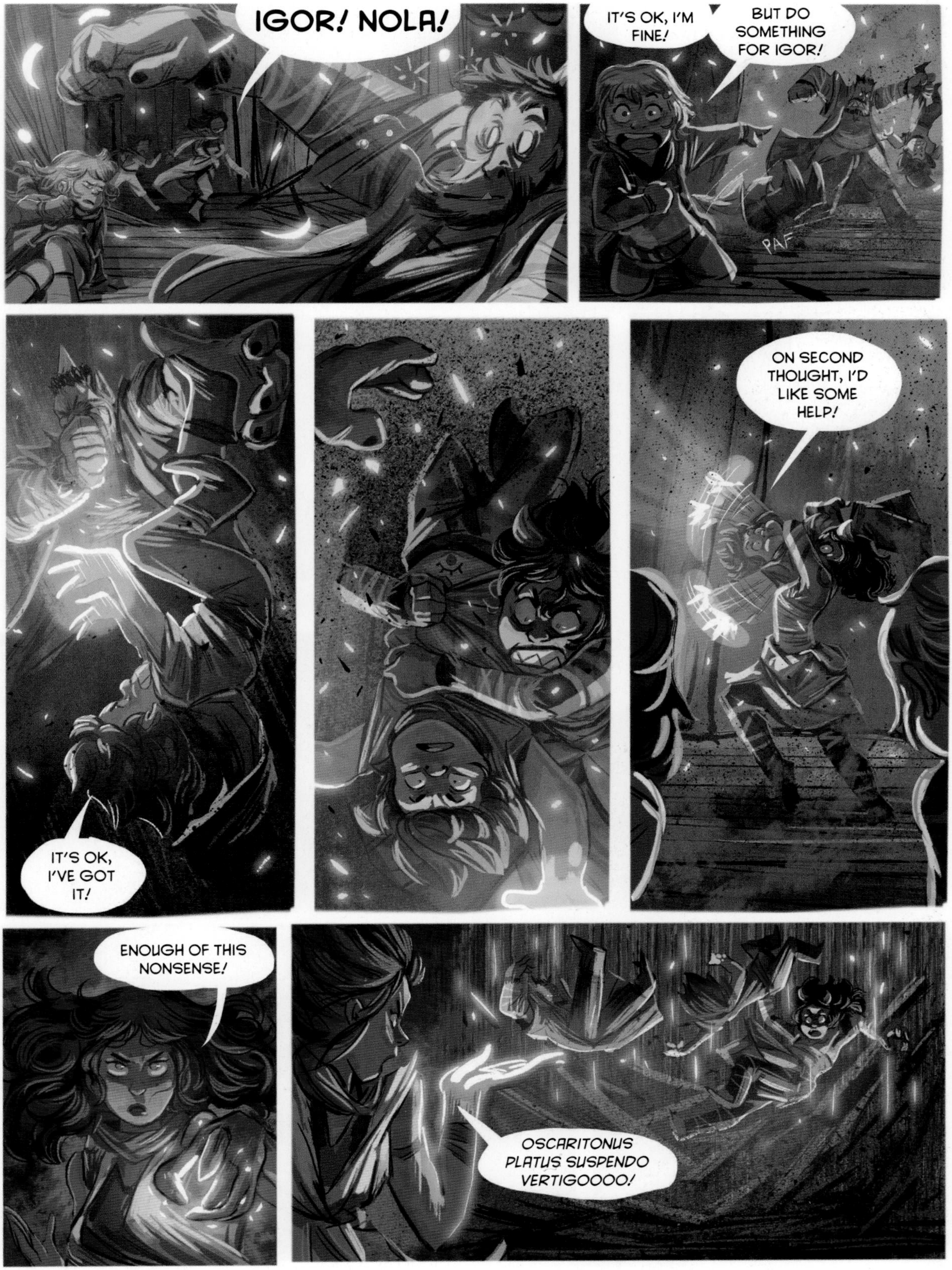
IGOR! NOLA!
IT'S OK, I'M FINE!
BUT DO SOMETHING FOR IGOR!
PAF
IT'S OK, I'VE GOT IT!
ON SECOND THOUGHT, I'D LIKE SOME HELP!
ENOUGH OF THIS NONSENSE!
OSCARITONUS PLATUS SUSPENDO VERTIGOOOO!

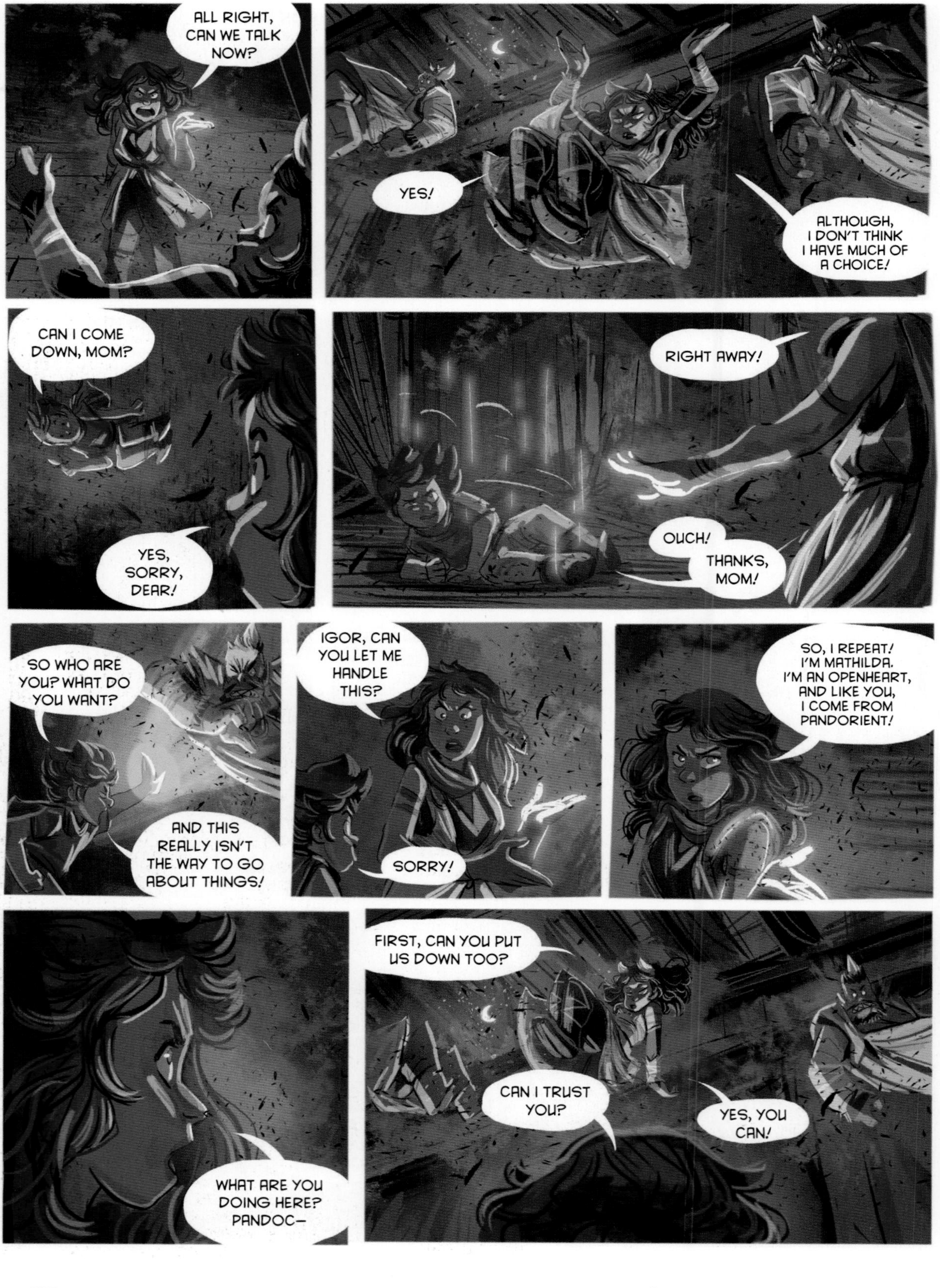
ALL RIGHT, CAN WE TALK NOW?
YES!
ALTHOUGH, I DON'T THINK I HAVE MUCH OF A CHOICE!
CAN I COME DOWN, MOM?
YES, SORRY, DEAR!
RIGHT AWAY!
OUCH!
THANKS, MOM!
SO WHO ARE YOU? WHAT DO YOU WANT?
AND THIS REALLY ISN'T THE WAY TO GO ABOUT THINGS!
IGOR, CAN YOU LET ME HANDLE THIS?
SORRY!
SO, I REPEAT! I'M MATHILDA. I'M AN OPENHEART, AND LIKE YOU, I COME FROM PANDORIENT!
WHAT ARE YOU DOING HERE? PANDOC—
FIRST, CAN YOU PUT US DOWN TOO?
CAN I TRUST YOU?
YES, YOU CAN!

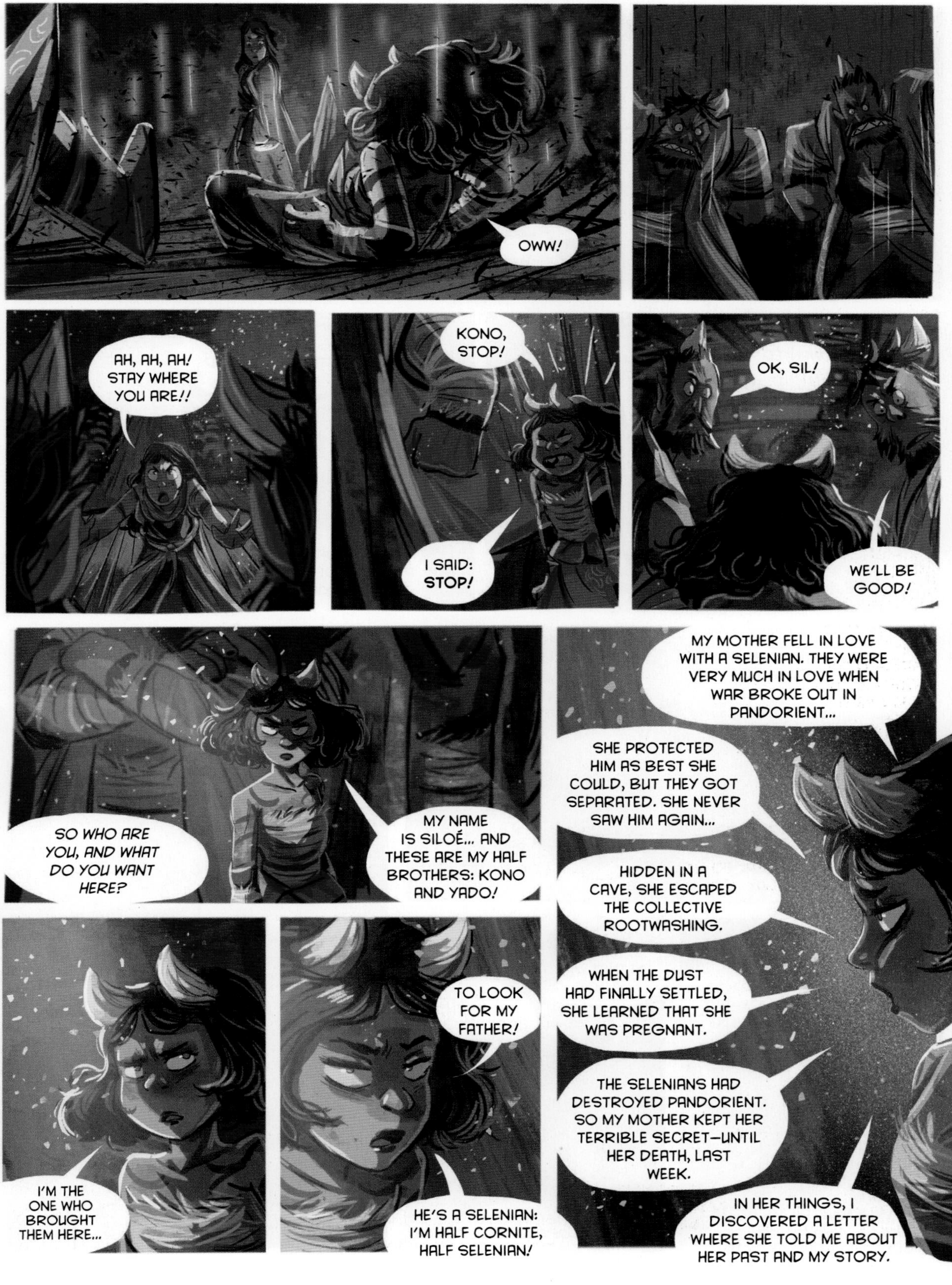
OWW!
AH, AH, AH! STAY WHERE YOU ARE!!
KONO, STOP!
I SAID: **STOP!**
OK, SIL!
WE'LL BE GOOD!
SO WHO ARE YOU, AND WHAT DO YOU WANT HERE?
MY NAME IS SILOÉ... AND THESE ARE MY HALF BROTHERS: KONO AND YADO!
I'M THE ONE WHO BROUGHT THEM HERE...
TO LOOK FOR MY FATHER!
HE'S A SELENIAN: I'M HALF CORNITE, HALF SELENIAN!
MY MOTHER FELL IN LOVE WITH A SELENIAN. THEY WERE VERY MUCH IN LOVE WHEN WAR BROKE OUT IN PANDORIENT...
SHE PROTECTED HIM AS BEST SHE COULD, BUT THEY GOT SEPARATED. SHE NEVER SAW HIM AGAIN...
HIDDEN IN A CAVE, SHE ESCAPED THE COLLECTIVE ROOTWASHING.
WHEN THE DUST HAD FINALLY SETTLED, SHE LEARNED THAT SHE WAS PREGNANT.
THE SELENIANS HAD DESTROYED PANDORIENT. SO MY MOTHER KEPT HER TERRIBLE SECRET—UNTIL HER DEATH, LAST WEEK.
IN HER THINGS, I DISCOVERED A LETTER WHERE SHE TOLD ME ABOUT HER PAST AND MY STORY.

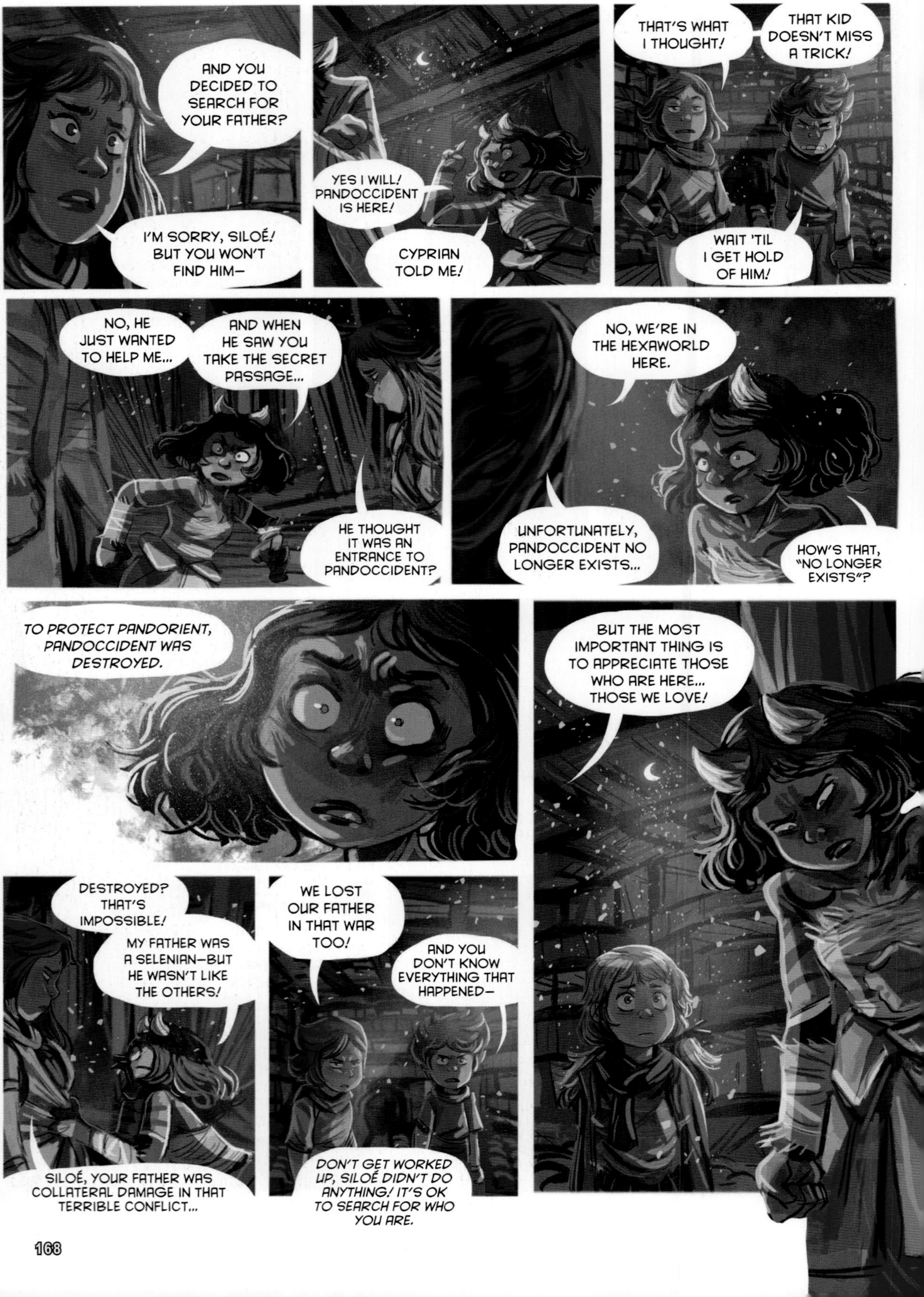

AND YOU DECIDED TO SEARCH FOR YOUR FATHER?
I'M SORRY, SILOÉ! BUT YOU WON'T FIND HIM—
YES I WILL! PANDOCCIDENT IS HERE!
CYPRIAN TOLD ME!
THAT'S WHAT I THOUGHT!
THAT KID DOESN'T MISS A TRICK!
WAIT 'TIL I GET HOLD OF HIM!
NO, HE JUST WANTED TO HELP ME...
AND WHEN HE SAW YOU TAKE THE SECRET PASSAGE...
HE THOUGHT IT WAS AN ENTRANCE TO PANDOCCIDENT?
NO, WE'RE IN THE HEXAWORLD HERE.
UNFORTUNATELY, PANDOCCIDENT NO LONGER EXISTS...
HOW'S THAT, "NO LONGER EXISTS"?
TO PROTECT PANDORIENT, PANDOCCIDENT WAS DESTROYED.
BUT THE MOST IMPORTANT THING IS TO APPRECIATE THOSE WHO ARE HERE... THOSE WE LOVE!
DESTROYED? THAT'S IMPOSSIBLE!
MY FATHER WAS A SELENIAN—BUT HE WASN'T LIKE THE OTHERS!
SILOÉ, YOUR FATHER WAS COLLATERAL DAMAGE IN THAT TERRIBLE CONFLICT...
WE LOST OUR FATHER IN THAT WAR TOO!
AND YOU DON'T KNOW EVERYTHING THAT HAPPENED—
DON'T GET WORKED UP, SILOÉ DIDN'T DO ANYTHING! IT'S OK TO SEARCH FOR WHO YOU ARE.

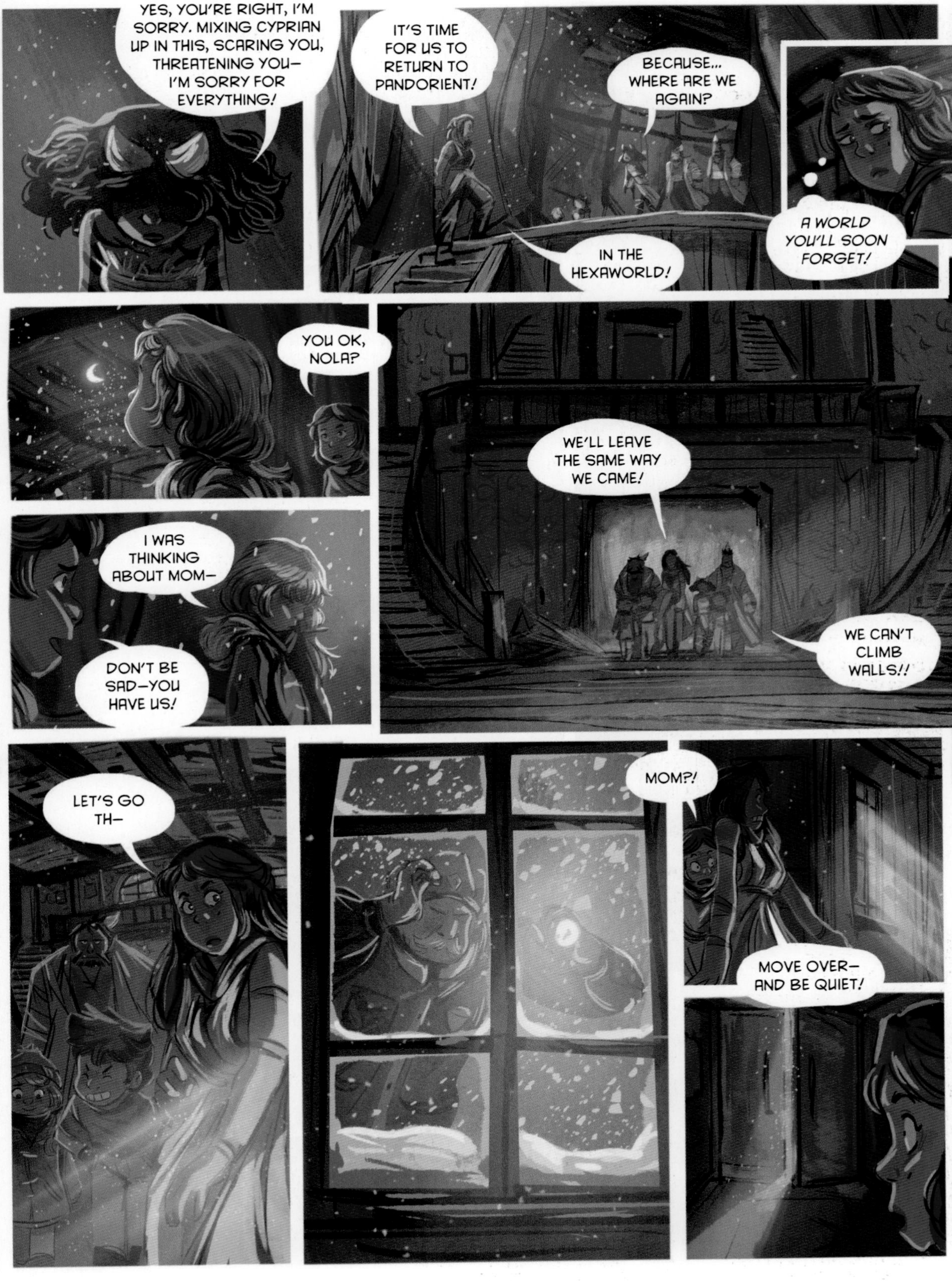
YES, YOU'RE RIGHT, I'M SORRY. MIXING CYPRIAN UP IN THIS, SCARING YOU, THREATENING YOU— I'M SORRY FOR EVERYTHING!
IT'S TIME FOR US TO RETURN TO PANDORIENT!
BECAUSE... WHERE ARE WE AGAIN?
IN THE HEXAWORLD!
A WORLD YOU'LL SOON FORGET!
YOU OK, NOLA?
I WAS THINKING ABOUT MOM—
DON'T BE SAD—YOU HAVE US!
WE'LL LEAVE THE SAME WAY WE CAME!
WE CAN'T CLIMB WALLS!!
LET'S GO TH—
MOM?!
MOVE OVER— AND BE QUIET!

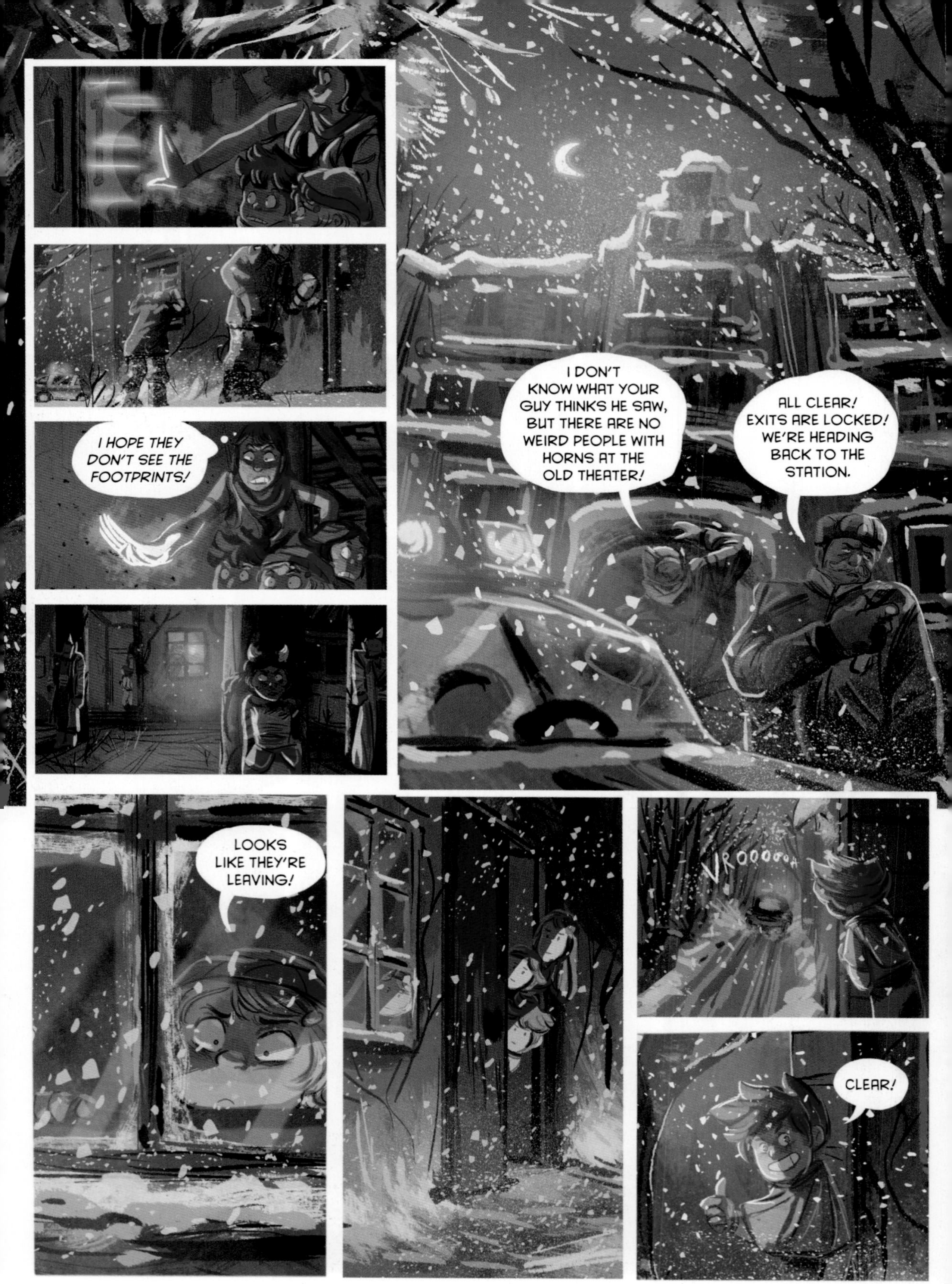
I HOPE THEY DON'T SEE THE FOOTPRINTS!
I DON'T KNOW WHAT YOUR GUY THINKS HE SAW, BUT THERE ARE NO WEIRD PEOPLE WITH HORNS AT THE OLD THEATER!
ALL CLEAR! EXITS ARE LOCKED! WE'RE HEADING BACK TO THE STATION.
LOOKS LIKE THEY'RE LEAVING!
VROOOOOM
CLEAR!

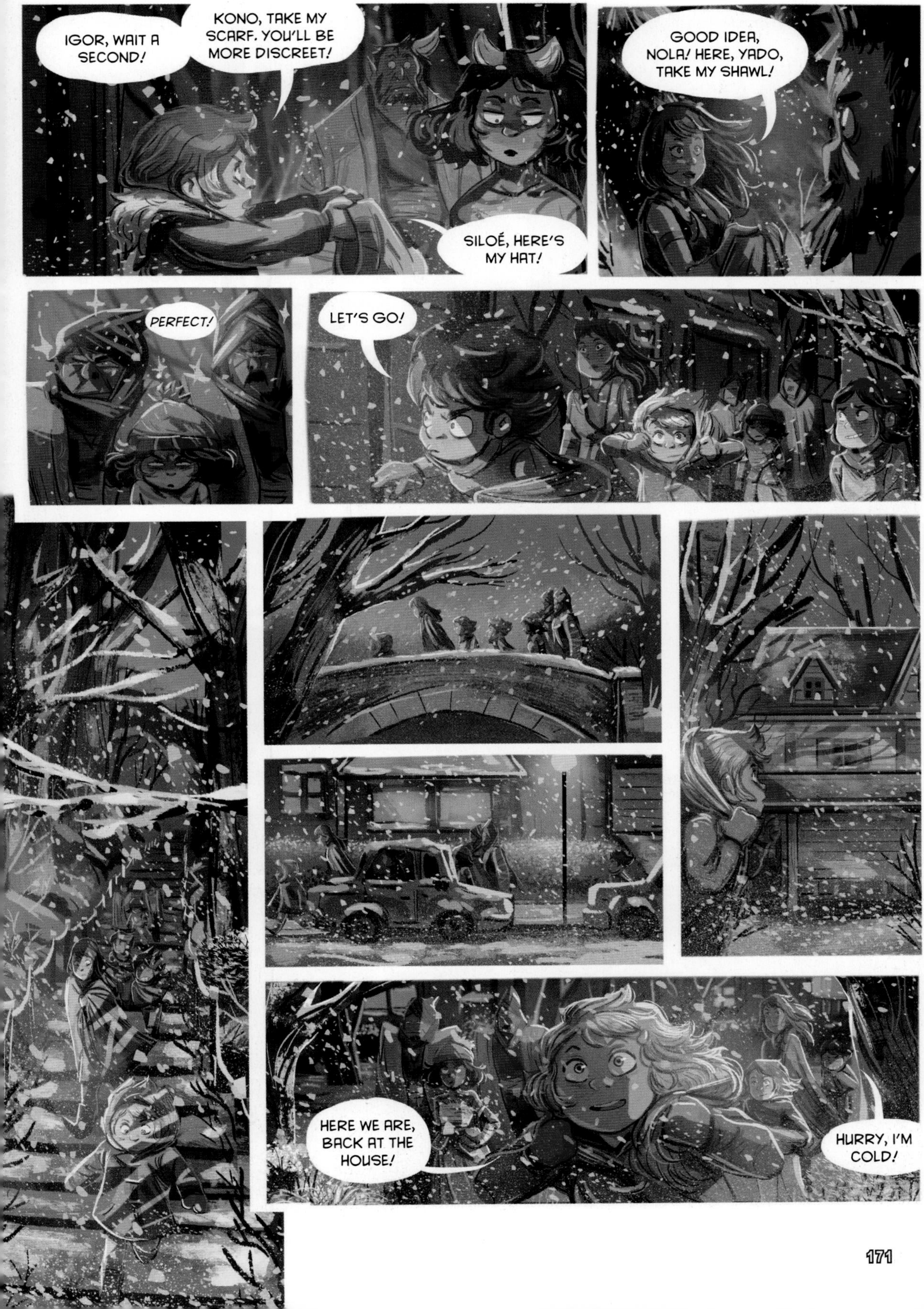

IGOR, WAIT A SECOND!
KONO, TAKE MY SCARF. YOU'LL BE MORE DISCREET!
SILOÉ, HERE'S MY HAT!
GOOD IDEA, NOLA! HERE, YADO, TAKE MY SHAWL!
PERFECT!
LET'S GO!
HERE WE ARE, BACK AT THE HOUSE!
HURRY, I'M COLD!

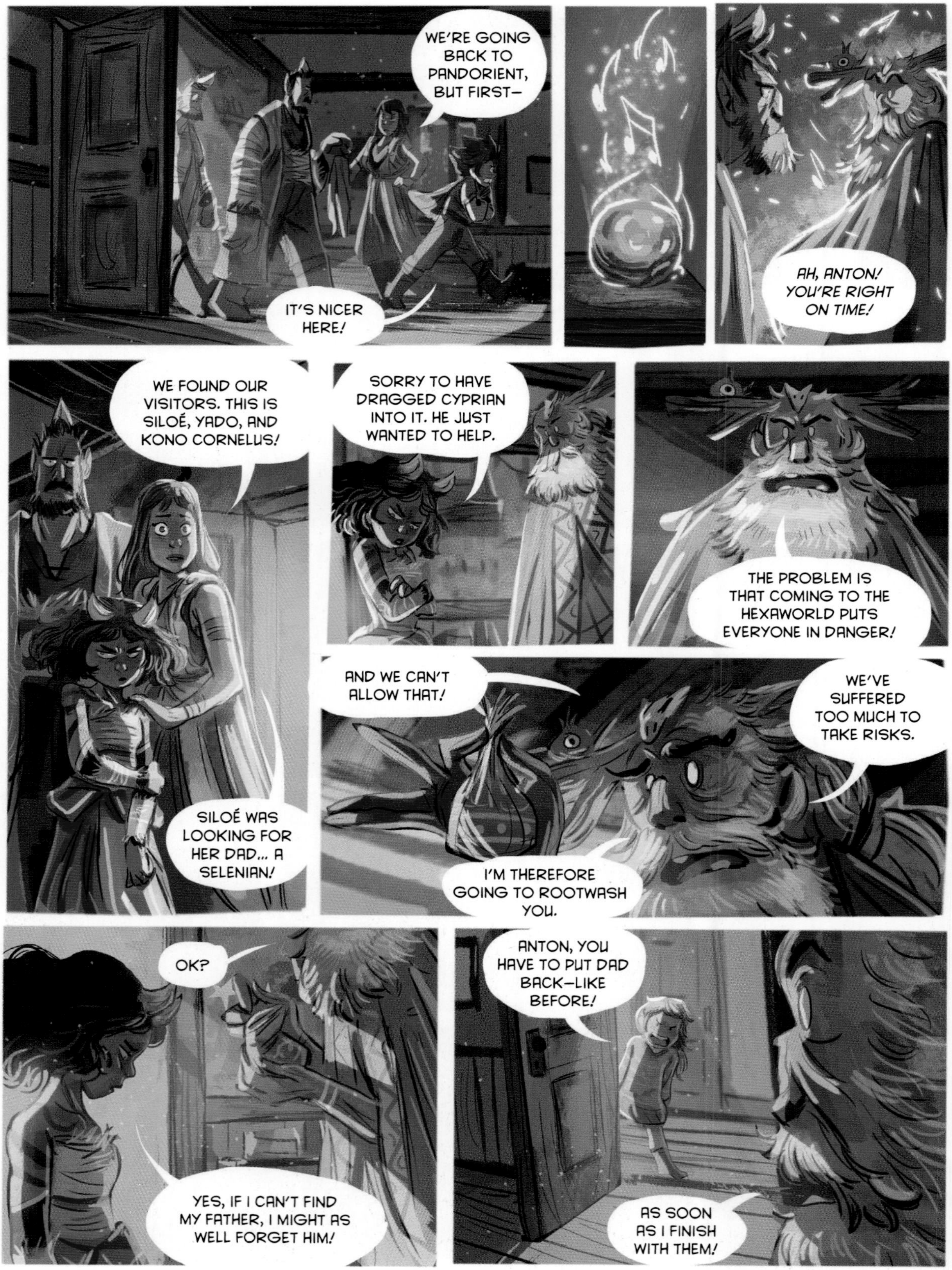
WE'RE GOING BACK TO PANDORIENT, BUT FIRST—
IT'S NICER HERE!
AH, ANTON! YOU'RE RIGHT ON TIME!
WE FOUND OUR VISITORS. THIS IS SILOÉ, YADO, AND KONO CORNELUS!
SILOÉ WAS LOOKING FOR HER DAD... A SELENIAN!
SORRY TO HAVE DRAGGED CYPRIAN INTO IT. HE JUST WANTED TO HELP.
THE PROBLEM IS THAT COMING TO THE HEXAWORLD PUTS EVERYONE IN DANGER!
AND WE CAN'T ALLOW THAT!
WE'VE SUFFERED TOO MUCH TO TAKE RISKS.
I'M THEREFORE GOING TO ROOTWASH YOU.
OK?
YES, IF I CAN'T FIND MY FATHER, I MIGHT AS WELL FORGET HIM!
ANTON, YOU HAVE TO PUT DAD BACK—LIKE BEFORE!
AS SOON AS I FINISH WITH THEM!

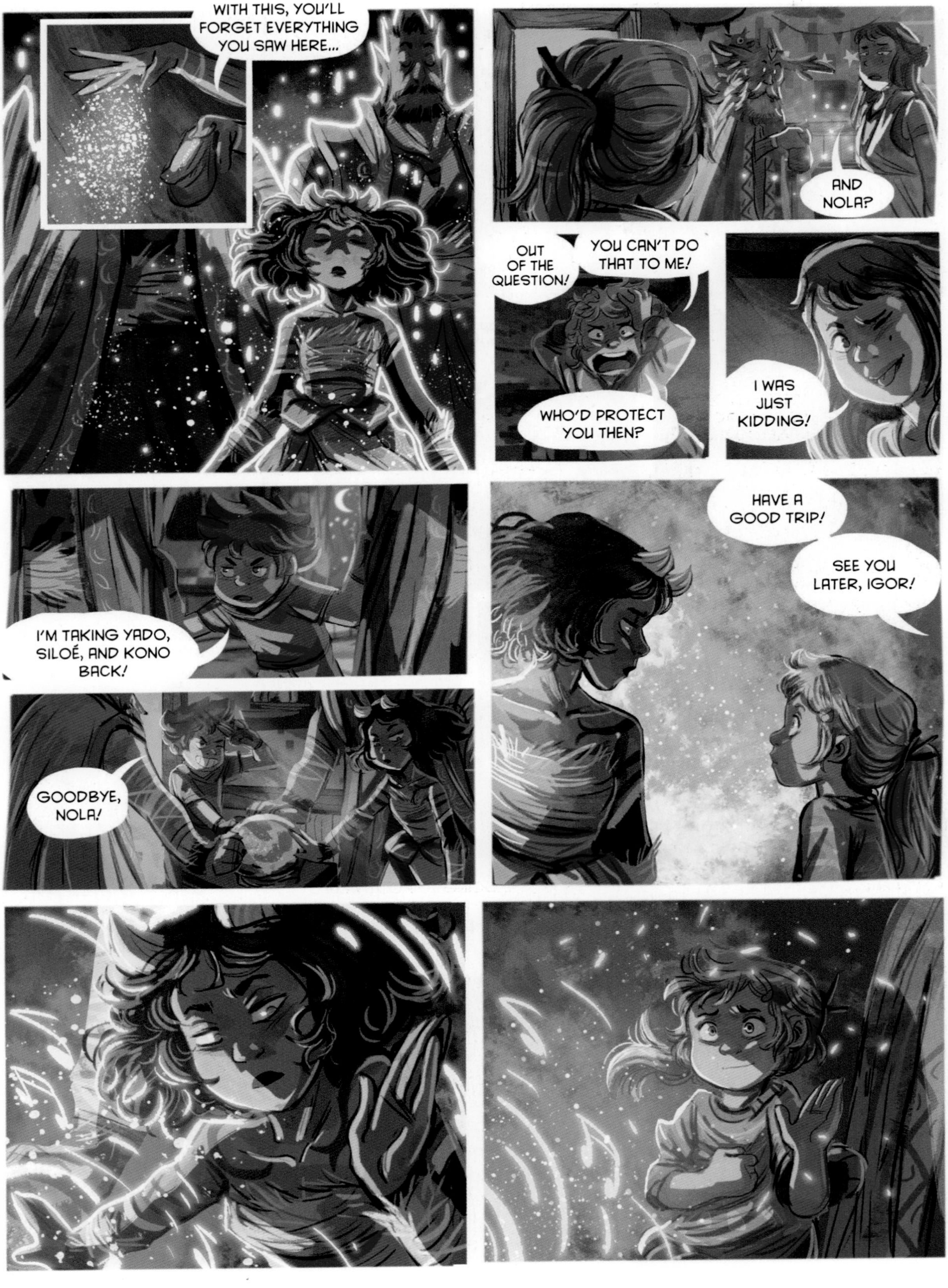
WITH THIS, YOU'LL FORGET EVERYTHING YOU SAW HERE...
AND NOLA?
YOU CAN'T DO THAT TO ME!
OUT OF THE QUESTION!
WHO'D PROTECT YOU THEN?
I WAS JUST KIDDING!
I'M TAKING YADO, SILOÉ, AND KONO BACK!
GOODBYE, NOLA!
HAVE A GOOD TRIP!
SEE YOU LATER, IGOR!

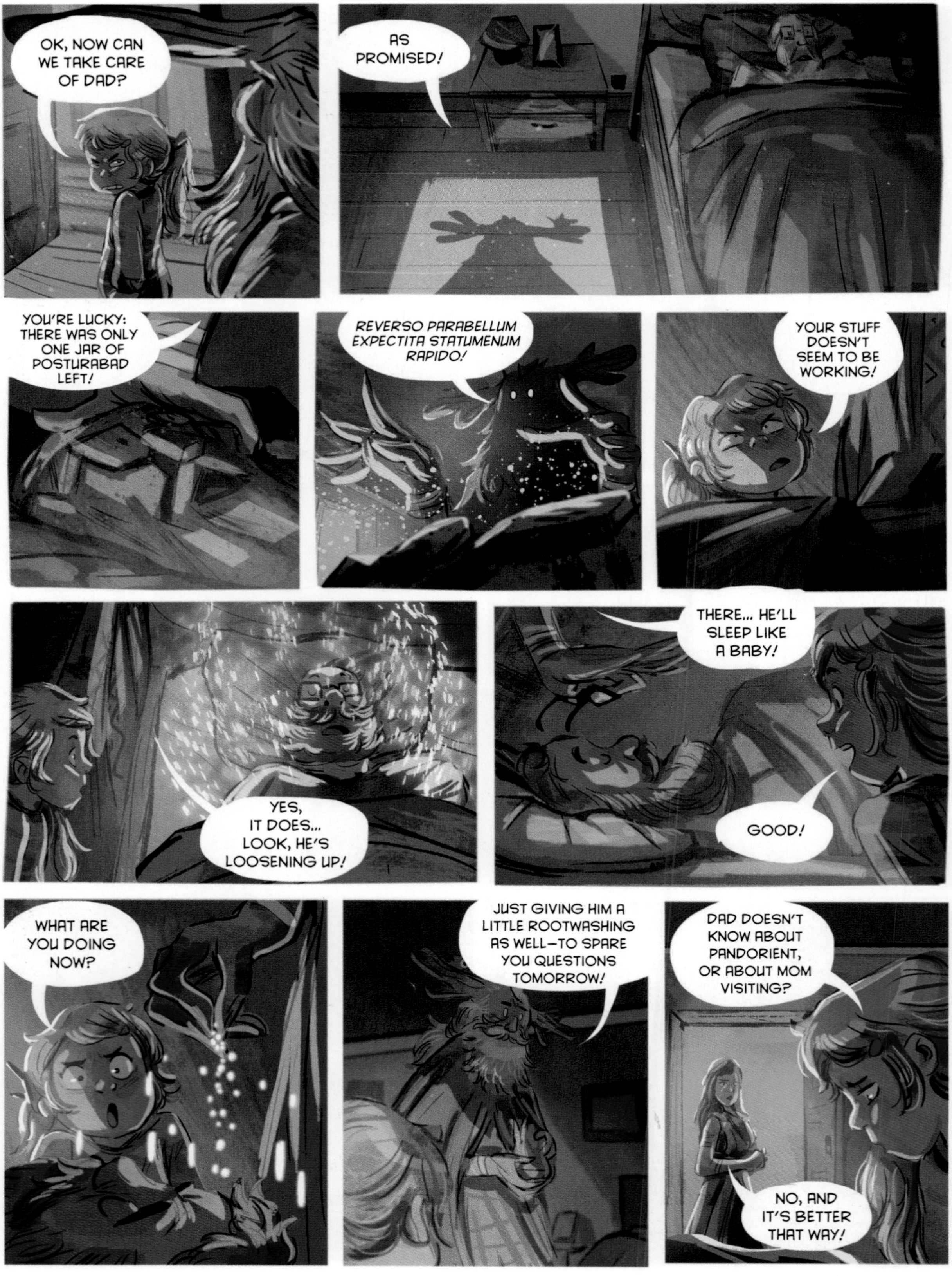

OK, NOW CAN WE TAKE CARE OF DAD?
AS PROMISED!
YOU'RE LUCKY: THERE WAS ONLY ONE JAR OF POSTURABAD LEFT!
REVERSO PARABELLUM EXPECTITA STATUMENUM RAPIDO!
YOUR STUFF DOESN'T SEEM TO BE WORKING!
YES, IT DOES... LOOK, HE'S LOOSENING UP!
THERE... HE'LL SLEEP LIKE A BABY!
GOOD!
WHAT ARE YOU DOING NOW?
JUST GIVING HIM A LITTLE ROOTWASHING AS WELL—TO SPARE YOU QUESTIONS TOMORROW!
DAD DOESN'T KNOW ABOUT PANDORIENT, OR ABOUT MOM VISITING?
NO, AND IT'S BETTER THAT WAY!

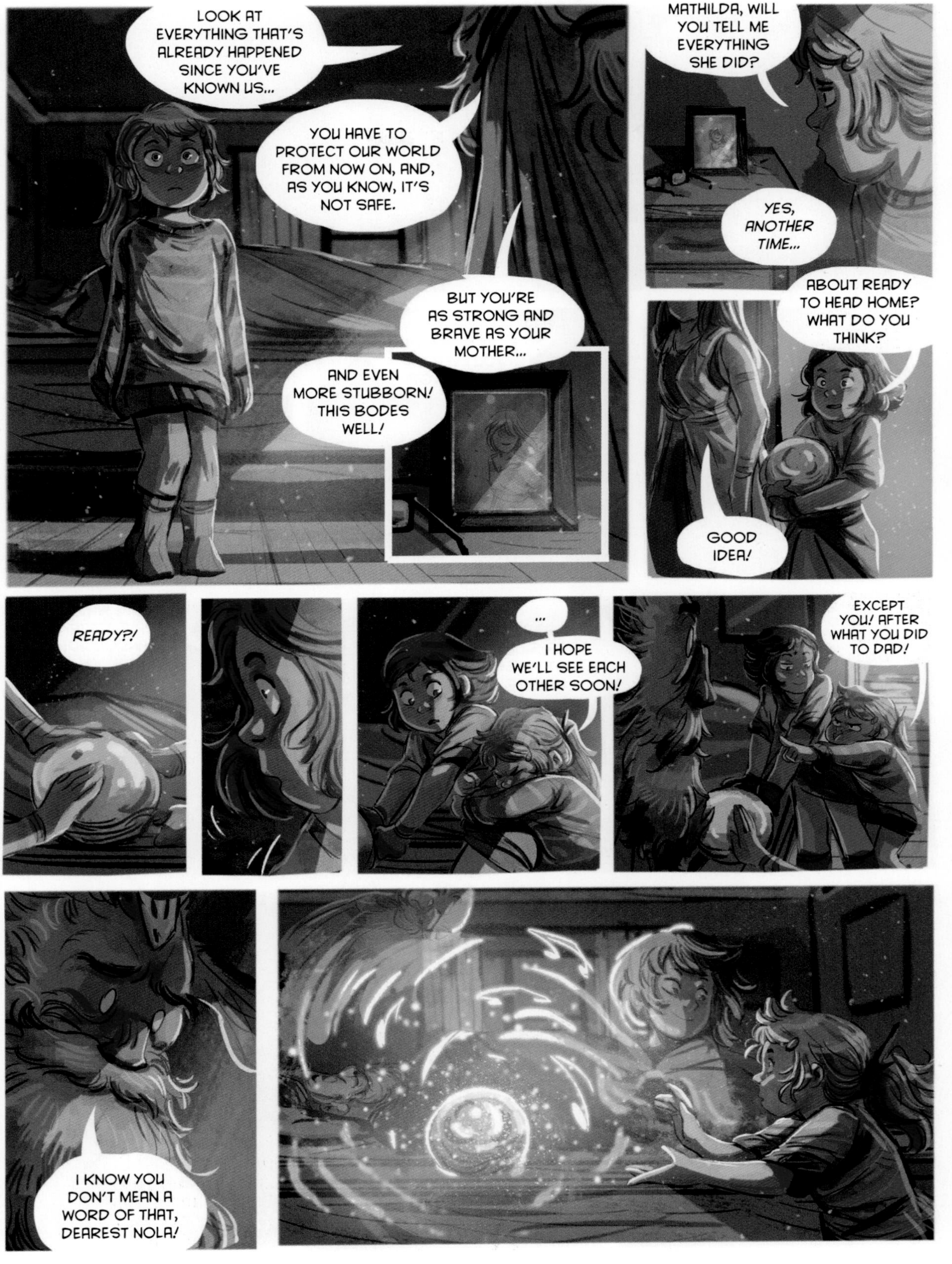
LOOK AT EVERYTHING THAT'S ALREADY HAPPENED SINCE YOU'VE KNOWN US...
YOU HAVE TO PROTECT OUR WORLD FROM NOW ON, AND, AS YOU KNOW, IT'S NOT SAFE.
BUT YOU'RE AS STRONG AND BRAVE AS YOUR MOTHER...
AND EVEN MORE STUBBORN! THIS BODES WELL!
MATHILDA, WILL YOU TELL ME EVERYTHING SHE DID?
YES, ANOTHER TIME...
ABOUT READY TO HEAD HOME? WHAT DO YOU THINK?
GOOD IDEA!
READY?!
...
I HOPE WE'LL SEE EACH OTHER SOON!
EXCEPT YOU! AFTER WHAT YOU DID TO DAD!
I KNOW YOU DON'T MEAN A WORD OF THAT, DEAREST NOLA!

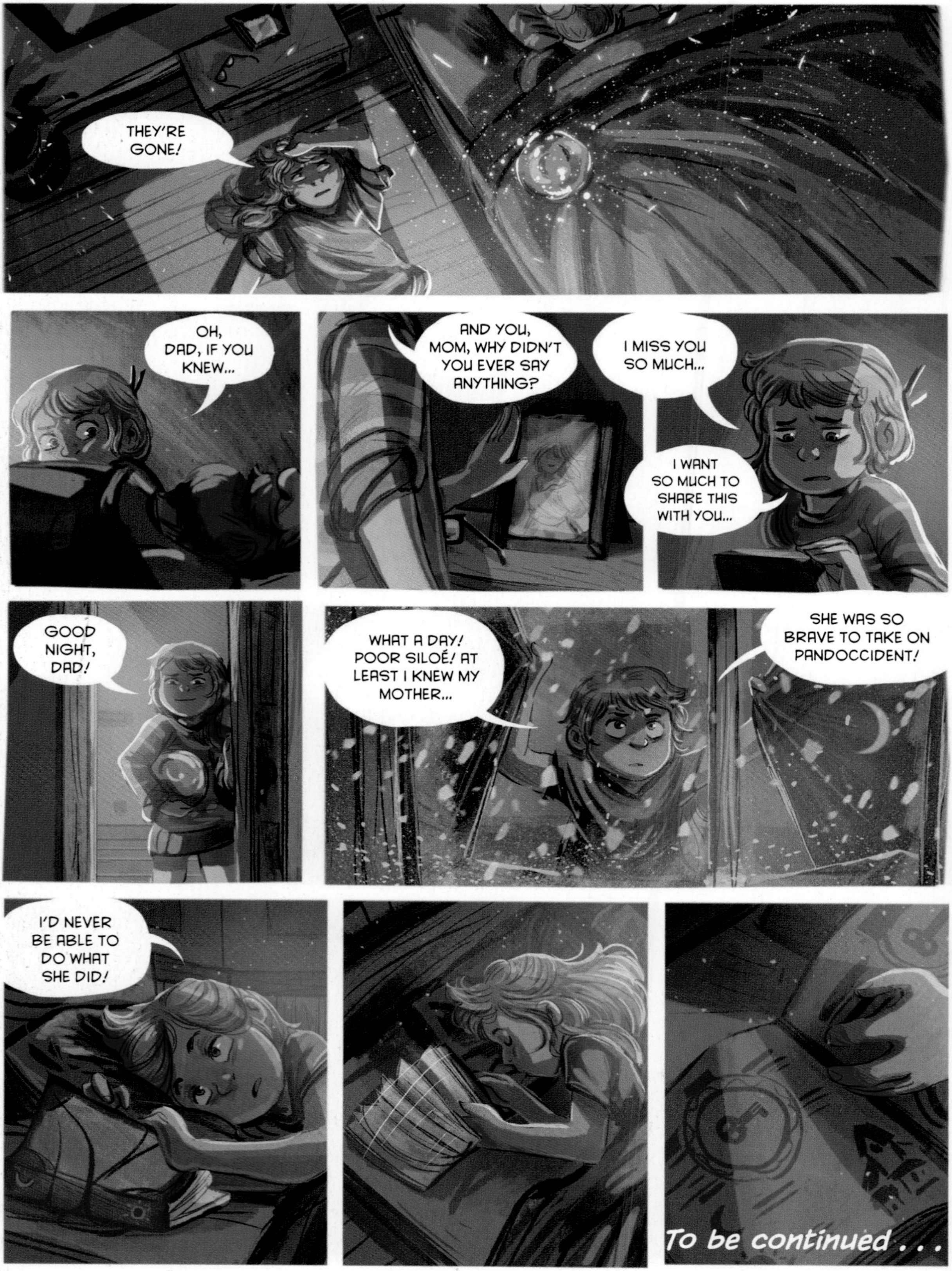
THEY'RE GONE!
OH, DAD, IF YOU KNEW...
AND YOU, MOM, WHY DIDN'T YOU EVER SAY ANYTHING?
I MISS YOU SO MUCH...
I WANT SO MUCH TO SHARE THIS WITH YOU...
GOOD NIGHT, DAD!
WHAT A DAY! POOR SILOÉ! AT LEAST I KNEW MY MOTHER...
SHE WAS SO BRAVE TO TAKE ON PANDOCCIDENT!
I'D NEVER BE ABLE TO DO WHAT SHE DID!
To be continued . . .

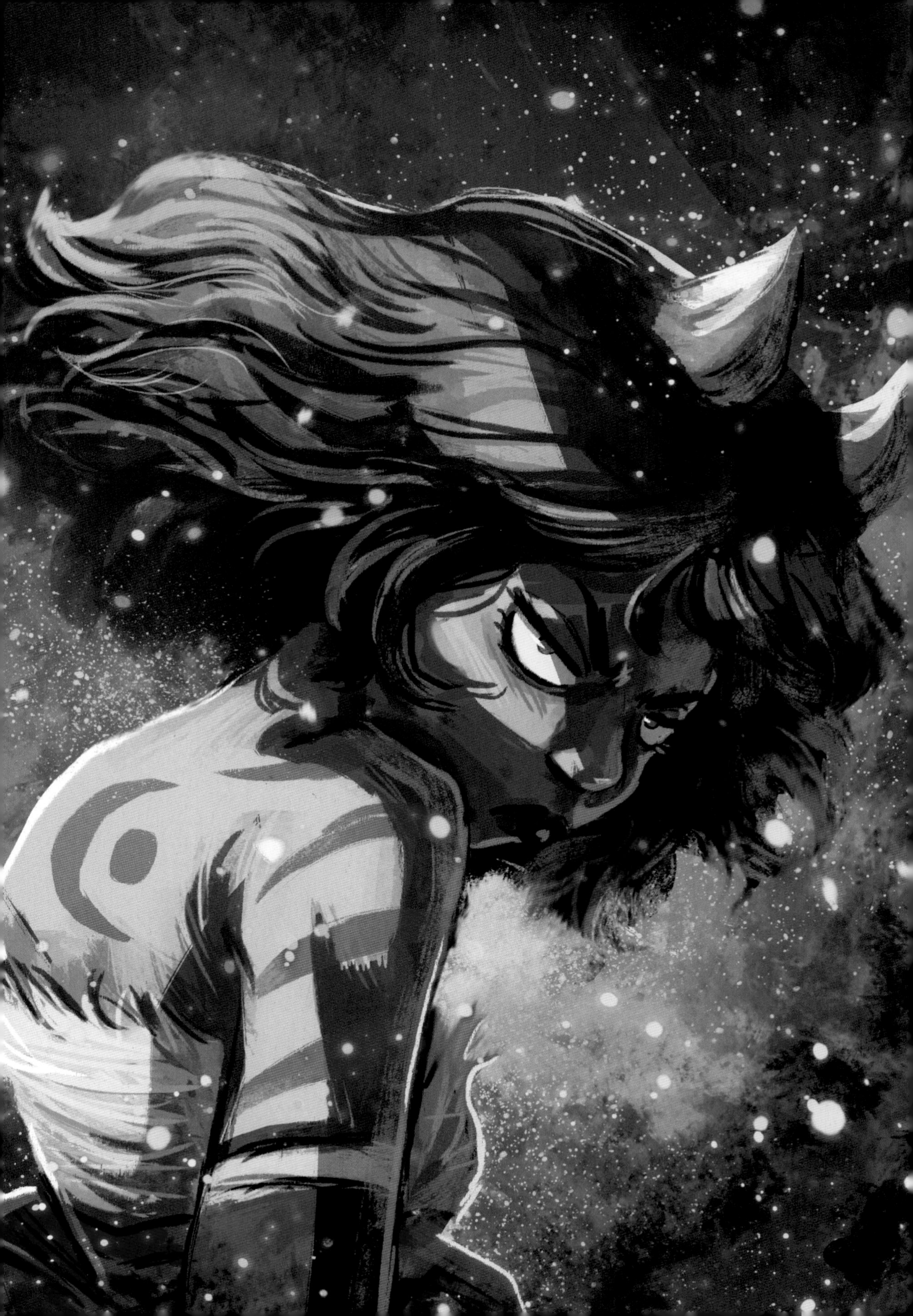

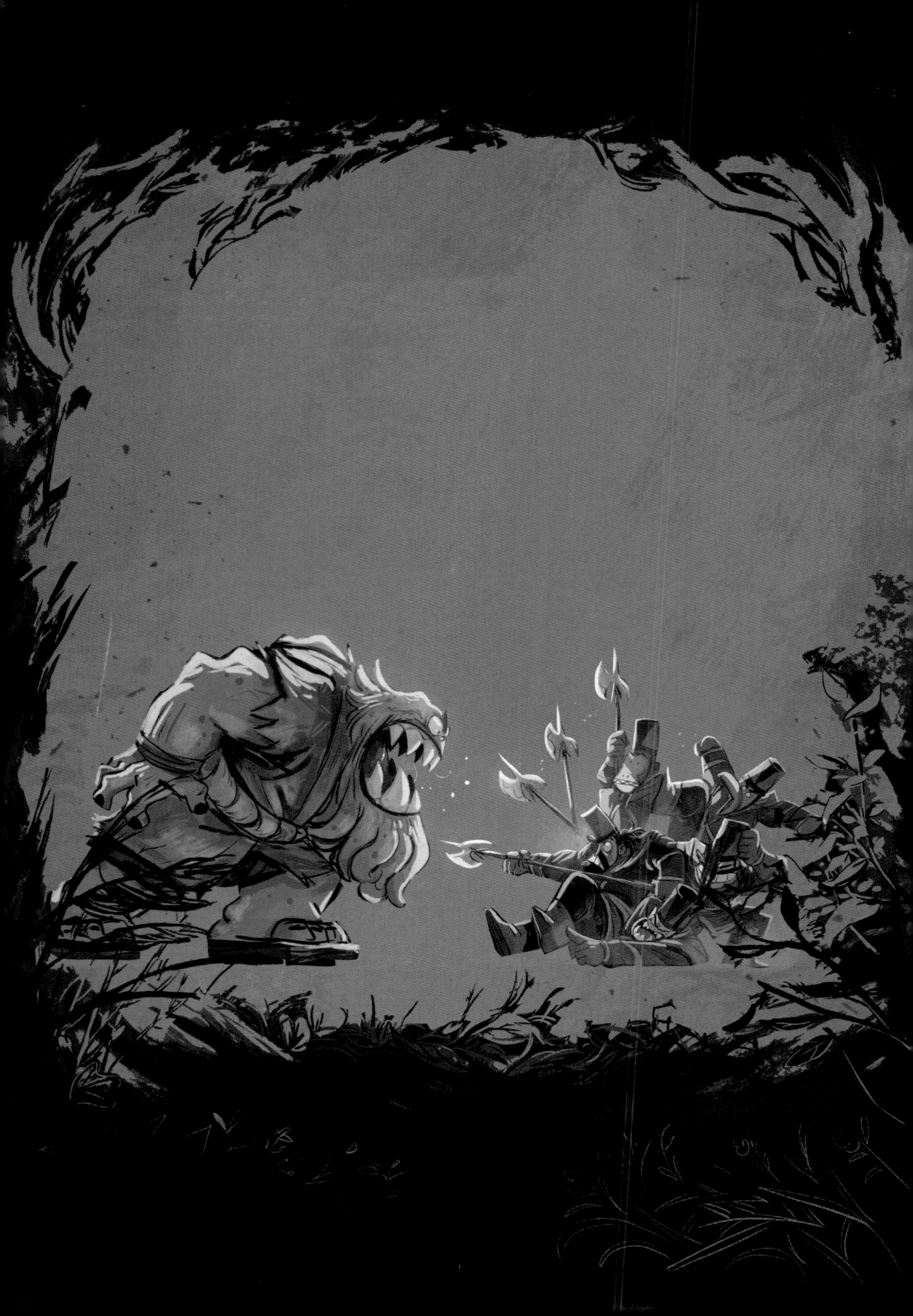

CHAPTER 4

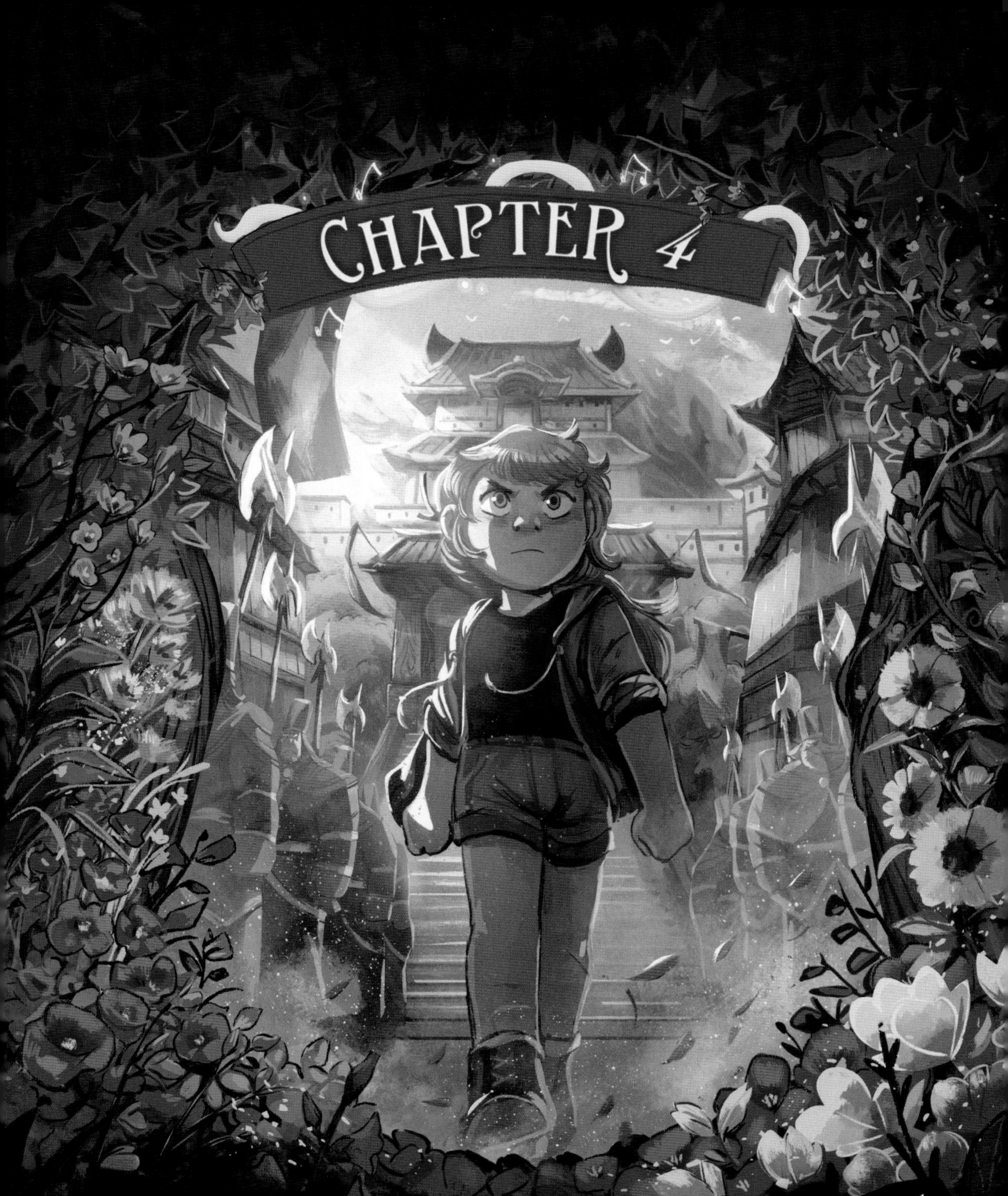

THE MYSTERIOUS DISAPPEARANCE

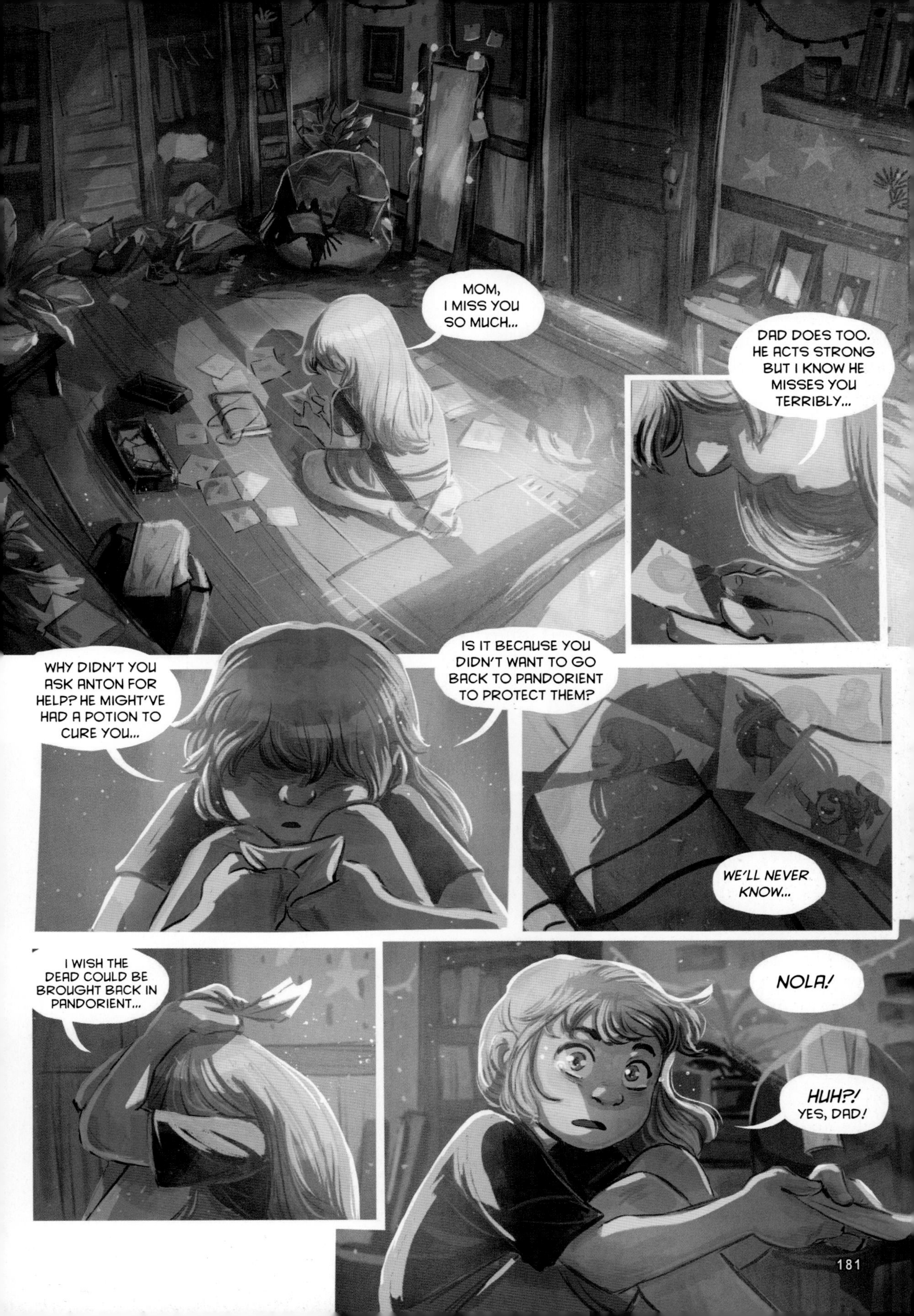

MOM, I MISS YOU SO MUCH...
DAD DOES TOO. HE ACTS STRONG BUT I KNOW HE MISSES YOU TERRIBLY...
WHY DIDN'T YOU ASK ANTON FOR HELP? HE MIGHT'VE HAD A POTION TO CURE YOU...
IS IT BECAUSE YOU DIDN'T WANT TO GO BACK TO PANDORIENT TO PROTECT THEM?
WE'LL NEVER KNOW...
I WISH THE DEAD COULD BE BROUGHT BACK IN PANDORIENT...
NOLA!
HUH?! YES, DAD!

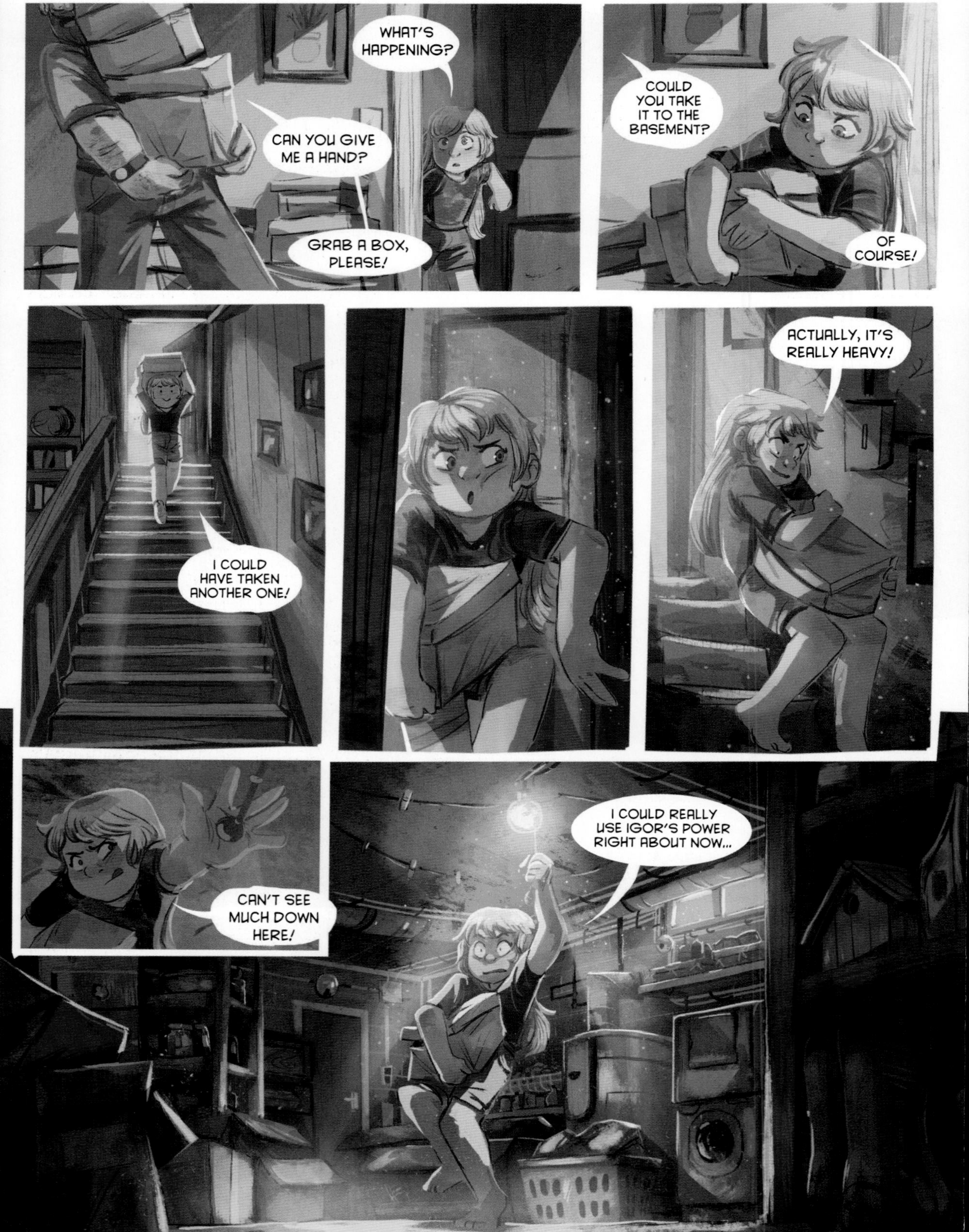
WHAT'S HAPPENING?
CAN YOU GIVE ME A HAND?
GRAB A BOX, PLEASE!
COULD YOU TAKE IT TO THE BASEMENT?
OF COURSE!
I COULD HAVE TAKEN ANOTHER ONE!
ACTUALLY, IT'S REALLY HEAVY!
CAN'T SEE MUCH DOWN HERE!
I COULD REALLY USE IGOR'S POWER RIGHT ABOUT NOW...

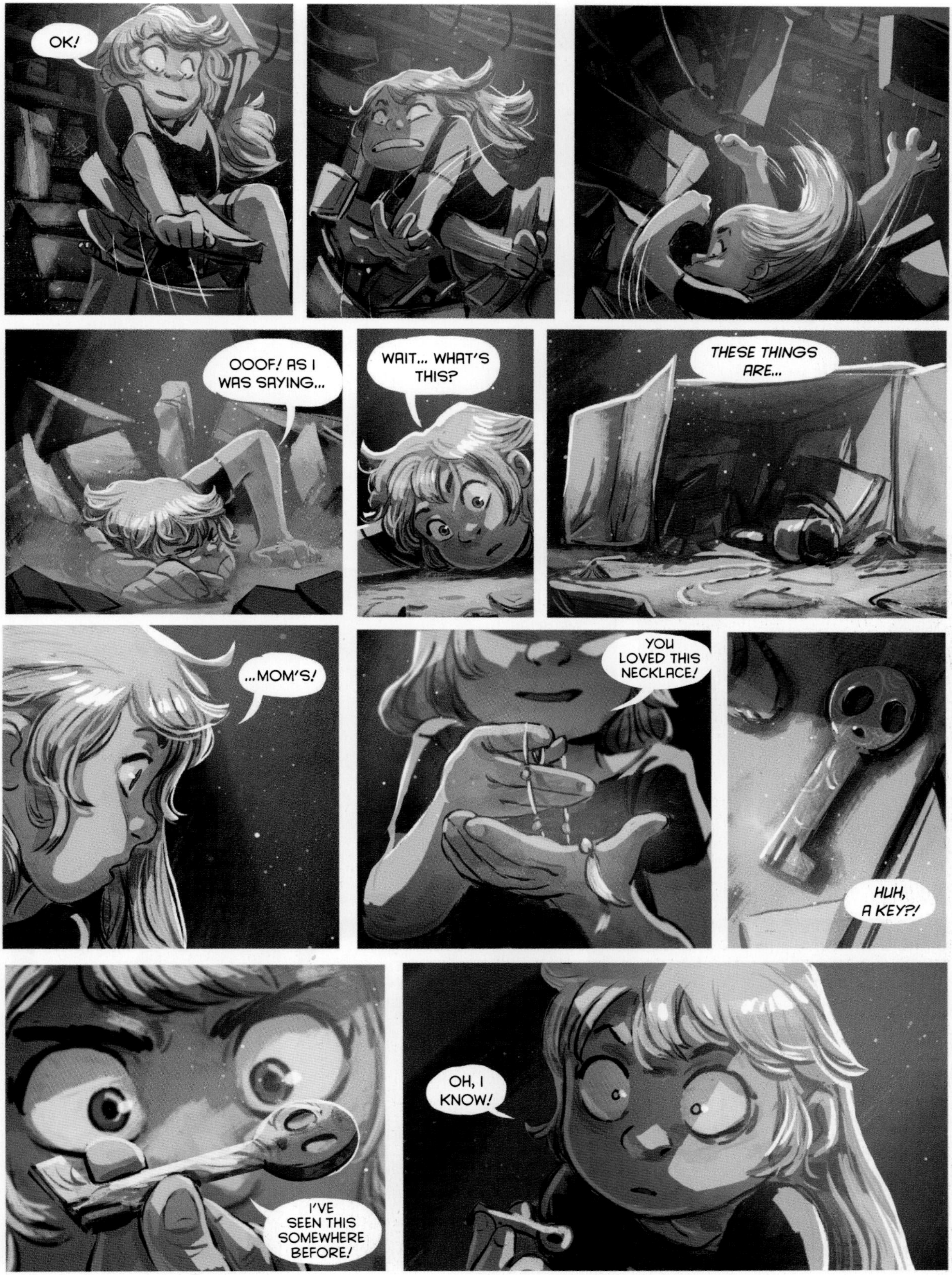
OK!
OOOF! AS I WAS SAYING...
WAIT... WHAT'S THIS?
THESE THINGS ARE...
...MOM'S!
YOU LOVED THIS NECKLACE!
HUH, A KEY?!
I'VE SEEN THIS SOMEWHERE BEFORE!
OH, I KNOW!

I'M PRETTY SURE IT WAS...

HERE! IN MOM'S BOOK!

BINGO!

LOOKS LIKE THE DRAWING, BUT WHO KNOWS WHAT IT OPENS?

WELL LITTLE KEY, IF YOU'RE IN MOM'S THINGS...

...AND IN THIS BOOK, IT MUST MEAN YOU'RE IMPORTANT!

WHAT'S YOUR SECRET?

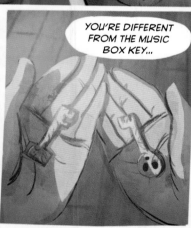

YOU'RE DIFFERENT FROM THE MUSIC BOX KEY...

I'LL TRY EVERYTHING...

...AND I'LL EVENTUALLY FIND OUT.

OR NOT!

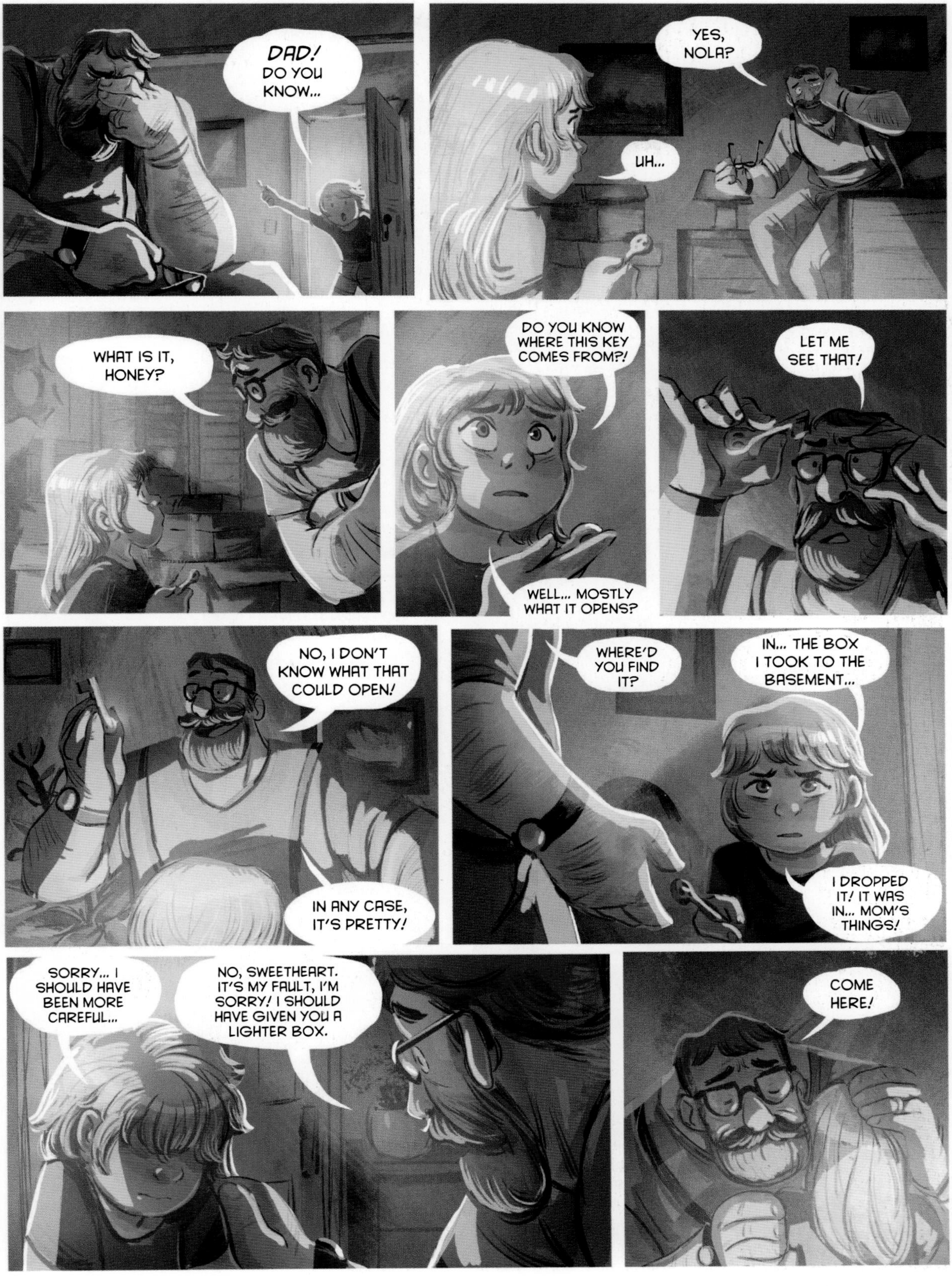
DAD! DO YOU KNOW...
YES, NOLA?
UH...
WHAT IS IT, HONEY?
DO YOU KNOW WHERE THIS KEY COMES FROM?!
WELL... MOSTLY WHAT IT OPENS?
LET ME SEE THAT!
NO, I DON'T KNOW WHAT THAT COULD OPEN!
IN ANY CASE, IT'S PRETTY!
WHERE'D YOU FIND IT?
IN... THE BOX I TOOK TO THE BASEMENT...
I DROPPED IT! IT WAS IN... MOM'S THINGS!
SORRY... I SHOULD HAVE BEEN MORE CAREFUL...
NO, SWEETHEART. IT'S MY FAULT, I'M SORRY! I SHOULD HAVE GIVEN YOU A LIGHTER BOX.
COME HERE!

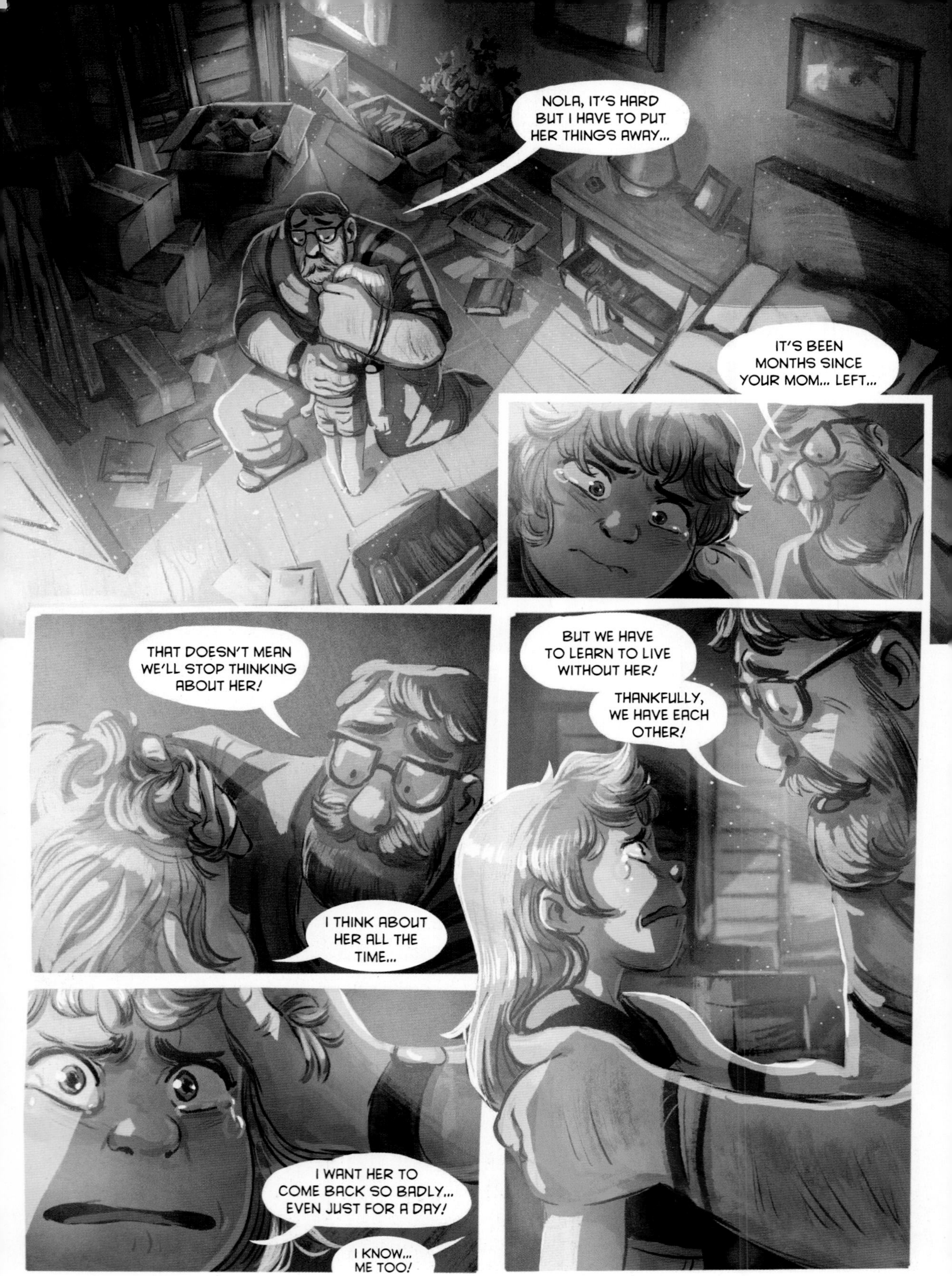
NOLA, IT'S HARD BUT I HAVE TO PUT HER THINGS AWAY...
IT'S BEEN MONTHS SINCE YOUR MOM... LEFT...
THAT DOESN'T MEAN WE'LL STOP THINKING ABOUT HER!
I THINK ABOUT HER ALL THE TIME...
BUT WE HAVE TO LEARN TO LIVE WITHOUT HER!
THANKFULLY, WE HAVE EACH OTHER!
I WANT HER TO COME BACK SO BADLY... EVEN JUST FOR A DAY!
I KNOW... ME TOO!

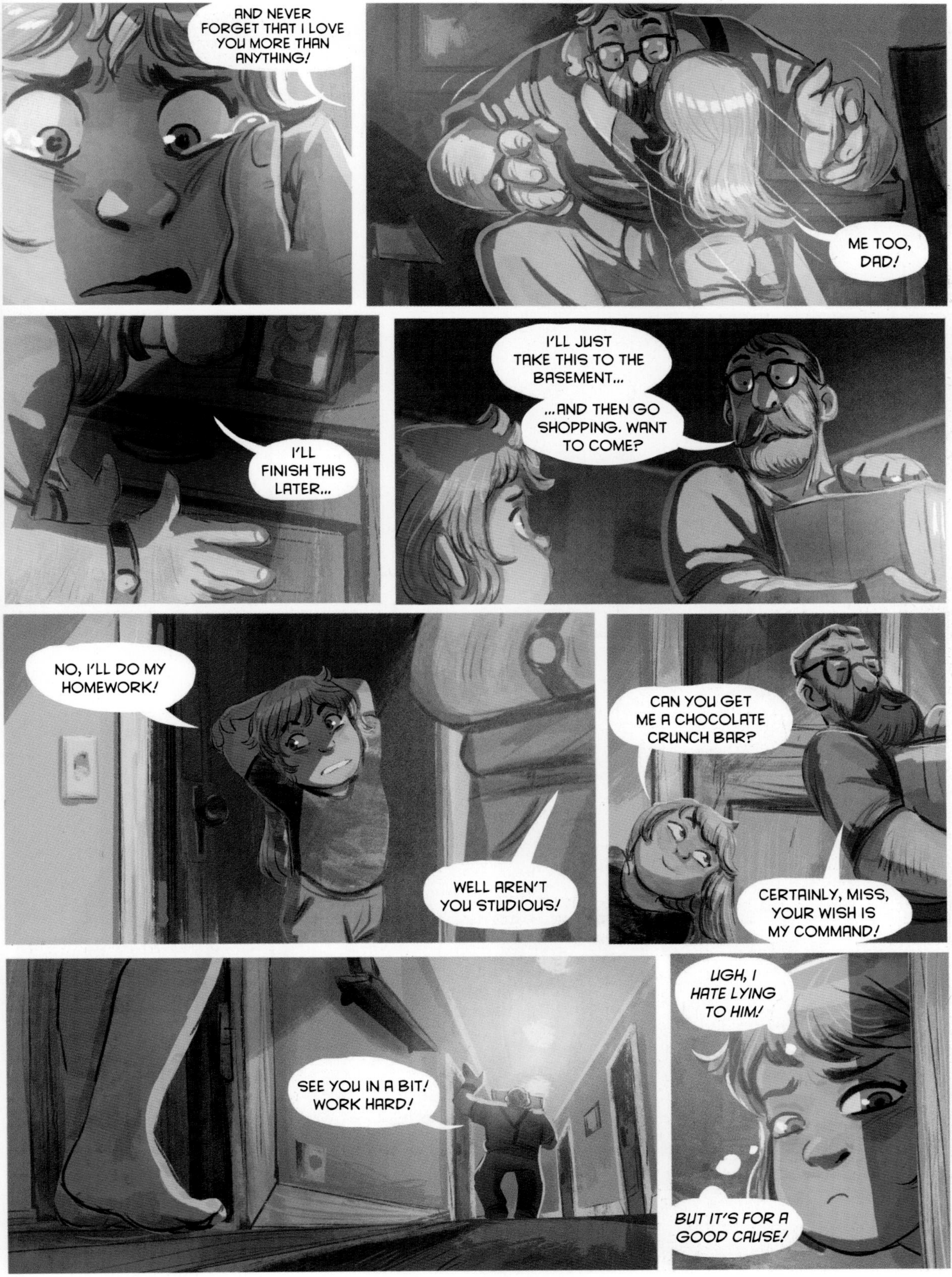
AND NEVER FORGET THAT I LOVE YOU MORE THAN ANYTHING!
ME TOO, DAD!
I'LL FINISH THIS LATER...
I'LL JUST TAKE THIS TO THE BASEMENT...
...AND THEN GO SHOPPING. WANT TO COME?
NO, I'LL DO MY HOMEWORK!
WELL AREN'T YOU STUDIOUS!
CAN YOU GET ME A CHOCOLATE CRUNCH BAR?
CERTAINLY, MISS, YOUR WISH IS MY COMMAND!
SEE YOU IN A BIT! WORK HARD!
UGH, I HATE LYING TO HIM!
BUT IT'S FOR A GOOD CAUSE!

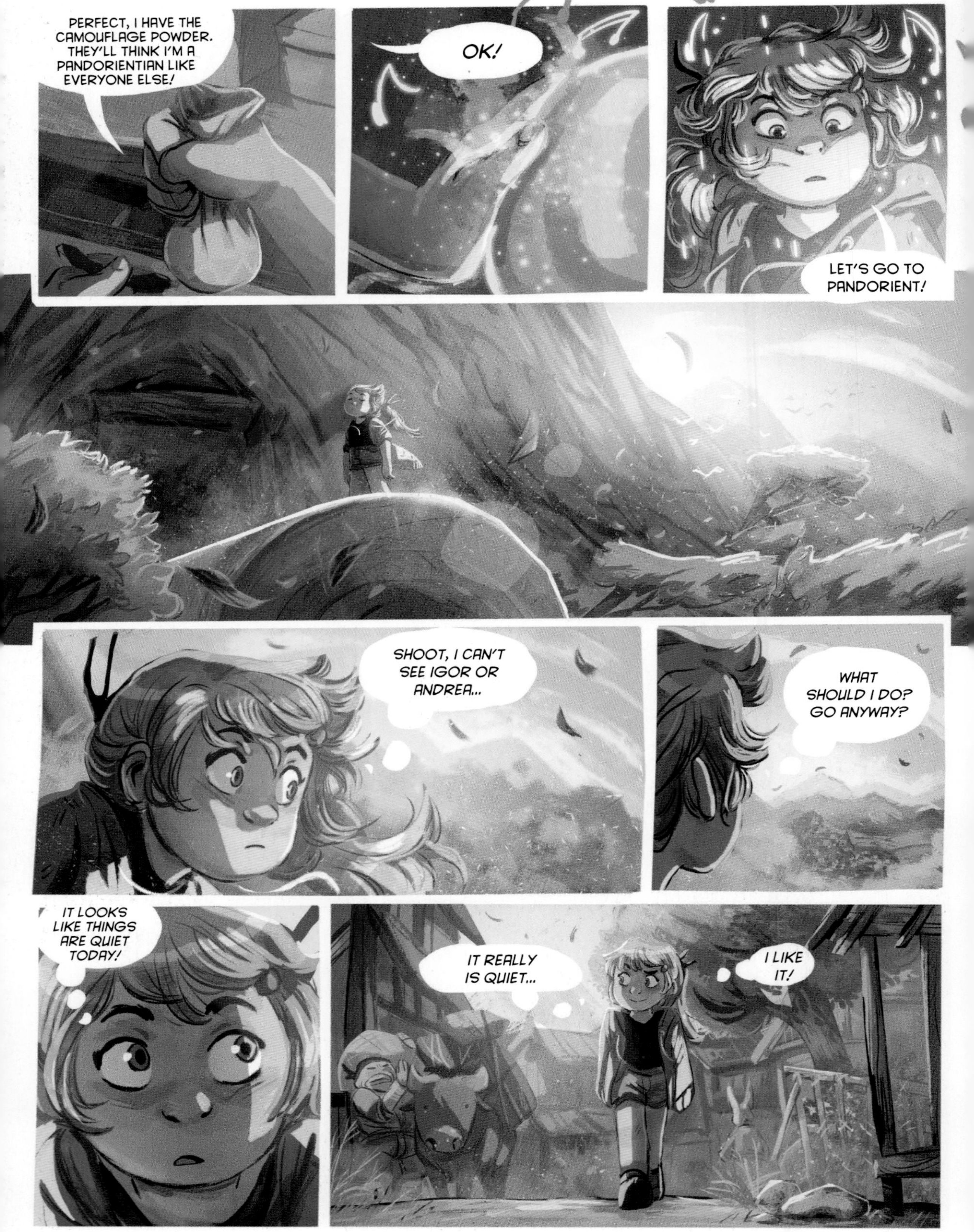
PERFECT, I HAVE THE CAMOUFLAGE POWDER. THEY'LL THINK I'M A PANDORIENTIAN LIKE EVERYONE ELSE!
OK!
LET'S GO TO PANDORIENT!
SHOOT, I CAN'T SEE IGOR OR ANDREA...
WHAT SHOULD I DO? GO ANYWAY?
IT LOOKS LIKE THINGS ARE QUIET TODAY!
IT REALLY IS QUIET...
I LIKE IT!

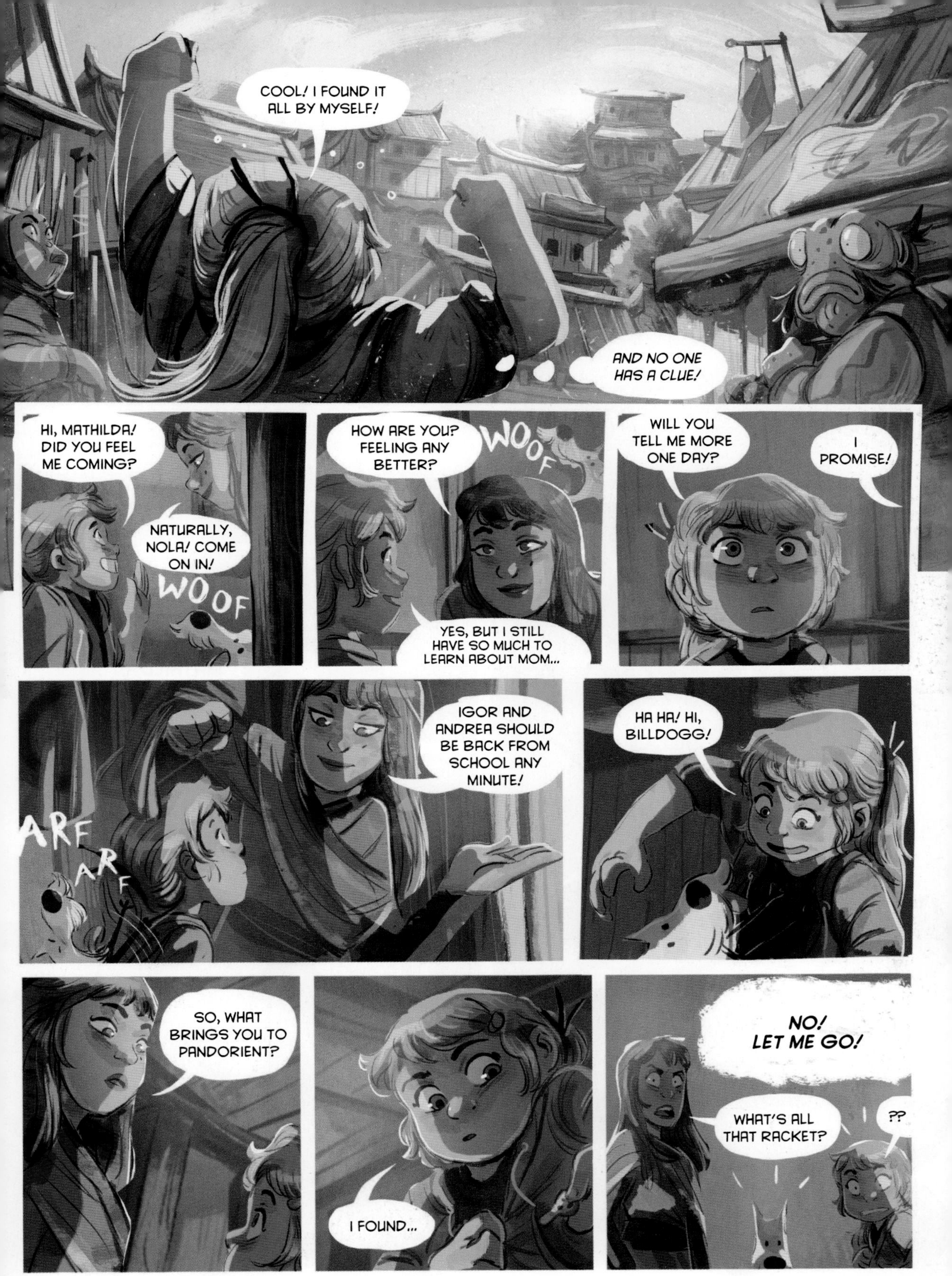
COOL! I FOUND IT ALL BY MYSELF!
AND NO ONE HAS A CLUE!
HI, MATHILDA! DID YOU FEEL ME COMING?
NATURALLY, NOLA! COME ON IN!
WOOF
HOW ARE YOU? FEELING ANY BETTER?
WOOF
YES, BUT I STILL HAVE SO MUCH TO LEARN ABOUT MOM...
WILL YOU TELL ME MORE ONE DAY?
I PROMISE!
IGOR AND ANDREA SHOULD BE BACK FROM SCHOOL ANY MINUTE!
ARF ARF
HA HA! HI, BILLDOGG!
SO, WHAT BRINGS YOU TO PANDORIENT?
I FOUND...
NO! LET ME GO!
WHAT'S ALL THAT RACKET?
??

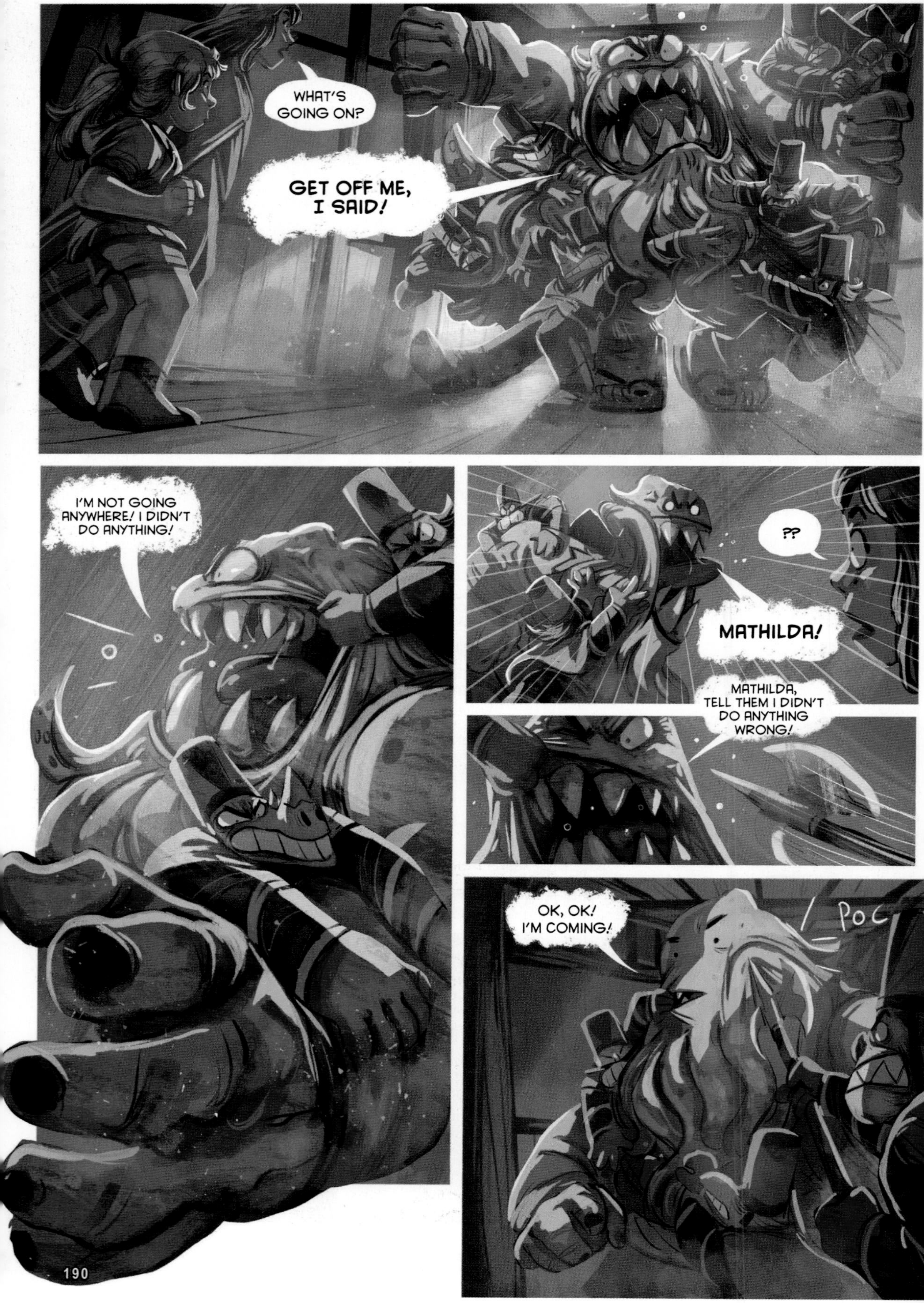

WHAT'S GOING ON?
GET OFF ME, I SAID!
I'M NOT GOING ANYWHERE! I DIDN'T DO ANYTHING!
??
MATHILDA!
MATHILDA, TELL THEM I DIDN'T DO ANYTHING WRONG!
OK, OK! I'M COMING!
POC

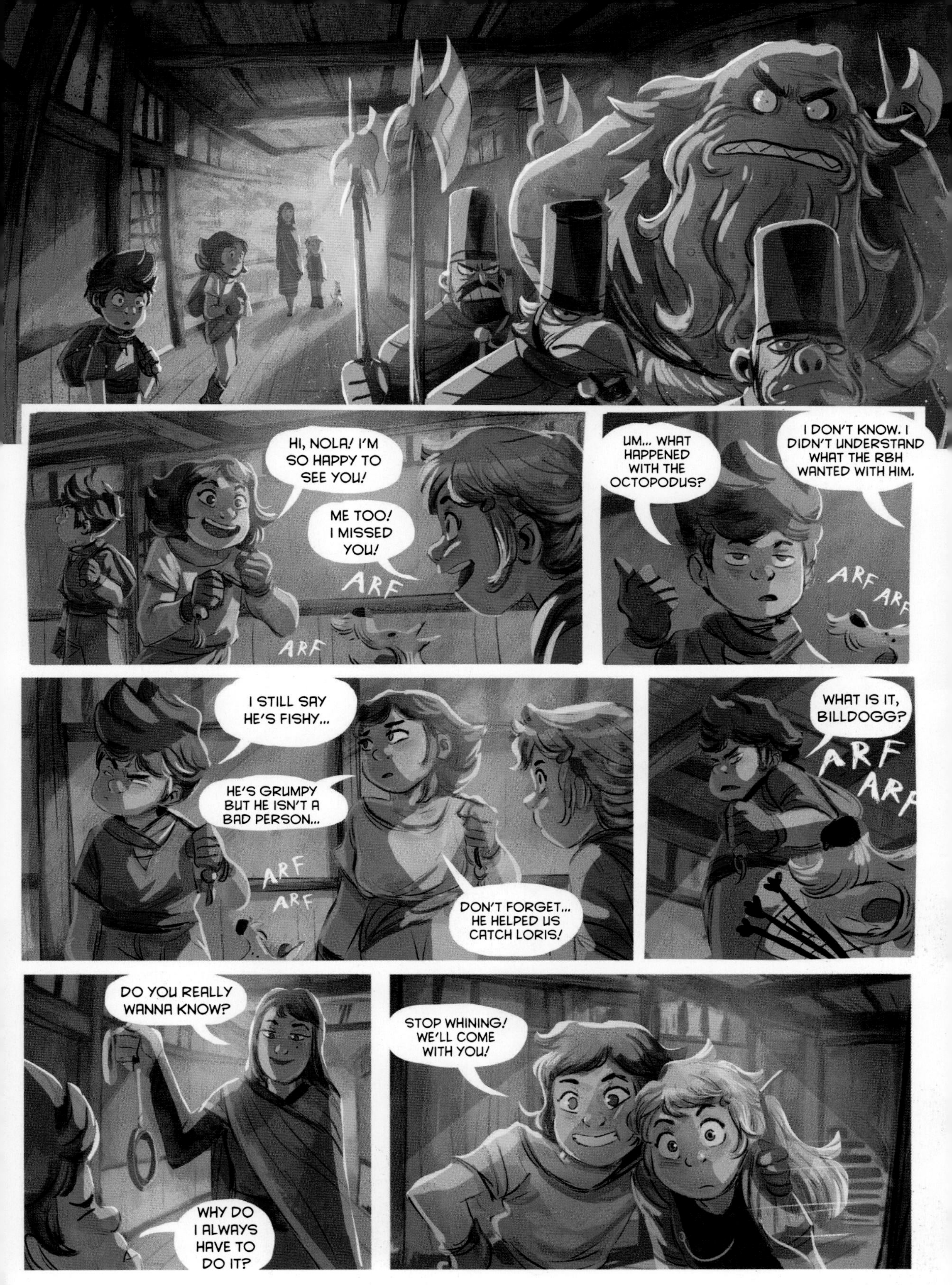
HI, NOLA! I'M SO HAPPY TO SEE YOU!
ME TOO! I MISSED YOU!
ARF
ARF
UM... WHAT HAPPENED WITH THE OCTOPODUS?
I DON'T KNOW. I DIDN'T UNDERSTAND WHAT THE RBH WANTED WITH HIM.
ARF ARF
I STILL SAY HE'S FISHY...
HE'S GRUMPY BUT HE ISN'T A BAD PERSON...
ARF ARF
DON'T FORGET... HE HELPED US CATCH LORIS!
WHAT IS IT, BILLDOGG?
ARF ARF
DO YOU REALLY WANNA KNOW?
WHY DO I ALWAYS HAVE TO DO IT?
STOP WHINING! WE'LL COME WITH YOU!

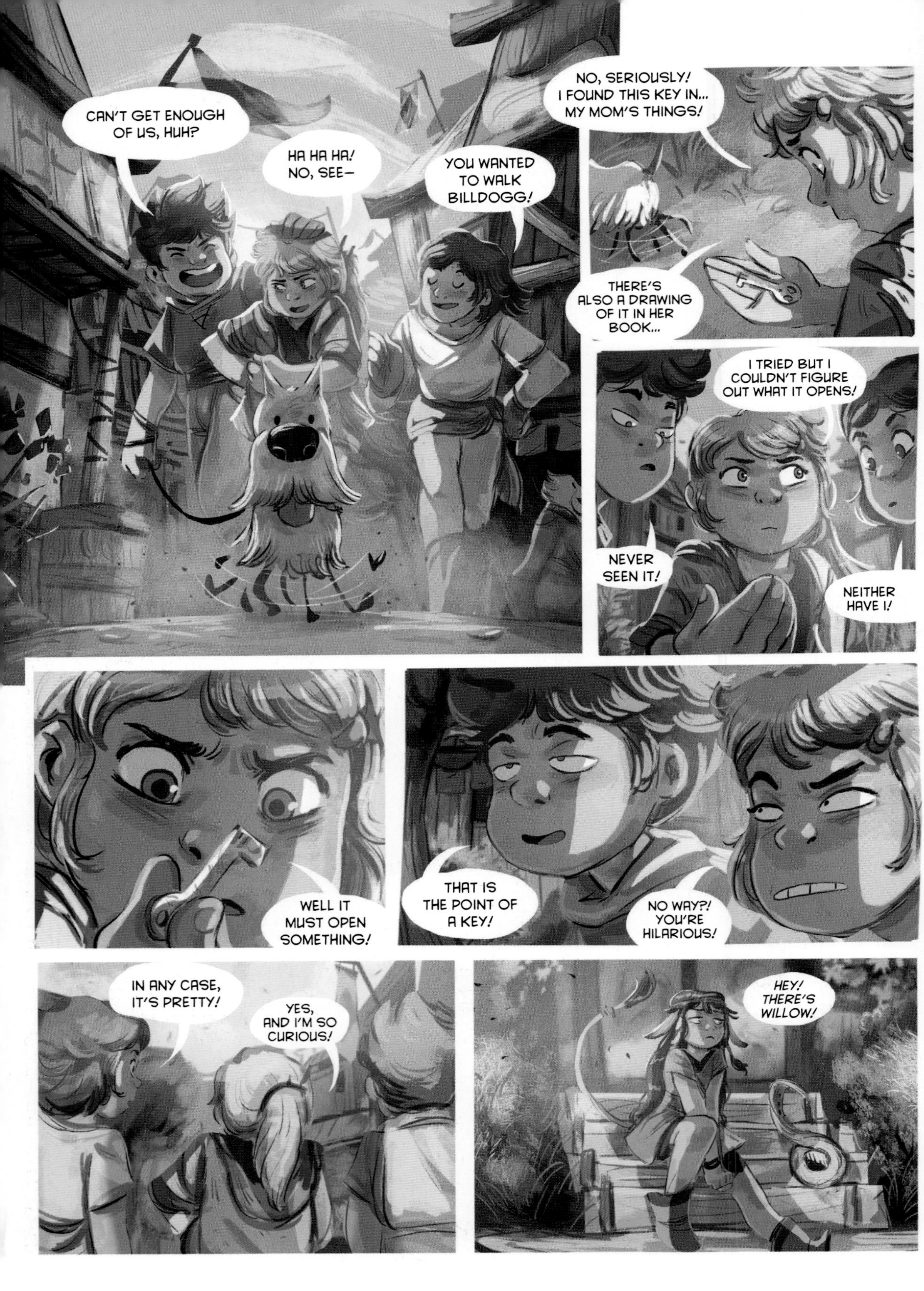
CAN'T GET ENOUGH OF US, HUH?
HA HA HA! NO, SEE—
YOU WANTED TO WALK BILLDOGG!
NO, SERIOUSLY! I FOUND THIS KEY IN... MY MOM'S THINGS!
THERE'S ALSO A DRAWING OF IT IN HER BOOK...
I TRIED BUT I COULDN'T FIGURE OUT WHAT IT OPENS!
NEVER SEEN IT!
NEITHER HAVE I!
WELL IT MUST OPEN SOMETHING!
THAT IS THE POINT OF A KEY!
NO WAY?! YOU'RE HILARIOUS!
IN ANY CASE, IT'S PRETTY!
YES, AND I'M SO CURIOUS!
HEY! THERE'S WILLOW!

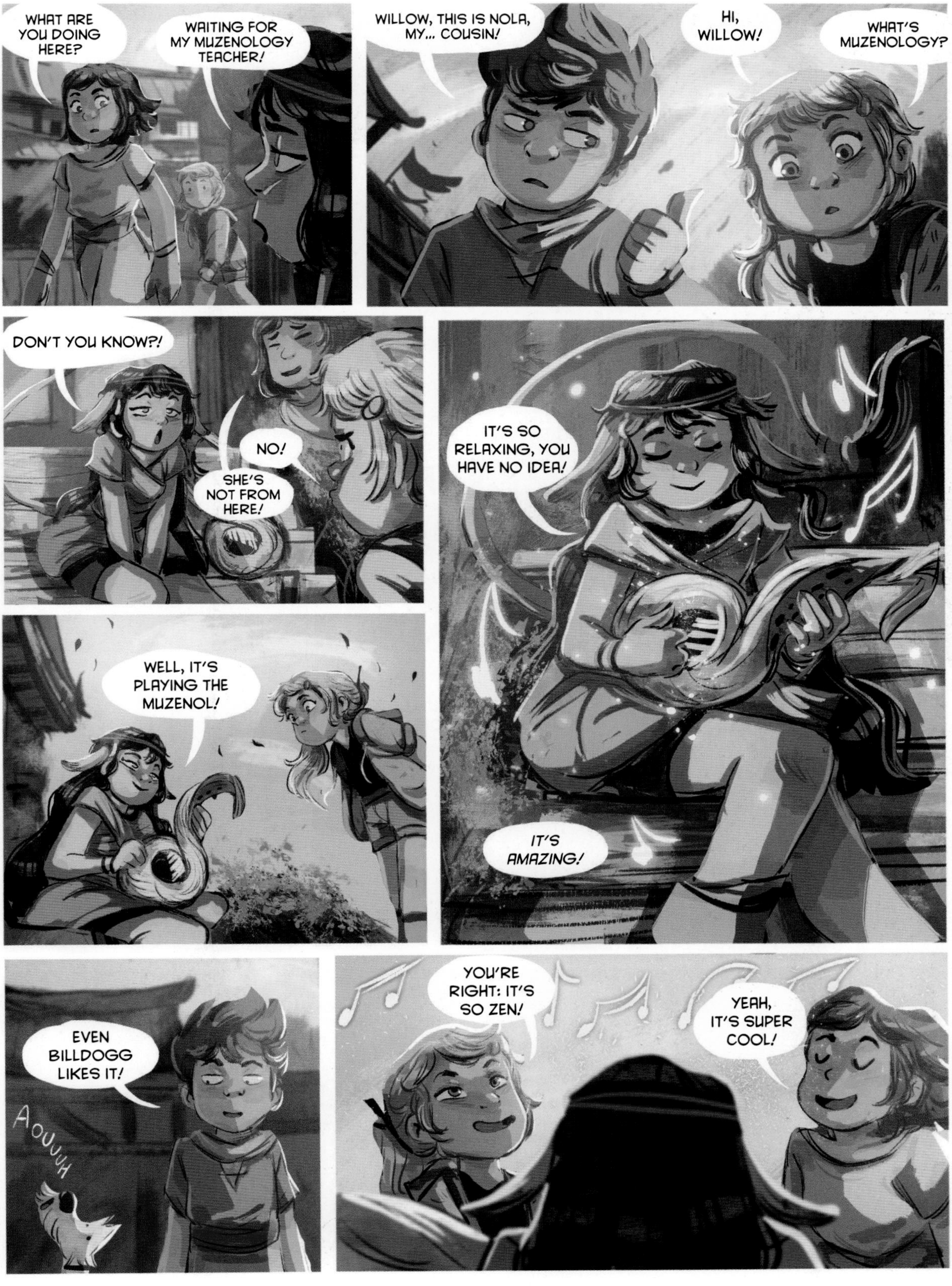
WHAT ARE YOU DOING HERE?
WAITING FOR MY MUZENOLOGY TEACHER!
WILLOW, THIS IS NOLA, MY... COUSIN!
HI, WILLOW!
WHAT'S MUZENOLOGY?
DON'T YOU KNOW?!
NO!
SHE'S NOT FROM HERE!
IT'S SO RELAXING, YOU HAVE NO IDEA!
IT'S AMAZING!
WELL, IT'S PLAYING THE MUZENOL!
EVEN BILLDOGG LIKES IT!
AOUUUH
YOU'RE RIGHT: IT'S SO ZEN!
YEAH, IT'S SUPER COOL!

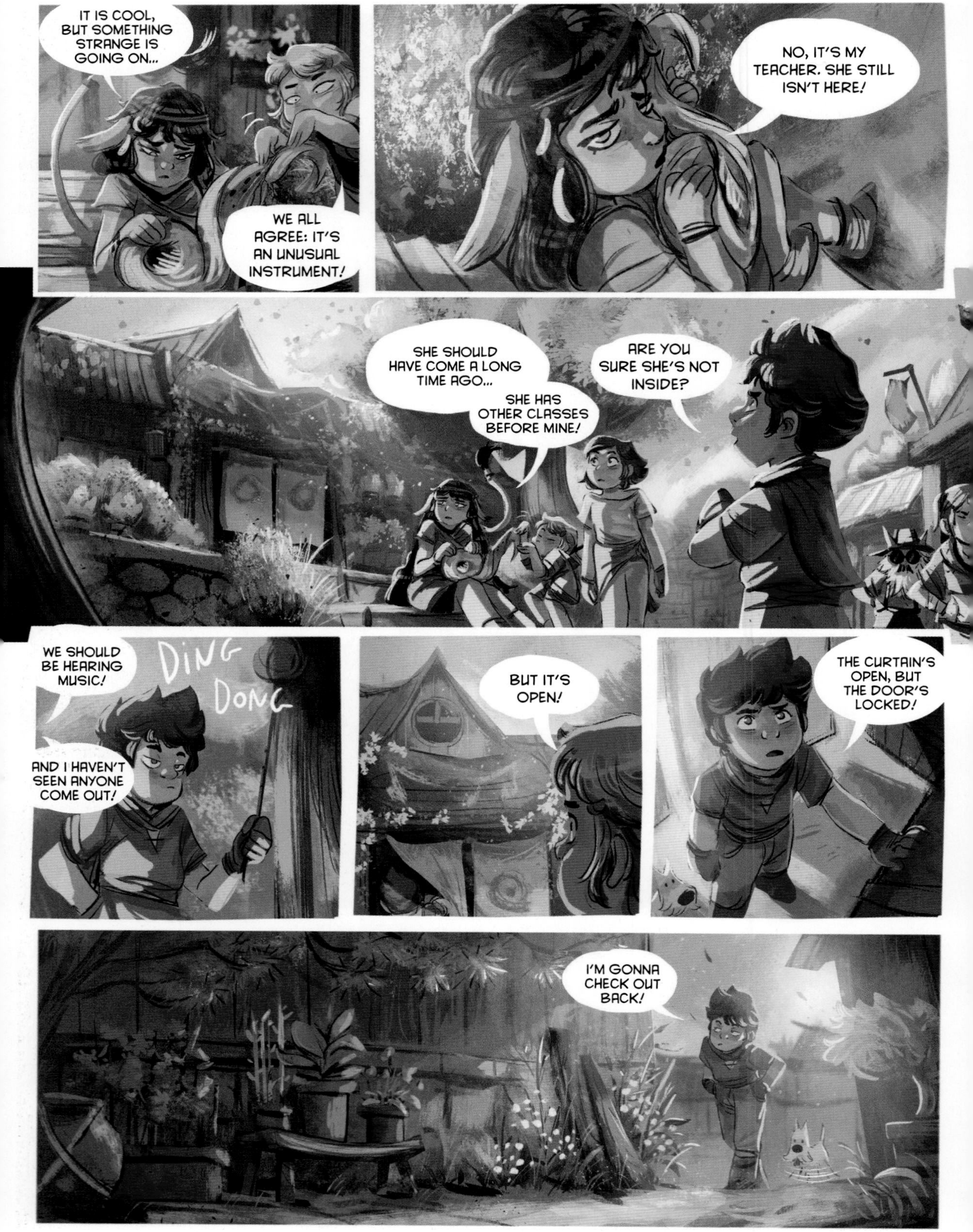
IT IS COOL, BUT SOMETHING STRANGE IS GOING ON...
WE ALL AGREE: IT'S AN UNUSUAL INSTRUMENT!
NO, IT'S MY TEACHER. SHE STILL ISN'T HERE!
SHE SHOULD HAVE COME A LONG TIME AGO...
SHE HAS OTHER CLASSES BEFORE MINE!
ARE YOU SURE SHE'S NOT INSIDE?
WE SHOULD BE HEARING MUSIC!
DING DONG
AND I HAVEN'T SEEN ANYONE COME OUT!
BUT IT'S OPEN!
THE CURTAIN'S OPEN, BUT THE DOOR'S LOCKED!
I'M GONNA CHECK OUT BACK!

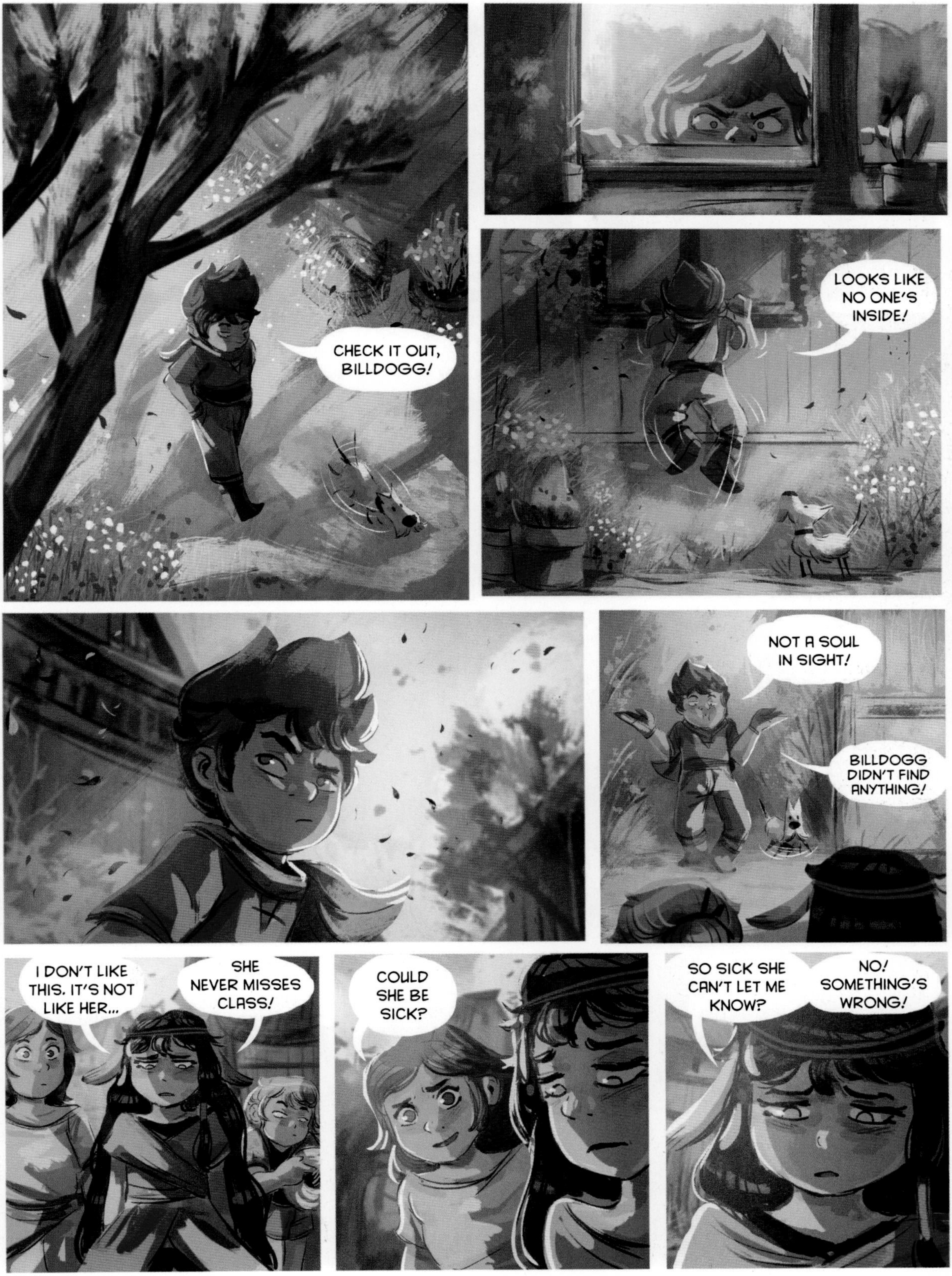
CHECK IT OUT, BILLDOGG!
LOOKS LIKE NO ONE'S INSIDE!
NOT A SOUL IN SIGHT!
BILLDOGG DIDN'T FIND ANYTHING!
I DON'T LIKE THIS. IT'S NOT LIKE HER...
SHE NEVER MISSES CLASS!
COULD SHE BE SICK?
SO SICK SHE CAN'T LET ME KNOW?
NO! SOMETHING'S WRONG!

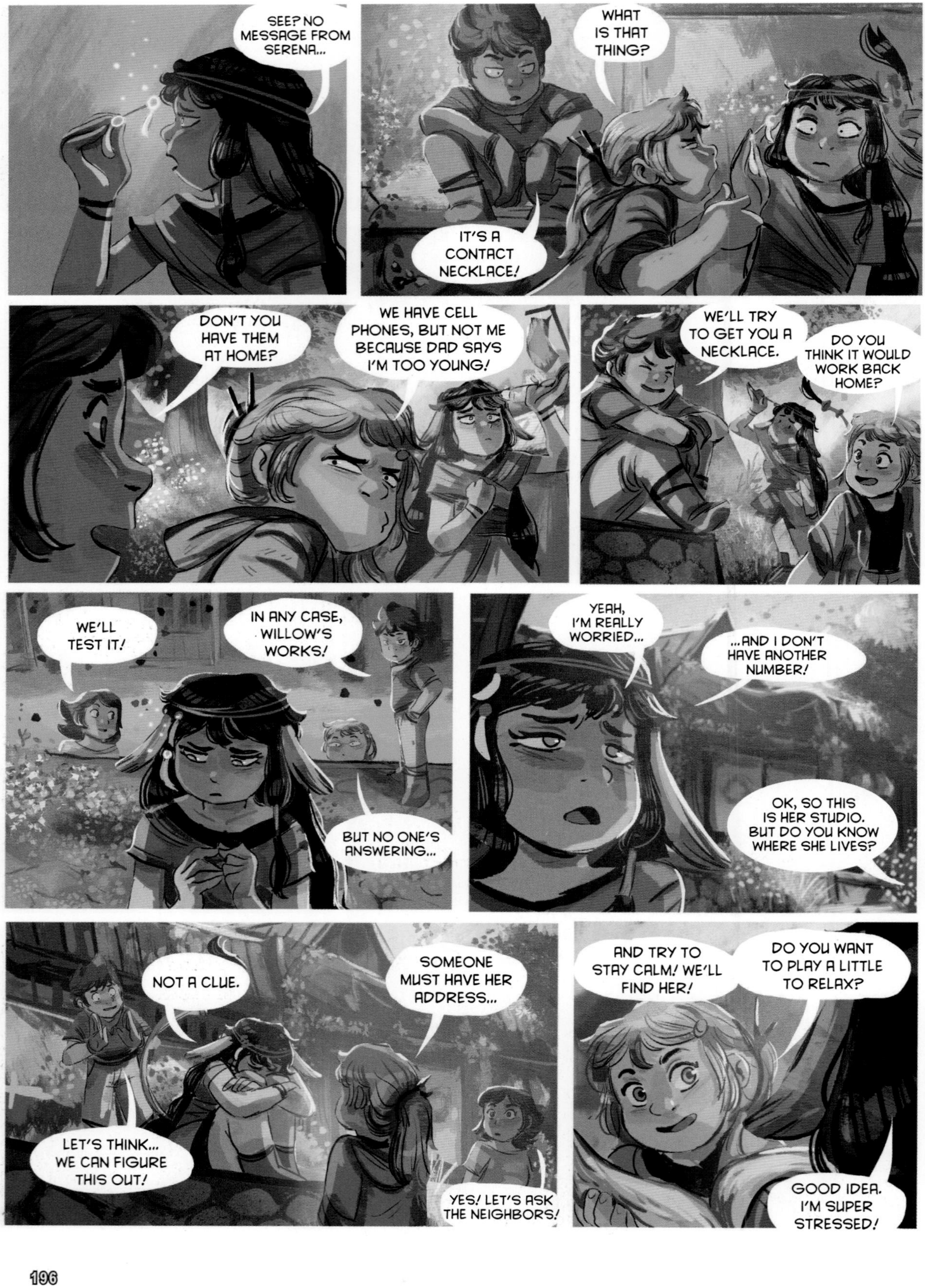
SEE? NO MESSAGE FROM SERENA...
WHAT IS THAT THING?
IT'S A CONTACT NECKLACE!
DON'T YOU HAVE THEM AT HOME?
WE HAVE CELL PHONES, BUT NOT ME BECAUSE DAD SAYS I'M TOO YOUNG!
WE'LL TRY TO GET YOU A NECKLACE.
DO YOU THINK IT WOULD WORK BACK HOME?
WE'LL TEST IT!
IN ANY CASE, WILLOW'S WORKS!
BUT NO ONE'S ANSWERING...
YEAH, I'M REALLY WORRIED...
...AND I DON'T HAVE ANOTHER NUMBER!
OK, SO THIS IS HER STUDIO. BUT DO YOU KNOW WHERE SHE LIVES?
NOT A CLUE.
SOMEONE MUST HAVE HER ADDRESS...
LET'S THINK... WE CAN FIGURE THIS OUT!
YES! LET'S ASK THE NEIGHBORS!
AND TRY TO STAY CALM! WE'LL FIND HER!
DO YOU WANT TO PLAY A LITTLE TO RELAX?
GOOD IDEA. I'M SUPER STRESSED!

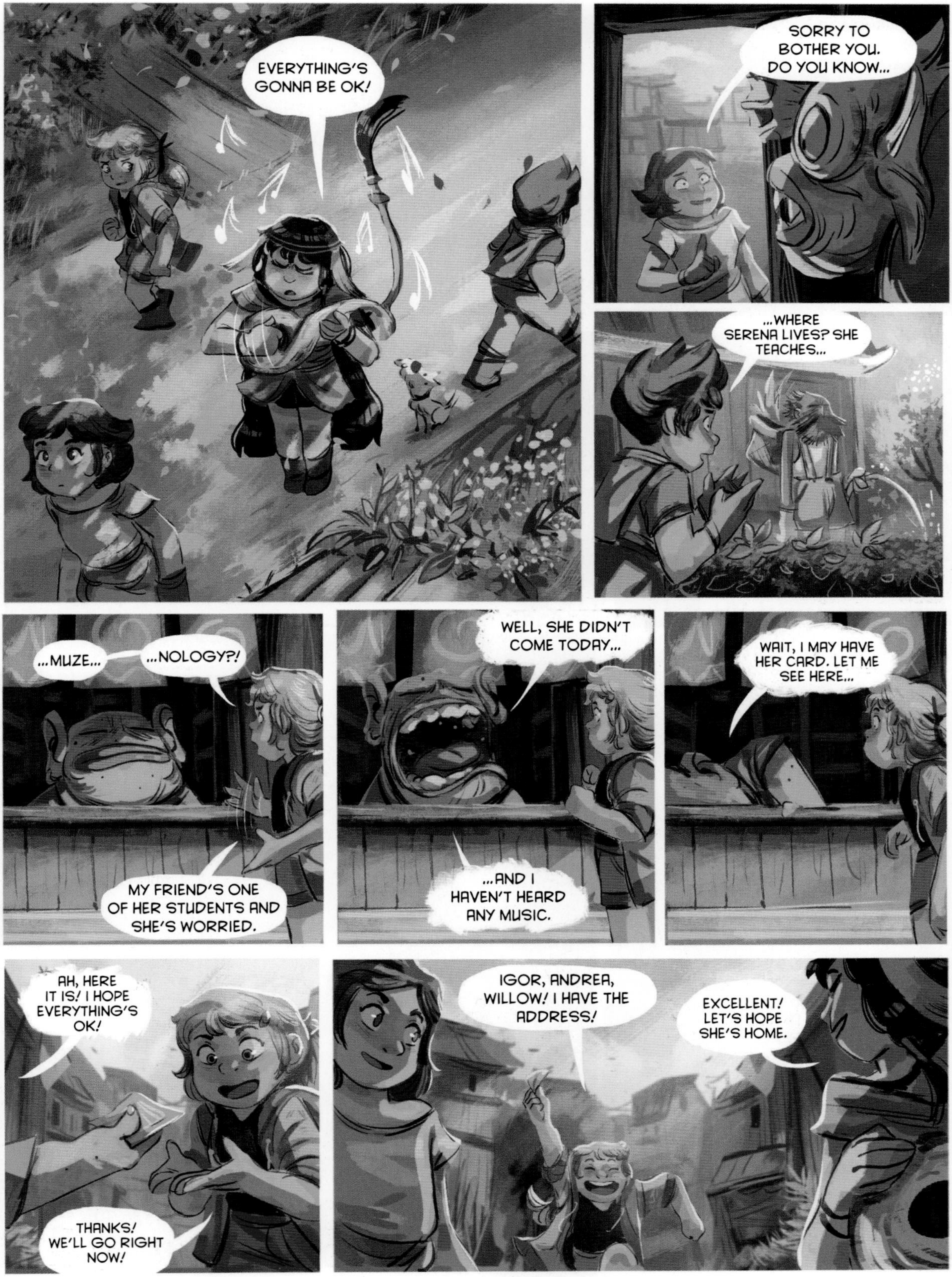
EVERYTHING'S GONNA BE OK!
SORRY TO BOTHER YOU. DO YOU KNOW...
...WHERE SERENA LIVES? SHE TEACHES...
...MUZE...
...NOLOGY?!
MY FRIEND'S ONE OF HER STUDENTS AND SHE'S WORRIED.
WELL, SHE DIDN'T COME TODAY...
...AND I HAVEN'T HEARD ANY MUSIC.
WAIT, I MAY HAVE HER CARD. LET ME SEE HERE...
AH, HERE IT IS! I HOPE EVERYTHING'S OK!
THANKS! WE'LL GO RIGHT NOW!
IGOR, ANDREA, WILLOW! I HAVE THE ADDRESS!
EXCELLENT! LET'S HOPE SHE'S HOME.

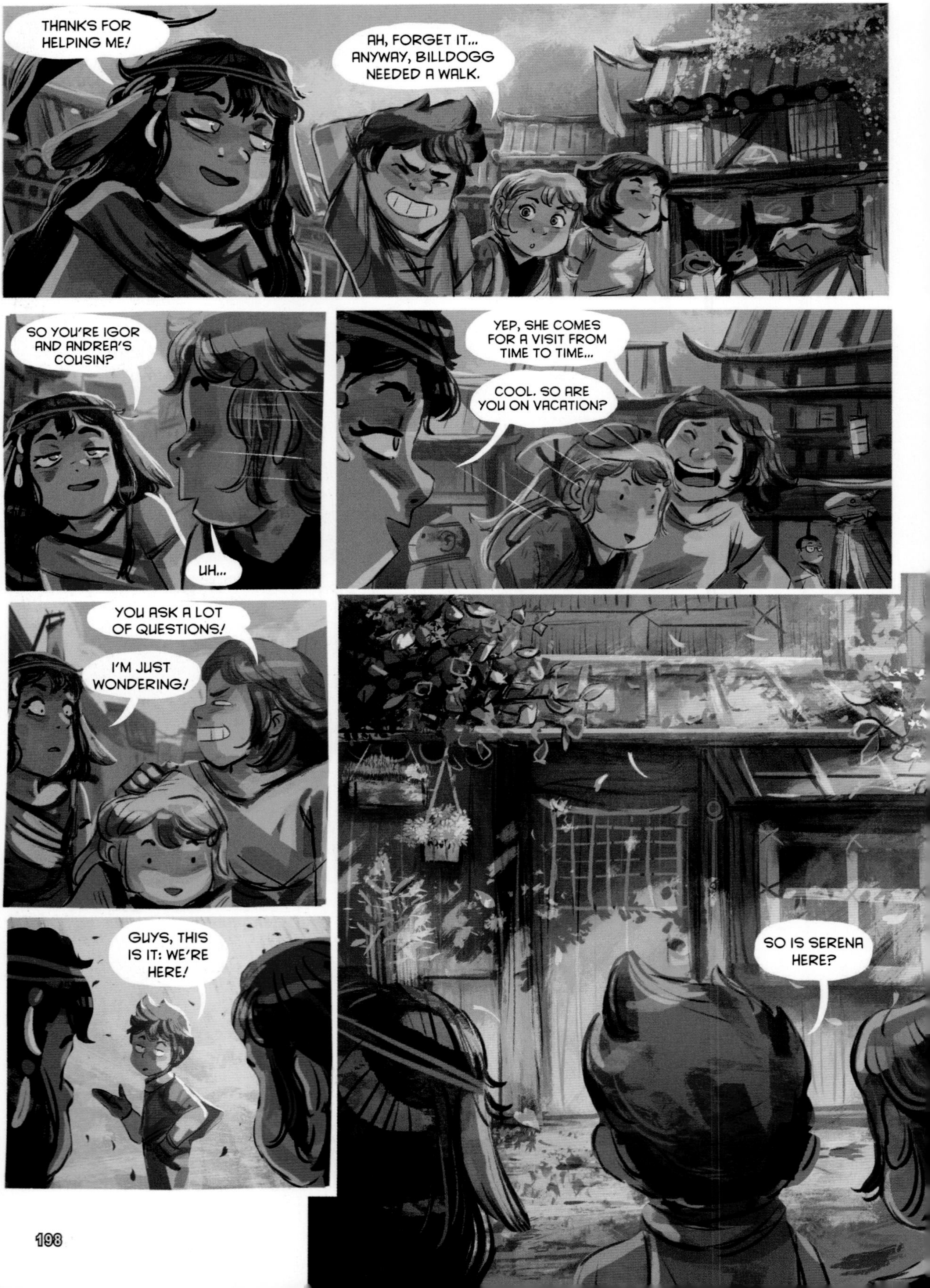

THANKS FOR HELPING ME!
AH, FORGET IT... ANYWAY, BILLDOGG NEEDED A WALK.
SO YOU'RE IGOR AND ANDREA'S COUSIN?
UH...
YEP, SHE COMES FOR A VISIT FROM TIME TO TIME...
COOL. SO ARE YOU ON VACATION?
YOU ASK A LOT OF QUESTIONS!
I'M JUST WONDERING!
GUYS, THIS IS IT: WE'RE HERE!
SO IS SERENA HERE?

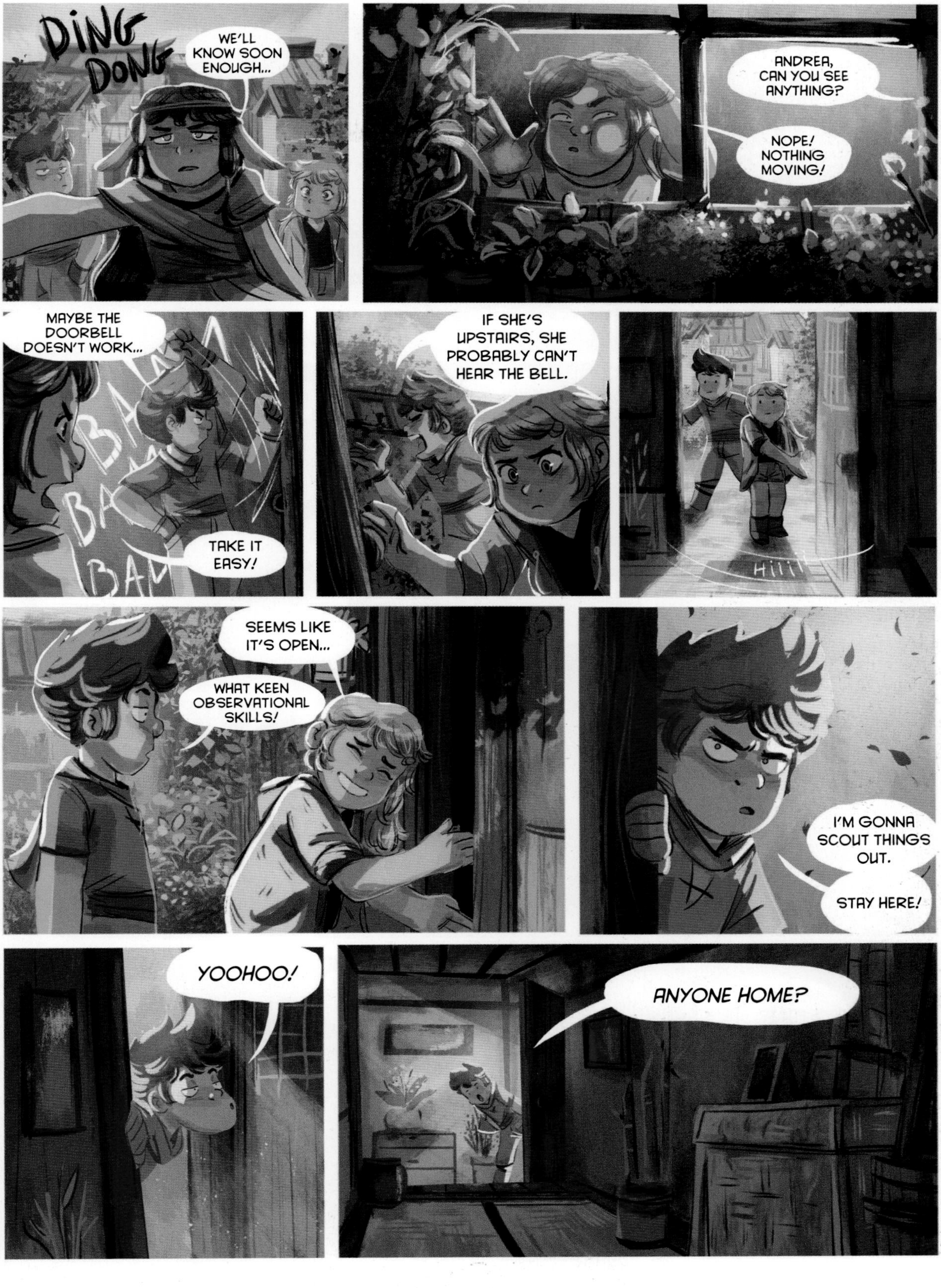
DING DONG
WE'LL KNOW SOON ENOUGH...
ANDREA, CAN YOU SEE ANYTHING?
NOPE! NOTHING MOVING!
MAYBE THE DOORBELL DOESN'T WORK...
BAM BAM BAM BAM
TAKE IT EASY!
IF SHE'S UPSTAIRS, SHE PROBABLY CAN'T HEAR THE BELL.
Hiiii
SEEMS LIKE IT'S OPEN...
WHAT KEEN OBSERVATIONAL SKILLS!
I'M GONNA SCOUT THINGS OUT.
STAY HERE!
YOOHOO!
ANYONE HOME?

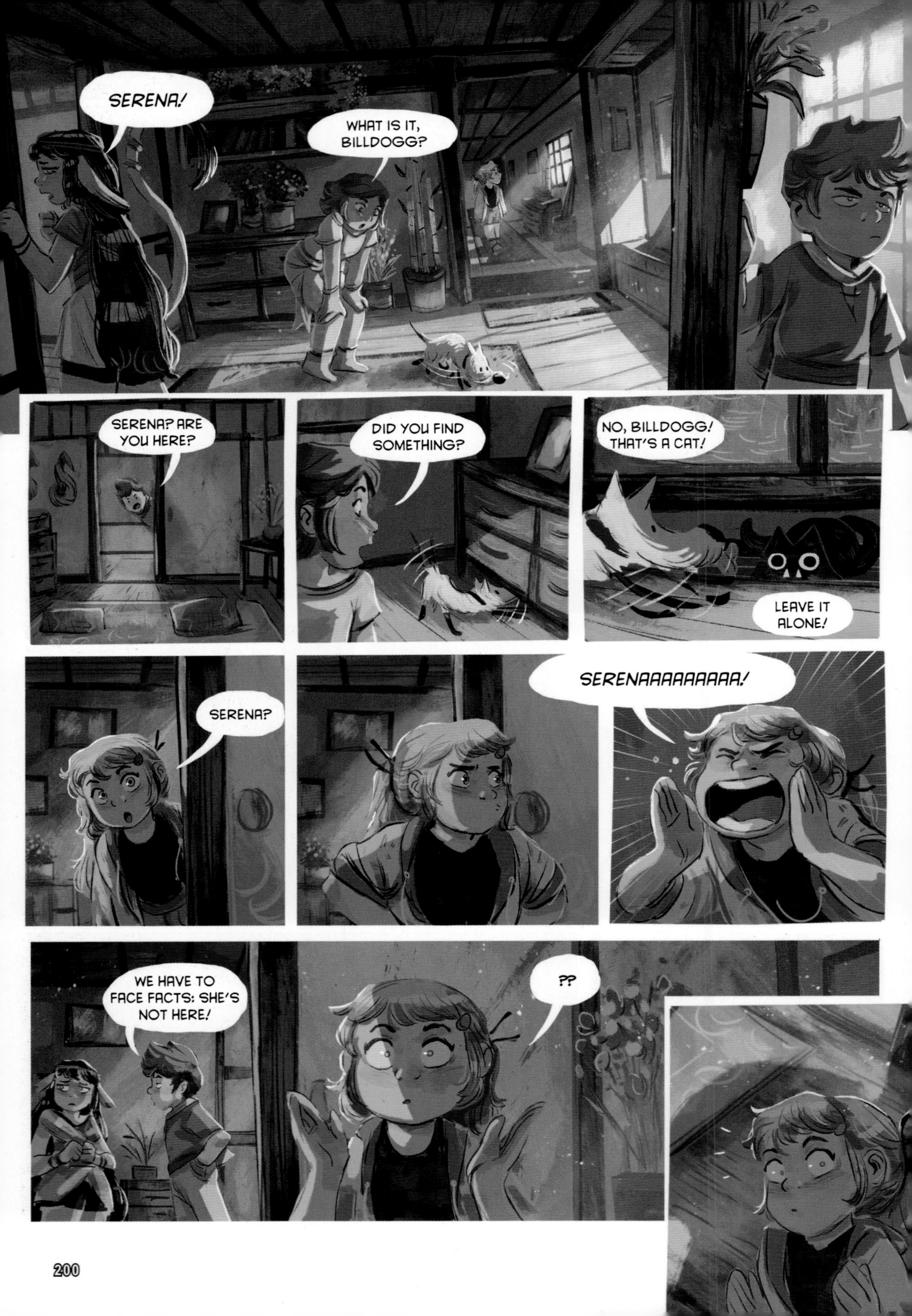
SERENA!
WHAT IS IT, BILLDOGG?
SERENA? ARE YOU HERE?
DID YOU FIND SOMETHING?
NO, BILLDOGG! THAT'S A CAT!
LEAVE IT ALONE!
SERENA?
SERENAAAAAAAAA!
WE HAVE TO FACE FACTS: SHE'S NOT HERE!
??

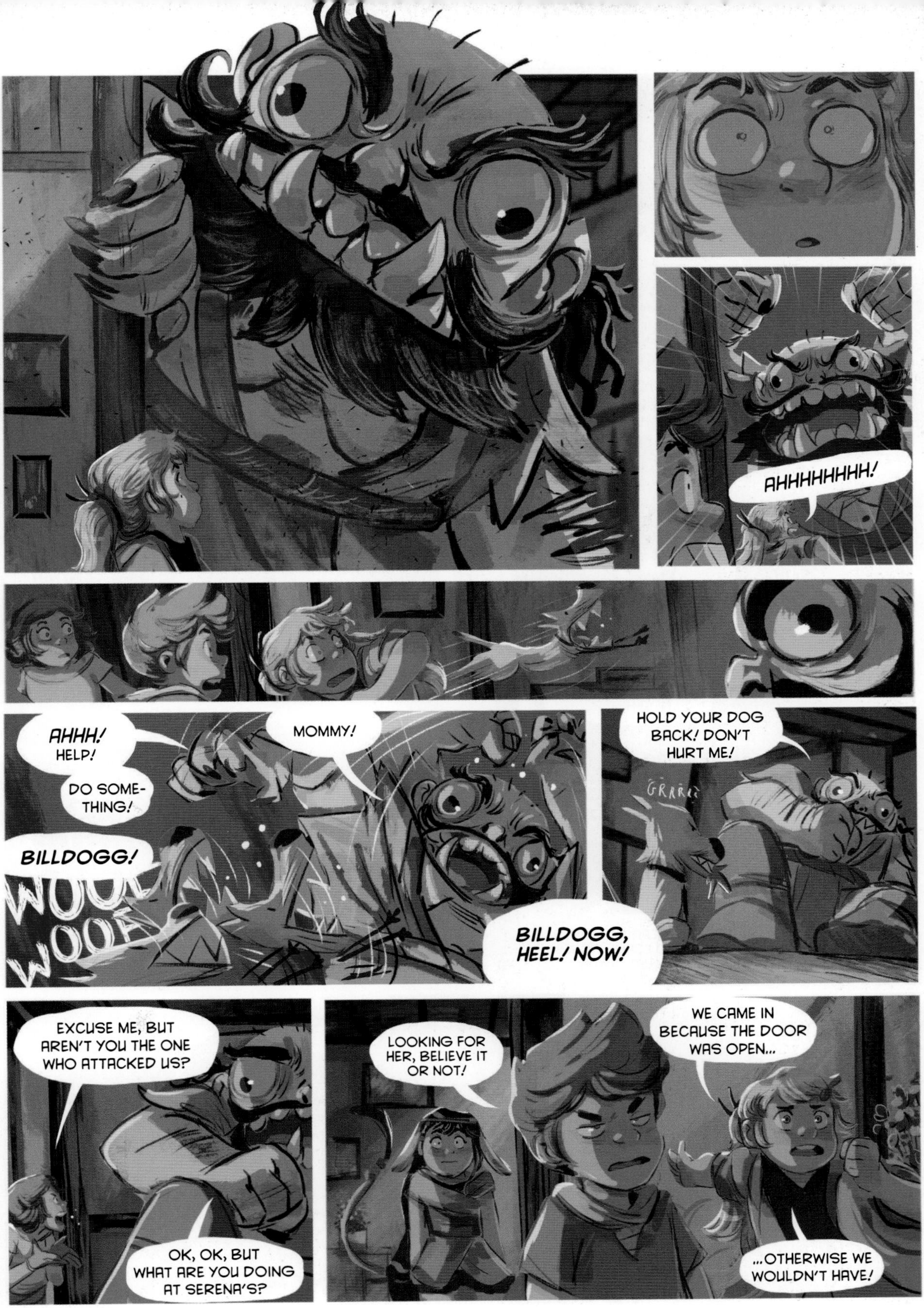
AHHHHHHHH!
AHHH! HELP!
DO SOME-THING!
MOMMY!
BILLDOGG!
WOOF WOOF
HOLD YOUR DOG BACK! DON'T HURT ME!
BILLDOGG, HEEL! NOW!
EXCUSE ME, BUT AREN'T YOU THE ONE WHO ATTACKED US?
OK, OK, BUT WHAT ARE YOU DOING AT SERENA'S?
LOOKING FOR HER, BELIEVE IT OR NOT!
WE CAME IN BECAUSE THE DOOR WAS OPEN...
...OTHERWISE WE WOULDN'T HAVE!

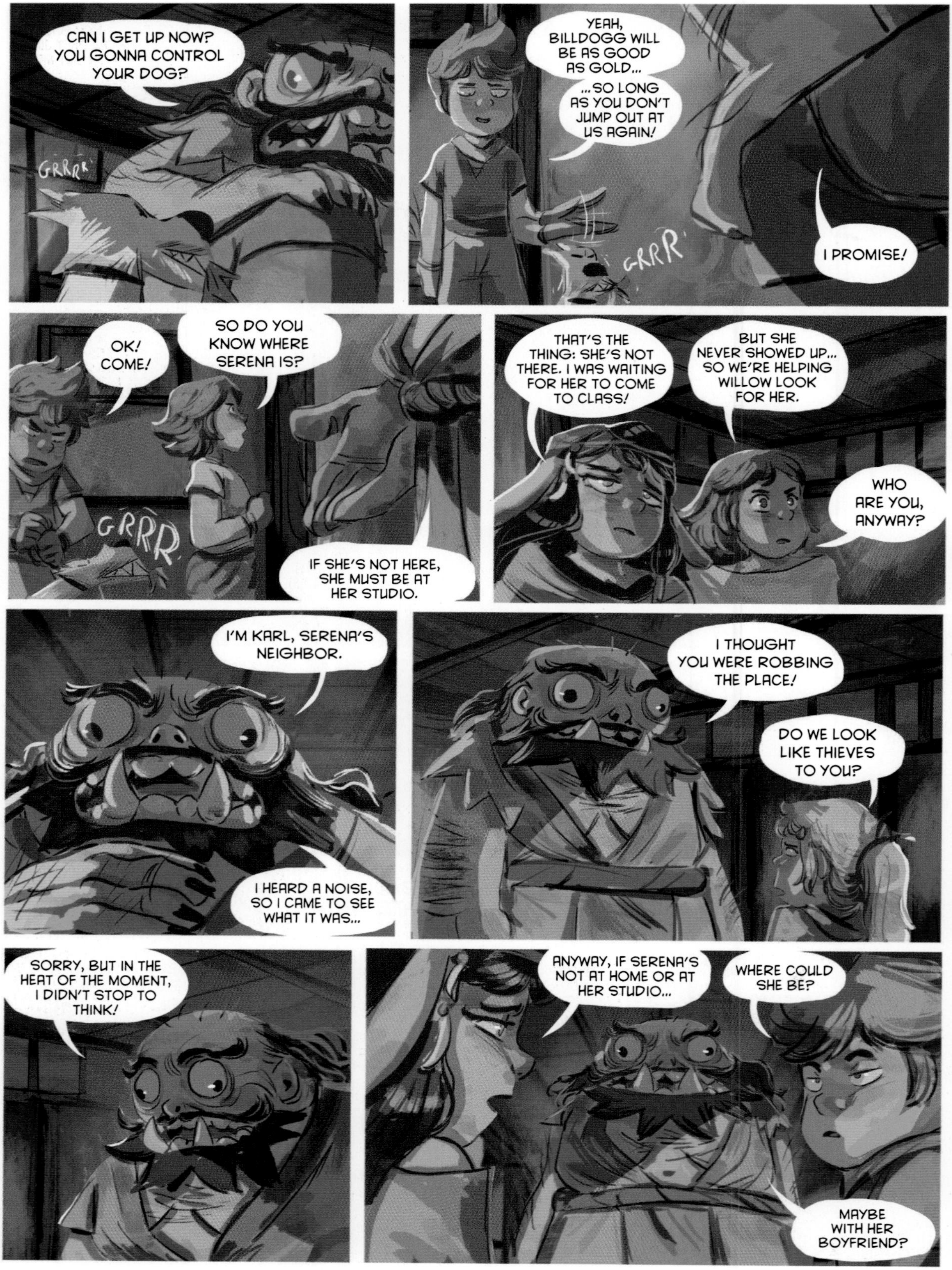
CAN I GET UP NOW? YOU GONNA CONTROL YOUR DOG?
GRRRR
YEAH, BILLDOGG WILL BE AS GOOD AS GOLD...
...SO LONG AS YOU DON'T JUMP OUT AT US AGAIN!
GRRR
I PROMISE!
OK! COME!
SO DO YOU KNOW WHERE SERENA IS?
GRRR
IF SHE'S NOT HERE, SHE MUST BE AT HER STUDIO.
THAT'S THE THING: SHE'S NOT THERE. I WAS WAITING FOR HER TO COME TO CLASS!
BUT SHE NEVER SHOWED UP... SO WE'RE HELPING WILLOW LOOK FOR HER.
WHO ARE YOU, ANYWAY?
I'M KARL, SERENA'S NEIGHBOR.
I HEARD A NOISE, SO I CAME TO SEE WHAT IT WAS...
I THOUGHT YOU WERE ROBBING THE PLACE!
DO WE LOOK LIKE THIEVES TO YOU?
SORRY, BUT IN THE HEAT OF THE MOMENT, I DIDN'T STOP TO THINK!
ANYWAY, IF SERENA'S NOT AT HOME OR AT HER STUDIO...
WHERE COULD SHE BE?
MAYBE WITH HER BOYFRIEND?

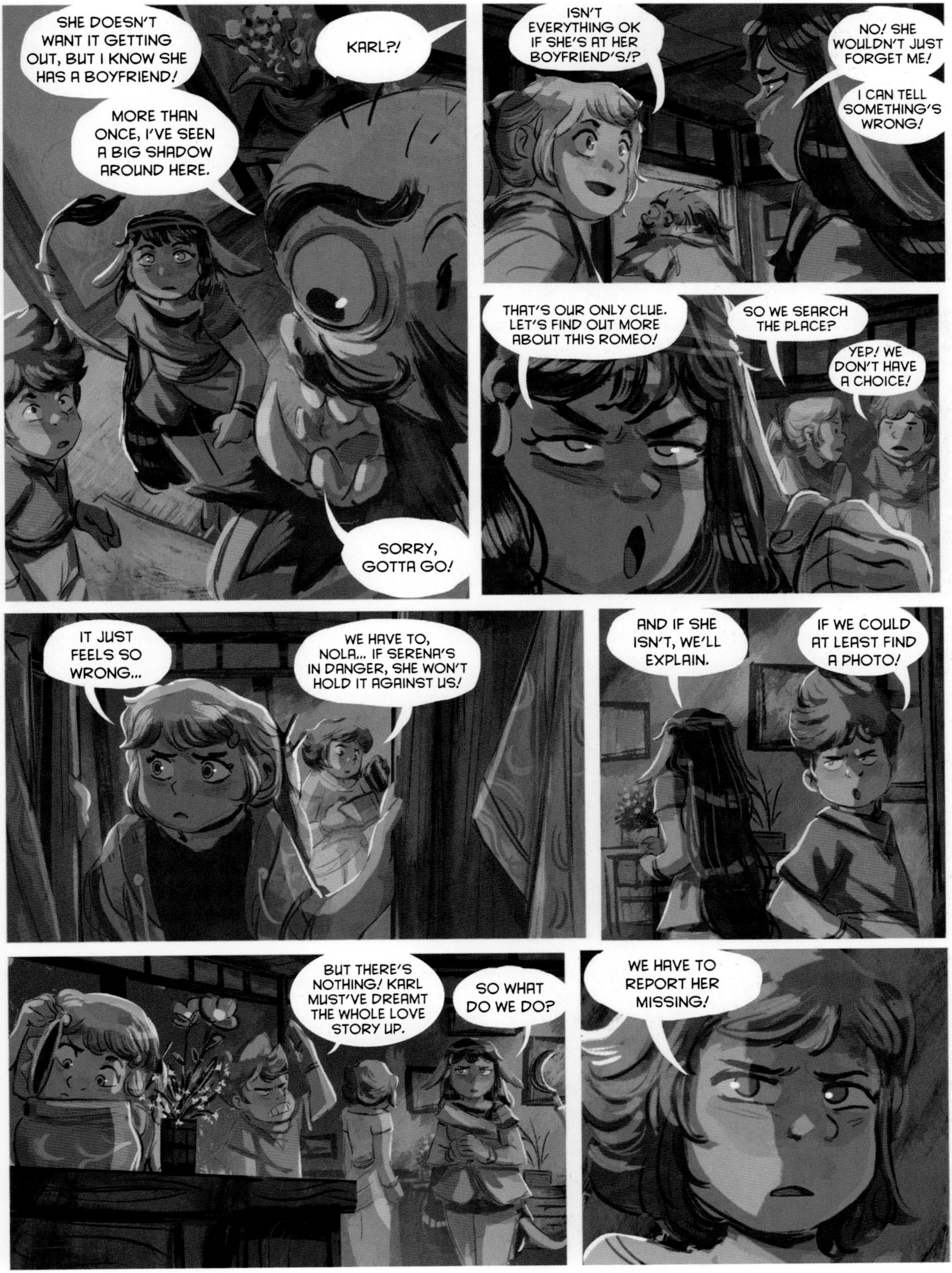

SHE DOESN'T WANT IT GETTING OUT, BUT I KNOW SHE HAS A BOYFRIEND!
MORE THAN ONCE, I'VE SEEN A BIG SHADOW AROUND HERE.
KARL?!
SORRY, GOTTA GO!
ISN'T EVERYTHING OK IF SHE'S AT HER BOYFRIEND'S!?
NO! SHE WOULDN'T JUST FORGET ME!
I CAN TELL SOMETHING'S WRONG!
THAT'S OUR ONLY CLUE. LET'S FIND OUT MORE ABOUT THIS ROMEO!
SO WE SEARCH THE PLACE?
YEP! WE DON'T HAVE A CHOICE!
IT JUST FEELS SO WRONG...
WE HAVE TO, NOLA... IF SERENA'S IN DANGER, SHE WON'T HOLD IT AGAINST US!
AND IF SHE ISN'T, WE'LL EXPLAIN.
IF WE COULD AT LEAST FIND A PHOTO!
BUT THERE'S NOTHING! KARL MUST'VE DREAMT THE WHOLE LOVE STORY UP.
SO WHAT DO WE DO?
WE HAVE TO REPORT HER MISSING!

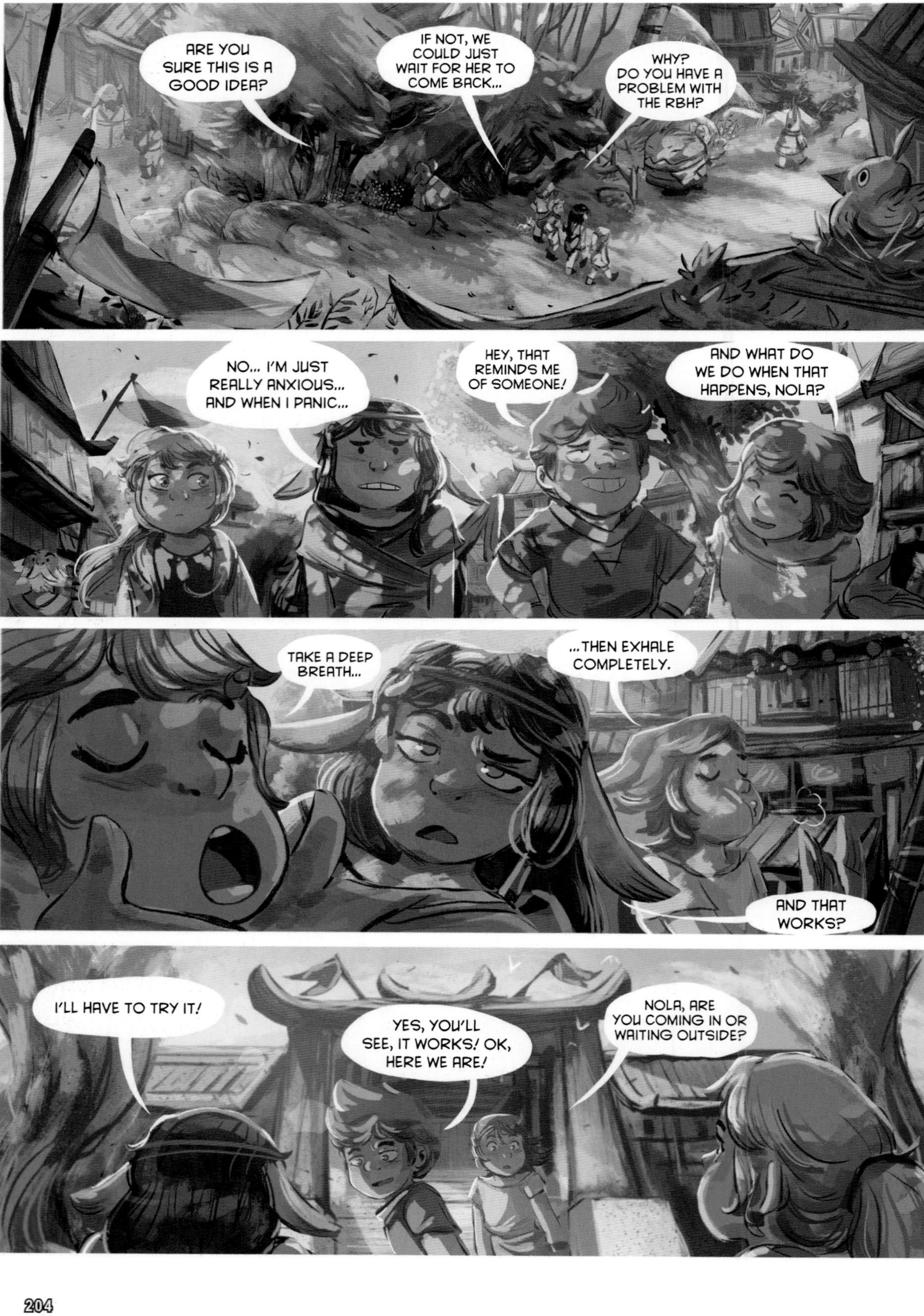
ARE YOU SURE THIS IS A GOOD IDEA?
IF NOT, WE COULD JUST WAIT FOR HER TO COME BACK...
WHY? DO YOU HAVE A PROBLEM WITH THE RBH?
NO... I'M JUST REALLY ANXIOUS... AND WHEN I PANIC...
HEY, THAT REMINDS ME OF SOMEONE!
AND WHAT DO WE DO WHEN THAT HAPPENS, NOLA?
TAKE A DEEP BREATH...
...THEN EXHALE COMPLETELY.
AND THAT WORKS?
I'LL HAVE TO TRY IT!
YES, YOU'LL SEE, IT WORKS! OK, HERE WE ARE!
NOLA, ARE YOU COMING IN OR WAITING OUTSIDE?

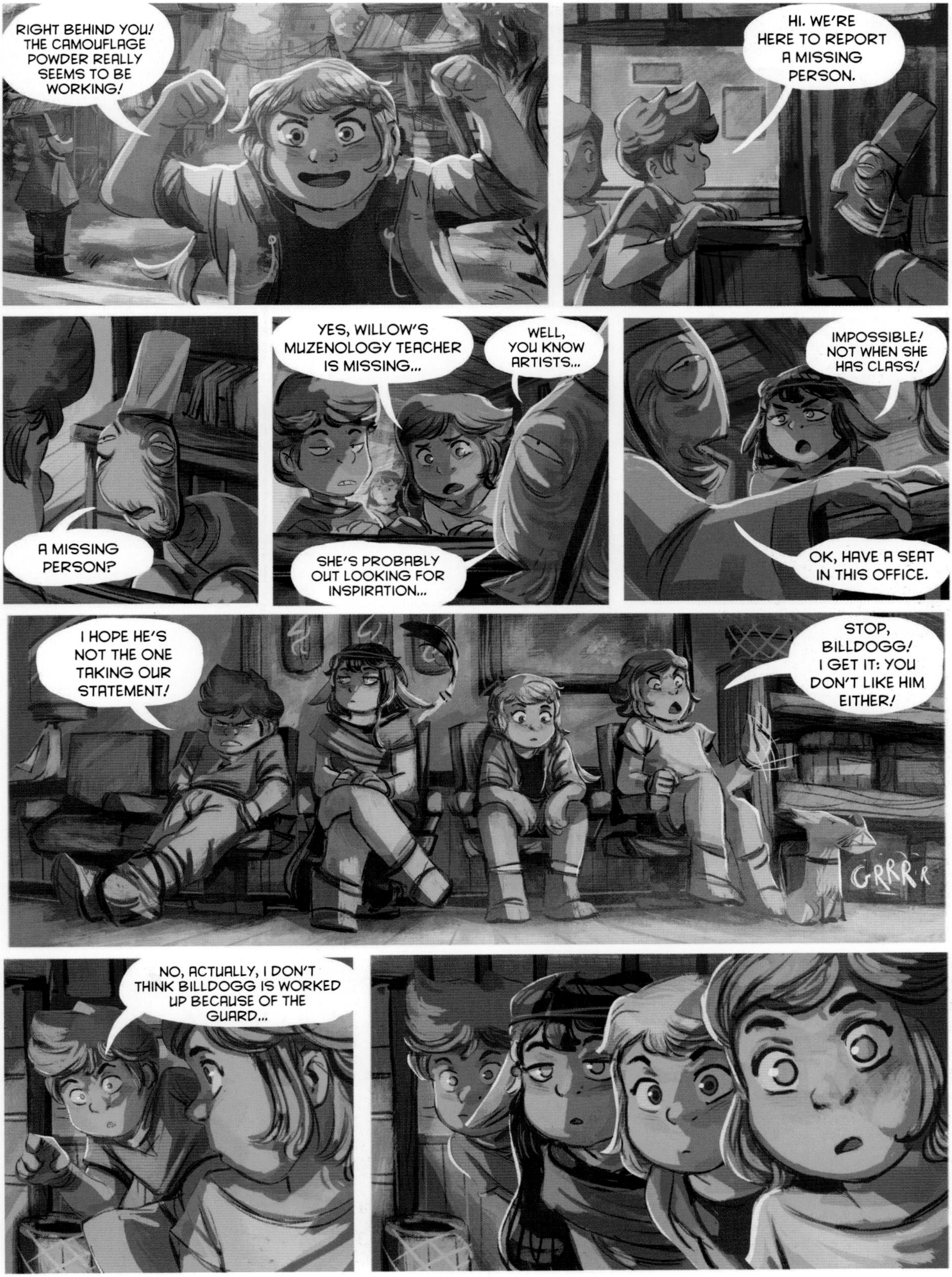
RIGHT BEHIND YOU! THE CAMOUFLAGE POWDER REALLY SEEMS TO BE WORKING!
HI. WE'RE HERE TO REPORT A MISSING PERSON.
A MISSING PERSON?
YES, WILLOW'S MUZENOLOGY TEACHER IS MISSING...
WELL, YOU KNOW ARTISTS...
SHE'S PROBABLY OUT LOOKING FOR INSPIRATION...
IMPOSSIBLE! NOT WHEN SHE HAS CLASS!
OK, HAVE A SEAT IN THIS OFFICE.
I HOPE HE'S NOT THE ONE TAKING OUR STATEMENT!
STOP, BILLDOGG! I GET IT: YOU DON'T LIKE HIM EITHER!
GRRRR
NO, ACTUALLY, I DON'T THINK BILLDOGG IS WORKED UP BECAUSE OF THE GUARD...

THE OCTOPODUS IS STILL HERE?!

THAT DOESN'T LOOK GOOD!

HELLO, YOUNGSTERS. WHAT CAN I DO FOR YOU?

WAS THAT THE OCTOPODUS? WHAT DID HE DO?

NON-COMPLIANCE WITH LAW 8612!

THE ONE ON THE NON-MIXING OF ETHNIC GROUPS?

THE VERY ONE!

PLEASE IGNORE MY NOSY BROTHER!

ANYWAY... DID YOU COME FOR NEWS ABOUT THE OCTOPODUS OR—

NO, ACTUALLY, WE'RE HERE BECAUSE...

...SERENA, MY MUZENOLOGY TEACHER, IS MISSING!

MISSING? WHAT MAKES YOU SO SURE?

BECAUSE SHE'S NEVER MISSED A SINGLE CLASS!

AND BECAUSE SHE LEFT WITHOUT LOCKING HER DOOR...

WHAT DOES YOUR TEACHER LOOK LIKE? CAN YOU DESCRIBE HER?

ACTUALLY, I HAVE A PHOTO FROM HER LAST GALA!

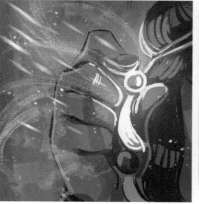

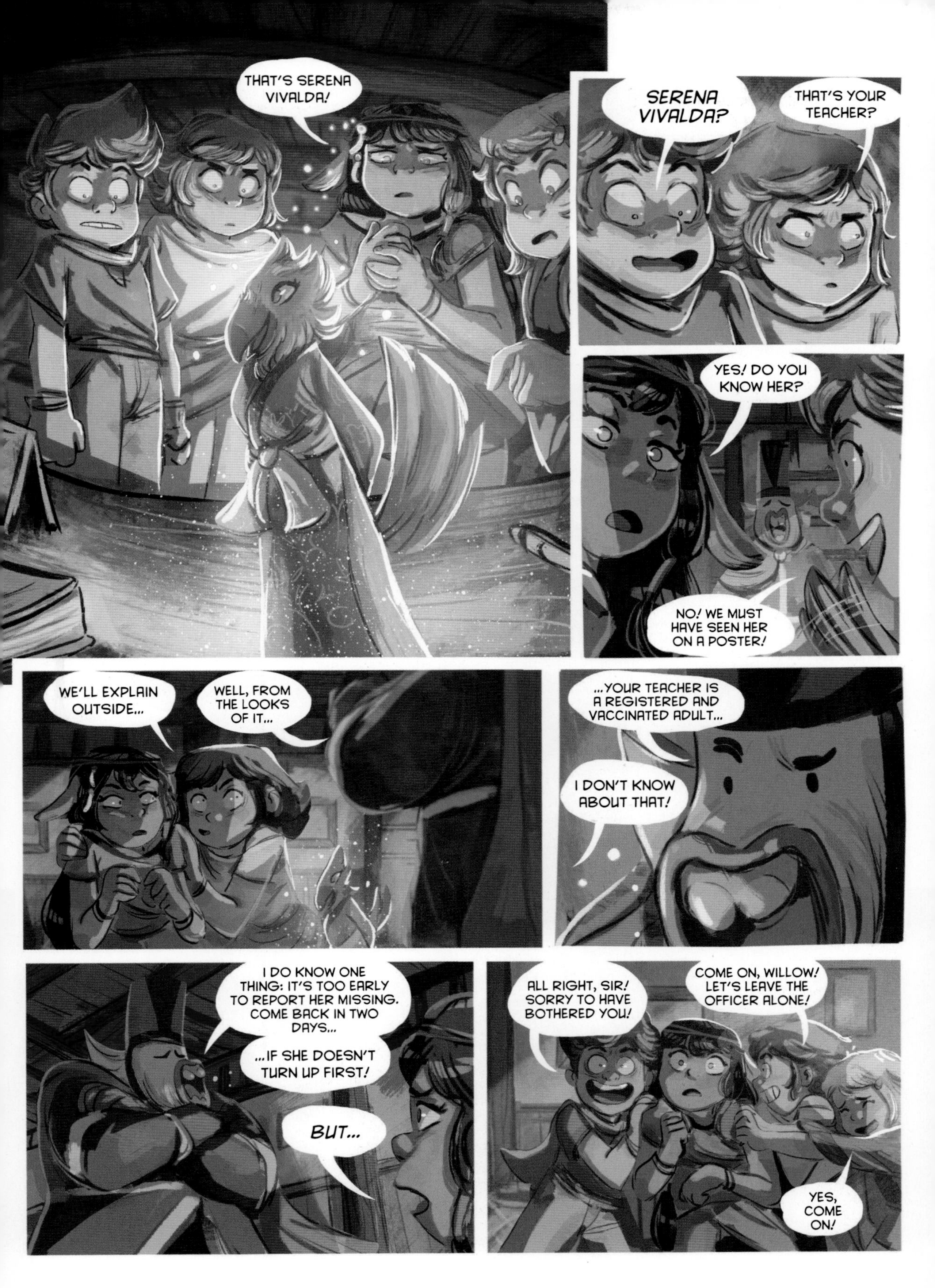
THAT'S SERENA VIVALDA!
SERENA VIVALDA?
THAT'S YOUR TEACHER?
YES! DO YOU KNOW HER?
NO! WE MUST HAVE SEEN HER ON A POSTER!
WE'LL EXPLAIN OUTSIDE...
WELL, FROM THE LOOKS OF IT...
...YOUR TEACHER IS A REGISTERED AND VACCINATED ADULT...
I DON'T KNOW ABOUT THAT!
I DO KNOW ONE THING: IT'S TOO EARLY TO REPORT HER MISSING. COME BACK IN TWO DAYS...
...IF SHE DOESN'T TURN UP FIRST!
BUT...
ALL RIGHT, SIR! SORRY TO HAVE BOTHERED YOU!
COME ON, WILLOW! LET'S LEAVE THE OFFICER ALONE!
YES, COME ON!

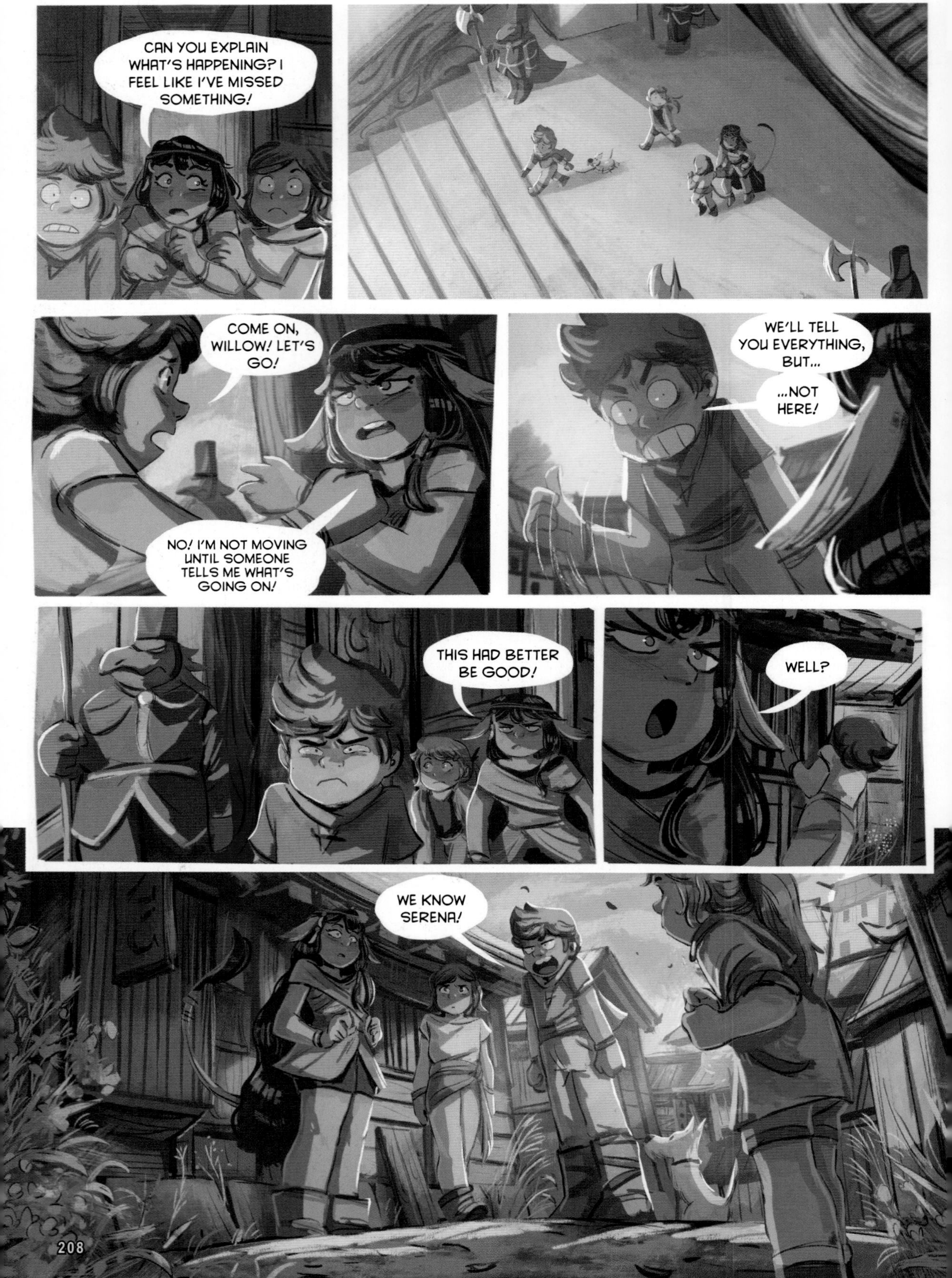
CAN YOU EXPLAIN WHAT'S HAPPENING? I FEEL LIKE I'VE MISSED SOMETHING!
COME ON, WILLOW! LET'S GO!
NO! I'M NOT MOVING UNTIL SOMEONE TELLS ME WHAT'S GOING ON!
WE'LL TELL YOU EVERYTHING, BUT...
...NOT HERE!
THIS HAD BETTER BE GOOD!
WELL?
WE KNOW SERENA!

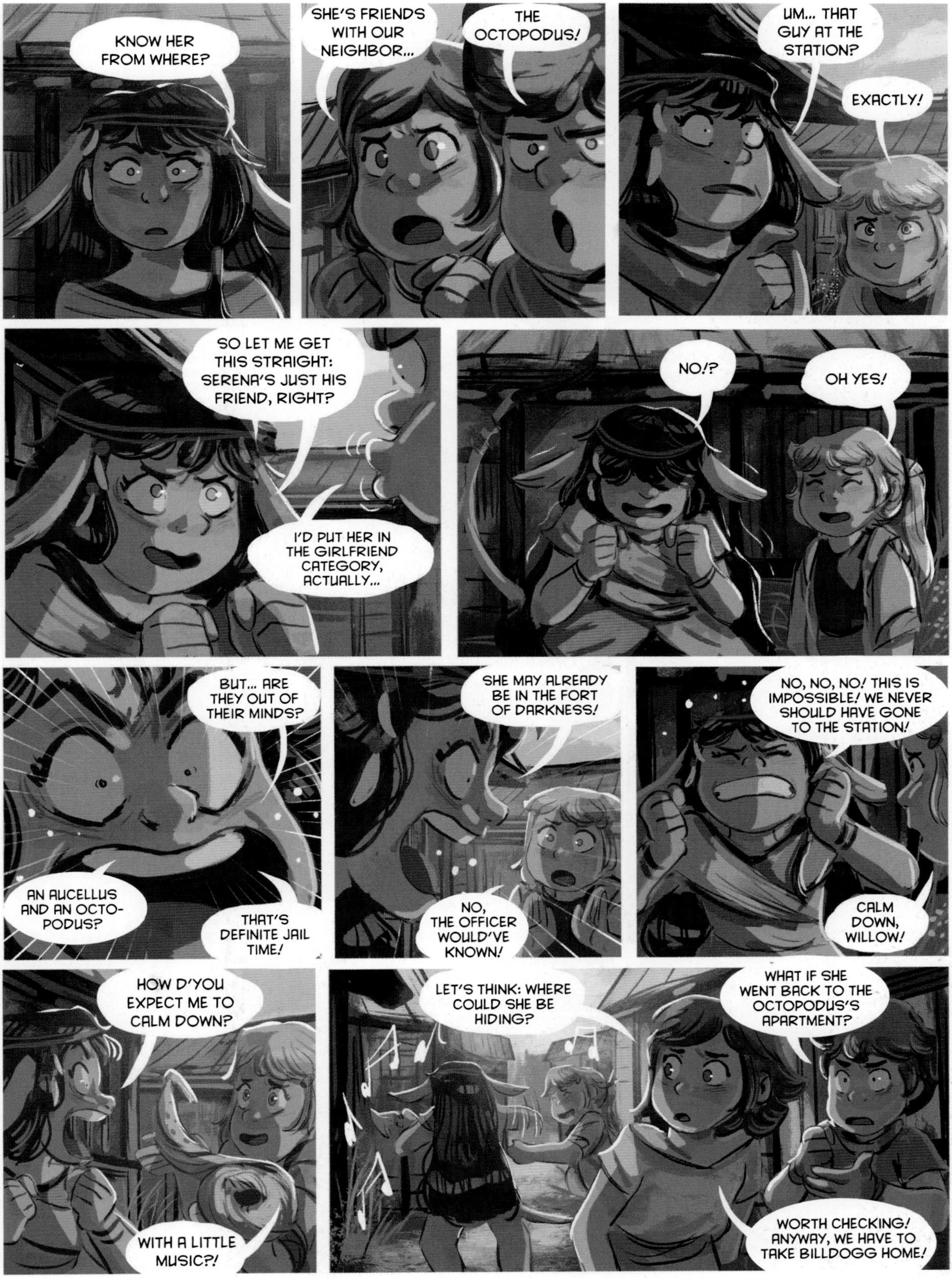
KNOW HER FROM WHERE?
SHE'S FRIENDS WITH OUR NEIGHBOR...
THE OCTOPODUS!
UM... THAT GUY AT THE STATION?
EXACTLY!
SO LET ME GET THIS STRAIGHT: SERENA'S JUST HIS FRIEND, RIGHT?
I'D PUT HER IN THE GIRLFRIEND CATEGORY, ACTUALLY...
NO!?
OH YES!
BUT... ARE THEY OUT OF THEIR MINDS?
AN AUCELLUS AND AN OCTO-PODUS?
THAT'S DEFINITE JAIL TIME!
SHE MAY ALREADY BE IN THE FORT OF DARKNESS!
NO, THE OFFICER WOULD'VE KNOWN!
NO, NO, NO! THIS IS IMPOSSIBLE! WE NEVER SHOULD HAVE GONE TO THE STATION!
CALM DOWN, WILLOW!
HOW D'YOU EXPECT ME TO CALM DOWN?
WITH A LITTLE MUSIC?!
LET'S THINK: WHERE COULD SHE BE HIDING?
WHAT IF SHE WENT BACK TO THE OCTOPODUS'S APARTMENT?
WORTH CHECKING! ANYWAY, WE HAVE TO TAKE BILLDOGG HOME!

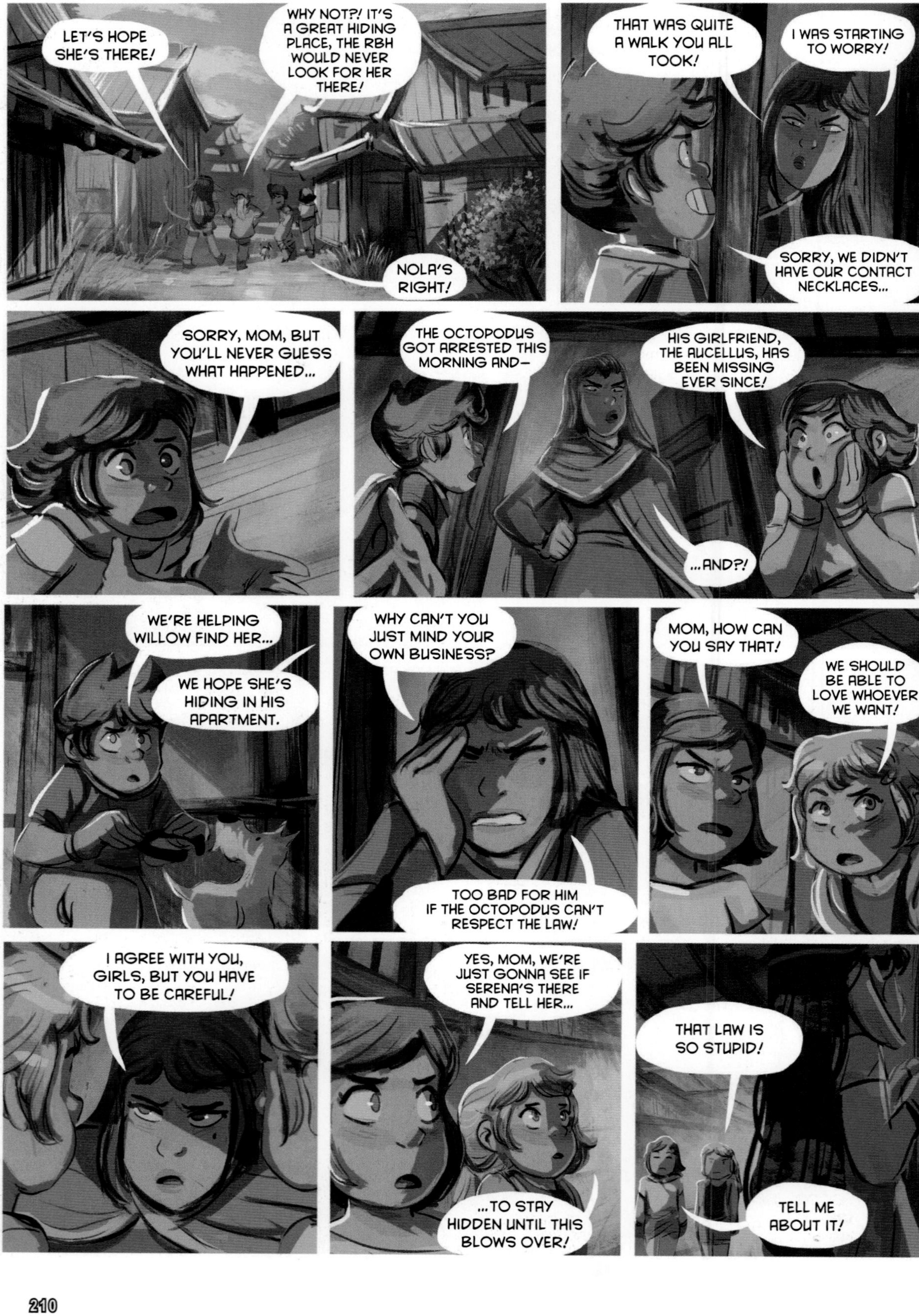

LET'S HOPE SHE'S THERE!
WHY NOT?! IT'S A GREAT HIDING PLACE, THE RBH WOULD NEVER LOOK FOR HER THERE!
NOLA'S RIGHT!
THAT WAS QUITE A WALK YOU ALL TOOK!
I WAS STARTING TO WORRY!
SORRY, WE DIDN'T HAVE OUR CONTACT NECKLACES...
SORRY, MOM, BUT YOU'LL NEVER GUESS WHAT HAPPENED...
THE OCTOPODUS GOT ARRESTED THIS MORNING AND—
HIS GIRLFRIEND, THE AUCELLUS, HAS BEEN MISSING EVER SINCE!
...AND?!
WE'RE HELPING WILLOW FIND HER...
WE HOPE SHE'S HIDING IN HIS APARTMENT.
WHY CAN'T YOU JUST MIND YOUR OWN BUSINESS?
TOO BAD FOR HIM IF THE OCTOPODUS CAN'T RESPECT THE LAW!
MOM, HOW CAN YOU SAY THAT!
WE SHOULD BE ABLE TO LOVE WHOEVER WE WANT!
I AGREE WITH YOU, GIRLS, BUT YOU HAVE TO BE CAREFUL!
YES, MOM, WE'RE JUST GONNA SEE IF SERENA'S THERE AND TELL HER...
...TO STAY HIDDEN UNTIL THIS BLOWS OVER!
THAT LAW IS SO STUPID!
TELL ME ABOUT IT!

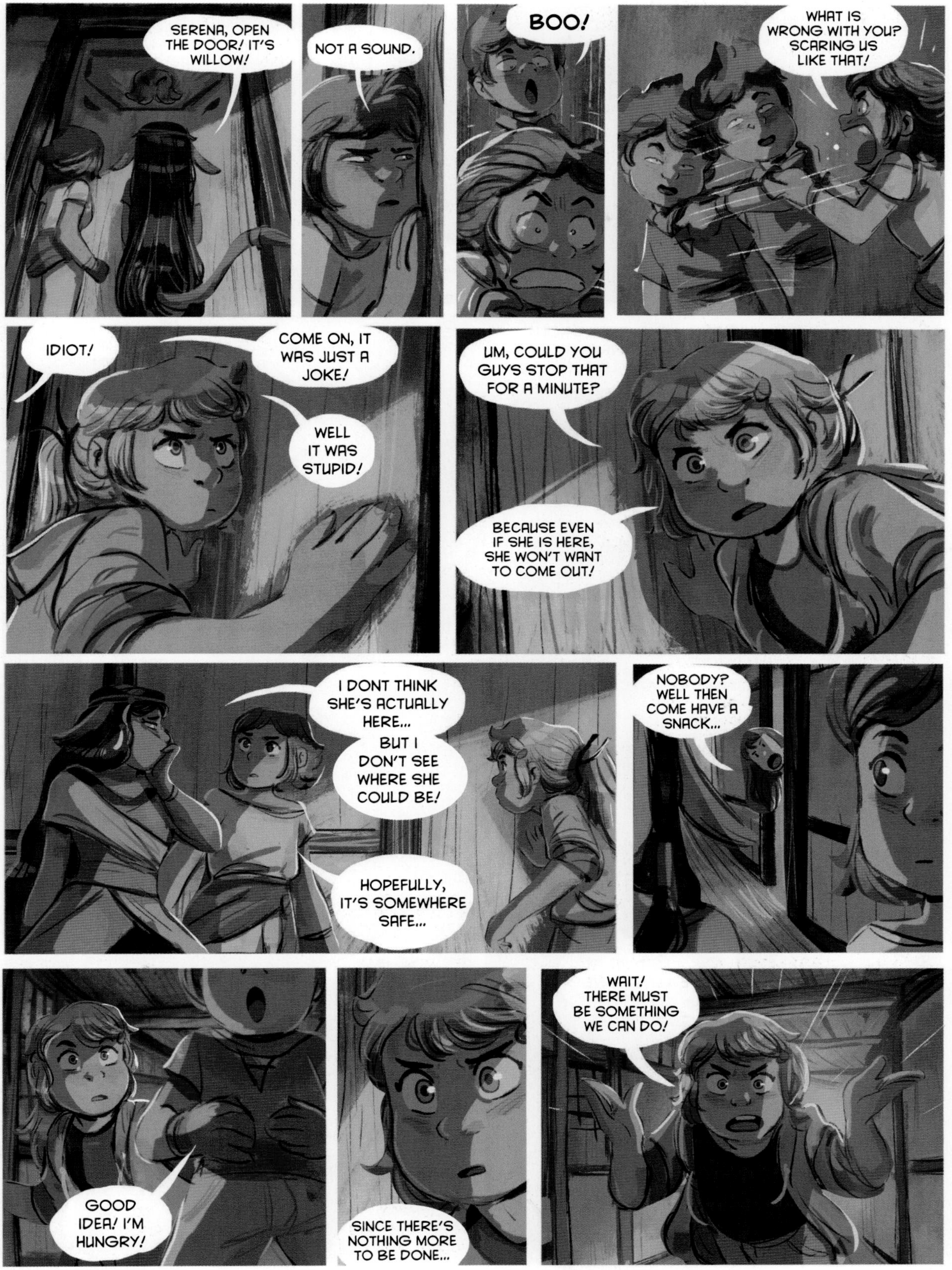
SERENA, OPEN THE DOOR! IT'S WILLOW!
NOT A SOUND.
BOO!
WHAT IS WRONG WITH YOU? SCARING US LIKE THAT!
IDIOT!
COME ON, IT WAS JUST A JOKE!
WELL IT WAS STUPID!
UM, COULD YOU GUYS STOP THAT FOR A MINUTE?
BECAUSE EVEN IF SHE IS HERE, SHE WON'T WANT TO COME OUT!
I DONT THINK SHE'S ACTUALLY HERE...
BUT I DON'T SEE WHERE SHE COULD BE!
HOPEFULLY, IT'S SOMEWHERE SAFE...
NOBODY? WELL THEN COME HAVE A SNACK...
GOOD IDEA! I'M HUNGRY!
SINCE THERE'S NOTHING MORE TO BE DONE...
WAIT! THERE MUST BE SOMETHING WE CAN DO!

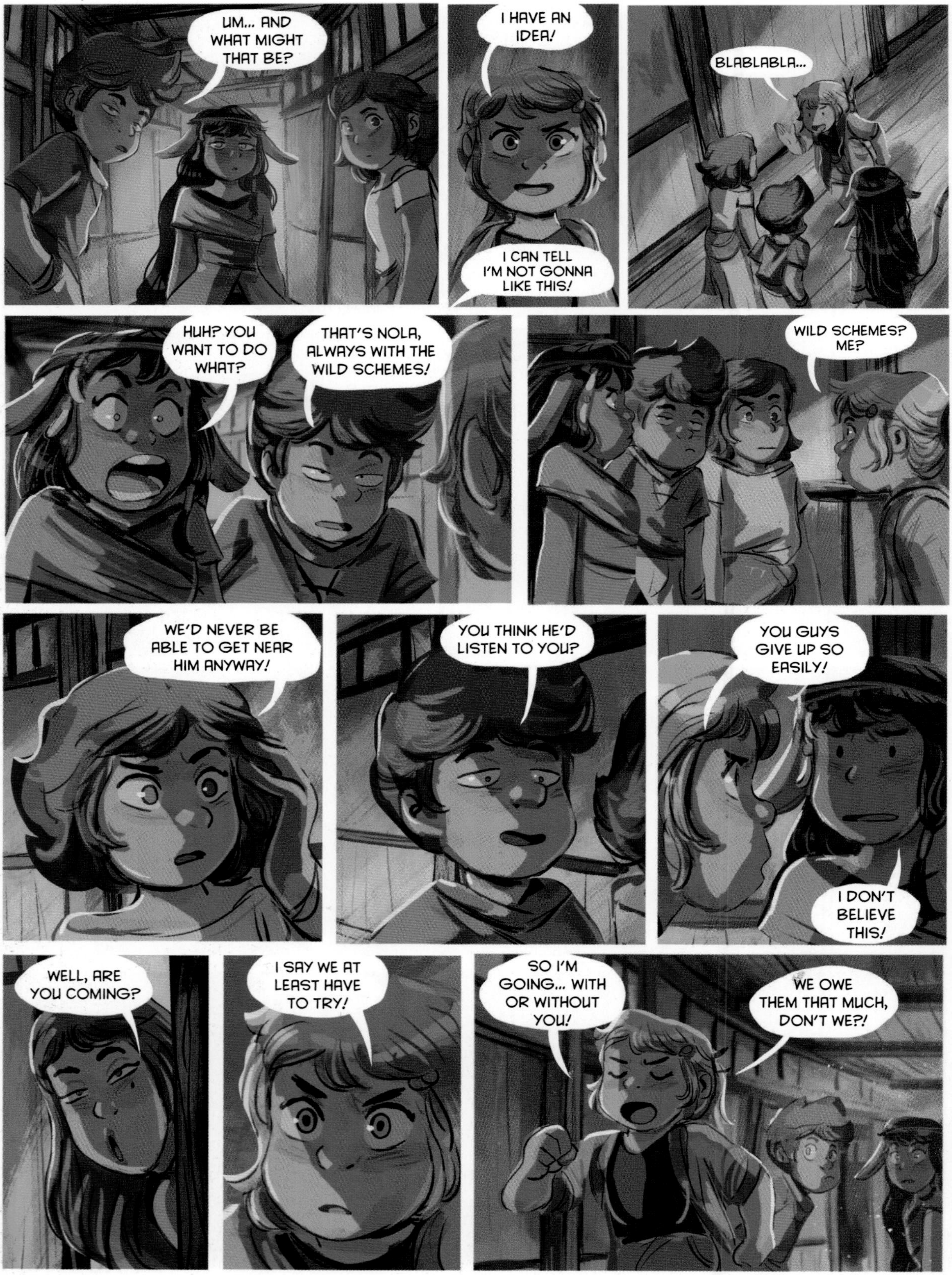
UM... AND WHAT MIGHT THAT BE?
I HAVE AN IDEA!
I CAN TELL I'M NOT GONNA LIKE THIS!
BLABLABLA...
HUH? YOU WANT TO DO WHAT?
THAT'S NOLA, ALWAYS WITH THE WILD SCHEMES!
WILD SCHEMES? ME?
WE'D NEVER BE ABLE TO GET NEAR HIM ANYWAY!
YOU THINK HE'D LISTEN TO YOU?
YOU GUYS GIVE UP SO EASILY!
I DON'T BELIEVE THIS!
WELL, ARE YOU COMING?
I SAY WE AT LEAST HAVE TO TRY!
SO I'M GOING... WITH OR WITHOUT YOU!
WE OWE THEM THAT MUCH, DON'T WE?!

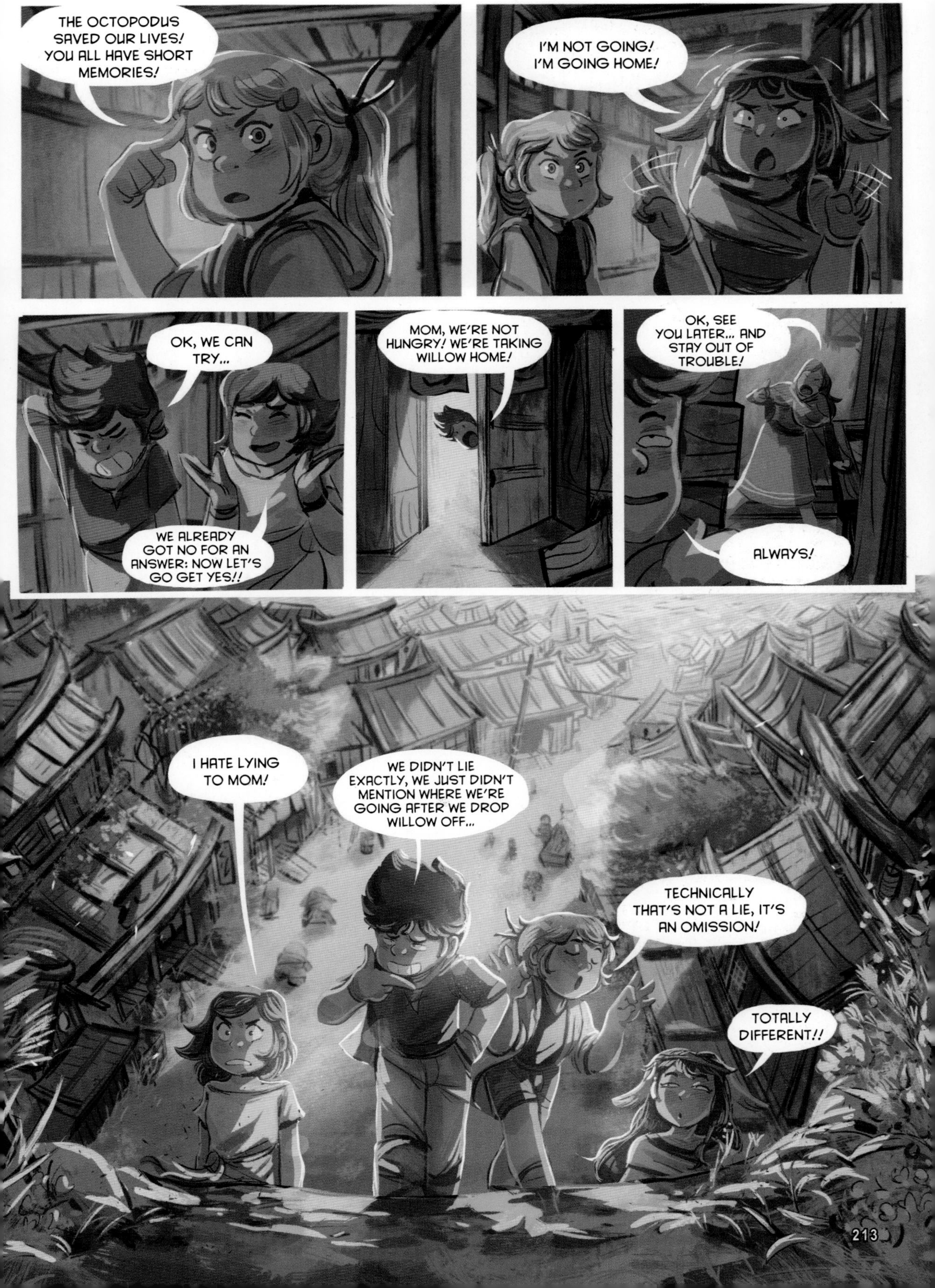
THE OCTOPODUS SAVED OUR LIVES! YOU ALL HAVE SHORT MEMORIES!
I'M NOT GOING! I'M GOING HOME!
OK, WE CAN TRY...
WE ALREADY GOT NO FOR AN ANSWER: NOW LET'S GO GET YES!!
MOM, WE'RE NOT HUNGRY! WE'RE TAKING WILLOW HOME!
OK, SEE YOU LATER... AND STAY OUT OF TROUBLE!
ALWAYS!
I HATE LYING TO MOM!
WE DIDN'T LIE EXACTLY, WE JUST DIDN'T MENTION WHERE WE'RE GOING AFTER WE DROP WILLOW OFF...
TECHNICALLY THAT'S NOT A LIE, IT'S AN OMISSION!
TOTALLY DIFFERENT!!

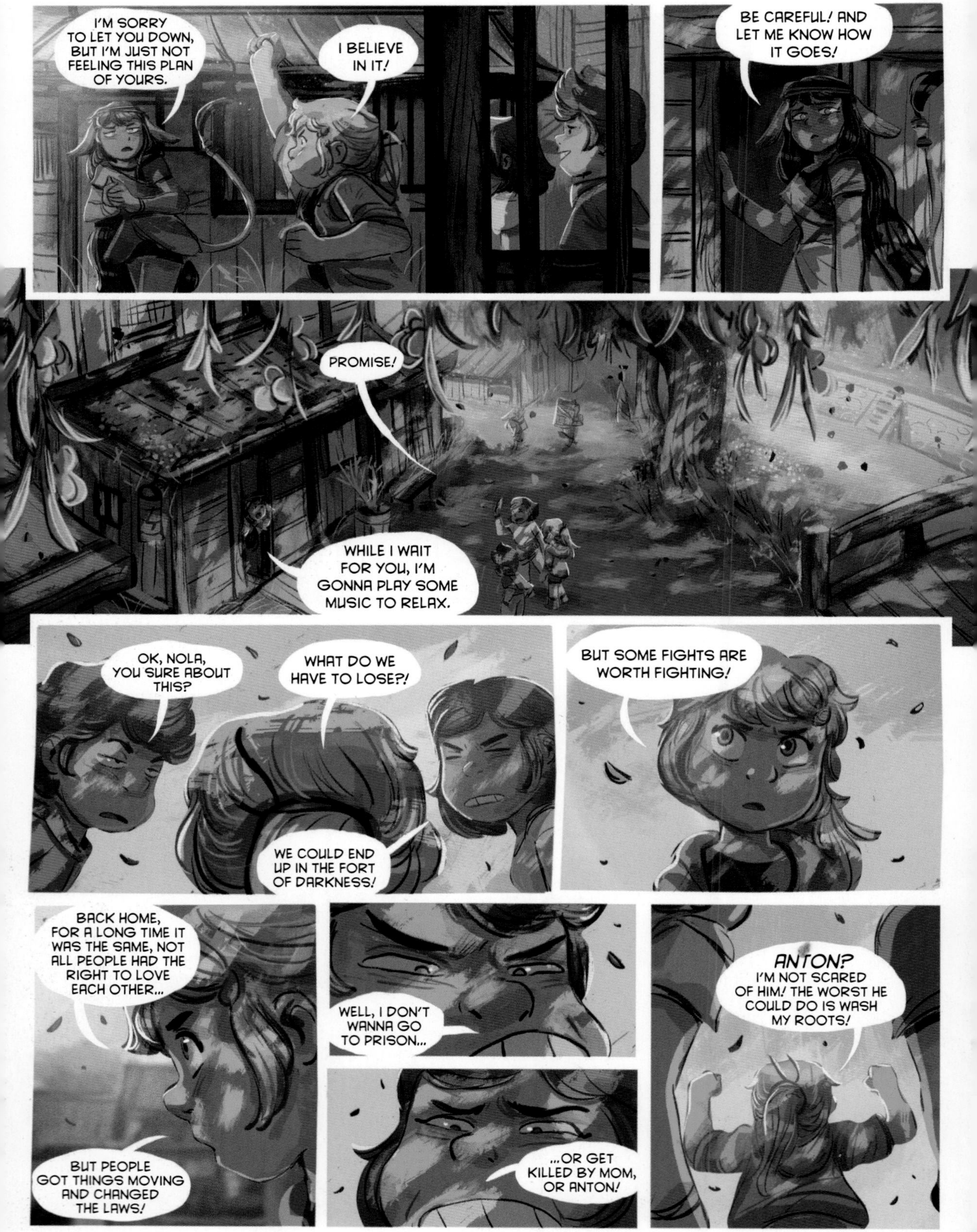
I'M SORRY TO LET YOU DOWN, BUT I'M JUST NOT FEELING THIS PLAN OF YOURS.
I BELIEVE IN IT!
BE CAREFUL! AND LET ME KNOW HOW IT GOES!
PROMISE!
WHILE I WAIT FOR YOU, I'M GONNA PLAY SOME MUSIC TO RELAX.
OK, NOLA, YOU SURE ABOUT THIS?
WHAT DO WE HAVE TO LOSE?!
WE COULD END UP IN THE FORT OF DARKNESS!
BUT SOME FIGHTS ARE WORTH FIGHTING!
BACK HOME, FOR A LONG TIME IT WAS THE SAME, NOT ALL PEOPLE HAD THE RIGHT TO LOVE EACH OTHER...
BUT PEOPLE GOT THINGS MOVING AND CHANGED THE LAWS!
WELL, I DON'T WANNA GO TO PRISON...
...OR GET KILLED BY MOM, OR ANTON!
ANTON? I'M NOT SCARED OF HIM! THE WORST HE COULD DO IS WASH MY ROOTS!

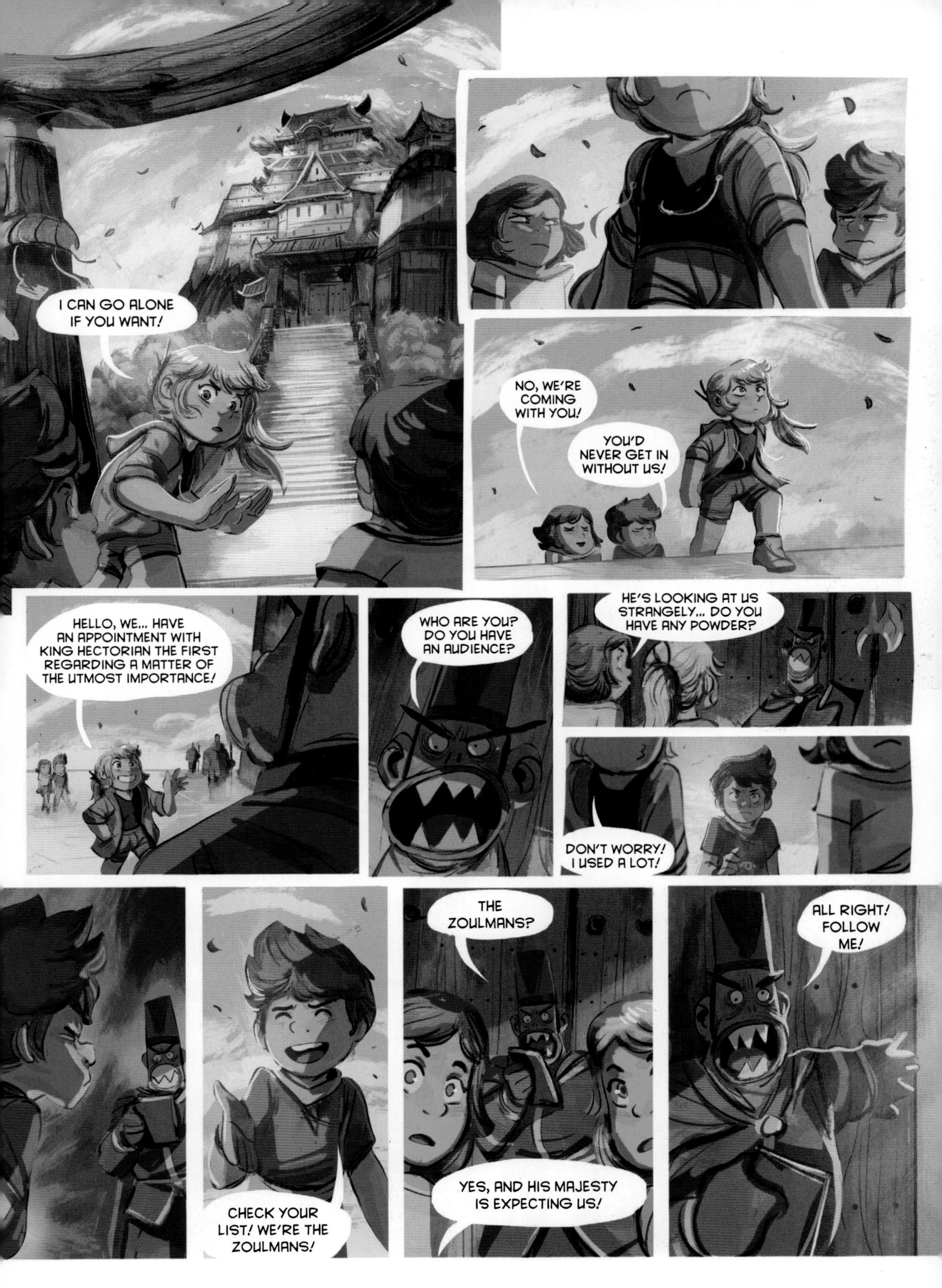
I CAN GO ALONE IF YOU WANT!
NO, WE'RE COMING WITH YOU!
YOU'D NEVER GET IN WITHOUT US!
HELLO, WE... HAVE AN APPOINTMENT WITH KING HECTORIAN THE FIRST REGARDING A MATTER OF THE UTMOST IMPORTANCE!
WHO ARE YOU? DO YOU HAVE AN AUDIENCE?
HE'S LOOKING AT US STRANGELY... DO YOU HAVE ANY POWDER?
DON'T WORRY! I USED A LOT!
CHECK YOUR LIST! WE'RE THE ZOULMANS!
THE ZOULMANS?
YES, AND HIS MAJESTY IS EXPECTING US!
ALL RIGHT! FOLLOW ME!

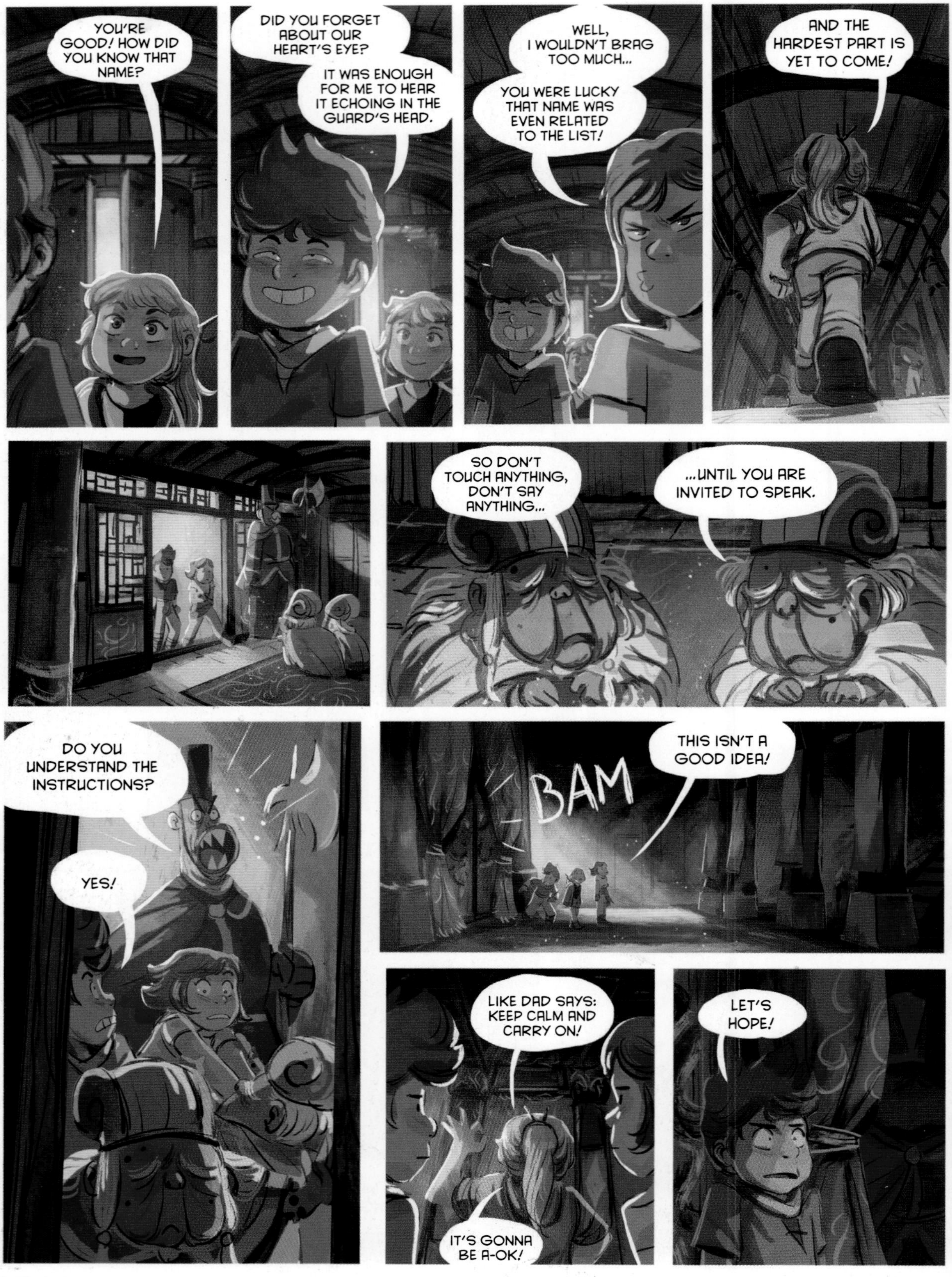
YOU'RE GOOD! HOW DID YOU KNOW THAT NAME?
DID YOU FORGET ABOUT OUR HEART'S EYE?
IT WAS ENOUGH FOR ME TO HEAR IT ECHOING IN THE GUARD'S HEAD.
WELL, I WOULDN'T BRAG TOO MUCH...
YOU WERE LUCKY THAT NAME WAS EVEN RELATED TO THE LIST!
AND THE HARDEST PART IS YET TO COME!
SO DON'T TOUCH ANYTHING, DON'T SAY ANYTHING...
...UNTIL YOU ARE INVITED TO SPEAK.
DO YOU UNDERSTAND THE INSTRUCTIONS?
YES!
BAM
THIS ISN'T A GOOD IDEA!
LIKE DAD SAYS: KEEP CALM AND CARRY ON!
IT'S GONNA BE A-OK!
LET'S HOPE!

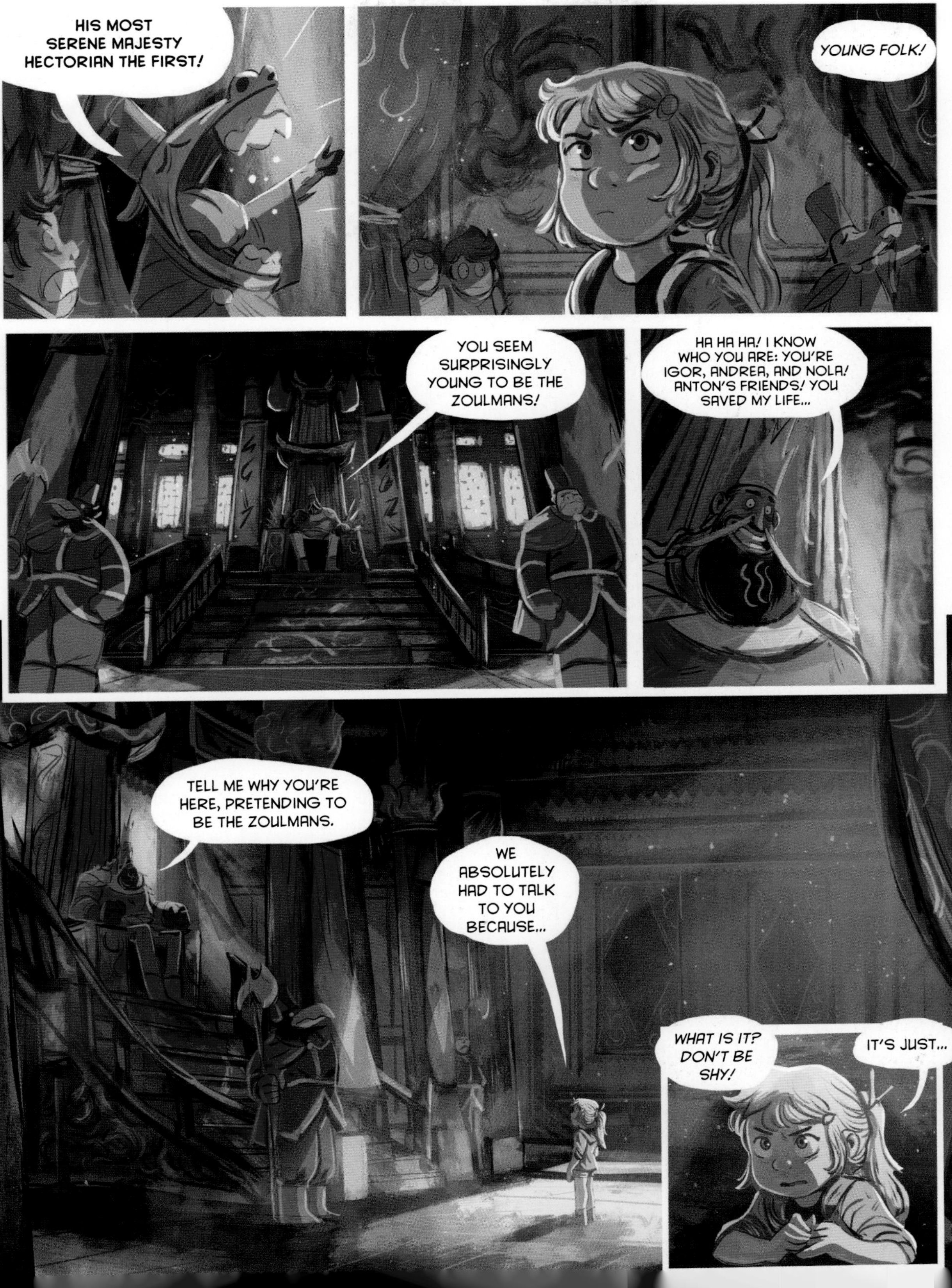
HIS MOST SERENE MAJESTY HECTORIAN THE FIRST!
YOUNG FOLK!
YOU SEEM SURPRISINGLY YOUNG TO BE THE ZOULMANS!
HA HA HA! I KNOW WHO YOU ARE: YOU'RE IGOR, ANDREA, AND NOLA! ANTON'S FRIENDS! YOU SAVED MY LIFE...
TELL ME WHY YOU'RE HERE, PRETENDING TO BE THE ZOULMANS.
WE ABSOLUTELY HAD TO TALK TO YOU BECAUSE...
WHAT IS IT? DON'T BE SHY!
IT'S JUST...

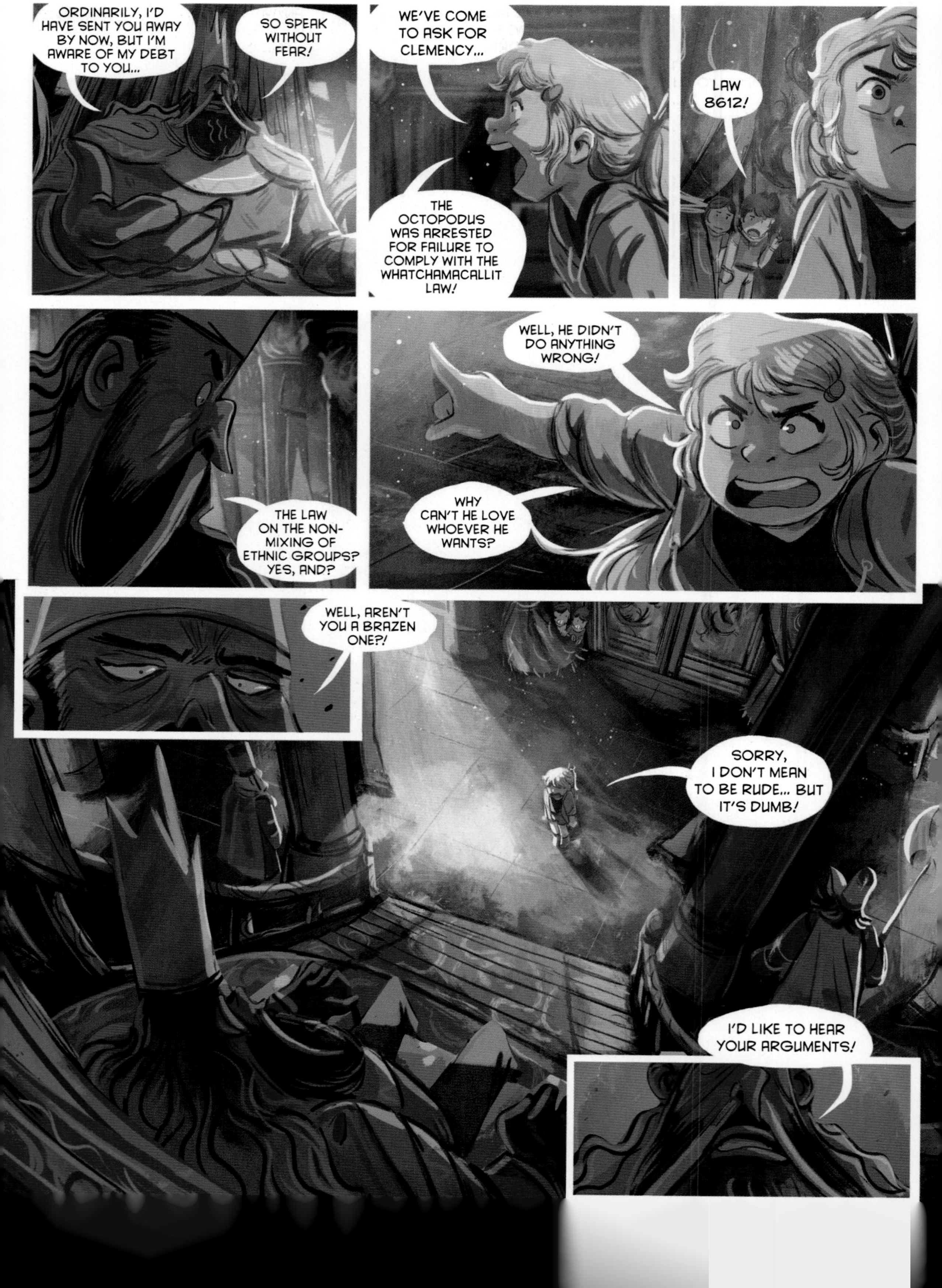
ORDINARILY, I'D HAVE SENT YOU AWAY BY NOW, BUT I'M AWARE OF MY DEBT TO YOU...
SO SPEAK WITHOUT FEAR!
WE'VE COME TO ASK FOR CLEMENCY...
THE OCTOPODUS WAS ARRESTED FOR FAILURE TO COMPLY WITH THE WHATCHAMACALLIT LAW!
LAW 8612!
THE LAW ON THE NON-MIXING OF ETHNIC GROUPS? YES, AND?
WELL, HE DIDN'T DO ANYTHING WRONG!
WHY CAN'T HE LOVE WHOEVER HE WANTS?
WELL, AREN'T YOU A BRAZEN ONE?!
SORRY, I DON'T MEAN TO BE RUDE... BUT IT'S DUMB!
I'D LIKE TO HEAR YOUR ARGUMENTS!

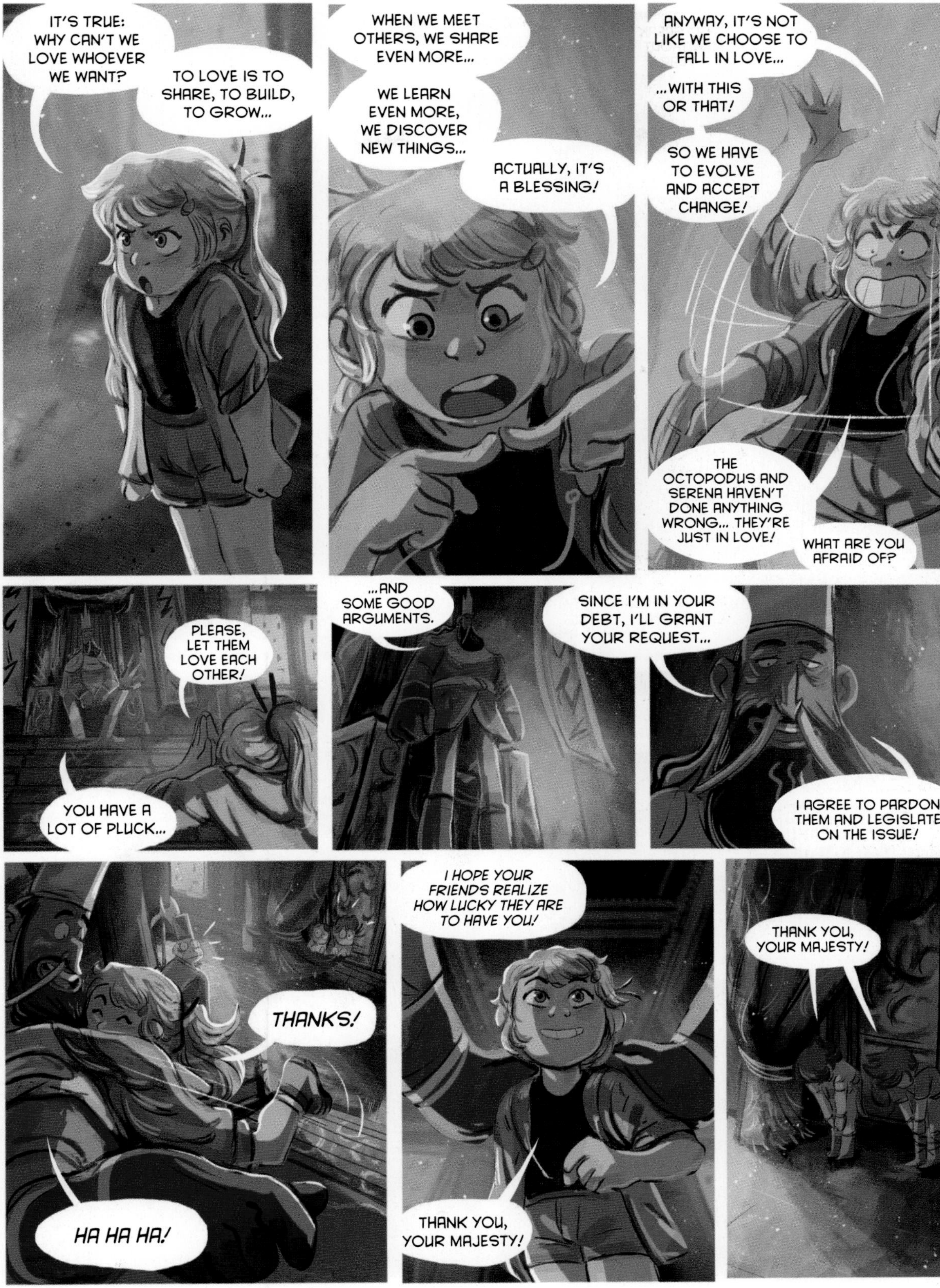
IT'S TRUE: WHY CAN'T WE LOVE WHOEVER WE WANT?
TO LOVE IS TO SHARE, TO BUILD, TO GROW...
WHEN WE MEET OTHERS, WE SHARE EVEN MORE...
WE LEARN EVEN MORE, WE DISCOVER NEW THINGS...
ACTUALLY, IT'S A BLESSING!
ANYWAY, IT'S NOT LIKE WE CHOOSE TO FALL IN LOVE...
...WITH THIS OR THAT!
SO WE HAVE TO EVOLVE AND ACCEPT CHANGE!
THE OCTOPODUS AND SERENA HAVEN'T DONE ANYTHING WRONG... THEY'RE JUST IN LOVE!
WHAT ARE YOU AFRAID OF?
PLEASE, LET THEM LOVE EACH OTHER!
YOU HAVE A LOT OF PLUCK...
...AND SOME GOOD ARGUMENTS.
SINCE I'M IN YOUR DEBT, I'LL GRANT YOUR REQUEST...
I AGREE TO PARDON THEM AND LEGISLATE ON THE ISSUE!
THANKS!
HA HA HA!
I HOPE YOUR FRIENDS REALIZE HOW LUCKY THEY ARE TO HAVE YOU!
THANK YOU, YOUR MAJESTY!
THANK YOU, YOUR MAJESTY!

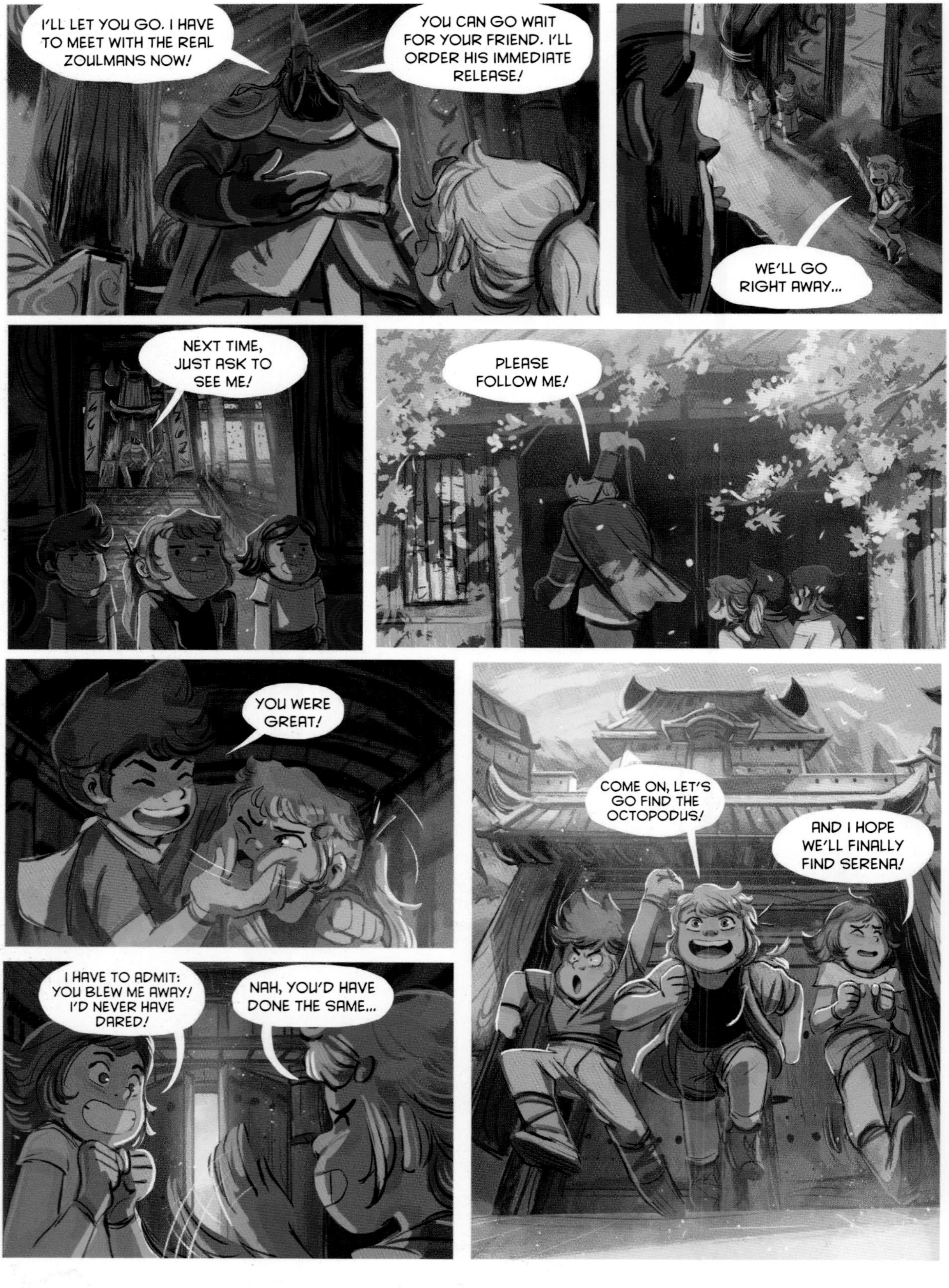
I'LL LET YOU GO. I HAVE TO MEET WITH THE REAL ZOULMANS NOW!
YOU CAN GO WAIT FOR YOUR FRIEND. I'LL ORDER HIS IMMEDIATE RELEASE!
WE'LL GO RIGHT AWAY...
NEXT TIME, JUST ASK TO SEE ME!
PLEASE FOLLOW ME!
YOU WERE GREAT!
I HAVE TO ADMIT: YOU BLEW ME AWAY! I'D NEVER HAVE DARED!
NAH, YOU'D HAVE DONE THE SAME...
COME ON, LET'S GO FIND THE OCTOPODUS!
AND I HOPE WE'LL FINALLY FIND SERENA!

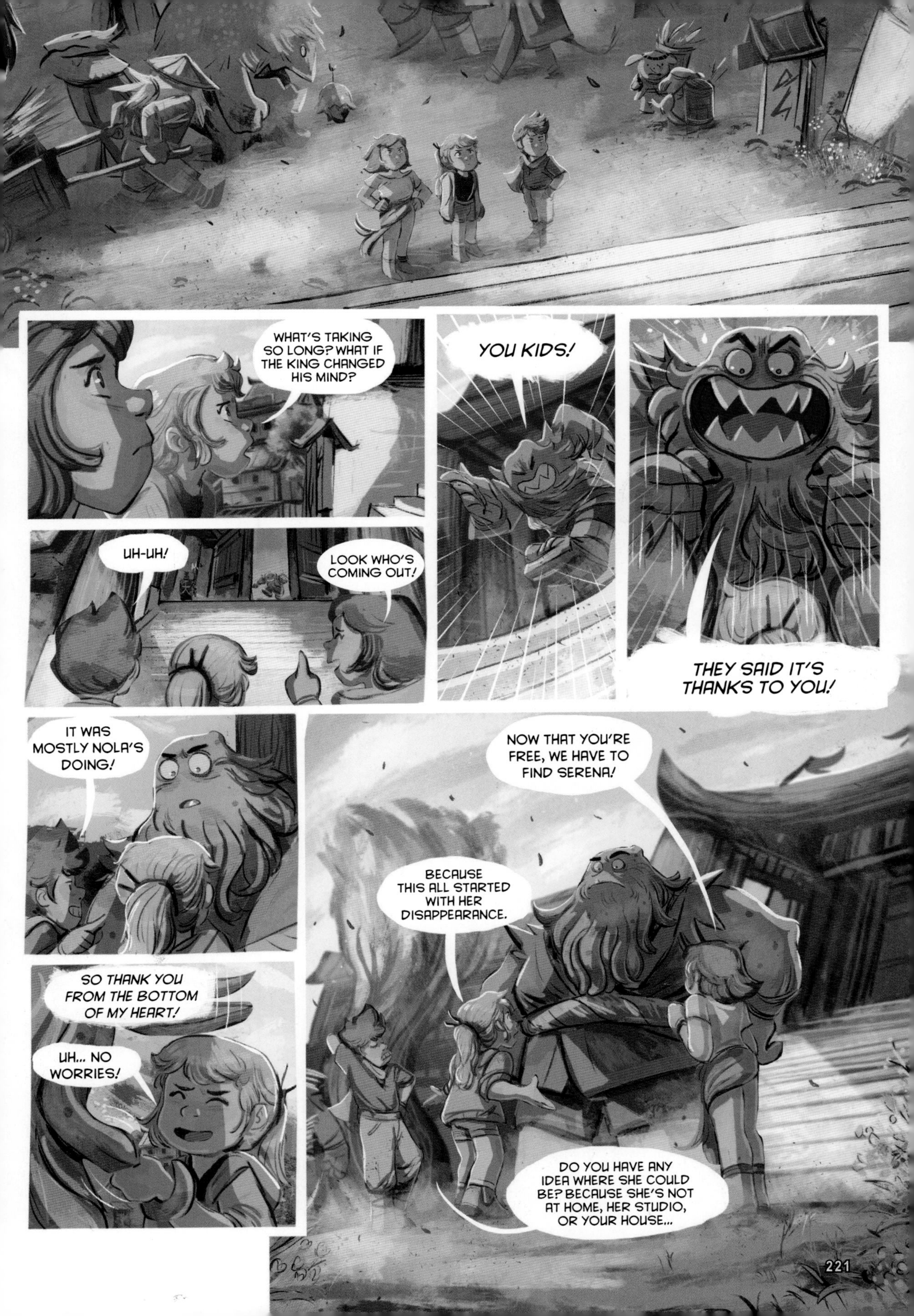
WHAT'S TAKING SO LONG? WHAT IF THE KING CHANGED HIS MIND?
UH-UH!
LOOK WHO'S COMING OUT!
YOU KIDS!
THEY SAID IT'S THANKS TO YOU!
IT WAS MOSTLY NOLA'S DOING!
SO THANK YOU FROM THE BOTTOM OF MY HEART!
UH... NO WORRIES!
NOW THAT YOU'RE FREE, WE HAVE TO FIND SERENA!
BECAUSE THIS ALL STARTED WITH HER DISAPPEARANCE.
DO YOU HAVE ANY IDEA WHERE SHE COULD BE? BECAUSE SHE'S NOT AT HOME, HER STUDIO, OR YOUR HOUSE...

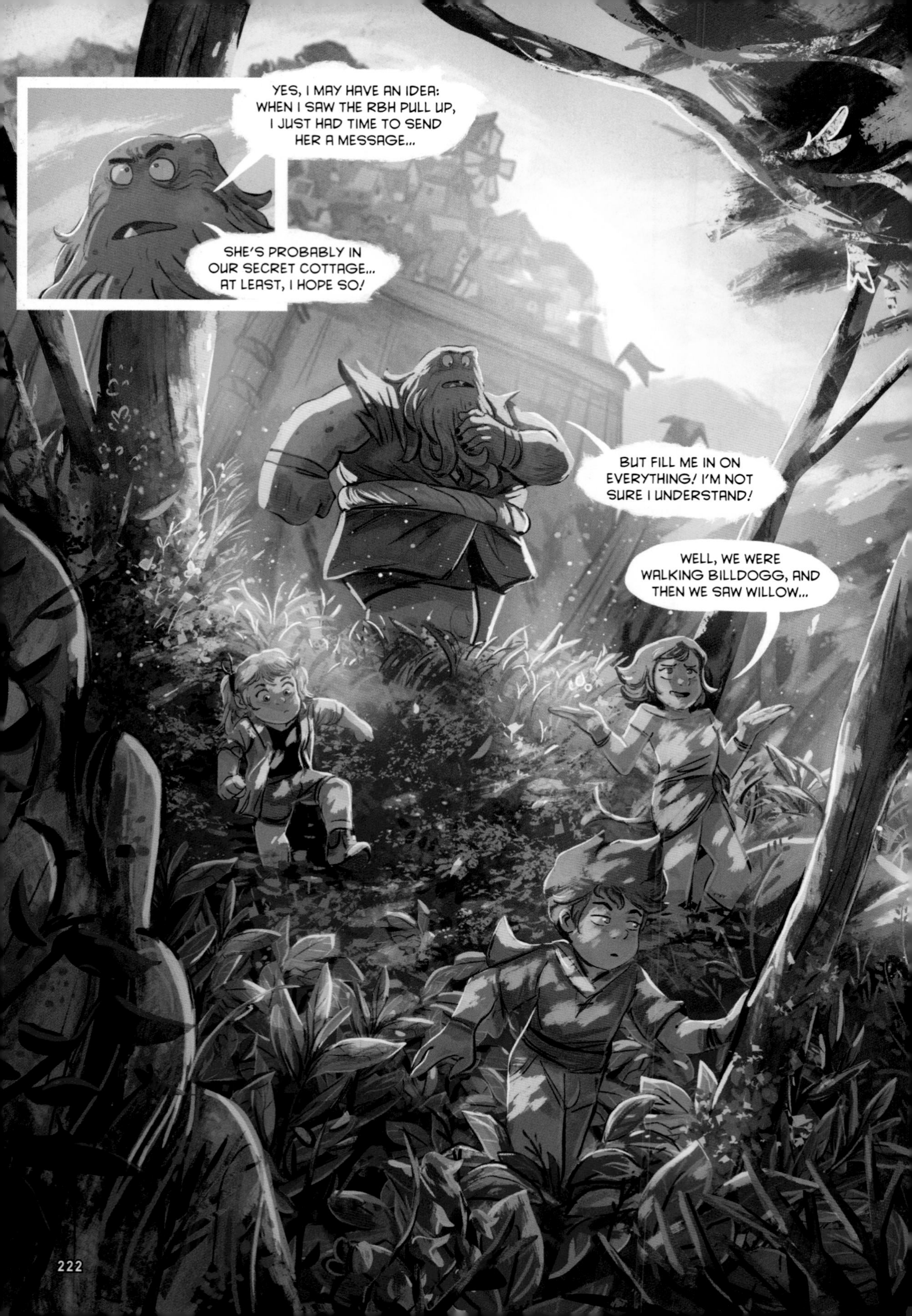

YES, I MAY HAVE AN IDEA: WHEN I SAW THE RBH PULL UP, I JUST HAD TIME TO SEND HER A MESSAGE...
SHE'S PROBABLY IN OUR SECRET COTTAGE... AT LEAST, I HOPE SO!
BUT FILL ME IN ON EVERYTHING! I'M NOT SURE I UNDERSTAND!
WELL, WE WERE WALKING BILLDOGG, AND THEN WE SAW WILLOW...

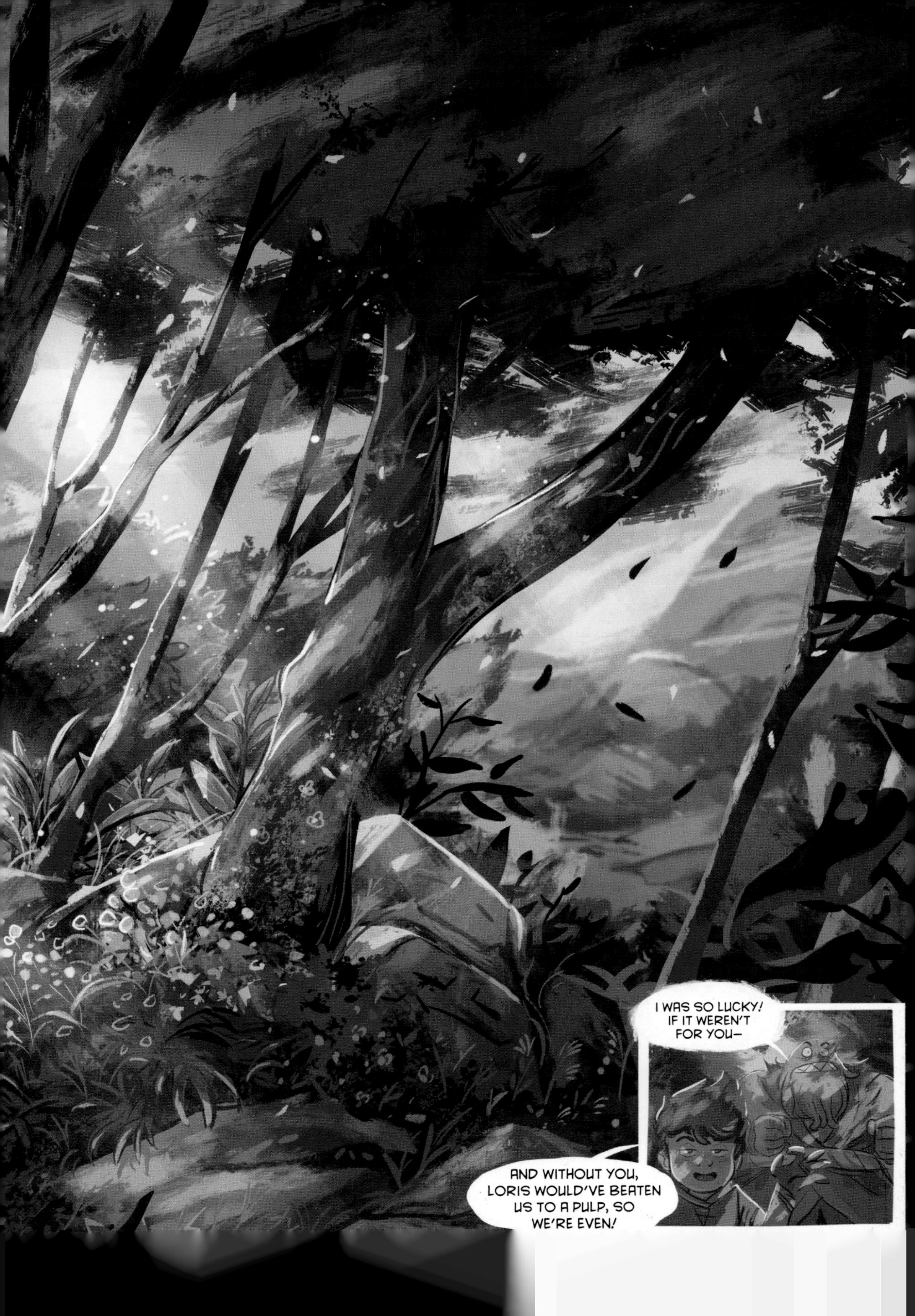
I WAS SO LUCKY! IF IT WEREN'T FOR YOU—
AND WITHOUT YOU, LORIS WOULD'VE BEATEN US TO A PULP, SO WE'RE EVEN!

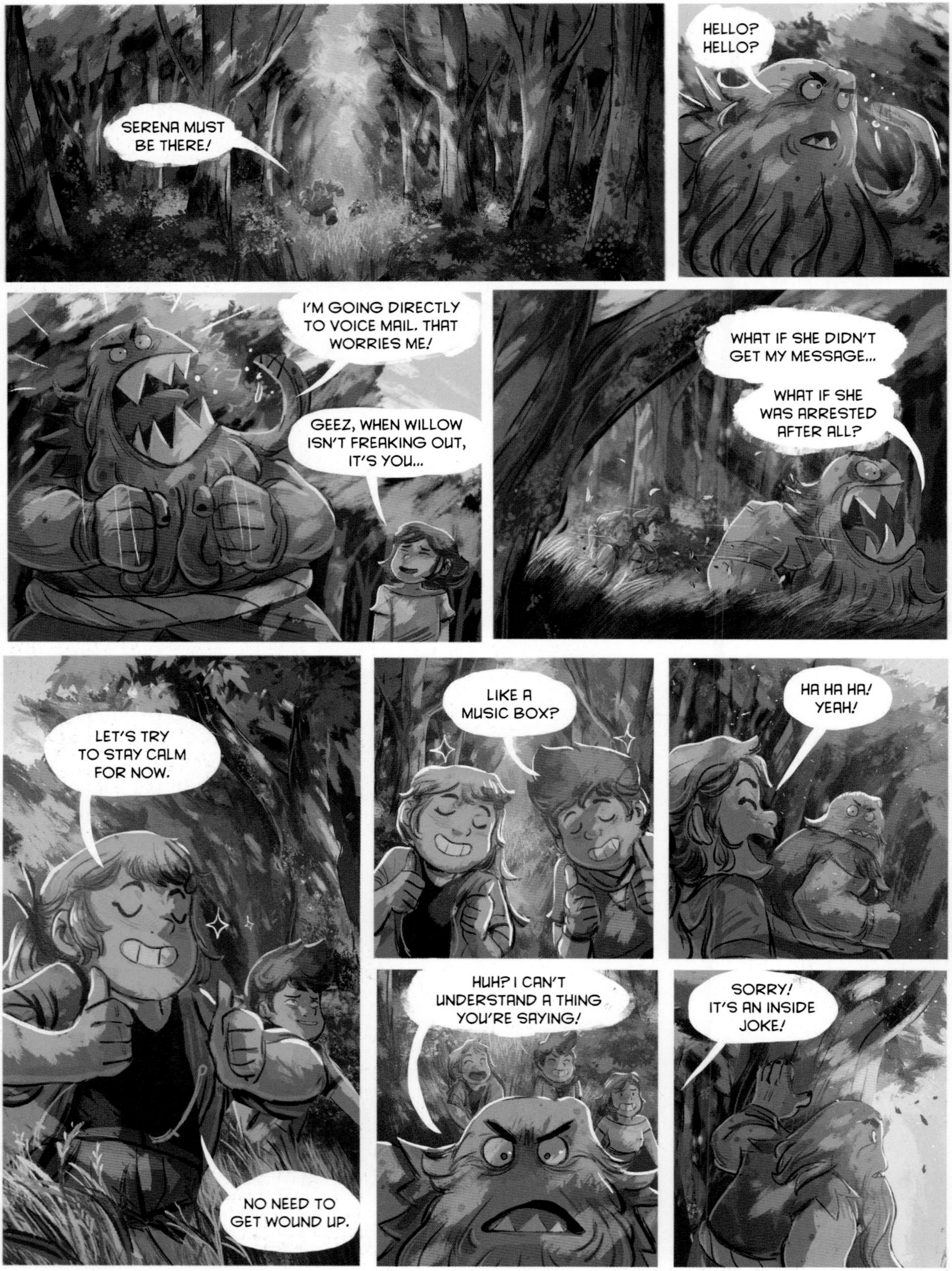

SERENA MUST BE THERE!
HELLO? HELLO?
I'M GOING DIRECTLY TO VOICE MAIL. THAT WORRIES ME!
GEEZ, WHEN WILLOW ISN'T FREAKING OUT, IT'S YOU...
WHAT IF SHE DIDN'T GET MY MESSAGE...
WHAT IF SHE WAS ARRESTED AFTER ALL?
LET'S TRY TO STAY CALM FOR NOW.
NO NEED TO GET WOUND UP.
LIKE A MUSIC BOX?
HA HA HA! YEAH!
HUH? I CAN'T UNDERSTAND A THING YOU'RE SAYING!
SORRY! IT'S AN INSIDE JOKE!

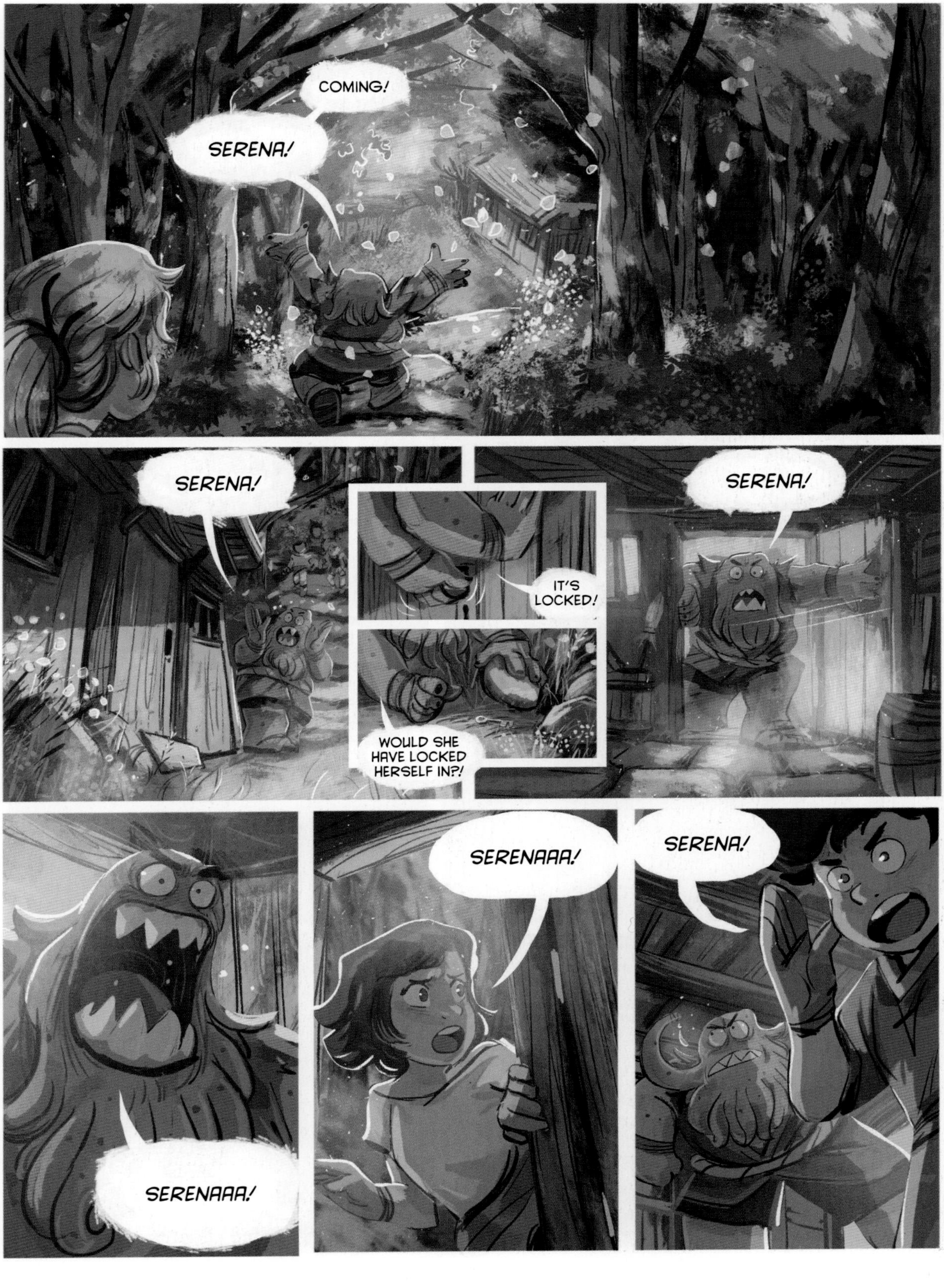
COMING!
SERENA!
SERENA!
IT'S LOCKED!
WOULD SHE HAVE LOCKED HERSELF IN?!
SERENA!
SERENAAA!
SERENAAA!
SERENA!

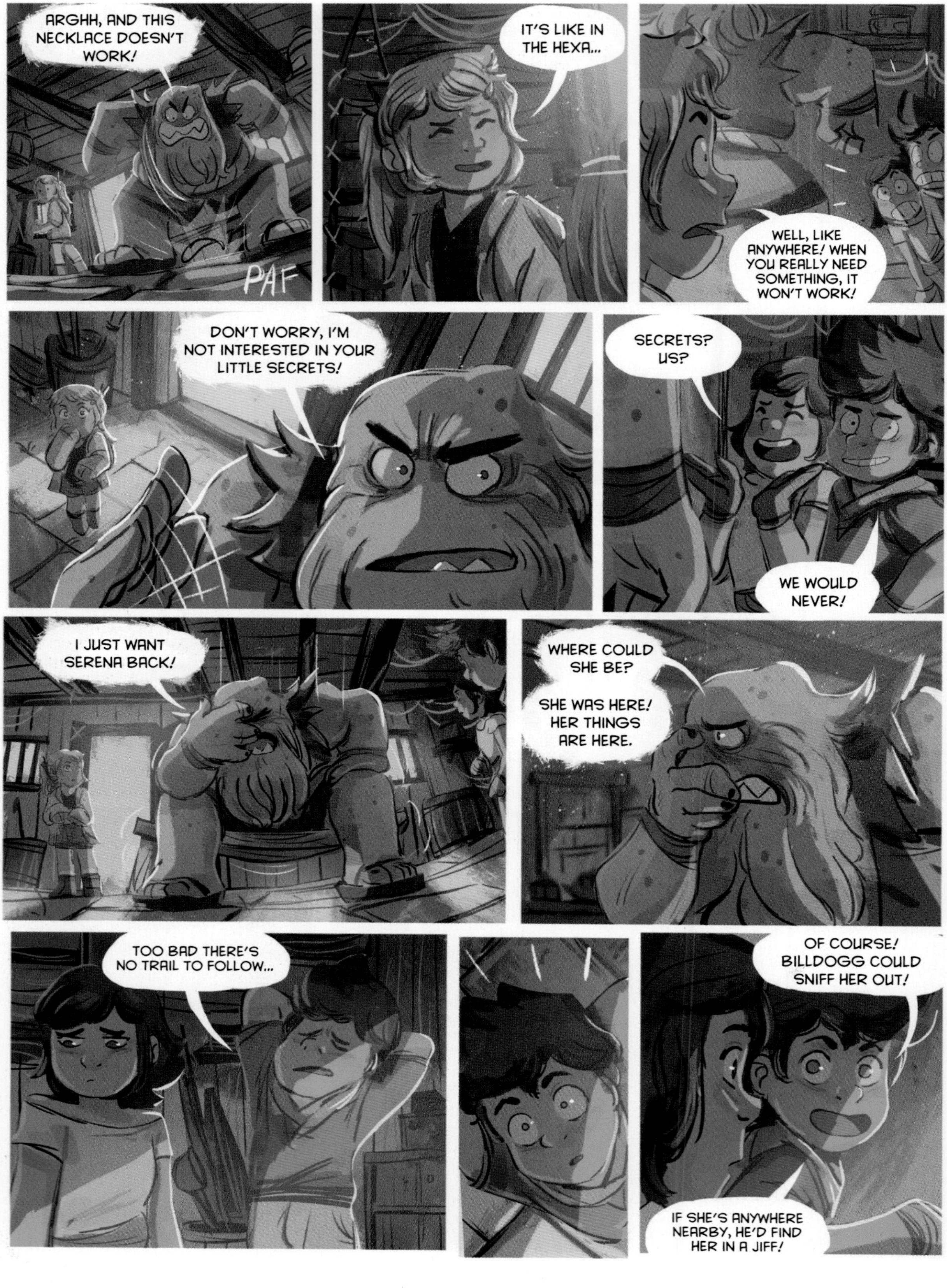
ARGHH, AND THIS NECKLACE DOESN'T WORK!
PAF
IT'S LIKE IN THE HEXA...
WELL, LIKE ANYWHERE! WHEN YOU REALLY NEED SOMETHING, IT WON'T WORK!
DON'T WORRY, I'M NOT INTERESTED IN YOUR LITTLE SECRETS!
SECRETS? US?
WE WOULD NEVER!
I JUST WANT SERENA BACK!
WHERE COULD SHE BE?
SHE WAS HERE! HER THINGS ARE HERE.
TOO BAD THERE'S NO TRAIL TO FOLLOW...
OF COURSE! BILLDOGG COULD SNIFF HER OUT!
IF SHE'S ANYWHERE NEARBY, HE'D FIND HER IN A JIFF!

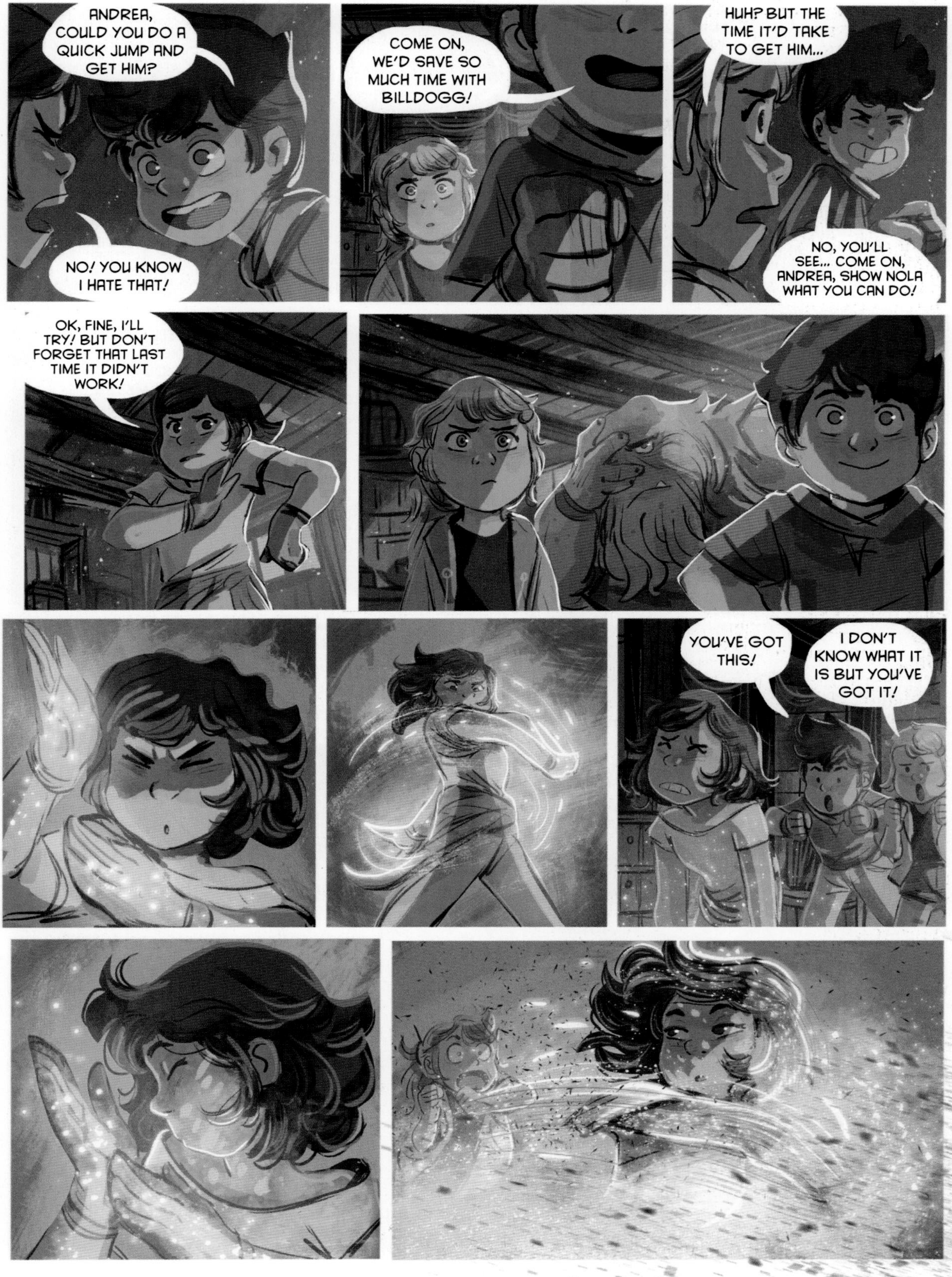
ANDREA, COULD YOU DO A QUICK JUMP AND GET HIM?
NO! YOU KNOW I HATE THAT!
COME ON, WE'D SAVE SO MUCH TIME WITH BILLDOGG!
HUH? BUT THE TIME IT'D TAKE TO GET HIM...
NO, YOU'LL SEE... COME ON, ANDREA, SHOW NOLA WHAT YOU CAN DO!
OK, FINE, I'LL TRY! BUT DON'T FORGET THAT LAST TIME IT DIDN'T WORK!
YOU'VE GOT THIS!
I DON'T KNOW WHAT IT IS BUT YOU'VE GOT IT!

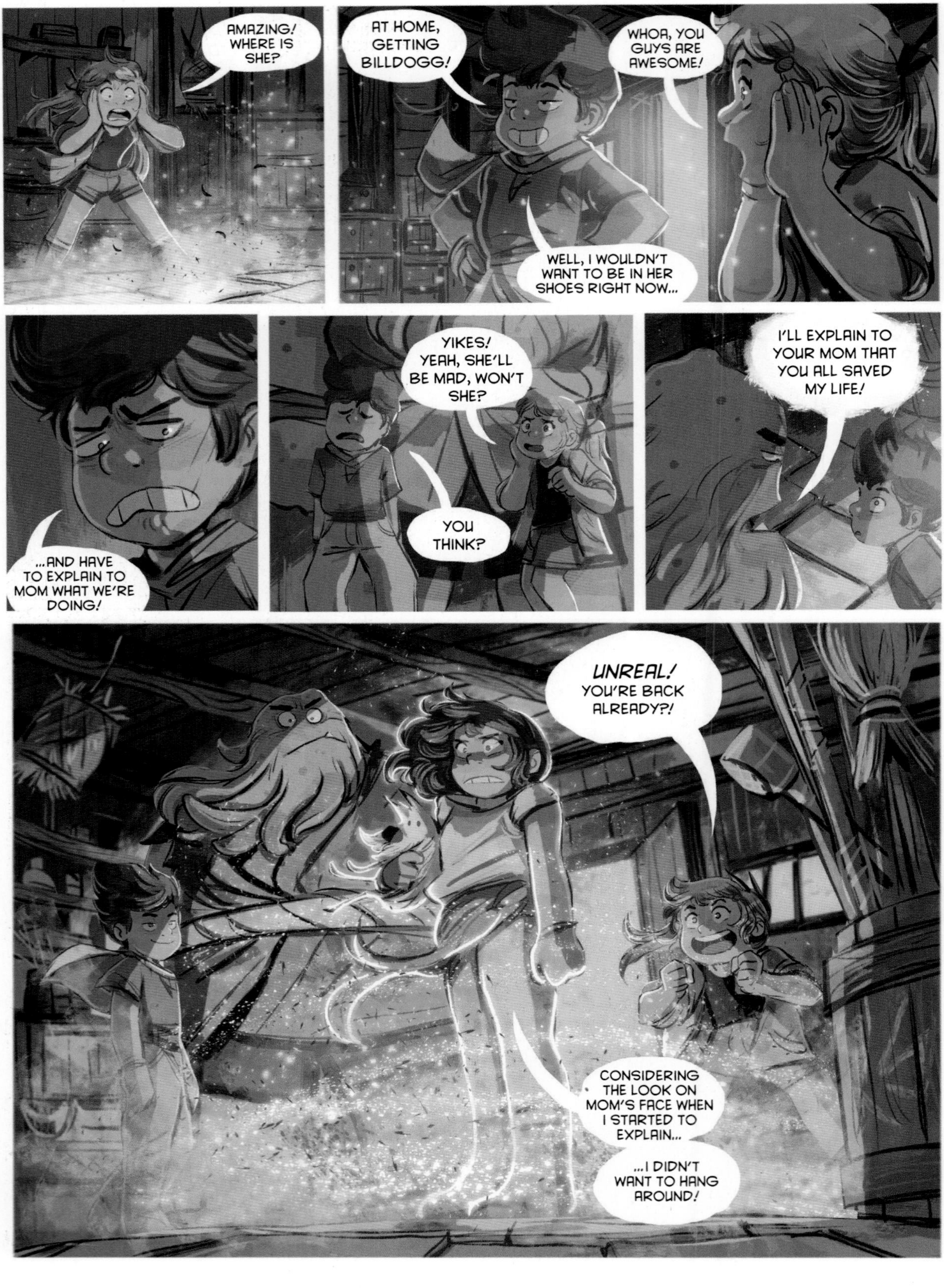
AMAZING! WHERE IS SHE?
AT HOME, GETTING BILLDOGG!
WHOA, YOU GUYS ARE AWESOME!
WELL, I WOULDN'T WANT TO BE IN HER SHOES RIGHT NOW...
...AND HAVE TO EXPLAIN TO MOM WHAT WE'RE DOING!
YIKES! YEAH, SHE'LL BE MAD, WON'T SHE?
YOU THINK?
I'LL EXPLAIN TO YOUR MOM THAT YOU ALL SAVED MY LIFE!
UNREAL! YOU'RE BACK ALREADY?!
CONSIDERING THE LOOK ON MOM'S FACE WHEN I STARTED TO EXPLAIN...
...I DIDN'T WANT TO HANG AROUND!

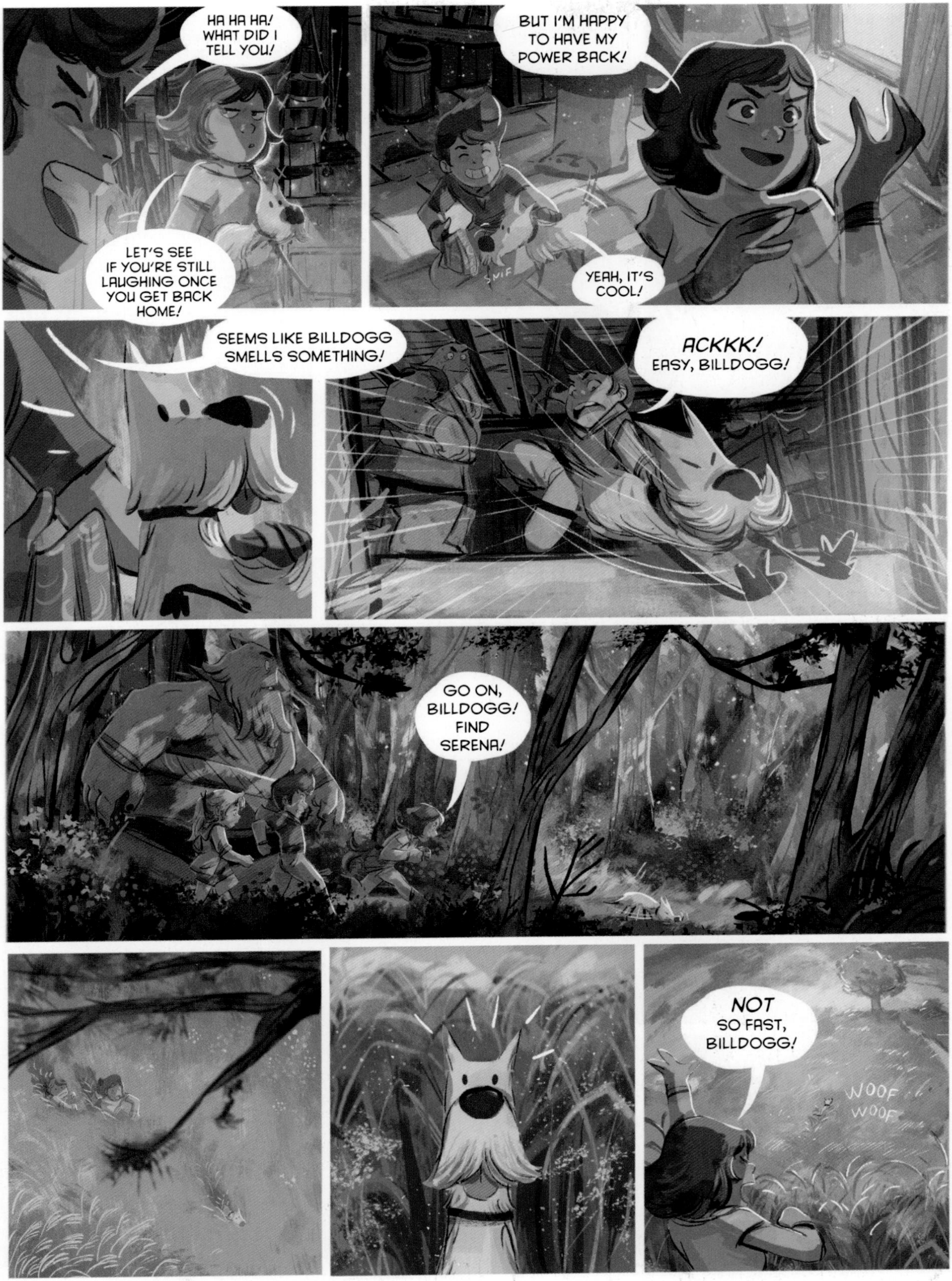
HA HA HA! WHAT DID I TELL YOU!
LET'S SEE IF YOU'RE STILL LAUGHING ONCE YOU GET BACK HOME!
BUT I'M HAPPY TO HAVE MY POWER BACK!
SNIF
YEAH, IT'S COOL!
SEEMS LIKE BILLDOGG SMELLS SOMETHING!
ACKKK! EASY, BILLDOGG!
GO ON, BILLDOGG! FIND SERENA!
NOT SO FAST, BILLDOGG!
WOOF WOOF

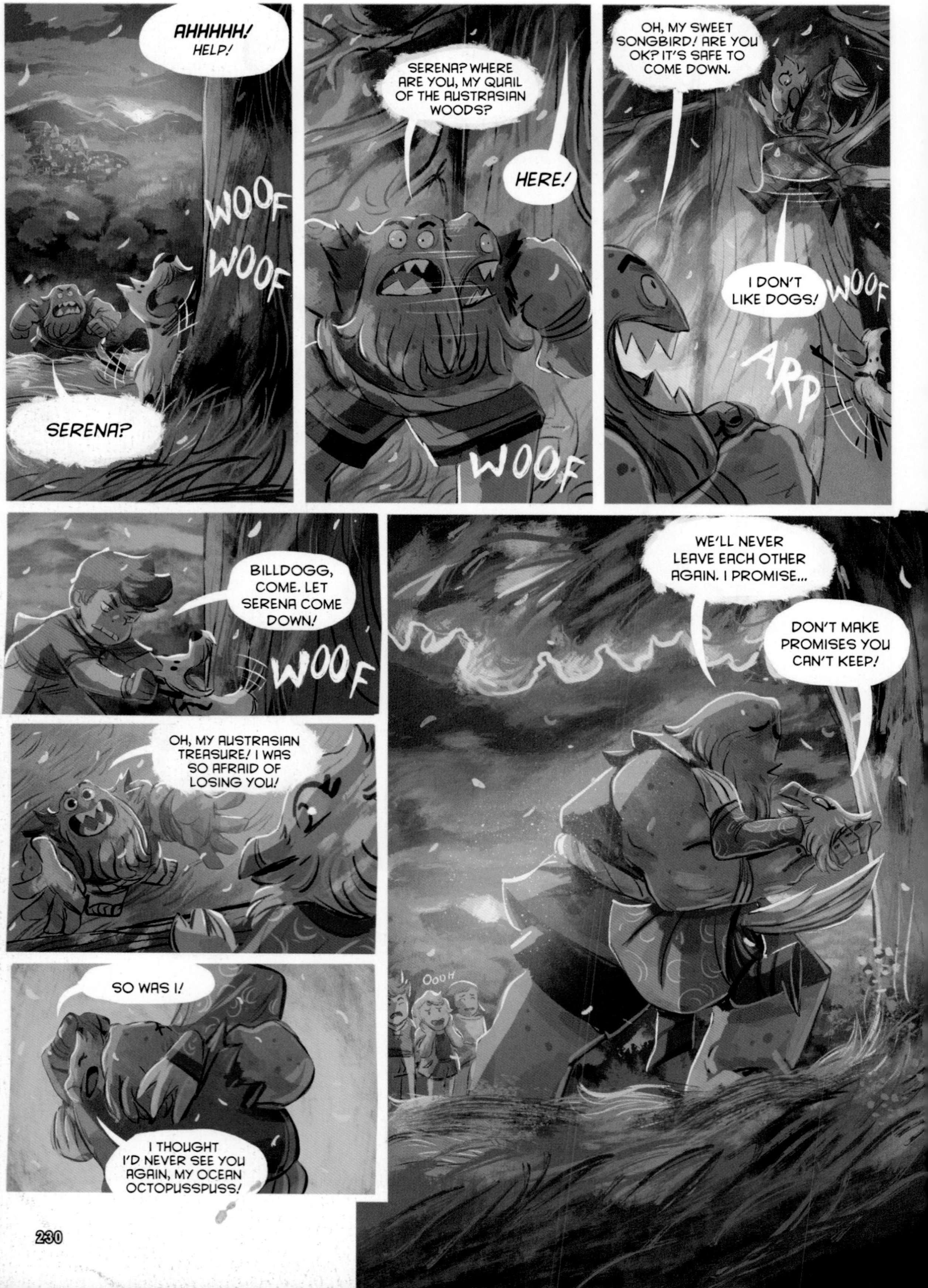
AHHHHH!
HELP!
WOOF
WOOF
SERENA?
SERENA? WHERE ARE YOU, MY QUAIL OF THE AUSTRASIAN WOODS?
HERE!
WOOF
OH, MY SWEET SONGBIRD! ARE YOU OK? IT'S SAFE TO COME DOWN.
I DON'T LIKE DOGS!
WOOF
ARP
BILLDOGG, COME. LET SERENA COME DOWN!
WOOF
OH, MY AUSTRASIAN TREASURE! I WAS SO AFRAID OF LOSING YOU!
SO WAS I!
I THOUGHT I'D NEVER SEE YOU AGAIN, MY OCEAN OCTOPUSSPUSS!
WE'LL NEVER LEAVE EACH OTHER AGAIN. I PROMISE...
DON'T MAKE PROMISES YOU CAN'T KEEP!
OOOH

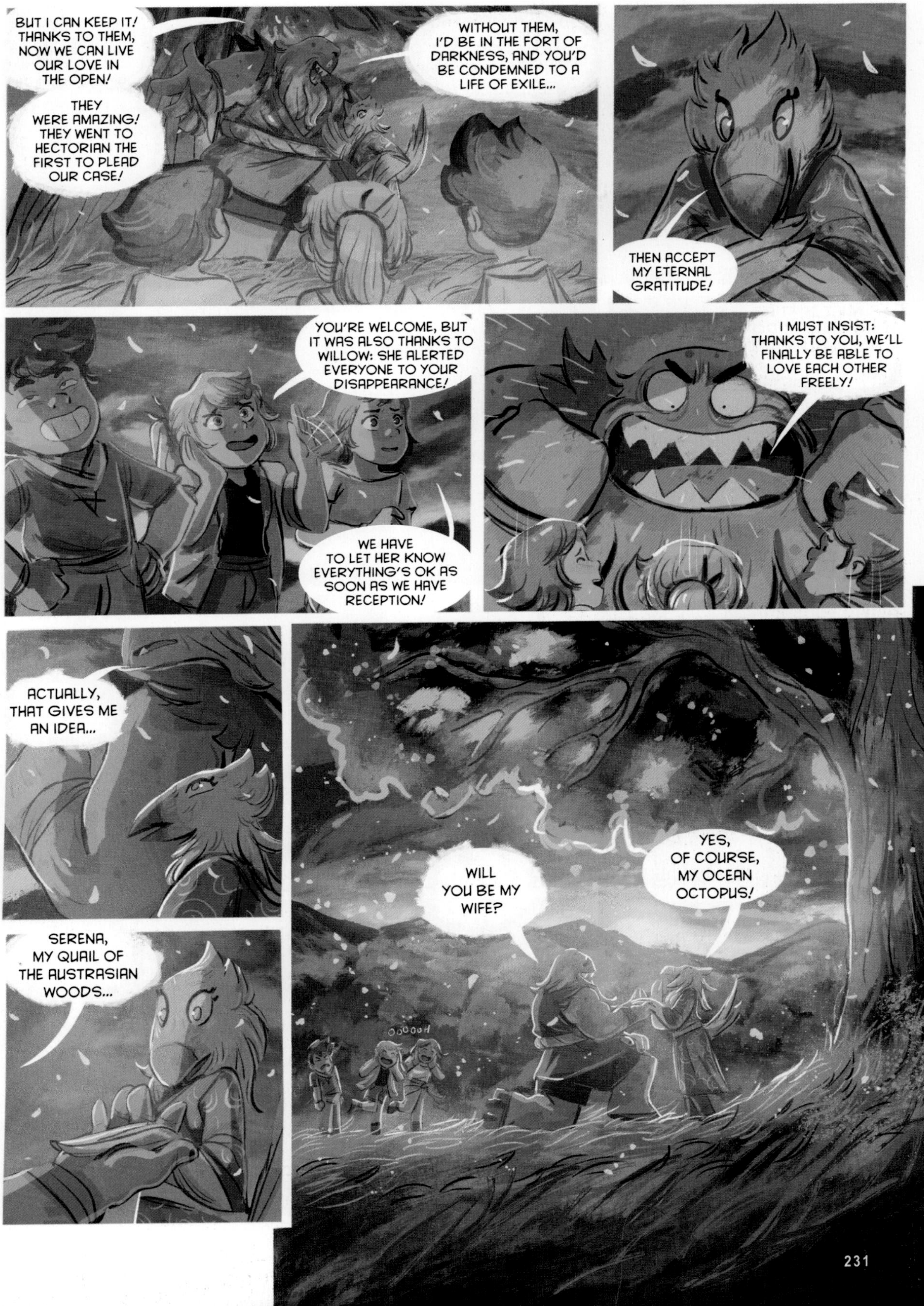
BUT I CAN KEEP IT! THANKS TO THEM, NOW WE CAN LIVE OUR LOVE IN THE OPEN!
THEY WERE AMAZING! THEY WENT TO HECTORIAN THE FIRST TO PLEAD OUR CASE!
WITHOUT THEM, I'D BE IN THE FORT OF DARKNESS, AND YOU'D BE CONDEMNED TO A LIFE OF EXILE...
THEN ACCEPT MY ETERNAL GRATITUDE!
YOU'RE WELCOME, BUT IT WAS ALSO THANKS TO WILLOW: SHE ALERTED EVERYONE TO YOUR DISAPPEARANCE!
WE HAVE TO LET HER KNOW EVERYTHING'S OK AS SOON AS WE HAVE RECEPTION!
I MUST INSIST: THANKS TO YOU, WE'LL FINALLY BE ABLE TO LOVE EACH OTHER FREELY!
ACTUALLY, THAT GIVES ME AN IDEA...
SERENA, MY QUAIL OF THE AUSTRASIAN WOODS...
OOOOOH
WILL YOU BE MY WIFE?
YES, OF COURSE, MY OCEAN OCTOPUS!

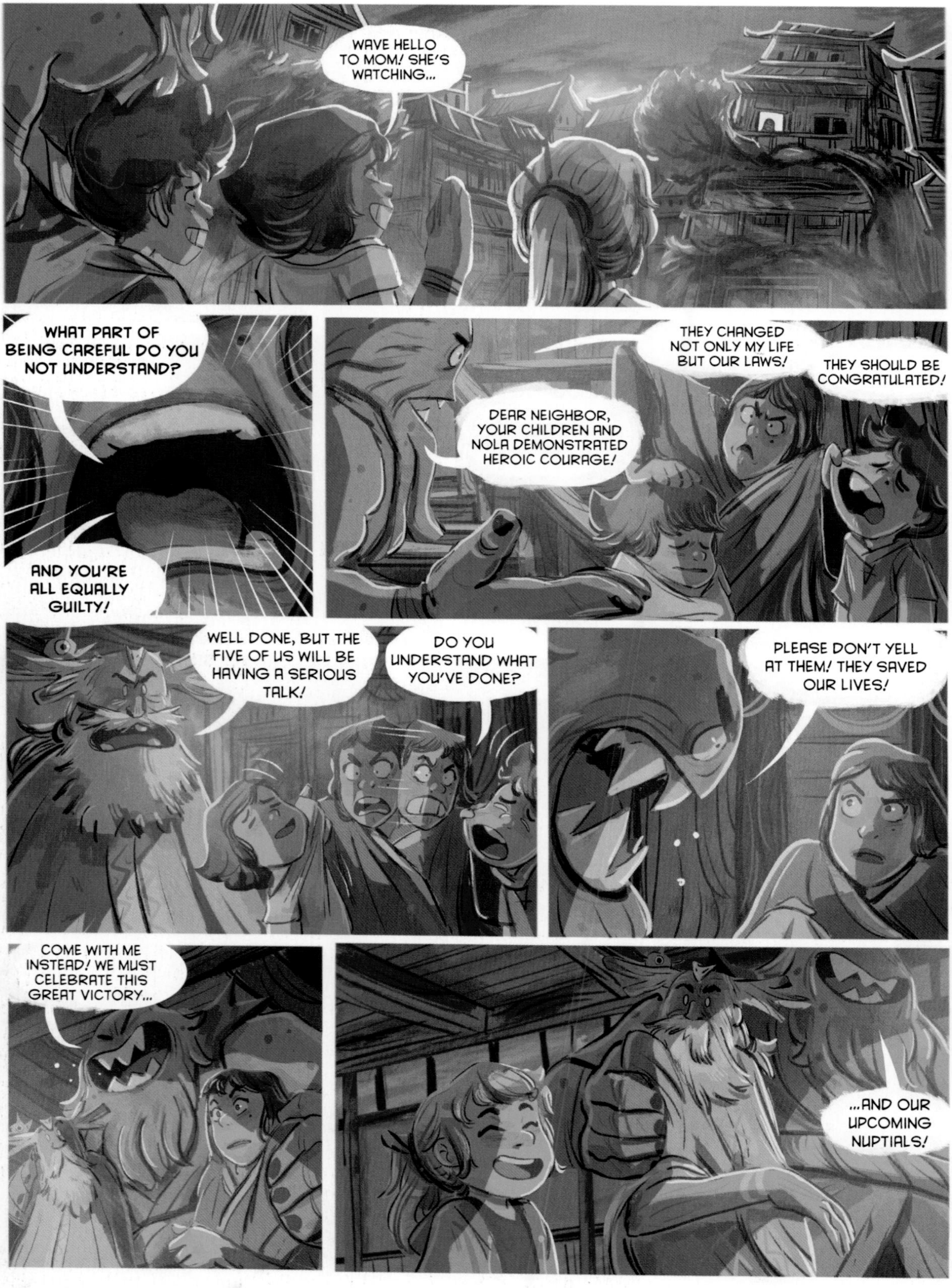
WAVE HELLO TO MOM! SHE'S WATCHING...
WHAT PART OF BEING CAREFUL DO YOU NOT UNDERSTAND?
AND YOU'RE ALL EQUALLY GUILTY!
DEAR NEIGHBOR, YOUR CHILDREN AND NOLA DEMONSTRATED HEROIC COURAGE!
THEY CHANGED NOT ONLY MY LIFE BUT OUR LAWS!
THEY SHOULD BE CONGRATULATED!
WELL DONE, BUT THE FIVE OF US WILL BE HAVING A SERIOUS TALK!
DO YOU UNDERSTAND WHAT YOU'VE DONE?
PLEASE DON'T YELL AT THEM! THEY SAVED OUR LIVES!
COME WITH ME INSTEAD! WE MUST CELEBRATE THIS GREAT VICTORY...
...AND OUR UPCOMING NUPTIALS!

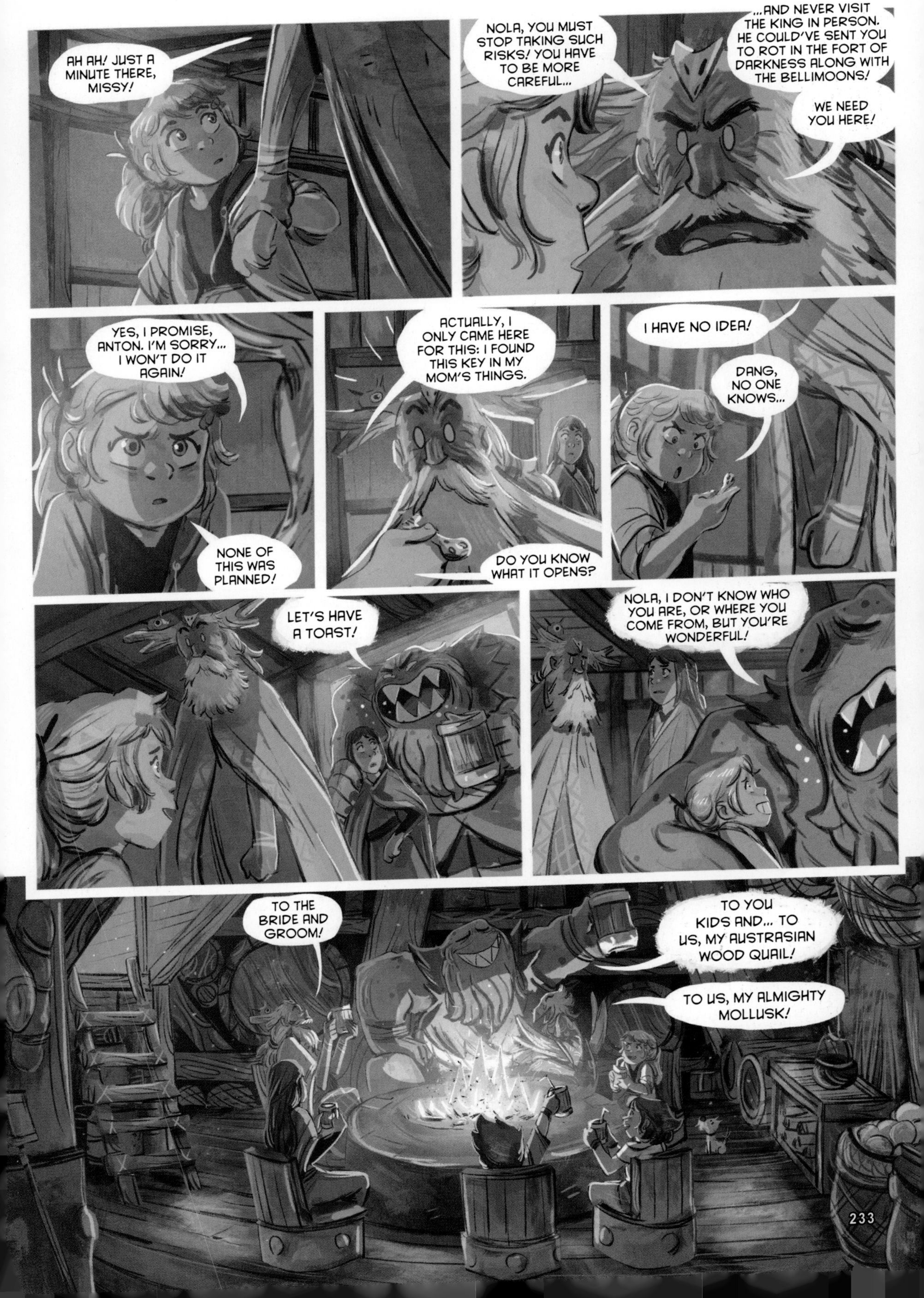
AH AH! JUST A MINUTE THERE, MISSY!
NOLA, YOU MUST STOP TAKING SUCH RISKS! YOU HAVE TO BE MORE CAREFUL...
...AND NEVER VISIT THE KING IN PERSON. HE COULD'VE SENT YOU TO ROT IN THE FORT OF DARKNESS ALONG WITH THE BELLIMOONS!
WE NEED YOU HERE!
YES, I PROMISE, ANTON. I'M SORRY... I WON'T DO IT AGAIN!
NONE OF THIS WAS PLANNED!
ACTUALLY, I ONLY CAME HERE FOR THIS: I FOUND THIS KEY IN MY MOM'S THINGS.
DO YOU KNOW WHAT IT OPENS?
I HAVE NO IDEA!
DANG, NO ONE KNOWS...
LET'S HAVE A TOAST!
NOLA, I DON'T KNOW WHO YOU ARE, OR WHERE YOU COME FROM, BUT YOU'RE WONDERFUL!
TO THE BRIDE AND GROOM!
TO YOU KIDS AND... TO US, MY AUSTRASIAN WOOD QUAIL!
TO US, MY ALMIGHTY MOLLUSK!

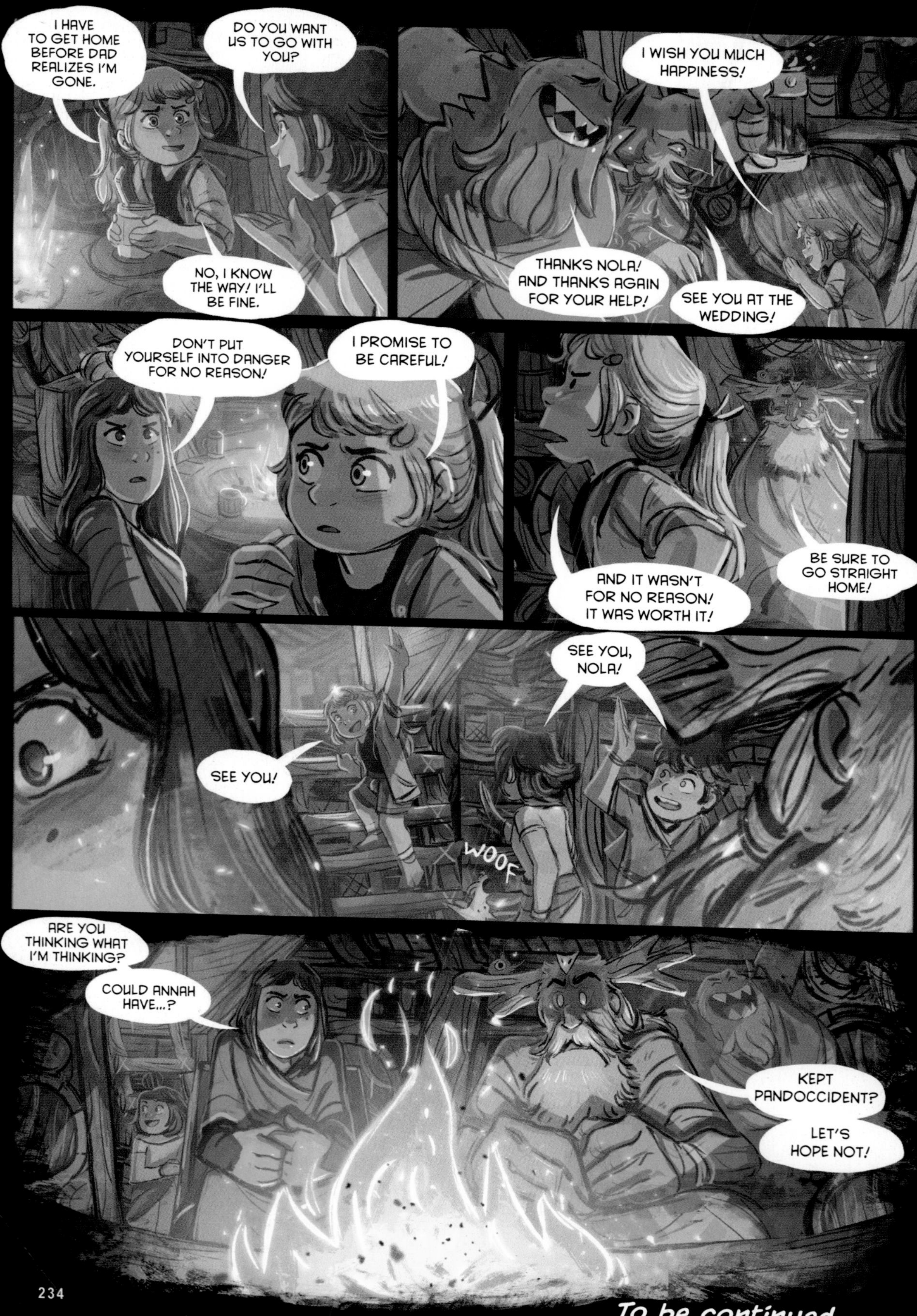
I HAVE TO GET HOME BEFORE DAD REALIZES I'M GONE.
DO YOU WANT US TO GO WITH YOU?
NO, I KNOW THE WAY! I'LL BE FINE.
I WISH YOU MUCH HAPPINESS!
THANKS NOLA! AND THANKS AGAIN FOR YOUR HELP!
SEE YOU AT THE WEDDING!
DON'T PUT YOURSELF INTO DANGER FOR NO REASON!
I PROMISE TO BE CAREFUL!
AND IT WASN'T FOR NO REASON! IT WAS WORTH IT!
BE SURE TO GO STRAIGHT HOME!
SEE YOU, NOLA!
SEE YOU!
WOOF
ARE YOU THINKING WHAT I'M THINKING?
COULD ANNAH HAVE...?
KEPT PANDOCCIDENT?
LET'S HOPE NOT!

To be continued . . .

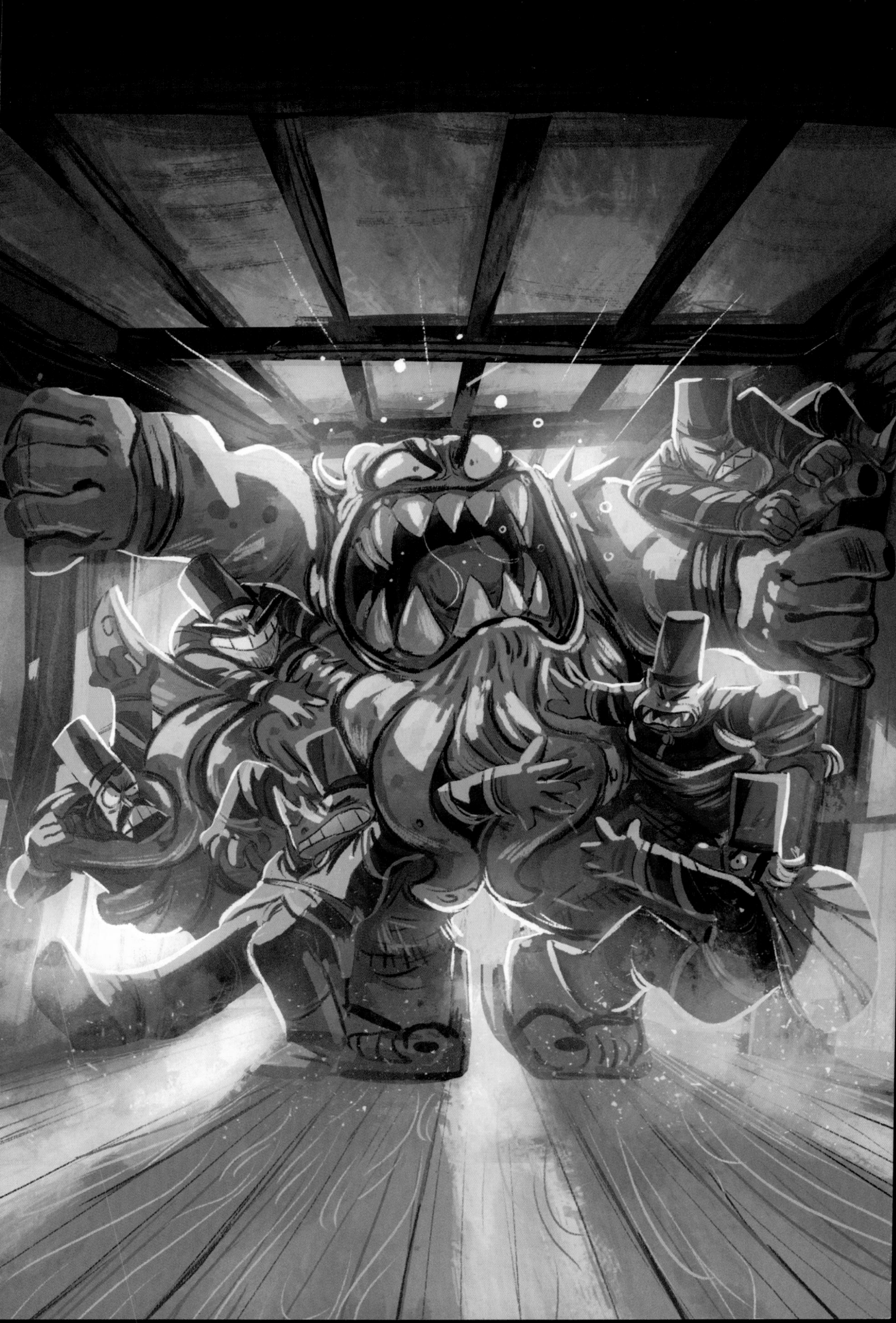

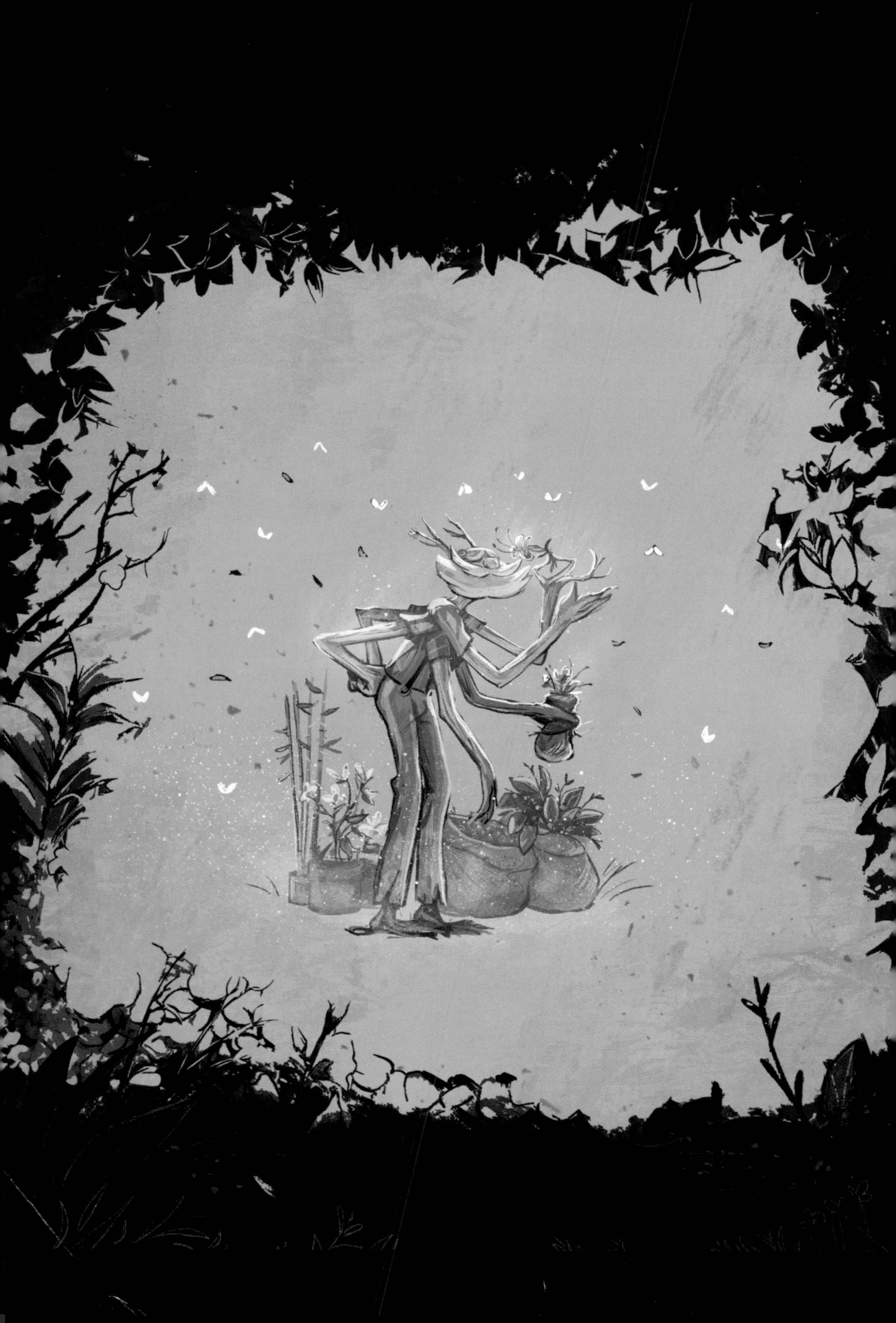

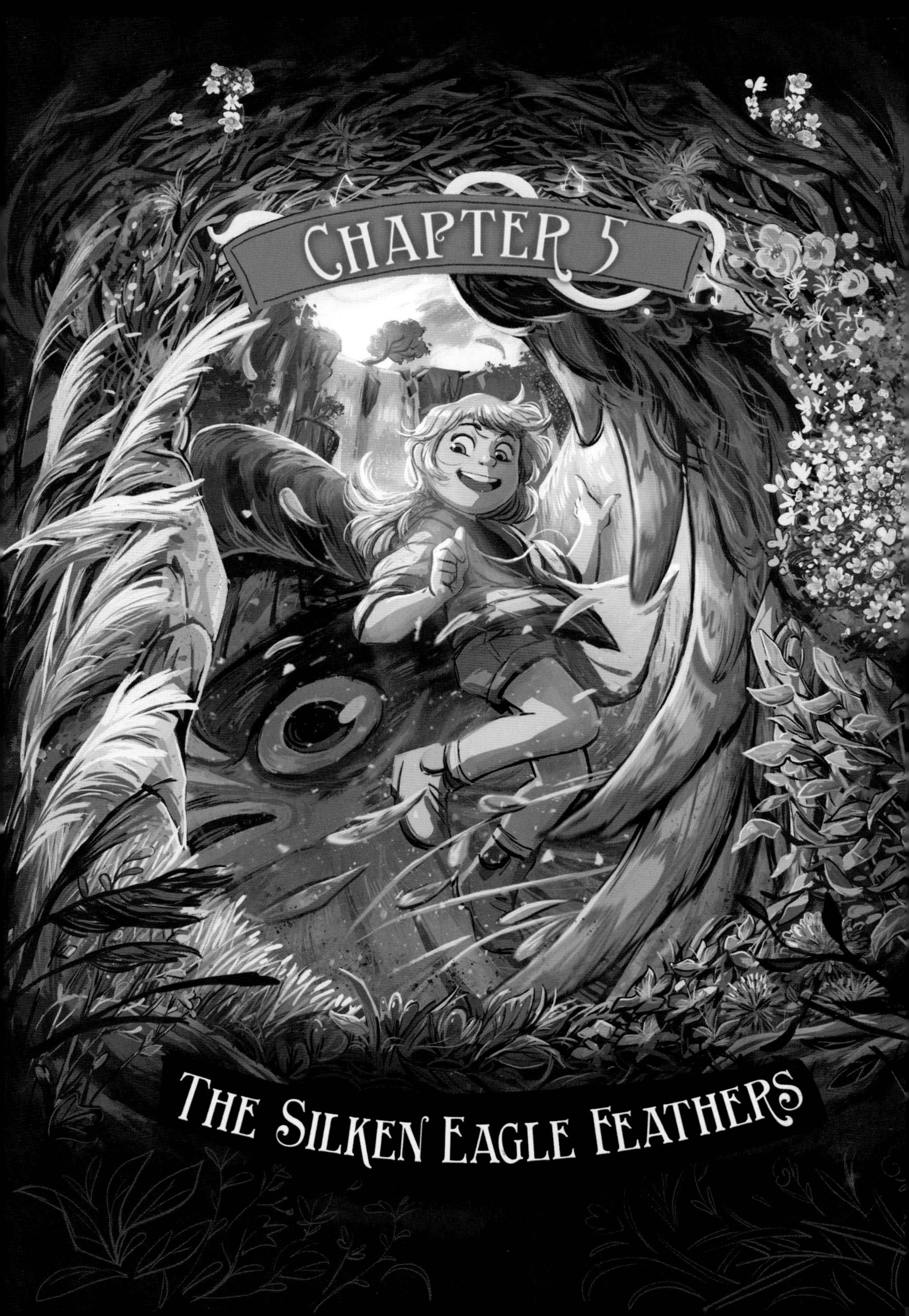
CHAPTER 5
THE SILKEN EAGLE FEATHERS

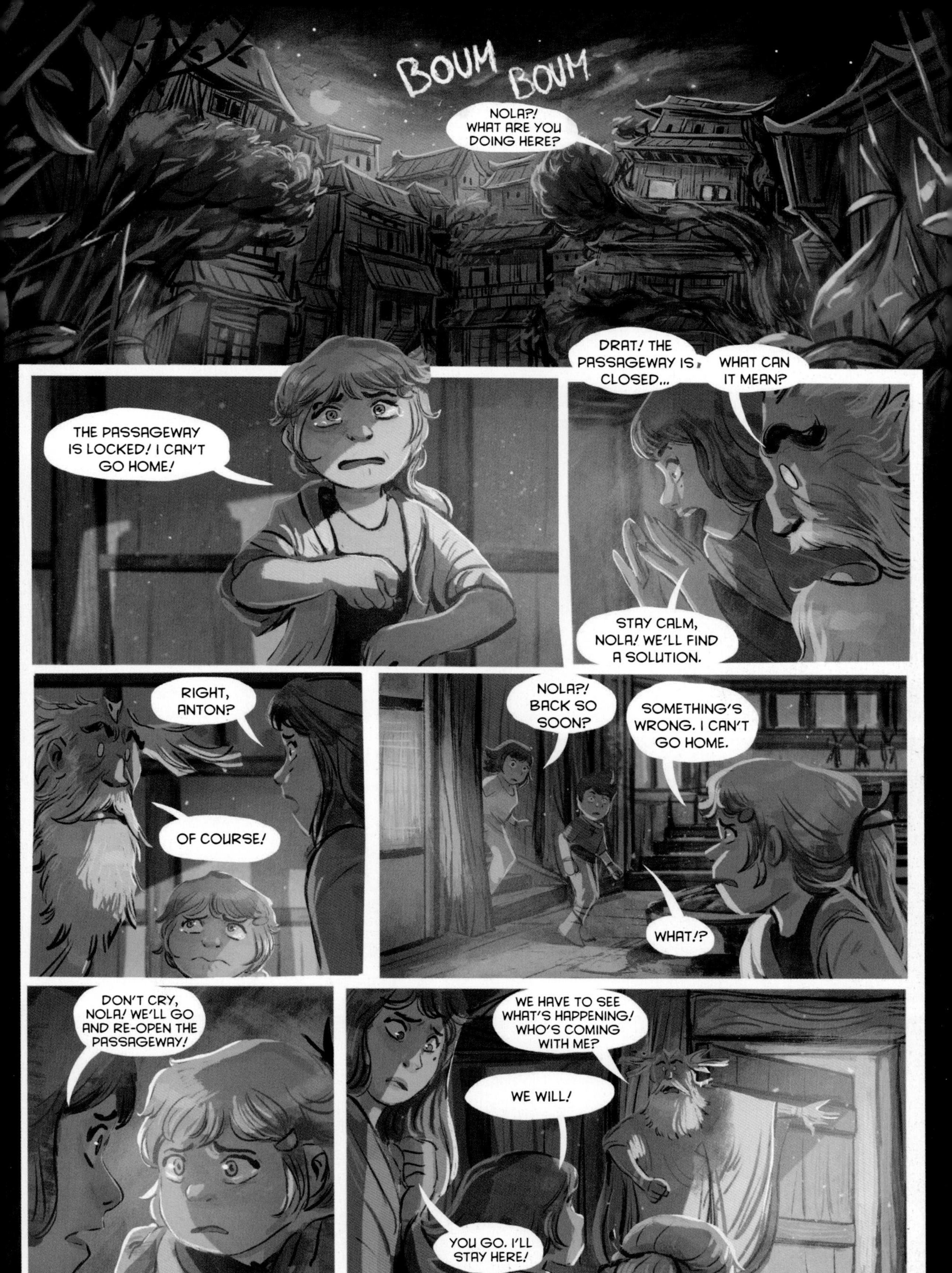
BOUM BOUM
NOLA?! WHAT ARE YOU DOING HERE?
THE PASSAGEWAY IS LOCKED! I CAN'T GO HOME!
DRAT! THE PASSAGEWAY IS CLOSED...
WHAT CAN IT MEAN?
STAY CALM, NOLA! WE'LL FIND A SOLUTION.
RIGHT, ANTON?
OF COURSE!
NOLA?! BACK SO SOON?
SOMETHING'S WRONG. I CAN'T GO HOME.
WHAT!?
DON'T CRY, NOLA! WE'LL GO AND RE-OPEN THE PASSAGEWAY!
WE HAVE TO SEE WHAT'S HAPPENING! WHO'S COMING WITH ME?
WE WILL!
YOU GO. I'LL STAY HERE!

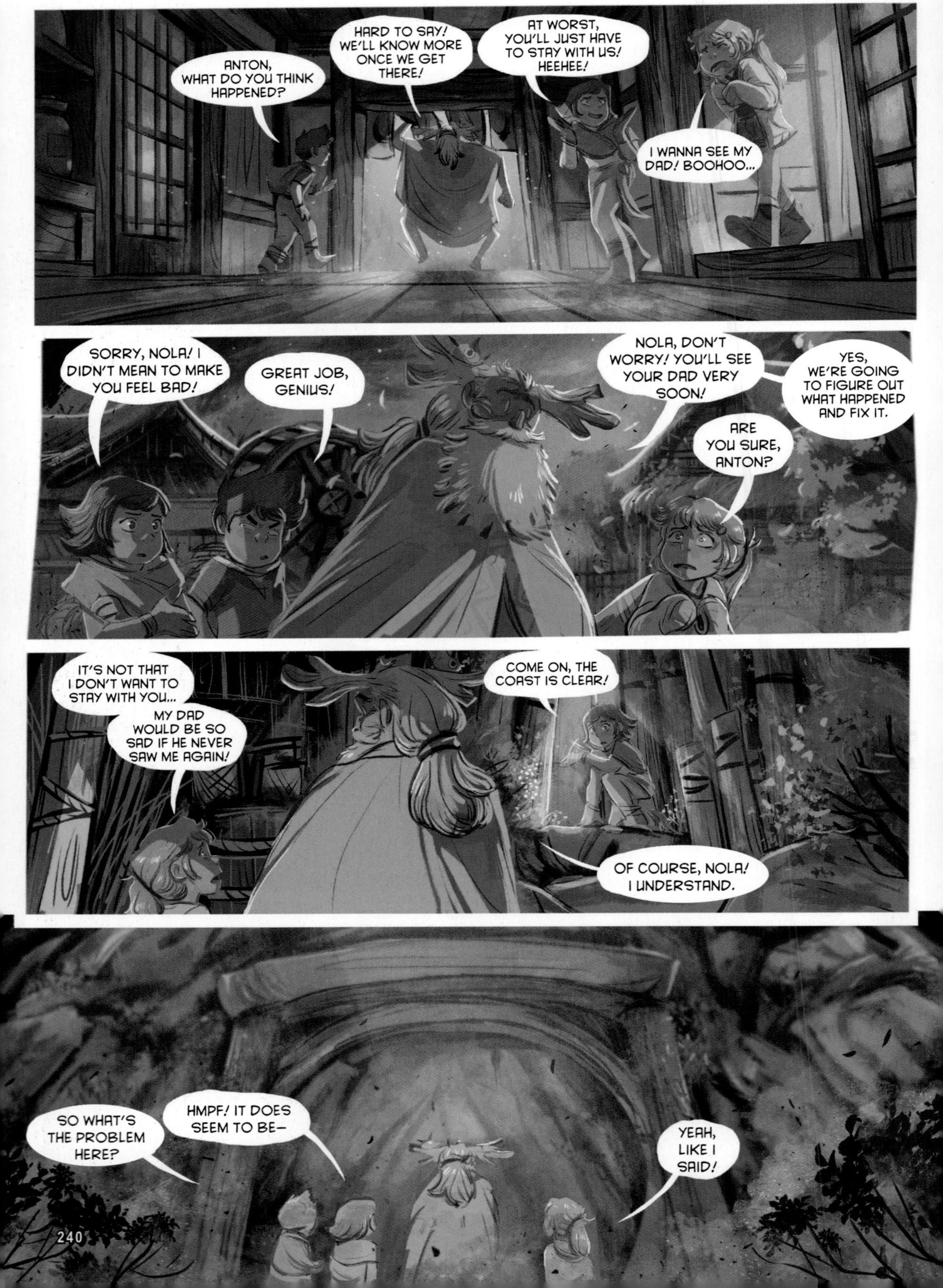
ANTON, WHAT DO YOU THINK HAPPENED?
HARD TO SAY! WE'LL KNOW MORE ONCE WE GET THERE!
AT WORST, YOU'LL JUST HAVE TO STAY WITH US! HEEHEE!
I WANNA SEE MY DAD! BOOHOO...
SORRY, NOLA! I DIDN'T MEAN TO MAKE YOU FEEL BAD!
GREAT JOB, GENIUS!
NOLA, DON'T WORRY! YOU'LL SEE YOUR DAD VERY SOON!
YES, WE'RE GOING TO FIGURE OUT WHAT HAPPENED AND FIX IT.
ARE YOU SURE, ANTON?
IT'S NOT THAT I DON'T WANT TO STAY WITH YOU...
MY DAD WOULD BE SO SAD IF HE NEVER SAW ME AGAIN!
COME ON, THE COAST IS CLEAR!
OF COURSE, NOLA! I UNDERSTAND.
SO WHAT'S THE PROBLEM HERE?
HMPF! IT DOES SEEM TO BE–
YEAH, LIKE I SAID!

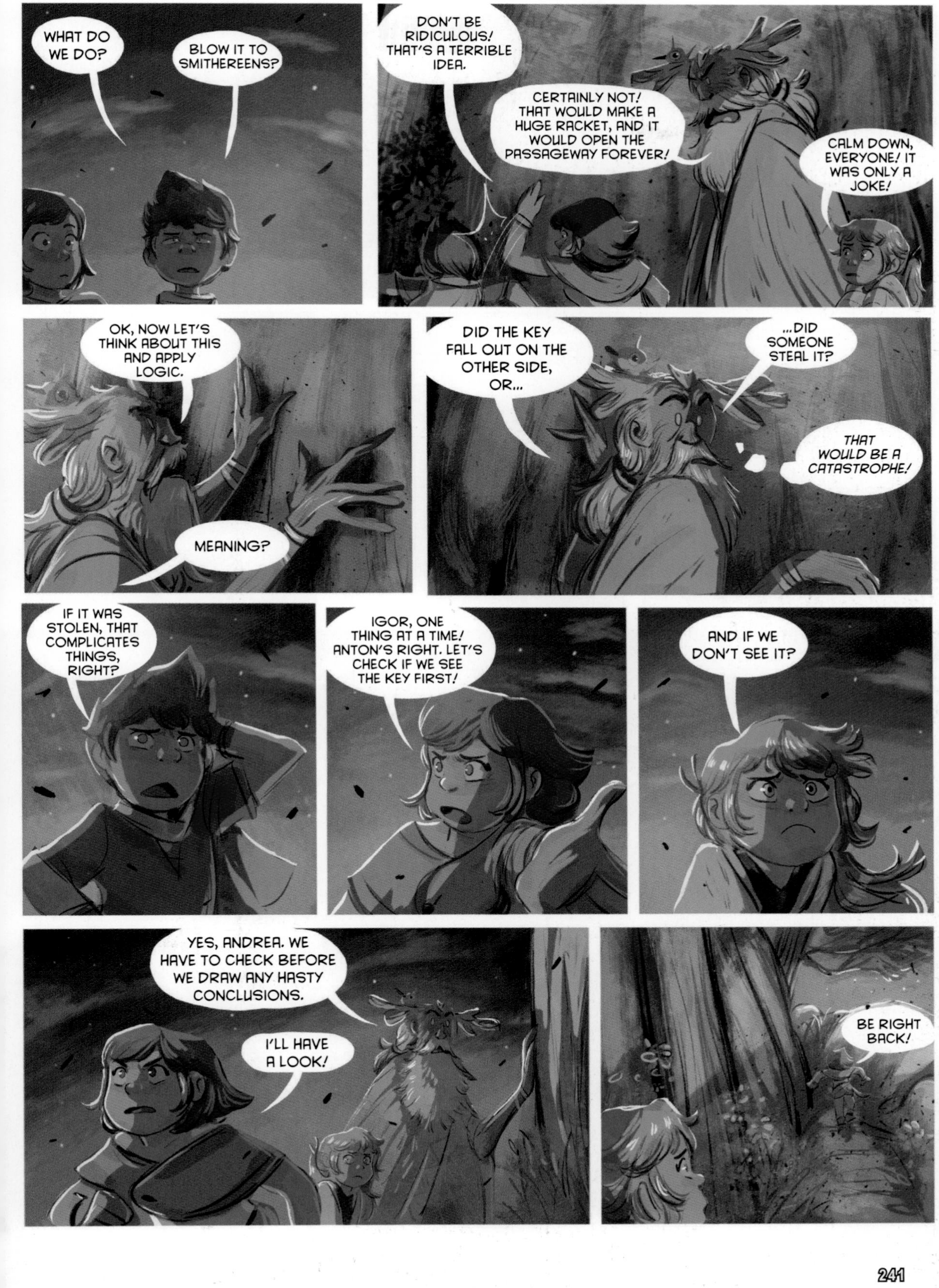
WHAT DO WE DO?
BLOW IT TO SMITHEREENS?
DON'T BE RIDICULOUS! THAT'S A TERRIBLE IDEA.
CERTAINLY NOT! THAT WOULD MAKE A HUGE RACKET, AND IT WOULD OPEN THE PASSAGEWAY FOREVER!
CALM DOWN, EVERYONE! IT WAS ONLY A JOKE!
OK, NOW LET'S THINK ABOUT THIS AND APPLY LOGIC.
MEANING?
DID THE KEY FALL OUT ON THE OTHER SIDE, OR...
...DID SOMEONE STEAL IT?
THAT WOULD BE A CATASTROPHE!
IF IT WAS STOLEN, THAT COMPLICATES THINGS, RIGHT?
IGOR, ONE THING AT A TIME! ANTON'S RIGHT. LET'S CHECK IF WE SEE THE KEY FIRST!
AND IF WE DON'T SEE IT?
YES, ANDREA. WE HAVE TO CHECK BEFORE WE DRAW ANY HASTY CONCLUSIONS.
I'LL HAVE A LOOK!
BE RIGHT BACK!

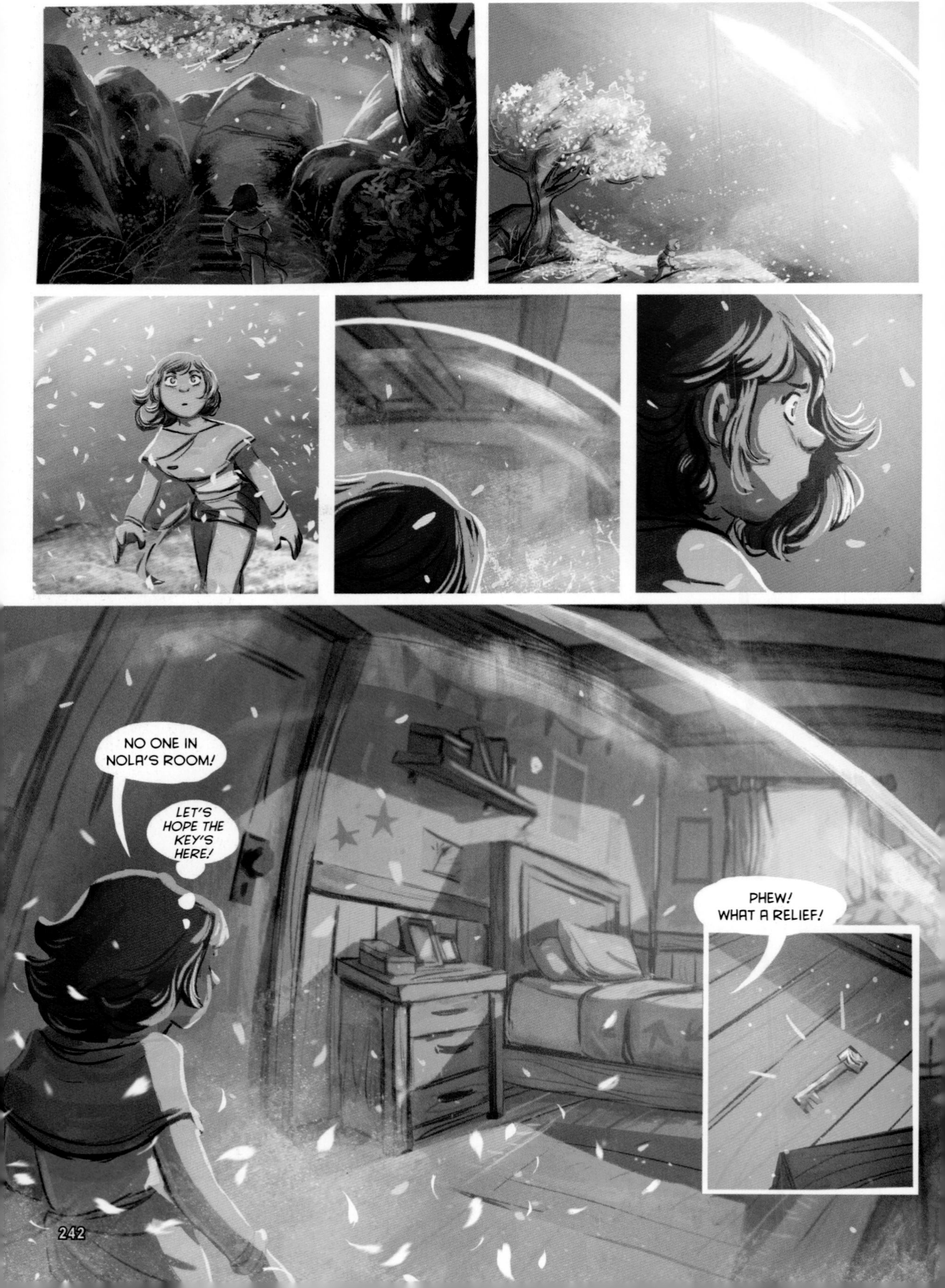
NO ONE IN NOLA'S ROOM!
LET'S HOPE THE KEY'S HERE!
PHEW! WHAT A RELIEF!

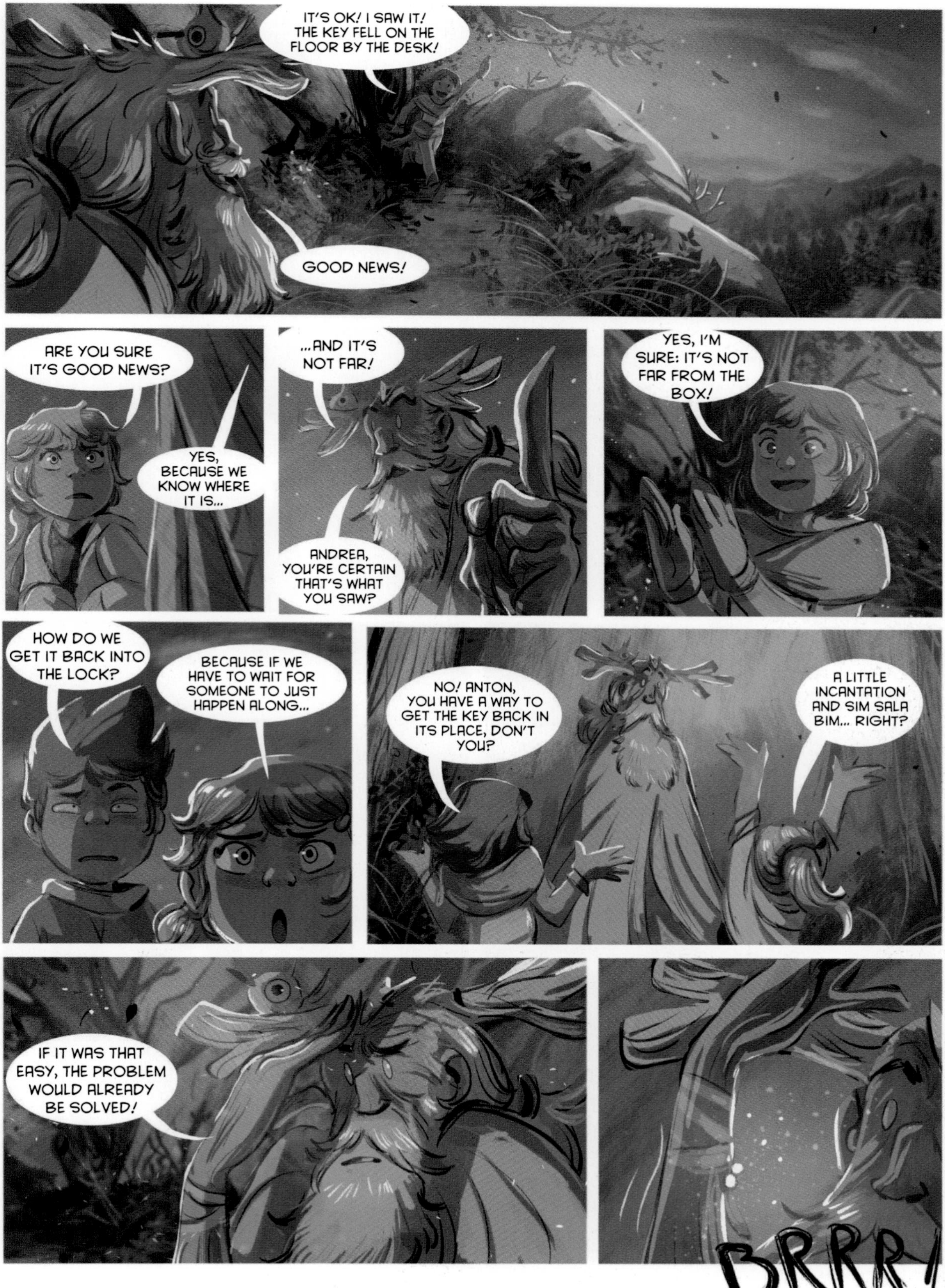
IT'S OK! I SAW IT! THE KEY FELL ON THE FLOOR BY THE DESK!
GOOD NEWS!
ARE YOU SURE IT'S GOOD NEWS?
YES, BECAUSE WE KNOW WHERE IT IS...
...AND IT'S NOT FAR!
ANDREA, YOU'RE CERTAIN THAT'S WHAT YOU SAW?
YES, I'M SURE: IT'S NOT FAR FROM THE BOX!
HOW DO WE GET IT BACK INTO THE LOCK?
BECAUSE IF WE HAVE TO WAIT FOR SOMEONE TO JUST HAPPEN ALONG...
NO! ANTON, YOU HAVE A WAY TO GET THE KEY BACK IN ITS PLACE, DON'T YOU?
A LITTLE INCANTATION AND SIM SALA BIM... RIGHT?
IF IT WAS THAT EASY, THE PROBLEM WOULD ALREADY BE SOLVED!
BRRR!

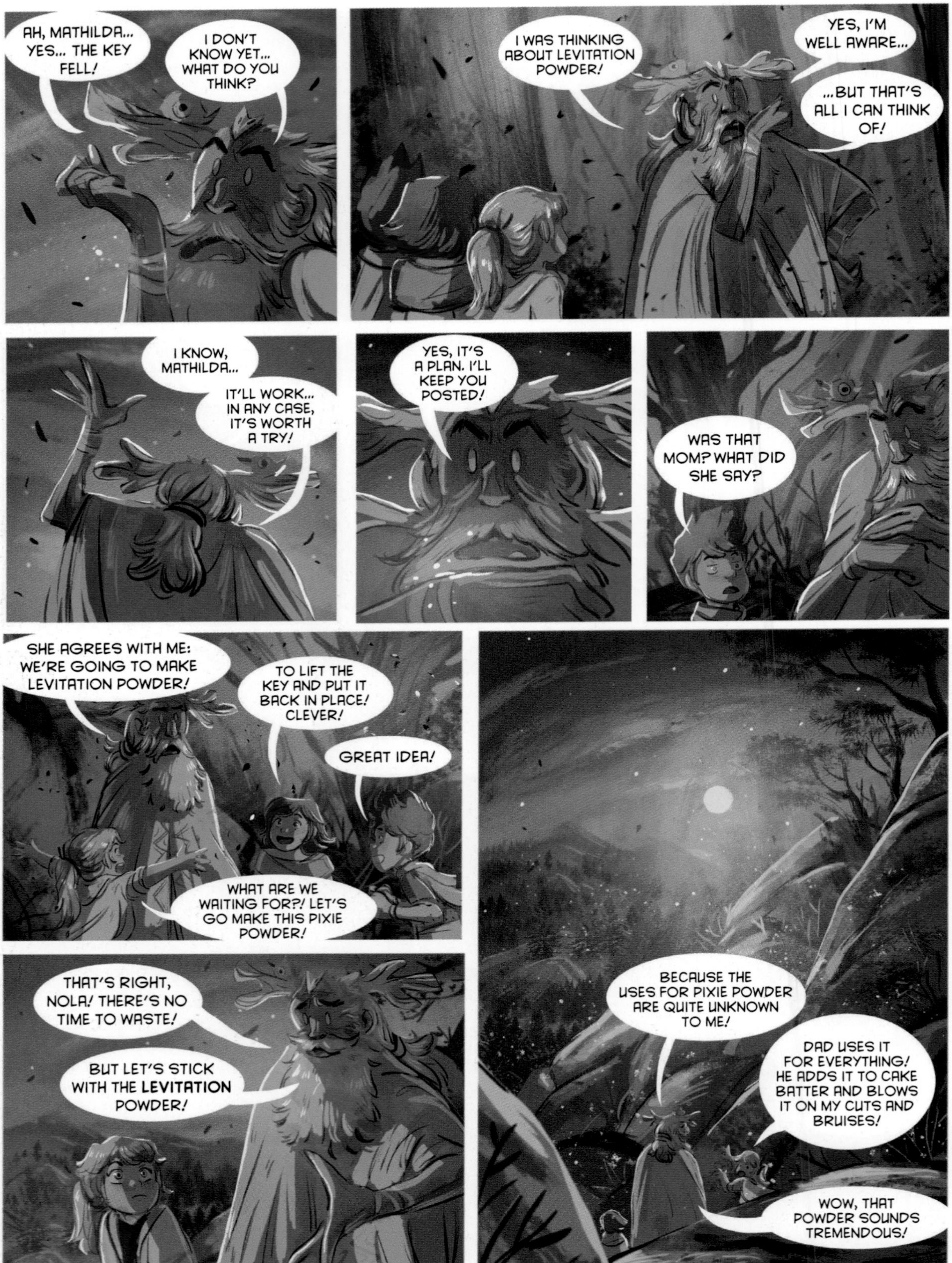
AH, MATHILDA... YES... THE KEY FELL!
I DON'T KNOW YET... WHAT DO YOU THINK?
I WAS THINKING ABOUT LEVITATION POWDER!
YES, I'M WELL AWARE...
...BUT THAT'S ALL I CAN THINK OF!
I KNOW, MATHILDA...
IT'LL WORK... IN ANY CASE, IT'S WORTH A TRY!
YES, IT'S A PLAN. I'LL KEEP YOU POSTED!
WAS THAT MOM? WHAT DID SHE SAY?
SHE AGREES WITH ME: WE'RE GOING TO MAKE LEVITATION POWDER!
TO LIFT THE KEY AND PUT IT BACK IN PLACE! CLEVER!
GREAT IDEA!
WHAT ARE WE WAITING FOR?! LET'S GO MAKE THIS PIXIE POWDER!
THAT'S RIGHT, NOLA! THERE'S NO TIME TO WASTE!
BUT LET'S STICK WITH THE LEVITATION POWDER!
BECAUSE THE USES FOR PIXIE POWDER ARE QUITE UNKNOWN TO ME!
DAD USES IT FOR EVERYTHING! HE ADDS IT TO CAKE BATTER AND BLOWS IT ON MY CUTS AND BRUISES!
WOW, THAT POWDER SOUNDS TREMENDOUS!

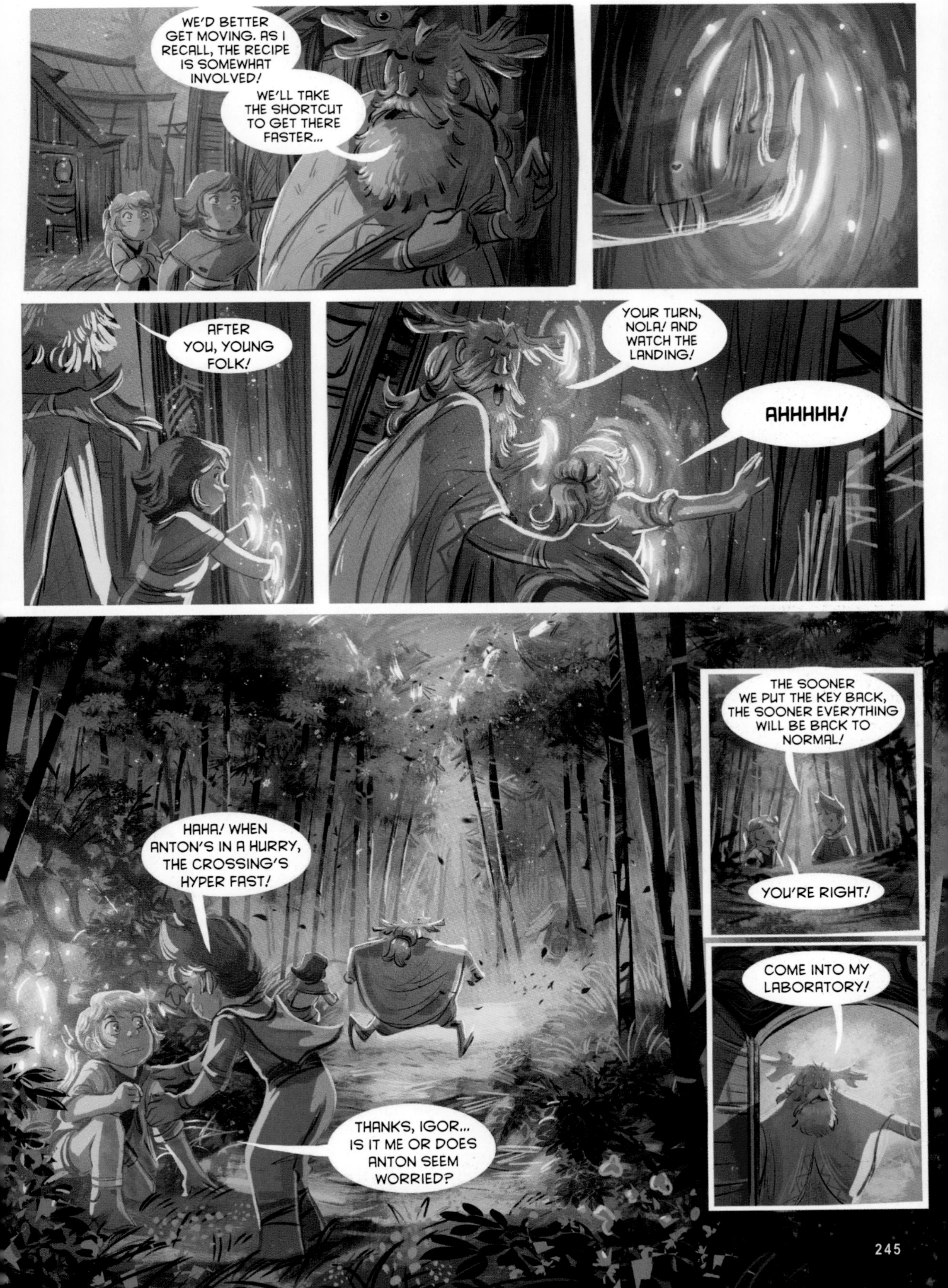
WE'D BETTER GET MOVING. AS I RECALL, THE RECIPE IS SOMEWHAT INVOLVED!
WE'LL TAKE THE SHORTCUT TO GET THERE FASTER...
AFTER YOU, YOUNG FOLK!
YOUR TURN, NOLA! AND WATCH THE LANDING!
AHHHHH!
HAHA! WHEN ANTON'S IN A HURRY, THE CROSSING'S HYPER FAST!
THANKS, IGOR... IS IT ME OR DOES ANTON SEEM WORRIED?
THE SOONER WE PUT THE KEY BACK, THE SOONER EVERYTHING WILL BE BACK TO NORMAL!
YOU'RE RIGHT!
COME INTO MY LABORATORY!

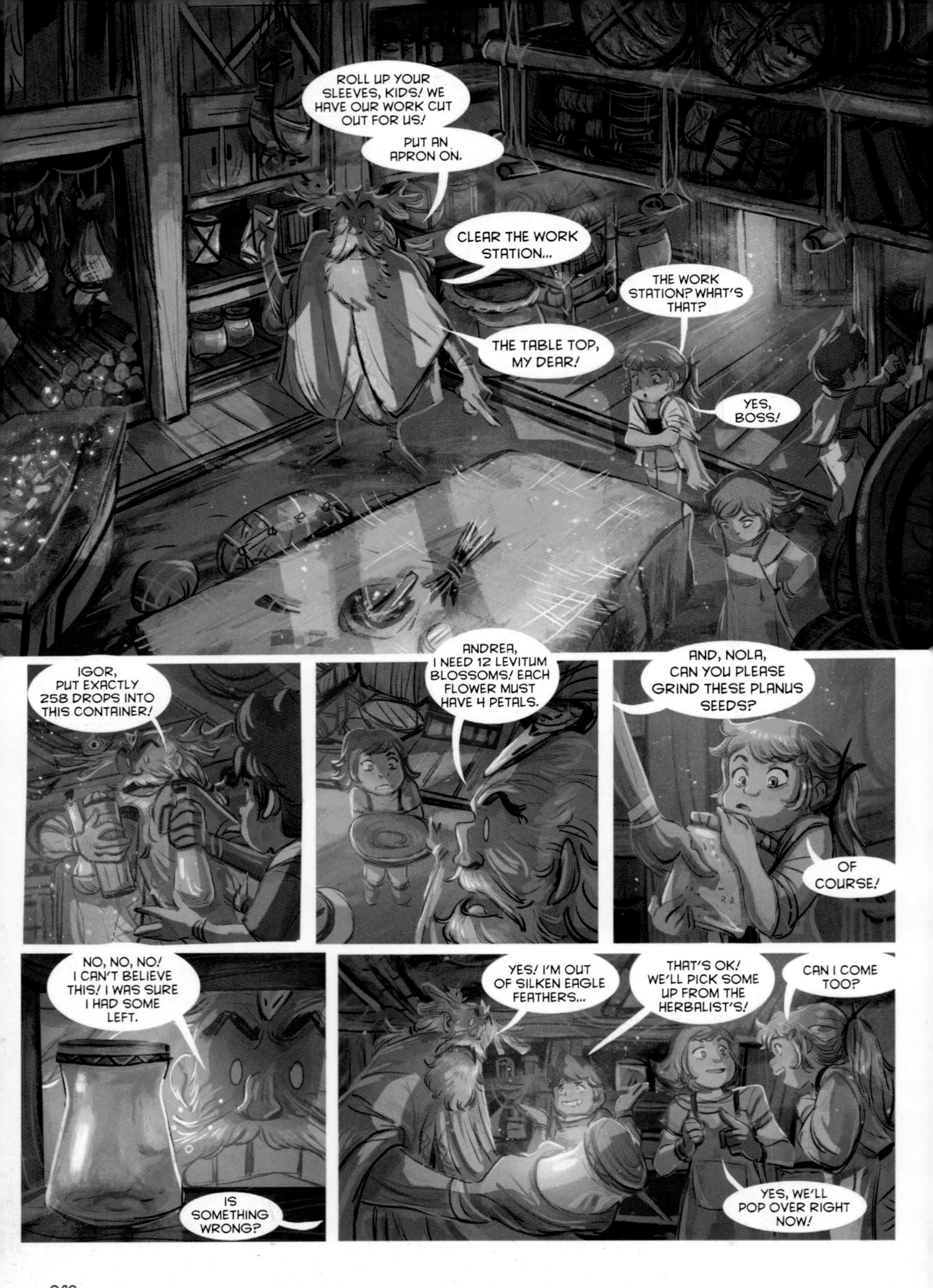
ROLL UP YOUR SLEEVES, KIDS! WE HAVE OUR WORK CUT OUT FOR US!
PUT AN APRON ON.
CLEAR THE WORK STATION...
THE WORK STATION? WHAT'S THAT?
THE TABLE TOP, MY DEAR!
YES, BOSS!
IGOR, PUT EXACTLY 258 DROPS INTO THIS CONTAINER!
ANDREA, I NEED 12 LEVITUM BLOSSOMS! EACH FLOWER MUST HAVE 4 PETALS.
AND, NOLA, CAN YOU PLEASE GRIND THESE PLANUS SEEDS?
OF COURSE!
NO, NO, NO! I CAN'T BELIEVE THIS! I WAS SURE I HAD SOME LEFT.
IS SOMETHING WRONG?
YES! I'M OUT OF SILKEN EAGLE FEATHERS...
THAT'S OK! WE'LL PICK SOME UP FROM THE HERBALIST'S!
CAN I COME TOO?
YES, WE'LL POP OVER RIGHT NOW!

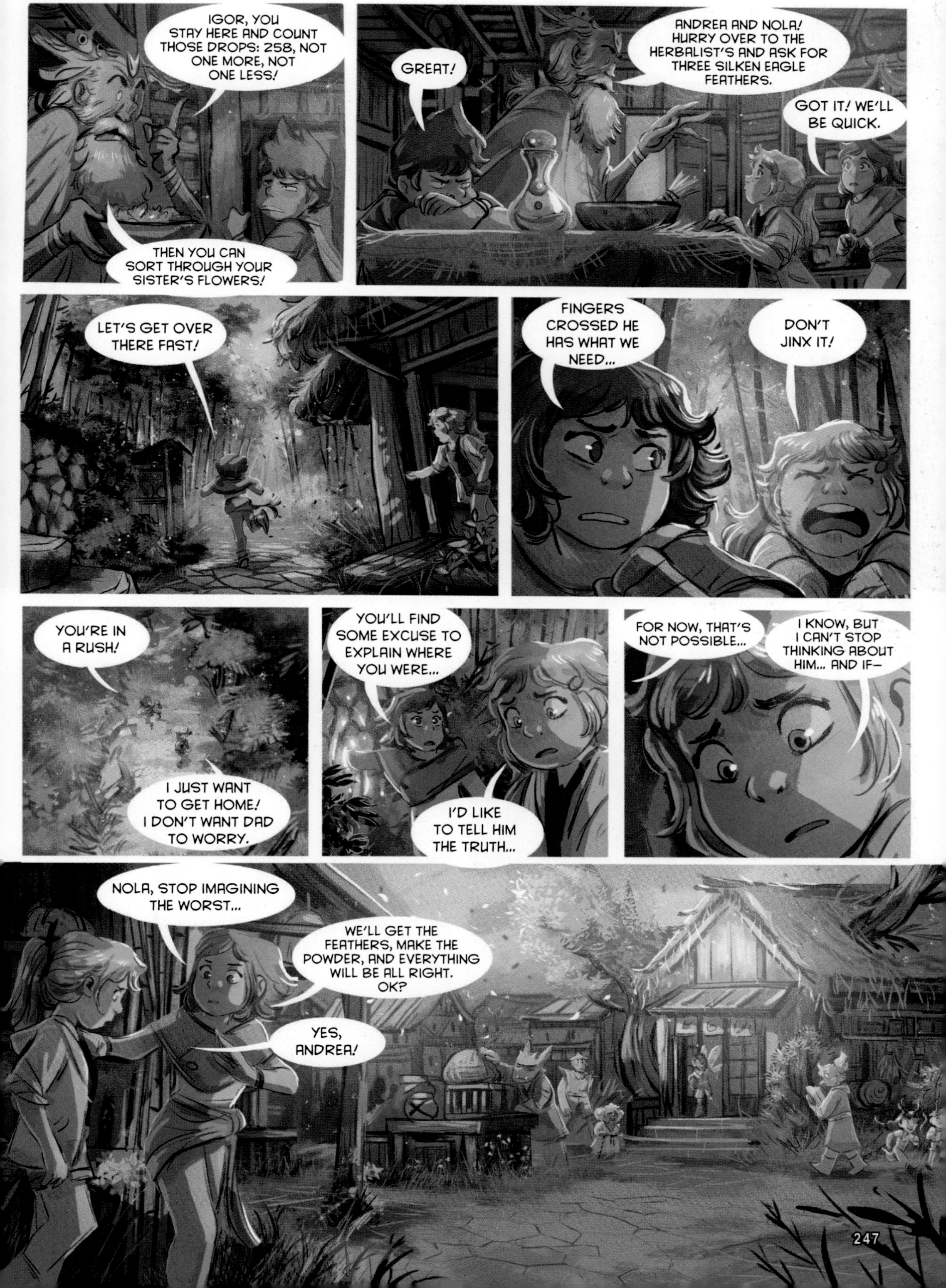
IGOR, YOU STAY HERE AND COUNT THOSE DROPS: 258, NOT ONE MORE, NOT ONE LESS!
THEN YOU CAN SORT THROUGH YOUR SISTER'S FLOWERS!
GREAT!
ANDREA AND NOLA! HURRY OVER TO THE HERBALIST'S AND ASK FOR THREE SILKEN EAGLE FEATHERS.
GOT IT! WE'LL BE QUICK.
LET'S GET OVER THERE FAST!
FINGERS CROSSED HE HAS WHAT WE NEED...
DON'T JINX IT!
YOU'RE IN A RUSH!
I JUST WANT TO GET HOME! I DON'T WANT DAD TO WORRY.
YOU'LL FIND SOME EXCUSE TO EXPLAIN WHERE YOU WERE...
I'D LIKE TO TELL HIM THE TRUTH...
FOR NOW, THAT'S NOT POSSIBLE...
I KNOW, BUT I CAN'T STOP THINKING ABOUT HIM... AND IF—
NOLA, STOP IMAGINING THE WORST...
WE'LL GET THE FEATHERS, MAKE THE POWDER, AND EVERYTHING WILL BE ALL RIGHT. OK?
YES, ANDREA!

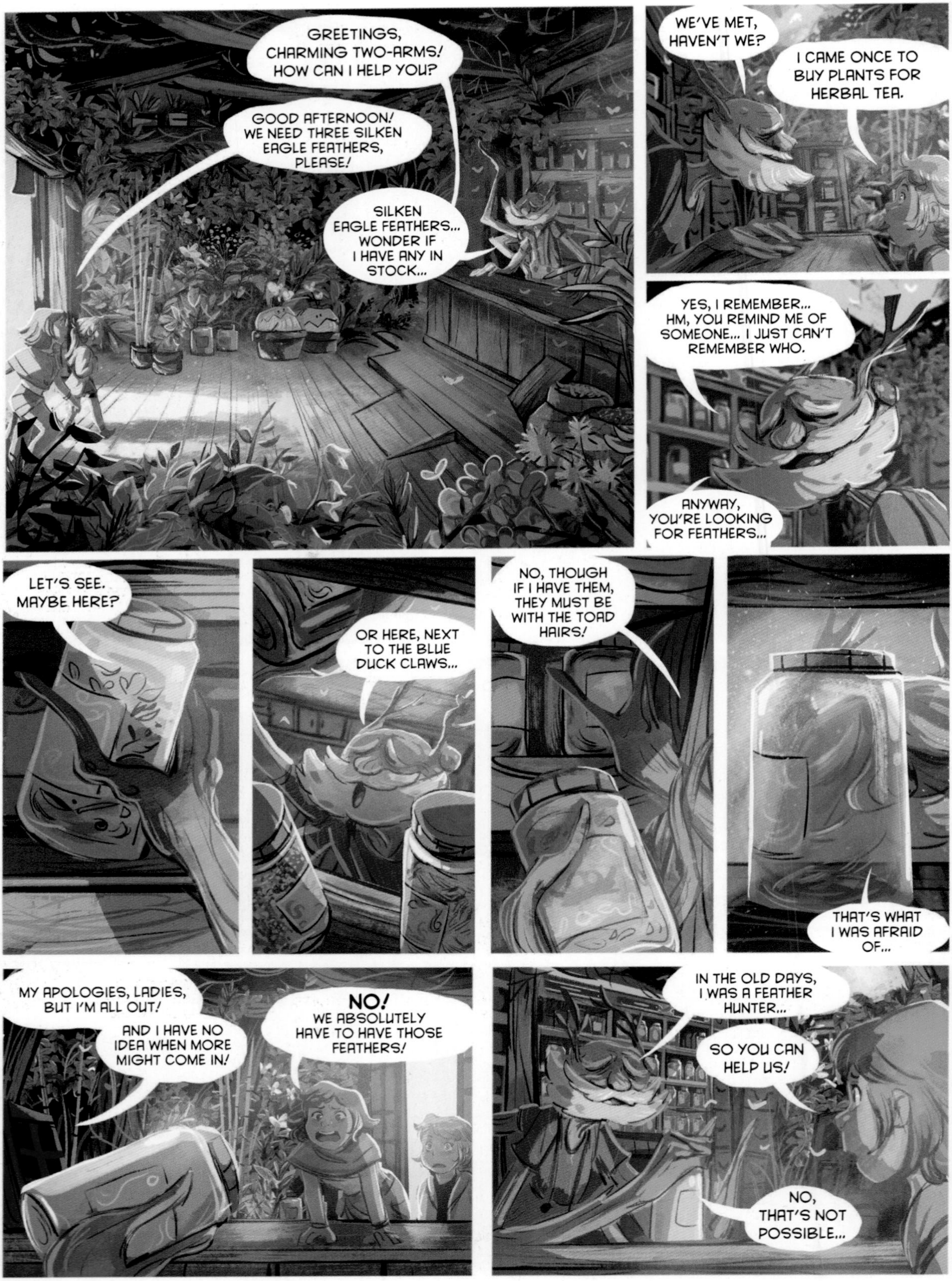
GREETINGS, CHARMING TWO-ARMS! HOW CAN I HELP YOU?
GOOD AFTERNOON! WE NEED THREE SILKEN EAGLE FEATHERS, PLEASE!
SILKEN EAGLE FEATHERS... WONDER IF I HAVE ANY IN STOCK...
WE'VE MET, HAVEN'T WE?
I CAME ONCE TO BUY PLANTS FOR HERBAL TEA.
YES, I REMEMBER... HM, YOU REMIND ME OF SOMEONE... I JUST CAN'T REMEMBER WHO.
ANYWAY, YOU'RE LOOKING FOR FEATHERS...
LET'S SEE. MAYBE HERE?
OR HERE, NEXT TO THE BLUE DUCK CLAWS...
NO, THOUGH IF I HAVE THEM, THEY MUST BE WITH THE TOAD HAIRS!
THAT'S WHAT I WAS AFRAID OF...
MY APOLOGIES, LADIES, BUT I'M ALL OUT!
AND I HAVE NO IDEA WHEN MORE MIGHT COME IN!
NO! WE ABSOLUTELY HAVE TO HAVE THOSE FEATHERS!
IN THE OLD DAYS, I WAS A FEATHER HUNTER...
SO YOU CAN HELP US!
NO, THAT'S NOT POSSIBLE...

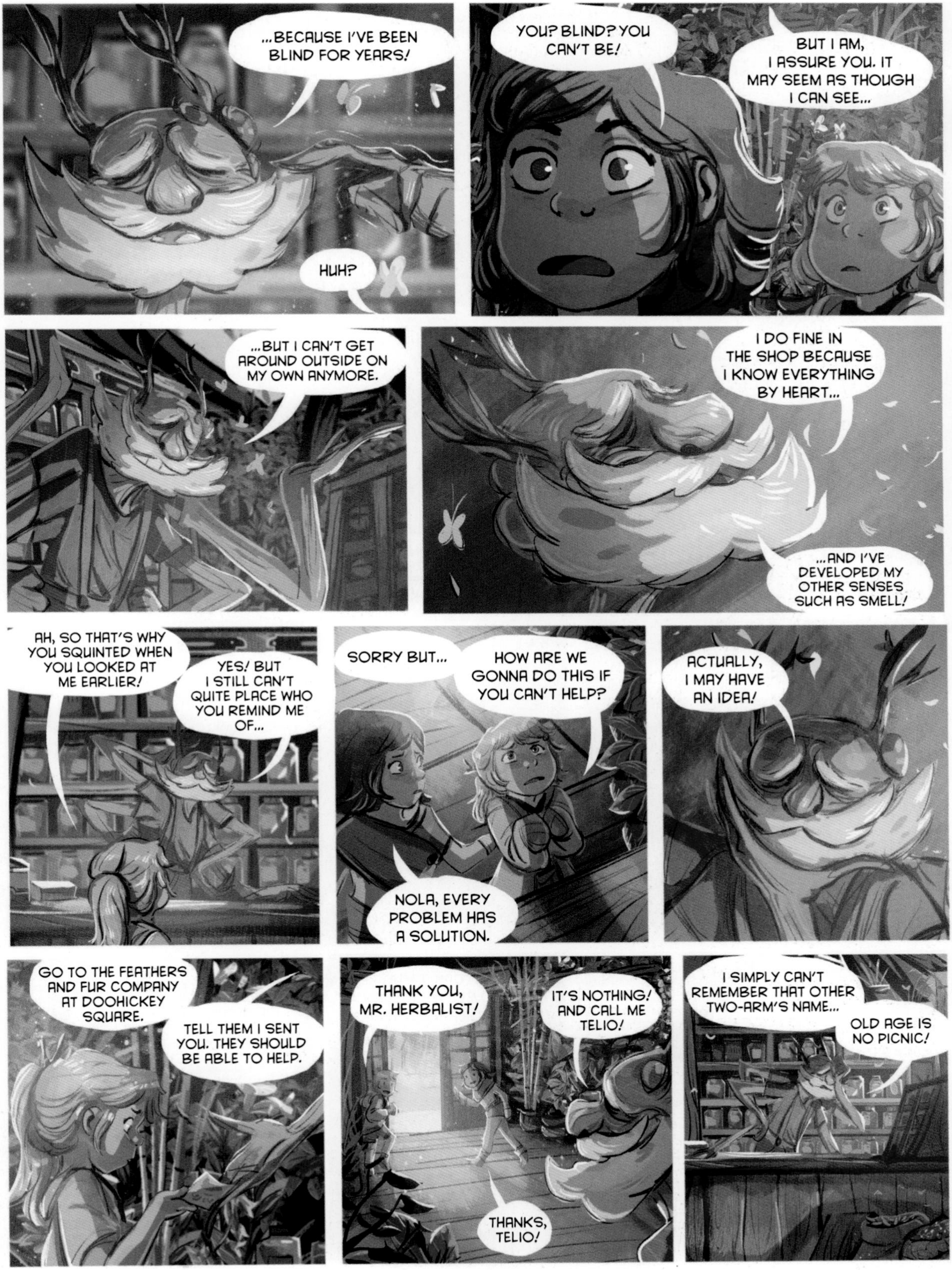
...BECAUSE I'VE BEEN BLIND FOR YEARS!
HUH?
YOU? BLIND? YOU CAN'T BE!
BUT I AM, I ASSURE YOU. IT MAY SEEM AS THOUGH I CAN SEE...
...BUT I CAN'T GET AROUND OUTSIDE ON MY OWN ANYMORE.
I DO FINE IN THE SHOP BECAUSE I KNOW EVERYTHING BY HEART...
...AND I'VE DEVELOPED MY OTHER SENSES SUCH AS SMELL!
AH, SO THAT'S WHY YOU SQUINTED WHEN YOU LOOKED AT ME EARLIER!
YES! BUT I STILL CAN'T QUITE PLACE WHO YOU REMIND ME OF...
SORRY BUT...
HOW ARE WE GONNA DO THIS IF YOU CAN'T HELP?
NOLA, EVERY PROBLEM HAS A SOLUTION.
ACTUALLY, I MAY HAVE AN IDEA!
GO TO THE FEATHERS AND FUR COMPANY AT DOOHICKEY SQUARE.
TELL THEM I SENT YOU. THEY SHOULD BE ABLE TO HELP.
THANK YOU, MR. HERBALIST!
IT'S NOTHING! AND CALL ME TELIO!
THANKS, TELIO!
I SIMPLY CAN'T REMEMBER THAT OTHER TWO-ARM'S NAME...
OLD AGE IS NO PICNIC!

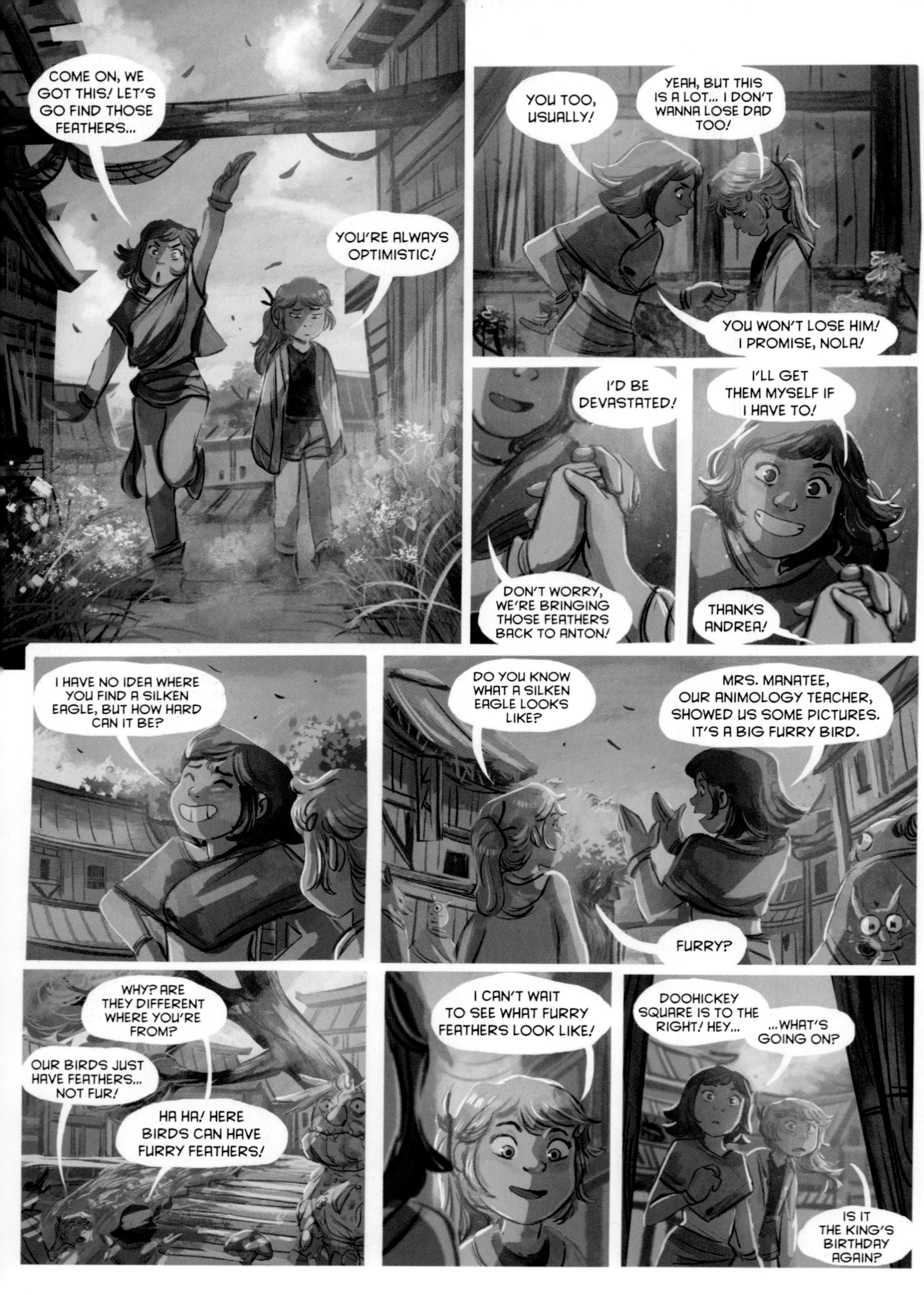
COME ON, WE GOT THIS! LET'S GO FIND THOSE FEATHERS...
YOU'RE ALWAYS OPTIMISTIC!
YOU TOO, USUALLY!
YEAH, BUT THIS IS A LOT... I DON'T WANNA LOSE DAD TOO!
YOU WON'T LOSE HIM! I PROMISE, NOLA!
I'D BE DEVASTATED!
DON'T WORRY, WE'RE BRINGING THOSE FEATHERS BACK TO ANTON!
I'LL GET THEM MYSELF IF I HAVE TO!
THANKS ANDREA!
I HAVE NO IDEA WHERE YOU FIND A SILKEN EAGLE, BUT HOW HARD CAN IT BE?
DO YOU KNOW WHAT A SILKEN EAGLE LOOKS LIKE?
MRS. MANATEE, OUR ANIMOLOGY TEACHER, SHOWED US SOME PICTURES. IT'S A BIG FURRY BIRD.
FURRY?
WHY? ARE THEY DIFFERENT WHERE YOU'RE FROM?
OUR BIRDS JUST HAVE FEATHERS... NOT FUR!
HA HA! HERE BIRDS CAN HAVE FURRY FEATHERS!
I CAN'T WAIT TO SEE WHAT FURRY FEATHERS LOOK LIKE!
DOOHICKEY SQUARE IS TO THE RIGHT! HEY...
...WHAT'S GOING ON?
IS IT THE KING'S BIRTHDAY AGAIN?

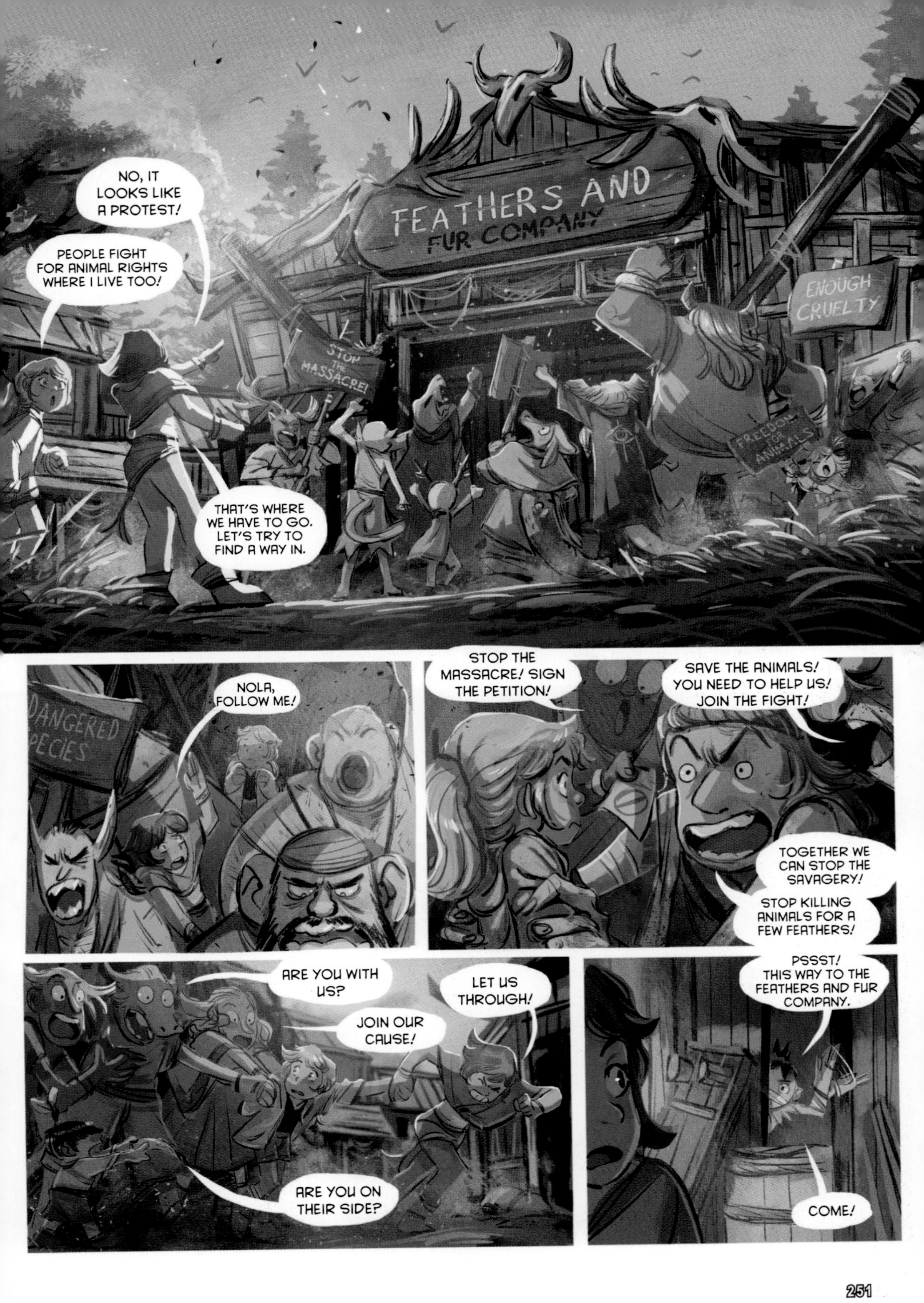
FEATHERS AND FUR COMPANY
NO, IT LOOKS LIKE A PROTEST!
PEOPLE FIGHT FOR ANIMAL RIGHTS WHERE I LIVE TOO!
STOP THE MASSACRE!
ENOUGH CRUELTY
FREEDOM FOR ANIMALS
THAT'S WHERE WE HAVE TO GO. LET'S TRY TO FIND A WAY IN.
NOLA, FOLLOW ME!
STOP THE MASSACRE! SIGN THE PETITION!
SAVE THE ANIMALS! YOU NEED TO HELP US! JOIN THE FIGHT!
TOGETHER WE CAN STOP THE SAVAGERY!
STOP KILLING ANIMALS FOR A FEW FEATHERS!
ARE YOU WITH US?
JOIN OUR CAUSE!
LET US THROUGH!
ARE YOU ON THEIR SIDE?
PSSST! THIS WAY TO THE FEATHERS AND FUR COMPANY.
COME!

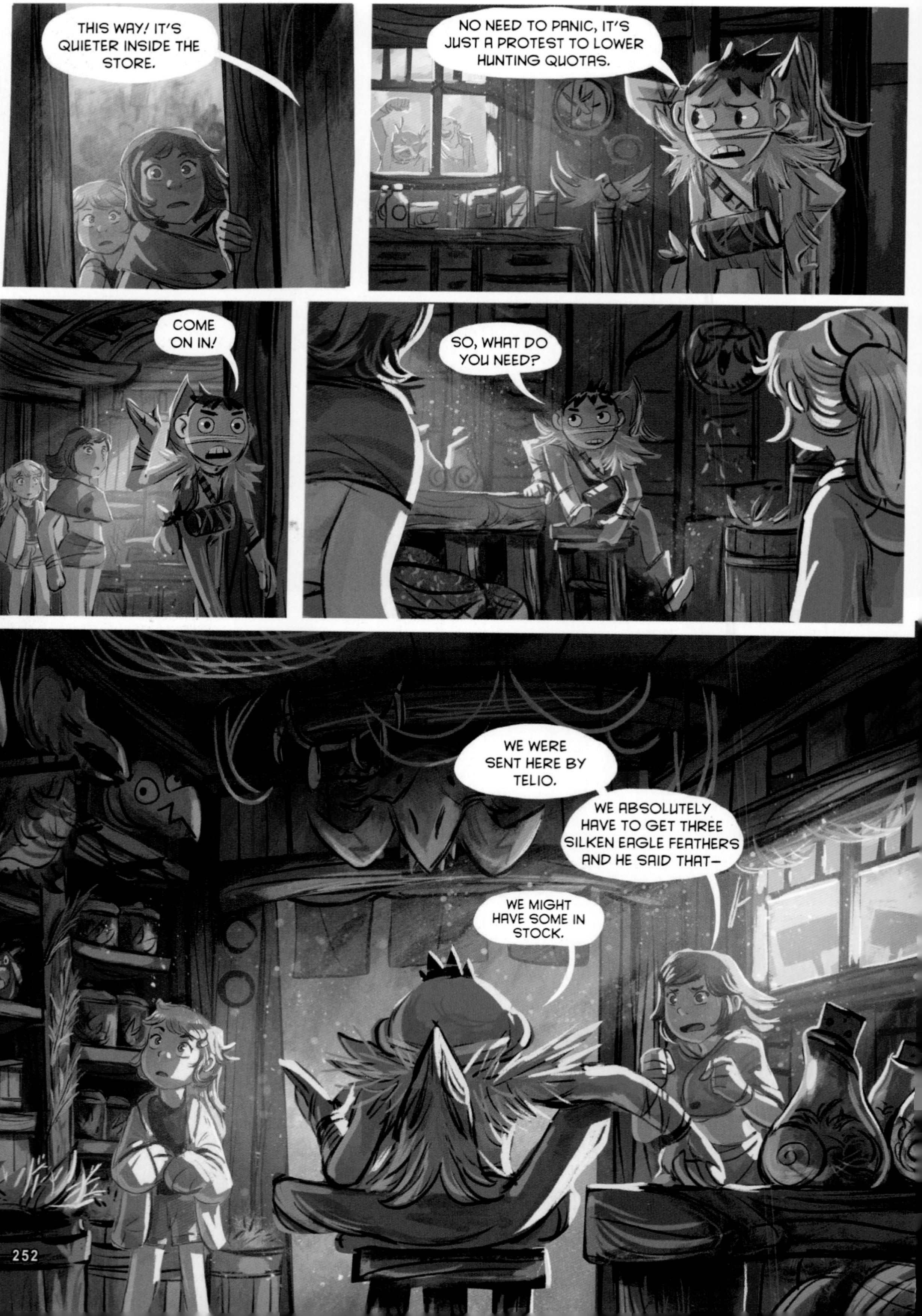
THIS WAY! IT'S QUIETER INSIDE THE STORE.
NO NEED TO PANIC, IT'S JUST A PROTEST TO LOWER HUNTING QUOTAS.
COME ON IN!
SO, WHAT DO YOU NEED?
WE WERE SENT HERE BY TELIO.
WE ABSOLUTELY HAVE TO GET THREE SILKEN EAGLE FEATHERS AND HE SAID THAT—
WE MIGHT HAVE SOME IN STOCK.

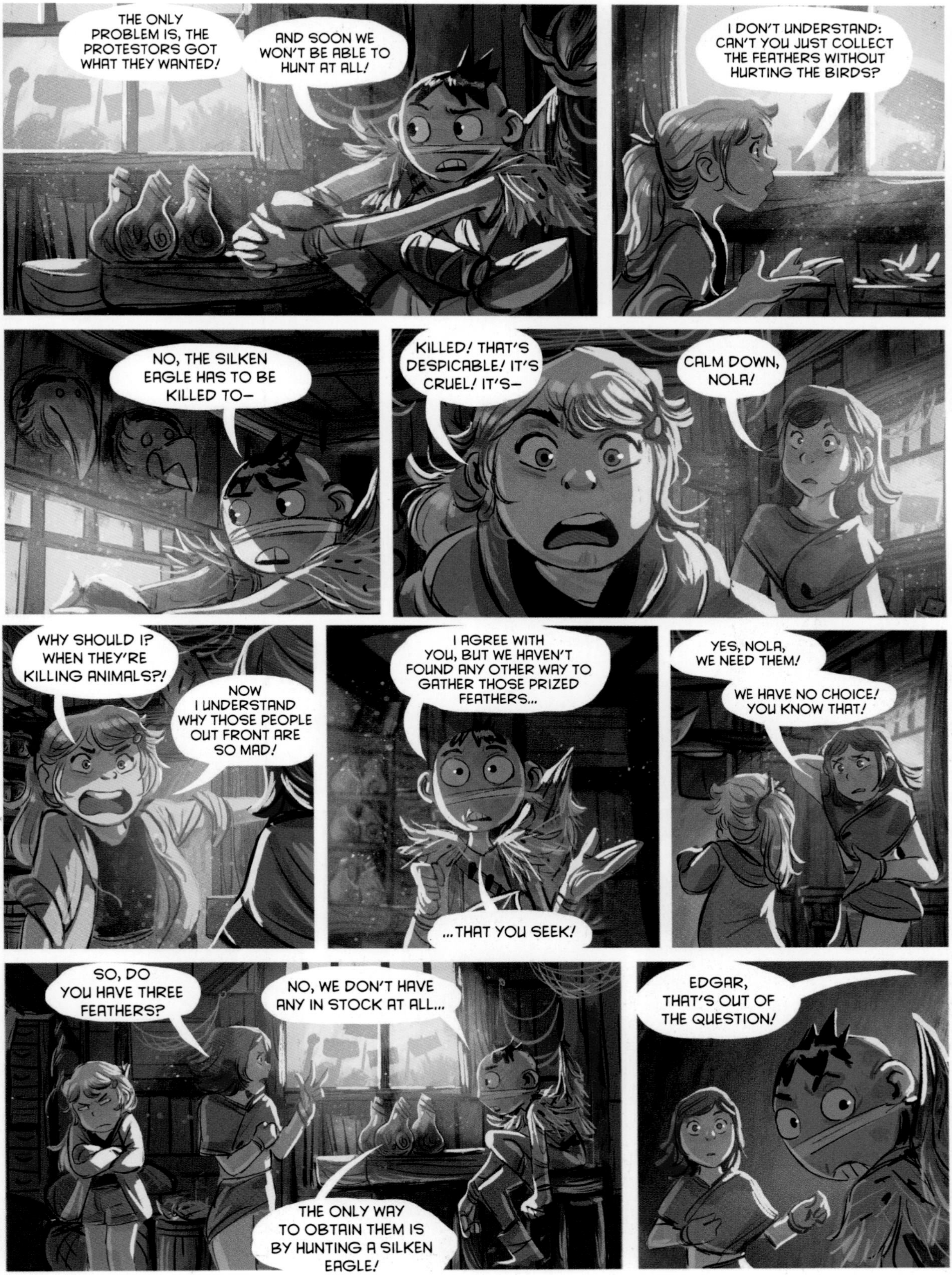
THE ONLY PROBLEM IS, THE PROTESTORS GOT WHAT THEY WANTED!
AND SOON WE WON'T BE ABLE TO HUNT AT ALL!
I DON'T UNDERSTAND: CAN'T YOU JUST COLLECT THE FEATHERS WITHOUT HURTING THE BIRDS?
NO, THE SILKEN EAGLE HAS TO BE KILLED TO—
KILLED! THAT'S DESPICABLE! IT'S CRUEL! IT'S—
CALM DOWN, NOLA!
WHY SHOULD I? WHEN THEY'RE KILLING ANIMALS?!
NOW I UNDERSTAND WHY THOSE PEOPLE OUT FRONT ARE SO MAD!
I AGREE WITH YOU, BUT WE HAVEN'T FOUND ANY OTHER WAY TO GATHER THOSE PRIZED FEATHERS...
...THAT YOU SEEK!
YES, NOLA, WE NEED THEM!
WE HAVE NO CHOICE! YOU KNOW THAT!
SO, DO YOU HAVE THREE FEATHERS?
NO, WE DON'T HAVE ANY IN STOCK AT ALL...
THE ONLY WAY TO OBTAIN THEM IS BY HUNTING A SILKEN EAGLE!
EDGAR, THAT'S OUT OF THE QUESTION!

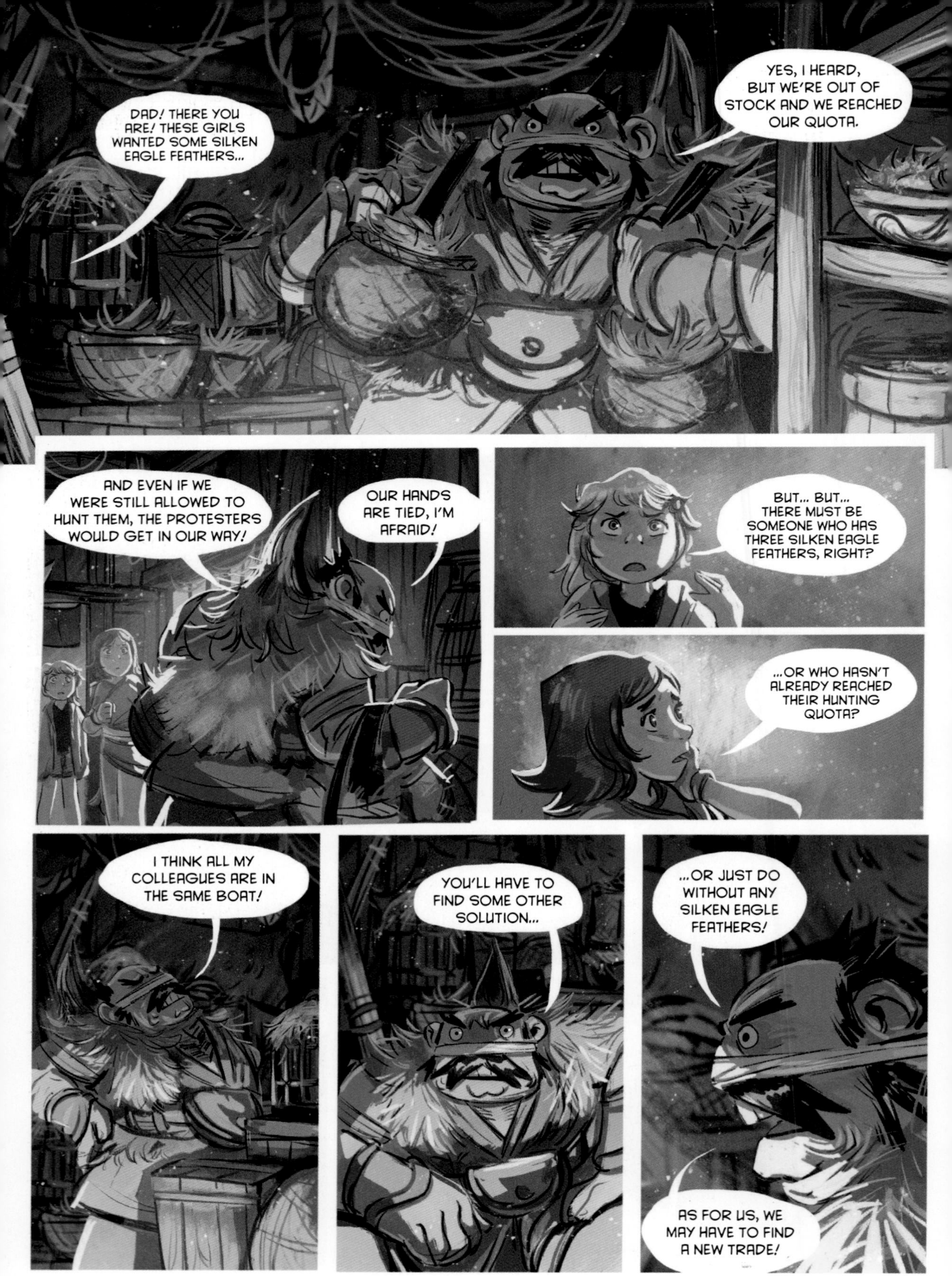
DAD! THERE YOU ARE! THESE GIRLS WANTED SOME SILKEN EAGLE FEATHERS...
YES, I HEARD, BUT WE'RE OUT OF STOCK AND WE REACHED OUR QUOTA.
AND EVEN IF WE WERE STILL ALLOWED TO HUNT THEM, THE PROTESTERS WOULD GET IN OUR WAY!
OUR HANDS ARE TIED, I'M AFRAID!
BUT... BUT... THERE MUST BE SOMEONE WHO HAS THREE SILKEN EAGLE FEATHERS, RIGHT?
...OR WHO HASN'T ALREADY REACHED THEIR HUNTING QUOTA?
I THINK ALL MY COLLEAGUES ARE IN THE SAME BOAT!
YOU'LL HAVE TO FIND SOME OTHER SOLUTION...
...OR JUST DO WITHOUT ANY SILKEN EAGLE FEATHERS!
AS FOR US, WE MAY HAVE TO FIND A NEW TRADE!

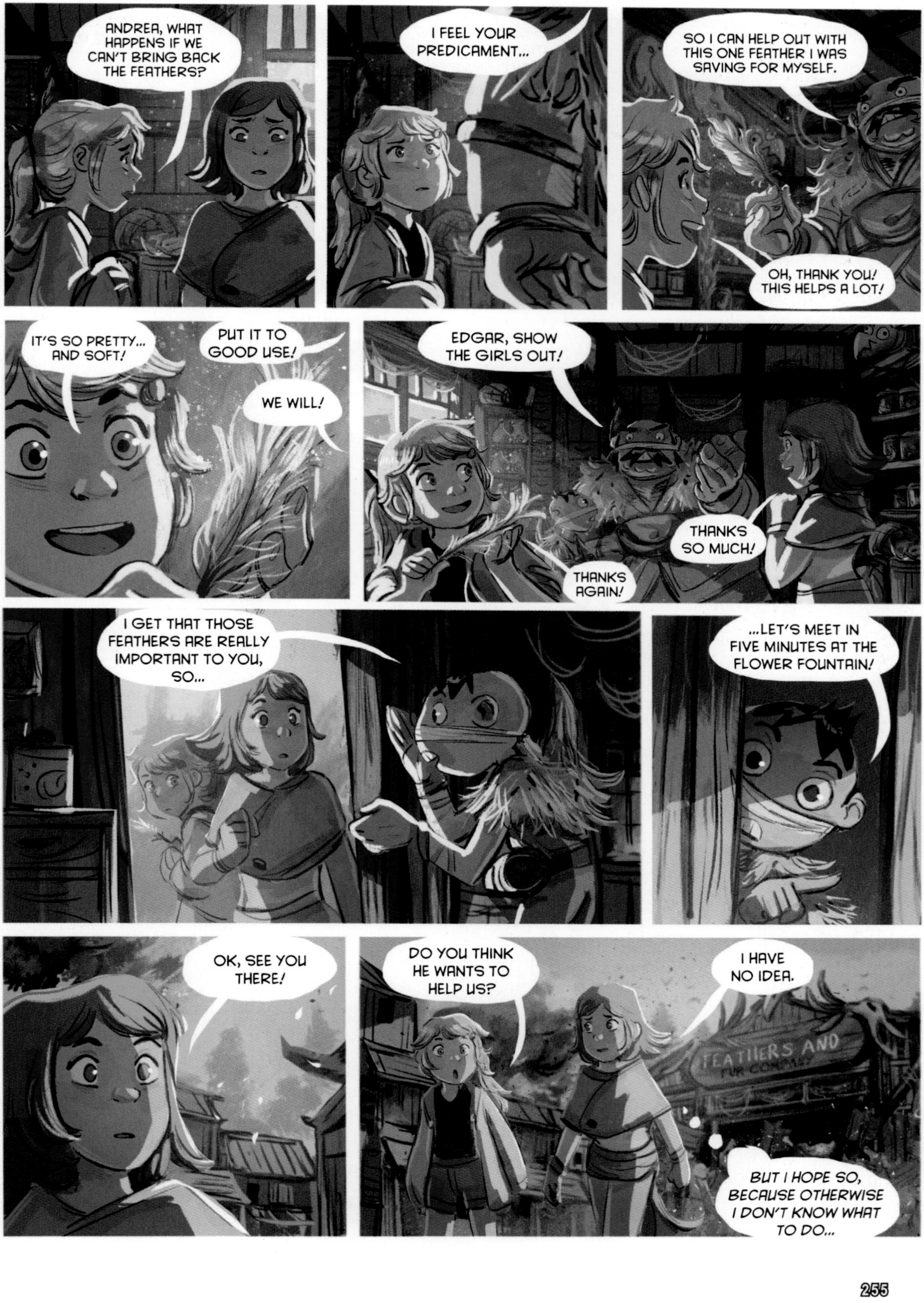
ANDREA, WHAT HAPPENS IF WE CAN'T BRING BACK THE FEATHERS?
I FEEL YOUR PREDICAMENT...
SO I CAN HELP OUT WITH THIS ONE FEATHER I WAS SAVING FOR MYSELF.
OH, THANK YOU! THIS HELPS A LOT!
IT'S SO PRETTY... AND SOFT!
PUT IT TO GOOD USE!
WE WILL!
EDGAR, SHOW THE GIRLS OUT!
THANKS SO MUCH!
THANKS AGAIN!
I GET THAT THOSE FEATHERS ARE REALLY IMPORTANT TO YOU, SO...
...LET'S MEET IN FIVE MINUTES AT THE FLOWER FOUNTAIN!
OK, SEE YOU THERE!
DO YOU THINK HE WANTS TO HELP US?
I HAVE NO IDEA.
FEATHERS AND
BUT I HOPE SO, BECAUSE OTHERWISE I DON'T KNOW WHAT TO DO...

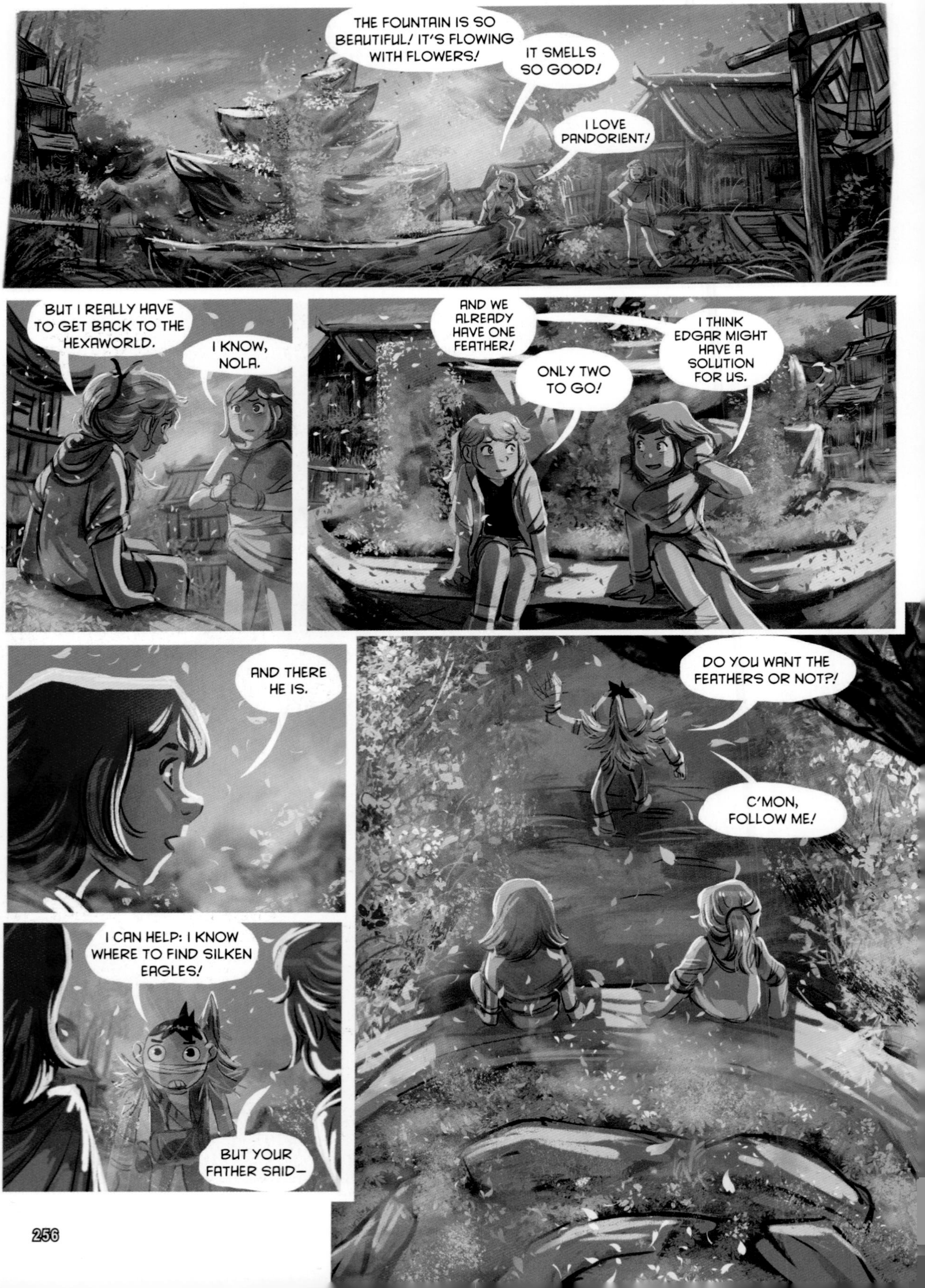
THE FOUNTAIN IS SO BEAUTIFUL! IT'S FLOWING WITH FLOWERS!
IT SMELLS SO GOOD!
I LOVE PANDORIENT!
BUT I REALLY HAVE TO GET BACK TO THE HEXAWORLD.
I KNOW, NOLA.
AND WE ALREADY HAVE ONE FEATHER!
ONLY TWO TO GO!
I THINK EDGAR MIGHT HAVE A SOLUTION FOR US.
AND THERE HE IS.
I CAN HELP: I KNOW WHERE TO FIND SILKEN EAGLES!
BUT YOUR FATHER SAID—
DO YOU WANT THE FEATHERS OR NOT?!
C'MON, FOLLOW ME!

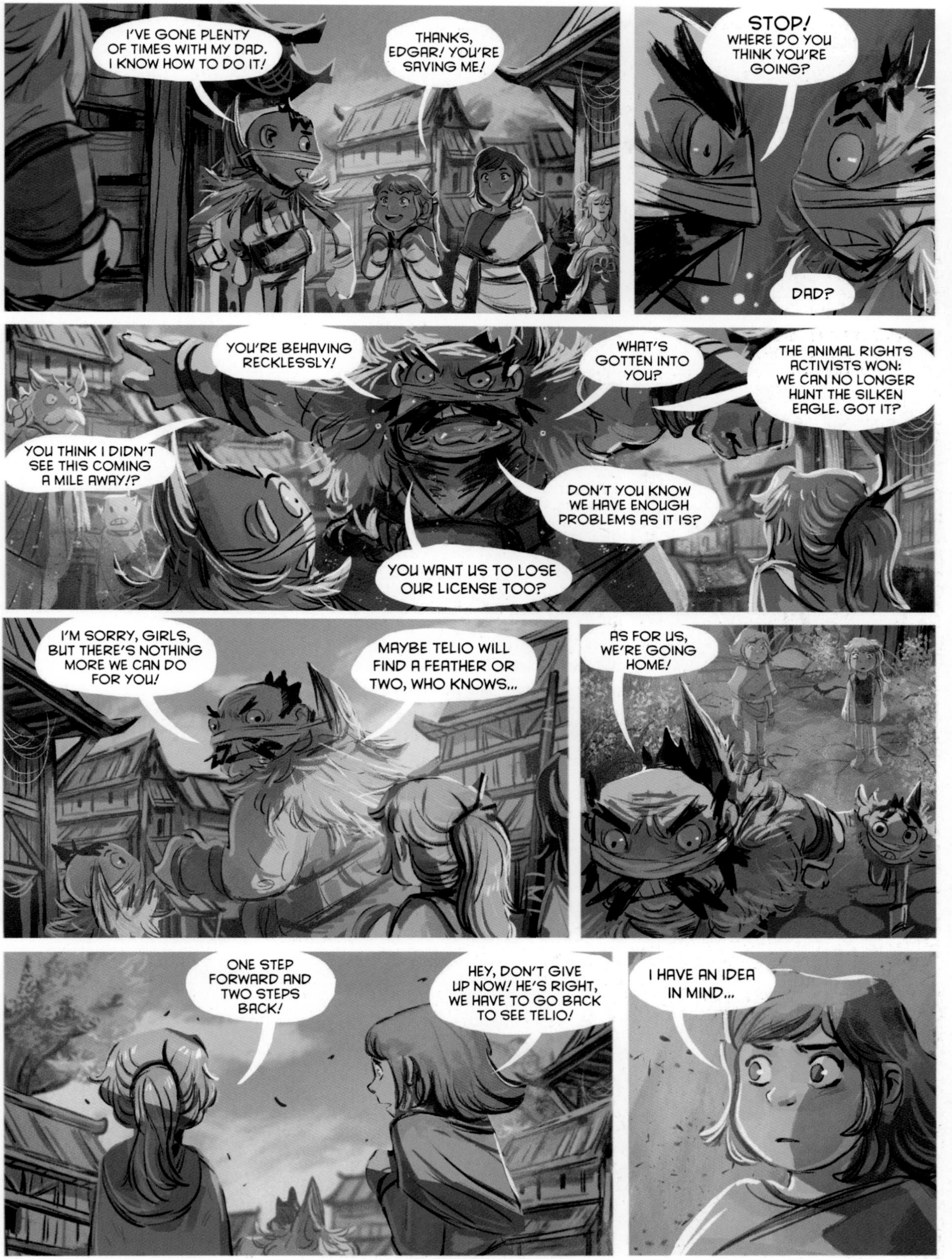
I'VE GONE PLENTY OF TIMES WITH MY DAD. I KNOW HOW TO DO IT!
THANKS, EDGAR! YOU'RE SAVING ME!
STOP! WHERE DO YOU THINK YOU'RE GOING?
DAD?
YOU'RE BEHAVING RECKLESSLY!
WHAT'S GOTTEN INTO YOU?
THE ANIMAL RIGHTS ACTIVISTS WON: WE CAN NO LONGER HUNT THE SILKEN EAGLE. GOT IT?
YOU THINK I DIDN'T SEE THIS COMING A MILE AWAY!?
DON'T YOU KNOW WE HAVE ENOUGH PROBLEMS AS IT IS?
YOU WANT US TO LOSE OUR LICENSE TOO?
I'M SORRY, GIRLS, BUT THERE'S NOTHING MORE WE CAN DO FOR YOU!
MAYBE TELIO WILL FIND A FEATHER OR TWO, WHO KNOWS...
AS FOR US, WE'RE GOING HOME!
ONE STEP FORWARD AND TWO STEPS BACK!
HEY, DON'T GIVE UP NOW! HE'S RIGHT, WE HAVE TO GO BACK TO SEE TELIO!
I HAVE AN IDEA IN MIND...

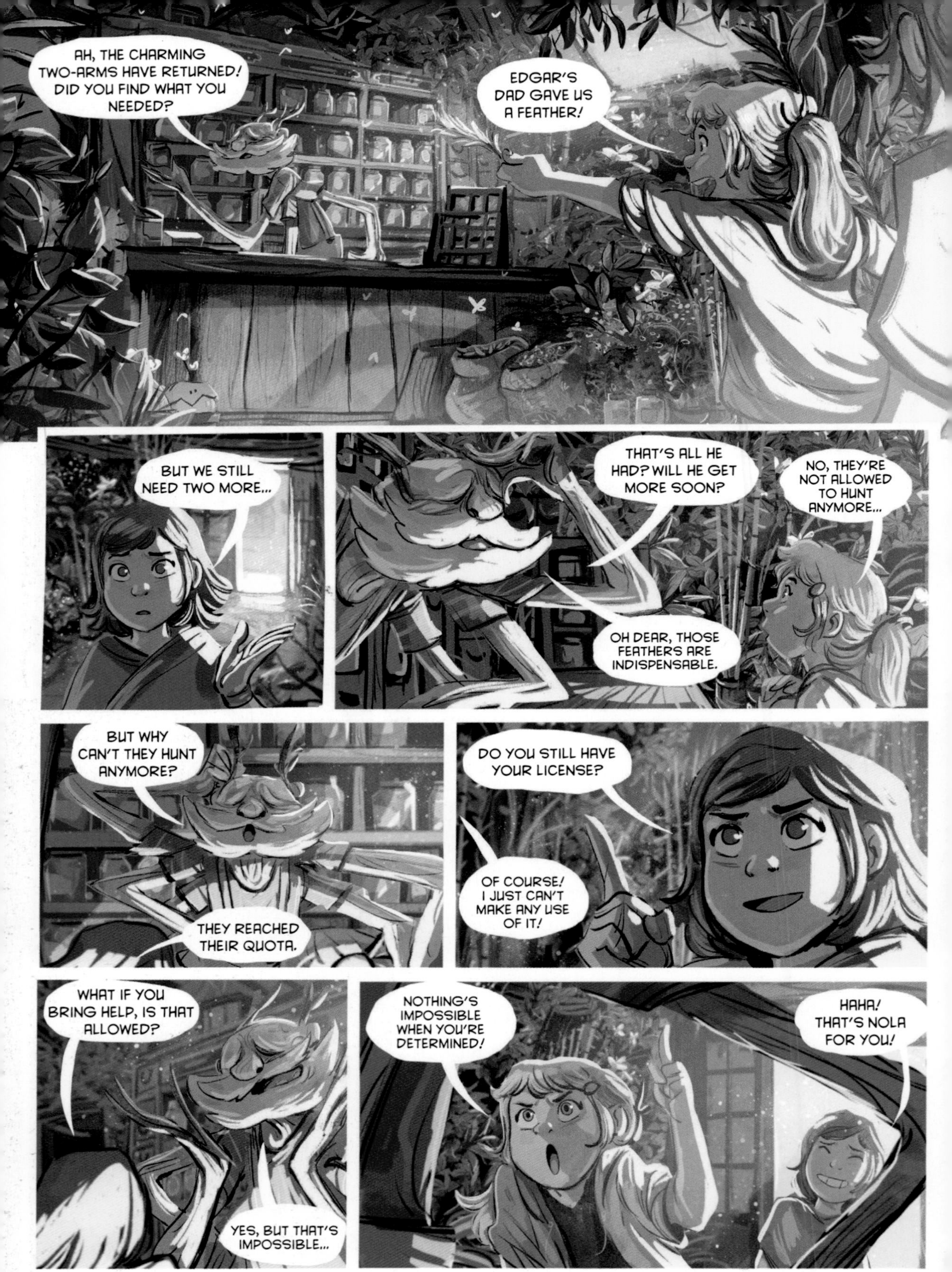
AH, THE CHARMING TWO-ARMS HAVE RETURNED! DID YOU FIND WHAT YOU NEEDED?
EDGAR'S DAD GAVE US A FEATHER!
BUT WE STILL NEED TWO MORE...
THAT'S ALL HE HAD? WILL HE GET MORE SOON?
NO, THEY'RE NOT ALLOWED TO HUNT ANYMORE...
OH DEAR, THOSE FEATHERS ARE INDISPENSABLE.
BUT WHY CAN'T THEY HUNT ANYMORE?
THEY REACHED THEIR QUOTA.
DO YOU STILL HAVE YOUR LICENSE?
OF COURSE! I JUST CAN'T MAKE ANY USE OF IT!
WHAT IF YOU BRING HELP, IS THAT ALLOWED?
YES, BUT THAT'S IMPOSSIBLE...
NOTHING'S IMPOSSIBLE WHEN YOU'RE DETERMINED!
HAHA! THAT'S NOLA FOR YOU!

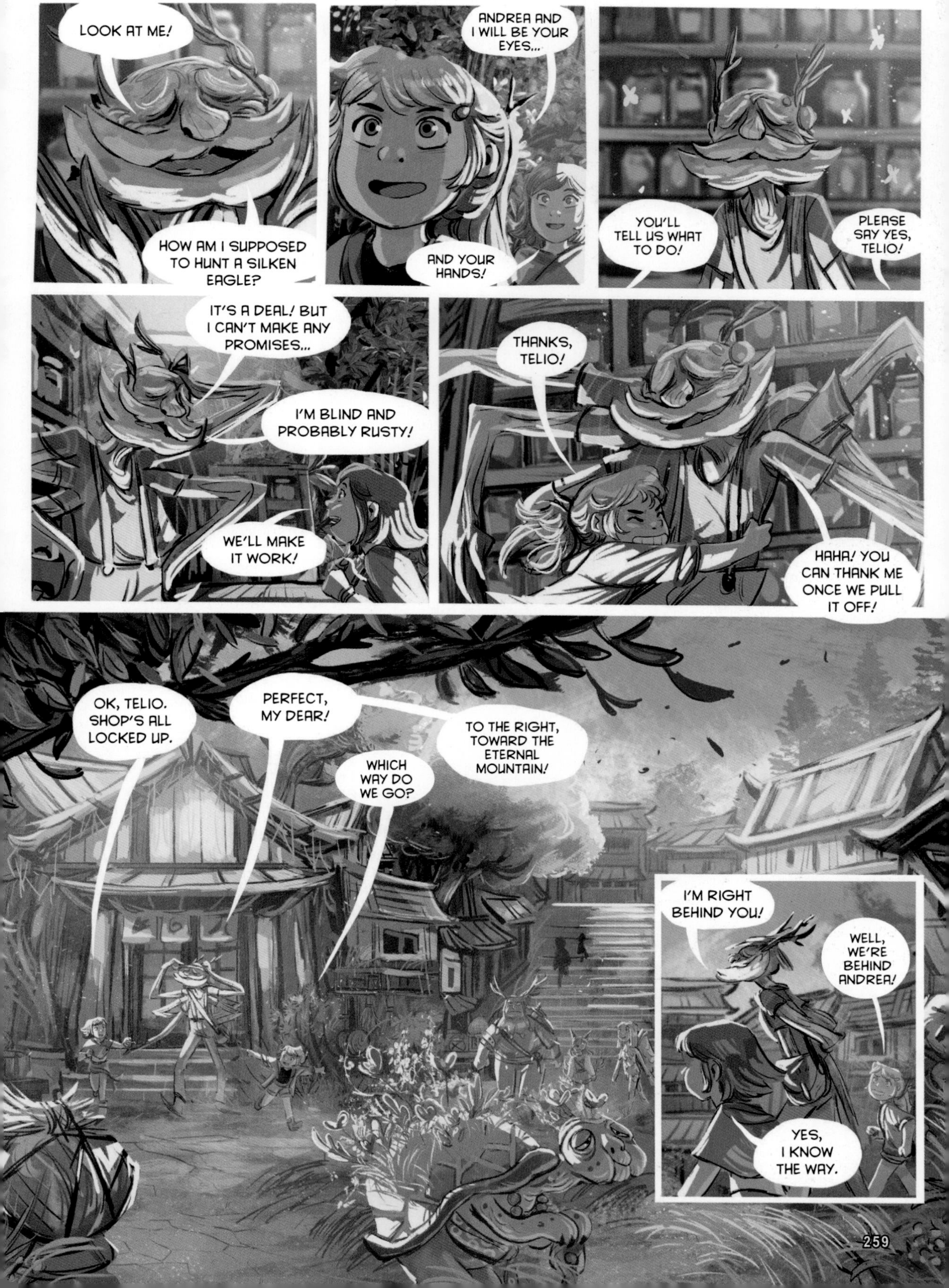
LOOK AT ME!
HOW AM I SUPPOSED TO HUNT A SILKEN EAGLE?
ANDREA AND I WILL BE YOUR EYES...
AND YOUR HANDS!
YOU'LL TELL US WHAT TO DO!
PLEASE SAY YES, TELIO!
IT'S A DEAL! BUT I CAN'T MAKE ANY PROMISES...
I'M BLIND AND PROBABLY RUSTY!
WE'LL MAKE IT WORK!
THANKS, TELIO!
HAHA! YOU CAN THANK ME ONCE WE PULL IT OFF!
OK, TELIO. SHOP'S ALL LOCKED UP.
PERFECT, MY DEAR!
WHICH WAY DO WE GO?
TO THE RIGHT, TOWARD THE ETERNAL MOUNTAIN!
I'M RIGHT BEHIND YOU!
WELL, WE'RE BEHIND ANDREA!
YES, I KNOW THE WAY.

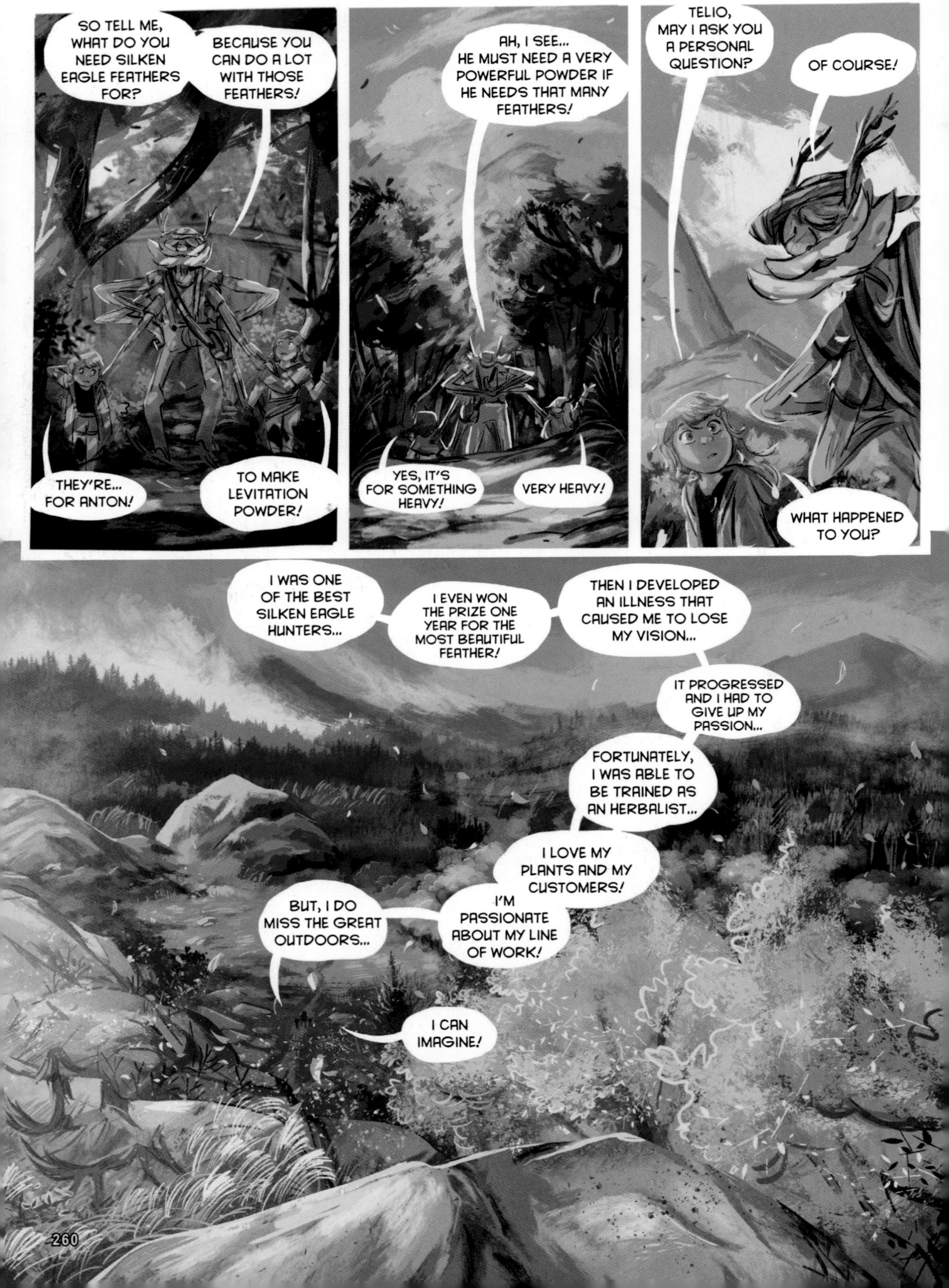
SO TELL ME, WHAT DO YOU NEED SILKEN EAGLE FEATHERS FOR?
BECAUSE YOU CAN DO A LOT WITH THOSE FEATHERS!
THEY'RE... FOR ANTON!
TO MAKE LEVITATION POWDER!
AH, I SEE... HE MUST NEED A VERY POWERFUL POWDER IF HE NEEDS THAT MANY FEATHERS!
YES, IT'S FOR SOMETHING HEAVY!
VERY HEAVY!
TELIO, MAY I ASK YOU A PERSONAL QUESTION?
OF COURSE!
WHAT HAPPENED TO YOU?
I WAS ONE OF THE BEST SILKEN EAGLE HUNTERS...
I EVEN WON THE PRIZE ONE YEAR FOR THE MOST BEAUTIFUL FEATHER!
THEN I DEVELOPED AN ILLNESS THAT CAUSED ME TO LOSE MY VISION...
IT PROGRESSED AND I HAD TO GIVE UP MY PASSION...
FORTUNATELY, I WAS ABLE TO BE TRAINED AS AN HERBALIST...
I LOVE MY PLANTS AND MY CUSTOMERS!
I'M PASSIONATE ABOUT MY LINE OF WORK!
BUT, I DO MISS THE GREAT OUTDOORS...
I CAN IMAGINE!

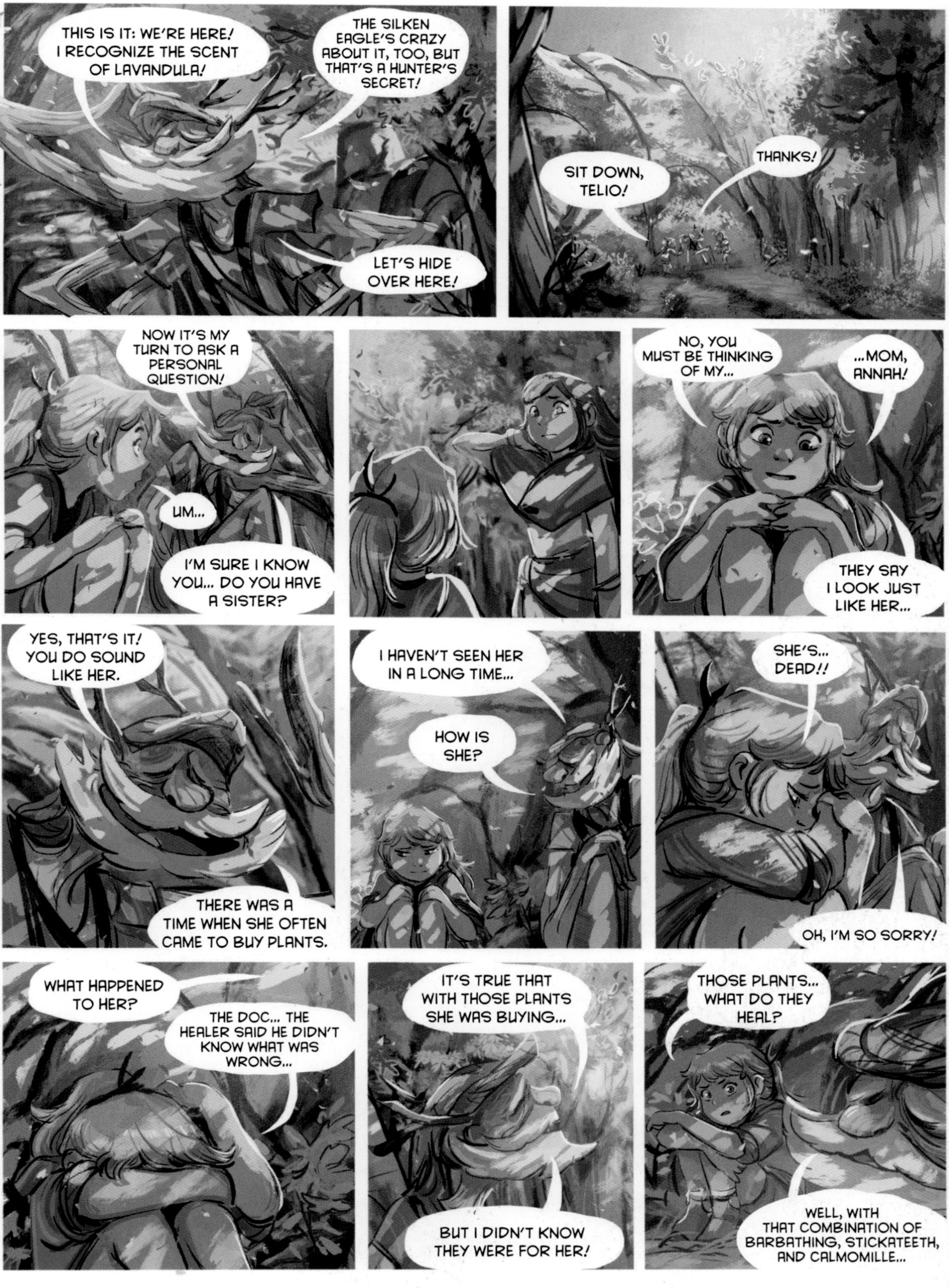

THIS IS IT: WE'RE HERE! I RECOGNIZE THE SCENT OF LAVANDULA!
THE SILKEN EAGLE'S CRAZY ABOUT IT, TOO, BUT THAT'S A HUNTER'S SECRET!
LET'S HIDE OVER HERE!
SIT DOWN, TELIO!
THANKS!
NOW IT'S MY TURN TO ASK A PERSONAL QUESTION!
UM...
I'M SURE I KNOW YOU... DO YOU HAVE A SISTER?
NO, YOU MUST BE THINKING OF MY...
...MOM, ANNAH!
THEY SAY I LOOK JUST LIKE HER...
YES, THAT'S IT! YOU DO SOUND LIKE HER.
THERE WAS A TIME WHEN SHE OFTEN CAME TO BUY PLANTS.
I HAVEN'T SEEN HER IN A LONG TIME...
HOW IS SHE?
SHE'S... DEAD!!
OH, I'M SO SORRY!
WHAT HAPPENED TO HER?
THE DOC... THE HEALER SAID HE DIDN'T KNOW WHAT WAS WRONG...
IT'S TRUE THAT WITH THOSE PLANTS SHE WAS BUYING...
BUT I DIDN'T KNOW THEY WERE FOR HER!
THOSE PLANTS... WHAT DO THEY HEAL?
WELL, WITH THAT COMBINATION OF BARBATHING, STICKATEETH, AND CALMOMILLE...

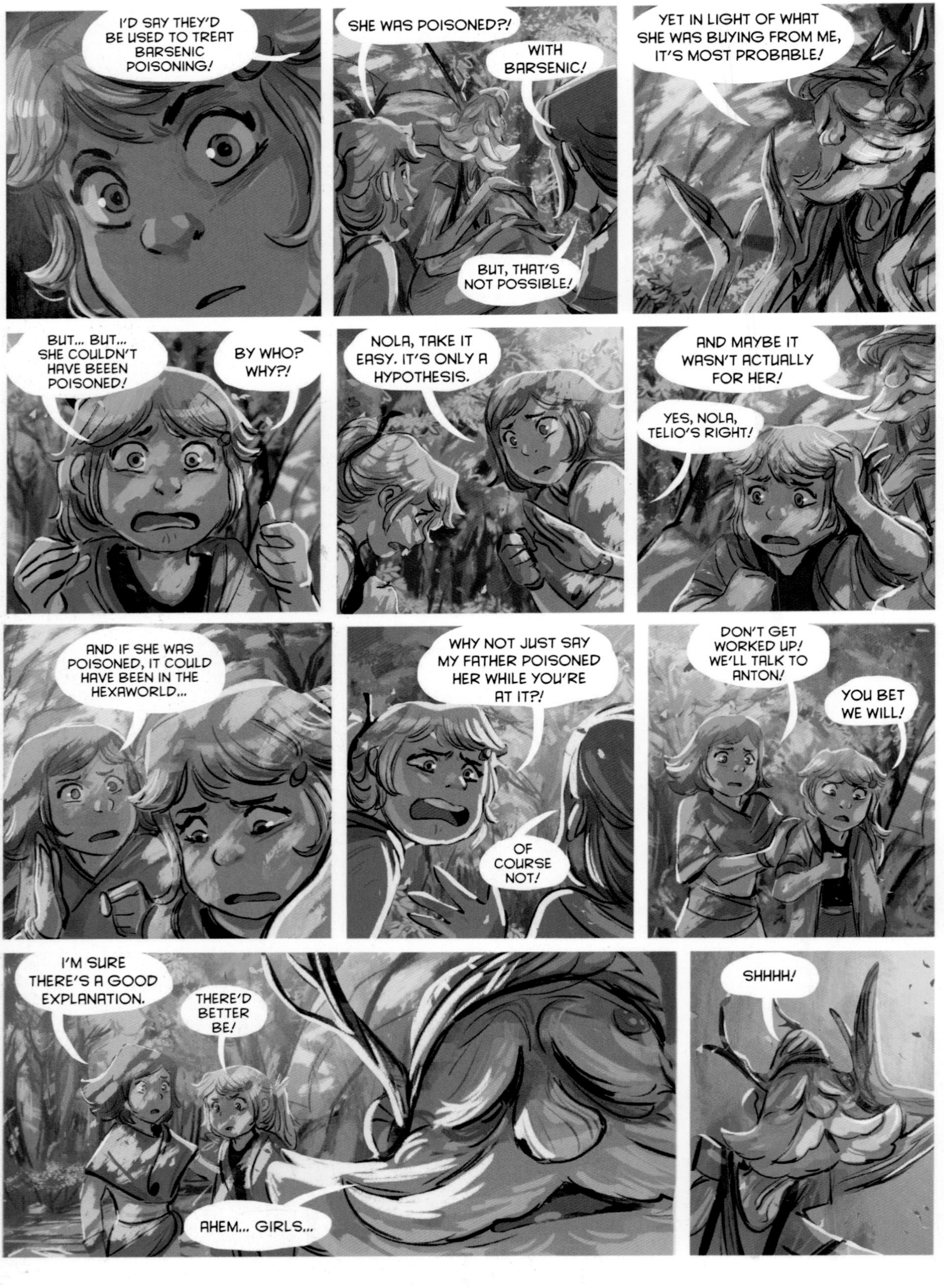

I'D SAY THEY'D BE USED TO TREAT BARSENIC POISONING!
SHE WAS POISONED?!
WITH BARSENIC!
BUT, THAT'S NOT POSSIBLE!
YET IN LIGHT OF WHAT SHE WAS BUYING FROM ME, IT'S MOST PROBABLE!
BUT... BUT... SHE COULDN'T HAVE BEEEN POISONED!
BY WHO? WHY?!
NOLA, TAKE IT EASY. IT'S ONLY A HYPOTHESIS.
AND MAYBE IT WASN'T ACTUALLY FOR HER!
YES, NOLA, TELIO'S RIGHT!
AND IF SHE WAS POISONED, IT COULD HAVE BEEN IN THE HEXAWORLD...
WHY NOT JUST SAY MY FATHER POISONED HER WHILE YOU'RE AT IT?!
OF COURSE NOT!
DON'T GET WORKED UP! WE'LL TALK TO ANTON!
YOU BET WE WILL!
I'M SURE THERE'S A GOOD EXPLANATION.
THERE'D BETTER BE!
AHEM... GIRLS...
SHHHH!

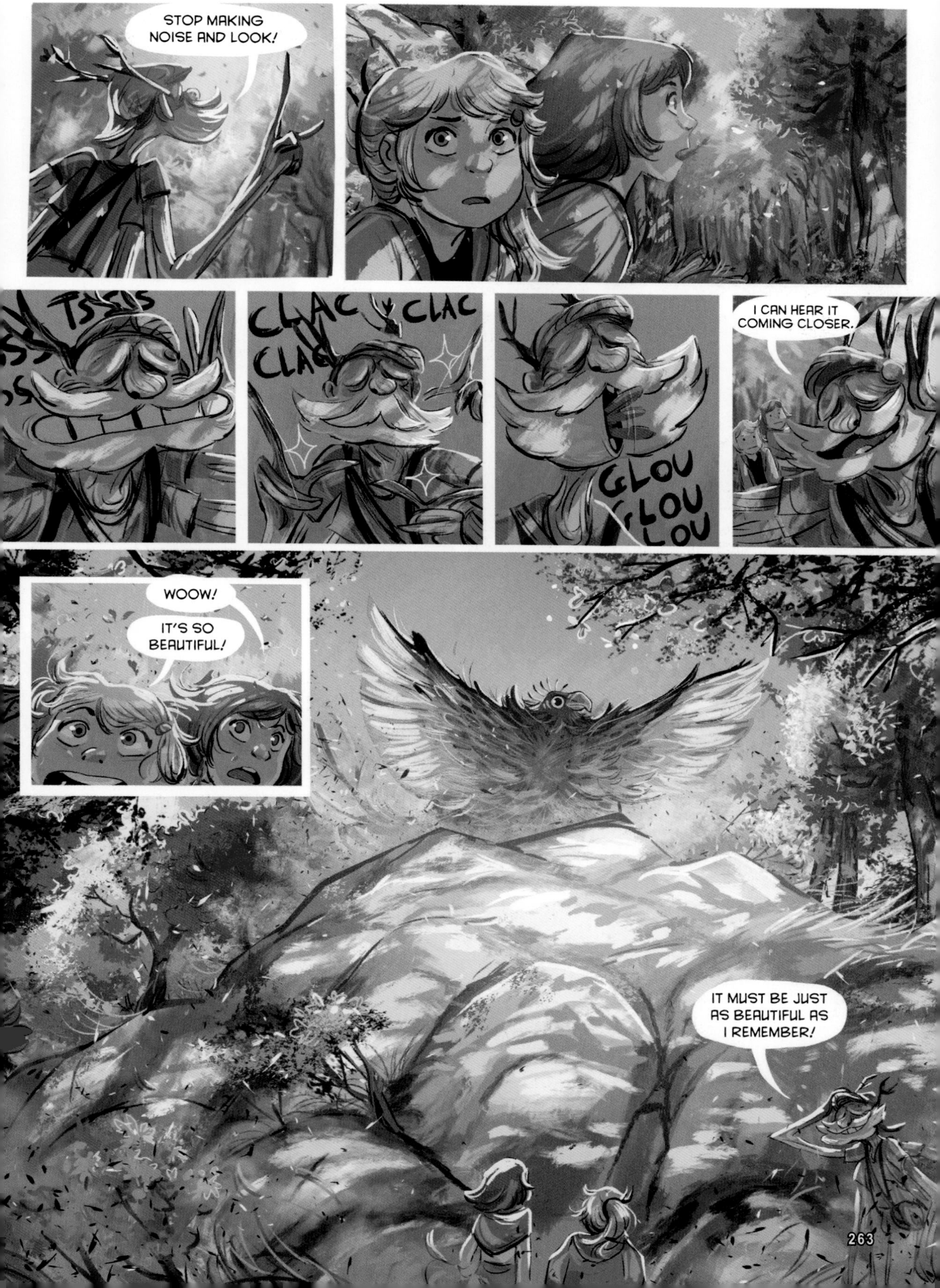
STOP MAKING NOISE AND LOOK!
TSSSS
CLAC CLAC CLAC
GLOU GLOU GLOU
I CAN HEAR IT COMING CLOSER.
WOOW!
IT'S SO BEAUTIFUL!
IT MUST BE JUST AS BEAUTIFUL AS I REMEMBER!

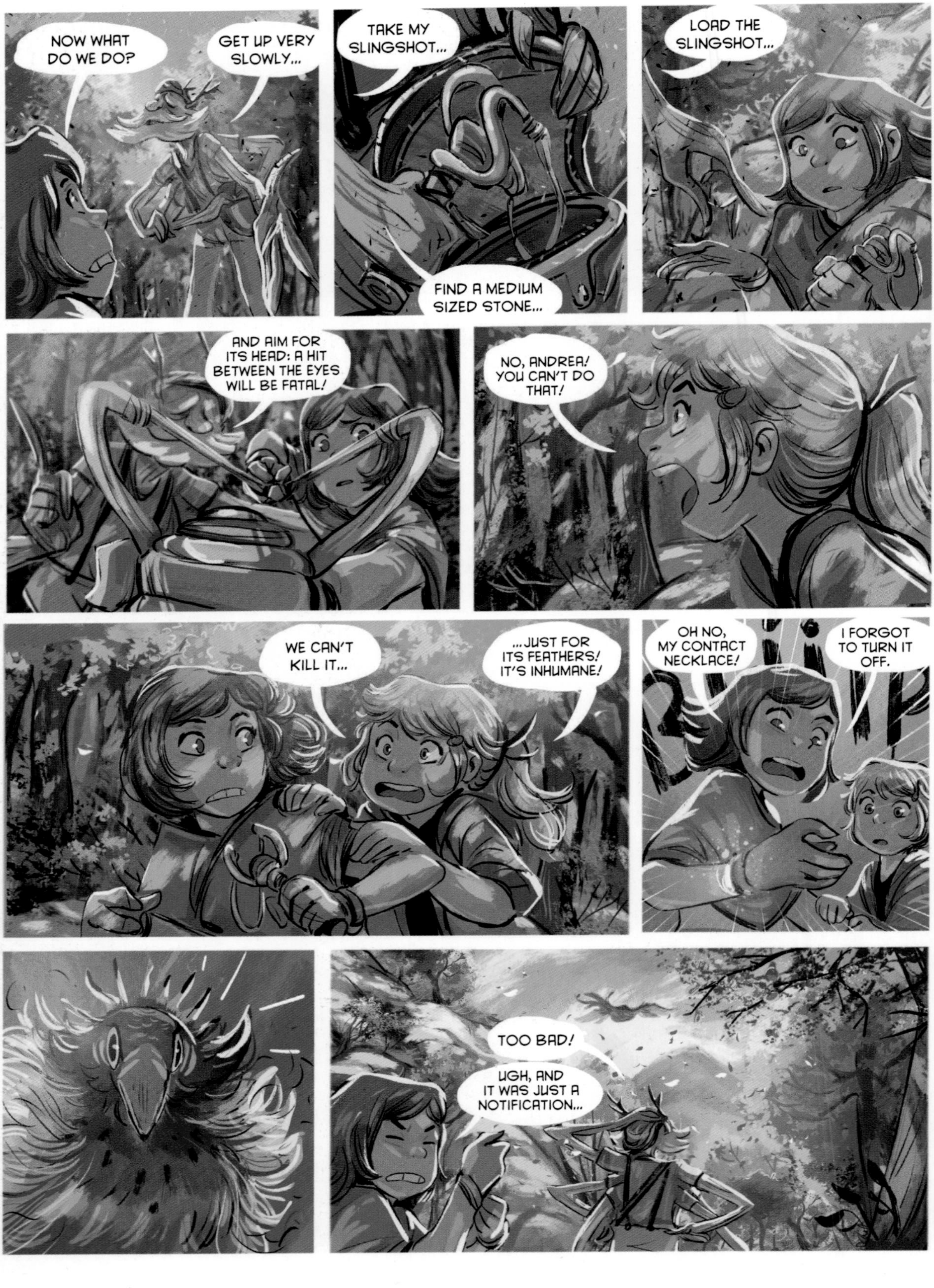

NOW WHAT DO WE DO?
GET UP VERY SLOWLY...
TAKE MY SLINGSHOT...
FIND A MEDIUM SIZED STONE...
LOAD THE SLINGSHOT...
AND AIM FOR ITS HEAD: A HIT BETWEEN THE EYES WILL BE FATAL!
NO, ANDREA! YOU CAN'T DO THAT!
WE CAN'T KILL IT...
...JUST FOR ITS FEATHERS! IT'S INHUMANE!
OH NO, MY CONTACT NECKLACE!
I FORGOT TO TURN IT OFF.
TOO BAD!
UGH, AND IT WAS JUST A NOTIFICATION...

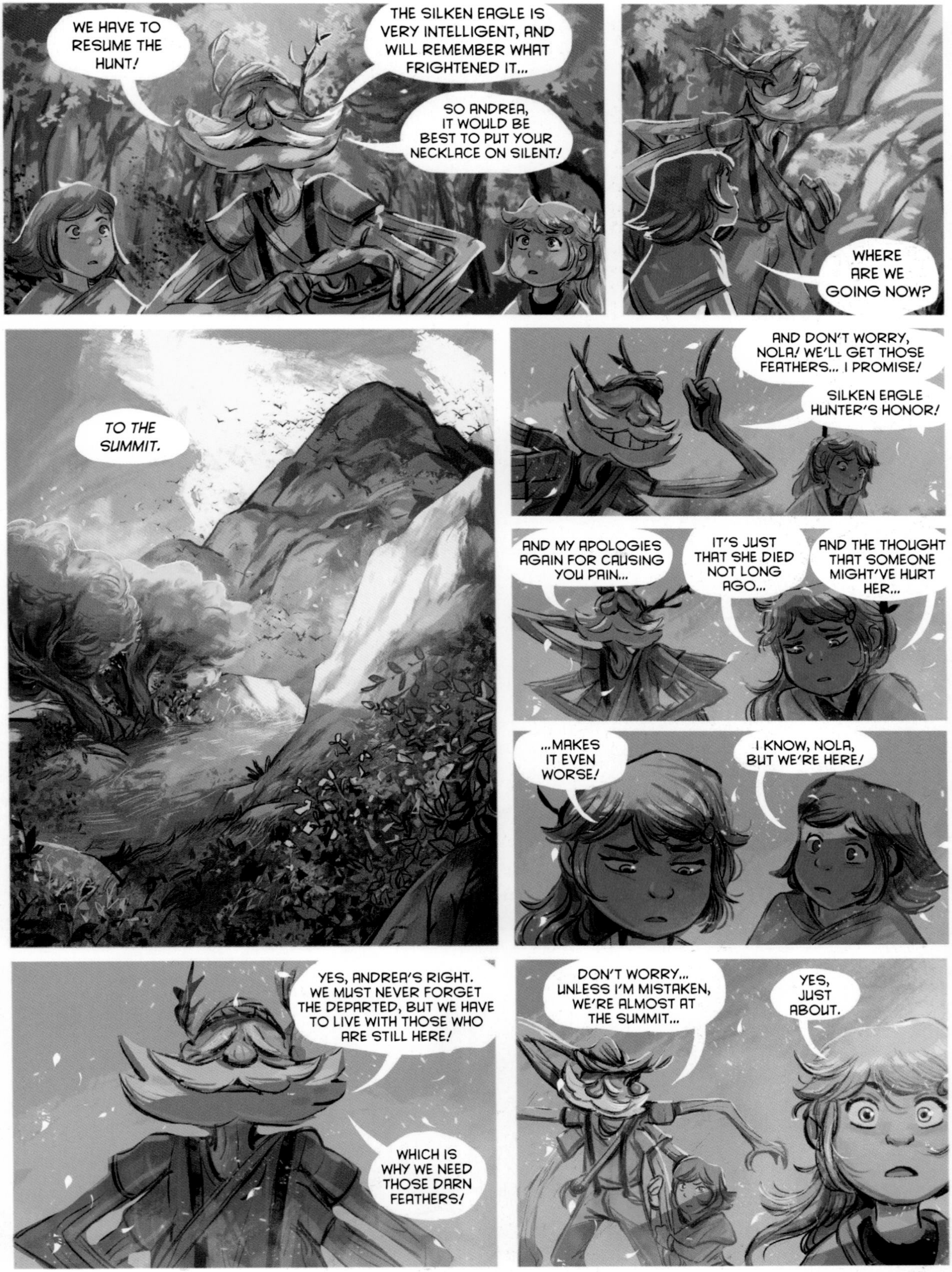
WE HAVE TO RESUME THE HUNT!
THE SILKEN EAGLE IS VERY INTELLIGENT, AND WILL REMEMBER WHAT FRIGHTENED IT...
SO ANDREA, IT WOULD BE BEST TO PUT YOUR NECKLACE ON SILENT!
WHERE ARE WE GOING NOW?
TO THE SUMMIT.
AND DON'T WORRY, NOLA! WE'LL GET THOSE FEATHERS... I PROMISE!
SILKEN EAGLE HUNTER'S HONOR!
AND MY APOLOGIES AGAIN FOR CAUSING YOU PAIN...
IT'S JUST THAT SHE DIED NOT LONG AGO...
AND THE THOUGHT THAT SOMEONE MIGHT'VE HURT HER...
...MAKES IT EVEN WORSE!
I KNOW, NOLA, BUT WE'RE HERE!
YES, ANDREA'S RIGHT. WE MUST NEVER FORGET THE DEPARTED, BUT WE HAVE TO LIVE WITH THOSE WHO ARE STILL HERE!
WHICH IS WHY WE NEED THOSE DARN FEATHERS!
DON'T WORRY... UNLESS I'M MISTAKEN, WE'RE ALMOST AT THE SUMMIT...
YES, JUST ABOUT.

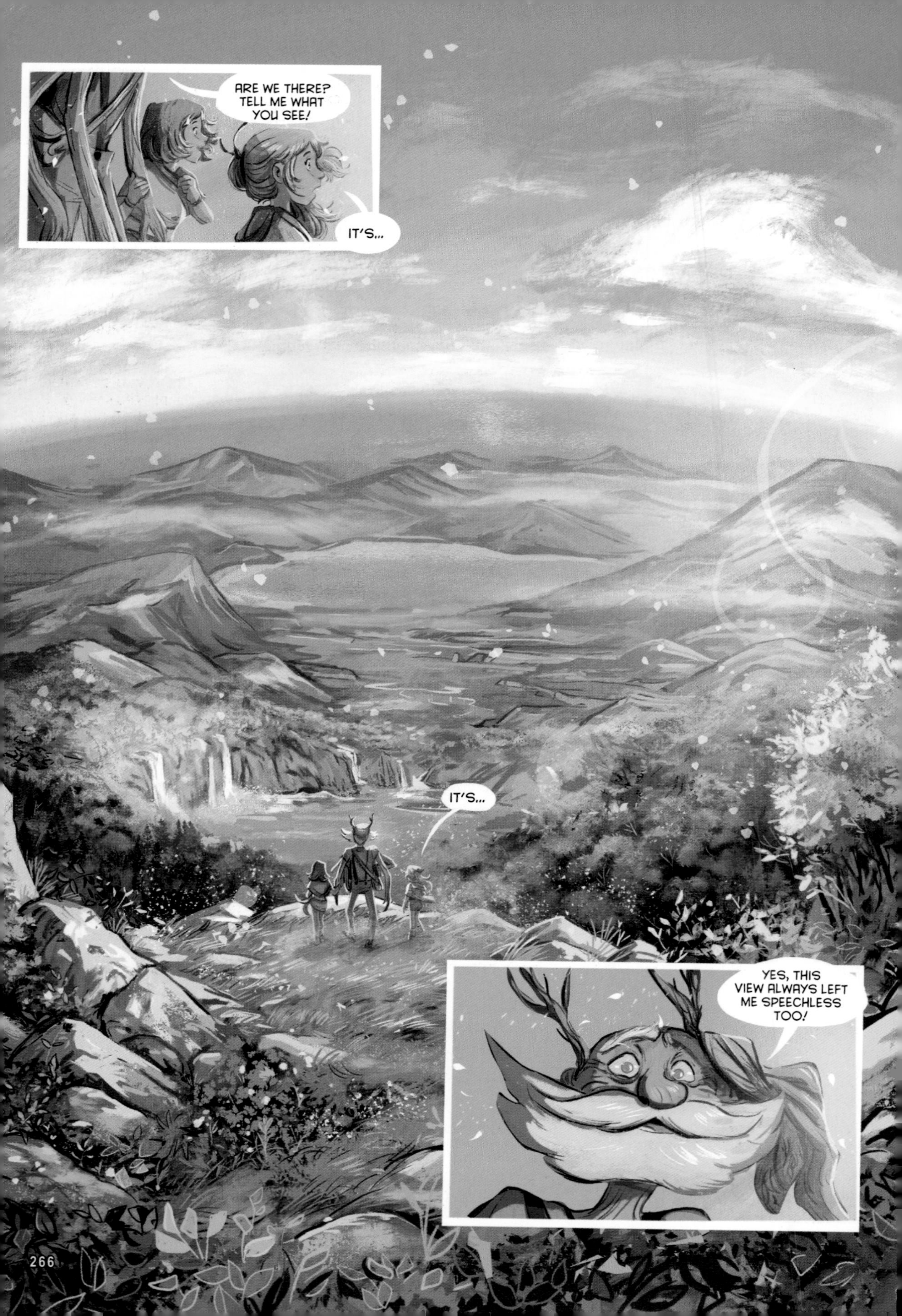
ARE WE THERE? TELL ME WHAT YOU SEE!
IT'S...
IT'S...
YES, THIS VIEW ALWAYS LEFT ME SPEECHLESS TOO!

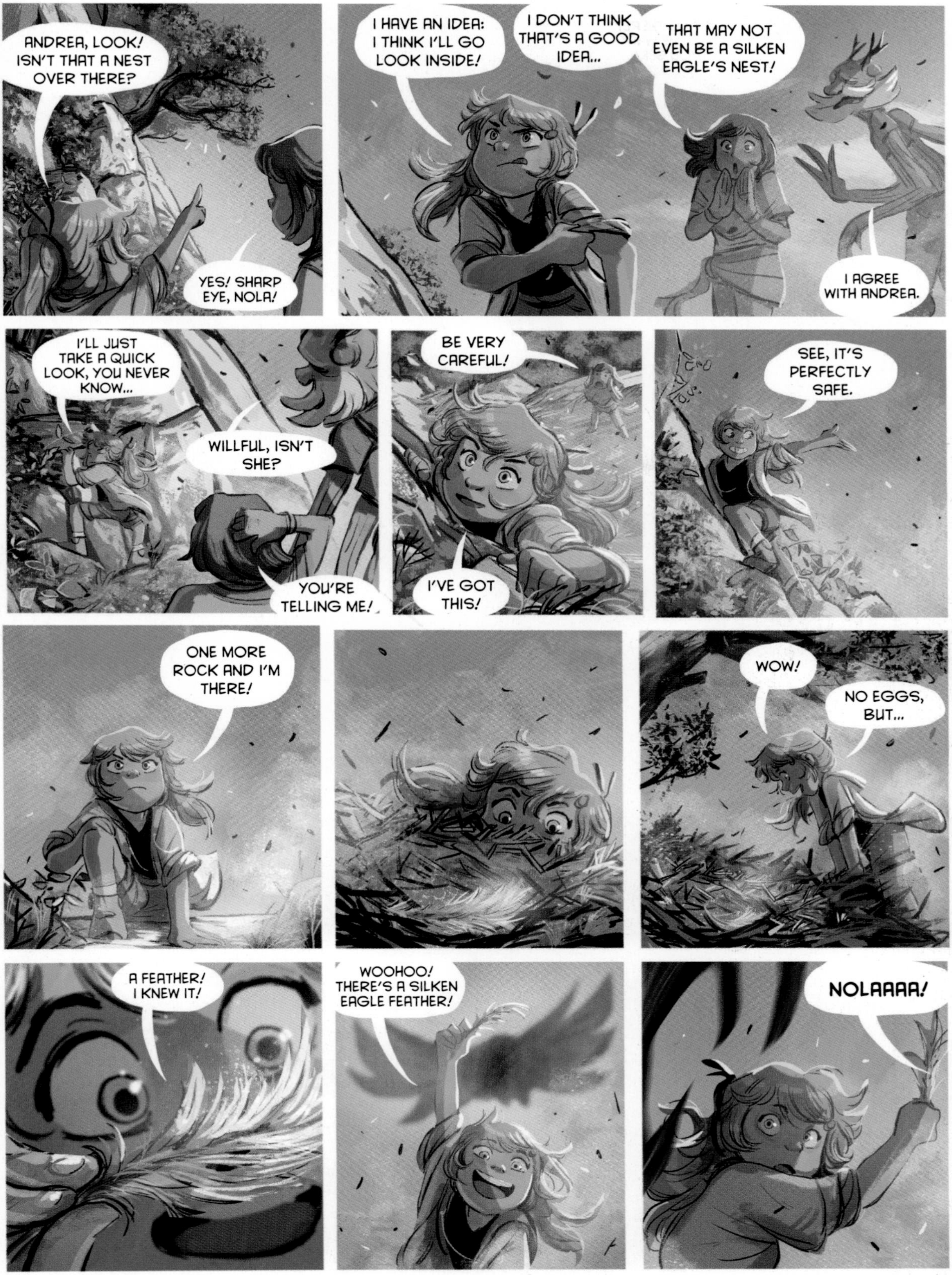
ANDREA, LOOK! ISN'T THAT A NEST OVER THERE?
YES! SHARP EYE, NOLA!
I HAVE AN IDEA: I THINK I'LL GO LOOK INSIDE!
I DON'T THINK THAT'S A GOOD IDEA...
THAT MAY NOT EVEN BE A SILKEN EAGLE'S NEST!
I AGREE WITH ANDREA.
I'LL JUST TAKE A QUICK LOOK, YOU NEVER KNOW...
WILLFUL, ISN'T SHE?
YOU'RE TELLING ME!
BE VERY CAREFUL!
I'VE GOT THIS!
SEE, IT'S PERFECTLY SAFE.
ONE MORE ROCK AND I'M THERE!
WOW!
NO EGGS, BUT...
A FEATHER! I KNEW IT!
WOOHOO! THERE'S A SILKEN EAGLE FEATHER!
NOLAAAA!

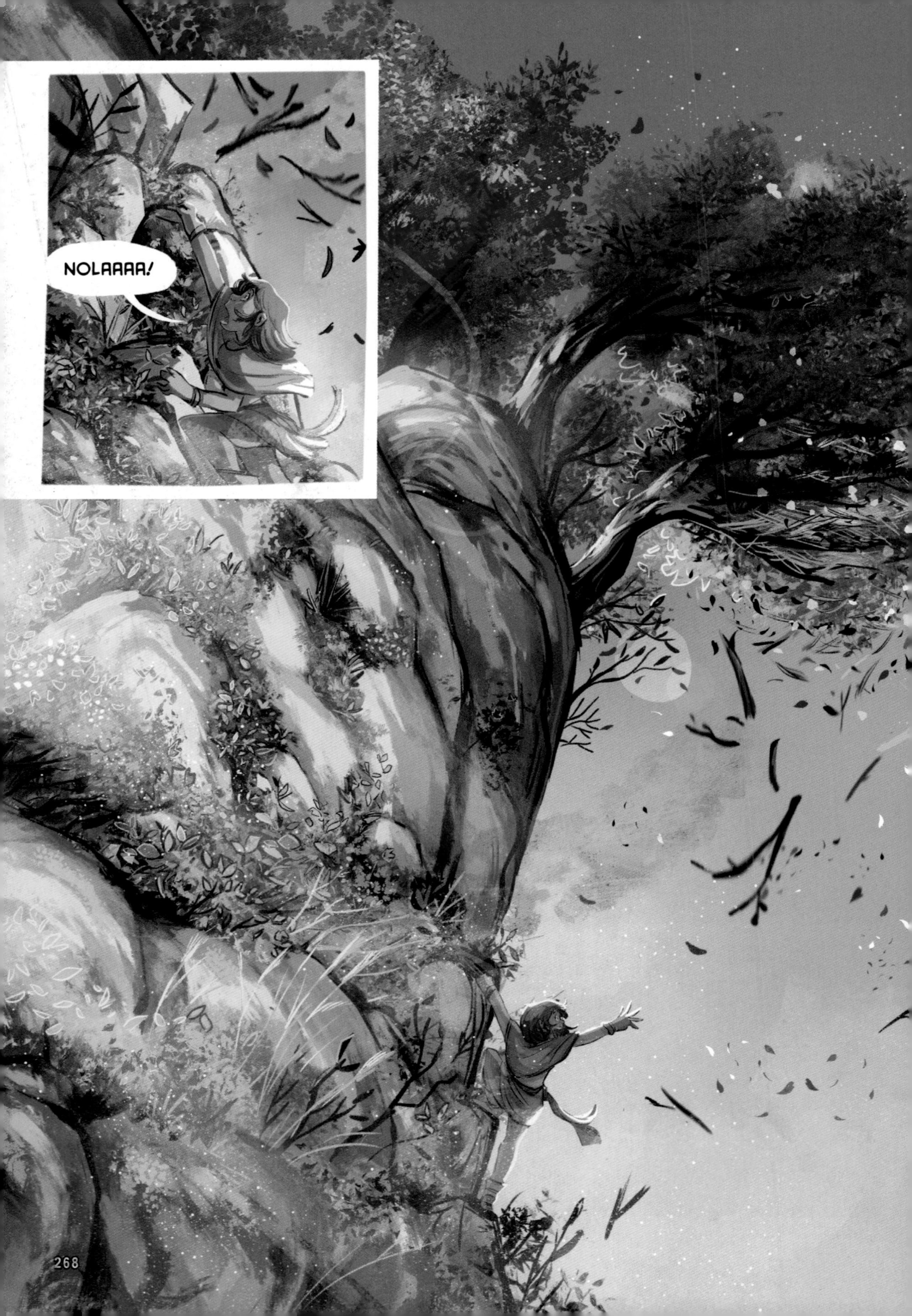
NOLAAAA!

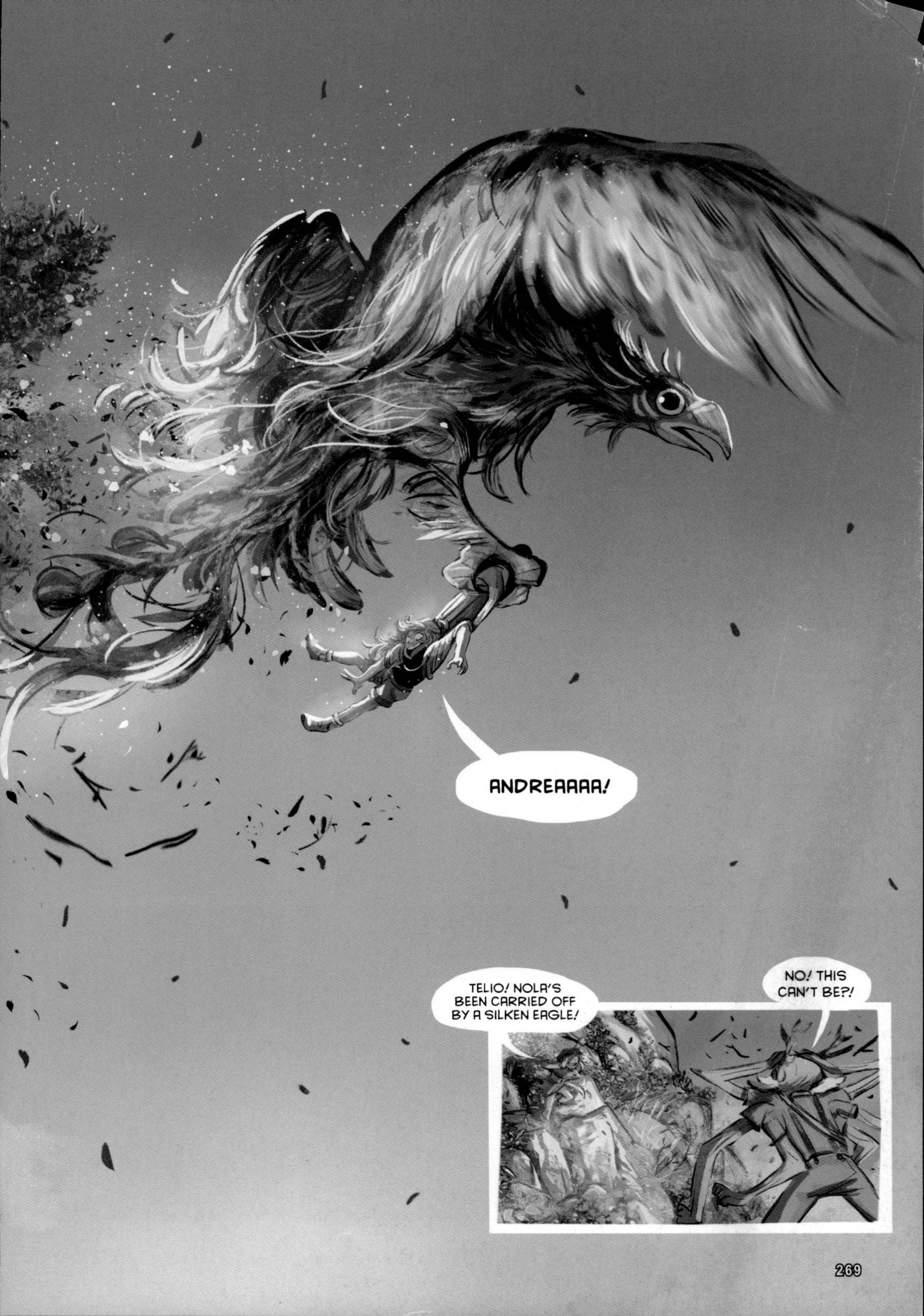
ANDREAAAA!
TELIO! NOLA'S BEEN CARRIED OFF BY A SILKEN EAGLE!
NO! THIS CAN'T BE?!

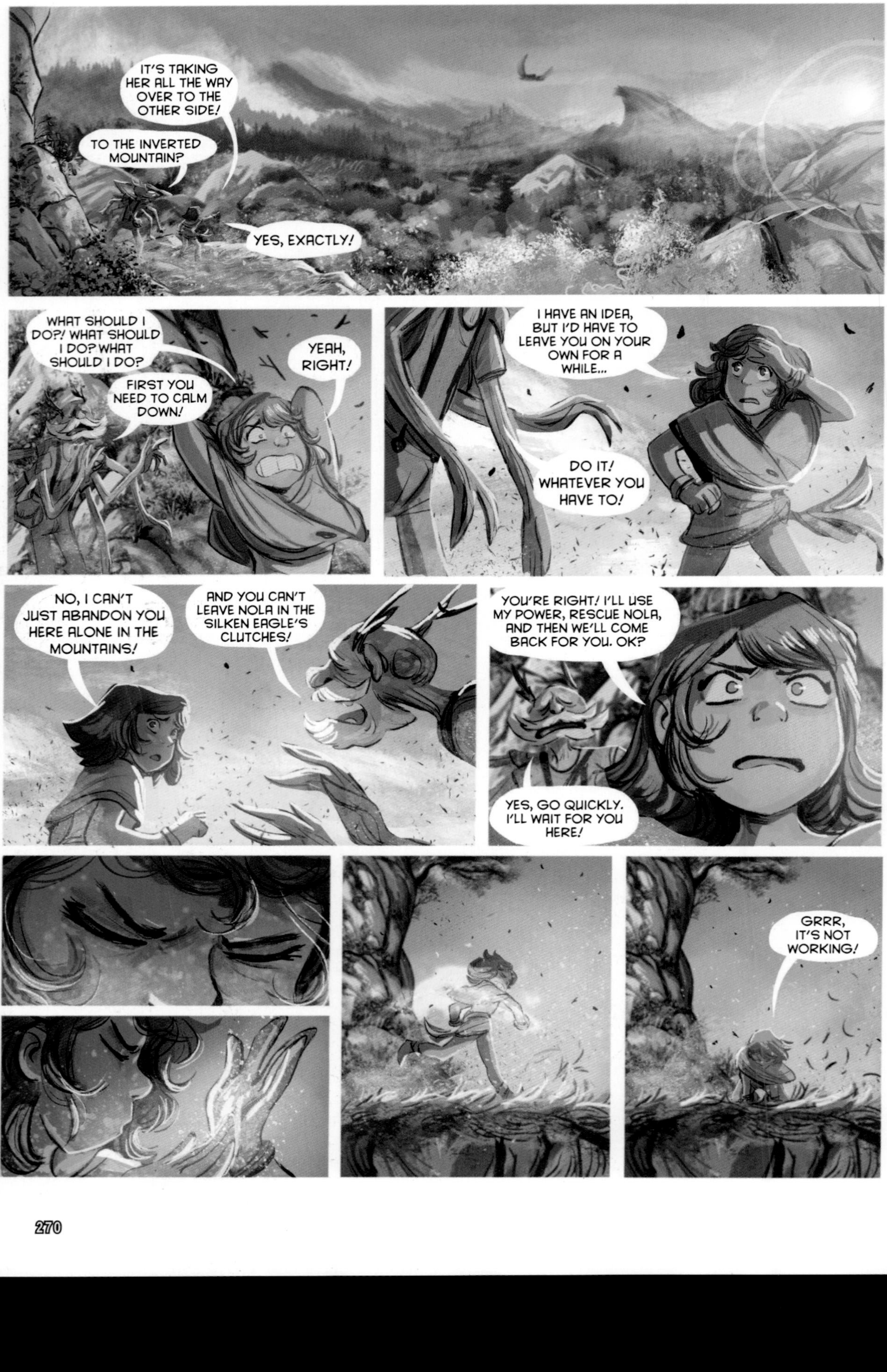
IT'S TAKING HER ALL THE WAY OVER TO THE OTHER SIDE!
TO THE INVERTED MOUNTAIN?
YES, EXACTLY!
WHAT SHOULD I DO?! WHAT SHOULD I DO? WHAT SHOULD I DO?
FIRST YOU NEED TO CALM DOWN!
YEAH, RIGHT!
I HAVE AN IDEA, BUT I'D HAVE TO LEAVE YOU ON YOUR OWN FOR A WHILE...
DO IT! WHATEVER YOU HAVE TO!
NO, I CAN'T JUST ABANDON YOU HERE ALONE IN THE MOUNTAINS!
AND YOU CAN'T LEAVE NOLA IN THE SILKEN EAGLE'S CLUTCHES!
YOU'RE RIGHT! I'LL USE MY POWER, RESCUE NOLA, AND THEN WE'LL COME BACK FOR YOU. OK?
YES, GO QUICKLY. I'LL WAIT FOR YOU HERE!
GRRR, IT'S NOT WORKING!

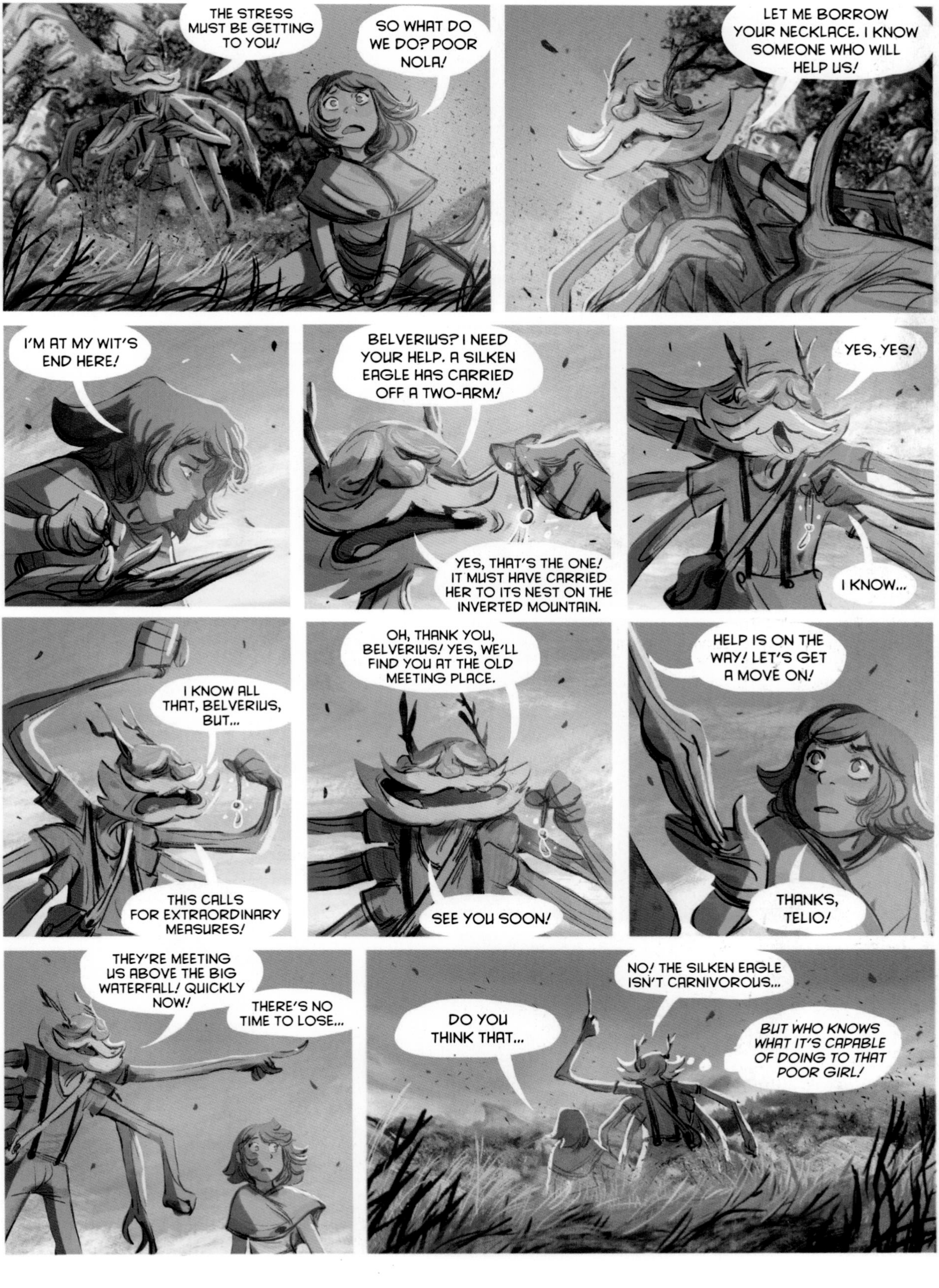
THE STRESS MUST BE GETTING TO YOU!
SO WHAT DO WE DO? POOR NOLA!
LET ME BORROW YOUR NECKLACE. I KNOW SOMEONE WHO WILL HELP US!
I'M AT MY WIT'S END HERE!
BELVERIUS? I NEED YOUR HELP. A SILKEN EAGLE HAS CARRIED OFF A TWO-ARM!
YES, THAT'S THE ONE! IT MUST HAVE CARRIED HER TO ITS NEST ON THE INVERTED MOUNTAIN.
YES, YES!
I KNOW...
I KNOW ALL THAT, BELVERIUS, BUT...
THIS CALLS FOR EXTRAORDINARY MEASURES!
OH, THANK YOU, BELVERIUS! YES, WE'LL FIND YOU AT THE OLD MEETING PLACE.
SEE YOU SOON!
HELP IS ON THE WAY! LET'S GET A MOVE ON!
THANKS, TELIO!
THEY'RE MEETING US ABOVE THE BIG WATERFALL! QUICKLY NOW!
THERE'S NO TIME TO LOSE...
DO YOU THINK THAT...
NO! THE SILKEN EAGLE ISN'T CARNIVOROUS...
BUT WHO KNOWS WHAT IT'S CAPABLE OF DOING TO THAT POOR GIRL!

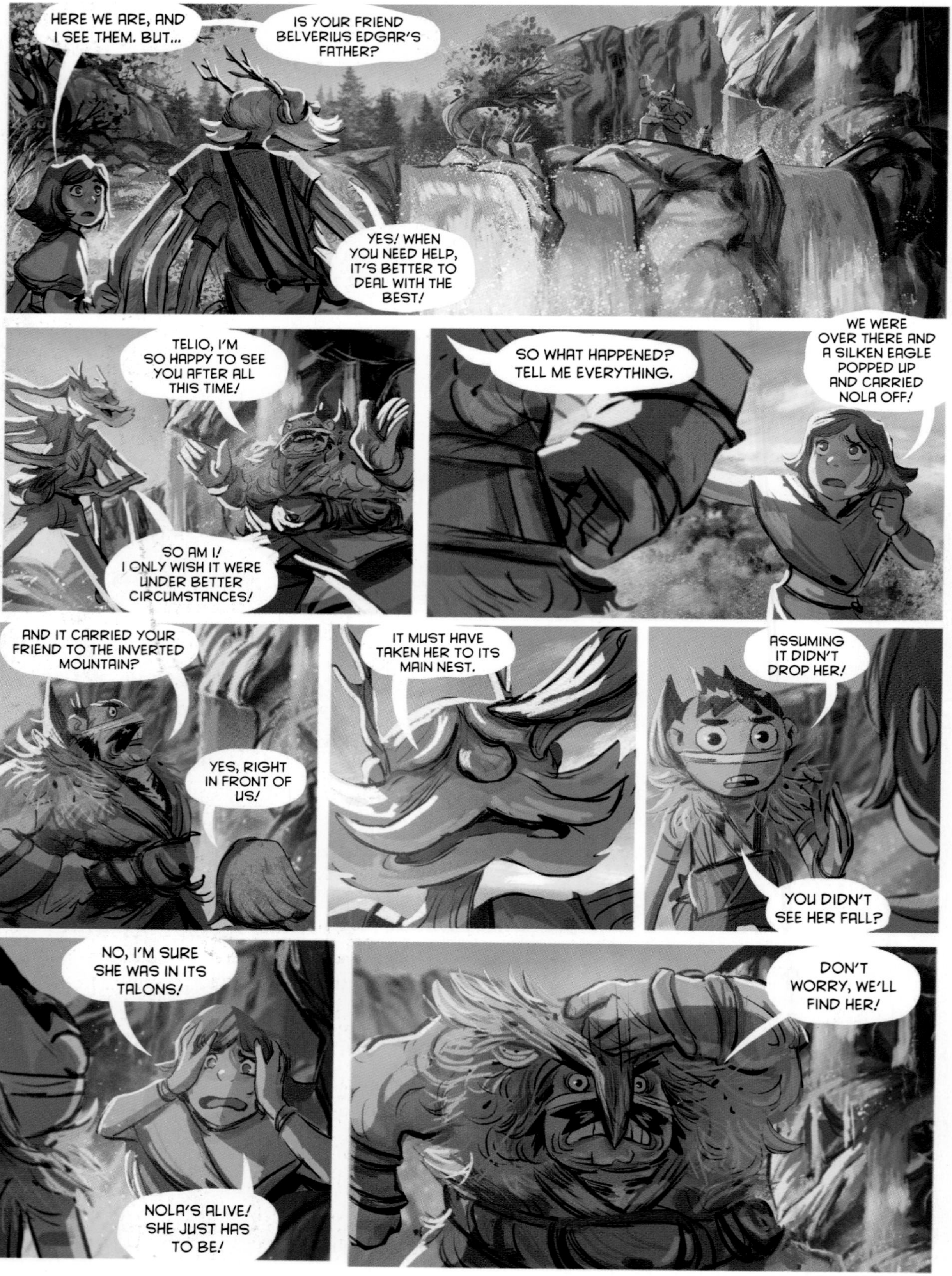
HERE WE ARE, AND I SEE THEM. BUT...
IS YOUR FRIEND BELVERIUS EDGAR'S FATHER?
YES! WHEN YOU NEED HELP, IT'S BETTER TO DEAL WITH THE BEST!
TELIO, I'M SO HAPPY TO SEE YOU AFTER ALL THIS TIME!
SO AM I! I ONLY WISH IT WERE UNDER BETTER CIRCUMSTANCES!
SO WHAT HAPPENED? TELL ME EVERYTHING.
WE WERE OVER THERE AND A SILKEN EAGLE POPPED UP AND CARRIED NOLA OFF!
AND IT CARRIED YOUR FRIEND TO THE INVERTED MOUNTAIN?
YES, RIGHT IN FRONT OF US!
IT MUST HAVE TAKEN HER TO ITS MAIN NEST.
ASSUMING IT DIDN'T DROP HER!
YOU DIDN'T SEE HER FALL?
NO, I'M SURE SHE WAS IN ITS TALONS!
NOLA'S ALIVE! SHE JUST HAS TO BE!
DON'T WORRY, WE'LL FIND HER!

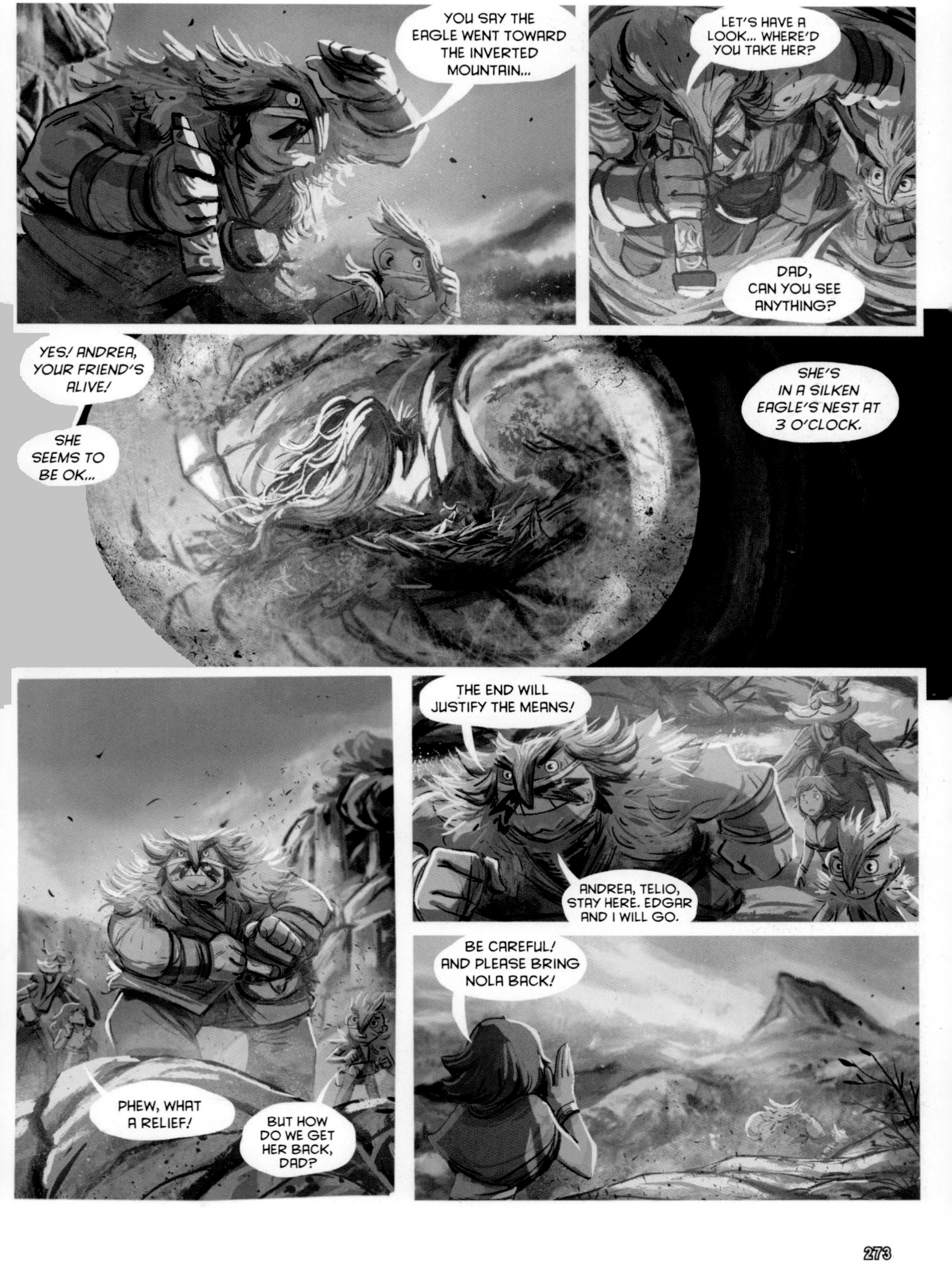
YOU SAY THE EAGLE WENT TOWARD THE INVERTED MOUNTAIN...
LET'S HAVE A LOOK... WHERE'D YOU TAKE HER?
DAD, CAN YOU SEE ANYTHING?
YES! ANDREA, YOUR FRIEND'S ALIVE!
SHE SEEMS TO BE OK...
SHE'S IN A SILKEN EAGLE'S NEST AT 3 O'CLOCK.
PHEW, WHAT A RELIEF!
BUT HOW DO WE GET HER BACK, DAD?
THE END WILL JUSTIFY THE MEANS!
ANDREA, TELIO, STAY HERE. EDGAR AND I WILL GO.
BE CAREFUL! AND PLEASE BRING NOLA BACK!

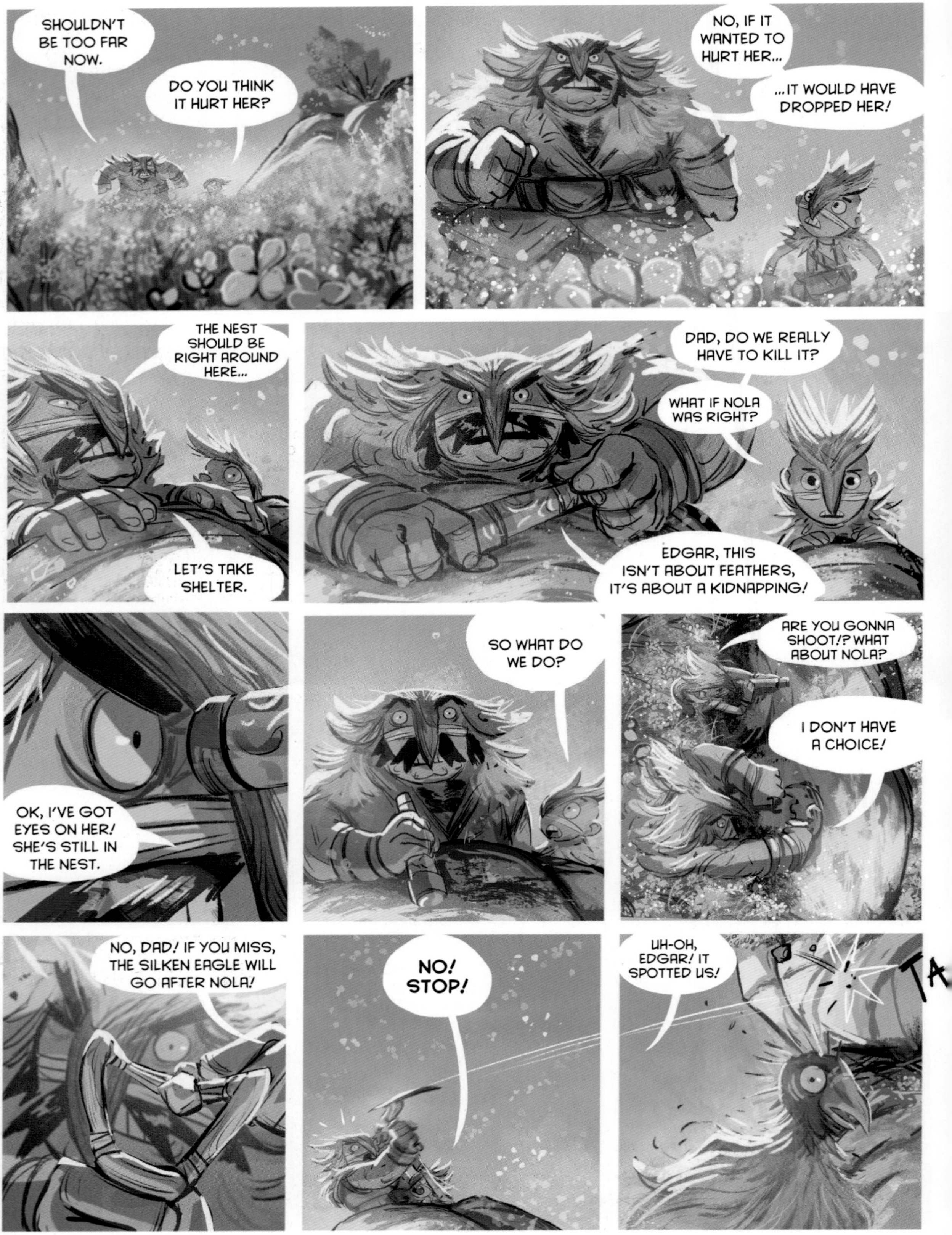
SHOULDN'T BE TOO FAR NOW.
DO YOU THINK IT HURT HER?
NO, IF IT WANTED TO HURT HER...
...IT WOULD HAVE DROPPED HER!
THE NEST SHOULD BE RIGHT AROUND HERE...
LET'S TAKE SHELTER.
DAD, DO WE REALLY HAVE TO KILL IT?
WHAT IF NOLA WAS RIGHT?
EDGAR, THIS ISN'T ABOUT FEATHERS, IT'S ABOUT A KIDNAPPING!
OK, I'VE GOT EYES ON HER! SHE'S STILL IN THE NEST.
SO WHAT DO WE DO?
ARE YOU GONNA SHOOT!? WHAT ABOUT NOLA?
I DON'T HAVE A CHOICE!
NO, DAD! IF YOU MISS, THE SILKEN EAGLE WILL GO AFTER NOLA!
NO! STOP!
UH-OH, EDGAR! IT SPOTTED US!
TA

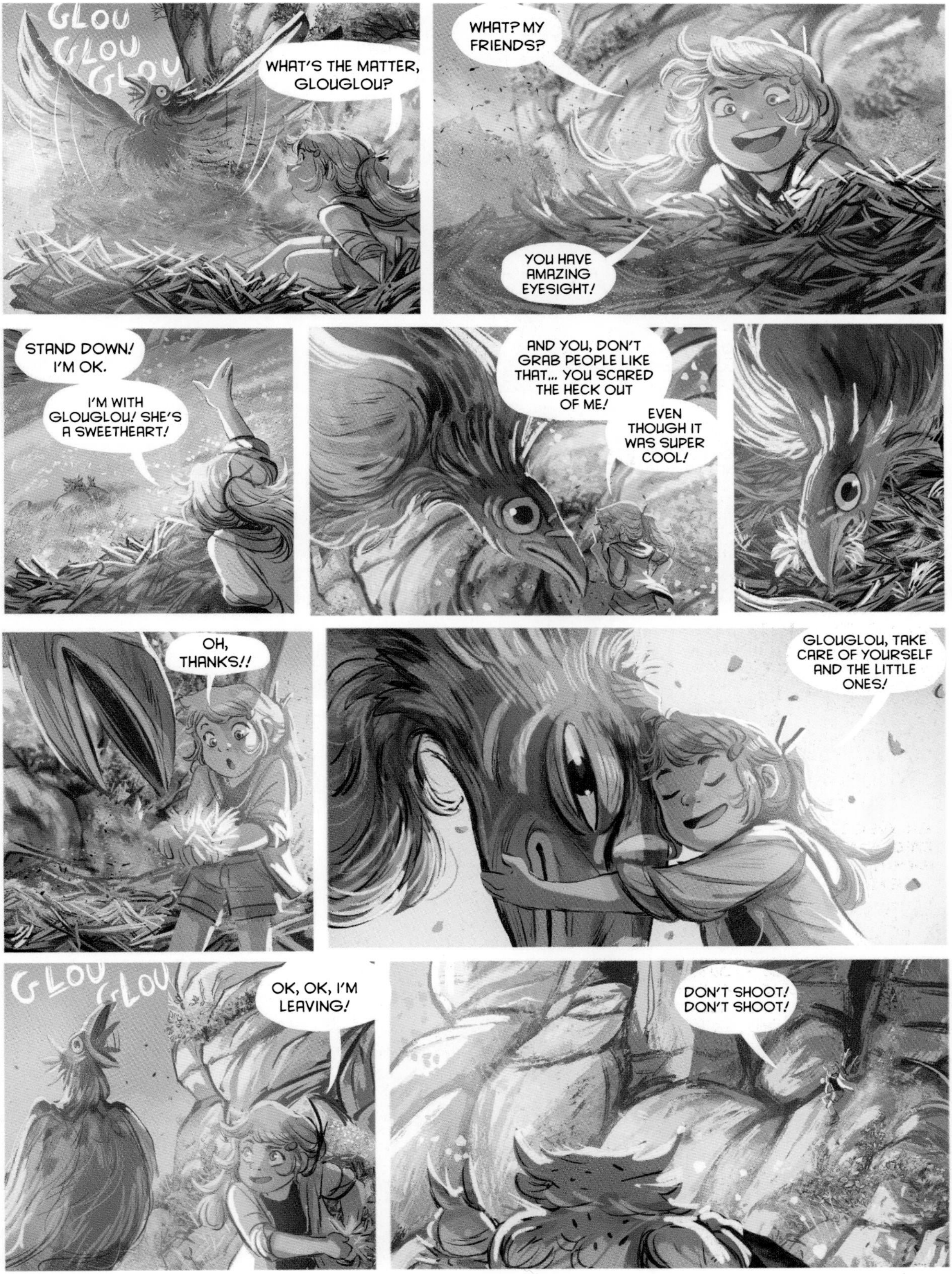
GLOU GLOU GLOU
WHAT'S THE MATTER, GLOUGLOU?
WHAT? MY FRIENDS?
YOU HAVE AMAZING EYESIGHT!
STAND DOWN! I'M OK.
I'M WITH GLOUGLOU! SHE'S A SWEETHEART!
AND YOU, DON'T GRAB PEOPLE LIKE THAT... YOU SCARED THE HECK OUT OF ME!
EVEN THOUGH IT WAS SUPER COOL!
OH, THANKS!!
GLOUGLOU, TAKE CARE OF YOURSELF AND THE LITTLE ONES!
GLOU GLOU
OK, OK, I'M LEAVING!
DON'T SHOOT! DON'T SHOOT!

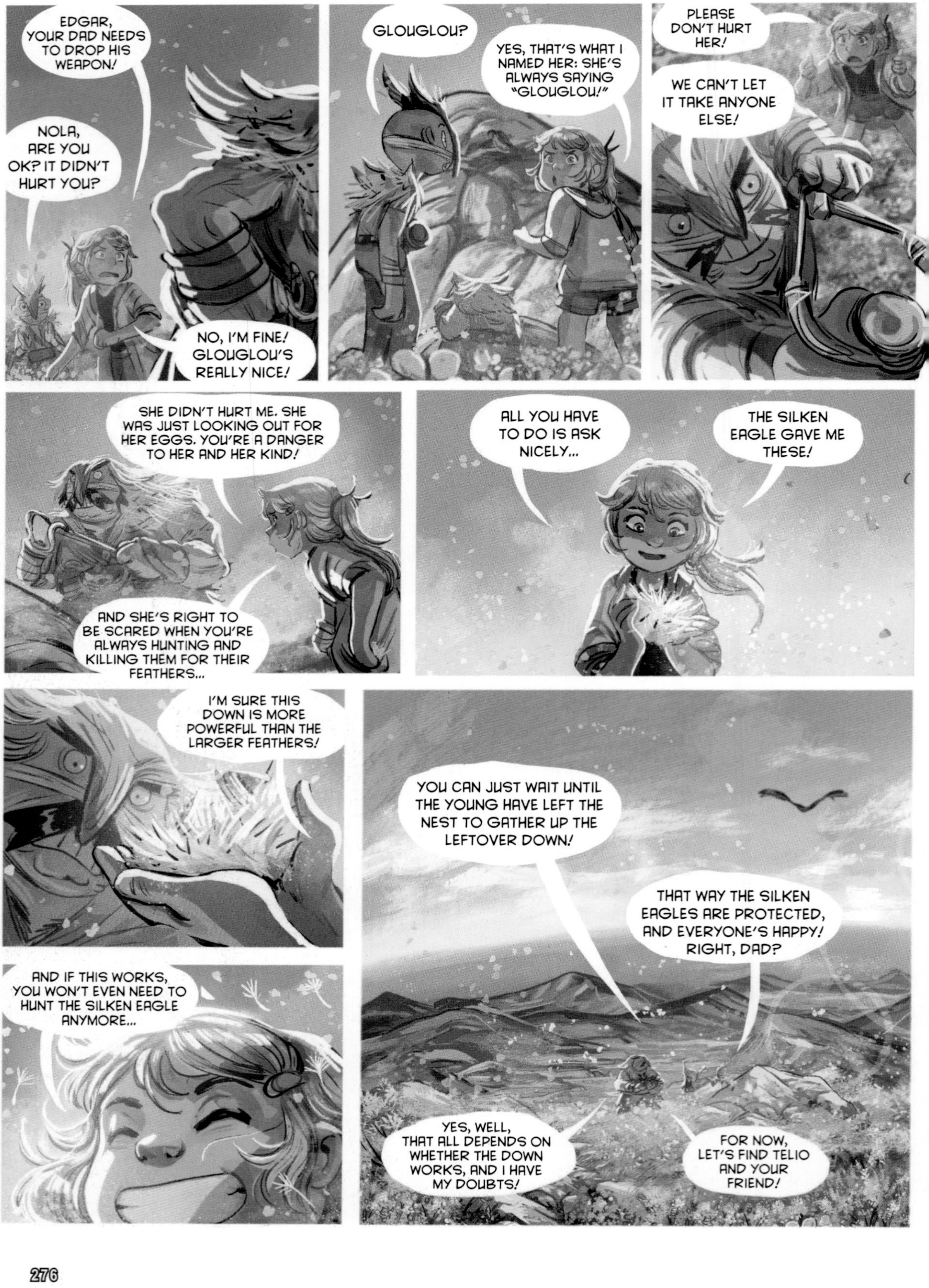
EDGAR, YOUR DAD NEEDS TO DROP HIS WEAPON!
NOLA, ARE YOU OK? IT DIDN'T HURT YOU?
NO, I'M FINE! GLOUGLOU'S REALLY NICE!
GLOUGLOU?
YES, THAT'S WHAT I NAMED HER: SHE'S ALWAYS SAYING "GLOUGLOU!"
PLEASE DON'T HURT HER!
WE CAN'T LET IT TAKE ANYONE ELSE!
SHE DIDN'T HURT ME. SHE WAS JUST LOOKING OUT FOR HER EGGS. YOU'RE A DANGER TO HER AND HER KIND!
AND SHE'S RIGHT TO BE SCARED WHEN YOU'RE ALWAYS HUNTING AND KILLING THEM FOR THEIR FEATHERS...
ALL YOU HAVE TO DO IS ASK NICELY...
THE SILKEN EAGLE GAVE ME THESE!
I'M SURE THIS DOWN IS MORE POWERFUL THAN THE LARGER FEATHERS!
AND IF THIS WORKS, YOU WON'T EVEN NEED TO HUNT THE SILKEN EAGLE ANYMORE...
YOU CAN JUST WAIT UNTIL THE YOUNG HAVE LEFT THE NEST TO GATHER UP THE LEFTOVER DOWN!
THAT WAY THE SILKEN EAGLES ARE PROTECTED, AND EVERYONE'S HAPPY! RIGHT, DAD?
YES, WELL, THAT ALL DEPENDS ON WHETHER THE DOWN WORKS, AND I HAVE MY DOUBTS!
FOR NOW, LET'S FIND TELIO AND YOUR FRIEND!

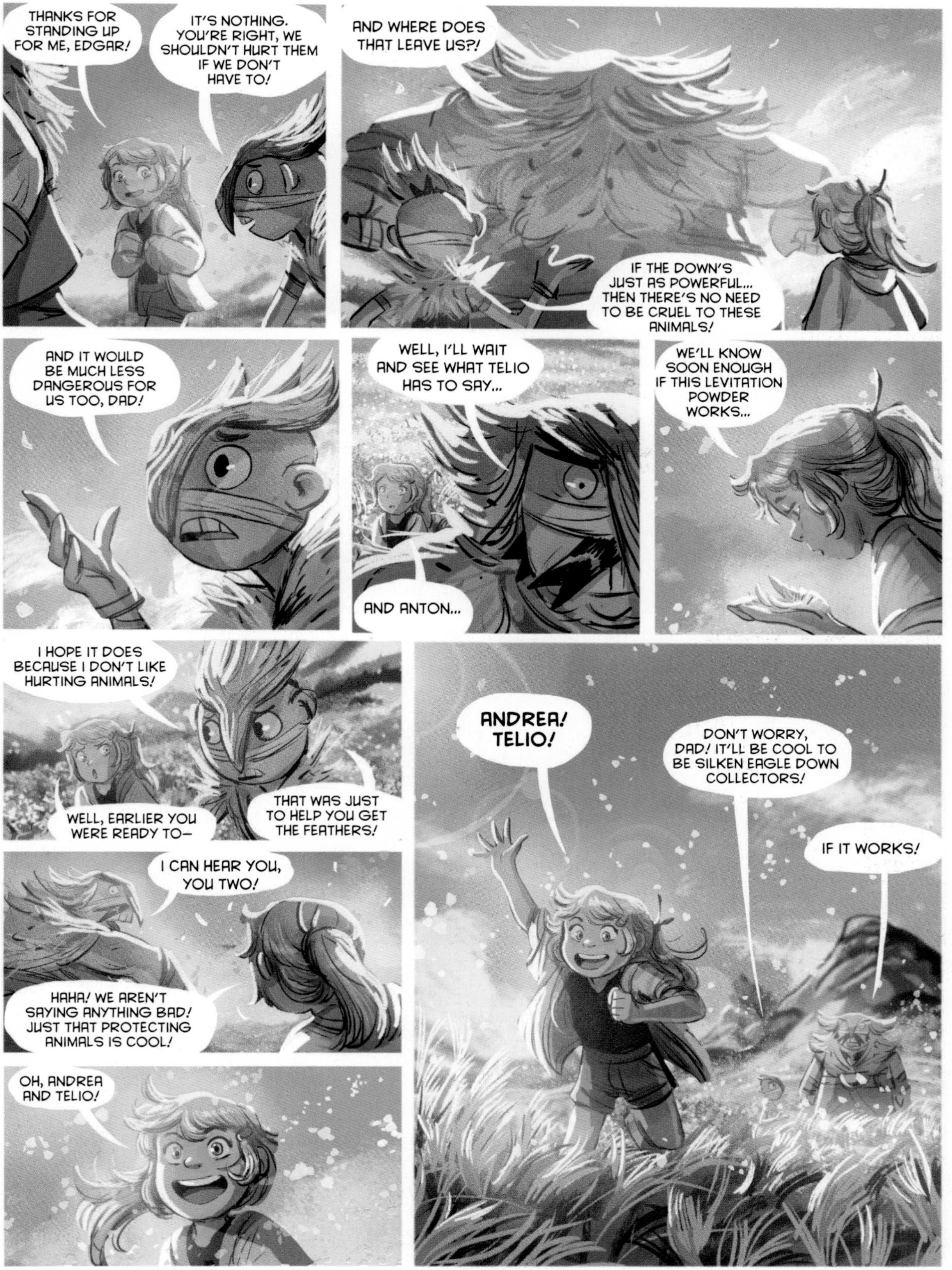

THANKS FOR STANDING UP FOR ME, EDGAR!
IT'S NOTHING. YOU'RE RIGHT, WE SHOULDN'T HURT THEM IF WE DON'T HAVE TO!
AND WHERE DOES THAT LEAVE US?!
IF THE DOWN'S JUST AS POWERFUL... THEN THERE'S NO NEED TO BE CRUEL TO THESE ANIMALS!
AND IT WOULD BE MUCH LESS DANGEROUS FOR US TOO, DAD!
WELL, I'LL WAIT AND SEE WHAT TELIO HAS TO SAY...
AND ANTON...
WE'LL KNOW SOON ENOUGH IF THIS LEVITATION POWDER WORKS...
I HOPE IT DOES BECAUSE I DON'T LIKE HURTING ANIMALS!
WELL, EARLIER YOU WERE READY TO–
THAT WAS JUST TO HELP YOU GET THE FEATHERS!
I CAN HEAR YOU, YOU TWO!
HAHA! WE AREN'T SAYING ANYTHING BAD! JUST THAT PROTECTING ANIMALS IS COOL!
OH, ANDREA AND TELIO!
ANDREA! TELIO!
DON'T WORRY, DAD! IT'LL BE COOL TO BE SILKEN EAGLE DOWN COLLECTORS!
IF IT WORKS!

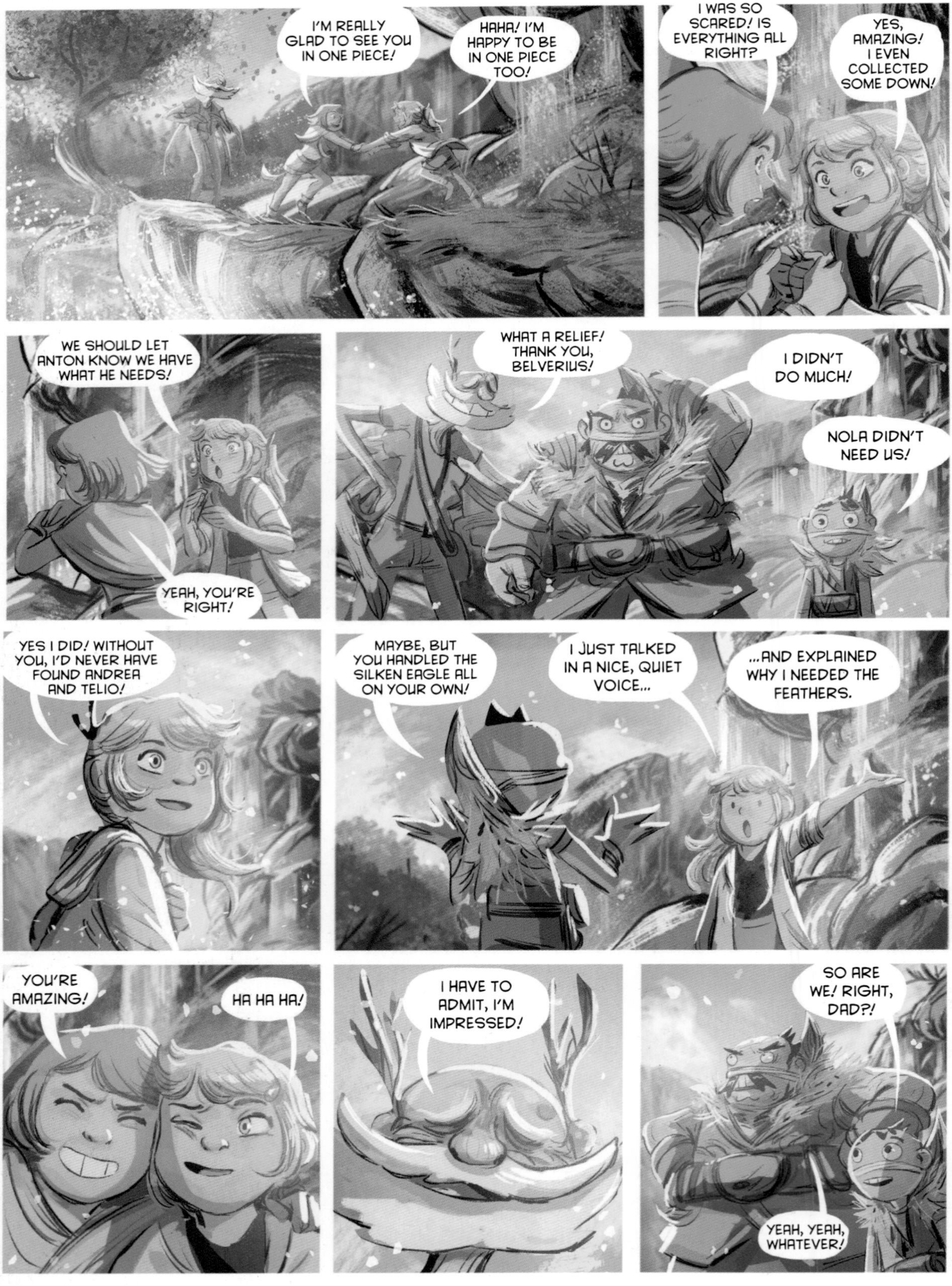

I'M REALLY GLAD TO SEE YOU IN ONE PIECE!
HAHA! I'M HAPPY TO BE IN ONE PIECE TOO!
I WAS SO SCARED! IS EVERYTHING ALL RIGHT?
YES, AMAZING! I EVEN COLLECTED SOME DOWN!
WE SHOULD LET ANTON KNOW WE HAVE WHAT HE NEEDS!
YEAH, YOU'RE RIGHT!
WHAT A RELIEF! THANK YOU, BELVERIUS!
I DIDN'T DO MUCH!
NOLA DIDN'T NEED US!
YES I DID! WITHOUT YOU, I'D NEVER HAVE FOUND ANDREA AND TELIO!
MAYBE, BUT YOU HANDLED THE SILKEN EAGLE ALL ON YOUR OWN!
I JUST TALKED IN A NICE, QUIET VOICE...
...AND EXPLAINED WHY I NEEDED THE FEATHERS.
YOU'RE AMAZING!
HA HA HA!
I HAVE TO ADMIT, I'M IMPRESSED!
SO ARE WE! RIGHT, DAD?!
YEAH, YEAH, WHATEVER!

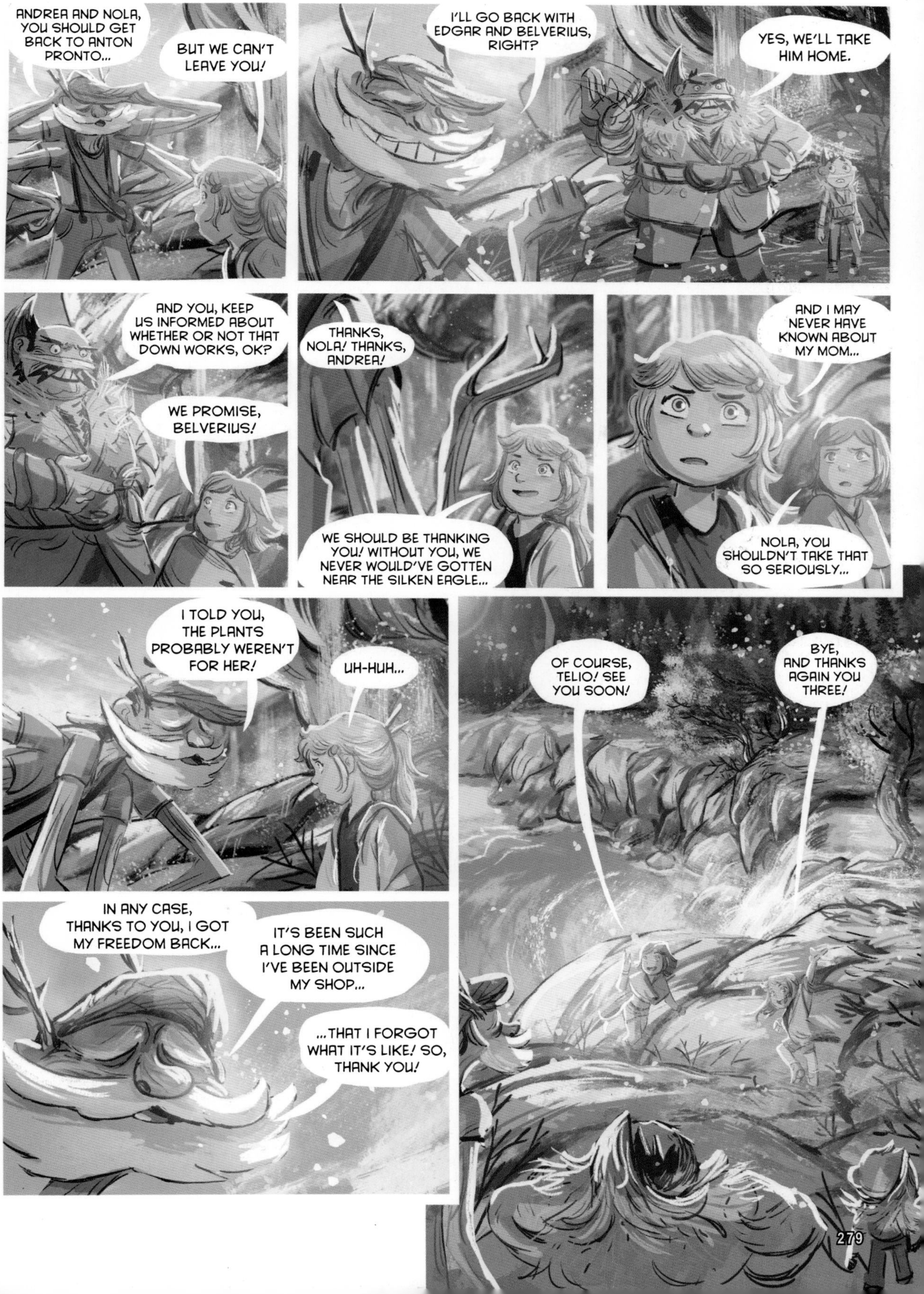
ANDREA AND NOLA, YOU SHOULD GET BACK TO ANTON PRONTO...
BUT WE CAN'T LEAVE YOU!
I'LL GO BACK WITH EDGAR AND BELVERIUS, RIGHT?
YES, WE'LL TAKE HIM HOME.
AND YOU, KEEP US INFORMED ABOUT WHETHER OR NOT THAT DOWN WORKS, OK?
WE PROMISE, BELVERIUS!
THANKS, NOLA! THANKS, ANDREA!
WE SHOULD BE THANKING YOU! WITHOUT YOU, WE NEVER WOULD'VE GOTTEN NEAR THE SILKEN EAGLE...
AND I MAY NEVER HAVE KNOWN ABOUT MY MOM...
NOLA, YOU SHOULDN'T TAKE THAT SO SERIOUSLY...
I TOLD YOU, THE PLANTS PROBABLY WEREN'T FOR HER!
UH-HUH...
IN ANY CASE, THANKS TO YOU, I GOT MY FREEDOM BACK...
IT'S BEEN SUCH A LONG TIME SINCE I'VE BEEN OUTSIDE MY SHOP...
...THAT I FORGOT WHAT IT'S LIKE! SO, THANK YOU!
OF COURSE, TELIO! SEE YOU SOON!
BYE, AND THANKS AGAIN YOU THREE!

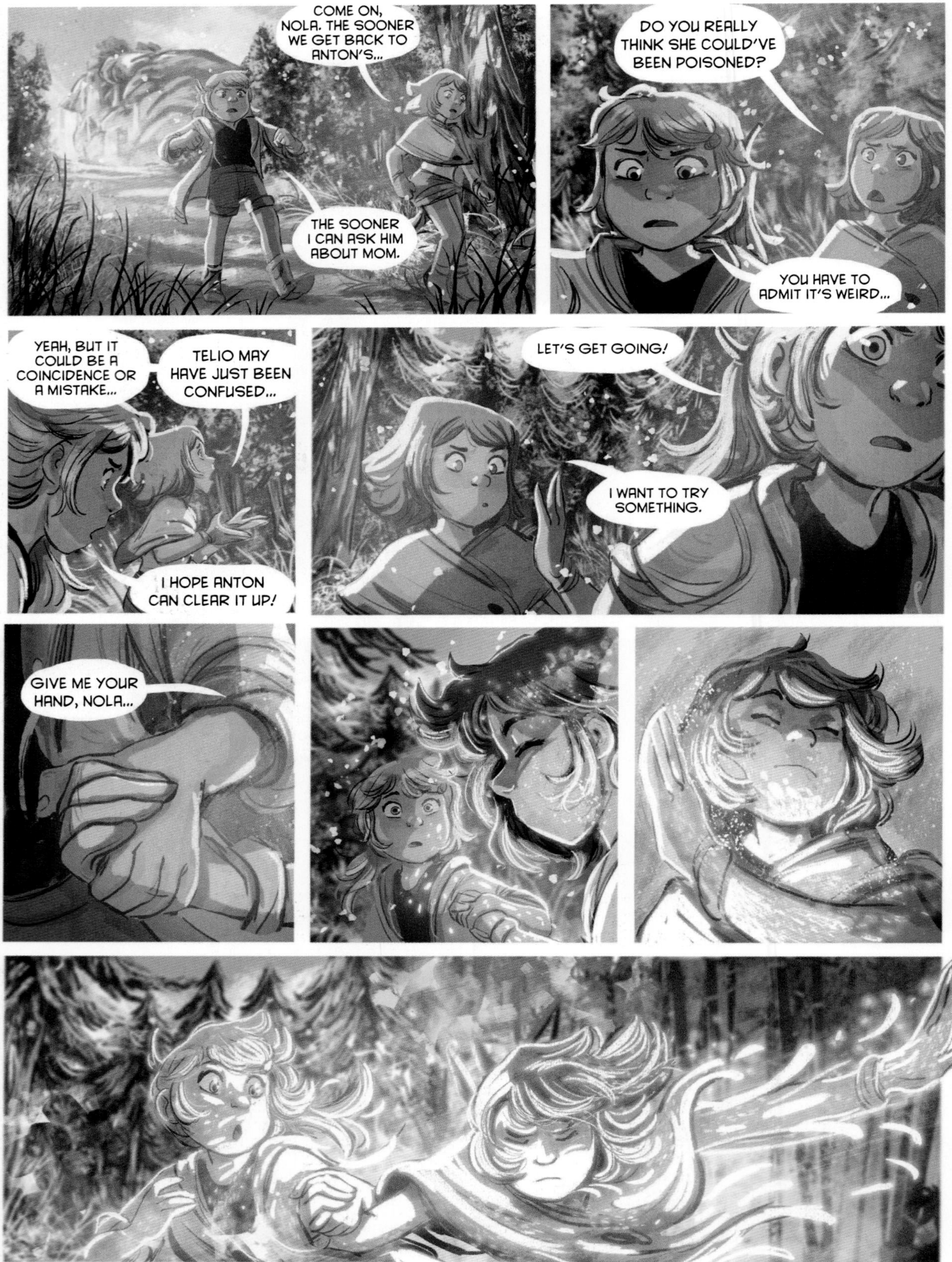
COME ON, NOLA. THE SOONER WE GET BACK TO ANTON'S...
THE SOONER I CAN ASK HIM ABOUT MOM.
DO YOU REALLY THINK SHE COULD'VE BEEN POISONED?
YOU HAVE TO ADMIT IT'S WEIRD...
YEAH, BUT IT COULD BE A COINCIDENCE OR A MISTAKE...
TELIO MAY HAVE JUST BEEN CONFUSED...
I HOPE ANTON CAN CLEAR IT UP!
LET'S GET GOING!
I WANT TO TRY SOMETHING.
GIVE ME YOUR HAND, NOLA...

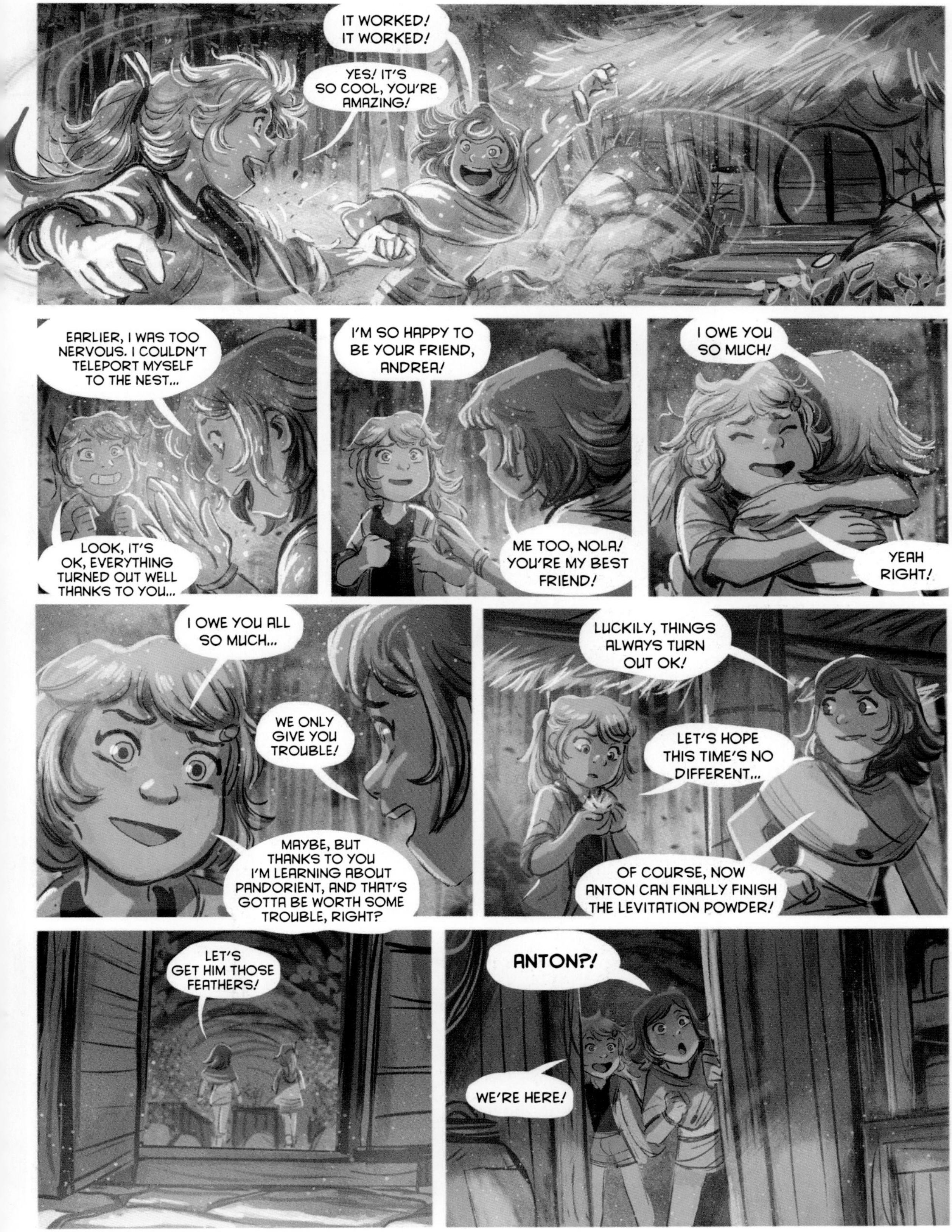
IT WORKED! IT WORKED!
YES! IT'S SO COOL, YOU'RE AMAZING!
EARLIER, I WAS TOO NERVOUS. I COULDN'T TELEPORT MYSELF TO THE NEST...
LOOK, IT'S OK, EVERYTHING TURNED OUT WELL THANKS TO YOU...
I'M SO HAPPY TO BE YOUR FRIEND, ANDREA!
ME TOO, NOLA! YOU'RE MY BEST FRIEND!
I OWE YOU SO MUCH!
YEAH RIGHT!
I OWE YOU ALL SO MUCH...
WE ONLY GIVE YOU TROUBLE!
MAYBE, BUT THANKS TO YOU I'M LEARNING ABOUT PANDORIENT, AND THAT'S GOTTA BE WORTH SOME TROUBLE, RIGHT?
LUCKILY, THINGS ALWAYS TURN OUT OK!
LET'S HOPE THIS TIME'S NO DIFFERENT...
OF COURSE, NOW ANTON CAN FINALLY FINISH THE LEVITATION POWDER!
LET'S GET HIM THOSE FEATHERS!
ANTON?!
WE'RE HERE!

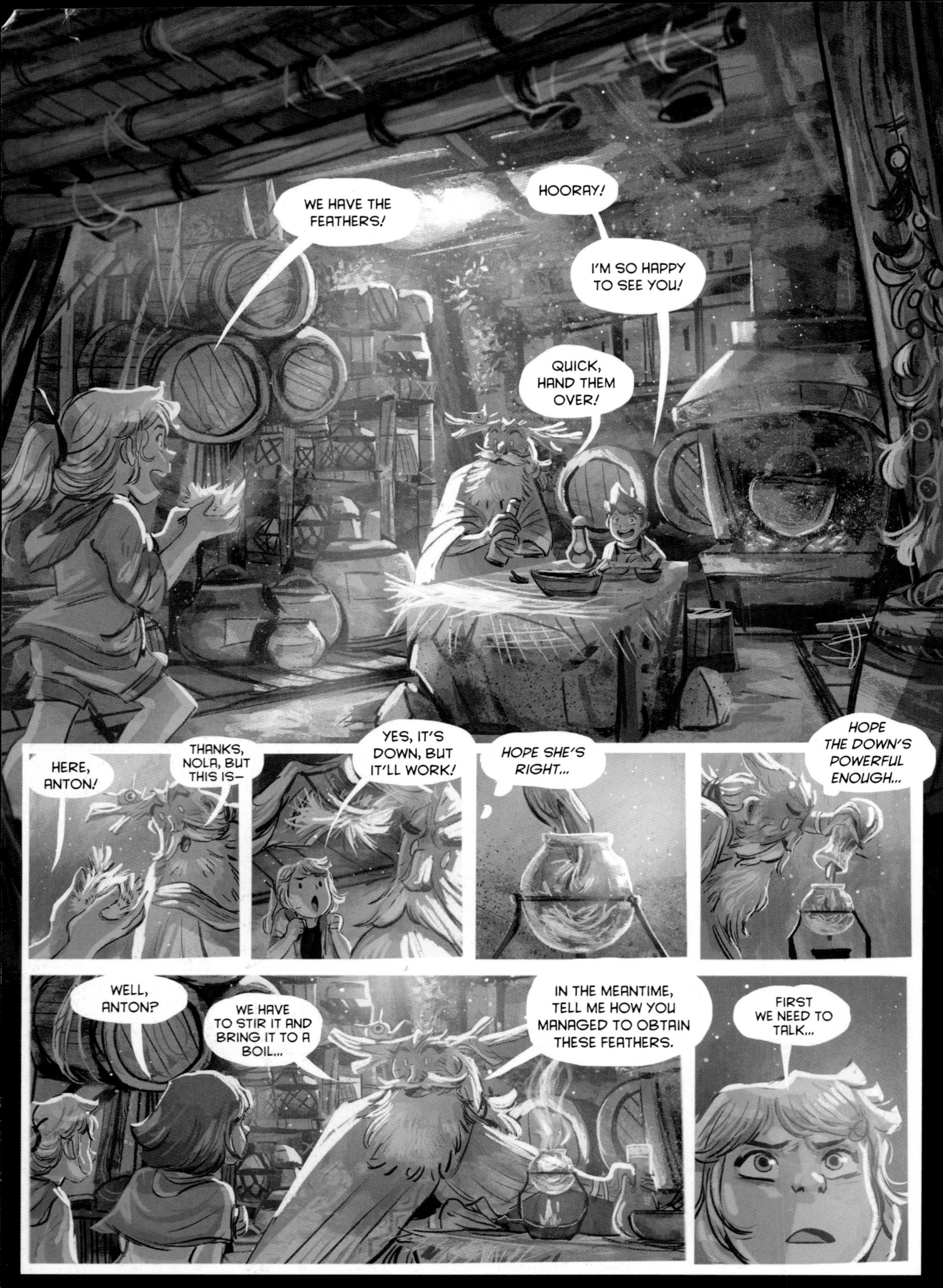
WE HAVE THE FEATHERS!
HOORAY!
I'M SO HAPPY TO SEE YOU!
QUICK, HAND THEM OVER!
HERE, ANTON!
THANKS, NOLA, BUT THIS IS–
YES, IT'S DOWN, BUT IT'LL WORK!
HOPE SHE'S RIGHT...
HOPE THE DOWN'S POWERFUL ENOUGH...
WELL, ANTON?
WE HAVE TO STIR IT AND BRING IT TO A BOIL...
IN THE MEANTIME, TELL ME HOW YOU MANAGED TO OBTAIN THESE FEATHERS.
FIRST WE NEED TO TALK...

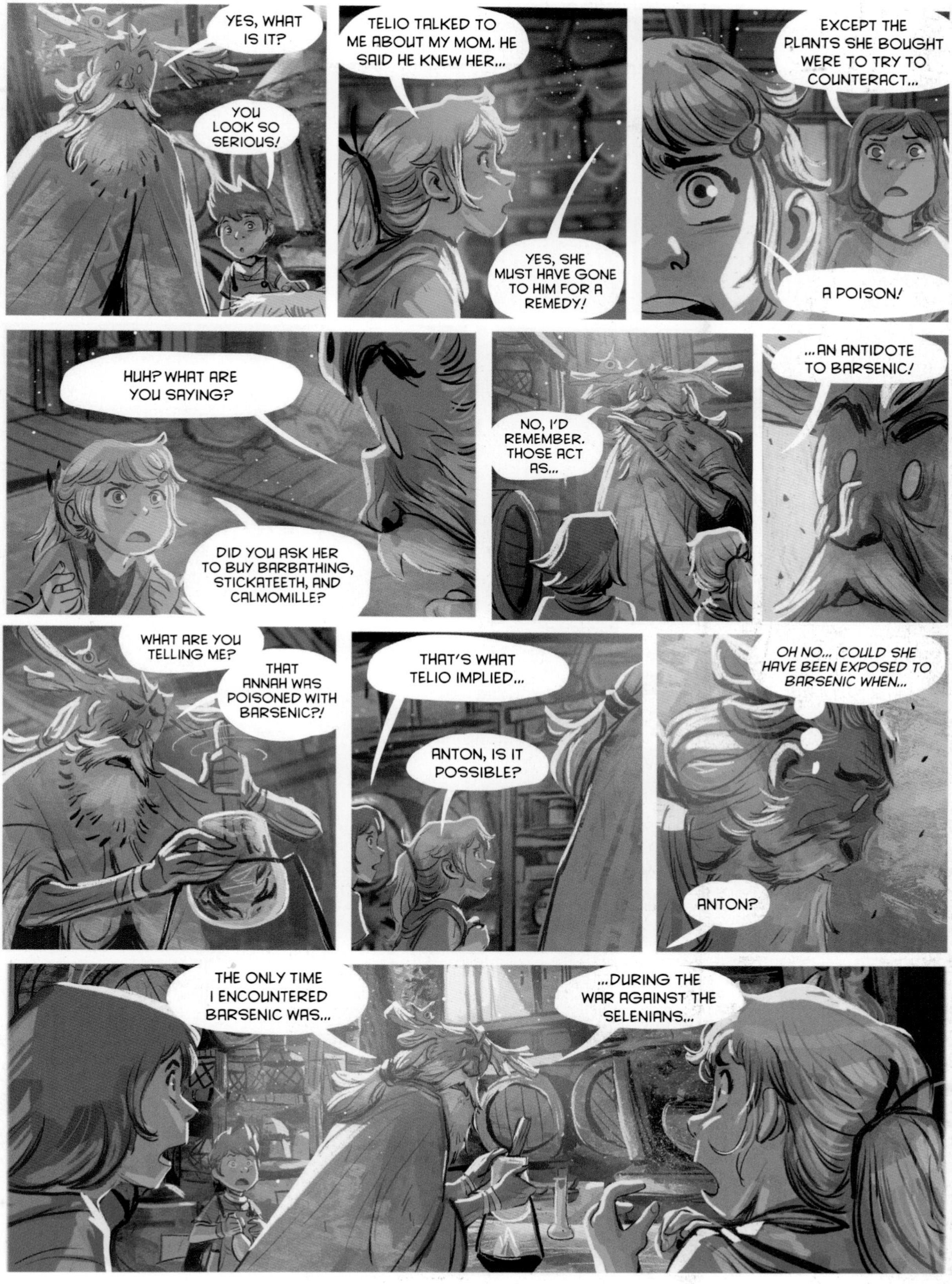
YES, WHAT IS IT?
YOU LOOK SO SERIOUS!
TELIO TALKED TO ME ABOUT MY MOM. HE SAID HE KNEW HER...
YES, SHE MUST HAVE GONE TO HIM FOR A REMEDY!
EXCEPT THE PLANTS SHE BOUGHT WERE TO TRY TO COUNTERACT...
A POISON!
HUH? WHAT ARE YOU SAYING?
DID YOU ASK HER TO BUY BARBATHING, STICKATEETH, AND CALMOMILLE?
NO, I'D REMEMBER. THOSE ACT AS...
...AN ANTIDOTE TO BARSENIC!
WHAT ARE YOU TELLING ME?
THAT ANNAH WAS POISONED WITH BARSENIC?!
THAT'S WHAT TELIO IMPLIED...
ANTON, IS IT POSSIBLE?
OH NO... COULD SHE HAVE BEEN EXPOSED TO BARSENIC WHEN...
ANTON?
THE ONLY TIME I ENCOUNTERED BARSENIC WAS...
...DURING THE WAR AGAINST THE SELENIANS...

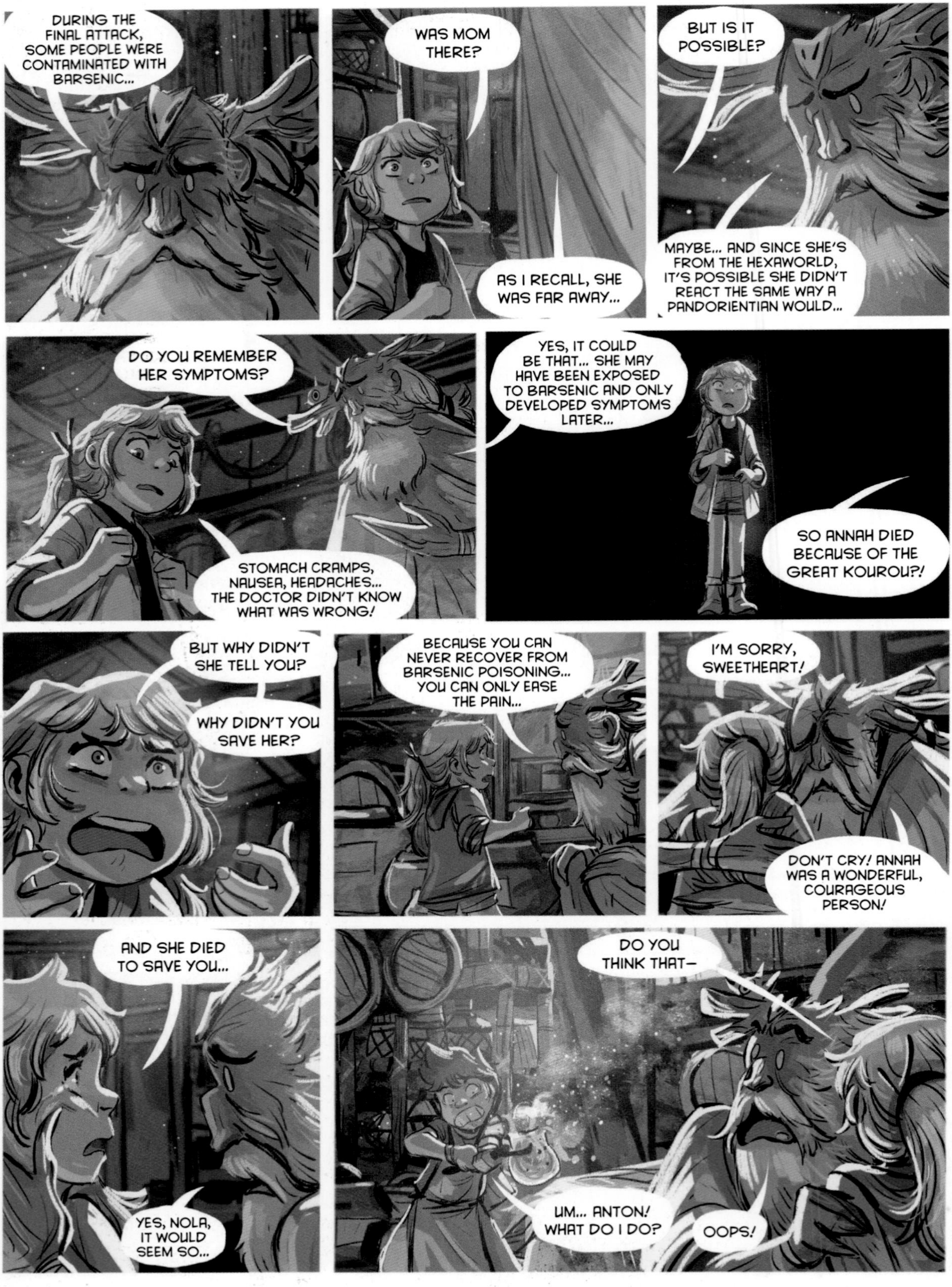
DURING THE FINAL ATTACK, SOME PEOPLE WERE CONTAMINATED WITH BARSENIC...
WAS MOM THERE?
AS I RECALL, SHE WAS FAR AWAY...
BUT IS IT POSSIBLE?
MAYBE... AND SINCE SHE'S FROM THE HEXAWORLD, IT'S POSSIBLE SHE DIDN'T REACT THE SAME WAY A PANDORIENTIAN WOULD...
DO YOU REMEMBER HER SYMPTOMS?
STOMACH CRAMPS, NAUSEA, HEADACHES... THE DOCTOR DIDN'T KNOW WHAT WAS WRONG!
YES, IT COULD BE THAT... SHE MAY HAVE BEEN EXPOSED TO BARSENIC AND ONLY DEVELOPED SYMPTOMS LATER...
SO ANNAH DIED BECAUSE OF THE GREAT KOUROU?!
BUT WHY DIDN'T SHE TELL YOU?
WHY DIDN'T YOU SAVE HER?
BECAUSE YOU CAN NEVER RECOVER FROM BARSENIC POISONING... YOU CAN ONLY EASE THE PAIN...
I'M SORRY, SWEETHEART!
DON'T CRY! ANNAH WAS A WONDERFUL, COURAGEOUS PERSON!
AND SHE DIED TO SAVE YOU...
YES, NOLA, IT WOULD SEEM SO...
DO YOU THINK THAT—
UM... ANTON! WHAT DO I DO?
OOPS!

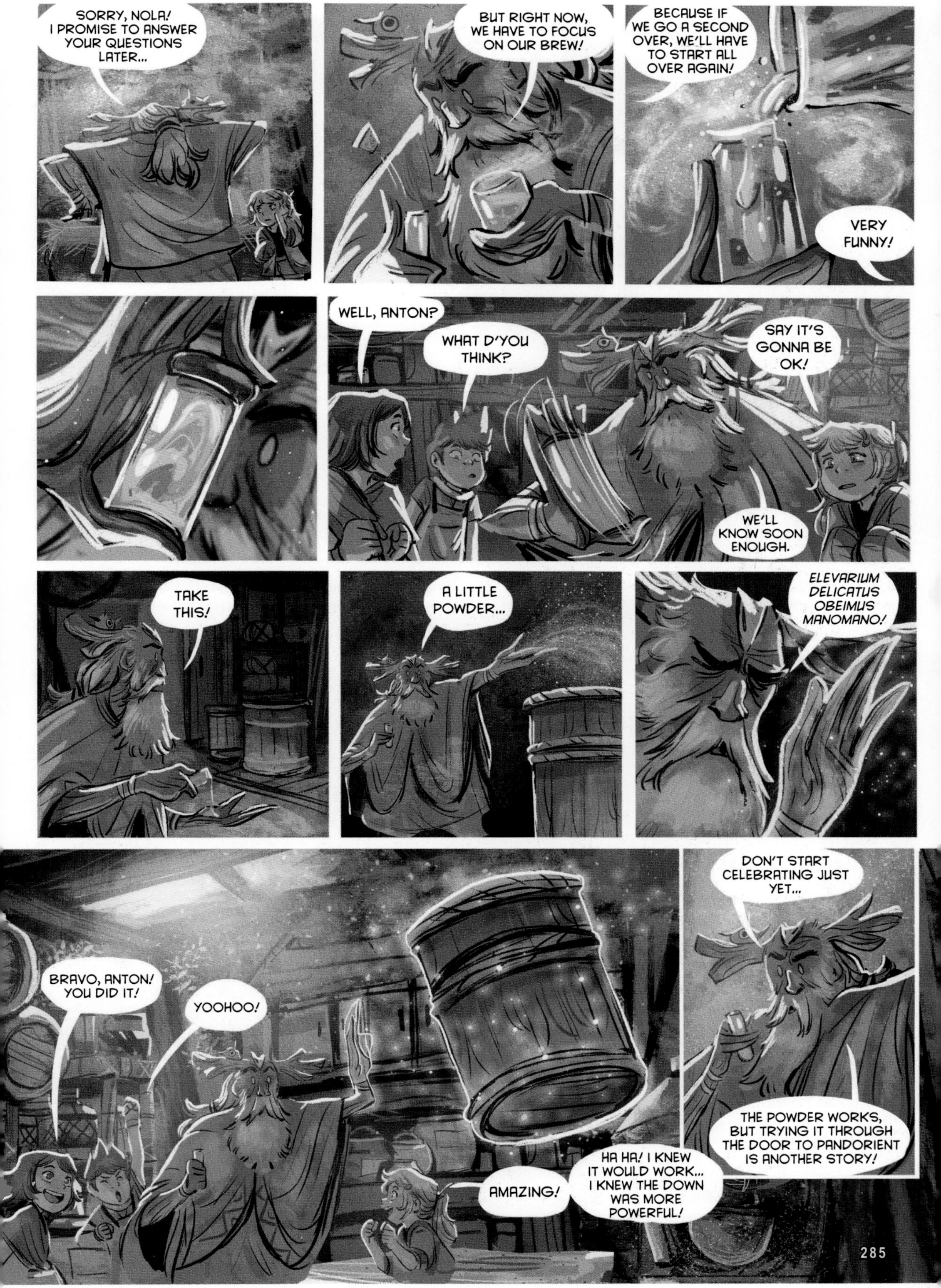
SORRY, NOLA! I PROMISE TO ANSWER YOUR QUESTIONS LATER...
BUT RIGHT NOW, WE HAVE TO FOCUS ON OUR BREW!
BECAUSE IF WE GO A SECOND OVER, WE'LL HAVE TO START ALL OVER AGAIN!
VERY FUNNY!
WELL, ANTON?
WHAT D'YOU THINK?
SAY IT'S GONNA BE OK!
WE'LL KNOW SOON ENOUGH.
TAKE THIS!
A LITTLE POWDER...
ELEVARIUM DELICATUS OBEIMUS MANOMANO!
BRAVO, ANTON! YOU DID IT!
YOOHOO!
AMAZING!
HA HA! I KNEW IT WOULD WORK... I KNEW THE DOWN WAS MORE POWERFUL!
DON'T START CELEBRATING JUST YET...
THE POWDER WORKS, BUT TRYING IT THROUGH THE DOOR TO PANDORIENT IS ANOTHER STORY!

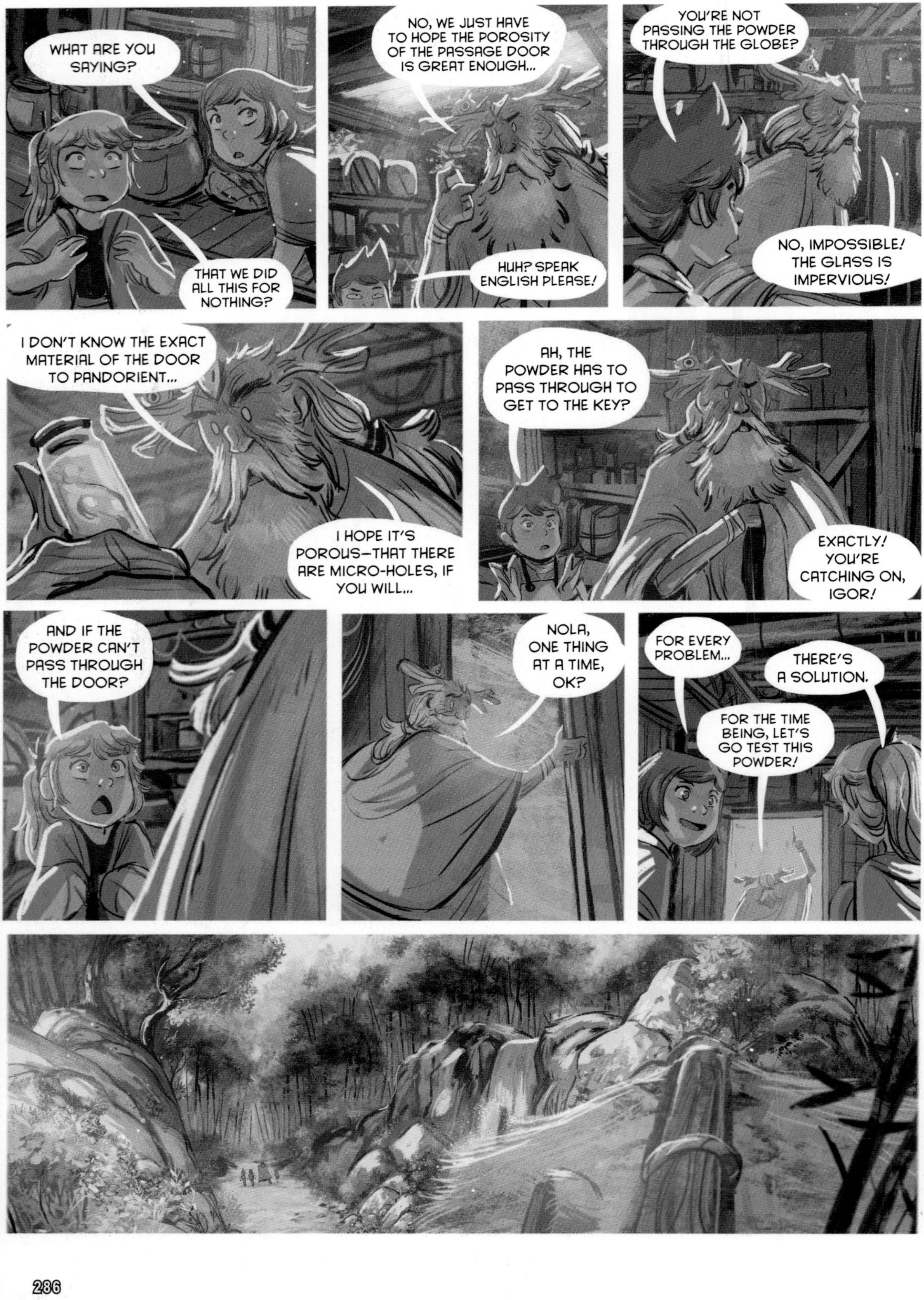
WHAT ARE YOU SAYING?
THAT WE DID ALL THIS FOR NOTHING?
NO, WE JUST HAVE TO HOPE THE POROSITY OF THE PASSAGE DOOR IS GREAT ENOUGH...
HUH? SPEAK ENGLISH PLEASE!
YOU'RE NOT PASSING THE POWDER THROUGH THE GLOBE?
NO, IMPOSSIBLE! THE GLASS IS IMPERVIOUS!
I DON'T KNOW THE EXACT MATERIAL OF THE DOOR TO PANDORIENT...
I HOPE IT'S POROUS—THAT THERE ARE MICRO-HOLES, IF YOU WILL...
AH, THE POWDER HAS TO PASS THROUGH TO GET TO THE KEY?
EXACTLY! YOU'RE CATCHING ON, IGOR!
AND IF THE POWDER CAN'T PASS THROUGH THE DOOR?
NOLA, ONE THING AT A TIME, OK?
FOR EVERY PROBLEM...
THERE'S A SOLUTION.
FOR THE TIME BEING, LET'S GO TEST THIS POWDER!

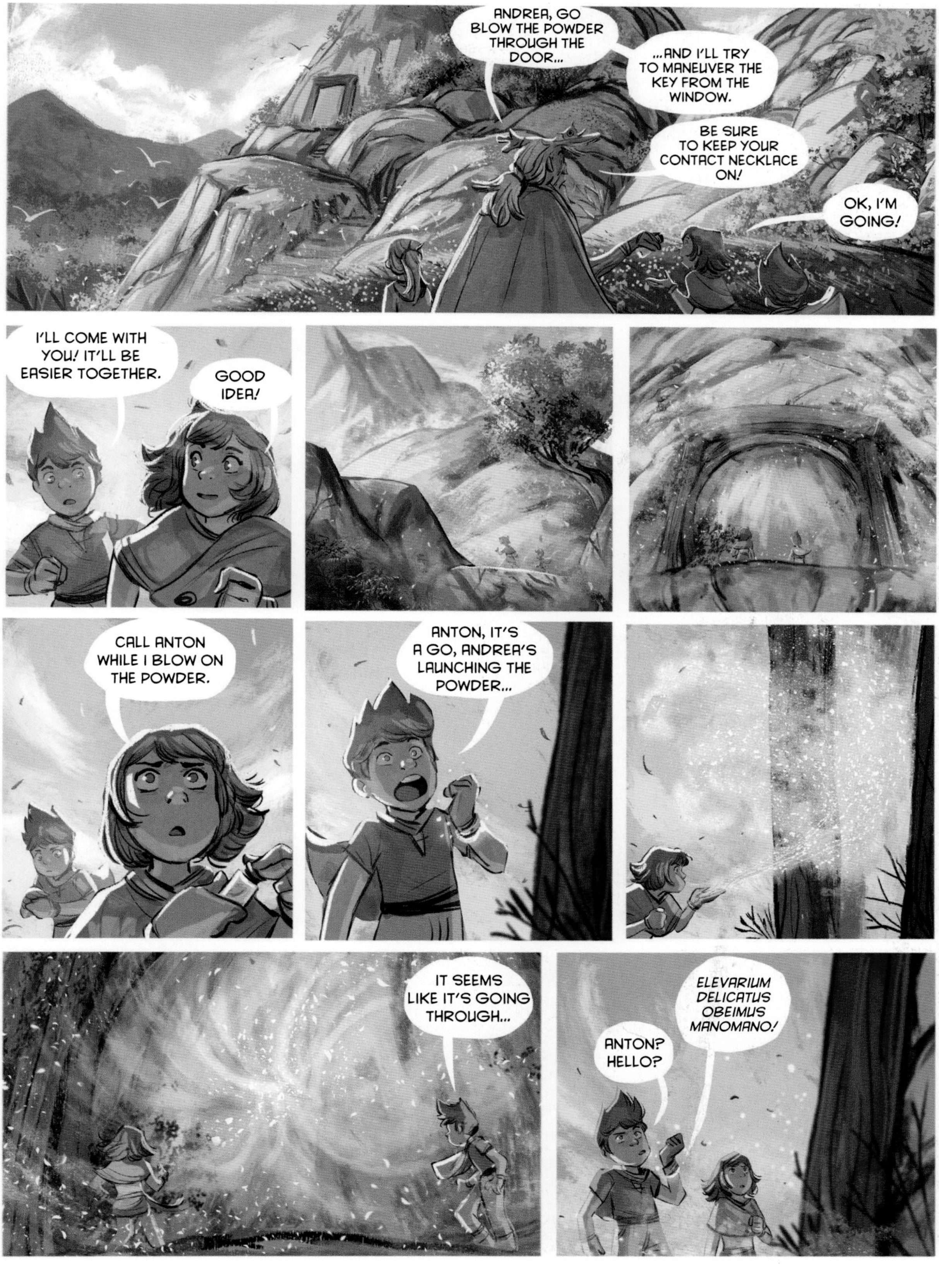
ANDREA, GO BLOW THE POWDER THROUGH THE DOOR...
...AND I'LL TRY TO MANEUVER THE KEY FROM THE WINDOW.
BE SURE TO KEEP YOUR CONTACT NECKLACE ON!
OK, I'M GOING!
I'LL COME WITH YOU! IT'LL BE EASIER TOGETHER.
GOOD IDEA!
CALL ANTON WHILE I BLOW ON THE POWDER.
ANTON, IT'S A GO, ANDREA'S LAUNCHING THE POWDER...
IT SEEMS LIKE IT'S GOING THROUGH...
ANTON? HELLO?
ELEVARIUM DELICATUS OBEIMUS MANOMANO!

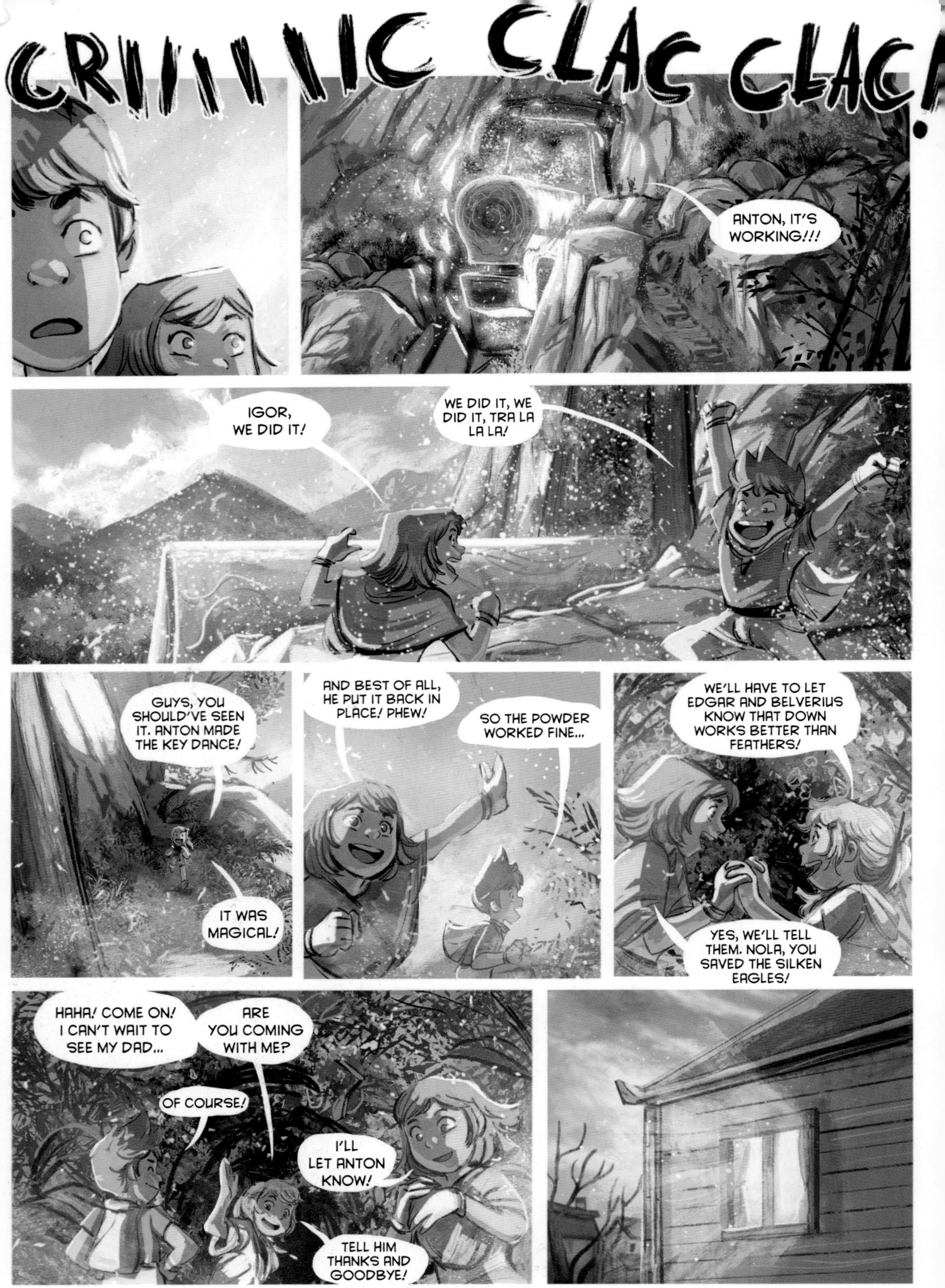
CRIIIIIIC CLAC CLAC!
ANTON, IT'S WORKING!!!
IGOR, WE DID IT!
WE DID IT, WE DID IT, TRA LA LA LA!
GUYS, YOU SHOULD'VE SEEN IT. ANTON MADE THE KEY DANCE!
IT WAS MAGICAL!
AND BEST OF ALL, HE PUT IT BACK IN PLACE! PHEW!
SO THE POWDER WORKED FINE...
WE'LL HAVE TO LET EDGAR AND BELVERIUS KNOW THAT DOWN WORKS BETTER THAN FEATHERS!
YES, WE'LL TELL THEM. NOLA, YOU SAVED THE SILKEN EAGLES!
HAHA! COME ON! I CAN'T WAIT TO SEE MY DAD...
ARE YOU COMING WITH ME?
OF COURSE!
I'LL LET ANTON KNOW!
TELL HIM THANKS AND GOODBYE!

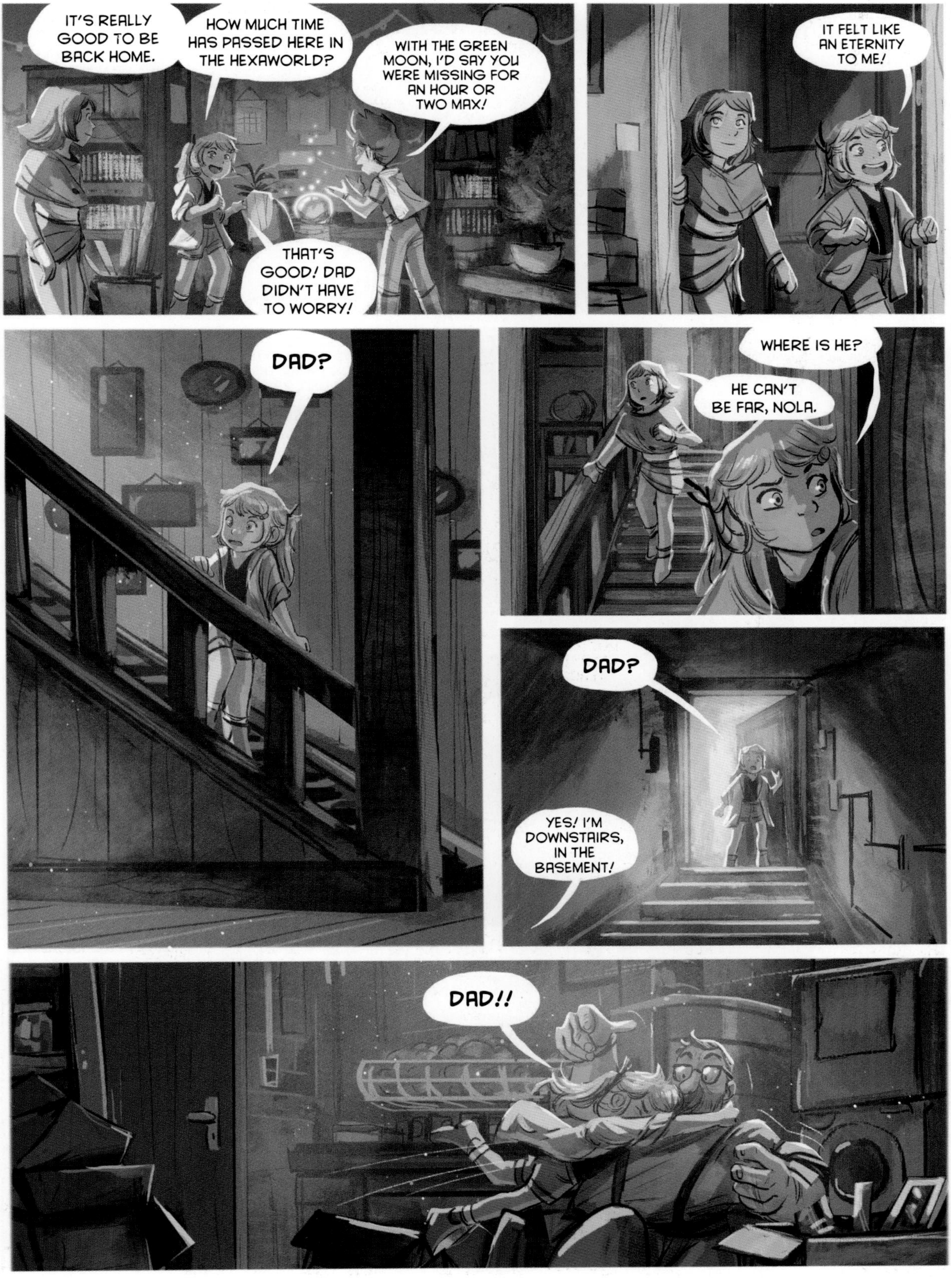
IT'S REALLY GOOD TO BE BACK HOME.
HOW MUCH TIME HAS PASSED HERE IN THE HEXAWORLD?
WITH THE GREEN MOON, I'D SAY YOU WERE MISSING FOR AN HOUR OR TWO MAX!
THAT'S GOOD! DAD DIDN'T HAVE TO WORRY!
IT FELT LIKE AN ETERNITY TO ME!
DAD?
WHERE IS HE?
HE CAN'T BE FAR, NOLA.
DAD?
YES! I'M DOWNSTAIRS, IN THE BASEMENT!
DAD!!

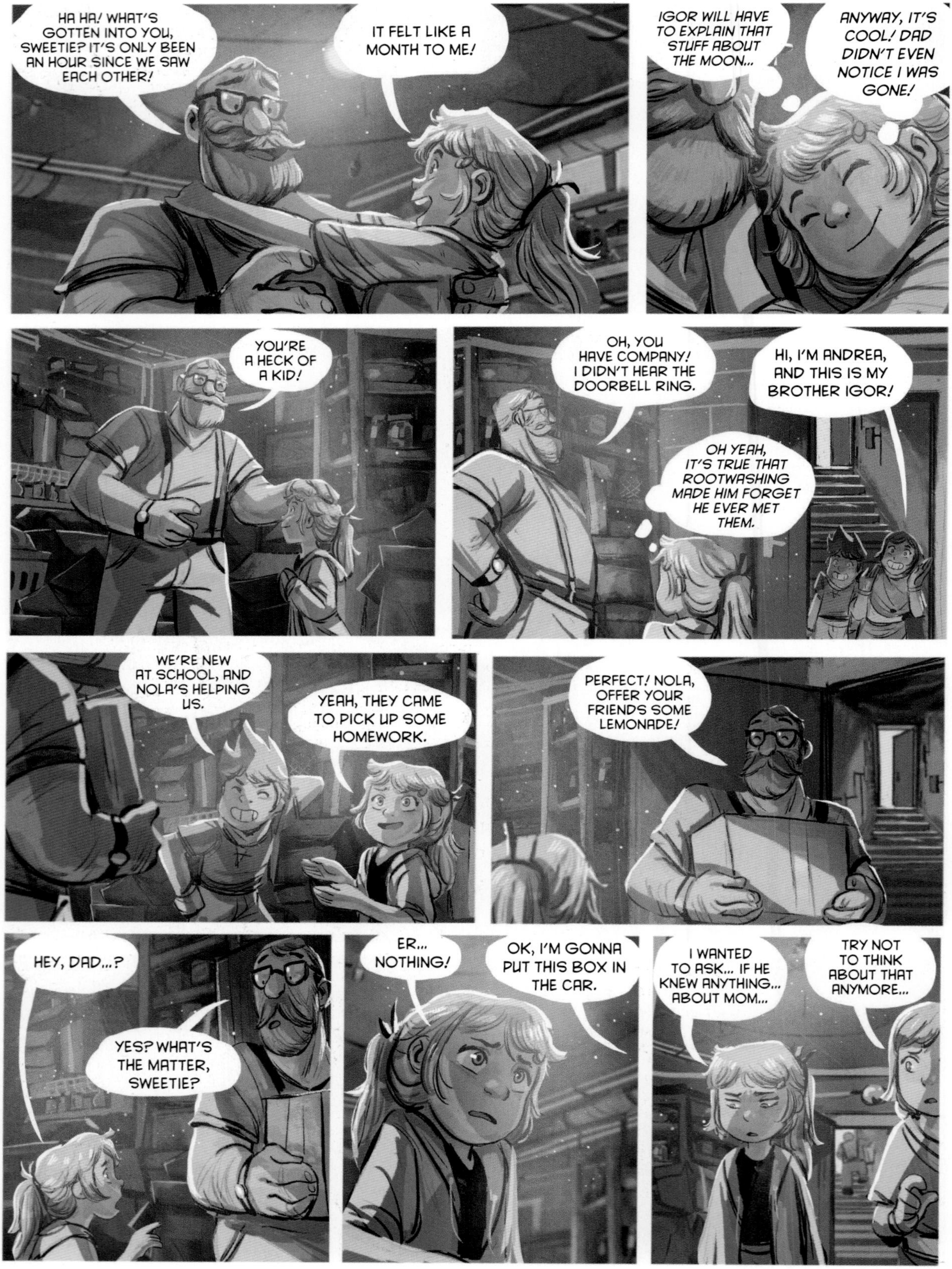
HA HA! WHAT'S GOTTEN INTO YOU, SWEETIE? IT'S ONLY BEEN AN HOUR SINCE WE SAW EACH OTHER!
IT FELT LIKE A MONTH TO ME!
IGOR WILL HAVE TO EXPLAIN THAT STUFF ABOUT THE MOON...
ANYWAY, IT'S COOL! DAD DIDN'T EVEN NOTICE I WAS GONE!
YOU'RE A HECK OF A KID!
OH, YOU HAVE COMPANY! I DIDN'T HEAR THE DOORBELL RING.
HI, I'M ANDREA, AND THIS IS MY BROTHER IGOR!
OH YEAH, IT'S TRUE THAT ROOTWASHING MADE HIM FORGET HE EVER MET THEM.
WE'RE NEW AT SCHOOL, AND NOLA'S HELPING US.
YEAH, THEY CAME TO PICK UP SOME HOMEWORK.
PERFECT! NOLA, OFFER YOUR FRIENDS SOME LEMONADE!
HEY, DAD...?
YES? WHAT'S THE MATTER, SWEETIE?
ER... NOTHING!
OK, I'M GONNA PUT THIS BOX IN THE CAR.
I WANTED TO ASK... IF HE KNEW ANYTHING... ABOUT MOM...
TRY NOT TO THINK ABOUT THAT ANYMORE...

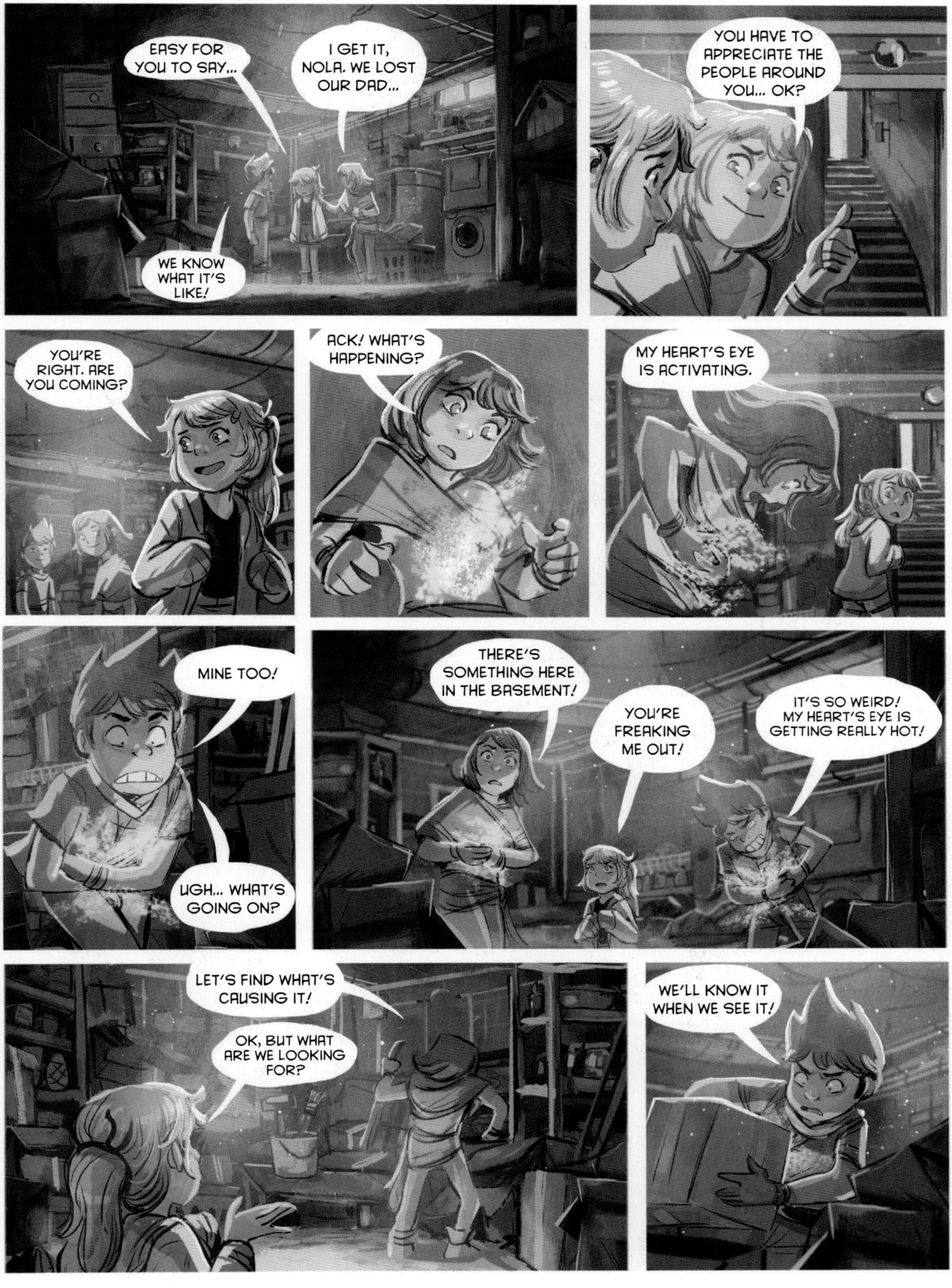
EASY FOR YOU TO SAY...
I GET IT, NOLA. WE LOST OUR DAD...
WE KNOW WHAT IT'S LIKE!
YOU HAVE TO APPRECIATE THE PEOPLE AROUND YOU... OK?
YOU'RE RIGHT. ARE YOU COMING?
ACK! WHAT'S HAPPENING?
MY HEART'S EYE IS ACTIVATING.
MINE TOO!
UGH... WHAT'S GOING ON?
THERE'S SOMETHING HERE IN THE BASEMENT!
YOU'RE FREAKING ME OUT!
IT'S SO WEIRD! MY HEART'S EYE IS GETTING REALLY HOT!
LET'S FIND WHAT'S CAUSING IT!
OK, BUT WHAT ARE WE LOOKING FOR?
WE'LL KNOW IT WHEN WE SEE IT!

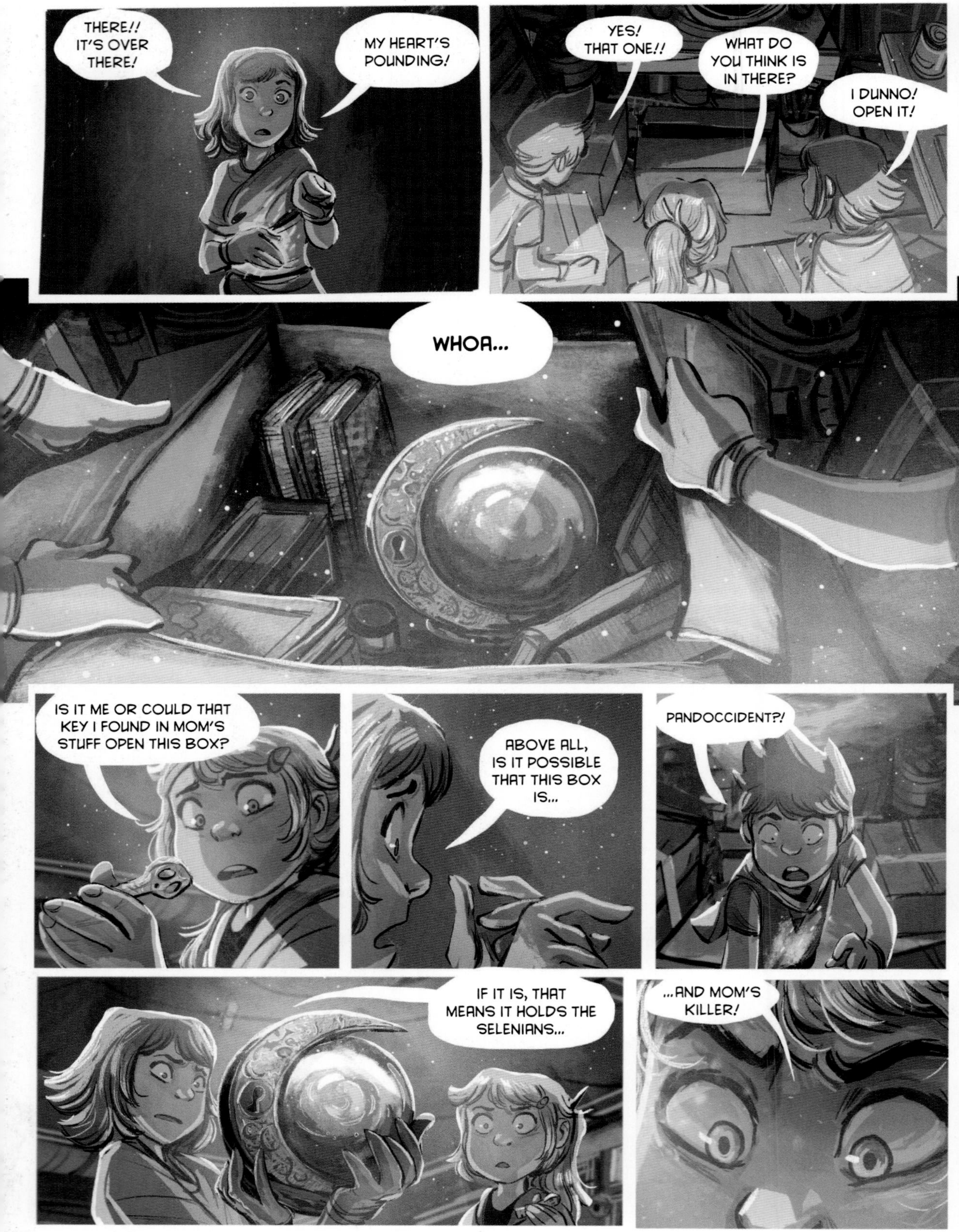
THERE!! IT'S OVER THERE!
MY HEART'S POUNDING!
YES! THAT ONE!!
WHAT DO YOU THINK IS IN THERE?
I DUNNO! OPEN IT!
WHOA...
IS IT ME OR COULD THAT KEY I FOUND IN MOM'S STUFF OPEN THIS BOX?
ABOVE ALL, IS IT POSSIBLE THAT THIS BOX IS...
PANDOCCIDENT?!
IF IT IS, THAT MEANS IT HOLDS THE SELENIANS...
...AND MOM'S KILLER!

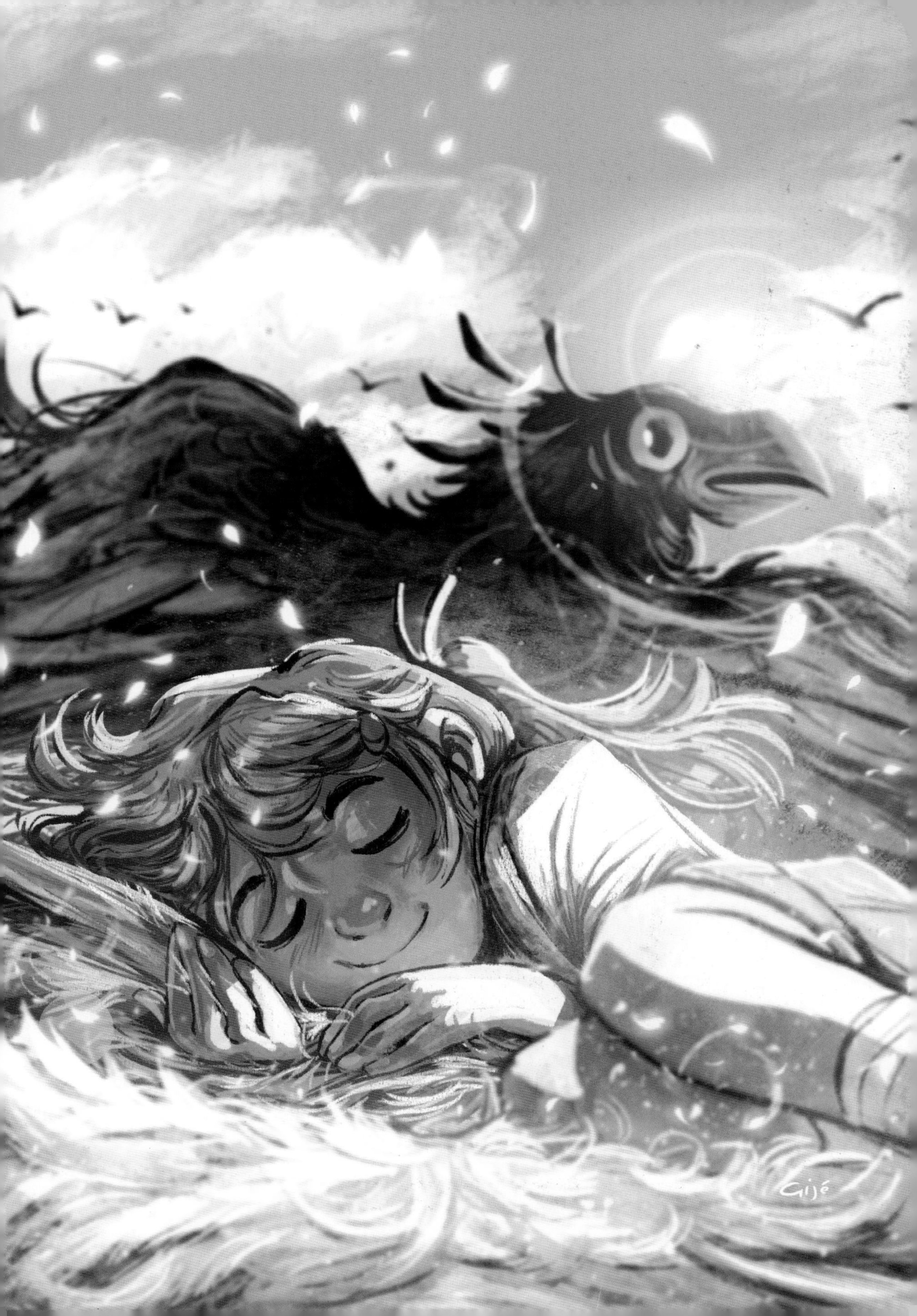
Gijé

WRITE YOUR OWN STORIES!

1. Imagine that an object you own has the power to transport you to another world. What would the object be and where would it take you? Write a short story about your own magical object and the adventure it sends you on.

2. Anton sprinkles camouflage powder on Nola so she can remain undetected in Pandorient. Imagine that you have a magic camouflage powder. Write about what you would use it for and where it would allow you to go in secret.

3. Mathilda uses her magic powers to unlock the door to the theater. Imagine that you have a magic power. Write a short story that reveals what your magic power is and how you use it to help others.

4. Andrea has the power to magically transport herself to other places. Imagine that you have the same power. Write about how you would use this power and where it would take you.

5. The silken eagle is large enough to carry Nola and fly away with her. Write a short story where a bird lifts you into the air and flies off. Describe where it would take you and how you would escape.

6. Imagine that you could make levitation powder like Anton does. Write about what you would do with your magical powder and how it could help you.

About the Author

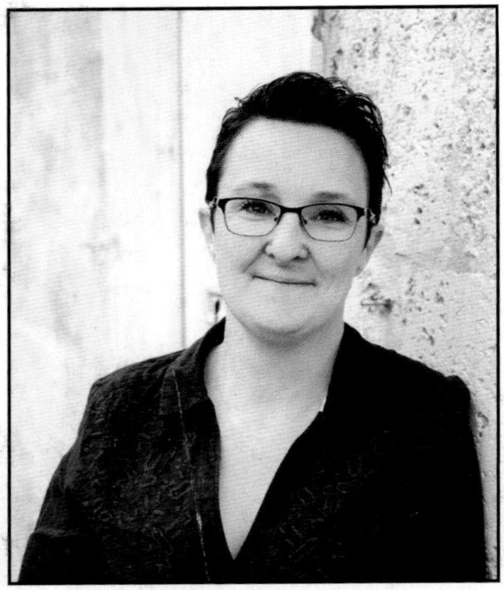

credit: © Chloé Vollmer Lo

Having always been drawn to the world of children, **Bénédicte Carboneill**, aka Carbone, made the logical choice by first becoming a teacher. After joining the teaching ranks in 1995, she went on to serve as a school principal before writing entered her life. Starting with publications on education, Carbone soon developed her own publishing house, Pas de l'échelle, which brought together comics and education. As an editor and author, she began writing for young children and teenagers. In 2015, she started writing comics with *Le Pass'Temps* and soon followed with *La boîte à musique* (*The Music Box*).

About the Illustrator

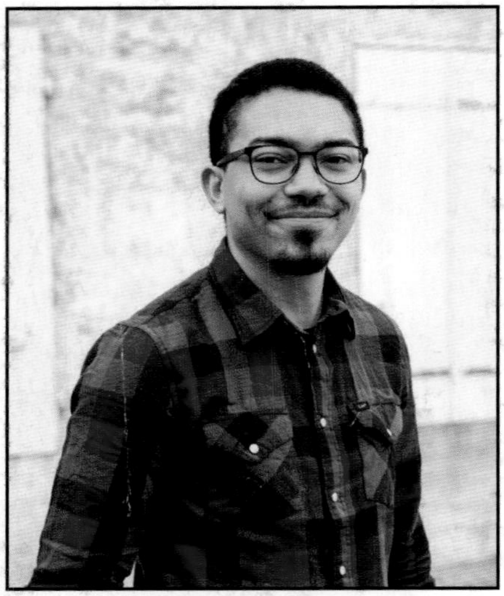

credit: © Chloé Vollmer Lo

Jérôme Gillet, aka Gijé, was born in 1988 in Lubumbashi (Congo). Following his studies in illustration at the Saint-Luc Institute in Liège (Belgium), he moved to Luxembourg to continue his training in animation. After graduating in 2012, Gijé started out as a freelance 2D artist before joining Zeilt Production as a computer graphics designer. While there, he gained valuable experience working on advertising, short films, and animated series. Then, in 2018, Gijé's career evolved once again as he turned to the comics world by illustrating *La boîte à musique* (*The Music Box*).